THE
COLLECTED
SHORT
STORIES

BY THE SAME AUTHOR

NOVELS

Not a Penny More, Not a Penny Less
Shall We Tell the President?
Kane and Abel
The Prodigal Daughter
First Among Equals
A Matter of Honor
As the Crow Flies
Honor Among Thieves
The Fourth Estate
The Eleventh Commandment

SHORT STORIES

A Quiver Full of Arrows
A Twist in the Tale
Twelve Red Herrings

PLAYS

Beyond Reasonable Doubt
Exclusive

THE
COLLECTED
SHORT
STORIES

JEFFREY ARCHER

HarperCollins*Publishers*

FIRST EDITION

Designed by Pagesetters, Inc.

Library of Congress Cataloging-in-Publication Data

Archer, Jeffrey, 1940–
[Short Stories]
The collected short stories/Jeffrey Archer.—1st ed.
p. cm.
ISBN 0–06–019224–0
I. Title.
PR6051.R285A15   1998
823'.914—DC21   98–17260

98 99 00 01 02 ❖/RRD 10 9 8 7 6 5 4 3 2 1

To John and Norma

CONTENTS

Contents

NEVER STOP
ON THE MOTORWAY

DIANA HAD BEEN HOPING to get away by 5:00, so she could be at the farm in time for dinner. She tried not to show her true feelings when at 4:37 her deputy, Phil Haskins, presented her with a complex twelve-page document that required the signature of a director before it could be sent out to the client. Haskins didn't hesitate to remind her that they had lost two similar contracts that week.

It was always the same on a Friday. The phones would go quiet in the middle of the afternoon and then, just as she thought she could slip away, an authorization would land on her desk. One glance at this particular document and Diana knew there would be no chance of escaping before 6:00.

The demands of being a single parent as well as a director of a small but thriving City company meant there were few moments left in any day to relax, so when it came to the one weekend in four that James and Caroline spent with her ex-husband, Diana would try to leave the office a little earlier than usual to avoid getting snarled up in the weekend traffic.

She read through the first page slowly and made a couple of emendations, aware that any mistake made hastily on a Friday evening could be regretted in the weeks to come. She glanced at the clock on her desk as she signed the final page of the document. It was just showing 5:51.

Diana gathered up her bag and walked purposefully toward the door, dropping the contract on Phil's desk without bothering to suggest that he have a good weekend. She suspected that the paperwork had been on his desk since 9:00 that morning, but that holding it until 4:37 was his only means of revenge now that she had been made head of department. Once she was

1

safely in the elevator, she pressed the button for the basement garage, calculating that the delay would probably add an extra hour to her journey.

She stepped out of the elevator, walked over to her Audi suburban, unlocked the door, and threw her bag onto the backseat. When she drove out into the street the stream of twilight traffic was just about keeping pace with the pinstriped pedestrians who, like worker ants, were hurrying toward the nearest hole in the ground.

She flicked on the six o'clock news. The chimes of Big Ben rang out before spokesmen from each of the three main political parties gave their views on the European election results. John Major was refusing to comment on his future. The Conservative Party's explanation for its poor showing was that only 36 percent of the country had bothered to go to the polls. Diana felt guilty—she was among the 64 percent who had failed to register their vote.

The newscaster moved on to say that the situation in Bosnia remained desperate, and that the UN was threatening dire consequences if Radovan Karadzic and the Serbs didn't come to an agreement with the other warring parties. Diana's mind began to drift—such a threat was hardly news any longer. She suspected that if she turned on the radio in a year's time they would probably be repeating it word for word.

As her car crawled round Russell Square, she began to think about the weekend ahead. It had been over a year since John had told her that he had met another woman and wanted a divorce. She still wondered why, after seven years of marriage, she hadn't been more shocked—or at least angry—at his betrayal. Since her appointment as a director, she had to admit they had spent less and less time together. And perhaps she had become anesthetized by the fact that a third of the married couples in Britain were now divorced or separated. Her parents had been unable to hide their disappointment, but then they had been married for forty-two years.

The divorce had been amicable enough, as John, who earned less than she did—one of their problems, perhaps—had given in to most of her demands. She had kept the apartment in Putney, the Audi suburban, and the children, to whom John was allowed access one weekend in four. He would have picked them up from school earlier that afternoon, and, as usual, he'd return them to the apartment in Putney around seven on Sunday evening.

Diana would go to almost any lengths to avoid being left on her own in Putney when they weren't around, and although she regularly grumbled about being saddled with the responsibility of bringing up two children without a father, she missed them desperately the moment they were out of sight.

She hadn't taken a lover, and she didn't sleep around. None of the senior staff at the office had ever gone further than asking her out to lunch. Perhaps because only three of them were unmarried—and not without reason. The one person she might have considered having a relationship with had made it abundantly clear that he only wanted to spend the night with her, not the days.

In any case, Diana had decided long ago that if she was to be taken seriously as the company's first woman director, an office affair, however casual or short-lived, could only end in tears. Men are so vain, she thought. A woman had to make only one mistake and she was immediately labeled as promiscuous. Then every other man on the premises either smirks behind your back, or treats your thigh as an extension of the arm on his chair.

Diana groaned as she came to a halt at yet another red light. In twenty minutes she hadn't covered more than a couple of miles. She opened the glove compartment on the passenger side and fumbled in the dark for a cassette. She found one and pressed it into the slot, hoping it would be Pavarotti, only to be greeted by the strident tones of Gloria Gaynor assuring her, "I will survive." She smiled and thought about Daniel as the light changed to green.

She and Daniel had majored in economics at Bristol University in the early 1980s, friends but never lovers. Then Daniel met Rachael, who had arrived a year after them, and from that moment he had never looked at another woman. They married the day he graduated, and after they returned from their honeymoon Daniel took over the management of his father's farm in Bedfordshire. Three children had followed in quick succession, and Diana had been proud when she was asked to be godmother to Sophie, the eldest. Daniel and Rachael had now been married for twelve years, and Diana felt confident that they wouldn't be disappointing *their* parents with any suggestion of a divorce. Although they were convinced that she led an exciting and fulfilling life, Diana often envied their gentle and uncomplicated existence.

She was regularly asked to spend the weekend with them in the country, but for every two or three invitations Daniel issued, she only accepted one—not because she wouldn't have liked to join them more often, but because since her divorce she had no desire to take advantage of their hospitality.

Although she enjoyed her work, it had been a bloody week. The two contracts had fallen through, James had been dropped from the school soccer team, and Caroline had never stopped telling her that her father didn't mind her watching television when she ought to be doing her homework.

Another traffic light changed to red.

It took Diana nearly an hour to travel the seven miles out of the city, and when she reached the first two-lane highway, she glanced up at the A1 sign, more out of habit than to seek guidance, because she knew every yard of the road from her office to the farm. She tried to increase her speed, but it was quite impossible, as both lanes remained obstinately crowded.

"Damn."

She had forgotten to get them a present, even a decent bottle of Bordeaux. "Damn," she repeated: Daniel and Rachael always did the giving. She began to wonder if she could pick something up on the way, then remembered there was nothing but service stations between here and the farm. She couldn't turn up with yet another box of chocolates they'd never eat. When she reached the traffic circle that led onto the A1, she managed to push the car over fifty for the first time. She began to relax, allowing her mind to drift with the music.

There was no warning. Although she immediately slammed

her foot on the brakes, it was already too late. There was a dull thump from the front bumper, and a slight shudder rocked the car.

A small black creature had shot across her path, and despite her quick reactions, she hadn't been able to avoid hitting it. Diana swung onto the hard shoulder and screeched to a halt, wondering if the animal could possibly have survived. She reversed slowly back to the spot where she thought she had hit it as the traffic roared past her.

And then she saw it, lying on the grass verge—a cat that had crossed the road for the tenth time. She stepped out of the car and walked toward the lifeless body. Suddenly Diana felt sick. She had two cats of her own, and she knew she would never be able to tell the children what she had done. She picked up the dead animal and laid it gently in the ditch by the roadside.

"I'm so sorry," she said, feeling a little silly. She gave it one last look before walking back to her car. Ironically, she had chosen the Audi for its safety features.

She climbed back into the car and switched on the ignition to find Gloria Gaynor still belting out her opinion of men. She turned her off and tried to stop thinking about the cat as she waited for a gap in the traffic large enough to allow her to ease her way back into the slow lane. She eventually succeeded but was still unable to erase the dead cat from her mind.

Diana had accelerated up to fifty again when she suddenly became aware of a pair of headlights shining through her rear windshield. She put up her arm and waved in her rearview mirror, but the lights continued to dazzle her. She slowed down to allow the vehicle to pass, but the driver showed no interest in doing so. Diana began to wonder if there was something wrong with her car. Was one of her lights not working? Was the exhaust billowing smoke? Was . . . ?

She decided to speed up and put some distance between herself and the vehicle behind, but it remained within a few yards of her bumper. She tried to snatch a look at the driver in her rearview mirror, but it was hard to see much in the harshness of the lights. As her eyes became more accustomed to the glare, she could make out the silhouette of a large black van bearing down on her, and what looked like a young man behind the wheel. He seemed to be waving at her.

Diana slowed down again as she approached the next traffic circle, giving him every chance to overtake her in the outside lane, but once again he didn't take the opportunity and just sat on her bumper, his headlights still undimmed. She waited for a small gap in the traffic coming from her right. When one appeared she slammed her foot on the accelerator, shot across the roundabout, and sped on up the A1.

She was rid of him at last. She was just beginning to relax and to think about Sophie, who always waited up so that she could read to her, when suddenly those high headlights were glaring through her rear windshield and blinding her once again. If anything, they were even closer to her than before.

She slowed down, he slowed down. She accelerated, he accelerated. She tried to think what she could do next, and began waving frantically at passing motorists as they sped by, but they remained oblivious to her predicament. She tried to think of other ways she might alert someone, and suddenly recalled that when she had joined the board of the company they had suggested she have a car phone installed. Diana had decided it could wait until the car went in for its next service, which should have been two weeks ago.

She brushed her hand across her forehead and removed a film of perspiration, thought for a moment, then maneuvered her car into the fast lane. The van swung across after her and hovered so close to her bumper that she became fearful that if she so much as touched her brakes she might unwittingly cause an enormous pile-up.

Diana took the car up to ninety, but the van wouldn't be shaken off. She pushed her foot further down on the accelerator and touched a hundred, but it still remained less than a car's length behind.

She flicked her headlights onto high, turned on her hazard lights, and blasted her horn at anyone who dared to remain in her path. She could only hope that the police might see her, wave her onto the hard shoulder, and book her for speeding. A fine would be infinitely preferable to a crash with a young tearaway, she thought, as the Audi suburban passed 110 for the first time in its life. But the black van couldn't be shaken off.

Without warning, she swerved back into the middle lane and took her foot off the accelerator, causing the van to pull up with her, which gave her a chance to look at the driver for the first time. He was wearing a black leather jacket and pointing menacingly at her. She shook her fist at him and accelerated away, but he simply swung across behind her like an Olympic runner determined not to allow his rival to break clear.

And then she remembered, and felt sick for a second time that night. "Oh my God!" she shouted aloud in terror. In a flood, the details of the murder that had taken place on the same road a few months before came rushing back to her. A woman had been raped before having her throat cut with a knife with a serrated edge and dumped in a ditch. For weeks there had been signs posted on the A1 appealing to passing motorists to phone a certain number if they had any information that might assist the police with their investigation. The signs had now disappeared, but the police were still searching for the killer. Diana began to tremble as she remembered their warning to all women drivers: "Never stop on the freeway."

A few seconds later she saw a road sign she knew well. She had reached it far sooner than she had anticipated. In three miles she would have to leave the motorway for the side road that led to the farm. She began to pray that if she took her usual turn, the black-jacketed man would continue up the A1 and she would finally be rid of him.

Diana decided that the time had come for her to speed him on his way. She swung back into the fast lane and once again put her foot down on the accelerator. She reached a hundred miles per hour for the second time as she sped past the two-mile sign. Her body was now covered in sweat, and the speedometer touched 110. She checked her rearview mirror, but he was still right behind her. She would have to pick the exact moment if she was to execute her plan successfully. With a mile to go, she began to look to her left, to be sure her timing would be perfect. She no longer needed to check in her mirror to know that he would still be there.

The next signpost showed three diagonal white lines, warning her that she ought to be on the inside lane if she intended to leave the freeway at the next junction. She kept the car in the outside lane at a hundred miles per hour until she spotted a large enough gap. Two white lines appeared by the roadside: Diana knew she would have only one chance to make her escape. As she passed the sign with a single white line on it, she suddenly swung across the road at ninety miles per hour, causing cars in the middle and inside lanes to throw on their brakes and blast out their angry opinions. But Diana didn't care what they thought of her, because she was now traveling down the side road to safety, and the black van was speeding on up the A1.

She laughed out loud with relief. To her right, she could see the steady flow of traffic on the motorway. But then her laugh turned to a scream as she saw the black van cut sharply across the freeway in front of a truck, mount the grass verge, and career onto the side road, swinging from side to side. It nearly drove over the edge and into a ditch but somehow managed to steady itself, ending up a few yards behind her, its lights once again glaring through her rear windshield.

When she reached the beginning of the side road, Diana turned left in the direction of the farm, frantically trying to work out what she should do next. The nearest town was about twelve miles away on the main road, and the farm was only seven, but five of those miles were down a winding unlit country lane. She checked her gas gauge. It was nearing empty, but there should still be enough in the tank for her to consider either option. There was less than a mile to go before she reached the turn, so she had only a minute in which to make up her mind.

With a hundred yards to go, she settled on the farm. Despite the unlit lane, she knew every twist and turn, and she felt confident that her pursuer wouldn't. Once she reached the farm she could be out of the car and inside the house long before he

could catch her. In any case, once he saw the farmhouse, surely he would flee.

The minute was up. Diana touched the brakes and skidded into a country road illuminated only by the moon.

Diana banged the palms of her hands on the steering wheel. Had she made the wrong decision? She glanced up at her rearview mirror. Had he given up? Of course he hadn't. The back of a Land Rover loomed up in front of her. Diana slowed down, waiting for a corner she knew well, where the road widened slightly. She held her breath, crashed into third gear, and overtook. Would a head-on collision be preferable to a cut throat? She rounded the bend and saw an empty road ahead of her. Once again she pressed her foot down, this time managing to put a clear seventy, perhaps even a hundred, yards between her and her pursuer, but this only offered her a few moments' respite. Before long the familiar headlights came bearing down on her once again.

With each bend Diana was able to gain a little time as the van continued to lurch from side to side, unfamiliar with the road, but she never managed a clear break of more than a few seconds. She checked the speedometer. From the turnoff on the main road to the farm was just over five miles, and she must have covered about two by now. She began to watch each tenth of a mile clicking up, terrified at the thought of the van overtaking her and forcing her into the ditch. She stuck determinedly to the center of the road.

Another mile passed, and still he clung to her. Suddenly she saw a car coming toward her. She switched her headlights to full and pressed on the horn. The other car retaliated by mimicking her actions, which caused her to slow down and brush against the hedgerow as they shot past each other. She checked the speedometer once again. Only two miles to go.

Diana would slow down and then speed up at each familiar bend in the road, making sure the van was never given enough room to pull up with her. She tried to concentrate on what she should do once the farmhouse came into sight. She reckoned that the drive leading up to the house must be about half a mile long. It was full of potholes and bumps that Daniel had

often explained he couldn't afford to have repaired. But at least it was only wide enough for one car.

The gate to the driveway was usually left open for her, though on the odd rare occasion Daniel had forgotten, and she'd had to get out of the car and open it for herself. She couldn't risk that tonight. If the gate was closed, she would have to travel on to the next town and stop outside the Crimson Kipper, which was always crowded at this time on a Friday night, or, if she could find it, at the steps of the local police station. She checked her gas gauge again. It was now touching red. "Oh my God," she said, realizing she might not have enough gas to reach the town.

She could only pray that Daniel had remembered to leave the gate open.

She swerved out of the next bend and speeded up, but once again she managed to gain only a few yards, and she knew that within seconds he would be back in place. He was. For the next few hundred yards they remained within feet of each other, and she felt certain he had to run into the back of her. She didn't once dare to touch her brakes—if they crashed in that lane, far from any help, she would have no hope of getting away from him.

She checked her speedometer. A mile to go.

"The gate must be open. It *must* be open," she prayed. As she swung around the next bend, she could make out the outline of the farmhouse in the distance. She almost screamed with relief when she saw that the lights were on in the downstairs rooms.

She shouted, "Thank God!" then remembered the gate again, and changed her plea to "Dear God, let it be open." She would know what needed to be done as soon as she came around the last bend. "Let it be open, just this once," she pleaded. "I'll never ask for anything again, ever." She swung round the final bend only inches ahead of the black van. "Please, please, please." And then she saw the gate.

It was open.

Her clothes were now drenched in sweat. She slowed down, wrenched the transmission into second, and threw the car

between the gap and into the bumpy driveway, hitting the gatepost on her right-hand side as she careered on up toward the house. The van didn't hesitate to follow her, and was still only inches behind as she straightened out. Diana kept her hand pressed down on the horn as the car bounced and lurched over the mounds and potholes.

Flocks of startled crows flapped out of overhanging branches, screeching as they shot into the air. Diana began screaming, "Daniel! Daniel!" Two hundred yards ahead of her, the porch light went on.

Her headlights were now shining onto the front of the house, and her hand was still pressed on the horn. With a hundred yards to go, she spotted Daniel coming out of the front door, but she didn't slow down, and neither did the van behind her. With fifty yards to go she began flashing her lights at Daniel. She could now make out the puzzled, anxious expression on his face.

With thirty yards to go she threw on her brakes. The heavy car skidded across the gravel in front of the house, coming to a halt in the flower bed just below the kitchen window. She heard the screech of brakes behind her. The leather-jacketed man, unfamiliar with the terrain, had been unable to react quickly enough, and as soon as his wheels touched the graveled forecourt he began to skid out of control. A second later the van came crashing into the back of her car, slamming it against the wall of the house and shattering the glass in the kitchen window.

Diana leaped out of the car screaming, "Daniel! Get a gun, get a gun!" She pointed back at the van. "That bastard's been chasing me for the last twenty miles!"

The man jumped out of the van and began limping toward them. Diana ran into the house. Daniel followed and grabbed a shotgun, normally reserved for rabbits, that was leaning against the wall. He ran back outside to face the unwelcome visitor, who had come to a halt by the back of Diana's Audi.

Daniel raised the shotgun to his shoulder and stared straight at him. "Don't move or I'll shoot," he said calmly. And then he remembered that the gun wasn't loaded. Diana ducked back out of the house but remained several yards behind him.

"Not me! Not me!" shouted the leather-jacketed youth, as Rachael appeared in the doorway.

"What's going on?" she asked nervously.

"Call the police," was all Daniel said, and his wife quickly disappeared back into the house.

Daniel advanced toward the terrified-looking young man, the gun aimed squarely at his chest.

"Not me! Not me!" he shouted again, pointing at the Audi. "He's in the car!" He quickly turned to face Diana. "I saw him get in when you were parked on the hard shoulder. What else could I have done? You just wouldn't pull over."

Daniel advanced cautiously toward the rear door of the car and ordered the young man to open it slowly, while he kept the gun aimed at his chest.

The youth opened the door and quickly took a pace backward. The three of them stared down at a man crouched on the floor of the car. In his right hand he held a long-bladed knife with a serrated edge. Daniel swung the barrel of the gun down to point at him but said nothing.

The sound of a police siren could just be heard in the distance.

OLD LOVE

SOME PEOPLE, IT IS said, fall in love at first sight, but that was not what happened to William Hatchard and Philippa Jameson. They hated each other from the moment they met. This mutual loathing commenced at the first tutorial of their freshman term. Both had arrived in the early thirties with major scholarships to read English language and literature, William at Merton, Philippa at Somerville. Each had been reliably assured by their schoolteachers that they would be the star pupil of their year.

Their tutor, Simon Jakes of New College, was both bemused and amused by the ferocious competition that so quickly developed between his two brightest pupils, and he used their enmity skillully to bring out the best in both of them without ever allowing either to indulge in outright abuse. Philippa, an attractive, slim redhead with a rather high-pitched voice, was the same height as William, so she conducted as many of her arguments as possible standing in newly acquired high-heeled shoes, while William, whose deep voice had an air of authority, would always try to expound his opinions from a sitting position. The more intense their rivalry became, the harder the one tried to outdo the other. By the end of their first year they were far ahead of their contemporaries while remaining neck and neck with each other. Simon Jakes told the Merton professor of Anglo-Saxon Studies that he had never had a brighter pair up in the same year and that it wouldn't be long before they were holding their own with him.

During the long vacation both worked to a grueling timetable, always imagining the other would be doing a little more. They stripped bare Blake, Wordsworth, Coleridge, Shelley, Byron, and went to bed only with Keats. When they returned

13

for the second year, they found that absence had made the heart grow even more hostile; and when they were both awarded A-plus for their essays on *Beowulf*, it didn't help. Simon Jakes remarked at New College high table one night that if Philippa Jameson had been born a boy, some of his tutorials would undoubtedly have ended in blows.

"Why don't you separate them?" asked the warden sleepily.

"What, and double my workload?" said Jakes. "They teach each other most of the time: I merely act as referee."

Occasionally the adversaries would seek his adjudication as to who was ahead of whom, and so confident was each of being the favored pupil that one would always ask in the other's hearing. Jakes was far too canny to be drawn; instead he would remind them that the examiners would be the final arbiters. So they began their own subterfuge by referring to each other, just within earshot, as "that silly woman" and "that arrogant man." By the end of their second year they were almost unable to remain in the same room together.

In the long vacation William took a passing interest in Al Jolson and a girl called Ruby, while Philippa flirted with the Charleston and a young naval lieutenant from Dartmouth. But when the term started in earnest these interludes were never admitted and soon forgotten.

At the beginning of their third year they both, on Simon Jakes's advice, applied for the Charles Oldham Shakespeare prize along with every other student in the year who was considered likely to gain a first. The Charles Oldham was awarded for an essay on a set aspect of Shakespeare's work, and Philippa and William both realized that this would be the only time in their academic lives that they would be tested against each other in closed competition. Surreptitiously, they worked their separate ways through the entire Shakespearean canon, from *Henry VI* to *Henry VIII*, and kept Jakes well beyond his appointed tutorial hours, demanding more and more refined discussion of more and more obscure points.

The chosen theme for the prize essay that year was "Satire in Shakespeare." *Troilus and Cressida* clearly called for the most attention, but both found there were nuances in virtually every one of the bard's thirty-seven plays. "Not to mention a gross of sonnets," wrote Philippa home to her father in a rare moment of self-doubt. As the year drew to a close it became obvious to all concerned that either William or Philippa had to win the prize while the other would undoubtedly come in second. Nevertheless no one was willing to venture an opinion as to who the victor would be. The New College porter, an expert in these matters, taking his usual bets for the Charles Oldham, made them both evens, ten to one against the rest of the field.

Before the prize essay submission date, they both had to take their final degree examinations. Philippa and William confronted the examination papers every morning and afternoon for two weeks with an appetite that bordered on the vulgar. It came as no surprise to anyone that they both achieved first-class degrees in the final honors school. Rumor spread around the university that the two rivals had been awarded As in every one of their nine papers.

"I would be willing to believe that is the case," Philippa told William. "But I feel I must point out to you that there is a considerable difference between an A-plus and an A-minus."

"I couldn't agree with you *more*," said William. "And when you discover who has won the Charles Oldham, you will know who was awarded *less*."

With only three weeks left before the prize essay had to be handed in, they both worked twelve hours a day, falling asleep over open textbooks, dreaming that the other was still beavering away. When the appointed hour came, they met in the marble-floored entrance hall of the Examination Schools, somber in the gloom.

"Good morning, William, I do hope your efforts will manage to secure a place in the first six."

"Thank you, Philippa. If they don't I shall look for the names C. S. Lewis, Nichol Smith, Nevil Coghill, Edmund Blunden, R. W. Chambers, and H. W. Garrard ahead of me. There's certainly no one else in the field to worry about."

"I am only pleased," said Philippa, as if she had not heard his reply, "that you were not seated next to me when I wrote my essay, thus ensuring for the first time in three years that you weren't able to copy from my notes."

"The only item I have ever copied from you, Philippa, was the Oxford-to-London timetable, and that I discovered later to be out-of-date, which was in keeping with the rest of your efforts."

They both handed in their twenty-five-thousand-word essays to the collector's office in the Examination Schools and left without a further word, returning to their respective colleges impatiently to await the result.

William tried to relax the weekend after submitting his essay, and for the first time in three years he played some tennis, against a girl from St. Anne's, failing to win a game, let alone a set. He nearly sank when he went swimming, and actually did so when punting. He was only relieved that Philippa had not been witness to any of his feeble physical efforts.

On Monday night after a resplendent dinner with the warden of Merton, he decided to take a walk along the banks of the Cherwell to clear his head before going to bed. The May evening was still light as he made his way down through the narrow confines of Merton Wall, across the meadows to the banks of the Cherwell. As he strolled along the winding path, he thought he spied his rival ahead of him under a tree, reading. He considered turning back but decided she might already have spotted him, so he kept on walking.

He had not seen Philippa for three days, although she had rarely been out of his thoughts: Once he had won the Charles Oldham, the silly woman would have to climb down from that high horse of hers. He smiled at the thought and decided to walk nonchalantly past her. As he drew nearer, he lifted his eyes from the path in front of him to steal a quick glance in her direction, and could feel himself reddening in anticipation of her inevitable well-timed insult. Nothing happened, so he looked more carefully, only to discover on closer inspection that she was not reading: Her head was bowed in her hands, and she appeared to be sobbing quietly. He slowed his progress to observe not the formidable rival who had for three years dogged his every step, but a forlorn and lonely creature who looked somewhat helpless.

William's first reaction was to think that the winner of the prize essay competition had been leaked to her and that he had indeed achieved his victory. On reflection, he realized that could not be the case: the examiners would only have received the essays that morning and since all the assessors read each submission, the results could not possibly be forthcoming until at least the end of the week. Philippa did not look up when he reached her side—he was even unsure whether she was aware of his presence. As he stopped to gaze at his adversary William could not help noticing how her long red hair curled just as it touched the shoulder. He sat down beside her, but still she did not stir.

"What's the matter?" he asked. "Is there anything I can do?"

She raised her head, revealing a face flushed from crying.

"No, nothing, William, except leave me alone. You deprive me of solitude without affording me company."

William was pleased that he immediately recognized the little literary allusion. "What's the matter, Madame de Sévigné?" he asked, more out of curiosity than concern, torn between sympathy and pleasure at catching her with her guard down.

It seemed a long time before she replied.

"My father died this morning," she said finally, as if speaking to herself.

It struck William as strange that after three years of seeing Philippa almost every day, he knew nothing about her home life.

"And your mother?" he said.

"She died when I was three. I don't even remember her. My father is—" she paused "—was a parish priest and brought me up, sacrificing everything he had to get me to Oxford, even the family silver. I wanted so much to win the Charles Oldham for him."

William put his arm tentatively on Philippa's shoulder.

"Don't be absurd. When you win the prize, they'll pronounce you the star pupil of the decade. After all, you will have had to beat me to achieve the distinction."

She tried to laugh. "Of course I wanted to beat you, William, but only for my father."

"How did he die?"

"Cancer, only he never let me know. He asked me not to go home before the summer term as he felt the break might interfere with my finals and the Charles Oldham. While all the time he must have been keeping me away because he knew if I saw the state he was in, that would have been the end of my completing any serious work."

"Where do you live?" asked William, again surprised that he did not know.

"Brockenhurst. In Hampshire. I'm going back there tomorrow morning. The funeral's on Wednesday."

"May I take you?" asked William.

Philippa looked up and was aware of a softness in her adversary's eyes that she had not seen before. "That would be kind, William."

"Come on then, you silly woman," he said. "I'll walk you back to your college."

"Last time you called me 'silly woman' you meant it."

William found it natural that they should hold hands as they walked along the riverbank. Neither spoke until they reached Somerville.

"What time shall I pick you up?" he asked, not letting go of her hand.

"I didn't know you had a car."

"My father presented me with an old MG when I was awarded a first. I have been longing to find some excuse to show the damn thing off to you. It has push-button ignition, you know."

"Obviously he didn't want to risk waiting to give you the car on the Charles Oldham results." William laughed more heartily than the little dig merited.

"Sorry," she said. "Put it down to habit. I shall look forward to seeing if you drive as appallingly as you write, in which case the journey may never come to any conclusion. I'll be ready for you at ten."

On the journey down to Hampshire, Philippa talked about

her father's work as a parish priest and inquired after William's family. They stopped for lunch at a pub in Winchester—rabbit stew and mashed potatoes.

"The first meal we've had together," said William.

No sardonic reply came flying back; Philippa simply smiled.

After lunch they traveled on to the village of Brockenhurst. William brought his car to an uncertain halt on the gravel outside the vicarage. An elderly maid, dressed in black, answered the door, surprised to see Miss Philippa with a man. Philippa introduced Annie to William and asked her to make up the spare room.

"I'm so glad you've found yourself such a nice young man," remarked Annie later. "Have you known him long?"

Philippa smiled. "No, we met for the first time yesterday."

Philippa cooked William dinner, which they ate by a fire he had laid in the front room. Although hardly a word passed between them for three hours, neither was bored. Philippa began to notice the way William's untidy fair hair fell over his forehead and thought how distinguished he would look in old age.

The next morning, she walked into the church on William's arm and stood bravely through the funeral. When the service was over William took her back to the vicarage, crowded with the many friends the parson had made.

"You mustn't think ill of us," said Mr. Crump, the vicar's warden, to Philippa. "You were everything to your father, and we were all under strict instructions not to let you know about his illness in case it should interfere with the Charles Oldham. That is the name of the prize, isn't it?"

"Yes," said Philippa. "But that all seems so unimportant now."

"She will win the prize in her father's memory," said William.

Philippa turned and looked at him, realizing for the first time that he actually wanted her to win the Charles Oldham.

They stayed that night at the vicarage and drove back to Oxford on the Thursday. On the Friday morning at ten o'clock William returned to Philippa's college and asked the porter if he could speak to Miss Jameson.

"Would you be kind enough to wait in the Horsebox, sir,"

said the porter as he showed William into a little room at the back of the lodge and then scurried off to find Miss Jameson. They returned together a few minutes later.

"What on earth are you doing here?"

"Come to take you to Stratford."

"But I haven't even had time to unpack the things I brought back from Brockenhurst."

"Just do as you are told for once; I'll give you fifteen minutes."

"Of course," she said. "Who am I to disobey the next winner of the Charles Oldham? I shall even allow you to come up to my room for one minute and help me unpack."

The porter's eyebrows nudged the edge of his cap, but he remained silent, in deference to Miss Jameson's recent bereavement. Again it surprised William to think that he had never been to Philippa's room during their three years. He had climbed the walls of all the women's colleges to be with a variety of girls of varying stupidity but never with Philippa. He sat down on the end of the bed.

"Not there, you thoughtless creature. The maid has only just made it. Men are all the same, you never sit in chairs."

"I shall one day," said William. "The chair of English Language and Literature."

"Not as long as I'm at this university, you won't," she said, as she disappeared into the bathroom.

"Good intentions are one thing but talent is quite another," he shouted at her retreating back, privately pleased that her competitive streak seemed to be returning.

Fifteen minutes later she came out of the bathroom in a yellow flowered dress with a neat white collar and matching cuffs. William thought she might even be wearing a touch of makeup.

"It will do our reputations no good to be seen together," she said.

"I've thought about that," said William. "If asked, I shall say you're my charity."

"Your charity?"

"Yes. This year I'm supporting distressed orphans."

Philippa signed out of college until midnight, and the two

scholars traveled down to Stratford, stopping off at Broadway for lunch. In the afternoon they rowed on the River Avon. William warned Philippa about his last disastrous outing in a punt. She admitted that she had already heard of the exhibition he had made of himself, but they arrived safely back at the shore: perhaps because Philippa took over the rowing. They went to see John Gielgud playing Romeo and dined at the Dirty Duck. Philippa was even quite rude to William during the meal.

They started their journey home just after eleven, and Philippa fell into a half sleep since they could hardly hear each other above the noise of the car engine. It must have been about twenty-five miles outside Oxford that the MG came to a halt.

"I thought," said William, "that when the gas gauge showed empty there was at least another gallon left in the tank."

"You're obviously wrong, and not for the first time, and because of such foresight you'll have to walk to the nearest garage all by yourself—you needn't imagine that I'm going to keep you company. I intend to stay put, right here in the warmth."

"But there isn't a garage between here and Oxford," protested William.

"Then you'll have to carry me. I am far too fragile to walk."

"I wouldn't be able to manage fifty yards after that sumptuous dinner and all that wine."

"It is no small mystery to me, William, how you could have managed a first-class honors degree in English when you can't even read a gas gauge."

"There's only one thing to do," said William. "We'll have to wait for the first bus in the morning."

Philippa clambered into the backseat and did not speak to him again before falling asleep. William donned his hat, scarf, and gloves, crossed his arms for warmth, and touched the tangled red mane of Philippa's hair as she slept. He then took off his coat and placed it so that it covered her.

Philippa woke first, a little after six, and groaned as she tried to stretch her aching limbs. She then shook William awake to ask him why his father hadn't been considerate enough to buy him a car with a comfortable backseat.

"But this is the niftiest thing going," said William, gingerly kneading his neck muscles before putting his coat back on.

"But it isn't going, and won't without gas," she replied, getting out of the car to stretch her legs.

"But I only let it run out for one reason," said William following her to the front of the car.

Philippa waited for a feeble punch line and was not disappointed.

"My father told me if I spent the night with a barmaid then I should simply order an extra pint of beer, but if I spent the night with the vicar's daughter, I would have to marry her."

Philippa laughed. William, tired, unshaven, and encumbered by his heavy coat, struggled to get down on one knee.

"What are you doing, William?"

"What do you think I'm doing, you silly woman? I am going to ask you to marry me."

"An invitation I am happy to decline, William. If I accepted such a proposal I might end up spending the rest of my life stranded on the road between Oxford and Stratford."

"Will you marry me if I win the Charles Oldham?"

"As there is absolutely no fear of that happening I can safely say yes. Now do get off your knee, William, before someone mistakes you for a straying stork."

The first bus arrived at 7:05 that Saturday morning and took Philippa and William back to Oxford. Philippa went to her rooms for a long hot bath while William filled a gas can and returned to his deserted MG. Having completed the task, he drove straight to Somerville and once again asked if he could see Miss Jameson. She came down a few minutes later.

"What! You again?" she said. "Am I not in enough trouble already?"

"Why so?"'

"Because I was out after midnight, unaccompanied."

"You were accompanied."

"Yes, and that's what's worrying them."

"Did you tell them we spent the night together?'

"No, I did not. I don't mind our contemporaries thinking I'm promiscuous, but I have strong objections to their believing that I have no taste. Now kindly go away, as I am contemplating the horror of your winning the Charles Oldham and my having to spend the rest of my life with you."

"You know I'm bound to win, so why don't you come live with me now?"

"I realize that it has become fashionable to sleep with just anyone nowadays, William, but if this is to be my last weekend of freedom I intend to savor it, especially since I may have to consider committing suicide."

"I love you."

"For the last time, William, go away. And if you haven't won the Charles Oldham don't ever show your face in Somerville again."

William left, desperate to know the result of the prize essay competition. Had he realized how much Philippa wanted him to win, he might have slept that night.

On Monday morning they both arrived early in the Examination Schools and stood waiting impatiently without speaking to each other, jostled by the other undergraduates of their year who had also been entered for the prize. On the stroke of ten the chairman of the examiners, in full academic dress, walking at a tortoiselike pace, arrived in the great hall and with a considerable pretense of indifference pinned a notice to the board. All the undergraduates who had entered for the prize rushed forward except for William and Philippa, who stood alone, aware that it was now too late to influence a result they were both dreading.

A girl shot out from the melee around the bulletin board and ran over to Philippa.

"Well done, Phil. You've won."

Tears came to Philippa's eyes as she turned toward William.

"May I add my congratulations," he said quickly. "You obviously deserved the prize."

"I wanted to say something to you on Saturday."

"You did. You said if I lost I must never show my face in Somerville again."

"No. I wanted to say: 'I do love nothing in the world so well as you; is not that strange?'"

He looked at her silently for a long moment. It was impossible to improve upon Beatrice's reply: "'As strange as the thing I know not,'" he said softly.

A college friend slapped him on the shoulder, took his hand, and shook it vigorously. *Proxime accessit* was obviously impressive in some people's eyes, if not in William's.

"Well done, William."

"Second place is not worthy of praise," said William disdainfully.

"But you won, Billy boy."

Philippa and William stared at each other.

"What do you mean?" said William.

"Exactly what I said. You've won the Charles Oldham."

Philippa and William ran to the board and studied the notice:

CHARLES OLDHAM MEMORIAL PRIZE
THE EXAMINERS FELT UNABLE ON THIS OCCASION TO AWARD THE
PRIZE TO ONE PERSON AND HAVE THEREFORE DECIDED THAT IT
SHOULD BE SHARED BY . . .

They gazed at the bulletin board in silence for some moments. Finally, Philippa bit her lip and said in a small voice: "Well, you didn't do too badly, considering the competition. I'm prepared to honor my undertaking, 'but, by this light, I take thee for pity.'"

William needed no prompting. "'I would not deny you; but, by this good day, I yield upon great persuasion, . . . for I was told you were in a consumption.'"

And to the delight of their peers and the amazement of the retreating don, they embraced under the bulletin board.

Rumor had it that from that moment on they were never apart for more than a few hours.

The marriage took place a month later in Philippa's family church at Brockenhurst. "Well, when you think about it," said William's roommate, "who else could she have married?" The contentious couple started their honeymoon in Athens arguing about the relative significance of Doric and Ionic architecture, of which neither knew any more than they had covertly read in a cheap tourist guidebook. They sailed on to Istanbul, where William prostrated himself at the front of every mosque he could find while Philippa stood on her own at the back fuming at the Turks' treatment of women.

"The Turks are a shrewd race," declared William. "So quick to appreciate real worth."

"Then why don't you embrace the Muslim religion, William, and I need only be in your presence once a year?"

"The misfortune of birth, a misplaced loyalty, and the signing of an unfortunate contract dictate that I spend the rest of my life with you."

Back at Oxford, with junior research fellowships at their respective colleges, they settled down to serious creative work. William embarked upon a massive study of word usage in Marlowe and, in his spare moments, taught himself statistics to assist his findings. Philippa chose as her subject the influence of the Reformation on seventeenth-century English writers and was soon drawn beyond literature into art and music. She bought herself a spinet and took to playing Dowland and Gibbons in the evening.

"For Christ's sake," said William, exasperated by the tinny sound. "You won't deduce their religious convictions from their key signatures."

"More informative than ifs and ands, my dear," she said, imperturbably, "and at night so much more relaxing than pots and pans."

Three years later, with well-received Ph.D.'s, they moved on, inexorably in tandem, to college teaching fellowships. As the long shadow of fascism fell across Europe, they read, wrote, criticized, and coached by quiet firesides in unchanging quadrangles.

"A rather dull Schools year for me," said William, "but I still managed five firsts from a field of eleven."

"An even duller one for me," said Philippa, "but somehow I squeezed three firsts out of six, and you won't have to invoke the binomial theorem, William, to work out that it's an arithmetical victory for me."

"The chairman of the examiners tells me," said William, "that a greater part of what your pupils say is no more than a recitation from memory."

"He told me," she retorted, "that yours have to make it up as they go along."

When they dined together in college, the guest list was always quickly filled, and as soon as grace had been said, the sharpness of their dialogue would flash across the candelabra.

"I hear a rumor, Philippa, that the college doesn't feel able to renew your fellowship at the end of the year?"

"I fear you speak the truth, William," she replied. "They decided they couldn't renew mine at the same time as offering me yours."

"Do you think they will ever make you a fellow of the British Academy, William?"

"I must say, with some considerable disappointment, never."

"I am sorry to hear that. Why not?"

"Because when they did invite me, I informed the president that I would prefer to wait to be elected at the same time as my wife."

Some nonuniversity guests sitting at high table for the first time took their verbal battles seriously; others could only be envious of such love.

One fellow uncharitably suggested they rehearsed their lines before coming to dinner for fear it might be thought they were getting on well together. During their early years as young dons, they became acknowledged as the leaders in their respective fields. Like magnets, they attracted the brightest undergraduates while apparently remaining poles apart themselves.

"Dr. Hatchard will be delivering half these lectures," Philippa announced at the start of the Michaelmas term of their joint lecture course on Arthurian legend. "But I can assure you it will not be the better half. You would be wise always to check which Dr. Hatchard is lecturing."

When Philippa was invited to give a series of lectures at Yale, William took a sabbatical so that he could be with her.

On the ship crossing the Atlantic, Philippa said, "Let's at least be thankful the journey is by sea, my dear, so we can't run out of gas."

"Rather let us thank God," replied William, "that the ship has an engine, because you would even take the wind out of Cunard's sails."

The only sadness in their lives was that Philippa could bear William no children, but if anything it drew the two closer together. Philippa lavished quasi-maternal affection on her tutorial pupils and allowed herself only the wry comment that she was spared the probability of producing a child with William's looks and William's brains.

At the outbreak of war William's expertise with handling words made a move into code-breaking inevitable. He was recruited by an anonymous gentleman who visited them at home with a briefcase chained to his wrist. Philippa listened shamelessly at the keyhole while they discussed the problems they had come up against and burst into the room and demanded to be recruited as well.

"Do you realize that I can complete *The Times* crossword puzzle in half the time my husband can?"

The anonymous man was only thankful that he wasn't chained to Philippa. He drafted them both to the Admiralty section to deal with encrypted wireless messages to and from German submarines.

The German signal manual was a four-letter codebook, and each message was recrypted, the substitution table changing daily. William taught Philippa how to evaluate letter frequencies, and she applied her new knowledge to modern German texts, coming up with a frequency analysis that was soon used by every code-breaking department in the Commonwealth.

Even so breaking the ciphers and building up the master signal book was a colossal task, which took them the best part of two years.

"I never knew your ifs and ands could be so informative," she said admiringly of her own work.

When the Allies invaded Europe, husband and wife could

together often break ciphers with no more than half a dozen lines of encrypted text to go on.

"They're an illiterate lot," grumbled William. "They don't encipher their umlauts. They deserve to be misunderstood."

"How can you give an opinion when you never dot your i's, William?"

"Because I consider the dot is redundant, and I hope to be responsible for removing it from the English language."

"Is that to be your major contribution to scholarship, William? If so I am bound to ask how anyone reading the essays of most of our undergraduates would be able to tell the difference between an *I* and an *i*."

"A feeble argument, my dear, which, if it had any conviction, would demand that you put a dot on top of an *n* so as to be sure it wasn't mistaken for an *h*."

"Keep working away at your theories, William, because I intend to spend my energy removing more than the dot and the *I* from Hitler."

In May 1945 they dined privately with Prime Minister and Mrs. Churchill at 10 Downing Street.

"What did the prime minister mean when he said to me that he could never understand what you were up to?" asked Philippa in the taxi to Paddington Station.

"The same as when he said to me that he knew exactly what you were capable of, I suppose," said William.

When the Merton professor of English retired in the early 1950s the whole university waited to see which Doctor Hatchard would be appointed to the chair.

"If the council invites you to take the chair," said William, putting his hand through his graying hair, "it will be because they are going to make me vice-chancellor."

"The only way you could ever be invited to hold a position so far beyond your ability would be nepotism, which would mean I was already vice-chancellor."

The general board, after several hours' discussion of the problem, offered two chairs and appointed William and Philippa full professors on the same day.

When the vice-chancellor was asked why precedent had been broken, he replied: "Simple. If I hadn't given them both a chair, one of them would have been after my job."

That night, after a celebration dinner, when they were walking home together along the banks of the Isis across Christ Church Meadows, in the midst a particularly heated argument about the quality of the last volume of Proust's monumental work, a policeman, noticing the affray, ran over to them and asked:

"Is everything all right, madam?'

"No, it is not," William interjected. "This woman has been attacking me for over thirty years, and to date the police have done deplorably little to protect me."

In the late fifties Harold Macmillan invited Philippa to join the board of the Independent Broadcasting Authority.

"I suppose you'll become what's known as a telly don," said William. "And as the average mental age of those who watch the box is seven you should feel quite at home."

"Agreed," said Philippa. "Twenty years of living with you has made me fully qualified to deal with infants."

The chairman of the BBC wrote to William a few weeks later inviting him to join its board of governors.

"Are you to replace *Hancock's Half Hour* or *Dick Barton, Special Agent*?" Philippa inquired.

"I am to give a series of twelve lectures."

"On what subject, pray?"

"Genius."

Philippa flicked through the *Radio Times*. "I see that *Genius* is to be broadcast at two o'clock on a Sunday morning, which is understandable, as that's when you are at your most brilliant."

When William was awarded an honorary doctorate at Princeton, Philippa attended the ceremony and sat proudly in the front row.

"I tried to secure a place in the back," she explained, "but it was filled with sleeping students who had obviously never heard of you."

"If that's the case, Philippa, I am only surprised you didn't mistake them for one of your tutorial lectures."

As the years went on, many anecdotes, only some of which were apocryphal, passed into the Oxford fabric. Everyone in the English school knew the stories about the "fighting Hatchards": how they spent their first night together, how they jointly won the Charles Oldham, how Phil would complete *The Times* crossword before Bill had finished shaving, how each had both been appointed to a professorial chair on the same day, and how they both worked longer hours than any of their contemporaries, as if they still had something to prove, if only to each other. It seemed almost required by the laws of symmetry that they should always be judged equals—until it was announced in the New Year's Honours that Philippa had been made a Dame of the British Empire.

"At least our dear queen has worked out which one of us is truly worthy of recognition," she said over the college dessert.

"Our dear queen," said William, selecting the Madeira, "knows only too well how little competition there is in the women's colleges: Sometimes one must encourage weaker candidates in the hope that it might inspire some real talent lower down."

After that, whenever they attended a public function together, Philippa would have the MC announce them as "Professor William and Dame Philippa Hatchard." She looked forward to many happy years of starting every official occasion one up on her husband, but her triumph lasted for only six months: William received a knighthood in the Queen's Birthday Honours. Philippa feigned surprise at the dear queen's uncharacteristic lapse of judgment and forthwith insisted on their being introduced in public as Sir William and Dame Philippa Hatchard.

"Understandable," said William. "The queen had to make you a dame first in order that no one should mistake you for a lady. When I married you, Philippa, you were a young fellow, and now I find I'm living with an old dame."

"It's no wonder," said Philippa, "that your poor pupils can't make up their minds whether you're homosexual or you simply have a mother fixation. Be thankful that I did not accept Girton's invitation: Then you would have been married to a mistress."

"I always have been, you silly woman."

As the years passed, they never let up their pretended belief in the other's mental feebleness. Philippa's books, "works of considerable distinction," she insisted, were published by Oxford University Press, while William's, "works of monumental significance," he declared, were printed at the presses of Cambridge University.

The tally of newly appointed professors of English they had taught as undergraduates soon reached double digits.

"If you count polytechnics, I shall have to throw in Maguire's readership in Kenya," said William.

"You did not teach the professor of English at Nairobi," said Philippa. "I did. You taught the head of state, which may well account for why the university is so highly thought of while the country is in such disarray."

In the early sixties they conducted a battle of letters in the *TLS* on the works of Philip Sidney without ever discussing the subject in each other's presence. In the end the editor said the correspondence must stop and adjudicated a draw.

They both declared him an idiot.

If there was one act that annoyed William in old age about Philippa, it was her continued determination each morning to complete *The Times* crossword before he arrived at the breakfast table. For a time, William ordered two copies of the paper until Philippa filled them both in while explaining to him it was a waste of money.

One particular morning in June at the end of their final academic year before retirement, William came down to breakfast to find only one space in the crossword left for him to complete. He studied the clue: "Skelton reported that this landed in the soup." He immediately filled in the eight little boxes.

Philippa looked over his shoulder. "There's no such word, you arrogant man," she said firmly. "You made it up to annoy me." She placed in front of him a very hard-boiled egg.

"Of course there is, you silly woman; look 'whymwham' up in the dictionary."

Philippa checked in the *Shorter Oxford* among the cookbooks in the kitchen, and trumpeted her delight that it was nowhere to be found.

"My dear Dame Philippa," said William, as if he were addressing a particularly stupid pupil, "you surely cannot imagine because you are old and your hair has become very white that you are a sage. You must understand that the *Shorter Oxford Dictionary* was cobbled together for simpletons whose command of the English language stretches to no more than one hundred thousand words. When I go to college this morning I shall confirm the existence of the word in the on my desk. Need I remind you that the *OED* is a serious work which, with over five hundred thousand words, was designed for scholars like myself?"

"Rubbish," said Philippa. "When I am proved right, you will repeat this story word for word, including your offensive non-word, at Somerville's Gaudy Feast."

"And you, my dear, will read the Collected Works of John Skelton and eat humble pie as your first course."

"We'll ask old Onions along to adjudicate."

"Agreed."

"Agreed."

With that, Sir William picked up his paper, kissed his wife on the cheek, and said with an exaggerated sigh, "It's at times like this that I wish I'd lost the Charles Oldham."

"You did, my dear. It was in the days when it wasn't fashionable to admit a woman had won anything."

"You won me."

"Yes, you arrogant man, but I was led to believe you were one of those prizes one could return at the end of the year. And now I find I shall have to keep you, even in retirement."

"Let us leave it to the *Oxford English Dictionary*, my dear, to decide the issue the Charles Oldham examiners were unable to determine," and with that he departed for his college.

"There's no such word," Philippa muttered as he closed the front door.

Heart attacks are known to be rarer among women than men. When Dame Philippa suffered hers in the kitchen that morning she collapsed on the floor calling hoarsely for William, but he was already out of earshot. It was the cleaning woman who found Dame Philippa on the kitchen floor and ran to fetch someone in authority. The bursar's first reaction was that she was probably pretending that Sir William had hit her with a frying pan, but nevertheless she hurried over to the Hatchards' house in Little Jericho just in case. The bursar checked Dame Philippa's pulse and called for the college doctor and then the principal. Both arrived within minutes.

The principal and the bursar stood waiting by the side of their illustrious academic colleague, but they already knew what the doctor was going to say.

"She's dead," he confirmed. "It must have been very sudden and with the minimum of pain." He checked his watch; the time was 9:47. He covered his patient with a blanket and called for an ambulance. He had taken care of Dame Philippa for over thirty years and he had told her so often to slow down that he might as well have made a record of it for all the notice she took.

"Who will tell Sir William?" asked the principal. The three of them looked at one another.

"I will," said the doctor.

It's a short walk from Little Jericho to Radcliffe Square. It was a long walk from Little Jericho to Radcliffe Square for the doctor that day. He never relished telling anyone of the death of a spouse, but this one was going to be the unhappiest of his career.

When he knocked on the professor's door, Sir William bade him enter. The great man was sitting at his desk poring over the *Oxford Dictionary*, humming to himself.

"I told her, but she wouldn't listen, the silly woman," he was saying to himself, and then he turned and saw the doctor standing silently in the doorway. "Doctor, you must be my guest at Somerville's Gaudy next Thursday week, where Dame Philippa will be eating humble pie. It will be nothing less than game, set, match and championship for me. A vindication of thirty years' scholarship."

The doctor did not smile, nor did he stir. Sir William walked over to him and gazed at his old friend intently. No words were necessary. The doctor said only, "I'm more sorry than I am able to express," and he left Sir William to his private grief.

Sir William's colleagues all knew within the hour. College lunch that day was spent in a silence broken only by the senior tutor inquiring of the warden if some food should be taken up to the Merton professor.

"I think not," said the warden. Nothing more was said.

Professors, fellows, and students alike crossed the front quadrangle in silence, and when they gathered for dinner that evening still no one felt like conversation. At the end of the meal the senior tutor suggested once again that something should be taken up to Sir William. This time the warden nodded his agreement, and a light meal was prepared by the college chef. The warden and the senior tutor climbed the worn stone steps to Sir William's room, and while one held the tray the other gently knocked on the door. There was no reply, so the warden, used to William's ways, pushed the door ajar and looked in.

The old man lay motionless on the wooden floor in a pool of blood, a small pistol by his side. The two men walked in and stared down. In his right hand, William was holding *The Collected Works of John Skelton*. The book was opened at "The Tunnyng of Elynour Rummyng," and the word *whymwham* was underlined.

> After the Sarasyns gyse,
> Woth a whymwham,
> Knyt with a trym tram,
> Upon her brayne pan.

Sir William, in his neat hand, had written a note in the margin: "Forgive me, but I had to let her know."

"Know what, I wonder?" said the warden softly to himself as he attempted to remove the book from Sir William's hand, but the fingers were already stiff and cold around it.

Legend has it that they were never apart for more than a few hours.

SHOESHINE BOY

TED BARKER WAS ONE of those members of Parliament who never sought high office. He'd had what was described by his fellow officers as a "good war"—in which he was awarded the Military Cross and reached the rank of major. After being demobilized in November 1945, he was happy to return to his wife, Hazel, and their home in Suffolk.

The family engineering business had also had a good war, under the diligent management of Ted's older brother, Ken. As soon as he arrived home, Ted was offered his old place on the board, which he happily accepted. But as the weeks passed by, the distinguished warrior became first bored and then disenchanted. There was no job for him at the factory that even remotely resembled active service.

It was around this time that he was approached by Ethel Thompson, the shop steward and—more important for the advancement of this tale—chairman of the Wedmore branch of the North Suffolk Conservative Association. The incumbent MP, Sir Dingle Lightfoot, known in the constituency as "Tiptoe," had made it clear that once the war was over they must look for someone to replace him.

"We don't want some clever clogs from London coming up here and telling us how to run this division," pronounced Mrs. Thompson. "We need someone who knows the district and understands the problems of the local people." Ted, she suggested, might be just right.

Ted confessed that he had never given such an idea a moment's thought, but promised Mrs. Thompson that he would take her proposal seriously, only asking for a week in which to consider his decision. He discussed the suggestion with his wife, and, having received her enthusiastic support, he paid a visit to Mrs. Thompson at her home the following Sunday afternoon. She was delighted to hear that Mr. Barker would be pleased to allow his name to go forward for consideration as the prospective parliamentary candidate for the division of North Suffolk.

The final shortlist included two "clever clogs" from London—one of whom later served in a Macmillan cabinet—and the local boy, Ted Barker. When the chairman announced the committee's decision to the local press, he said that it would be improper to reveal the number of votes each candidate had polled. In fact, Ted had comfortably outscored his two rivals put together.

Six months later the prime minister called a general election, and after a lively three-week campaign, Ted was elected as the member of Parliament for North Suffolk with a majority of more than seven thousand. He quickly became respected and popular with colleagues on both sides of the House, though he never pretended to be anything other than, in his own words, "an amateur politician."

As the years passed, Ted's popularity with his constituents grew, and he increased his majority with each succeeding general election. After fourteen years of diligent service to the party nationally and locally, the prime minister of the day, Harold Macmillan, recommended to the Queen that Ted should receive a knighthood.

By the end of the 1960s, Sir Ted (he was never known as Sir Edward) felt that the time was fast approaching when the division should start looking for a younger candidate, and he made it clear to the local chairman that he did not intend to run in the next election. He and Hazel quietly prepared for a peaceful retirement in their beloved East Anglia.

Shortly after the election, Ted was surprised to receive a call from 10 Downing Street: "The prime minister would like to see Sir Ted at 11:30 tomorrow morning."

Ted couldn't imagine why Edward Heath should want to see him. Although he had of course visited Number 10 on several occasions when he was a member of Parliament, those visits had only been for cocktail parties, receptions, and the occasional dinner for a visiting head of state. He admitted to Hazel that he was a little nervous.

Ted presented himself at the front door of Number 10 at 11:17 the next day. The duty clerk accompanied him down the long corridor on the ground floor and asked him to take a seat in the small waiting area that adjoins the Cabinet Room. By now Ted's nervousness was turning to apprehension. He felt like an errant schoolboy about to come face to face with his headmaster.

After a few minutes a private secretary appeared. "Good morning, Sir Ted. The prime minister will see you now." He accompanied Ted into the Cabinet Room, where Mr. Heath stood to greet him. "How kind of you to come at such short notice, Ted." Ted had to suppress a smile, because he knew the prime minister knew that it would have taken the scurvy or a local hurricane to stop him from answering such a summons.

"I'm hoping you can help me with a delicate matter, Ted," continued the prime minister, a man not known for wasting time on smalltalk. "I'm about to appoint the next governor of St. George's, and I can't think of anyone better qualified for the job than you."

Ted recalled the day when Mrs. Thompson had asked him to think about running for Parliament. But on this occasion he didn't require a week to consider his reply—even if he couldn't quite bring himself to admit that although he'd heard of St. George's, he certainly couldn't have located it on a map. Once he'd caught his breath, he simply said, "Thank you, Prime Minister. I'd be honored."

During the weeks that followed Sir Ted paid several visits to the Foreign and Colonial Offices to receive briefings on various aspects of his appointment. Thereafter he assiduously read every book, pamphlet, and government paper the mandarins supplied.

After a few weeks of boning up on his new subject, the governor-in-waiting had discovered that St. George's was a tiny group of islands in the middle of the North Atlantic. It had been colonized by the British in 1643, and thereafter had a long history of imperial rule, the islanders having scorned every offer of independence. They were one of Her Majesty's sovereign colonies, and that was how they wished to remain.

Even before he set out on his adventure, Ted had become used to being addressed as "Your Excellency." But after being fitted up by Alan Bennett of Savile Row with two different full-dress uniforms, Ted feared that he looked—what was that modern expression?—"over the top." In winter he was expected to wear an outfit of dark blue doeskin with scarlet collar and cuffs embroidered with silver oakleaves, while in the summer he was to be adorned in white cotton drill with a gold-embroidered collar and gold shoulder cords. The sight of him in either uniform caused Hazel to laugh out loud.

Ted didn't laugh when the tailors sent him the bill, especially after he learned that he would be unlikely to wear either uniform more than twice a year. "Still, think what a hit you'll be at fancy dress parties once you've retired," was Hazel's only comment.

The newly appointed governor and commander in chief of St. George's and his lady flew out to take up their post on January 12, 1971. They were greeted by the prime minister, as the colony's first citizen, and the chief justice, as the legal representative of the queen. After the new governor had taken the salute from six off-duty policemen standing vaguely to attention, the town band gave a rendering of the national anthem. The Union Jack was raised on the roof of the airport terminal, and a light smattering of applause broke out among the assembled gathering of twenty or thirty local dignitaries.

Sir Ted and Lady Barker were then driven to the official residence in a spacious but aging Rover that had already served the two previous governors. When they reached Government House, the driver brought the car to a halt and leaped out to open the gates. As they continued up the drive, Ted and Hazel saw their new home for the first time.

The colonial mansion was magnificent by any standards. Obviously built at the height of the British Empire, it was vastly out of proportion to either the importance of the island or

Britain's current position in the real world. But size, as the governor and his wife were quickly to discover, didn't necessarily equate with efficiency or comfort.

The air-conditioning didn't work, the plumbing was unreliable, Mrs. Rogers, the daily maid, was regularly out sick, and the only thing Ted's predecessor had left behind was an elderly black Labrador. Worse, the Foreign Office had no funds available to deal with any of these problems, and whenever Ted mentioned them in dispatches, he was met only with suggestions for cutbacks.

After a few weeks, Ted and Hazel began to think of St. George's as being rather like a great big parliamentary constituency, split into several islands, the two largest being Suffolk and Edward Islands. This heartened Ted, who even wondered if that was what had given the prime minister the idea of offering him the post in the first place.

The governor's duties could hardly have been described as onerous: He and Hazel spent most of their time visiting hospitals, delivering speeches at school prize-givings and judging flower shows. The highlight of the year was undoubtedly the queen's official birthday in June, when the governor held a garden party for local dignitaries at Government House and Suffolk played Edward Island at cricket—an opportunity for most of the colony's citizens to spend two days getting thoroughly drunk.

Ted and Hazel accepted the local realpolitik and settled down for five years of relaxed diplomacy among delightful people in a heavenly climate, seeing no cloud on the horizon that could disturb their blissful existence.

Until the phone call came.

It was a Thursday morning, and the governor was in his study with that Monday's *Times*. He was putting off reading a long article on the summit meeting taking place in Washington until he had finished the crossword, and was just about to fill in the answer to 12 across—"Erring herd twists to create this diversion (3,7)"—when his private secretary, Charles Roberts, came rushing into his office without knocking.

Ted realized it had to be something important, because he

had never known Charles to rush anywhere, and certainly he had never known him to enter the study without the courtesy of a knock.

"It's Mountbatten on the line," Charles blurted out. He could hardly have looked more anxious had he been reporting that the Germans were about to land on the north shore of the island. The governor raised an eyebrow. "Admiral of the Fleet Earl Mountbatten of Burma," said Charles, as if Ted hadn't understood.

"Then put him through," said Ted quietly, folding up his copy of *The Times* and placing it on the desk in front of him. He had met Mountbatten three times over the past twenty years but doubted if the great man would recall any of these encounters. Indeed, on the third occasion Ted had found it necessary to slip out of the function the admiral was addressing, as he was feeling a little queasy. He couldn't imagine what Mountbatten would want to speak to him about, and he had no time to consider the problem, as the phone on his desk was already ringing.

As Ted picked up the receiver he was still wondering whether to call Mountbatten "My Lord" since he was an earl, "Commander in Chief," since he was a former chief of the Defense Staff, or "Admiral," since Admiral of the Fleet is a life appointment. He settled for "Good morning, sir."

"Good morning, Your Excellency. I hope I find you well?"

"Yes, thank you, sir," replied Ted.

"Because if I remember correctly, when we last met you were suffering from a tummy bug."

"That's right, sir," said the surprised governor. He was reasonably confident that the purpose of Mountbatten's call wasn't to inquire about his health after all these years.

"Governor, you must be curious to know why I am calling."

"Yes, sir."

"I am presently in Washington attending the summit, and I had originally planned to return to London tomorrow morning."

"I understand, sir," said Ted, not understanding at all.

"But I thought I might make a slight detour and drop in to see you. I do enjoy visiting our colonies whenever I get the

41

chance. It gives me the opportunity to brief Her Majesty on what's happening. I hope that such a visit would not be inconvenient."

"Not at all, sir," said Ted. "We would be delighted to welcome you."

"Good," said Mountbatten. "Then I would be obliged if you could warn the airport authorities to expect my aircraft around four tomorrow afternoon. I would like to stay overnight, but if I'm to keep to my schedule I will need to leave you fairly early the following morning."

"Of course, sir. Nothing could be easier. My wife and I will be at the airport to welcome you at four o'clock tomorrow afternoon."

"That's kind of you, Governor. By the way, I'd rather things were left fairly informal. Please don't put yourself to any trouble." The line went dead.

Once he had replaced the receiver, it was Ted's turn to run for the first time in several months. He found Charles striding down the long corridor toward him, having obviously listened in on the extension.

"Find my wife and get yourself a notepad—and then both of you join me in my office immediately. Immediately," Ted repeated as he scuttled back into his study.

Hazel arrived a few minutes later, clutching a bunch of dahlias, followed by the breathless private secretary.

"Why the rush, Ted? What's the panic?"

"Mountbatten's coming."

"When?" Hazel asked quietly.

"Tomorrow afternoon. Four o'clock."

"That is a good reason to panic," Hazel admitted. She dumped the flowers in a vase on the windowsill and took a seat opposite her husband on the other side of his desk. "Perhaps this isn't the best time to let you know that Mrs. Rogers is out sick."

"You have to admire her timing," said Ted. "Right, we'll just have to bluff it."

"What *do* you mean, 'bluff it'?" asked Hazel.

"Well, let's not forget that Mountbatten's a member of the

royal family, a former chief of the Defense Staff, and an Admiral of the Fleet. The last colonial post he held was Viceroy of India, with three regiments under his command and a personal staff of over a thousand. So I can't imagine what he'll expect to find when he turns up here."

"Then let's begin by making a list of things that will have to be done," said Hazel briskly.

Charles removed a pen from his inside pocket, turned over the cover of his pad, and waited to write down his master's instructions.

"If he's arriving at the airport, the first thing he will expect is a red carpet," said Hazel.

"But we don't have a red carpet," said Ted.

"Yes, we do. There's the one that leads from the dining room to the drawing room. We'll have to use that, and hope we can get it back in place before he visits that part of the house. Charles, you will have to roll it up and take it to the airport—" she paused "—and then bring it back."

Charles scowled, but began writing furiously.

"And Charles, can you also see that it's cleaned by tomorrow?" interjected the governor. "I hadn't even realized it was red. Now, what about an honor guard?"

"We haven't got an honor guard," said Hazel. "If you remember, when we arrived on the island we were met by the prime minister, the chief justice, and six off-duty policemen."

"True," said Ted. "Then we'll just have to rely on the Territorial Army."

"You mean Colonel Hodges and his band of hopeful warriors? They don't even all have matching uniforms. And as for their rifles . . . "

"Hodges will just have to get them into some sort of shape by four o'clock tomorrow afternoon. Leave that one to me," said Ted, making a note on his pad. "I'll phone him later this morning. Now, what about a band?"

"Well there's the town band," said Charles. "And, of course, the police band."

"On this occasion they'll have to combine," said Hazel, "so we don't offend either of them."

43

"But they only know three tunes between them," said Ted.

"They only need to know one," said Hazel. "The national anthem."

"Right," said the governor. "Since there are sure to be a lot of musical feathers that will need unruffling, I'll leave you to deal with them, Hazel. Our next problem is how we transport him from the airport to Government House."

"Certainly not in the old Rover," said Hazel. "It's broken down three times in the last month, and it smells like a kennel."

"Henry Bendall has a Rolls-Royce," said Ted. "We'll just have to commandeer that."

"As long as no one tells Mountbatten that it's owned by the local undertaker, and what it was used for the morning before he arrived."

"Mick Flaherty also has an old Rolls," piped up Charles. "A Silver Shadow, if I remember correctly."

"But he loathes the British," said Hazel.

"Agreed," said Ted, "but he'll still want to have dinner at Government House when he discovers the guest of honor is a member of the royal family."

"Dinner?" said Hazel, her voice rising in horror.

"Of course we will have to give a dinner in his honor," said Ted. "And, worse, everyone who is anyone will expect to be invited. How many can the dining room hold?" He and Hazel turned to the private secretary.

"Sixty, if pushed," replied Charles, looking up from his notes.

"We're pushed," said Ted.

"We certainly are," said Hazel. "Because we don't have sixty plates, let alone sixty coffee cups, sixty teaspoons, sixty . . . "

"We still have that Royal Worcester service presented by the late king after his visit in 1947," said Ted. "How many pieces of that are fit for use?"

"Enough for about fourteen settings, at the last count," said Hazel.

"Right, then that's dealt with how many people will be at the top table."

"What about the menu?" asked Charles.

"And, more important, who is going to cook it?" added Ted.

"We'll have to ask Dotty Cuthbert if she can spare Mrs. Travis for the evening," said Hazel. "No one on the island is a better cook."

"And we'll also need her butler, not to mention the rest of her staff," added Ted.

By now Charles was on his third page.

"You'd better deal with Lady Cuthbert, my dear," said Ted. "I'll try to square Mick Flaherty."

"Our next problem will be the drinks," said Hazel. "Don't forget, the last governor emptied the cellar a few days before he left."

"And the Foreign Office refuses to restock it," Ted reminded her. "Jonathan Fletcher has the best cellar on the island . . . "

"And, God bless him, he won't expect to be at the top table," said Hazel.

"If we're limited to fourteen places, the top table's looking awfully crowded already," said Ted.

"Dotty Cuthbert, the Bendalls, the Flahertys, the Hodgeses," said Hazel, writing down the names. "Not to mention the prime minister, the chief justice, the mayor, the chief of police, plus their wives—let's hope that some of them are indisposed or abroad." She was beginning to sound desperate.

"Where's he going to sleep?" asked Charles innocently.

"God, I hadn't thought of him sleeping," said Ted.

"He'll have to take our bedroom. It's the only one with a bed that doesn't sink in the middle," said Hazel.

"We'll move into the Nelson Room for the night, and suffer those dreadful woodwormed beds and their ancient horsehair mattresses."

"Agreed," said Hazel. "I'll make sure all our things are out of the Queen Victoria Room by this evening."

"And Charles," said the governor, "phone the Foreign Office, would you, and find out Mountbatten's likes and dislikes. Food, drink, eccentric habits—anything you can discover. They're sure to have a file on him, and this is one gentleman I don't want to catch me making a mistake."

The private secretary turned over yet another page of his pad, and continued scribbling.

For the next hour, the three of them went over any and every problem that might arise during the visit, and after a sandwich lunch, departed in their different directions to spend the afternoon making begging calls all around the island.

It was Charles's idea that the governor should appear on the local television station's early-evening news, to let the citizens know that a member of the royal family would be visiting the island the following day. Sir Ted ended his broadcast by saying that he hoped as many people as possible would be at the airport to welcome "the great war leader" when his plane touched down at four the following afternoon.

While Hazel spent the evening cleaning every room the great war leader might conceivably enter, Charles, with the aid of a flashlight, tended to the flower beds that lined the driveway, and Ted supervised the shuttling of plates, cutlery, food, and wine from different parts of the island to Government House.

"Now, what have we forgotten?" said Ted, as he climbed into bed at two o'clock that morning.

"Heaven only knows," Hazel said wearily before turning out the light. "But whatever it is, let's hope Mountbatten never finds out."

The governor, dressed in his summer uniform, with gold piping down the sides of his white trousers, decorations and campaign medals across his chest, and an old-fashioned Wolseley helmet with a plume of red-over-white swan's feathers on his head, walked out onto the landing to join his wife. Hazel was wearing the green summer frock she had bought for the governor's garden party two years earlier, and was checking the flowers in the entrance hall.

"Too late for that," said Ted, as she rearranged a sprig that had strayed half an inch. "It's time we left for the airport."

They descended the steps of Government House to find two Rolls-Royces, one black, one white, and their old Rover standing in line. Charles followed closely behind them, carrying the red carpet, which he dropped into the trunk of the Rover as his master stepped into the back of the leading Rolls-Royce.

The first thing the governor needed to check was the chauffeur's name.

"Bill Simmons," he was informed.

"All you have to remember, Bill, is to look as if you've been doing this job all your life."

"Right, Guv."

"No," said Ted firmly. "In front of the admiral, you must address me as 'Your Excellency,' and Lord Mountbatten as 'My Lord.' If in any doubt, say nothing."

"Right, Guv, Your Excellency."

Bill started the car and drove toward the gates at what he evidently considered was a stately pace, before turning right and taking the road to the airport. When they reached the terminal fifteen minutes later a policeman ushered the tiny motorcade out onto the tarmac, where the combined bands were playing a medley from *West Side Story*—at least, that was what Ted charitably thought it might be.

As he stepped out of the car Ted came face to face with three ranks of soldiers from the Territorial Army standing at ease, sixty-one of them, aged from seventeen to seventy. Ted had to admit that, although they weren't the Grenadier Guards, they weren't like something from TV's "Dad's Army" either. And they had two advantages: a real-live colonel in full-dress uniform, and a genuine sergeant-major, with a voice to match.

Charles had already begun rolling out the red carpet when the governor turned his attention to the hastily erected barriers, behind which he was delighted to see a larger crowd than he had ever witnessed on the island, even at the annual football derby between Suffolk and Edward Islands.

Many of the islanders were waving Union Jacks, and some were holding up pictures of the queen. Ted smiled and checked his watch. The plane was due in seventeen minutes.

The prime minister, the local mayor, the chief justice, the commissioner of police, and their wives were lining up at the end of the red carpet. The sun beat down from a cloudless sky. As Ted turned in a slow circle to take in the scene, he could see for himself that everyone had made a special effort.

Suddenly the sound of engines could be heard, and the crowd began to cheer. Ted looked up, shielded his eyes, and saw an Andover of the Queen's Flight descending toward the airport. It touched down on the far end of the runway at three minutes before the hour, and taxied up to the red carpet as four chimes struck on the clock above the flight control tower.

The door of the plane opened, and there stood Admiral of the Fleet the Earl Mountbatten of Burma, KG, PC, GCB, OM, GCSI, GCIE, GCVO, DSO, FRS, DCL (Hon.), LL.D. (Hon.), attired in the full dress uniform of an Admiral of the Fleet (summer wear).

"If that's what he means by 'fairly informal,' I suppose we should be thankful that he didn't ask us to lay on an official visit," murmured Hazel as she and Ted walked to the bottom of the steps that had been quickly wheeled into place.

As Mountbatten slowly descended the stairway, the crowd cheered even louder. Once he stepped onto the red carpet the governor took a pace forward, removed his plumed hat, and bowed. The admiral saluted, and at that moment the combined bands of town and police struck up the national anthem. The crowd sang "God Save the Queen" so lustily that the occasional uncertain note was smothered by their exuberance.

When the anthem came to an end, the governor said, "Welcome to St. George's, sir."

"Thank you, Governor," replied Mountbatten.

"May I present my wife, Hazel." The governor's wife took a pace forward, did a full curtsey, and shook hands with the admiral.

"How good to see you again, Lady Barker. This is indeed a pleasure."

The governor guided his guest to the end of the red carpet and introduced him to the prime minister and his wife, Sheila; the local mayor and his wife, Caroline; the chief justice and his wife, Janet; and the commissioner of police and his latest wife, whose name he couldn't remember.

"Perhaps you'd care to inspect the honor guard before we leave for Government House," suggested Ted, steering Mountbatten in the direction of Colonel Hodges and his men.

"Absolutely delighted," said the admiral, waving to the crowd as the two of them proceeded across the tarmac toward the waiting guard. When they still had some twenty yards to go, the colonel sprang to attention, took three paces forward, saluted and said crisply, "Honor guard ready for inspection, sir."

Mountbatten came to a halt and returned a naval salute, which was a sign for the sergeant major, standing at attention six paces behind his colonel, to bellow out the words: "Commanding officer on parade! General salute, pre–sent arms!"

The front row, in possession of the unit's entire supply of weapons, presented arms, while the second and third rows came rigidly to attention.

Mountbatten marched dutifully up and down the ranks, as gravely as if he were inspecting a full brigade of Life Guards. When he had passed the last soldier in the back row, the colonel came to attention and saluted once again. Mountbatten returned the salute and said, "Thank you, Colonel. First-class effort. Well done."

The governor then guided Mountbatten toward the white Rolls-Royce, where Bill was standing at what he imagined was attention, while at the same time holding open the back door. Mountbatten stepped in as the governor hurried round to the other side, opened the door for himself, and joined his guest on the back seat. Hazel and the admiral's ADC took their places in the black Rolls-Royce, while Charles and the admiral's secretary had to make do with the Rover. The governor only hoped that Mountbatten hadn't seen two members of the airport staff rolling up the red carpet and placing it in the Rover's trunk. Hazel was only praying that they had enough sheets left over for the bed in the Green Room. If not, the ADC would be wondering about their sleeping habits.

The island's two police motorcycles, with white-uniformed outriders, preceded the three cars as they made their way towards the exit. The crowd waved and cheered lustily as the motorcade began its short journey to Government House. So successful had Ted's television appearance the previous evening been that the ten-mile route was lined with well-wishers.

As they approached the open gates two policemen sprang to

attention and saluted as the leading car passed through. In the distance Ted could see a butler, two underbutlers, and several maids, all smartly clad, standing on the steps awaiting their arrival. "Damn it," he almost said aloud as the car came to a halt at the bottom of the steps. "I don't know the butler's name."

The car door was smartly opened by one of the underbutlers while the second supervised the unloading of the luggage from the boot.

The butler took a pace forward as Mountbatten stepped out of the car. "Carruthers, M'lord," he said, bowing. "Welcome to the residence. If you would be kind enough to follow me, I will direct you to your quarters." The admiral, accompanied by the governor and Lady Barker, climbed the steps into Government House and followed Carruthers up the main staircase.

"Magnificent, these old government residences," said Mountbatten as they reached the top of the stairs. Carruthers opened the door to the Queen Victoria Room and stood to one side, as if he had done so a thousand times before.

"How charming," said the admiral, taking in the governor's private suite. He walked over to the window and looked out onto the newly mowed lawn. "How very pleasant. It reminds me of Broadlands, my home in Hampshire."

Lady Barker smiled at the compliment but didn't allow herself to relax.

"Is there anything you require, M'lord?' asked Carruthers, as an under-butler began to supervise the unpacking of the cases.

Hazel held her breath.

"No, I don't think so," said Mountbatten. "Everything looks just perfect."

"Perhaps you'd care to join Hazel and me for tea in the drawing room when you're ready, sir," suggested Ted.

"How thoughtful of you," said the admiral. "I'll be down in about thirty minutes, if I may."

The governor and his wife left the room, closing the door quietly behind them.

"I think he suspects something," whispered Hazel as they tiptoed down the staircase.

"You may be right," said Ted, placing his plumed hat on the

stand in the hall, "but that's all the more reason to check we haven't forgotten anything. I'll start with the dining room. You ought to go and see how Mrs. Travis is getting on in the kitchen."

When Hazel entered the kitchen she found Mrs. Travis preparing the vegetables, and one of the maids peeling a mound of potatoes. She thanked Mrs. Travis for taking over at such short notice, and admitted she had never seen the kitchen so full of exotic foods, or the surfaces so immaculately clean. Even the floor was spotless. Realizing that her presence was superfluous, Hazel joined her husband in the dining room, where she found him admiring the expertise of the second underbutler, who was laying out the place settings for that evening, as a maid folded napkins to look like swans.

"So far, so good," said Hazel. They left the dining room and entered the drawing room, where Ted paced up and down, trying to think if there was anything he had forgotten while they waited for the great man to join them for tea.

A few minutes later, Mountbatten walked in. He was no longer dressed in his admiral's uniform but had changed into a dark gray double-breasted suit.

"Damn it," thought Ted, immediately aware of what he'd forgotten to do.

Hazel rose to greet her guest and guided him to a large, comfortable chair.

"I must say, Lady Barker, your butler is a splendid chap," said Mountbatten. "He even knew the brand of whiskey I prefer. How long have you had him?"

"Not very long," admitted Hazel.

"Well, if he ever wants a job in England, don't hesitate to let me know—though I'm bound to say you'd be a fool to part with him," he added, as a maid came in carrying a beautiful Wedgwood tea service Hazel had never set eyes on before.

"Earl Grey, if I remember correctly," said Hazel.

"What a memory you have, Lady Barker," said the admiral, as the maid began to pour.

"Thank God for the Foreign Office briefing," Hazel thought, as she accepted the compliment with a smile.

"And how did the conference go, sir?' asked Ted, as he dropped a lump of sugar—the one thing he felt might be their own—into his cup of tea.

"For the British, quite well," said Mountbatten. "But it would have gone better if the French hadn't been up to their usual tricks. Giscard seems to regard himself as a cross between Charlemagne and Joan of Arc." His hosts laughed politely. "No, the real problem we're facing at the moment, Ted, is quite simply . . . "

By the time Mountbatten had dealt with the outcome of the summit, given his undiluted views of James Callaghan and Ted Heath, covered the problem of finding a wife for Prince Charles and mulled over the long-term repercussions of Watergate, it was almost time for him to change.

"Are we dressing for dinner?"

"Yes, sir—if that meets with your approval."

"Full decorations?" Mountbatten asked, sounding hopeful.

"I thought that would be appropriate, sir," replied Ted, remembering the Foreign Office's advice about the Admiral's liking for dressing up at the slightest opportunity.

Mountbatten smiled as Carruthers appeared silently at the door. Ted raised an eyebrow.

"I have laid out the full dress uniform, M'lord. I took the liberty of pressing the trousers. The bedroom maid is drawing a bath for you."

Mountbatten smiled. "Thank you," he said as he rose from his chair. "Such a splendid tea," he added turning to face his hostess. "And such wonderful staff. Hazel, I don't know how you do it."

"Thank you, sir," said Hazel, trying not to blush.

"What time would you like me to come down for dinner, Ted?" Mountbatten asked.

"The first guests should be arriving for drinks at about 7:30, sir. We were hoping to serve dinner at eight, if that's convenient for you."

"Couldn't be better," declared Mountbatten. "How many are you expecting?"

"Around sixty, sir. You'll find a guest list on your bedside table. Perhaps Hazel and I could come and fetch you at 7:50?"

"You run a tight ship, Ted," said Mountbatten with approval. "You'll find me ready the moment you appear," he added as he followed Carruthers out of the room.

Once the door was closed behind him, Hazel said to the maid, "Molly, can you clear away the tea things, please?" She hesitated for a moment. "It is Molly, isn't it?"

"Yes, ma'am," said the girl.

"I think he knows," said Ted, looking a little anxious.

"Maybe, but we haven't time to worry about that now," said Hazel, already on her way to carry out a further inspection of the kitchen.

The mound of potatoes had diminished to a peeled heap. Mrs. Travis, who was preparing the sauces, was calling for more pepper and for some spices to be fetched from a shop in town. Aware once again that she wasn't needed in the kitchen, Hazel moved on to the dining room, where she found Ted. The top table was now fully laid with the King's dinner service, three sets of wine glasses, crested linen napkins, and a glorious centerpiece of a silver pheasant, which gave added sparkle.

"Who lent us that?" she asked.

"I have no idea," replied Ted. "But one thing's for certain—it will have flown home by the morning."

"If we keep the lighting low enough," whispered Hazel, "he might not notice that the other tables all have different cutlery."

"Heavens, just look at the time," said Ted.

They left the dining room and walked quickly up the stairs. Ted nearly barged straight into Mountbatten's room, but remembered just in time.

The governor rather liked his dark blue doeskin uniform with the scarlet collar and cuffs. He was admiring the ensemble in the mirror when Hazel entered the room in a pink Hardy Amies outfit, which she had originally thought a waste of money because she never expected it to be given a proper outing.

"Men are so vain," she remarked as her husband continued to inspect himself in the mirror. "You do realize you're only meant to wear that in winter."

"I am well aware of that," said Ted peevishly, "but it's the only other uniform I've got. In any case, I bet Mountbatten will outdo us both." He flicked a piece of fluff from his trousers, which he had just finished pressing.

The governor and his wife left the Nelson Room and walked down the main staircase just before 7:20, to find yet another under-butler stationed by the front door, and two more maids standing opposite him carrying silver trays laden with glasses of champagne. Hazel introduced herself to the three of them, and again checked the flowers in the entrance hall.

As 7:30 struck on the long-case clock in the lobby the first guest walked in.

"Henry," said the governor. "Lovely to see you. Thank you so much for the use of the Rolls. And Bill, come to that," he added in a stage whisper.

"My pleasure, Your Excellency," Henry Bendall replied. "I must say, I like the uniform."

Lady Cuthbert came bustling through the front door. "Can't stop," she said. "Ignore me. Just pretend I'm not here."

"Dotty, I simply don't know what we would have done without you," Hazel said, chasing after her across the hall.

"Delighted to lend a hand," said Lady Cuthbert. "I thought I'd come bang on time, so I could spend a few minutes in the kitchen with Mrs. Travis. By the way, Benson is standing out in the drive, ready to rush home if you find you're still short of anything."

"You are a saint, Dotty. I'll take you through . . ."

"No, don't worry," said Lady Cuthbert. "I know my way around. You just carry on greeting your guests."

"Good evening, Mr. Mayor," said Ted, as Lady Cuthbert disappeared in the direction of the kitchen.

"Good evening, Your Excellency. How kind of you to invite us to such an auspicious occasion."

"And what a lovely dress, Mrs. Janson," said the governor.

"Thank you, Your Excellency," said the Mayor's wife.

"Would you care for a glass of champagne?" said Hazel as she arrived back at her husband's side.

By 7:45 most of the guests had arrived, and Ted was chatting to Mick Flaherty when Hazel touched him on the elbow. He glanced toward her.

"I think we should go and fetch him now," she whispered.

Ted nodded, and asked the chief justice to take over the welcoming of the guests. They wove a path through the chattering throng, and climbed the great staircase. When they reached the door of the Queen Victoria Room, they paused and looked at each other.

Ted checked his watch—7:50. He leaned forward and gave a gentle tap. Carruthers immediately opened the door to reveal Mountbatten attired in his third outfit of the day: full ceremonial uniform of an Admiral of the Fleet, three stars, a gold and blue sash and eight rows of campaign decorations.

"Good evening, Your Excellency," said Mountbatten.

"Good evening, sir," said the governor, star struck.

The Admiral took three paces forward and came to a halt at the top of the staircase. He stood to attention. Ted and Hazel waited on either side of him. As he didn't move, they didn't.

Carruthers proceeded slowly down the stairs in front of them, stopping on the third step. He cleared his throat and waited for the assembled guests to fall silent.

"Your Excellency, Prime Minister, Mr. Mayor, ladies and gentlemen," he announced. "The Right Honorable the Earl Mountbatten of Burma."

Mountbatten descended the stairs slowly as the waiting guests applauded politely. As he passed Carruthers, the butler gave a deep bow. The governor, with Hazel on his arm, followed two paces behind.

"He must know," whispered Hazel.

"You may be right. But does he know we know?" said Ted.

Mountbatten moved deftly around the room, as Ted introduced him to each of the guests in turn. They bowed and curtsied, listening attentively to the few words the admiral had to say to them. The one exception was Mick Flaherty, who didn't stop talking, and remained more upright than Ted had ever seen him before.

At eight o'clock one of the under-butlers banged a gong, which until then neither the governor nor his wife had even realized existed. As the sound died away, Carruthers announced, "My Lord, Your Excellency, Prime Minister, Mr. Mayor, ladies and gentlemen, dinner is served."

If there was a better cook on St. George's than Mrs. Travis, no one at the top table had ever been fed by her, and that evening she had excelled herself.

Mountbatten chatted and smiled, making no secret of how much he was enjoying himself. He spent a long time talking to Lady Cuthbert, whose husband had served under him at Portsmouth, and to Mick Flaherty, to whom he listened with polite interest.

Each course surpassed the one before: soufflé, followed by lamb cutlets, and an apricot hazelnut meringue to complete the feast. Mountbatten remarked on every one of the wines, and even called for a second glass of port.

After dinner, he joined the guests for coffee in the drawing room, and managed to have a word with everyone, even though Colonel Hodges tried to buttonhole him about defense cuts.

The guests began to leave a few minutes before midnight, and Ted was amused to see that when Mick Flaherty bade farewell to the Admiral, he bowed low and said, "Good night, My Lord. It has been an honor to meet you."

Dotty was among the last to depart, and she curtsied low to the guest of honor. "You've helped to make this such a pleasant evening, Lady Cuthbert," Mountbatten told her.

"If you only knew just how much," thought Hazel.

After the under-butler had closed the door on the last guest, Mountbatten turned to his hostess and said, "Hazel, I must thank you for a truly memorable occasion. The head chef at the Savoy couldn't have produced a finer banquet. Perfect in every part."

"You are very kind, sir. I will pass your thanks on to the staff." She just stopped herself from saying "my staff." "Is there anything else we can do for you before you retire?"

"No, thank you," Mountbatten replied. "It has been a long day, and with your permission, I'll turn in now."

"And at what time would you like breakfast, sir?" asked the governor.

"Would 7:30 be convenient?" Mountbatten asked. "That will give me time to fly out at nine."

"Certainly," said Ted. "I'll see that Carruthers brings a light breakfast up to your room at 7:30—unless you'd like something cooked."

"A light breakfast will be just the thing," Mountbatten said. "A perfect evening. Your staff could not have done more, Hazel. Good night, and thank you, my dear."

The Governor bowed and his lady curtsied as the great man ascended the staircase two paces behind Carruthers. When the butler closed the door of the Queen Victoria Room, Ted put his arm around his wife and said, "He knows we know."

"You may be right," said Hazel. "But does he know we know he knows?'

"I'll have to think about that," said Ted.

Arm in arm, they returned to the kitchen, where they found Mrs. Travis packing dishes into a crate under the supervision of Lady Cuthbert, the long lace sleeves of whose evening dress were now firmly rolled up.

"How did you get back in, Dotty?" asked Hazel.

"Just walked round to the back yard and came in the servants' entrance," replied Lady Cuthbert.

"Did you spot anything that went badly wrong?' Hazel asked anxiously.

"I don't think so," replied Lady Cuthbert. "Not unless you count Mick Flaherty failing to get a fourth glass of Muscat de Venise."

"Mrs. Travis," said Ted, "the head chef at the Savoy couldn't have produced a finer banquet. Perfect in every part. I do no more than repeat Lord Mountbatten's exact words."

"Thank you, Your Excellency," said Mrs. Travis. "He's got a big appetite, hasn't he?" she added with a smile.

A moment later, Carruthers entered the kitchen. He checked round the room, which was spotless once again, then turned to Ted and said, "With your permission, sir, we will take our leave."

"Of course," said the governor. "And may I thank you, Carruthers, for the role you and your amazing team have played.

You all did a superb job. Lord Mountbatten never stopped remarking on it."

"His Lordship is most kind, sir. At what time would you like us to return in the morning to prepare and serve his breakfast?"

"Well, he asked for a light breakfast in his room at 7:30."

"Then we will be back by 6:30," said Carruthers.

Hazel opened the kitchen door to let them all out, and they humped crates full of crockery and baskets full of food to the waiting cars. The last person to leave was Dotty, who was clutching the silver pheasant. Hazel kissed her on both cheeks as she departed.

"I don't know how you feel, but I'm exhausted," said Ted, bolting the kitchen door.

Hazel checked her watch. It was seventeen minutes past one.

"Shattered," she admitted. "So, let's try and grab some sleep, because *we'll* also have to be up by seven to make sure everything is ready before he leaves for the airport."

Ted put his arm back around his wife's waist. "A personal triumph for you, my dear."

They strolled into the hall and wearily began to climb the stairs, but didn't utter another word, for fear of disturbing their guest's repose. When they reached the landing, they came to an abrupt halt, and stared down in horror at the sight that greeted them. Three pairs of black leather shoes had been placed neatly in line outside the Queen Victoria Room.

"Now I'm certain he knows," said Hazel.

Ted nodded and, turning to his wife, whispered, "You or me?"

Hazel pointed a finger firmly at her husband. "Definitely you, my dear," she said sweetly, before disappearing in the direction of the Nelson Room.

Ted shrugged his shoulders, picked up the admiral's shoes, and returned downstairs to the kitchen.

His excellency the governor and commander in chief of St. George's spent a considerable time polishing those three pairs of shoes, as he realized that not only must they pass inspection by an Admiral of the Fleet, but they must look as if the job had been carried out by Carruthers.

When Mountbatten returned to the Admiralty in Whitehall the following Monday, he made a full written report on his visit to St George's. Copies were sent to the queen and the foreign secretary.

The Admiral told the story of his visit at a family gathering that Saturday evening at Windsor Castle, and once the laughter had died down, the queen asked him, "When did you first become suspicious?"

"It was Carruthers who gave it away. He knew everything about Sir Ted, except which regiment he had served in. That's just not possible for an old soldier."

The queen had one further question: "Do you think the governor knew you knew?"

"I can't be certain, Lillibet," replied Mountbatten after some thought. "But I intend to leave him in no doubt that I did."

The Foreign Secretary laughed uproariously when he read Mountbatten's report, and appended a note to the last sheet asking for clarification on two points:

A. How can you be certain that the staff who served dinner were not part of the governor's entourage?

B. Do you think Sir Ted knew that you knew?

The admiral replied by return:

A. After dinner, one of the maids asked Lady Barker if she took sugar in her coffee, but a moment later she gave Lady Cuthbert two lumps, without needing to ask.

B. Possibly not. But he certainly will on Christmas Day.

Sir Ted was pleased to receive a Christmas card from Lord Mountbatten, signed, "Best wishes, Dickie. Thank you for a memorable stay." It was accompanied by a gift.

Hazel unwrapped the little parcel to discover a tin of Cherry Blossom shoe polish (black). Her only comment was, "So now we know he knew."

"Agreed," said Ted with a grin. "But did he know we knew he knew? That's what I'd like to know."

CHEAP AT
HALF THE PRICE

WOMEN ARE NATURALLY SUPERIOR to men, and Consuela
Rosenheim was no exception.

Victor Rosenheim, an American banker, was Consuela's third
husband, and the gossip columns on both sides of the Atlantic
were suggesting that, like a chain smoker with cigarettes, the
former Colombian model was already searching for her next
spouse before she had extracted the last gasp from the old one.
Her first two husbands—one an Arab, the other a Jew (Consuela showed no racial prejudice when it came to signing marriage contracts)—had not quite left her in a position that would
guarantee her financial security once her natural beauty had
faded. But two more divorce settlements would sort that out.
With this in mind, Consuela estimated that she only had
another five years before the final vow must be taken.

The Rosenheims flew into London from their home in New
York—or, to be more accurate, from their homes in New York.
Consuela had traveled to the airport by chauffeur-driven car
from their house in the Hamptons, while her husband had
been taken from his Wall Street office in a second chauffeur-
driven car. They met in the Concorde lounge at JFK. When they
had landed at Heathrow another limousine transported them
to the Ritz, where they were escorted to their usual suite without any suggestion of having to sign forms or register.

The purpose of their trip was twofold. Mr. Rosenheim was
hoping to take over a small merchant bank that had not bene-
fited from the recession, while Mrs. Rosenheim intended to
occupy her time looking for a suitable birthday present—for
herself. Despite considerable research I have been unable to

discover exactly which birthday Consuela would officially be celebrating.

After a sleepless night induced by jet lag, Victor Rosenheim was whisked away to an early-morning meeting in the City, while Consuela remained in bed toying with her breakfast. She managed one piece of thin unbuttered toast and a stab at a boiled egg.

Once the breakfast tray had been removed, Consuela made a couple of phone calls to confirm luncheon dates for the two days she would be in London. She then disappeared into the bathroom.

Fifty minutes later she emerged from her suite dressed in a pink Olaganie suit with a dark blue collar, her fair hair bouncing on her shoulders. Few of the men she passed between the elevator and the revolving doors failed to turn their heads, so Consuela judged that the previous fifty minutes had not been wasted. She stepped out of the hotel and into the morning sun to begin her search for the birthday present.

Consuela began her quest in New Bond Street. As in the past, she had no intention of straying more than a few blocks north, south, east, or west from that comforting landmark, while a chauffeur-driven car hovered a few yards behind her.

She spent some time in Asprey's considering the latest slim-line watches, a gold statue of a tiger with jade eyes, and a Fabergé egg, before moving on to Cartier, where she dismissed a crested silver salver, a platinum watch, and a Louis XIV long-case clock. From there she walked another few yards to Tiffany's, which, despite a determined salesman who showed her almost everything the shop had to offer, she still left empty-handed.

Consuela stood on the pavement and checked her watch. It was 12:52, and she had to accept that it had been a fruitless morning. She instructed her chauffeur to drive her to Harry's Bar, where she found Mrs. Stavros Kleanthis waiting for her at their usual table. Consuela greeted her friend with a kiss on both cheeks, and took the seat opposite her.

Mrs. Kleanthis, the wife of a not unknown shipowner—the Greeks preferring one wife and several liaisons—had for the last few minutes been concentrating her attention on the menu to be sure that the restaurant served the few dishes that her latest diet would permit. Between them the two women had read every book that had reached number one on the *New York Times* bestseller list that included the words "youth," "orgasm," "slimming," "fitness," or "immortality" in its title.

"How's Victor?" asked Maria, once she and Consuela had ordered their meals.

Consuela paused to consider her response, and decided on the truth.

"Fast reaching his sell-by date," she replied. "And Stavros?'

"Well past his, I'm afraid," said Maria. "But as I have neither your looks nor your figure, not to mention the fact that I have three teenage children, I don't suppose I'll be returning to the market to select the latest brand."

Consuela smiled as a salade niçoise was placed in front of her.

"So, what brings you to London—other than to have lunch with an old friend?" asked Maria.

"Victor has his eye on another bank," replied Consuela, as if she were discussing a child who collected stamps. "And I'm in search of a suitable birthday present."

"And what are you expecting Victor to come up with this time?" asked Maria. "A house in the country? A thoroughbred racehorse? Or perhaps your own Learjet?"

"None of the above," said Consuela, placing her fork by the half-finished salad. "I need something that can't be bargained over at a future date, so my gift must be one that any court, in any state, will acknowledge is unquestionably mine."

"Have you found anything appropriate yet?" asked Maria.

"Not yet," admitted Consuela. "Asprey's yielded nothing of interest, Cartier's cupboard was almost bare, and the only attractive thing in Tiffany's was the salesman, who was undoubtedly penniless. I shall have to continue my search this afternoon."

The salad plates were deftly removed by a waiter whom Maria considered far too young and far too thin. Another waiter with the same problem poured them both a cup of fresh decaffeinated coffee. Consuela refused the proffered cream and sugar, though her companion was not quite so disciplined.

The two ladies grumbled on about the sacrifices they were having to make because of the recession until they were the only diners left in the room. At this point a fatter waiter presented them with the bill—an extraordinarily long ledger considering that neither of them had ordered a second course, or had requested more than Evian from the wine waiter.

On the pavement of South Audley Street they kissed again on both cheeks before going their separate ways, one to the east and the other to the west.

Consuela climbed into the back of her chauffeur-driven car in order to be returned to New Bond Street, a distance of no more than half a mile.

Once she was back on familiar territory, she began to work her way steadily down the other side of the street, stopping at Bentley's, where it appeared that they hadn't sold anything since last year, and moving rapidly on to Adler, who seemed to be suffering from much the same problem. She cursed the recession once again, and blamed it all on Bill Clinton, who Victor had assured her was the cause of most of the world's current problems.

Consuela was beginning to despair of finding anything worthwhile in Bond Street, and reluctantly began her journey back toward the Ritz, feeling she might even have to consider an expedition to Knightsbridge the following day, when she came to a sudden halt outside the House of Graff. Consuela could not recall the shop from her last visit to London some six months before, and as she knew Bond Street better than she had ever known any of her three husbands, she concluded that it must be a new establishment.

She gazed at the stunning gems in their magnificent settings, heavily protected behind the bulletproof windows. When she reached the third window her mouth opened wide, like a newborn chick demanding to be fed. From that moment she knew that no further excursions would be necessary, for there, hanging around a slender marble neck, was a peerless diamond-and-ruby necklace. She felt that she had seen the magnificent piece of jewelry somewhere before, but she quickly dismissed the thought from her mind and continued to study the exquisitely set rubies surrounded by perfectly cut diamonds, making up a necklace of unparalleled beauty. Without giving a moment's thought to how much the object might cost, Consuela walked slowly toward the thick glass door at the entrance to the shop, and pressed a discreet ivory button on the wall. The House of Graff obviously had no interest in passing trade.

The door was unlocked by a security officer who needed no more than a glance at Mrs. Rosenheim to know that he should usher her quickly through to the inner portals, where a second door was opened and Consuela came face to face with a tall, imposing man in a long black coat and pinstriped trousers.

"Good afternoon, madam," he said, bowing slightly. Consuela noticed that he surreptitiously admired her rings as he did so. "Can I be of assistance?"

Although the room was full of treasures that might in normal circumstances have deserved hours of her attention, Consuela's mind was focused on only one object.

"Yes. I would like to study more closely the diamond-and-ruby necklace on display in the third window."

"Certainly, madam," the manager replied, pulling out a chair for his customer. He nodded almost imperceptibly to an assistant, who silently walked over to the window, unlocked a little door, and extracted the necklace. The manager slipped behind the counter and pressed a concealed button. Four floors above, a slight burr sounded in the private office of Mr. Laurence Graff, warning the proprietor that a customer had inquired about a particularly expensive item, and that he might wish to deal with them personally.

Laurence Graff glanced up at the television screen on the wall to his left, which showed him what was taking place on the ground floor.

"Ah," he said, once he saw the lady in the pink suit seated at the Louis XIV table. "Mrs. Consuela Rosenheim, if I'm not mistaken." Just as the Speaker of the House of Commons can identify every one of its 650 members, so Laurence Graff recognized the 650 customers who might be able to afford the most extravagant of his treasures. He quickly stepped from behind his desk, walked out of his office, and took the waiting elevator to the ground floor.

Meanwhile, the manager had laid out a black velvet cloth on the table in front of Mrs. Rosenheim, and the assistant placed the necklace delicately on top of it. Consuela stared down at the object of her desire, mesmerized.

"Good afternoon, Mrs. Rosenheim," said Laurence Graff as he stepped out of the elevator and walked across the thick pile carpet toward his would-be customer. "How nice to see you again."

He had in truth only seen her once before—at a shoulder-to-shoulder cocktail party in Manhattan. But after that, he could have spotted her at a hundred paces on a moving escalator.

"Good afternoon, Mr. . . . " Consuela hesitated, feeling unsure of herself for the first time that day.

"Laurence Graff," he said, offering his hand. "We met at Sotheby–Parke Bernet last year—a charity function in aid of the Red Cross, if I remember correctly."

"Of course," said Mrs. Rosenheim, unable to recall him, or the occasion.

Mr. Graff bowed reverently toward the diamond-and-ruby necklace.

"The Kanemarra heirloom," he purred, then paused, before taking the manager's place at the table. "Fashioned in 1936 by Silvio di Larchi," he continued. "All the rubies were extracted from a single mine in Burma, over a period of twenty years. The diamonds were purchased from De Beers by an Egyptian merchant who, after the necklace had been made for him, offered the unique piece to King Farouk—for services rendered. When the monarch married Princess Farida, he presented it to her on their wedding day, and she in return bore him four heirs, none of whom, alas, was destined to succeed to the throne." Graff looked up from one object of beauty and gazed on another.

"Since then it has passed through several hands before arriving at the House of Graff," continued the proprietor. "Its most recent owner was an actress, whose husband's oil wells unfortunately dried up."

The flicker of a smile crossed the face of Consuela Rosenheim as she finally recalled where she had previously seen the necklace.

"Quite magnificent," she said, giving it one final look. "I will be back," she added as she rose from her chair. Graff accompanied her to the door. Nine out of ten customers who make such a claim have no intention of returning, but he could always sense the tenth.

"May I ask the price?" Consuela asked indifferently as he held the door open for her.

"One million pounds, madam," Graff replied, as casually as if she had inquired about the cost of a plastic keyring at a seaside gift shop.

Once she had reached the sidewalk, Consuela dismissed her chauffeur. Her mind was now working at a speed that would have impressed her husband. She slipped across the street, calling first at the White House, then Yves Saint-Laurent, and finally at Chanel, emerging some two hours later with all the weapons she required for the battle that lay ahead. She did not arrive back at her suite at the Ritz until a few minutes before six.

Consuela was relieved to find that her husband had not yet returned from the bank. She used the time to take a long bath, and to contemplate how the trap should be set. Once she was dry and powdered, she dabbed a suggestion of a new scent on her throat, then slipped into some of her newly acquired clothes.

She was checking herself once again in the full-length mirror when Victor entered the room. He stopped on the spot, dropping his briefcase on the carpet. Consuela turned to face him.

"You look stunning," he declared, with the same look of desire she had lavished on the Kanemarra heirloom a few hours before.

"Thank you, darling," she replied. "And how did your day go?"

"A triumph. The takeover has been agreed, and at half the price it would have cost me only a year ago."

Consuela smiled. An unexpected bonus.

"Those of us who are still in possession of cash need have no fear of the recession," Victor added with satisfaction.

Over a quiet supper in the Ritz's dining room, Victor described to his wife in great detail what had taken place at the bank that day. During the occasional break in this monologue Consuela indulged her husband by remarking, "How clever of you, Victor," "How amazing," "How you managed it I will never understand." When he finally ordered a large brandy, lit a cigar, and leaned back in his chair, she began to run her elegantly stockinged right foot gently along the inside of his thigh. For the first time that evening, Victor stopped thinking about the takeover.

As they left the dining room and strolled toward the elevator, Victor placed an arm around his wife's slim waist. By the time the elevator had reached the sixth floor he had already taken off his jacket, and his hand had slipped a few inches further down. Consuela giggled. Long before they had reached the door of their suite, he had begun tugging off his tie.

When they entered the room, Consuela placed the Do Not Disturb sign on the outside doorknob. For the next few minutes Victor was transfixed to the spot as he watched his slim wife slowly remove each garment she had purchased that afternoon. He quickly pulled off his own clothes, and wished once again that he had carried out his New Year's resolution.

Forty minutes later, Victor lay exhausted on the bed. After a few moments of sighing, he began to snore. Consuela pulled the sheet over their naked bodies, but her eyes remained wide open. She was already going over the next step in her plan.

Victor awoke the following morning to discover his wife's hand gently stroking the inside of his leg. He rolled over to face her, the memory of the previous night still vivid in his mind. They made love a second time, something they had not done for as long as he could recall.

It was not until he stepped out of the shower that Victor remembered that it was his wife's birthday, and that he had promised to spend the morning with her selecting a gift. He only hoped that her eye had already settled on something she wanted, as he needed to spend most of the day closeted in the City with his lawyers, going over the offer document line by line.

"Happy birthday, darling," he said as he padded back into the bedroom. "By the way, did you have any luck finding a present?" he added as he scanned the front page of the *Financial Times*, which was already speculating on the possible takeover, describing it as a coup. A smile of satisfaction appeared on Victor's face for the second time that morning.

"Yes, my darling," Consuela replied. "I did come across one little bauble that I rather liked. I just hope it isn't too expensive."

"And how much is this 'little bauble'?" Victor asked. Consuela turned to face him. She was wearing only two garments, both of them black, and both of them remarkably skimpy.

Victor started to wonder if he still had the time, but then he remembered the lawyers, who had been up all night and would be waiting patiently for him at the bank.

"I didn't ask the price," Consuela replied. "You're so much cleverer than I am at that sort of thing," she added, as she slipped into a navy silk blouse.

Victor glanced at his watch. "How far away is it?" he asked.

"Just across the road, in Bond Street, my darling," Consuela replied. "I shouldn't have to delay you for too long." She knew exactly what was going through her husband's mind.

"Good. Then let's go and look at this little bauble without delay," he said as he buttoned his shirt.

While Victor finished dressing, Consuela, with the help of the *Financial Times*, skillfully guided the conversation back to his triumph of the previous day. She listened once more to the details of the takeover as they left the hotel and strolled up Bond Street together arm in arm.

"Probably saved myself several million," he told her yet again. Consuela smiled as she led him to the door of the House of Graff.

"Several million?" she gasped. "How clever you are, Victor."

The security guard quickly opened the door, and this time Consuela found that Mr. Graff was already standing by the table waiting for her. He bowed low, then turned to Victor. "May I offer my congratulations on your brilliant coup, Mr. Rosenheim." Victor smiled. "How may I help you?"

"My husband would like to see the Kanemarra heirloom," said Consuela, before Victor had a chance to reply.

"Of course, madam," said the proprietor. He stepped behind the table and spread out the black velvet cloth. Once again the assistant removed the magnificent necklace from its stand in the third window, and carefully laid it out on the center of the velvet cloth to show the jewels to their best advantage. Mr. Graff was about to embark on the piece's history, when Victor simply said, "How much is it?"

Mr. Graff raised his head. "This is no ordinary piece of jewelry. I feel . . . "

"How much?" repeated Victor.

"Its provenance alone warrants . . . "

"How much?"

"The sheer beauty, not to mention the craftsmanship involved . . . "

"How much?" asked Victor, his voice now rising.

"The word 'unique' would not be inappropriate."

"You may be right, but I still need to know how much it's going to cost me," said Victor, who was beginning to sound exasperated.

"One million pounds, sir," Graff said in an even tone, aware that he could not risk another superlative.

"I'll settle at half a million, no more," came back the immediate reply.

"I am sorry to say, sir," said Graff, "that with this particular piece, there is no room for bargaining."

"There's always room for bargaining, whatever one is selling," said Victor. "I repeat my offer. Half a million."

"I fear that in this case, sir . . . "

"I feel confident that you'll see things my way, given time," said Victor. "But I don't have that much time to spare this morning, so I'll write out a check for half a million, and leave *you* to decide whether you wish to cash it or not."

"I fear you are wasting your time, sir," said Graff. "I cannot let the Kanemarra heirloom go for less than one million."

Victor took a checkbook from his inside pocket, unscrewed the top of his fountain pen, and wrote out the words "Five hundred thousand pounds only" below the name of the bank that bore his name. His wife took a discreet pace backward.

Graff was about to repeat his previous comment when he glanced up and observed Mrs. Rosenheim silently pleading with him to accept the check.

A look of curiosity came over his face as Consuela continued her urgent mime.

Victor tore out the check and left it on the table. "I'll give you twenty-four hours to decide," he said. "We return to New York tomorrow morning—with or without the Kanemarra heirloom. It's your decision."

Graff left the check on the table as he accompanied Mr. and Mrs. Rosenheim to the front door and bowed them out onto Bond Street.

"You were brilliant, my darling," said Consuela as the chauffeur opened the car door for his master.

"The bank," Rosenheim instructed as he fell into the back seat. "You'll have your little bauble, Consuela. He'll cash the check before the twenty-four hours are up, of that I'm sure." The chauffeur closed the back door, and the window purred down as Victor added with a smile, "Happy birthday, darling."

Consuela returned his smile, and blew him a kiss as the car pulled out into the traffic and edged its way toward Piccadilly. The morning had not turned out quite as she had planned, because she felt unable to agree with her husband's judgment—but then, she still had twenty-four hours to play with.

Consuela returned to the suite at the Ritz, undressed, took a shower, opened another bottle of perfume, and slowly began to change into the second outfit she had purchased the previous day. Before she left the room she turned to the commodities section of the *Financial Times*, and checked the price of green coffee.

She emerged from the Arlington Street entrance of the Ritz wearing a double-breasted navy blue Yves Saint-Laurent suit and a wide-brimmed red-and-white hat. Ignoring her chauffeur, she hailed a taxi, instructing the driver to take her to a small, discreet hotel in Knightsbridge. Fifteen minutes later she entered the foyer with her head bowed and, after giving the name of her host to the manager, was accompanied to a suite on the fourth floor. Her luncheon companion stood as she entered the room, walked forward, kissed her on both cheeks, and wished her a happy birthday.

After an intimate lunch, and an even more intimate hour spent in the adjoining room, Consuela's companion listened to her request and, having first checked his watch, agreed to accompany her to Mayfair. He didn't mention to her that he would have to be back in his office by four o'clock to take an important call from South America. Since the downfall of the Brazilian president, coffee prices had gone through the roof.

As the car traveled down Brompton Road, Consuela's companion telephoned to check the latest spot price of green coffee in New York (only her skill in bed had managed to stop him from calling earlier). He was pleased to learn that it was up another two cents, but not as pleased as she was. Eleven minutes later, the car deposited them outside the House of Graff.

When they entered the shop together arm in arm, Mr. Graff didn't so much as raise an eyebrow.

"Good afternoon, Mr. Carvalho," he said. "I do hope that your estates yielded an abundant crop this year."

Mr. Carvalho smiled and replied, "I cannot complain."

"And how may I assist you?" inquired the proprietor.

"We would like to see the diamond necklace in the third window," said Consuela, without a moment's hesitation.

"Of course, madam," said Graff, as if he were addressing a complete stranger.

Once again the black velvet cloth was laid out on the table, and once again the assistant placed the Kanemarra heirloom in its centre.

This time Mr. Graff was allowed to relate its history before Carvalho politely inquired after the price.

"One million pounds," said Graff.

After a moment's hesitation, Carvalho said, "I'm willing to pay half a million."

"This is no ordinary piece of jewelry," replied the proprietor. "I feel . . . "

"Possibly not, but half a million is my best offer," said Carvalho.

"The sheer beauty, not to mention the craftsmanship involved . . . "

"Nevertheless, I am not willing to go above half a million."

"The word 'unique' would not be inappropriate."

"Half a million, and no more," insisted Carvalho.

"I am sorry to say, sir," said Graff, "that with this particular piece there is no room for bargaining."

"There's always room for bargaining, whatever one is selling," the coffee grower insisted.

"I fear that is not true in this case, sir. You see . . . "

"I suspect you will come to your senses in time," said Carvalho. "But, regrettably, I do not have any time to spare this afternoon. I will write out a check for half a million pounds, and leave *you* to decide whether you wish to cash it."

Carvalho took a checkbook from his inside pocket, unscrewed the top of his fountain pen, and wrote out the words "Five hundred thousand pounds only." Consuela looked on silently.

Carvalho tore out the check and left it on the counter.

"I'll give you twenty-four hours to decide. I leave for Chicago on the early evening flight tomorrow. If the check has not been presented by the time I reach my office . . . "

Graff bowed his head slightly, and left the check on the table. He accompanied them to the door and bowed again when they stepped out onto the sidewalk.

"You were brilliant, my darling," said Consuela as the chauffeur opened the car door for his employer.

"The Exchange," said Carvalho. Turning back to face his mistress, he added, "You'll have your necklace before the day is out, of that I'm certain, my darling."

Consuela smiled and waved as the car disappeared in the

direction of Piccadilly, and on this occasion she felt able to agree with her lover's judgment. Once the car had turned the corner, she slipped back into the House of Graff.

The proprietor smiled and handed over the smartly wrapped gift. He bowed low and simply said, "Happy birthday, Mrs. Rosenheim."

BROKEN ROUTINE

SEPTIMUS HORATIO CORNWALLIS DID not live up to his name. With such a name he should have been a cabinet minister, an admiral, or at least a rural dean. In fact, Septimus Horatio Cornwallis was a claims adjuster at the head office of the Prudential Assurance Company Limited, 172 Holborn Bars, London EC1.

Septimus's names could be blamed on his father, who had a small knowledge of Nelson; on his mother, who was superstitious; and on his great-great-great-grandfather, who was alleged to have been a second cousin of the illustrious governor-general of India. On leaving school Septimus, a thin, anemic, prematurely balding young man, joined the Prudential Assurance Company; his careers adviser having told him that it was an ideal opening for a young man with his qualifications. Some time later, when Septimus reflected on the advice, it worried him, because even he realized that he had no qualifications. Despite this setback, Septimus rose slowly over the years from office boy to claims adjuster (not so much climbing the ladder as resting on each rung for some considerable time), which afforded him the grandiose title of assistant deputy manager (claims department).

Septimus spent his day in a glass cubicle on the sixth floor, adjusting claims and recommending payments of anything up to one million pounds. He felt that if he "kept his nose clean" (one of Septimus's favorite expressions), he would, after another twenty years, become a manager (claims department) and have walls around him that you couldn't see through and a carpet that wasn't laid in small squares of slightly differing shades of green. He might even become one of those signatures on the million-pound checks.

Septimus resided in Sevenoaks with his wife, Norma, and his two children, Winston and Elizabeth, who attended the local comprehensive school. They would have gone to the grammar school, he regularly informed his colleagues, but the Labour government had stopped all that.

Septimus operated his daily life by means of a set of invariable subroutines, like a primitive microprocessor, while he supposed himself to be a great follower of tradition and discipline. For if he was nothing, he was at least a creature of habit. Had, for some inexplicable reason, the KGB wanted to assassinate Septimus, all they would have had to do was put him under surveillance for seven days and they would have known his every movement throughout the working year.

Septimus rose every morning at 7:15 and donned one of his two pinhead-patterned dark suits. He left his home at 47 Palmerston Drive at 7:55, having consumed his invariable breakfast of one soft-boiled egg, two pieces of toast, and two cups of tea. On arriving at platform one at Sevenoaks station, he would purchase a copy of the *Daily Express* before boarding the 8:27 to Cannon Street. During the journey Septimus would read his newspaper and smoke two cigarettes, arriving at Cannon Street at 9:07. He would then walk to the office and be sitting at his desk in his glass cubicle on the sixth floor, confronting the first claim to be adjusted, by 9:30. He took his coffee break at 11:00, allowing himself the luxury of two more cigarettes, when once again he would regale his colleagues with the imagined achievements of his children. At 11:15 he returned to work.

At one o'clock he would leave the "great Gothic cathedral" (another of his expressions) for one hour, which he passed at a pub called the Havelock, where he would drink a half pint of Carlsberg lager with a dash of lime and eat the dish of the day. After he finished his lunch, he would once again smoke two cigarettes. At 1:55 he returned to the insurance records until the fifteen-minute tea break at four o'clock, which was another ritual occasion for two more cigarettes. On the dot of 5:30, Septimus would pick up his umbrella and reinforced steel briefcase with the initials S.H.C. in silver on the side and leave, double-locking his glass cubicle. As he walked through the typing pool, he would announce with a mechanical jauntiness, "See you same time tomorrow, girls," hum a few bars from *The Sound of Music* in the descending elevator, and then walk out into the torrent of office workers surging down High Holborn. He would stride purposefully toward Cannon Street station, umbrella tapping away on the pavement, while he rubbed shoulders with bankers, shippers, oil men, and brokers, not discontent to think himself part of the great City of London.

Once he reached the station, Septimus would purchase a copy of the *Evening Standard* and a pack of ten Benson & Hedges cigarettes from Smith's newsstand, placing both on the top of his Prudential documents already in the briefcase. He would board the fourth carriage of the train on platform five at 5:30, and secure his favored window seat in a closed compartment facing the engine, next to the balding gentleman with the inevitable *Financial Times*, and opposite the smartly dressed secretary who read long romantic novels to somewhere beyond Sevenoaks. Before sitting down he would extract the *Evening Standard* and the new pack of Benson & Hedges from his briefcase, put them both on the armrest of his seat, and place the briefcase and his rolled umbrella on the rack above him. Once settled, he would open the pack of cigarettes and smoke the first of the two allocated for the journey while reading the *Evening Standard*. This would leave him eight to be smoked before catching the 5:50 the following evening.

As the train pulled into Sevenoaks station, he would mumble good night to his fellow passengers (the only word he ever spoke during the entire journey) and leave, making his way straight to the semidetached at 47 Palmerston Drive, arriving at the front door a little before 6:45. Between 6:45 and 7:30 he would finish reading his paper or check over his children's homework with a *tut-tut* when he spotted a mistake, or a sigh when he couldn't fathom the new math. At 7:30 his "good lady" (another of his favored expressions) would place on the kitchen table in front of him the *Woman's Own* dish of the day or his favorite dinner of three fish fingers, peas, and french fries. He would then say, "If God had meant fish to have fingers, he would have given them hands," laugh, and cover the oblong fish with tomato sauce, consuming the meal to the accompaniment of his wife's recital of the day's events. At 9:00 he watched the news on BBC 1 (he never watched ITV), and at 10:30 he retired to bed.

This routine was adhered to year in year out with breaks only for holidays, for which Septimus naturally also had a routine. Alternate Christmases were spent with Norma's parents in Watford, and the ones in between with Septimus's sister and brother-in-law in Epsom, while in the summer, their high spot of the year, the family took a two-week vacation in the Olympic Hotel, Corfu.

Septimus not only liked his lifestyle, but was distressed if for any reason his routine met with the slightest interference. This humdrum existence seemed certain to last him from womb to tomb, for Septimus was not the stuff on which authors base two-hundred-thousand-word sagas. Nevertheless, there was one occasion when Septimus's routine was not merely interfered with, but frankly shattered.

One evening at 5:27, when Septimus was closing the file on the last claim for the day, his immediate superior, the deputy manager, called him in for a consultation. Owing to this gross lack of consideration, Septimus did not manage to get away from the office until a few minutes after six. Although everyone had left the typing pool, still he saluted the empty desks and silent typewriters with the invariable "See you same time tomorrow, girls," and hummed a few bars of "Edelweiss" to the descending elevator. As he stepped out of the great Gothic cathedral it started to rain. Septimus reluctantly undid his neatly rolled umbrella and, putting it up, dashed through the puddles, hoping that he would be in time to catch the 6:32. On arrival at Cannon Street, he lined up for his paper and cigarettes and put them in his briefcase before rushing on to platform five. To add to his annoyance, the loudspeaker was announcing with perfunctory apology that three trains had already been taken off that evening because of a go-slow.

Septimus eventually fought his way through the dripping,

bustling crowds to the sixth carriage of a train that was not scheduled on any timetable. He discovered that it was filled with people he had never seen before and, worse, almost every seat was already occupied. In fact, the only place he could find to sit was in the middle of the train with his back to the engine. He threw his briefcase and creased umbrella onto the rack above him and reluctantly squeezed himself into the seat before looking around the carriage. There was not a familiar face among the other six occupants. A woman with three children more than filled the seat opposite him, while an elderly man was sleeping soundly on his left. On the other side of him, leaning over and looking out of the window, was a young man of about twenty.

When Septimus first laid eyes on the boy he couldn't believe what he saw. The youth was clad in a black leather jacket and skin-tight jeans and was whistling to himself. His dark, creamed hair was combed up at the front and down at the sides, while the only two colors of the young man's outfit that matched were his jacket and fingernails. But worst of all to one of Septimus's sensitive nature was the slogan printed in boot studs on the back of his jacket. "Heil Hitler" it declared unashamedly over a white-painted Nazi sign and, as if that were not enough, below the swastika in gold shone the words: "Up yours." What was the country coming to? thought Septimus. They ought to bring back National Service for delinquents like that. Septimus himself had not been eligible for National Service on account of his flat feet.

Septimus decided to ignore the creature, and, picking up the pack of Benson & Hedges on the armrest by his side, he lit one and began to read the *Evening Standard*. He then replaced the pack of cigarettes on the armrest, as he always did, knowing he would smoke one more before reaching Sevenoaks. When the train eventually moved out of Cannon Street, the darkly clad youth turned toward Septimus and, glaring at him, picked up the pack of cigarettes, took one, lit it, and started to puff away. Septimus could not believe what was happening. He was about to protest when he realized that none of his regulars was in the carriage to back him up. He considered the situation for a moment and decided that "discretion was the better part of valor" (yet another of the sayings of Septimus).

When the train stopped at Petts Wood, Septimus put down the newspaper although he had scarcely read a word, and as he nearly always did, took his second cigarette. He lit it, inhaled, and was about to retrieve the *Evening Standard* when the youth grabbed at the corner, and they ended up with half the paper each. This time Septimus did look around the carriage for support. The children opposite started giggling, while their mother consciously averted her eyes from what was taking place, obviously not wanting to become involved; the old man on Septimus's left was now snoring. Septimus was about to secure the pack of cigarettes by putting them in his pocket when the youth pounced on them, removed another and lit it, inhaled deeply, and then blew the smoke quite deliberately across Septimus's face before placing the cigarettes back on the armrest. Septimus's answering glare expressed as much malevolence as he was able to project through the gray haze. Grinding his teeth in fury, he returned to the *Evening Standard*, only to discover that he had ended up with the help wanted, used cars, and sports sections, subjects in which he had absolutely no interest. His one compensation, however, was his certainty that sports was the only section the lout really wanted. Septimus was now, in any case, incapable of reading the paper, trembling as he was at the outrages perpetrated by his neighbor.

His thoughts were now turning to revenge, and gradually a plan began to form in his mind with which he was confident the youth would be left in no doubt that "virtue can sometimes be more than its own reward" (a variation on a saying of Septimus). He smiled thinly, and, breaking his routine, he took a third cigarette and defiantly placed the pack back on the armrest. The youth stubbed out his own cigarette and, as if taking up the challenge, picked up the pack, removed another one, and lit it. Septimus was by no means beaten; he puffed his way quickly through the weed, stubbed it out, a quarter unsmoked, took a fourth and lit it immediately. The race was on, for there were now only two cigarettes left. But Septimus, despite a great deal of puffing and coughing, managed to finish his fourth cigarette ahead of the youth. He leaned across the leather jacket and stubbed his cigarette out in the window ashtray. The carriage was now filled with smoke, but the youth was still puffing as fast as he could. The children opposite were coughing, and the woman was waving her arms around like a windmill. Septimus ignored her and kept his eye on the pack of cigarettes while pretending to read about Arsenal's chances in the Football Association Cup.

Septimus then recalled Montgomery's maxim that surprise and timing in the final analysis are the weapons of victory. As the youth finished his fourth cigarette and was stubbing it out the train pulled slowly into Sevenoaks station. The youth's hand was raised, but Septimus was quicker. He had anticipated the enemy's next move and now seized the cigarette pack. He took out the ninth cigarette and, placing it between his lips, lit it slowly and luxuriously, inhaling as deeply as he could before blowing the smoke out straight into the face of the enemy. The youth stared up at him in dismay. Septimus then removed the last cigarette from the pack and crumpled the tobacco into shreds between his first finger and thumb, allowing the little flakes to fall back into the empty pack. Then he closed the pack neatly, and with a flourish replaced the little gold box on the armrest. In the same movement he picked up from his vacant seat the sports section of the *Evening Standard*, tore the paper in half, in quarters, in eighths, and finally in sixteenths, placing the little squares in a neat pile on the youth's lap.

The train came to a halt at Sevenoaks. A triumphant Septimus, having struck his blow for the silent majority, retrieved his umbrella and briefcase from the rack above him and turned to leave.

As he picked up his briefcase it knocked against the armrest in front of him, and the lid sprang open. Everyone in the carriage stared at its contents. For there, on top of his Prudential documents, was a neatly folded copy of the *Evening Standard* and an unopened pack of ten Benson & Hedges cigarettes.

AN EYE FOR
AN EYE

Sir Matthew Roberts, QC, closed the file and placed it on the desk in front of him. He was not a happy man. He was quite willing to defend Mary Banks, but he was not at all confident about her plea of not guilty.

Sir Matthew leaned back in his deep leather chair to consider the case while he awaited the arrival of the instructing solicitor, who had briefed him, and the junior counsel he had selected for the case. As he gazed out over the Middle Temple courtyard, he only hoped he had made the right decision.

On the face of it, the case of *Regina* v. *Banks* was a simple one of murder; but after what Bruce Banks had subjected his wife to during the eleven years of their marriage, Sir Matthew was confident not only that he could get the charge reduced to manslaughter, but that if the jury was packed with women, he might even secure an acquittal. There was, however, a complication.

He lit a cigarette and inhaled deeply, something his wife had always chided him for. He looked at Victoria's photograph on the desk in front of him. It reminded him of his youth: But then, Victoria would always be young—death had ensured that.

Reluctantly he forced his mind back to his client and her plea of mitigation. He reopened the file. Mary Banks was claiming that she couldn't possibly have chopped her husband up with an ax and buried him under the pigsty, because at the time of his death she was not only a patient in the local hospital, but was also blind. As Sir Matthew inhaled deeply once again, there was a knock on the door.

"Come in," he bellowed—not because he liked the sound of his own voice, but because the doors of his chambers were so thick that if he didn't holler, no one would ever hear him.

Sir Matthew's clerk opened the door and announced Mr. Bernard Casson and Mr. Hugh Witherington. Two very different men, thought Sir Matthew as they entered the room, but each would serve the purpose he had planned for them in this particular case.

Bernard Casson was a solicitor of the old school—formal, punctilious, and always painstakingly correct. His conservatively tailored herringbone suit never seemed to change from one year to the next; Matthew often wondered if he had purchased half a dozen such suits in a closing-down sale and wore a different one every day of the week. He peered up at Casson over his half-moon spectacles. The solicitor's thin mustache and neatly parted hair gave him an old-fashioned look that had fooled many an opponent into thinking he had a second-class mind. Sir Matthew regularly gave thanks that his friend was no orator, because if Bernard had been a barrister, Matthew would not have relished the prospect of opposing him in court.

A pace behind Casson stood his junior counsel for this brief, Hugh Witherington. The Lord must have been feeling particularly ungenerous on the day Witherington entered the world, as he had given him neither looks nor brains. If he had bestowed any other talents on him, they were yet to be revealed. After several attempts Witherington had finally been called to the bar, but for the number of briefs he was offered, he would have had a more regular income had he signed on for welfare. Sir Matthew's clerk had raised an eyebrow when the name of Witherington had been mooted as junior counsel in the case, but Sir Matthew just smiled, and had not offered an explanation.

Sir Matthew rose, stubbed out his cigarette, and ushered the two men toward the vacant chairs on the other side of his desk. He waited for both of them to settle before he proceeded.

"Kind of you to attend chambers, Mr. Casson," he said, although they both knew that the solicitor was doing no more than holding with the traditions of the bar.

"My pleasure, Sir Matthew," replied the elderly solicitor, nodding slightly to show that he still appreciated the old courtesies.

"I don't think you know Hugh Witherington, my junior in this case," said Sir Matthew, gesturing toward the undistinguished young barrister.

Witherington nervously touched the silk handkerchief in his breast pocket.

"No, I hadn't had the pleasure of Mr. Witherington's acquaintance until we met in the corridor a few moments ago," said Casson. "May I say how delighted I am that you have been willing to take on this case, Sir Matthew?"

Matthew smiled at his friend's formality. He knew Bernard would never dream of calling him by his first name while junior counsel was present. "I'm only too happy to be working with you again, Mr. Casson. Even if you have presented me on this occasion with something of a challenge."

The conventional pleasantries over, the elderly solicitor removed a brown file from his battered Gladstone bag. "I have had a further consultation with my client since I last saw you," he said as he opened the file, "and I took the opportunity to pass on your opinion. But I fear Mrs. Banks remains determined to plead not guilty."

"So she is still protesting her innocence?"

"Yes, Sir Matthew. Mrs. Banks emphatically claims that she couldn't have committed the murder because she had been blinded by her husband some days before he died, and in any case, at the time of his death she was registered as a patient at the local hospital."

"The pathologist's report is singularly vague about the time of death," Sir Matthew reminded his old friend. "After all, they didn't discover the body for at least a couple of weeks. As I understand it, the police feel the murder could have been committed twenty-four or even forty-eight hours before Mrs. Banks was taken to the hospital."

"I have also read their report, Sir Matthew," Casson replied, "and informed Mrs. Banks of its contents. But she remains adamant that she is innocent, and that the jury will be persuaded of it. 'Especially with Sir Matthew Roberts as my defender,' were the exact words she used, if I remember correctly," he added with a smile.

"I am not seduced, Mr. Casson," said Sir Matthew, lighting another cigarette.

"You did promise Victoria—" interjected the solicitor, lowering his shield, but only for a moment.

"So, I have one last chance to convince her," said Sir Matthew, ignoring his friend's comment.

"And Mrs. Banks has one last chance to convince you," said Mr. Casson.

"Touché," said Sir Matthew, nodding his appreciation of the solicitor's neat riposte as he stubbed out his almost untouched cigarette. He felt he was losing this fencing match with his old friend, and that the time had come to go on the attack.

He returned to the open file on his desk. "First," he said, looking straight at Casson, as if his colleague were in the witness box, "when the body was dug up, there were traces of your client's blood on the collar of the dead man's shirt."

"My client accepts that," said Casson, calmly checking his own notes. "But—"

"Second," said Sir Matthew before Casson had a chance to reply, "when the instrument that had been used to chop up the body, an ax, was found the following day, a hair from Mrs. Banks's head was discovered lodged in its handle."

"We won't be denying that," said Casson.

"We don't have a lot of choice," said Sir Matthew, rising from his seat and beginning to pace around the room. "And third, when the spade that was used to dig the victim's grave was finally discovered, your client's fingerprints were found all over it."

"We can explain that as well," said Casson.

"But will the jury accept our explanation," asked Sir Matthew, his voice rising, "when they learn that the murdered man had a long history of violence, that your client was regularly seen in the local village either bruised, or with a black eye, sometimes bleeding from cuts around the head—once even nursing a broken arm?"

"She has always stated that those injuries were sustained when working on the farm where her husband was manager."

"That places a strain on my credulity which it's quite unable to withstand," said Sir Matthew, as he finished circling the room and returned to his chair. "And we are not helped by the fact that the only person known to have visited the farm regularly was the postman. Apparently everyone else in the village refused to venture beyond the front gate." He flicked over another page of his notes.

"That might have made it easier for someone to come in and kill Banks," suggested Witherington.

Sir Matthew was unable to hide his surprise as he looked across at his junior, having almost forgotten that he was in the room. "Interesting point," he said, unwilling to stamp on Witherington while he still had it in his power to play the one trump card in this case.

"The next problem we face," he went on, "is that your client claims that she went blind after her husband struck her with a hot frying pan. Rather convenient, Mr. Casson, wouldn't you say?"

"The scar can still be seen clearly on the side of my client's face," said Casson. "And the doctor remains convinced that she is indeed blind."

"Doctors are easier to convince than prosecuting counsels and world-weary judges, Mr. Casson," said Sir Matthew, turning another page of his file. "Next, when samples from the body were examined—and God knows who was willing to carry out that particular task—the quantity of strychnine found in the blood would have felled a bull elephant."

"That was only the opinion of the Crown's pathologists," said Mr. Casson.

"And one I will find hard to refute in court," said Sir Matthew, "because counsel for the prosecution will undoubtedly ask Mrs. Banks to explain why she purchased four grams of strychnine from an agricultural supplier in Reading shortly before her husband's death. If I were in his position, I would repeat that question over and over again."

"Possibly," said Casson, checking his notes, "but she has explained that they had been having a problem with rats, which had been killing the chickens, and she feared for the other animals on the farm, not to mention their nine-year-old son."

"Ah, yes, Rupert. But he was away at boarding school at the time, was he not?" Sir Matthew paused. "You see, Mr. Casson, my problem is a simple one." He closed his file. "I don't believe her."

Casson raised an eyebrow.

"Unlike her husband, Mrs. Banks is a very clever woman. Witness the fact that she has already fooled several people into believing this incredible story. But I can tell you, Mr. Casson, that she isn't going to fool me."

"But what can we do, Sir Matthew, if Mrs. Banks insists that this is her case, and asks us to defend her accordingly?" asked Casson.

Sir Matthew rose again and paced around the room silently, coming to a halt in front of the solicitor. "Not a lot, I agree," he said, reverting to a more conciliatory tone. "But I do wish I could convince the dear lady to plead guilty to manslaughter. We'd be certain to gain the sympathy of any jury, after what she's been put through. And we can always rely on some women's group or other to picket the court throughout the hearing. Any judge who passed a harsh sentence on Mary Banks would be described as chauvinistic and sexually discriminatory by every newspaper editorial writer in the land. I'd have her out of prison in a matter of weeks. No, Mr. Casson, we *must* get her to change her plea."

"But how can we hope to do that, when she remains so adamant that she is innocent?" asked Casson.

A smile flickered across Sir Matthew's face. "Mr. Witherington and I have a plan, don't we, Hugh?" he said, turning to Witherington for a second time.

"Yes, Sir Matthew," replied the young barrister, sounding

pleased to at last have his opinion sought, even in this rudimentary way. As Sir Matthew volunteered no clue as to the plan, Casson did not press the point.

"So, when do I come face to face with our client?" asked Sir Matthew, turning his attention back to the solicitor.

"Would eleven o'clock on Monday morning be convenient?" asked Casson.

"Where is she at the moment?" asked Sir Matthew, thumbing through his diary.

"Holloway," replied Casson.

"Then we will be at Holloway at eleven on Monday morning," said Sir Matthew. "And to be honest with you, I can't wait to meet Mrs. Mary Banks. That woman must have real guts, not to mention imagination. Mark my words, Mr. Casson, she'll prove a worthy opponent for any counsel."

When Sir Matthew entered the interviewing room of Holloway Prison and saw Mary Banks for the first time, he was momentarily taken aback. He knew from his file on the case that she was thirty-seven, but the frail, gray-haired woman who sat with her hands resting in her lap looked nearer fifty. Only when he studied her fine cheekbones and slim figure did he see that she might once have been a beautiful woman.

Sir Matthew allowed Casson to take the seat opposite her at a plain Formica table in the center of an otherwise empty, cream-painted brick room. There was a small, barred window halfway up the wall that threw a shaft of light onto their client. Sir Matthew and his junior took their places on either side of the instructing solicitor. Leading counsel noisily poured himself a cup of coffee.

"Good morning, Mrs. Banks," said Casson.

"Good morning, Mr. Casson," she replied, turning slightly to face the direction from which the voice had come. "You have brought someone with you."

"Yes, Mrs. Banks, I am accompanied by Sir Matthew Roberts, QC, who will be acting as your defense counsel."

She gave a slight bow of the head as Sir Matthew rose from

his chair, took a pace forward, and said, "Good morning, Mrs. Banks," then suddenly thrust out his right hand.

"Good morning, Sir Matthew," she replied, without moving a muscle, still looking in Casson's direction. "I'm delighted that you will be representing me."

"Sir Matthew would like to ask you a few questions, Mrs. Banks," said Casson, "so that he can decide what might be the best approach in your case. He will assume the role of counsel for the prosecution, so that you can get used to what it will be like when you go into the witness seat."

"I understand," replied Mrs. Banks. "I shall be happy to answer any of Sir Matthew's questions. I'm sure it won't prove difficult for someone of his eminence to show that a frail, blind woman would be incapable of chopping up a vicious sixteen-stone man."

"Not if that vicious sixteen-stone man was poisoned before he was chopped up," said Sir Matthew quietly.

"Which would be quite an achievement for someone lying in a hospital bed five miles from where the crime was committed," replied Mrs. Banks.

"If indeed that *was* when the crime was committed," responded Sir Matthew. "You claim your blindness was caused by a blow to the side of your head."

"Yes, Sir Matthew. My husband picked up the frying pan from the stove while I was cooking breakfast and struck me with it. I ducked, but the edge of the pan caught me on the left side of my face." She touched a scar above her left eye that looked as if it would remain with her for the rest of her life.

"And then what happened?"

"I passed out and collapsed onto the kitchen floor. When I came to, I could sense someone else was in the room. But I had no idea who it was until he spoke, when I recognized the voice of Jack Pembridge, our postman. He carried me to his van and drove me to the local hospital."

"And it was while you were in the hospital that the police discovered your husband's body?"

"That is correct, Sir Matthew. After I had been in Parkmead

for nearly two weeks, I asked the vicar, who had been to visit me every day, to try and find out how Bruce was coping without me."

"Did you not think it surprising that your husband hadn't been to see you once during the time you were in the hospital?" asked Sir Matthew, who began slowly pushing his cup of coffee toward the edge of the table.

"No. I had threatened to leave him on several occasions, and I don't think—" The cup fell off the table and shattered noisily on the stone floor. Sir Matthew's eyes never left Mrs. Banks.

She jumped nervously, but did not turn to look in the direction of the broken cup.

"Are you all right, Mr. Casson?" she asked.

"My fault," said Sir Matthew. "How clumsy of me."

Casson suppressed a smile. Witherington remained unmoved.

"Please continue," said Sir Matthew as he bent down and began picking up the pieces of china scattered across the floor. "You were saying, 'I don't think . . .'"

"Oh, yes," said Mrs. Banks. "I don't think Bruce would have cared whether I returned to the farm or not."

"Quite so," said Sir Matthew after he had placed the broken pieces on the table. "But can you explain to me why the police found one of your hairs on the handle of the ax that was used to dismember your husband's body?"

"Yes, Sir Matthew, I can. I was chopping up some wood for the stove before I prepared his breakfast."

"Then I am bound to ask why there were no fingerprints on the handle of the ax, Mrs. Banks."

"Because I was wearing gloves, Sir Matthew. If you had ever worked on a farm in mid-October, you would know only too well how cold it can be at five in the morning."

This time Casson did allow himself to smile.

"But what about the blood found on your husband's collar? Blood that was shown by the Crown's forensic scientist to match your own."

"You will find my blood on many things in that house, should you care to look closely, Sir Matthew."

"And the spade, the one with your fingerprints all over it?

Had you also been doing some digging before breakfast that morning?"

"No, but I would have had cause to use it every day the previous week."

"I see," said Sir Matthew. "Let us now turn our attention to something I suspect you didn't do every day, namely the purchase of strychnine. First, Mrs. Banks, why did you need such a large amount? And second, why did you have to travel twenty-seven miles to Reading to purchase it?"

"I shop in Reading every other Thursday," Mrs. Banks explained. "There isn't an agricultural supplier any nearer."

Sir Matthew frowned and rose from his chair. He began slowly to circle Mrs. Banks, while Casson watched her eyes. They never moved.

When Sir Matthew was directly behind his client, he checked his watch. It was 11:17. He knew his timing had to be exact, because he had become uncomfortably aware that he was dealing not only with a clever woman but also an extremely cunning one. Mind you, he reflected, anyone who had lived for eleven years with such a man as Bruce Banks would have had to be cunning simply to survive.

"You still haven't explained why you needed such a large amount of strychnine," he said, remaining behind his client.

"We had been losing a lot of chickens," Mrs. Banks replied, still not moving her head. "My husband thought it was rats, so he told me to get a large quantity of strychnine to finish them off. 'Once and for all' were his exact words."

"But as it turned out, it was he who was finished off, once and for all—and undoubtedly with the same poison," said Sir Matthew quietly.

"I also feared for Rupert's safety," said Mrs. Banks, ignoring her counsel's sarcasm.

"But your son was away at school at the time, am I not correct?"

"Yes, you are, Sir Matthew, but he was due back for half term that weekend."

"Have you ever used that supplier before?"

"Regularly," said Mrs. Banks, as Sir Matthew completed his

circle and returned to face her once again. "I go there at least once a month, as I'm sure the manager will confirm." She turned her head and faced a foot or so to his right.

Sir Matthew remained silent, resisting the temptation to look at his watch. He knew it could only be a matter of seconds. A few moments later the door on the far side of the interview room swung open, and a boy of about nine years of age entered. The three of them watched their client closely as the child walked silently toward her. Rupert Banks came to a halt in front of his mother and smiled but received no response. He waited for a further ten seconds, then turned and walked back out, exactly as he had been instructed to do. Mrs. Banks's eyes remained fixed somewhere between Sir Matthew and Mr. Casson.

The smile on Casson's face was now almost one of triumph.

"Is there someone else in the room?" asked Mrs. Banks. "I thought I heard the door open."

"No," said Sir Matthew. "Only Mr. Casson and I are in the room." Witherington still hadn't moved a muscle.

Sir Matthew began to circle Mrs. Banks for what he knew had to be the last time. He had almost come to believe that he might have misjudged her. When he was directly behind her once again, he nodded to his junior, who remained seated in front of her.

Witherington removed the silk handkerchief from his breast pocket, slowly unfolded it, and laid it out flat on the table in front of him. Mrs. Banks showed no reaction. Witherington stretched out the fingers of his right hand, bowed his head slightly, and paused before placing his right hand over his left eye. Without warning he plucked the eye out of its socket and placed it in the middle of the silk handkerchief. He left it on the table for a full thirty seconds, then began to polish it. Sir Matthew completed his circle, and observed beads of perspiration appearing on Mrs. Banks's forehead as he sat down. When Witherington had finished cleaning the almond-shaped glass object, he slowly raised his head until he was staring directly at her, then eased the eye back into its socket. Mrs. Banks momentarily turned away. She quickly tried to compose herself, but it was too late.

Sir Matthew rose from his chair and smiled at his client. She returned the smile.

"I must confess, Mrs. Banks," he said, "I would feel much more confident about a plea of guilty to manslaughter."

THE LUNCHEON

SHE WAVED AT ME across a crowded room of the St. Regis Hotel in New York. I waved back, realizing I knew the face but unable to place it. She squeezed past waiters and guests and had reached me before I had a chance to ask anyone who she was. I racked that section of my brain that is meant to store people, but it transmitted no reply. I realized I would have to resort to the old party trick of carefully worded questions until her answers jogged my memory.

"How *are* you, darling?" she cried, and threw her arms around me, an opening that didn't help, since we were at a Literary Guild cocktail party, and anyone will throw their arms around you on such occasions, even the directors of the Book-of-the-Month Club. From her accent she was clearly American, and she looked to be approaching forty but thanks to the genius of modern makeup might even have overtaken it. She wore a long white cocktail dress and her blond hair was done up in one of those buns that looks like a brioche. The overall effect made her appear somewhat like a chess queen. Not that the cottage loaf helped, because she might have had dark hair flowing to her shoulders when we last met. I do wish women would realize that when they change their hairstyle they often achieve exactly what they set out to do: look completely different to any unsuspecting male.

"I'm well, thank you," I said to the white queen. "And you?" I inquired as my opening gambit.

"I'm just fine, darling," she replied, taking a glass of champagne from a passing waiter.

"And how's the family?" I asked, not sure if she even had one.

"They're all well," she replied. No help there. "And how is Louise?" she enquired.

"Blooming," I said. So she knew my wife. But then, not necessarily, I thought. Most American women are experts at remembering the names of men's wives. They have to be, when on the New York circuit they change so often it becomes a greater challenge than the *Times* crossword.

"Have you been to London lately?" I roared above the babble. A brave question, as she might never have been to Europe.

"Only once since we had lunch together." She looked at me quizzically. "You don't remember who I am, do you?" she asked as she devoured a cocktail sausage.

I smiled.

"Don't be silly, Susan," I said. "How could I ever forget?"

She smiled.

I confess that I remembered the white queen's name in the nick of time. Although I still had only vague recollections of the lady, I certainly would never forget the lunch.

I had just had my first book published, and the critics on both sides of the Atlantic had been complimentary, even if the checks from my publishers were less so. My agent had told me on several occasions that I shouldn't write if I wanted to make money. This created a dilemma, because I couldn't see how to make money if I didn't write.

It was around this time that the lady who was now facing me and chattering on, oblivious to my silence, telephoned from New York to heap lavish praise on my novel. There is no writer who does not enjoy receiving such calls, although I confess to having been less than captivated by an eleven-year-old girl who called me collect from California to say she had found a spelling mistake on page 47 and warned that she would call again if she discovered another. However, this particular lady might have ended her transatlantic congratulations with nothing more than good-bye if she had not dropped her own name. It was one of those names that can, on the spur of the moment, always book a table at a chic restaurant or a seat at the opera, which mere mortals like myself would have found impossible to attain given a month's notice. To be fair, it was her husband's name that had achieved the reputation, as one of the world's most distinguished film producers.

"When I'm next in London you must have lunch with me," came crackling down the phone.

"No," said I gallantly, "you must have lunch with *me*."

"How perfectly charming you English always are," she said.

I have often wondered how much American women get away with when they say those few words to an Englishman. Nevertheless, the wife of an Oscar-winning producer does not phone one every day.

"I promise to call you when I'm next in London," she said.

And indeed she did, for almost six months to the day she telephoned again, this time from the Connaught Hotel, to declare how much she was looking forward to our meeting.

"Where would you like to have lunch?" I said, realizing a second too late, when she replied with the name of one of the most exclusive restaurants in town, that I should have made sure it was I who chose the venue. I was glad she couldn't see my forlorn face as she added airily, "Monday, one o'clock. Leave the booking to me—I'm known there."

On the day in question I donned my one respectable suit, a new shirt I had been saving for a special occasion since Christmas, and the only tie that looked as if it hadn't previously been used to hold up my trousers. I then strolled over to my bank and asked for a statement of my current account. The teller handed me a long piece of paper unworthy of its amount. I studied the figure as one who has to make a major financial decision. The bottom line stated in black lettering that I was in credit to the sum of thirty-seven pounds and sixty-three pence. I wrote out a check for thirty-seven pounds. I feel that a gentleman should always leave his account in credit, and I might add it was a belief that my bank manager shared with me. I then walked up to Mayfair for my luncheon date.

As I entered the restaurant I observed too many waiters and plush seats for my liking. You can't eat either, but you can be charged for them. At a corner table for two sat a woman who, although not young, was elegant. She wore a blouse of powder blue crepe-de-chine, and her blond hair was rolled away from her face in a style that reminded me of the war years and had once again become fashionable. It was clearly my transatlantic admirer, and she greeted me in the same "I've known you all my life" fashion as she was to do at the Literary Guild cocktail party years later. Although she had a drink in front of her, I didn't order an apéritif, explaining that I never drank before lunch—and I would have liked to add, "but as soon as your husband makes a film of my novel, I will."

She launched immediately into the latest Hollywood gossip, not so much dropping names as reciting them, while I ate my way through the potato chips from the bowl in front of me. A few minutes later a waiter materialized by the table and presented us with two large embossed leather menus, considerably better bound than my novel. The place positively reeked of unnecessary expense. I opened the menu and studied the first chapter with horror; it was eminently put-downable. I had no idea that simple food obtained from Covent Garden that morning could cost quite so much by merely being transported to Mayfair. I could have bought her the same dishes for a quarter of the price at my favorite bistro, a mere one hundred yards away, and to add to my discomfort I observed that it was one of those restaurants where the guest's menu made no mention of the prices. I settled down to study the long list of French dishes, which only served to remind me that I hadn't eaten well for more than a month, a state of affairs that was about to be prolonged by a further day. I remembered my bank balance and morosely reflected that I would probably have to wait until my agent sold the Icelandic rights of my novel before I could afford a square meal again.

"What would you like?" I said gallantly.

"I always enjoy a light lunch," she volunteered. I sighed with premature relief, only to find that "light" did not necessarily mean inexpensive.

She smiled sweetly up at the waiter, who looked as if *he* wouldn't be wondering where his next meal might be coming from, and ordered just a sliver of smoked salmon, followed by two tiny tender lamb cutlets. Then she hesitated, but only for a moment, before adding "and a side salad."

I studied the menu with some caution, running my finger down the prices, not the dishes.

"I also eat lightly at lunch," I said mendaciously. "The chef's salad will be quite enough for me." The waiter was obviously affronted but left peaceably.

She chatted of Coppola and Preminger, of Pacino and Redford, and of Garbo as if she saw her all the time. She was kind enough to stop for a moment and ask what I was working on at present. I would have liked to have replied, "On how I'm going to explain to my wife that I only have sixty-three pence left in the bank," but I actually discussed my ideas for another novel. She seemed impressed but still made no reference to her husband. Should I mention him? No. Mustn't sound pushy, or as though I needed the money.

The food arrived, or that is to say her smoked salmon did, and I sat silently watching her eat my bank account while I nibbled a roll. I looked up only to discover a wine waiter hovering by my side.

"Would you care for some wine?" said I, recklessly.

"No, I don't think so," she said. I smiled a little too soon: "Well, perhaps a little something white and dry."

The wine waiter handed over a second leather-bound book, this time with golden grapes embossed on the cover. I searched down the pages for half bottles, explaining to my guest that I never drank at lunch. I chose the cheapest. The wine waiter reappeared a moment later with a large silver bucket full of ice in which the half bottle looked drowned, and, like me, completely out of its depth. A junior waiter cleared away the empty plate while another wheeled a large trolley to the side of our table and served the lamb cutlets and the chef's salad. At the same time a third waiter made up an exquisite side salad for my guest that ended up bigger than my complete order. I didn't feel I could ask her to swap.

To be fair, the chef's salad was superb—although I confess it was hard to appreciate such food fully while trying to work out a plot that would be convincing if I found the bill came to over thirty-seven pounds.

"How silly of me to ask for white wine with lamb," she said, having nearly finished the half bottle. I ordered a half bottle of the house red without calling for the wine list.

She finished the white wine and then launched into the theater, music, and other authors. All those who were still alive she seemed to know, and those who were dead she hadn't read. I might have enjoyed the performance if it hadn't been for the fear of wondering if I would be able to afford it when the curtain came down. When the waiter cleared away the empty dishes he asked my guest if she would care for anything else.

"No, thank you," she said—I nearly applauded. "Unless you have one of your famous apple surprises."

"I fear the last one may have gone, madam, but I'll go and see."

"Don't hurry," I wanted to say, but instead I just smiled as the rope tightened around my neck. A few moments later the waiter strode back in triumph, weaving between the tables holding the apple surprise in the palm of his hand, high above his head. I prayed to Newton that the apple would obey his law. It didn't.

"The last one, madam."

"Oh, what luck," she declared.

"Oh, what luck," I repeated, unable to face the menu and discover the price. I was now attempting some mental arithmetic as I realized it was going to be a close-run thing.

"Anything else, madam?" the ingratiating waiter inquired.

I took a deep breath.

"Just coffee," she said.

"And for you, sir?"

"No, no, not for me." He left us. I couldn't think of an explanation for why I didn't drink coffee.

She then produced from the large Gucci bag by her side a copy of my novel, which I signed with a flourish, hoping the headwaiter would see, and feel I was the sort of man who should be allowed to sign the bill as well, but he resolutely remained at the far end of the room while I wrote the words "An unforgettable meeting" and appended my signature.

While the dear lady was drinking her coffee I picked at another roll and called for the bill, not because I was in any particular hurry, but like a guilty defendant at the Old Bailey, I preferred to wait no longer for the judge's sentence. A man in a smart green uniform whom I had never seen before appeared carrying a silver tray with a folded piece of paper on it, looking not unlike my bank statement. I pushed back the edge of the bill slowly and read the figure: thirty-six pounds and forty pence. I casually put my hand into my inside pocket and withdrew my life's possessions, then placed the crisp new notes on the silver tray. They were whisked away. The man in the green uniform returned a few moments later with my sixty pence change, which I pocketed, since it was the only way I was going to get a bus home. The waiter gave me a look that would have undoubtedly won him a character part in any film produced by the lady's distinguished husband.

My guest rose and walked across the restaurant, waving at, and occasionally kissing, people I had previously seen only in glossy magazines. When she reached the door she stopped to retrieve her coat, a mink. I helped her on with the fur, again failing to leave a tip. As we stood on the Curzon Street sidewalk, a dark blue Rolls-Royce drew up beside us and a liveried chauffeur leaped out and opened the rear door. She climbed in.

"Good-bye, darling," she said as the electric window slid down. "Thank you for such a lovely lunch."

"Good-bye," I said and, summoning up my courage, added: "I do hope when you are next in town I shall have the opportunity of meeting your distinguished husband."

"Oh, darling, didn't you know?" she said.

"Know what?"

"We were divorced ages ago."

"Divorced?" said I.

"Oh, yes," she said gaily, "I haven't spoken to him for years."

I just stood there looking helpless.

"Oh, don't worry yourself on my account," she said. "He's no loss. In any case, I recently married again"—another film producer, I prayed—"in fact, I quite expected to bump into my husband today—you see, he owns the restaurant."

Without another word the electric window purred up and the Rolls-Royce glided effortlessly out of sight, leaving me to walk to the nearest bus stop.

As I stood surrounded by Literary Guild guests, staring at the white queen with the brioche bun, I could still see her drifting away in that blue Rolls-Royce. I tried to concentrate on her words.

"I knew you wouldn't forget me, darling," she was saying. "After all, I did take you to lunch, didn't I?"

THE COUP

THE BLUE-AND-SILVER BOEING 707, displaying a large *P* on its tail, taxied to a halt at the north end of Lagos International Airport. A fleet of six black Mercedeses drove up to the side of the aircraft and waited in a line resembling a land-bound crocodile. Six sweating, uniformed drivers leaped out and stood at attention. When the driver of the front car opened his rear door, Colonel Usman of the Federal Guard stepped out and walked quickly to the bottom of the passenger steps, which had been hurriedly pushed into place by four of the airport staff.

The front section cabin door swung back, and the colonel stared up into the gap, to see, framed against the dark interior of the cabin, a slim, attractive hostess dressed in a blue suit with silver piping. On her jacket lapel was a large *P*. She turned and nodded in the direction of the cabin. A few seconds later, an immaculately dressed tall man with thick black hair and deep brown eyes replaced her in the doorway. The man had an air of effortless style about him that self-made millionaires would have paid a considerable part of their fortune to possess. The colonel saluted as Senhor Eduardo Francisco de Silveira, head of the Prentino empire, gave a curt nod.

De Silveira emerged from the coolness of his air-conditioned 707 into the burning Nigerian sun without showing the slightest sign of discomfort. The colonel guided the tall, elegant Brazilian, who was accompanied only by his private secretary, to the front Mercedes while the rest of the Prentino staff filed down the back stairway of the aircraft and filled the other five cars. The driver, a corporal who had been detailed to be available night and day for the honored guest, opened the rear door of the front car and saluted. Eduardo de Silveira showed no sign of acknowledgment. The corporal smiled nervously, revealing the largest set of white teeth the Brazilian had ever seen.

"Welcome to Lagos," the corporal volunteered. "Hope you make very big deal while you are in Nigeria."

Eduardo did not comment as he settled back into his seat and stared out of the tinted window to watch some passengers of a British Airways 707 that had landed just before him form a long line on the hot tarmac as they waited patiently to clear customs. The driver put the car into first gear, and the black crocodile proceeded on its journey. Colonel Usman, who was now in the front seat beside the corporal, soon discovered that the Brazilian guest did not care for smalltalk, and the secretary who was seated by his employer's side never once opened his mouth. The colonel, used to doing things by example, remained silent, leaving de Silveira to consider his plan of campaign.

Eduardo Francisco de Silveira had been born in the small village of Rebeti, a hundred miles north of Rio de Janeiro, heir to one of the two most powerful family fortunes in Brazil. He had been educated privately in Switzerland before attending the University of California at Los Angeles. He went on to complete his education at the Harvard Business School. After Harvard he returned from America to work in Brazil, where he started at neither the top nor the bottom of the firm but in the middle, managing his family's mining interests in Minas Gerais. He quickly worked his way to the top, even faster than his father had planned, but then the boy turned out to be not so much a chip as a chunk off the old block. At twenty-nine he married Maria, eldest daughter of his father's closest friend, and when, twelve years later, his father died, Eduardo succeeded to the Prentino throne. There were seven sons in all: the second son, Alfredo, was now in charge of banking; João ran shipping; Carlos organized construction; Manoel arranged food and supplies; Jaime managed the family newspapers, and little Antonio, the last—and certainly the least—ran the family farms. All the brothers reported to Eduardo before making any major decision, for he was still chairman of the largest private company in Brazil, despite the boastful claims of his old family enemy, Manuel Rodrigues.

When General Castelo Branco's military regime overthrew the civilian government in 1964, the generals agreed that they could not kill off all the de Silveiras or the Rodrigueses, so they had better learn to live with the two rival families. The de Silveiras for their part had always had enough sense never to involve themselves in politics other than by making payments to every government official, military or civilian, according to his rank. This ensured that the Prentino empire grew alongside whatever faction came to power. One of the reasons Eduardo de Silveira had allocated three days in his crowded schedule for a visit to Lagos was that the Nigerian system of government seemed to resemble so closely that of Brazil, and at least on this project he had cut the ground from under Manuel Rodrigues's feet, which would more than make up for losing the Rio airport tender to him. Eduardo smiled at the thought of Rodrigues not realizing that he was in Nigeria to close a deal that could make him twice the size of his rival.

As the black Mercedes moved slowly through the teeming, noisy streets, paying no attention to traffic lights, red or green, Eduardo thought back to his first meeting with General Mohammed, the Nigerian head of state, on the occasion of the president's official visit to Brazil. Speaking at the dinner given in General Mohammed's honor, President Ernesto Geisel declared a hope that the two countries would move toward closer cooperation in politics and commerce. Eduardo agreed with his unelected leader and was happy to leave the politics to the resident if he allowed him to get on with the commerce. General Mohammed made his reply, on behalf of the guests, in an English accent that normally would only be associated with Oxford. The general talked at length of the project that was most dear to his heart—the building of a new Nigerian capital in Abuja, a city that he considered might even rival Brasilia. After the speeches were over, the general took de Silveira on one side and spoke in greater detail of the Abuja city project, asking him if he might consider a private tender. Eduardo smiled and wished only that his enemy, Rodrigues, could hear the intimate conversation he was having with the Nigerian head of state.

Eduardo studied carefully the outline proposal sent to him a week later, after the general had returned to Nigeria, and agreed to his first request by dispatching a research team of seven men to fly to Lagos and complete a feasibility study on Abuja.

One month later, the team's detailed report was in de Silveira's hands. Eduardo came to the conclusion that the potential profitability of the project was worthy of a full proposal to the Nigerian government. He contacted General Mohammed personally to find that he was in full agreement and authorized the go-ahead. This time twenty-three men were dispatched to Lagos, and three months and 170 pages later, Eduardo signed and sealed the proposal, designated "A New Capital for Nigeria." He made only one alteration to the final document. The cover of the proposal was in blue and silver with the Prentino logo in the center: Eduardo had that changed to green and white, the national colors of Nigeria, with the national emblem of an eagle astride two horses. He realized it was the little things that impressed generals and often tipped the scales. He sent ten copies of the feasibility study to Nigeria's head of state with an invoice for one million dollars.

When General Mohammed had studied the proposal he invited Eduardo de Silveira to visit Nigeria as his guest, in order to discuss the next stage of the project. De Silveira telexed back, provisionally accepting the invitation, and pointing out politely but firmly that he had not yet received reimbursement for the one million dollars spent on the initial feasibility study. The money was telexed by return from the Central Bank of Nigeria, and de Silveira managed to find four consecutive days in his diary for "the New Federal Capital project": His schedule demanded that he arrive in Lagos on a Monday morning because he had to be in Paris by the Thursday night at the latest.

While these thoughts were going through Eduardo's mind, the Mercedeses drew up outside Dodan Barracks. The iron gates swung open, and a full armed guard gave the general salute, an honor normally accorded only to a visiting head of state. The black Mercedeses drove slowly through the gates and came to a halt outside the president's private residence. A brigadier waited on the steps to escort de Silveira through to the president.

The two men had lunch together in a small room that closely resembled a British officers' mess. The meal consisted of a steak that would not have been acceptable to any South American cowhand, surrounded by vegetables that reminded Eduardo of his schooldays. Still, Eduardo had never yet met a soldier who understood that a good chef was every bit as important as a good orderly. During the lunch they talked in overall terms about the problems of building a whole new city in the middle of an equatorial jungle.

The provisional estimate of the cost of the project had been one thousand million dollars, but when de Silveira warned the president that the final outcome might well end up nearer three thousand million, the president's jaw dropped slightly. De Silveira had to admit that the project would be the most ambitious that Prentino International had ever tackled, but he was quick to point out to the president that the same would be true of any construction company in the world.

De Silveira, not a man to play his best card early, waited until the coffee to slip into the conversation that he had just been awarded, against heavy opposition (that had included Rodrigues), the contract to build an eight-lane highway through the Amazonian jungle, which would eventually link up with the Pan-American Highway, a contract second in size only to the one they were now contemplating in Nigeria. The president was impressed and inquired if the venture would not prevent de Silveira from involving himself in the new capital project.

"I'll know the answer to that question in three days' time," replied the Brazilian, and undertook to have a further discussion with the head of state at the end of his visit, when he would let him know if he was prepared to continue with the scheme.

After lunch Eduardo was driven to the Federal Palace Hotel, where the entire sixth floor had been placed at his disposal. Several complaining guests who had come to Nigeria to close deals involving mere millions had been asked to vacate their rooms at short notice to make way for de Silveira and his staff. Eduardo knew nothing of these goings-on, since there was always a room available for him wherever he arrived in the world.

The six Mercedeses drew up outside the hotel and the colonel guided his charge through the swinging doors and past reception. Eduardo had not checked himself into a hotel for the past fourteen years except on those occasions when he chose to register under an assumed name, not wanting anyone to know the identity of the woman he was with.

The chairman of Prentino International walked down the center of the hotel's main corridor and stepped into a waiting elevator. His legs went weak, and he suddenly felt sick. In the corner of the elevator stood a stubby, balding, overweight man, who was dressed in a pair of old jeans and a T-shirt, his mouth continually opening and closing as he chewed gum. The two men stood as far apart as possible, neither showing any sign of recognition. The elevator stopped at the fifth floor, and Manuel Rodrigues, chairman of Rodrigues International SA, stepped out, leaving behind him the man who had been his bitter rival for thirty years.

Eduardo held on to the rail in the elevator to steady himself, for he still felt dizzy. How he despised that uneducated self-made upstart whose family of four half-brothers, all by different fathers, claimed that they now ran the largest construction company in Brazil. Both men were as interested in the other's failure as they were in their own success.

Eduardo was somewhat puzzled to know what Rodrigues could possibly be doing in Lagos, since he felt certain that his rival had not come into contact with the Nigerian president. After all, Eduardo had never collected the rent on a small house in Rio that was occupied by the mistress of a very senior official in the government's protocol department. And the man's only task was to be certain that Rodrigues was never

invited to any function attended by a visiting dignitary in
Brazil. The continual absence of Rodrigues from these state
occasions ensured the absent-mindedness of Eduardo's rent
collector in Rio.

Eduardo would never have admitted to anyone that
Rodrigues's presence worried him, but he nevertheless resolved
to find out immediately what had brought his old enemy to
Nigeria. Once he reached his suite de Silveira instructed his
private secretary to check what Manuel Rodrigues was up to.
Eduardo was prepared to return to Brazil immediately if
Rodrigues turned out to be involved in any way with the new
capital project, while one young lady in Rio would suddenly
find herself looking for alternative accommodation.

Within an hour, his private secretary returned with the information his chairman had requested. Rodrigues, he had discovered, was in Nigeria to tender for the contract to construct a
new port in Lagos and was apparently not involved in any way
with the new capital; in fact, he was still trying to arrange a
meeting with the president.

"Which minister is in charge of the ports and when am I due
to see him?" asked de Silveira.

The secretary delved into his appointments file. "The trans-
portation minister," the secretary said. "You have an appointment with him at nine o'clock on Thursday morning." The
Nigerian civil service had mapped out a four-day schedule of
meetings for de Silveira that included every cabinet minister
involved in the new city project. "It's the last meeting before
your final discussion with the president. You then fly on to
Paris."

"Excellent. Remind me of this conversation five minutes
before I see the minister and again when I talk to the president."

The secretary made a note in the file and left.

Eduardo sat alone in his suite, going over the reports on the
new capital project submitted by his experts. Some of his team
were already showing signs of nervousness. One particular anxiety that always came up with a large construction contract was
the principal's ability to pay, and pay on time. Failure to do so

was the quickest route to bankruptcy, but since the discovery of oil in Nigeria there seemed to be no shortage of income—and certainly no shortage of people willing to spend that money on behalf of the government. These anxieties did not worry de Silveira, who always insisted on a substantial payment in advance; otherwise he wouldn't move himself or his vast staff one centimeter out of Brazil. However, the massive scope of this particular contract made the circumstances somewhat unusual. Eduardo realized that it would be most damaging to his international reputation if he started the assignment and then was seen not to complete it. He reread the reports over a quiet dinner in his room and retired to bed early, having wasted an hour vainly trying to place a call to his wife.

De Silveira's first appointment the next morning was with the governor of the Central Bank of Nigeria. Eduardo wore a newly pressed suit, fresh shirt, and highly polished shoes: For four days no one would see him in the same clothes. At 8:45 there was a quiet knock on the door of his suite, and the secretary opened it to find Colonel Usman standing to attention, waiting to escort Eduardo to the bank. As they were leaving the hotel Eduardo again saw Manuel Rodrigues, wearing the same pair of jeans, the same crumpled T-shirt, and probably chewing the same gum as he stepped into a BMW. De Silveira only stopped scowling at the disappearing BMW when he remembered his Thursday-morning appointment with the minister in charge of ports, followed by a meeting with the president.

The governor of the Central Bank of Nigeria was in the habit of proposing how payment schedules would be met and completion orders would be guaranteed. He had never been told by anyone that if the payment was seven days overdue he could consider the contract null and void, and they could take it or leave it. The minister would have made some comment if Abuja had not been the president's pet project. That position established, de Silveira went on to check the bank's reserves, long-term deposits, overseas commitments, and estimated oil revenues for the next five years. He left the governor in what could only be described as a jellylike state: glistening and wobbly. Eduardo's next appointment was an unavoidable courtesy call on the Brazilian ambassador for lunch. He hated these functions, believing embassies to be fit only for cocktail parties and discussion of out-of-date trivia, neither of which he cared for. The food in such establishments was invariably bad and the company worse. It turned out to be no different on this occasion, and the only profit (Eduardo considered everything in terms of profit and loss) to be derived from the encounter was the information that Manuel Rodrigues was on a shortlist of three for the building of the new port in Lagos, and was expecting to have an audience with the president on Friday if he was awarded the contract. By Thursday morning that will be a shortlist of two and there will be no meeting with the president, de Silveira promised himself, considering that that was the most he was likely to gain from the lunch, until the ambassador added: "Rodrigues seems most keen on you being awarded the new city contract at Abuja. He's singing your praises to every minister he meets. Funny," the ambassador continued. "I always thought you two didn't see eye to eye."

Eduardo made no reply as he tried to fathom what trick Rodrigues could be up to by promoting his cause.

Eduardo spent the afternoon with the minister of finance and confirmed the provisional arrangements he had made with the governor of the bank. The minister of finance had been forewarned by the governor what he was to expect from an encounter with Eduardo de Silveira, and that he was not to be taken aback by the Brazilian's curt demands. De Silveira, aware that this warning would have taken place, let the poor man bargain a little and even gave way on a few minor points that he would be able to tell the President about at the next meeting of the Supreme Military Council. Eduardo left the smiling minister believing that he had scored a point or two against the formidable South American.

That evening, Eduardo dined privately with his senior advisers, who themselves were already dealing with the ministers' officials. Each was now coming up with daily reports about the problems that would have to be faced if they worked in Nigeria. His chief engineer was quick to emphasize that skilled labor could not be hired at any price because the Germans had already cornered the market for their extensive road projects. The financial advisers also presented a gloomy report, of international companies waiting six months or more for their checks to be cleared by the central bank. Eduardo made notes on the views they expressed but never ventured an opinion himself. His staff left him a little after eleven, and he decided to take a stroll around the hotel grounds before retiring to bed. On his walk through the luxuriant tropical gardens he only just avoided a face-to-face confrontation with Manuel Rodrigues by darting behind a large Iroko plant. The little man passed by champing away at his gum, oblivious to Eduardo's baleful glare. Eduardo informed a chattering gray parrot of his most secret thoughts: by Thursday afternoon, Rodrigues, you will be on your way back to Brazil with a suitcase full of plans that can be filed under "aborted projects." The parrot cocked his head and screeched at him as if he had been let in on the secret. Eduardo allowed himself a smile and returned to his room.

Colonel Usman arrived on the dot of 8:45 again the next day and Eduardo spent the morning with the Minister of Supplies and Co-operatives—or lack of them, as he commented to his private secretary afterwards. The afternoon was spent with the Minister of Labour checking over the availability of unskilled workers and the total lack of skilled operatives. Eduardo was fast reaching the conclusion that, despite the professed optimism of the ministers concerned, this was going to be the toughest contract he had ever tackled. There was more to be lost than money if the whole international business world stood watching him fall flat on his face. In the evening his staff reported to him once again, having solved a few old problems and unearthed some new ones. Tentatively, they had come to the conclusion that if the present regime stayed in power, there need be no serious concern over payment, as the President had earmarked the new city as a priority project. They had even heard a rumor that the army would be willing to lend-lease part of the Service Corps if there turned out to be a shortage of skilled labor. Eduardo made a note to have this point confirmed in writing by the head of state during their final meeting the next day. But the labor problem was not what was occupying Eduardo's thoughts as he put on his silk pajamas that night. He was chuckling at the idea of Manuel Rodrigues's imminent and sudden departure for Brazil. Eduardo slept well.

He rose with renewed vigor the next morning, showered, and put on a fresh suit. The four days were turning out to be well worth while and a single stone might yet kill two birds. By 8:45, he was waiting impatiently for the previously punctual colonel. The colonel did not show up at 8:45 and had still not appeared when the clock on his mantelpiece struck 9:00. De Silveira sent his private secretary off to find out where he was while he paced angrily backward and forward through the hotel suite. His secretary returned a few minutes later in a panic, with the information that the hotel was surrounded by armed guards. Eduardo did not panic. He had been through eight coups in his life from which he had learned one golden rule: The new regime never kills visiting foreigners as it needs their money every bit as much as the last government. Eduardo picked up the telephone but no one answered him, so he switched on the radio. A tape recording was playing:

"This is Radio Nigeria, this is Radio Nigeria. There has been a coup. General Mohammed has been overthrown and Lieutenant Colonel Dimka has assumed leadership of the new revolutionary government. Do not be afraid; remain at home and everything will be back to normal in a few hours. This is Radio Nigeria, this is Radio Nigeria. There has been a . . . "

Eduardo switched off the radio as two thoughts flashed through his mind: Coups always held up everything and caused chaos, so undoubtedly he had wasted the four days. But worse, would it now be possible for him even to get out of Nigeria and carry on his normal business with the rest of the world?

By lunchtime, the radio was playing martial music interspersed with the tape-recorded message he now knew off by heart. Eduardo detailed all his staff to find out anything they could and to report back to him direct. They all returned with the same story: that it was impossible to get past the soldiers surrounding the hotel, so no new information could be unearthed. Eduardo swore for the first time in months. To add to his inconvenience, the hotel manager rang to say that regretably Mr. de Silveira would have to eat in the main dining room as there would be no room service until further notice. Eduardo went down to the dining room somewhat reluctantly, only to discover that the headwaiter showed no interest in who he was and placed him unceremoniously at a small table already occupied by three Italians. Manuel Rodrigues was seated only two tables away: Eduardo stiffened at the thought of the other man enjoying his discomfiture and then remembered it was that morning he was supposed to have seen the minister of ports. He ate his meal quickly despite being served slowly, and when the Italians tried to make conversation with him he waved them away with his hand, feigning lack of understanding, despite the fact that he spoke their language fluently. As soon as he had finished the second course he returned to his room. His staff had only gossip to pass on and they had been unable to make contact with the Brazilian Embassy to lodge an official protest. "A lot of good an official protest will do us," said Eduardo, slumping down in his chair. "Who do you send it to, the new regime or the old one?"

He sat alone in his room for the rest of the day, interrupted only by what he thought was the sound of gunfire in the distance. He read the New Federal Capital project proposal and his advisers' reports for a third time.

The next morning Eduardo, dressed in the same suit he had worn on the day of his arrival, was greeted by his secretary with the news that the coup had been crushed; after fierce street fighting, he informed his unusually attentive chairman, the old regime had regained power but not without losses; among those killed in the uprising had been General Mohammed, the head of state. The secretary's news was officially confirmed on Radio Nigeria later that morning. The ringleader of the abortive coup had been one Lieutenant Colonel Dimka: Dimka, along with one or two junior officers, had escaped, and the government had ordered a dusk-to-dawn curfew until the evil criminals were apprehended.

Pull off a coup and you're a national hero; fail and you're an evil criminal. In business it's the same difference between bankruptcy and making a fortune, considered Eduardo as he listened to the news report. He was beginning to form plans in his mind for an early departure from Nigeria when the newscaster made an announcement that chilled him to the very marrow.

"While Lieutenant Colonel Dimka and his accomplices remain on the run, airports throughout the country will be closed until further notice."

When the newscaster had finished his report, martial music was played in memory of the late General Mohammed.

Eduardo went downstairs in a flaming temper. The hotel was still surrounded by armed guards. He stared at the fleet of six empty Mercedeses, which was parked only ten yards beyond the soldiers' rifles. He marched back into the foyer, irritated by the babble of different tongues coming at him from every direction. Eduardo looked around him: It was obvious that many people had been stranded in the hotel overnight and had ended up sleeping in the lounge or the bar. He checked the paperback rack in the lobby for something to read, but there were only four copies left of a tourist guide to Lagos; everything had been sold. Authors who had not been read for years were now changing hands at a premium. Eduardo returned to his room, which was fast assuming the character of a prison, and balked at reading the New Federal Capital project for a fourth time. He tried again to make contact with the Brazilian ambassador to discover if he could obtain special permission to leave the country as he had his own aircraft. No one answered the embassy phone. He went down for an early lunch only to find the dining room was once again packed to capacity. Eduardo was placed at a table with some Germans who were worrying about a contract that had been signed by the government the previous week, before the aborted coup. They were wondering if it would still be honored. Manuel Rodrigues entered the room a few minutes later and was placed at the next table.

During the afternoon, de Silveira ruefully examined his schedule for the next seven days. He had been due in Paris that morning to see the minister of the interior, and from there should have flown on to London to confer with the chairman of the Steel Board. His calendar was fully booked for the next ninety-two days until his family vacation in May. "I'm having this year's vacation in Nigeria," he commented wryly to an assistant.

What annoyed Eduardo most about the coup was the lack of communication it afforded with the outside world. He wondered what was going on in Brazil and he hated not being able to telephone or telex Paris or London to explain his absence personally. He listened addictively to Radio Nigeria on the hour every hour for any new scrap of information. At five o'clock, he learned that the Supreme Military Council had elected a new President who would address the nation on television and radio at nine o'clock that night.

Eduardo de Silveira switched on the television at 8:45. Normally an assistant would have put it on for him at one minute to nine. He sat watching a Nigerian woman giving a talk on dressmaking, followed by the weather forecast man who supplied Eduardo with the revealing information that the temperature would continue to be hot for the next month. Eduardo's knee was twitching up and down nervously as he waited for the address by the new president. At nine o'clock, after the national anthem had been played, the new head of state, General Obasanjo, appeared on the screen in full-dress uniform. He spoke first of the tragic death and sad loss for the nation of the late president, and went on to say that his government would continue to work in the best interest of Nigeria. He looked ill at ease as he apologized to all foreign visitors who were inconvenienced by the attempted coup but went on to make it clear that the dusk-to-dawn curfew would continue until the rebel leaders were tracked down and brought to justice. He confirmed that all airports would remain closed until Lieutenant Colonel Dimka was in safe custody. The new president ended his statement by saying that all other forms of communication would be opened up again as soon as possible. The national anthem was played for a second time, while Eduardo thought of the millions of dollars that might be lost to him by his incarceration in that hotel room, while his private plane sat idly on the tarmac only a few miles away. One of his senior managers started to take bets on how long it would take for the authorities to capture Lieutenant Colonel Dimka; he did not tell de Silveira how short the odds were on a month.

Eduardo went down to the dining room in the suit he had worn the day before. A junior waiter placed him at a table with some Frenchmen who had been hoping to win a contract to drill bore holes in the Niger state. Again Eduardo waved a languid hand when they tried to include him in their conversation. At that very moment he was meant to be with the French minister of the interior, not with some French hole borers. He tried to concentrate on his watered-down soup, wondering how much longer it would be before it would be just water. The headwaiter appeared by his side, gesturing to the one remaining seat at the table, in which he placed Manuel Rodrigues. Still neither man gave any sign of recognizing the other. Eduardo debated with himself whether he should leave the table or carry on as if his oldest rival were still in Brazil. He decided the latter was more dignified. The Frenchmen began an argument among themselves as to when they would be able to get out of Lagos. One of them declared emphatically that he had heard on the highest authority that the government intended to track down every last one of those involved in the coup before they opened the airports and that might take up to a month.

"What?" said the two Brazilians together, in English.

"I can't stay here for a month," said Eduardo.

"Neither can I," said Manuel Rodrigues.

"You'll have to, at least until Dimka is captured," said one of the Frenchmen, breaking into English. "So you must both relax yourselves, yes?"

The two Brazilians continued their meal in silence. When Eduardo had finished he rose from the table and without looking directly at Rodrigues said good night in Portuguese. The old rival inclined his head in reply to the salutation.

The next day brought forth no new information. The hotel remained surrounded with soldiers and by the evening Eduardo had lost his temper with every member of staff with whom he had come into contact. He went down to dinner on his own and as he entered the dining room he saw Manuel

Rodrigues sitting alone at a table in the corner. Rodrigues looked up, seemed to hesitate for a moment, and then beckoned to Eduardo. Eduardo himself hesitated before walking slowly toward Rodrigues and taking the seat opposite him. Rodrigues poured him a glass of wine. Eduardo, who rarely drank, drank it. Their conversation was stilted to begin with, but as both men consumed more wine so they each began to relax in the other's company. By the time coffee had arrived, Manuel was telling Eduardo what he could do with this godforsaken country.

"You will not stay on, if you are awarded the port contract?" inquired Eduardo.

"Not a hope," said Rodrigues, who showed no surprise that de Silveira knew of his interest in the port contract. "I withdrew from the shortlist the day before the coup. I had intended to fly back to Brazil that Thursday morning."

"Can you say why you withdrew?"

"Labor problems mainly, and then the congestion of the ports."

"I am not sure I understand," said Eduardo, understanding full well but curious to learn if Rodrigues had picked up some tiny detail his own staff had missed.

Manuel Rodrigues paused to ingest the fact that the man he had viewed as his most dangerous enemy for more than thirty years was now listening to his own inside information. He considered the situation for a moment while he sipped his coffee. Eduardo didn't speak.

"To begin with, there's a terrible shortage of skilled labor, and on top of that there's this insane quota system."

"Quota system?" said Eduardo innocently.

"The percentage of people from the contractor's country which the government will allow to work in Nigeria."

"Why should that be a problem?" said Eduardo, leaning forward.

"By law, you have to employ at a ratio of fifty nationals to one foreigner, so I could only have brought over twenty-five of my top men to organize a fifty-million-dollar contract, and I'd have had to make do with Nigerians at every other level. The government is cutting its own throat with the wretched system; they can't expect unskilled men, black or white, to become experienced engineers overnight. It's all to do with their national pride. Someone must tell them they can't afford that sort of pride if they want to complete the job at a sensible price. That path is the surest route to bankruptcy. On top of that, the Germans have already rounded up all the best skilled labor for their road projects."

"But surely," said Eduardo, "you charge according to the rules, however stupid, thus covering all eventualities, and as long as you're certain that payment is guaranteed . . . "

Manuel raised his hand to stop Eduardo's flow: "That's another problem. You can't be certain. The government reneged on a major steel contract only last month. In so doing," he explained, "they had bankrupted a distinguished international company. So they are perfectly capable of trying the same trick with me. And if they don't pay up, who do you sue? The Supreme Military Council?"

"And the port problem?"

"The port is totally congested. There are 170 ships desperate to unload their cargo with a waiting time of anything up to six months. On top of that, there is a demurrage charge of five thousand dollars a day, and only perishable foods are given any priority."

"But there's always a way around that sort of problem," said Eduardo, rubbing a thumb twice across the top of his fingers.

"Bribery? It doesn't work, Eduardo. How can you possibly jump the line when all 170 ships have already bribed the harbor master? And don't imagine that fixing the rent on apartment for one of his mistresses would help either," said Rodrigues, grinning. "With that man you will have to supply the mistress as well."

Eduardo held his breath but said nothing.

"Come to think of it," continued Rodrigues, "if the situation becomes any worse, the harbor master will be the one man in the country who is richer than you."

Eduardo laughed for the first time in three days.

"I tell you, Eduardo, we could make a bigger profit building a salt mine in Siberia."

Eduardo laughed again, and some of the Prentino and Rodrigues staff dining at other tables stared in disbelief at their masters.

"You were in for the big one, the new city of Abuja?" said Manuel.

"That's right," admitted Eduardo.

"I have done everything in my power to make sure you were awarded that contract," said the other quietly.

"What?" said Eduardo in disbelief. "Why?"

"I thought Abuja would give the Prentino empire more headaches than even you could cope with, Eduardo, and that might possibly leave the field wide open for me at home. Think about it. Every time there's a cutback in Nigeria, what will be the first head to roll off the chopping block? 'The unnecessary city,' as the locals all call it."

"The unnecessary city?" repeated Eduardo.

"Yes, and it doesn't help when you say you won't move without advance payment. You know as well as I do, you will need one hundred of your best men here full time to organize such a massive enterprise. They'll need feeding, salaries, housing, perhaps even a school and a hospital. Once they are settled down here, you can't just pull them off the job every two weeks because the government is running late clearing the checks. It's not practical, and you know it." Rodrigues poured Eduardo de Silveira another glass of wine.

"I had already taken that into consideration," Eduardo said, as he sipped the wine, "but I thought that with the support of the head of state . . . "

"The late head of state."

"I take your point, Manuel."

"Maybe the next head of state will also back you, but what about the one after that? Nigeria has had three coups in the past three years."

Eduardo remained silent for a moment.

"Do you play backgammon?"

"Yes. Why do you ask?"

"I must make *some* money while I'm here." Manuel laughed.

"Why don't you come to my room," continued de Silveira. "Though I must warn you I always manage to beat my staff."

"Perhaps they always manage to lose," said Manuel, as he rose and grabbed the half empty bottle of wine by its neck. Both men were laughing as they left the dining room.

After that, the two chairmen had lunch and dinner together every day. Within a week, their staff were eating at the same tables. Eduardo could be seen in the dining room without a tie, while Manuel wore a shirt for the first time in years. By the end of two weeks, the two rivals had played each other at table tennis, backgammon, and bridge with the stakes set at one hundred dollars a point. At the end of each day Eduardo always seemed to end up owing Manuel about a million dollars, which Manuel happily traded for the best bottle of wine left in the hotel's cellar.

Although Lieutenant Colonel Dimka had been sighted by about forty thousand Nigerians in about as many different places, he still remained resolutely uncaptured. As the new president had insisted, airports remained closed but communications were opened which at least allowed Eduardo to telephone and telex Brazil. His brothers and wife were sending replies by the hour, imploring Eduardo to return home at any cost: Decisions on major contracts throughout the world were being held up by his absence. But Eduardo's message back to Brazil was always the same: As long as Dimka is on the loose, the airports will remain closed.

It was on a Tuesday night during dinner that Eduardo took the trouble to explain to Manuel why Brazil had lost the World Cup. Manuel dismissed Eduardo's outrageous claims as ill informed and prejudiced. It was the only subject on which they hadn't agreed in the past three weeks.

"I blame the whole fiasco on Zagalo," said Eduardo.

"No, no, you cannot blame the manager," said Manuel. "The fault lies with our stupid selectors, who know even less about football than you do. They should never have dropped Leao from goal, and in any case we should have learned from the

Argentinian defeat last year that our methods are now out of date. You must attack, attack, if you want to score goals."

"Rubbish. We still have the surest defense in the world."

"Which means the best result you can hope for is a 0–0 draw."

"Never . . ." began Eduardo.

"Excuse me, sir." Eduardo looked up to see his private secretary standing by his side looking anxiously down at him.

"Yes, what's the problem?"

"An urgent telex from Brazil, sir."

Eduardo read the first paragraph and then asked Manuel if he would be kind enough to excuse him for a few minutes. The latter nodded politely. Eduardo left the table, and as he marched through the dining room seventeen other guests left unfinished meals and followed him quickly to his suite on the top floor, where the rest of his staff was already assembled. He sat down in the corner of the room on his own. No one spoke as he read through the telex carefully, suddenly realizing how many days he had been imprisoned in Lagos.

The telex was from his brother Carlos, and the contents concerned the Pan-American road project, an eight-lane highway that would stretch from Brazil to Mexico. Prentino's had tendered for the section that ran through the middle of the Amazon jungle and had to have the bank guarantees signed and certified by midday tomorrow, Tuesday. But Eduardo had quite forgotten which Tuesday it was, and the document he was committed to sign by the following day's deadline.

"What's the problem?" Eduardo asked his private secretary. "The Banco do Brasil has already agreed with Alfredo to act as guarantors. What's stopping Carlos signing the agreement in my absence?"

"The Mexicans are now demanding that responsibility for the contract be shared because of the insurance problems: Lloyd's of London will not cover the entire risk if only one company is involved. The details are all on page seven of the telex."

Eduardo flicked quickly through the pages. He read that his brothers had already tried to put pressure on Lloyd's, but to no avail. That's like trying to bribe a maiden aunt into taking part in a public orgy, thought Eduardo, and he would have told them as much if he had been back in Brazil. The Mexican government was therefore insisting that the contract be shared with an international construction company acceptable to Lloyd's if the legal documents were to be signed by the midday deadline the following day.

"Stay put," said Eduardo to his staff, and he returned to the dining room alone, trailing the long telex behind him. Rodrigues watched him as he scurried back to their table.

"You look like a man with a problem."

"I am," said Eduardo. "Read that."

Manuel's experienced eye ran down the telex, picking out the salient points. He had tendered for the Amazon road project himself and could still recall the details. At Eduardo's insistence, he reread page seven.

"Mexican bandits," he said as he returned the telex to Eduardo. "Who do they think they are, telling Eduardo de Silveira how he must conduct his business. Telex them back immediately and inform them you're chairman of the greatest construction company in the world and they can roast in hell before you will agree to their pathetic terms. You know it's far too late for them to go out to tender again with every other section of the highway ready to begin work. They would lose millions. Call their bluff, Eduardo."

"I think you may be right, Manuel, but any holdup now can only waste my time and money, so I intend to agree to their demand and look for a partner."

"You'll never find one at such short notice."

"I will."

"Who?"

Eduardo de Silveira hesitated only for a second. "You, Manuel. I want to offer Rodrigues International SA fifty percent of the Amazon road contract."

Manuel Rodrigues looked up at Eduardo. It was the first time that he had not anticipated his old rival's next move. "I suppose it might help cover the millions you owe me in table tennis debts."

The two men laughed, then Rodrigues stood up and they

shook hands gravely. De Silveira left the dining room on the run and wrote out a telex for his manager to transmit.

"Sign, accept terms, fifty per cent partner will be Rodrigues International Construction SA, Brazil."

"If I telex that message, sir, you do realize that it's legally binding?"

"Send it," said Eduardo.

Eduardo returned once again to the dining room, where Manuel had ordered the finest bottle of champagne in the hotel. Just as they were calling for a second bottle, and singing a spirited version of *Esta Cheganda a Hora*, Eduardo's private secretary appeared by his side again, this time with two telexes, one from the President of the Banco do Brasil and a second from his brother Carlos. Both wanted confirmation of the agreed partner for the Amazon road project. Eduardo uncorked the second bottle of champagne without looking up at his private secretary.

"Confirm Rodrigues International Construction to the president of the bank and my brother," he said as he filled Manuel's empty glass. "And don't bother me again tonight."

"Yes, sir," said the private secretary and left without another word.

Neither man could recall what time he climbed into bed that night, but de Silveira was abruptly awakened from a deep sleep by his secretary early the next morning. Eduardo took a few minutes to digest the news. Lieutenant Colonel Dimka had been caught in Kano at three o'clock that morning, and all the airports were now open again. Eduardo picked up the phone and dialed three digits.

"Manuel, you've heard the news? Good. Then you must fly back with me in my 707 or it may be days before you get out. One hour's time in the lobby. See you then."

At 8:45 there was a quiet knock on the door, and Eduardo's secretary opened it to find Colonel Usman standing to attention, just as he had done in the days before the coup. He held a note in his hand. Eduardo tore open the envelope to find an invitation to lunch that day with the new head of state, General Obasanjo.

"Please convey my apologies to your president," said Eduardo, "and be kind enough to explain that I have pressing commitments to attend to in my own country."

The colonel retired reluctantly. Eduardo dressed in the suit, shirt, and tie he had worn on his first day in Nigeria and took the lift downstairs to the lobby where he joined Manuel, who was once more wearing jeans and a T-shirt. The two chairmen left the hotel and climbed into the back of the leading Mercedes and the motorcade of six began its journey to the airport. The colonel, who now sat in front with the driver, did not venture to speak to either of the distinguished Brazilians for the entire journey. The two men, he would be able to tell the new president later, seemed to be preoccupied with a discussion on an Amazon road project and how the responsibility should be divided between their two companies.

Customs were bypassed as neither man had anything they wanted to take out of the country other than themselves, and the fleet of cars came to a halt at the side of Eduardo's blue and silver 707. The staff of both companies climbed aboard the rear section of the aircraft, also engrossed in discussion on the Amazon road project.

A corporal jumped out of the lead car and opened the back door, to allow the two chairmen to walk straight up the steps and board the front section of the aircraft.

As Eduardo stepped out of the Mercedes, the Nigerian driver saluted smartly. "Good-bye, sir," he said, revealing the large set of white teeth once again.

Eduardo said nothing.

"I hope," said the corporal politely, "you made very big deal while you were in Nigeria."

THE PERFECT
MURDER

IF I HADN'T CHANGED my mind that night I would never have found out the truth.

I couldn't believe that Carla had slept with another man, that she had lied about her love for me—and that I might be second or even third in her affections.

Carla had phoned me at the office during the day, something I had told her not to do, but since I also warned her never to call me at home she hadn't been left with a lot of choice. As it turned out, all she had wanted to let me know was that she wouldn't be able to make it for what the French so decorously call a *cinq à sept*. She had to visit her sister in Fulham who had been taken ill, she explained.

I was disappointed. It had been another depressing day, and now I was being asked to forgo the one thing that would have made it bearable.

"I thought you didn't get on well with your sister," I said tartly.

There was no immediate reply from the other end. Eventually Carla asked, "Shall we make it next Tuesday, the usual time?"

"I don't know if that's convenient," I said. "I'll call you on Monday when I know what my plans are." I put down the receiver.

Wearily, I phoned my wife to let her know I was on the way home—something I usually did from the phone booth outside Carla's apartment. It was a trick I often used to make Elizabeth feel she knew where I was every moment of the day.

Most of the office staff had already left for the night, so I gathered together some papers I could work on at home. Since the new company had taken us over six months ago, the management had not only fired my number two in the accounts department but expected me to cover his work as well as my own. I was hardly in a position to complain, since my new boss made it abundantly clear that if I didn't like the arrangement I should feel free to seek employment elsewhere. I might have, too, but I couldn't think of many firms that would readily take on a man who had reached that magic age somewhere between the sought-after and the available.

As I drove out of the office parking lot and joined the evening rush hour I began to regret having been so sharp with Carla. After all, the role of the other woman was hardly one she delighted in. The feeling of guilt persisted, so that when I reached the corner of Sloane Square, I jumped out of my car and ran across the road.

"A dozen roses," I said, fumbling with my wallet.

A man who must have made his profit from lovers selected twelve unopened buds without comment. My choice didn't show a great deal of imagination, but at least Carla would know I'd tried.

I drove on toward her flat, hoping she had not yet left for her sister's, that perhaps we might even find time for a quick drink. Then I remembered that I had already told my wife I was on the way home. A few minutes' delay could be explained by a traffic jam, but that lame excuse could hardly cover my staying on for a drink.

When I arrived at Carla's home I had the usual trouble finding a parking space, until I spotted a gap that would just take a Rover opposite the newsstand. I stopped and would have backed into the space had I not noticed a man coming out of the entrance to her apartment house. I wouldn't have given it a second thought if Carla hadn't followed him a moment later. She stood there in the doorway, wearing a loose blue housecoat. She leaned forward to give her departing visitor a kiss that could hardly have been described as sisterly. As she closed the door I drove my car around the corner and double-parked.

I watched the man in my rearview mirror as he crossed the street, went to the newsstand, and a few moments later reappeared with an evening paper and what looked like a pack of cigarettes. He walked to his car, a blue BMW, stopped to remove a parking ticket from his windshield, and appeared to curse. How long had the BMW been there? I even began to wonder if he had been with Carla when she phoned to tell me not to come around.

The man climbed into the BMW, fastened his seat belt, and lit a cigarette before driving off. I took his parking space in part payment for my woman. I didn't consider it a fair exchange. I checked up and down the street, as I always did, before getting out and walking over to the apartment house. It was already dark, and no one gave me a second glance. I pressed the bell marked "Moorland."

When Carla opened the front door I was greeted with a huge smile that quickly turned into a frown, then just as quickly back to a smile. The first smile must have been meant for the BMW man. I often wondered why she wouldn't give me a front-door key. I stared into those blue eyes that had first captivated me so many months ago. Despite her smile, those eyes now revealed a coldness I had never seen before.

She turned to reopen the door and let me into her ground-floor apartment. I noticed that under her housecoat she was wearing the wine-red negligee I had given her for Christmas. Once inside the flat I found myself checking round the room I knew so well. On the glass table in the center of the room stood the "Snoopy" coffee mug I usually drank from, empty. By its side was Carla's mug, also empty, and a dozen roses arranged in a vase. The buds were just beginning to open.

I have always been quick to chide, and the sight of the flowers made it impossible for me to hide my anger.

"And who was the man who just left?" I asked.

"An insurance broker," she replied, removing the mugs from the table.

"And what was he insuring?" I asked. "Your love life?"

"Why do you automatically assume he's my lover?" Her voice had begun to rise.

"Do you usually have coffee with an insurance broker in your negligee? Come to think of it, *my* negligee."

"I'll have coffee with whom I damn well please," she said, "and wearing what I damn well please, especially when you are on your way home to your wife."

"But I had wanted to come to you—"

"And then return to your wife. In any case, you're always telling me I should lead my own life and not rely on you," she added, an argument Carla often fell back on when she had something to hide.

"You know it's not that easy."

"I know it's easy enough for you to jump into bed with me whenever it suits you. That's all I'm good for, isn't it?"

"That's not fair."

"Not fair? Weren't you hoping for your usual at six so you could still be home at seven in time for supper with Elizabeth?"

"I haven't made love to my wife in years!" I shouted.

"We only have your word for that," she spit out with scorn.

"I have been utterly faithful to you."

"Which means I always have to be to you, I suppose?"

"Stop behaving like a whore."

Carla's eyes flashed as she leaped forward and slapped me across the face with all the strength she could muster.

I was still slightly off balance when she raised her arm a second time, but as her hand came swinging toward me I blocked it and was even able to push her back against the mantelpiece. She recovered quickly and came flying at me again.

In a moment of uncontrolled fury, just as she was about to launch herself at me, I clenched my fist and took a swing at her. I caught her on the side of the chin, and she wheeled back from the impact. I watched her put an arm out to break her fall. But before she had the chance to leap back up and retaliate, I turned and strode out, slamming the apartment door behind me.

I ran down the hall, out onto the street, jumped into my car, and drove off quickly. I couldn't have been with her for more than ten minutes. Although I felt like murdering her at the time, I regretted having hit her long before I reached home. Twice I nearly turned back. Everything she had complained about was fair, and I wondered if I dared phone her from home. Although Carla and I had only been lovers for a few months, she must have known how much I cared.

If Elizabeth had intended to comment on my being late, she changed her mind the moment I handed her the roses. She began to arrange them in a vase while I poured myself a large whiskey. I waited for her to say something, since I rarely drank before dinner, but she seemed preoccupied with the flowers. Although I had already made up my mind to phone Carla and try to make amends, I decided I couldn't do it from home. In any case, if I waited until the morning when I was back in the office, she might by then have calmed down a little.

I woke early the next day and lay in bed, considering what form my apology should take. I decided to invite her to lunch at the little French bistro she liked so much, halfway between my office and hers. Carla always appreciated seeing me in the middle of the day, when she knew it couldn't be for sex. After I had shaved and dressed I joined Elizabeth for breakfast, and seeing there was nothing interesting on the front page, I turned to the financial section. The company's stock had fallen again, following City forecasts of poor interim profits. Millions would undoubtedly be wiped off our stock value following such a bad piece of publicity. I already knew that when it came to publishing the annual accounts, it would be a miracle if the company didn't declare a loss.

After gulping down a second cup of coffee, I kissed my wife on the cheek and made for the car. It was then that I decided to drop a note into Carla's mailbox rather than cope with the embarrassment of a phone call.

"Forgive me," I wrote. "Marcel's, one o'clock. *Sole Véronique* on a Friday. Love, Casaneva." I rarely wrote to Carla, and when I did I only ever signed it with her chosen nickname.

I took a short detour so that I could pass her home but was held up by a traffic jam. As I approached the apartment I could see that the holdup was being caused by some sort of accident. It had to be quite a serious one because there was an ambulance blocking the other side of the road and delaying the flow of oncoming vehicles. A traffic officer was trying to help, but she was only slowing things down even more. It was obvious that it was going to be impossible to park anywhere near Carla's appartment, so I resigned myself to phoning her from the office. I did not relish the prospect.

I felt a sinking feeling moments later when I saw that the ambulance was parked only a few yards from the front door to her apartment house. I knew I was being irrational, but I began to fear the worst. I tried to convince myself it was probably a road accident and had nothing to do with Carla.

It was then that I spotted the police car tucked in behind the ambulance.

As I drew up with the two vehicles I saw that Carla's front door was wide open. A man in a long white coat came scurrying out and opened the back of the ambulance. I stopped my car to observe more carefully what was going on, hoping the man behind me would not become impatient. Drivers coming from the other direction raised a hand to thank me for allowing them to pass. I thought I could let a dozen or so through before anyone would start to complain. The traffic officer helped by urging them on.

Then a stretcher appeared at the end of the hall. Two uniformed orderlies carried a shrouded body out onto the road and placed it in the back of the ambulance. I was unable to see the face because it was covered by the sheet, but a third man, who could only have been a detective, walked immediately behind the stretcher. He was carrying a plastic bag, inside which I could make out a red garment that I feared was the negligee I had given Carla.

I vomited my breakfast all over the passenger seat, my head finally resting on the steering wheel. A moment later they closed the ambulance door, a siren started up, and the traffic officer began waving me on. The ambulance moved quickly off, and the man behind me started to press his horn. He was, after all, only an innocent bysitter. I lurched forward and later couldn't recall any part of my journey to the office.

Once I had reached the office parking lot, I cleared up the mess on the passenger seat as best I could and left a window open before taking an elevator to the washroom on the seventh floor. I tore my lunch invitation to Carla into little pieces and flushed them down the lavatory. I walked into my room on the twelfth floor a little after eight-thirty, to find the managing director pacing up and down in front of my desk, obviously waiting for me. I had quite forgotten that it was Friday, and he always expected the latest completed figures to be ready for his consideration.

This Friday it turned out he also wanted the projected accounts for the months of May, June, and July. I promised they would be on his desk by midday. The one thing I needed was a clear morning, and I was not going to be allowed it.

Every time the phone rang, the door opened, or anyone even spoke to me, my heart missed a beat—I assumed it could only be the police. By midday I had finished some sort of report for the managing director, but I knew he would find it neither adequate nor accurate. As soon as I had deposited the papers with his secretary, I left for an early lunch. I realized I wouldn't be able to eat anything, but at least I could get hold of the first edition of the *Standard* and search for any news they might have picked up about Carla's death.

I sat in the corner of my local pub, where I knew I couldn't be seen from behind the bar. A tomato juice by my side, I began slowly to turn the pages of the paper.

She hadn't made page one. She hadn't made the second, third, or fourth page. And on page five she rated only a tiny paragraph. "Miss Carla Moorland, aged 31, was found dead at her home in Pimlico earlier this morning." I remember thinking at the time they hadn't even got her age right. "Detective Inspector Simmons, who has been put in charge of the case, said that an investigation was being carried out and they were awaiting the pathologist's report but to date they had no reason to suspect foul play."

After that piece of news I even managed a little soup and a roll. Once I had read the report a second time I made my way back to the office parking lot and sat in my car. I wound down the other front window to allow more fresh air in before turning on *The World at One* on the radio. Carla didn't even get a mention. In the age of semiautomatics, drugs, AIDS, and gold bullion robberies the death of a thirty-two-year-old industrial personal assistant had passed unnoticed by the BBC.

I returned to my office to find on my desk a memo containing a series of questions that had been fired back by the managing director, leaving me in no doubt as to how he felt about my report. I was able to deal with nearly all his queries and return the answers to his secretary before I left the office that night, despite spending most of the afternoon trying to convince myself that whatever had caused Carla's death must have happened after I left and could not possibly have been connected with my hitting her. But that red negligee kept returning to my thoughts. Was there any way they could trace it back to me? I had bought it at Harrods—an extravagance, but I felt certain it couldn't be unique, and it was still the only serious present I'd ever given her. But the note that was attached—had Carla destroyed it? Would they discover who Casaneva was?

I drove directly home that evening, aware that I would never again be able to travel down the street Carla had lived on. I listened to the end of the *PM* program on my car radio, and as soon as I reached home switched on the six o'clock news. I turned to Channel Four at seven and back to the BBC at nine. I returned to ITV at ten and even ended up watching *Newsnight.*

Carla's death, in their combined editorial opinion, must have been less important than a Third Division football result between Reading and Walsall. Elizabeth continued reading her latest library book, oblivious to my possible peril.

I slept fitfully that night, and as soon as I heard the papers pushed through the mail slot the next morning I ran downstairs to check the headlines.

DUKAKIS NOMINATED AS CANDIDATE stared up at me from the front page of *The Times.*

I found myself wondering, irrelevantly, if he would ever be president. "President Dukakis" didn't sound quite right to me.

I picked up my wife's *Daily Express* and the three-word headline filled the top of the page: LOVERS' TIFF MURDER.

My legs gave way, and I fell to my knees. I must have made a strange sight, crumpled up on the floor trying to read that opening paragraph. I couldn't make out the words of the second paragraph without my glasses. I stumbled back upstairs with the papers and grabbed the glasses from the table on my side of the bed. Elizabeth was still sleeping soundly. Even so, I locked myself in the bathroom, where I could read the story slowly and without fear of interruption.

> Police are now treating as murder the death of a beautiful Pimlico secretary, Carla Moorland, 32, who was found dead in her flat early yesterday morning. Detective Inspector Simmons of Scotland Yard, who is in charge of the case, initially considered Carla Moorland's death to be due to natural causes, but an X-ray has revealed a broken jaw which could have been caused in a fight.
>
> An inquest will be held on April 19th.
>
> Miss Moorland's daily, Maria Lucia (48), said—exclusively to the *Express*—that her employer had been with a man friend when she had left the flat at five o'clock on the night in question. Another witness, Mrs. Rita Johnson, who lives in the adjoining block of flats, stated she had seen a man leaving Miss Moorland's flat at around six, before entering the newsagents opposite and later driving away. Mrs. Johnson added that she couldn't be sure of the make of the car but it might have been a Rover . . . .

"Oh, my God," I exclaimed in such a loud voice that I was afraid it might have woken Elizabeth. I shaved and showered quickly, trying to think as I went along. I was dressed and ready to leave for work even before my wife was awake. I kissed her on the cheek but she only turned over, so I scribbled a note and left it on her side of the bed, explaining that I had to spend the morning in the office as I had an important report to complete.

On my journey to work I rehearsed exactly what I was going to say. I went over it again and again. I arrived on the twelfth floor a little before eight and left my door wide open so I would be aware of the slightest intrusion. I felt confident that I had a clear fifteen, even twenty minutes before anyone else could be expected to arrive.

Once again I went over exactly what I needed to say. I found the number in the L–R directory and scribbled it down on a pad in front of me before writing five headings in block capitals, something I always did before a board meeting.

> BUS STOP
> COAT
> NO. 19
> BMW
> TICKET

Then I dialled the number.

I took off my watch and placed it in front of me. I had read somewhere that the location of a telephone call can be traced in about three minutes.

A woman's voice said, "Scotland Yard."

"Inspector Simmons, please," was all I volunteered.

"Can I tell him who's calling?"

"No, I would prefer not to give my name."

"Yes, of course, sir," she said, evidently used to such callers.

Another ringing tone. My mouth went dry as a man's voice announced, "Simmons," and I heard the detective speak for the first time. I was taken aback to find that a man with so English a name could have such a strong Glaswegian accent.

"Can I help you?" he asked.

"No, but I think I can help you," I said in a quiet tone which I pitched considerably lower than my natural speaking voice.

"How can you help me, sir?"

"Are you the officer in charge of the Carla-whatever-her-name-is case?"

"Yes, I am. But how can you help?" he repeated.

The second hand showed one minute had already passed.

"I saw a man leaving her flat that night."

"Where were you at the time?"

"At the bus stop on the same side of the road."

"Can you give me a description of the man?" Simmons's tone was every bit as casual as my own.

"Tall. I'd say five eleven, six feet. Well built. Wore one of those posh City coats—you know, the black ones with a velvet collar."

"How can you be so sure about the coat?" the detective asked.

"It was so cold standing out there waiting for the No. 19 that I wished it had been me who was wearing it."

"Do you remember anything in particular that happened after he left the apartment?"

"Only that he went to the newsstand opposite before getting into his car and driving away."

"Yes, we know that much," said the detective inspector. "I don't suppose you recall what make of car it was?"

Two minutes had now passed, and I began to watch the second hand more closely.

"I think it was a BMW," I said.

"Do you remember the color, by any chance?"

"No, it was too dark for that." I paused. "But I saw him tear a parking ticket off the windshield, so it shouldn't be too hard for you to trace him."

"And at what time did all this take place?"

"Around six-fifteen to six-thirty, Inspector," I said.

"And can you tell me . . . ?"

Two minutes, fifty-eight seconds. I hung up. My whole body broke out in a sweat.

"Good to see you in the office on a Saturday morning," said the managing director grimly as he passed my door. "Soon as you're finished whatever you're doing I'd like a word with you."

I left my desk and followed him along the corridor into his office. For the next hour he went over my projected figures, but however hard I tried I couldn't concentrate. It wasn't long before he stopped trying to disguise his impatience.

"Have you got something else on your mind?" he asked as he closed his file. "You seem preoccupied."

"No," I insisted, "just been doing a lot of overtime lately," and stood up to leave.

Once I had returned to my office, I burned the piece of paper with the five headings and left to go home. In the first edition of the afternoon paper, the "Lovers' Tiff" story had been moved back to page seven. They had nothing new to report.

The rest of Saturday seemed interminable, but my wife's *Sunday Express* finally brought me some relief.

"Following up information received in the Carla Moorland 'Lovers' Tiff' murder, a man is helping the police with their inquiries." The commonplace expressions I had read so often in the past suddenly took on a real meaning.

I scoured the other Sunday papers, listened to every news bulletin, and watched each news item on television. When my wife became curious I explained that there was a rumor in the office that the company might be taken over again, which meant I could lose my job.

By Monday morning the *Daily Express* had named the man in "The Lovers' Tiff murder" as Paul Menzies, fifty-one, an insurance broker from Sutton. His wife was in a hospital in Epsom under sedation while he was being held in the cells of Brixton Prison under arrest. I began to wonder if Mr. Menzies had told Carla the truth about *his* wife and what *his* nickname might be. I poured myself a strong black coffee and left for the office.

Later that morning, Menzies appeared before the magistrates at the Horseferry Road court, charged with the murder of Carla Moorland. The police had been successful in opposing bail, the *Standard* reassured me.

It takes six months, I was to discover, for a case of this gravity to reach the Old Bailey. Paul Menzies passed those months on remand in Brixton Prison. I spent the same period fearful of every telephone call, every knock on the door, every unexpected visitor. Each one created its own nightmare. Innocent people have no idea how many such incidents occur every day. I went about my job as best I could, often wondering if Menzies knew of my relationship with Carla, if he knew my name, or if he even knew of my existence.

It must have been a couple of months before the trial was due to begin that the company held its annual general meeting. It had taken some considerable creative accountancy on my part to produce a set of figures that showed us managing any profit at all. We certainly didn't pay our stockholders a dividend that year.

I came away from the meeting relieved, almost elated. Six months had passed since Carla's death, and not one incident had occurred during that period to suggest that anyone suspected I had even known her, let alone been the cause of her death. I still felt guilty about Carla, even missed her, but after six months I was now able to go for a whole day without fear entering my mind. Strangely, I felt no guilt about Menzies's plight. After all, it was he who had become the instrument that was going to keep me from a lifetime spent in prison. So when the blow came it had double the impact.

It was on August 26—I shall never forget it—that I received a letter that made me realize it might be necessary to follow every word of the trial. However much I tried to convince myself I should explain why I couldn't do it, I knew I wouldn't be able to resist.

That same morning, a Friday—I suppose these things always happen on a Friday—I was called in for what I assumed was to be a routine weekly meeting with the managing director, only to be informed that the company no longer needed me.

"Frankly, in the last few months your work has gone from bad to worse," I was told.

I didn't feel able to disagree with him.

"And you have left me with no choice but to replace you." A polite way of saying, "You're fired."

"Your desk will be cleared by five this evening," the managing director continued, "when you will receive a cheque from the accounts department for 17,500 pounds."

I raised an eyebrow.

"Six months' compensation, as stipulated in your contract when we took over the company," he explained.

When the managing director stretched out his hand it was not to wish me luck but to ask for the keys of my Rover.

I remember my first thought when he informed me of his decision: At least I would be able to attend every day of the trial without any hassle.

Elizabeth took the news of my firing badly but only asked what plans I had for finding a new job. During the next month I pretended to look for a position in another company but realized I couldn't hope to settle down to anything until the case was over.

On the morning of the trial all the popular papers had colorful background pieces. The *Daily Express* even displayed on its front page a flattering picture of Carla in a swimsuit on the beach at Marbella: I wondered how much her sister in Fulham had been paid for that particular item. Alongside it was a profile photo of Paul Menzies that made him look as if he were already a convict.

I was among the first to be told in which court at the Old Bailey the case of the *Crown* v. *Menzies* would be tried. A uniformed policeman gave me detailed directions, and along with several others I made my way to Court No. 4.

Once I had reached the courtroom I filed in and made sure that I sat on the end of my row. I looked round thinking everyone would stare at me, but to my relief no one showed the slightest interest.

I had a good view of the defendant as he stood in the dock. Menzies was a frail man who looked as if he had recently lost a lot of weight; fifty-one, the newspapers had said, but he looked nearer seventy. I began to wonder how much I must have aged over the past few months.

Menzies wore a smart dark blue suit that hung loosely on him, a clean shirt, and what I thought must be a regimental tie. His gray thinning hair was swept straight back; a small silver moustache gave him a military air. He certainly didn't look like a murderer or much of a catch as a lover, but anyone glancing toward me would probably have come to the same conclusion. I searched around the sea of faces for Mrs. Menzies but no one in the court fitted the newspaper description of her.

We all rose when Mr. Justice Buchanan came in. "The *Crown* v. *Menzies*," the clerk of the court read out.

The judge leaned forward to tell Menzies that he could be seated and then turned slowly toward the jury box.

He explained that, although there had been considerable press interest in the case, their opinion was all that mattered because they alone would be asked to decide if the prisoner were guilty or not guilty of murder. He also advised the jury against reading any newspaper articles concerning the trial or listening to anyone else's views, especially those who had not been present in court: Such people, he said, were always the first to have an immutable opinion on what the verdict should be. He went on to remind the jury how important it was to concentrate on the evidence because a man's life was at stake. I found myself nodding in agreement.

I glanced around the court hoping there was nobody there who would recognize me. Menzies's eyes remained fixed firmly on the judge, who was turning back to face the prosecuting counsel.

Even as Sir Humphrey Mountcliff rose from his place on the bench, I was thankful he was against Menzies and not me. A man of dominating height with a high forehead and silver gray hair, he commanded the court not only with his physical presence but with a voice that was never less than authoritative.

To a silent assembly he spent the rest of the morning setting out the case for the prosecution. His eyes rarely left the jury box except occasionally to peer down at his notes.

He reconstructed the events as he imagined they had happened that evening in April.

The opening address lasted two and a half hours, shorter than I'd expected. The judge then suggested a break for lunch and asked us all to be back in our places by ten past two.

After lunch Sir Humphrey called his first witness, Detective Inspector Simmons. I was unable to look directly at the policeman while he presented his evidence. Each reply he gave was as if he were addressing me personally. I wondered if he suspected all along that there was another man. Simmons gave a highly professional account of himself as he described in detail how they had found the body and later traced Menzies through two witnesses and the damning parking ticket. By the time Sir Humphrey sat down, few people in that court could have felt that Simmons had arrested the wrong man.

Menzies's defense counsel, who rose to cross-examine the detective inspector, could not have been in greater contrast to

Sir Humphrey. Mr. Robert Scott, QC, was short and stocky, with thick bushy eyebrows. He spoke slowly and without inflection. I was happy to observe that one member of the jury was having difficulty in staying awake.

For the next twenty minutes Scott took the detective inspector painstakingly back over his evidence but was unable to make Simmons retract anything substantial. As the inspector stepped out of the witness seat, I felt confident enough to look him straight in the eye.

The next witness was a Home Office pathologist, Dr. Anthony Mallins, who, after answering a few preliminary questions to establish his professional status, moved on to answer an inquiry from Sir Humphrey that took everyone by surprise. The pathologist informed the court that there was clear evidence to suggest that Miss Moorland had had sexual intercourse shortly before her death.

"How can you be so certain, Dr. Mallins?"

"Because I found traces of blood group B on the deceased's upper thigh, while Miss Moorland was later found to be blood group O. There were also traces of seminal fluid on the negligee she was wearing at the time of her death."

"Are these common blood groups?" Sir Humphrey asked.

"Blood group O is common," Dr. Mallins admitted. "Group B, however, is fairly unusual."

"And what would you say was the cause of her death?" Sir Humphrey asked.

"A blow or blows to the head, which caused a broken jaw, and lacerations at the base of the skull which may have been delivered by a blunt instrument."

I wanted to stand up and say, "I can tell you which!" when Sir Humphrey said, "Thank you, Dr. Mallins. No more questions. Please wait there."

Mr. Scott treated the doctor with far more respect than he had Inspector Simmons, despite Mallins's being the defendant's witness.

"Could the blow on the back of Miss Moorland's head have been caused by a fall?" he asked.

The doctor hesitated. "Possibly," he agreed. "But that wouldn't explain the broken jaw."

Mr. Scott ignored the comment and pressed on.

"What percentage of people in Britain are blood group B?"

"About five, six percent," volunteered the doctor.

"Two and a half million people," said Mr. Scott, and waited for the figure to sink in before he suddenly changed tack.

But as hard as he tried he could not shift the pathologist on the time of death or on the fact that sexual intercourse must have taken place around the hours his client had been with Carla.

When Mr. Scott sat down, the judge asked Sir Humphrey if he wished to reexamine.

"I do, My Lord. Dr. Mallins, you told the court that Miss Moorland suffered from a broken jaw and lacerations on the back of her head. Could the lacerations have been caused by falling on to a blunt object after the jaw had been broken?"

"I must object, My Lord," said Mr. Scott, rising with unusual speed. "This is a leading question."

Mr. Justice Buchanan leaned forward and peered down at the doctor. "I agree, Mr. Scott, but I would like to know if Dr. Mallins found blood group O, Miss Moorland's blood group, on any other object in the room?"

"Yes, My Lord," replied the doctor. "On the edge of the glass table in the center of the room."

"Thank you, Dr. Mallins," said Sir Humphrey. "No more questions."

Sir Humphrey's next witness was Mrs. Rita Johnson, the lady who claimed she had seen everything.

"Mrs. Johnson, on the evening of April 7, did you see a man leave the apartment house where Miss Moorland lived?" Sir Humphrey asked.

"Yes, I did."

"At about what time was that?"

"A few minutes after six."

"Please tell the court what happened next."

"He walked across the road, removed a parking ticket, got into his car, and drove away."

"Do you see that man in the court today?"

"Yes," she said firmly, pointing to Menzies, who at this suggestion shook his head vigorously.

"No more questions."

Mr. Scott rose slowly again.

"What did you say was the make of the car the man got into?"

"I can't be sure," Mrs. Johnson said, "but I think it was a BMW."

"Not a Rover, as you first told the police the following morning?"

The witness did not reply.

"And did you actually see the man in question remove a parking ticket from the car windshield?" Mr. Scott asked.

"I think so, sir, but it all happened so quickly."

"I'm sure it did," said Mr. Scott. "In fact, I suggest to you that it happened so quickly that you've got the wrong man and the wrong car."

"No, sir," she replied, but without the same conviction with which she had delivered her earlier replies.

Sir Humphrey did not reexamine Mrs. Johnson. I realized that he wanted her evidence to be forgotten by the jury as quickly as possible. As it was, when she left the witness box she also left everyone in court in considerable doubt.

Carla's daily cleaing woman, Maria Lucia, was far more convincing. She stated unequivocally that she had seen Menzies in the living room of the apartment that afternoon when she arrived a little before five. However, she had, she admitted, never seen him before that day.

"But isn't it true," asked Sir Humphrey, "that you usually only work in the mornings?"

"Yes," she replied. "Although Miss Moorland was in the habit of bringing work home on a Thursday afternoon, so it was convenient for me to come in and collect my wages."

"And how was Miss Moorland dressed that afternoon?" asked Sir Humphrey.

"In her blue robe," replied the cleaning woman.

"Is this how she usually dressed on a Thursday afternoon?"

"No, sir, but I assumed she was going to have a bath before going out that evening."

"But when you left the apartment was she still with Mr. Menzies?"

"Yes, sir."

"Do you remember anything else she was wearing that day?"

"Yes, sir. Underneath the morning coat she wore a red negligee."

My negligee was duly produced, and Maria Lucia identified it. At this point I stared directly at the witness, but she showed not a flicker of recognition. I thanked all the gods in the pantheon that I had never once been to visit Carla in the morning.

"Please wait there," were Sir Humphrey's final words to Miss Lucia.

Mr. Scott rose to cross-examine.

"Miss Lucia, you have told the court that the purpose of the visit was to collect your wages. How long were you at the apartment on this occasion?"

"I did a little cleaning up in the kitchen and ironed a blouse, perhaps twenty minutes."

"Did you see Miss Moorland during this time?"

"Yes, I went into the living room to ask if she would like some more coffee, but she said no."

"Was Mr. Menzies with her at the time?"

"Yes, he was."

"Were you at any time aware of a quarrel between the two of them or even raised voices?"

"No, sir."

"When you saw them together did Miss Moorland show any signs of distress or need of help?"

"No, sir."

"Then what happened?"

"Miss Moorland joined me in the kitchen a few minutes later and gave me my wages, and I let myself out."

"When you were alone in the kitchen with Miss Moorland, did she give any sign of being afraid of her guest?"

143

"No, sir."

"No more questions, My Lord."

Sir Humphrey did not reexamine Maria Lucia and informed the judge that he had completed the case for the prosecution. Mr. Justice Buchanan nodded and said he felt that was enough for the day; but I wasn't convinced it was enough to convict Menzies.

When I got home that night Elizabeth did not ask me where I had been, and I did not volunteer any information. I spent the evening pretending to go over job applications.

The following morning I had a late breakfast and read the papers before returning to my place at the end of a row in Court No. 4, only a few moments before the judge made his entrance.

Mr. Justice Buchanan, having sat down, adjusted his wig before calling on Mr. Scott to open the case for the defence. Mr. Scott, QC, was once again slow to rise—a man paid by the hour, I thought uncharitably. He started by promising the court that his opening address would be brief, and he then remained on his feet for the next two and a half hours.

He began the case for the defense by going over in detail the relevant parts, as he saw them, of Menzies's past. He assured us all that those who wished to dissect it later would only find an unblemished record. Paul Menzies was a happily married man who lived in Sutton with his wife and three children—Polly, aged twenty-one; Michael, nineteen; and Sally, sixteen. Two of the children were now in college and the youngest had just graduated from high school. Doctors had advised Mrs. Menzies not to attend the trial, following her recent release from the hospital. I noticed two of the women on the jury smile sympathetically.

Mr. Menzies, Mr. Scott continued, had been with the same firm of insurance brokers in the City of London for the past six years and, although he had not been promoted, he was a much respected member of the staff. He was a pillar of his local community, having served with the Territorial Army, and on the committee of the local camera club. He had once even run for

144

the Sutton council. He could hardly be described as a serious candidate as a murderer.

Mr. Scott then went on to the actual day of the killing and confirmed that Mr. Menzies had had an appointment with Miss Moorland on the afternoon in question, but in a strictly professional capacity with the sole purpose of helping her with a personal insurance plan. There could have been no other reason to visit Miss Moorland during office hours. He did not have sexual intercourse with her, and he certainly did not murder her.

The defendant had left his client a few minutes after six. He understood she had intended to change before going out to dinner with her sister in Fulham. He had arranged to see her the following Wednesday at his office for the purpose of drawing up the completed policy. The defense, Mr. Scott went on, would later produce a diary entry that would establish the truth of this statement.

The charge against the accused was, he submitted, based almost completely on circumstantial evidence. He felt confident that, when the trial reached its conclusion, the jury would be left with no choice but to release his client back into the bosom of his loving family. "You must end this nightmare," Mr. Scott concluded. "It has gone on far too long for an innocent man."

At this point the judge suggested a break for lunch. During the meal I was unable to concentrate or even take in what was being said around me. The majority of those who had an opinion to give now seemed convinced that Menzies was innocent.

As soon as we returned, at ten past two, Mr. Scott called his first witness: the defendant himself.

Paul Menzies left the dock and walked slowly over to the witness box. He took a copy of the New Testament in his right hand and haltingly read the words of the oath, from a card he held in his left.

Every eye was fixed on him while Mr. Scott began to guide his client carefully through the minefield of evidence.

Menzies became progressively more confident in his delivery as the day wore on, and when at four-thirty the judge told the court, "That's enough for today," I was convinced that he would get off, even if only by a majority verdict.

I spent a fitful night before returning to my place on the third day fearing the worst. Would Menzies be released, and would they then start looking for me?

Mr. Scott opened the third morning as gently as he had begun the second, but he repeated so many questions from the previous day that it became obvious he was only steadying his client in preparation for prosecuting counsel. Before he finally sat down he asked Menzies for a third time, "Did you ever have sexual intercourse with Miss Moorland?"

"No, sir. I had only met her for the first time that day," Menzies replied firmly.

"And did you murder Miss Moorland?"

"Certainly not, sir," said Menzies, his voice now strong and confident.

Mr. Scott resumed his place, a look of quiet satisfaction on his face.

In fairness to Menzies, very little that takes place in normal life could have prepared anyone for cross-examination by Sir Humphrey Mountcliff. I could not have asked for a better advocate.

"I'd like to start, if I may, Mr. Menzies," he began, "with what your counsel seems to set great store by as proof of your innocence."

Menzies's thin lips remained in a firm straight line.

"The pertinent entry in your diary that suggests that you made a second appointment to see Miss Moorland, the murdered woman"—three words Sir Humphrey was to repeat again and again during his cross-examination—"for the Wednesday after she had been killed."

"Yes, sir," said Menzies.

"This entry was made—correct me if I'm wrong—following your Thursday meeting at Miss Moorland's apartment."

"Yes, sir," said Menzies, obviously tutored not to add anything that might later help prosecuting counsel.

"So when did you make that entry?" Sir Humphrey asked.

"On the Friday morning."

"After Miss Moorland had been killed?"

"Yes, but I didn't know."

"Do you carry a diary on you, Mr. Menzies?"

"Yes, but only a small pocket diary, not my large desk one."

"Do you have it with you today?"

"I do."

"May I be allowed to see it?"

Reluctantly Menzies took a small green diary out of his jacket pocket and handed it over to the clerk of the court, who in turn passed it to Sir Humphrey. Sir Humphrey began to leaf through the pages.

"I see that there is no entry for your appointment with Miss Moorland for the afternoon on which she was murdered?"

"No, sir," said Menzies. "I put office appointments only in my desk diary; personal appointments are restricted to my pocket diary."

"I understand," said Sir Humphrey. He paused and looked up. "But isn't it strange, Mr. Menzies, that you agreed to an appointment with a client to discuss further business and you then trusted it to memory, when you so easily could have put it in the diary you carry around with you all the time before transferring it?"

"I might have written it down on a slip of paper at the time, but as I explained, that's a personal diary."

"Is it?" said Sir Humphrey as he flicked back a few more pages. "Who is David Paterson?" he asked.

Menzies looked as if he were trying to place him.

"Mr. David Paterson, 112 City Road, 11:30, January 9 this year," Sir Humphrey read out to the court. Menzies looked anxious. "We could subpoena Mr. Paterson if you can't recall the meeting," said Sir Humphrey helpfully.

"He's a client of my firm," said Menzies in a quiet voice.

"A client of your firm," Sir Humphrey repeated slowly. "I wonder how many of those I could find if I went through your diary at a more leisurely pace?" Menzies bowed his head as Sir Humphrey passed the diary back to the clerk, having made his point.

"Now I should like to turn to some more important questions . . . "

"Not until after lunch, Sir Humphrey," the judge intervened. "It's nearly one, and I think we'll take a break now."

"As you wish, My Lord," came back the courteous reply.

I left the court in a more optimistic mood, even though I couldn't wait to discover what could be more important than that diary. Sir Humphrey's emphasis on little lies, although they did not prove Menzies was a murderer, did show he was hiding something. I became anxious that during the break Mr. Scott might advise Menzies to admit to his affair with Carla, and thus make the rest of his story appear more credible. To my relief, over the meal I learned that Menzies could not consult his counsel while he was still in the witness box. I noticed when we returned to court that Mr. Scott's smile had disappeared.

Sir Humphrey rose to continue his cross-examination.

"You have stated under oath, Mr. Menzies, that you are a happily married man."

"I am, sir," said the defendant with feeling.

"Was your first marriage as happy, Mr. Menzies?" asked Sir Humphrey casually. The defendant's cheeks drained of their color. I quickly looked over toward Mr. Scott, who could not mask that this was information with which he had not been entrusted.

"Take your time before you answer," said Sir Humphrey.

All eyes turned to the man in the witness seat.

"No," said Menzies and quickly added, "but I was very young at the time. It was many years ago and all a ghastly mistake."

"All a ghastly mistake?" repeated Sir Humphrey, looking straight at the jury. "And how did that marriage end?"

"In divorce," Menzies said quite simply.

"And what were the grounds for that divorce?"

"Cruelty," said Menzies, "but . . . "

"But . . . would you like me to read out to the jury what your first wife swore under oath in court that day?"

Menzies stood there shaking. He knew that "No" would damn him and "Yes" would hang him.

"Well, since you seem unable to advise us, I will, with your permission, My Lord, read the statement made before Mr. Justice Rodger on June 9, 1961, at the Swindon County Court by the first Mrs. Menzies." Sir Humphrey cleared his throat. "'He used to hit me again and again, and it became so bad that I had to run away for fear he might one day kill me.'" Sir Humphrey emphasized the last five words.

"She was exaggerating!" shouted Menzies from the witness box.

"How unfortunate that poor Miss Carla Moorland cannot be with us today to let us know if your story about her is also an exaggeration."

"I object, My Lord," said Mr. Scott. "Sir Humphrey is harassing the witness."

"I agree," said the judge. "Tread more carefully in future, Sir Humphrey."

"I apologize, My Lord," said Sir Humphrey, sounding singularly unapologetic. He closed the file to which he had been referring and replaced it on the desk in front of him before taking up a new one. He opened it slowly, making sure all in the court were following every movement before he extracted a single sheet of paper.

"How many mistresses have you had since you were married to the second Mrs. Menzies?"

"Objection, My Lord. How can this be relevant?"

"My Lord, it *is* relevant, I respectfully suggest. I intend to show that this was not a business relationship that Mr. Menzies was conducting with Miss Moorland but a highly personal one."

"The question can be put to the defendant," ruled the judge.

Menzies said nothing as Sir Humphrey held up the sheet of paper in front of him and studied it.

"Take your time because I want the exact number," Sir Humphrey said, looking over the top of his glasses.

The seconds ticked on as we all waited.

"Hmm—three, I think," Menzies said eventually in a voice that just carried. The members of the press began scribbling furiously.

"Three," said Sir Humphrey, staring at his piece of paper in disbelief.

"Well, perhaps four."

"And was the fourth Miss Carla Moorland?" Sir Humphrey asked. "Because you had sexual intercourse with her that evening, didn't you?"

"No, I did not," said Menzies, but by this time few in that courtroom could have believed him.

"Very well then," continued Sir Humphrey, as he placed the piece of paper on the bench in front of him. "But before I return to your relationship with Miss Moorland, let us discover the truth about the other four."

I stared at the piece of paper from which Sir Humphrey had been reading. From where I was seated I could see that there was nothing written on it at all. A blank white sheet lay before him.

I was finding it hard to keep a grin off my face. Menzies's adulterous background was an unexpected bonus for me and the press—and I couldn't help wondering how Carla would have reacted if she had known about it.

Sir Humphrey spent the rest of the day making Menzies relate the details of his relationships with the previous four mistresses. The court was agog, and the journalists continued to scribble away, knowing they were about to have a field day. When the court adjourned, Mr. Scott's eyes were closed.

I drove home that night feeling not a little pleased with myself; like a man who had just completed a good day's work.

On entering the courtroom the following morning I noticed people were beginning to acknowledge other regulars and nod. I found myself falling into the same pattern and greeted people silently as I took my regular position at the end of the bench.

Sir Humphrey spent the morning going over some of Menzies's other misdemeanors. We discovered that he had served in the Territorial Army for only five months and left after a misunderstanding with his commanding officer over how many hours he should have been spending on exercises during weekends and how much he had claimed in expenses for those hours. We also learned that his attempts to get on the local council sprang more from anger at being refused planning permission to build on a piece of land adjoining his house than from an altruistic desire to serve his fellow men. To be fair, Sir Humphrey could have made the Archangel Gabriel look like a soccer hooligan; but his trump card was still to come.

"Mr. Menzies, I should now like to return to your version of what happened on the night Miss Moorland was killed."

"Yes," sighed Menzies in a tired voice.

"When you visit a client to discuss one of your policies, how long would you say such a consultation usually lasts?"

"Usually half an hour, an hour at the most," said Menzies.

"And how long did the consultation with Miss Moorland take?"

"A good hour," said Menzies.

"And you left her, if I remember your evidence correctly, a little after six o'clock."

"That is correct."

"And what time was your appointment?"

"At five o'clock, as was shown clearly in my desk diary," said Menzies.

"Well, Mr. Menzies, if you arrived at about five to keep your appointment with Miss Moorland and left a little after six, how did you manage to get a parking fine?"

"I didn't have any small change for the meter at the time," said Menzies confidently. "As I was already a couple of minutes late, I just risked it."

"You just risked it," repeated Sir Humphrey slowly. "You are obviously a man who takes risks, Mr. Menzies. I wonder if you would be good enough to look at the parking ticket in question."

The clerk handed it up to Menzies.

"Would you read out to the court the hour and minute that the traffic warden has written in the little boxes to show when the offence occurred."

Once again Menzies took a long time to reply.

"Four-sixteen to four-thirty," he said eventually.

"I didn't hear that," said the judge.

"Would you be kind enough to repeat what you said for the judge?" Sir Humphrey asked.

Menzies repeated the damning figures.

"So now we have established that you were in fact with Miss Moorland some time before four-sixteen, and not, as I suggest you later wrote in your diary, five o'clock. That was just another lie, wasn't it?"

"No," said Menzies. "I must have arrived a little earlier than I realized."

"At least an hour earlier, it seems. And I also suggest to you that you arrived at that early hour because your interest in Carla Moorland was not simply professional?"

"That's not true."

"Then it wasn't your intention that she should become your mistress?"

Menzies hesitated long enough for Sir Humphrey to answer his own question. "Because the business part of your meeting finished in the usual half hour, did it not, Mr. Menzies?" He waited for a response but still none was forthcoming.

"What is your blood group, Mr. Menzies?"

"I have no idea."

Sir Humphrey changed tack without warning: "Have you heard of DNA, by any chance?"

"No," came back the puzzled reply.

"Deoxyribonucleic acid testing is a technique that shows genetic information unique to every individual. Blood or semen samples can be matched. Semen, Mr. Menzies, is as unique as any fingerprint. With such a sample we would know immediately if you raped Miss Moorland."

"I didn't rape her," Menzies said indignantly.

"Nevertheless, sexual intercourse did take place, didn't it?" said Sir Humphrey quietly.

Menzies remained silent.

"Shall I recall the Home Office pathologist and ask him to carry out a DNA test?"

Menzies still made no reply.

"And check your blood group?" Sir Humphrey paused. "I will ask you once again, Mr. Menzies. Did sexual intercourse between you and the murdered woman take place that Thursday afternoon?"

"Yes, sir," said Menzies in a whisper.

"Yes, sir," repeated Sir Humphrey so that the whole court could hear it.

"But it wasn't rape," Menzies shouted back at Sir Humphrey.

"Wasn't it?" said Sir Humphrey.

"And I swear I didn't kill her."

I must have been the only person in that courtroom who knew he was telling the truth. All Sir Humphrey said was, "No more questions, My Lord."

Mr. Scott tried manfully to resurrect his client's credibility during reexamination, but the fact that Menzies had been caught lying about his relationship with Carla made everything he had said previously appear doubtful.

If only Menzies had told the truth about being Carla's lover, his story might well have been accepted. I wondered why he had gone through the charade—in order to protect his wife? Whatever the motive, it had only ended by making him appear guilty of a crime he hadn't committed.

I went home that night and ate the largest meal I had had for several days.

The following morning Mr. Scott called two more witnesses. The first turned out to be the vicar of St. Peter's, Sutton, who was there as a character witness to prove what a pillar of the community Menzies was. After Sir Humphrey had finished his cross-examination the vicar ended up looking like a rather kind, unworldly old man, whose knowledge of Menzies was based on the latter's occasional attendance at Sunday matins.

The second was Menzies's superior at the company they worked for in the City. He was a far more impressive figure, but he was unable to confirm that Miss Moorland had ever been a client of the company.

Mr. Scott put up no more witnesses and informed Mr. Justice Buchanan that he had completed the case for the defense. The judge nodded and, turning to Sir Humphrey, told him he would not be required to begin his final address until the following morning.

That heralded the signal for the court to adjourn.

Another long evening and an even longer night had to be endured by Menzies and myself. As on every other day during the trial, I made sure I was in my place the next morning before the judge entered.

Sir Humphrey's closing speech was masterful. Every little untruth was logged, so that one began to accept that very little of Menzies's testimony could be relied on.

"We will never know for certain," said Sir Humphrey, "for what reason poor young Carla Moorland was murdered. Refusal to succumb to Menzies's advances? A fit of temper that ended with a blow that caused her to fall and later die alone? But there are, however, some things, members of the jury, of which we can be quite certain.

"We can be certain that Menzies was with the murdered woman that day before the hour of four-sixteen because of the evidence of the damning parking ticket.

"We can be certain that he left a little after six because we have a witness who saw him drive away, and he does not himself deny this evidence.

"And we can be certain that he wrote a false entry in his diary to make you believe he had a business appointment with the murdered woman at five, rather than a personal assignation some time before.

"And we can now be certain that he lied about having sexual intercourse with Miss Moorland a short time before she was killed, though we cannot be certain if intercourse took place before or after her jaw had been broken." Sir Humphrey's eyes rested on the jury before he continued.

"We can, finally, establish, beyond reasonable doubt, from the pathologist's report, the time of death and that, therefore, Menzies was the last person who could possibly have seen Carla Moorland alive.

"Therefore no one else could have killed Carla Moorland—for do not forget Inspector Simmons's evidence—and if you accept that, you can be in no doubt that only Menzies could have been responsible for her death. And how damning you must have found it that he tried to hide the existence of a first wife who had left him on the grounds of his cruelty, and the four mistresses who left him we know not why or how. Only one less than Bluebeard," Sir Humphrey added with feeling.

"For the sake of every young girl who lives on her own in our capital, you must carry out your duty, however painful that duty might be. And find Menzies guilty of murder."

When Sir Humphrey sat down I wanted to applaud.

The judge sent us away for another break. Voices all around me were now damning Menzies. I listened contentedly without offering an opinion. I knew that if the jury convicted Menzies the file would be closed and no eyes would ever be turned in my direction. I was seated in my place before the judge appeared at ten past two. He called on Mr. Scott.

Menzies's counsel put up a spirited defense of his client, pointing out that almost all the evidence that Sir Humphrey had come up with had been circumstantial, and that it was even possible someone else could have visited Carla Moorland after his client had left that night. Mr. Scott's bushy eyebrows seemed almost to have a life of their own as he energetically emphasized that it was the prosecution's responsibility to prove their case beyond reasonable doubt and not his to disprove it, and that, in his opinion, his learned friend, Sir Humphrey, had failed to do so.

During his summing-up Scott avoided any mention of diary entries, parking tickets, past mistresses, sexual intercourse, or questions of his client's role in the community. A latecomer listening only to the closing speeches might have been forgiven for thinking the two learned gentlemen were summarizing different cases.

Mr. Scott's expression became grim as he turned to face the jury for his summation. "The twelve of you," he said, "hold the fate of my client in your hands. You must, therefore, be certain, I repeat, certain beyond reasonable doubt that Paul Menzies could have committed such an evil crime as murder.

"This is not a trial about Mr. Menzies's lifestyle, his position in the community, or even his sexual habits. If adultery were a crime I feel confident Mr. Menzies would not be the only person in this courtroom to be in the dock today." He paused as his eyes swept up and down the jury.

"For this reason I feel confident that you will find it in your hearts to release my client from the torment he has been put through during the last seven months. He has surely been shown to be an innocent man deserving of your compassion."

Mr. Scott sank down on the bench having, I felt, given his client a glimmer of hope.

The judge told us that he would not begin his own summing-up until Monday morning.

The weekend seemed interminable to me. By Monday I had convinced myself that enough members of the jury would feel there just had not been sufficient evidence to convict.

As soon as the trial resumed, the judge began by explaining once again that it was the jury alone who must make the ultimate decision. It was not his job to let them know how he felt, but only to advise them on the law.

He went back over all the evidence, trying to put it in perspective, but he never gave so much as a hint as to his own opinions. When he had completed his summing-up late that afternoon he sent the jury away to consider their verdict.

I waited with nearly as much anxiety as Menzies must have done while I listened to others giving their opinion as the minutes ticked by in that little room. Then, four hours later, a note was sent up to the judge.

He immediately asked the jury to return to their places while the press flooded back into the courtroom, making it look like the House of Commons on budget day. The clerk dutifully handed up the note to Mr. Justice Buchanan. He opened it and read what only twelve other people in the courtroom could have known.

He handed it back to the clerk, who then read the note to a silent court.

Mr. Justice Buchanan frowned before asking if there were any chance of a unanimous verdict being reached if he allowed more time. Once he had learned that it was proving impossible, he reluctantly nodded his agreement to a majority verdict.

The jury disappeared downstairs again to continue its deliberations, and did not return for another three hours. I could sense the tension in the court as neighbors sought to give each other opinions in noisy whispers. The clerk called for silence as the judge waited for everyone to settle before he instructed the clerk to proceed.

When the clerk rose, I could hear the person next to me breathing.

"Would the foreman please stand?"

I rose from my place.

"Have you reached a verdict on which at least ten of you are agreed?"

"We have, sir."

"Do you find the defendant, Paul Menzies, guilty or not guilty?"

"Guilty," I replied.

YOU'LL NEVER LIVE
TO REGRET IT

AND SO IT WAS agreed: David would leave everything to Pat. If one of them had to die, at least the other would be financially secure for the rest of their life. David felt it was the least he could do for someone who'd stood by him for so many years, especially as he was the one who had been unfaithful.

They had known each other almost all their lives, because their parents had been close friends for as long as either of them could remember. Both families had hoped David might end up marrying Pat's sister Ruth, and they were unable to hide their surprise—and in Pat's father's case his disapproval—when the two of them started living together, especially as Pat was three years older than David.

For some time David had been putting it off and hoping for a miracle cure, despite a pushy insurance broker from Geneva Life called Marvin Roebuck who had been pressing him to "take a meeting" for the past nine months. On the first Monday of the tenth month he phoned again, and this time David reluctantly agreed to see him. He chose a date when he knew Pat would be on night duty at the hotel, and asked Roebuck to come round to their apartment—that way, he felt, it would look as if it was the broker who had done the chasing.

David was watering the scarlet *Clupea harengus* on the hall table when Marvin Roebuck pressed the buzzer on the front door. Once he had poured his visitor a Coke, David told him he had every type of insurance he could possibly need: theft, accident, car, property, health, even vacation.

"But what about life?" asked Marvin, licking his lips.

"That's one I don't need," said David. "I earn a good salary, I have more than enough security, and on top of that, my parents will leave everything to me."

"But wouldn't it be prudent to have a lump sum that comes to you automatically on your sixtieth or sixty-fifth birthday?" asked Marvin, as he continued to push at a door that he had no way of knowing was already wide open. "After all, you can never be sure what disaster might lie around the corner."

David knew exactly what disaster lay around the corner, but he still innocently asked, "What sort of figure are you talking about?"

"Well, that would depend on how much you are currently earning," said Marvin.

"A hundred twenty thousand a year," said David, trying to sound casual, as it was almost double his real income. Marvin was obviously impressed, and David remained silent as he carried out some rapid calculations in his head.

"Well," said Marvin eventually, "I'd suggest half a million dollars—as a ballpark figure. After all," he added, quickly running a finger down a page of actuarial tables he had extracted from his aluminium briefcase, "you're only twenty-seven, so the payments would be well within your means. In fact, you might even consider a larger sum if you're confident your income will continue to rise over the next few years."

"It has done so every year for the past seven," said David, this time truthfully.

"What kind of business are you in, my friend?" asked Marvin.

"Stocks and bonds," replied David, not offering any details of the small firm he worked for, or the junior position he held.

Marvin licked his lips again, even though they had told him not to do so on countless refresher courses, especially when going in for the kill.

"So, what amount do you think I should go for?" asked David, continuing to make sure it was always Marvin who took the lead.

"Well, a million is comfortably within your credit range," said Marvin, once again checking his little book of tables. "The monthly payments might seem a bit steep to begin with, but as the years go by, what with inflation and your continual salary increases, you can expect that in time they will become almost insignificant."

"How much would I have to pay each month to end up getting a million?" asked David, attempting to give the impression he might have been hooked.

"Assuming we select your sixtieth birthday for terminating the contract, a little over a thousand dollars a month," said Marvin, trying to make it sound a mere pittance. "And don't forget, sixty percent of it is tax deductible, so in real terms you'll only be paying around fifteen dollars a day, while you end up getting a million, just at the time when you most need it. And by the way, that one thousand is constant, it never goes up. In fact it's inflation-proof." He let out a dreadful shrill laugh.

"But would I still receive the full sum, whatever happens to the market?"

"One million dollars on your sixtieth birthday," confirmed Marvin, "whatever happens, short of the world coming to an end. Even I can't write a policy for that," he said, letting out another shrill laugh. "However, my friend, if unhappily you were to die before your sixtieth birthday—which God forbid—your dependents would receive the full amount immediately."

"I don't have any dependents," said David, trying to look bored.

"There must be someone you care about," said Marvin. "A good-looking guy like you."

"Why don't you leave the forms with me, Mr. Roebuck, and I'll think about it over the weekend. I promise I'll get back to you."

Marvin looked disappointed. He didn't need a refresher course to be told that you're supposed to nail the client to the wall at the first meeting, not let them get away, because that only gave them time to think things over. His lips felt dry.

Pat returned from the evening shift in the early hours of the morning, but David had stayed awake so he could go over what had happened at the meeting with Marvin. Pat was apprehensive and uncertain about the plan. David had always taken care of any problems they had had in the past, especially financial ones, and Pat wasn't sure how it would all work out once David was no longer around to give his advice. Thank God it was David who'd had to deal with Marvin—Pat couldn't even say no to a door-to-door salesman.

"So, what do we do next?" asked Pat.

"Wait."

"But you promised Marvin you'd get back to him."

"I know, but I have absolutely no intention of doing so," said David, placing his arm around Pat's shoulders. "I'd bet a hundred dollars on Marvin phoning me first thing on Monday morning. And don't forget, I still need it to look as if he's the one who's doing the pushing."

As they climbed into bed, Pat felt an attack of asthma coming on, and decided now was not the time to ask David to go over the details again. After all, as David had explained again and again, there would never be any need for Pat to meet Marvin.

Marvin phoned at 8:30 on Monday morning.

"Hoped to catch you before you went off to sell those stocks and bonds," he said. "Have you come to a decision?"

"Yes, I have," said David. "I discussed the whole idea with my mother over the weekend, and she thinks I should go for the million, because five hundred thousand may not turn out to be such a large sum of money by the time I reach sixty."

Marvin was glad that David couldn't see him licking his lips. "Your mother's obviously a shrewd woman," was his only comment.

"Can I leave you to handle all the paperwork?" asked David, trying to sound as if he didn't want to deal with any of the details.

"You bet," said Marvin. "Don't even think about it, my friend. Just leave all that hassle to me. I know you've made the right decision, David. I promise you, you'll never live to regret it."

The following day Marvin phoned again to say that the paperwork had been completed, and all that was now required was for David to have a medical—"routine" was the word he kept repeating. But because of the size of the sum insured, it would have to be with the company's doctor in New York.

David made a fuss about having to travel to New York, adding that perhaps he'd made the wrong decision, but after more pleading from Marvin, mixed with some unctuous persuasion, he finally gave in.

Marvin brought all the forms around to the apartment the following evening after Pat had left for work.

David scribbled his signature on three separate documents between two penciled X's. His final act was to print Pat's name in a little box Marvin had indicated with his stubby finger. "As your sole dependent," the broker explained, "should you pass away before September 1, 2027—God forbid. Are you married to Pat?"

"No, we just live together," replied David.

After a few more "my friends" and even more "you'll never live to regret it"s, Marvin left the apartment, clutching the forms.

"All you have to do now is keep your nerve," David told Pat once he had confirmed that the paperwork had been completed. "Just remember, no one knows me as well as you do, and once it's all over, you'll collect a million dollars."

When they eventually went to bed that night, Pat desperately wanted to make love to David, but they both accepted it was no longer possible.

The two of them traveled down to New York together the following Monday to keep the appointment David had made with Geneva Life's senior medical consultant. They parted a block away from the insurance company's head office, since they didn't want to run the risk of being seen together. They hugged each other once again, but as they parted David was still worried about whether Pat would be able to go through with it.

A couple of minutes before twelve, he arrived at the doctor's office. A young woman in a long white coat smiled up at him from behind her desk.

"Good morning," he said. "My name is David Kravits. I have an appointment with Dr. Royston."

"Oh, yes, Mr. Kravits," said the nurse. "Dr. Royston is expecting you. Please follow me." She led him down a long, bleak corridor to the last room on the left. A small brass plaque read "Dr. Royston." She knocked, opened the door, and said, "Mr. Kravits, Doctor."

Dr. Royston turned out to be a short, elderly man with only a few strands of hair left on his shiny sunburned head. He wore horn-rimmed glasses, and had a look on his face which suggested that his own life insurance policy might not be far from reaching maturity. He rose from his chair, shook his patient by the hand, and said, "It's for a life insurance policy, if I remember correctly."

"Yes, that's right."

"Shouldn't take us too long, Mr. Kravits. Fairly routine, but the company does like to be sure you're fit and well if they're going to be liable for such a large amount of money. Do have a seat," he said, pointing to the other side of his desk.

"I thought the sum was far too high myself. I would have been happy to settle for half a million, but the broker was very persuasive . . . "

"Any serious illness during the past ten years?" the doctor asked, obviously not interested in the broker's views.

"No. The occasional cold, but nothing I'd describe as serious," he replied.

"Good. And in your immediate family, any history of heart attacks, cancer, liver complaints?"

"Not that I'm aware of."

"Father still alive?"

"Very much so."

"And he's fit and well?"

"Jogs every morning, and pumps weights at the local gym on weekends."

"And your mother?"

"Doesn't do either, but I wouldn't be surprised if she outlives him comfortably."

The doctor laughed. "Any of your grandparents still living?"

"All except one. My dad's father died two years ago."

"Do you know the cause of death?"

"He just passed away, I think. At least, that was how the priest described it at his funeral."

"And how old was he?" the doctor asked. "Do you remember?"

"Eighty-one, eighty-two."

"Good," repeated Dr Royston, checking another little box on the form in front of him. "Have you ever suffered from any of these?" he asked, holding out a clipboard. The list began with arthritis and ended eighteen lines later with tuberculosis.

He ran an eye slowly down the long list before replying. "No, none of them," was all he said, not admitting to asthma on this occasion.

"Do you smoke?"

"Never."

"Drink?"

"Socially—I enjoy the occasional glass of wine with dinner, but I never drink spirits."

"Excellent," said the doctor and checked the last of the little boxes. "Now, let's check your height and weight. Come over here, please, Mr. Kravits, and climb onto this scale."

The doctor had to stand on his toes in order to push the wooden marker up until it was flat across his patient's head. "Six feet one inch," he declared, then looked down at the scale and flicked the little weight across until it just balanced. "A hundred and seventy-nine pounds. Not bad." He filled in two more lines of his report. "Perhaps just a little overweight."

"Now I need a urine sample, Mr. Kravits. If you would be kind enough to take this plastic container next door, fill it about halfway up, leave it on the ledge when you've finished, and then come back to me."

The doctor wrote out some more notes while his patient left the room. He returned a few moments later.

"I've left the container on the ledge," was all he said.

"Good. The next thing I need is a blood sample. Could you roll up your right sleeve?" The doctor placed a rubber pad around his right bicep and pumped until the veins stood out clearly. "A tiny prick," he said. "You'll hardly feel a thing." The needle went in, and he turned away as the doctor drew his blood. Dr. Royston cleaned the wound and fixed a small circular Band-Aid over the broken skin. The doctor then bent over and placed a cold stethoscope on different parts of the patient's chest, occasionally asking him to breathe in and out.

"Good," he kept repeating. Finally he said, "That just about wraps it up, Mr. Kravits. You'll need to spend a few minutes down the corridor with Dr. Harvey, so she can take a chest X ray and have some fun with her electric pads, but after that you'll be through, and you can go home to"—he checked his pad— "New Jersey. The company will be in touch in a few days, as soon as we've had the results."

"Thank you, Dr. Royston," he said as he buttoned his shirt. The doctor pressed a buzzer on his desk and the nurse reappeared and led him to another room, with a plaque on the door that read "Dr. Mary Harvey." Dr. Harvey, a smartly dressed middle-aged woman with her gray hair cropped short, was waiting for him. She smiled at the tall, handsome man and asked him to take off his shirt again and to step up onto the platform and stand in front of the X-ray unit.

"Place your arms behind your back and breathe in. Thank you." Next she asked him to lie down on the examining table in the corner of the room. She leaned over his chest, smeared blodges of gel on his skin, and fixed little pads to them. While he stared up at the white ceiling she flicked a switch and concentrated on a tiny television screen on the corner of her desk. Her expression gave nothing away.

After she had removed the gel with a damp cloth, she said, "You can put your shirt back on, Mr. Kravits. You are now free to leave."

Once he was fully dressed, the young man hurried out of the building and down the steps, and ran all the way to the corner where they had parted. They hugged each other again.

"Everything go all right?"

"I think so," he said. "They told me I'd be hearing from them in the next few days, once they've had the results of all their tests."

"Thank God it hasn't been a problem for you."

"I only wish it weren't for you."

"Let's not even think about it," said David, holding tightly onto the one person he loved.

Marvin rang a week later to let David know that Dr. Royston had given him a clean bill of health. All he had to do now was send the first installment of $1,100 to the insurance company. David mailed a check to Geneva Life the following morning. Thereafter his payments were made by automatic debit on the first day of each month.

Nineteen days after the seventh payment had been cleared, David Kravits died of AIDS.

Pat tried to remember the first thing he was supposed to do once the will had been read. He was to contact a Mr. Levy, David's lawyer, and leave everything in his hands. David had warned him not to become involved in any way himself. Let Levy, as his executor, make the claim from the insurance company, he had said, and then pass the money on to him. "If in any doubt, say nothing," was the last piece of advice David had given Pat before he died.

Ten days later Pat received a letter from a claims representative at Geneva Life requesting an interview with the beneficiary of the policy. Pat passed the letter straight to David's lawyer. Mr. Levy wrote back agreeing to an interview, which would take place, at his client's request, at the offices of Levy, Goldberg & Levy in Manhattan.

"Is there anything you haven't told me, Patrick?" Levy asked him a few minutes before the insurance company's claims representative was due to arrive. "Because if there is, you'd better tell me now."

"No, Mr. Levy, there's nothing more to tell you," Pat replied, carrying out David's instructions to the letter.

From the moment the meeting began, the representative of Geneva Life, his eyes continually boring into Pat's bowed head, left Mr. Levy in no doubt that he was not happy about paying out on this particular claim. But the lawyer stonewalled every question, strengthened by the knowledge that eight months before, when rigorous tests had been taken, Geneva Life's doctors had found no sign of David's being HIV positive.

Levy kept repeating, "However much noise you make, your company will have to pay up in the end." He added for good measure, "If I have not received the full amount due to my client within thirty days, I will immediately instigate proceedings against Geneva Life." The claims representative asked Levy if he would consider a deal. Levy glanced at Pat, who bowed his head even lower, and replied, "Certainly not."

Pat arrived back at the apartment two hours later, exhausted and depressed, fearing that an attack of asthma might be coming on. He tried to prepare some supper before he went to work, but everything seemed so pointless without David. He was already wondering if he should have agreed to a settlement.

The phone rang only once during the evening. Pat rushed to pick it up, hoping it might be either his mother or his sister Ruth. It turned out to be Marvin, who bleated, "I'm in real trouble, Pat. I'm probably going to lose my job over that policy I made out for your friend David."

Pat said how sorry he was, but felt there was nothing he could do to help.

"Yes, there is," insisted Marvin. "For a start, you could take out a policy yourself. That might just save my skin."

"I don't think that would be wise," said Pat, wondering what David would have advised.

"Surely David wouldn't have wanted to see me fired," Marvin pleaded. "Have mercy on me, my friend. I just can't afford another divorce."

"How much would it cost me?" asked Pat, desperate to find some way of getting Marvin off the line.

"You're going to get a million dollars in cash," Marvin almost shouted, "and you're asking me what it's going to cost? What's a thousand dollars a month to someone as rich as you?"

"But I can't be sure that I am going to get the million," Pat protested.

"That's all been settled," Marvin told him, his voice falling by several decibels. "I'm not supposed to let you know this, but you'll be receiving the check on the thirtieth of the month. The company knows that your lawyer's got them by the balls— you wouldn't even have to make the first payment until after you'd received the million."

"All right," said Pat, desperate to be rid of him. "I'll do it, but not until I've received the check."

"Thank you, my friend. I'll drop around with the paperwork tomorrow night."

"No, that's not possible," said Pat. "I'm working nights this month. You'd better make it tomorrow afternoon."

"You won't be working nights once you've received that check, my friend," said Marvin, letting out one of his dreadful shrill laughs. "Lucky man," he added before he put the phone down.

By the time Marvin came around to the apartment the following afternoon, Pat was already having second thoughts. If he had to visit Dr. Royston again, they would immediately realize the truth. But once Marvin had assured him that the medical could be with any doctor of his choice, and that the first payment would be postdated, he caved in and signed all the forms between the penciled X's, making Ruth his sole beneficiary. He hoped David would have approved of that decision, at least.

"Thank you, my friend. I won't be bothering you again," promised Marvin. His final words as he closed the door behind him were, "I promise you, you'll never live to regret it."

Pat saw his doctor a week later. The examination didn't take long, as Pat had recently had a complete check-up. On that occasion, as the doctor recalled, Pat had appeared quite nervous, and couldn't hide his relief when he'd phoned to give him the all-clear. "Not much wrong with you, Patrick," he said, "apart from the asthma, which doesn't seem to be getting any worse."

Marvin called a week later to let Pat know that the doctor had given him a clean bill of health, and that he had held on to his job with Geneva Life.

"I'm pleased for you," said Pat. "But what about my check?"

"It will be paid out on the last day of the month. Only a matter of processing it now. Should be with you twenty-four hours before the first payment is due on your policy. Just like I said, you win both ways."

Pat called David's lawyer on the last day of the month to ask if he had received the check from Geneva Life.

"There was nothing in this morning's mail," Levy told him, "but I'll phone the other side right now, in case it's already been issued and is on its way. If not, I'll start proceedings against them immediately."

Pat wondered if he should tell Levy that he had signed a check for $1,100, which was due to be cleared the following day, and that he only just had sufficient funds in his account to cover it—certainly not enough to see him through until his next paycheck. All his surplus cash had gone to help with David's monthly payments to Geneva Life. He decided not to mention it. David had repeatedly told him that if he was in any doubt, he should say nothing.

"I'll phone you at close of business tonight and let you know exactly what the position is," said Levy.

"No, that won't be possible," said Pat. "I'm on night duty all this week. In fact I have to leave for work right now. Perhaps you could call me first thing tomorrow morning?"

"Will do," promised the lawyer.

When Pat returned home from work in the early hours, he couldn't get to sleep. He tossed and turned, worrying how he would survive for the rest of the month if his check was presented to the bank that morning, and he still hadn't received the million dollars from Geneva Life.

His phone rang at 9:31. Pat grabbed it, and was relieved to hear Mr. Levy's voice on the other end of the line.

"Patrick, I had a call from Geneva Life yesterday evening while you were at work, and I must tell you that you've broken Levy's golden rule."

"Levy's golden rule?" asked Pat, mystified.

"Yes, Levy's golden rule. It's quite simple really, Patrick. By all means drop anything you like, on anyone you like, but don't *ever* drop it all over your own lawyer."

"I don't understand," said Pat.

"Your doctor has supplied Geneva Life with a sample of your blood and urine, and they just happen to be identical to the ones Dr. Royston has in his laboratory in the name of David Kravits."

Pat felt the blood draining from his head as he realized the trick Marvin must have played on him. His heart began beating faster and faster. Suddenly his legs gave way, and he collapsed on the floor, gasping for breath.

"Did you hear me, Patrick?" asked Levy. "Are you still there?"

A paramedic team broke into the apartment twenty minutes later, but, moments before they reached him, Pat had died of a heart attack brought on by a suffocating bout of asthma.

Mr. Levy did nothing until he was able to confirm with Pat's bankers that his client's check for $1,100 had been cleared by the insurance company.

Nineteen months later Pat's sister Ruth received a payment of one million dollars from Geneva Life, but not until they had gone through a lengthy court battle with Levy, Goldberg & Levy.

The jury finally accepted that Pat had died of natural causes, and that the insurance policy was in existence at the time of his death.

I promise you, Marvin Roebuck lived to regret it.

THE FIRST MIRACLE

TOMORROW IT WOULD BE A.D. 1, but nobody had told him.

If anyone had, he wouldn't have understood, because he thought it was the forty-third year of the reign of the emperor. And in any case, he had more important things on his mind.

His mother was still angry with him, and he had to admit that he'd been naughty that day, even by the standards of a normal thirteen-year-old. He hadn't meant to drop the pitcher when she had sent him to the well for water. He had tried to explain to her that it wasn't his fault he had tripped over a stone—that bit at least was true. What he hadn't told her was that he had been chasing a stray dog at the time. And then there was that pomegranate: How was he to know that it was the last one, and that his father had taken a liking to them?

The young Roman was now dreading his father's return and the possibility that he might be given another leathering. He could still recall the last one: He hadn't been able to sit down for two days without being reminded of the pain, and the thin red scars hadn't completely disappeared for three weeks.

He sat on the window ledge in a shaded corner of his room, trying to think of some way he could redeem himself in his mother's eyes. He had spilled cooking oil all over his tunic and she had thrown him out of the kitchen. "Go and play outside," she had snapped, but playing outside wasn't much fun if you were only allowed to play by yourself. Pater had forbidden him to mix with the local boys.

How he hated this uncivilized country! If only he could be back home among his friends, there would be so much for him to do. Still, only another three weeks and he would . . .

The door swung open and his mother bustled into the room. She was dressed in the thin black garments favored by locals: it was the only way to keep cool, she had explained to her husband when he had seen her wearing them for the first time. He had grunted his disapproval, so now she always changed back into imperial dress before he returned in the evening.

"Can't you find anything useful to do?" she asked, addressing the sulking figure of her son.

"I was just . . . "

"Daydreaming as usual. Well, it's time for you to wake up, because I need you to go into the village and fetch some food."

"Yes, Mater, I'll go at once," the boy said. He jumped off the window ledge, and started running toward the door.

"At least wait until you've heard what I want."

"Sorry, Mater," he said, coming to an abrupt halt.

"Now listen, and listen carefully," she began, counting on her fingers as she spoke. "I need a chicken, some raisins, figs, dates, and . . . ah, yes, two pomegranates."

The boy's face reddened at the mention of the pomegranates. He stared down at the stone floor, hoping she might have forgotten. His mother put her hand into the leather purse that hung from her waist and removed two small coins, but before she handed them over she made her son repeat her instructions.

"One chicken, some raisins, figs, dates, and two pomegranates," he recited, as he might the modern poet Virgil.

"And be sure to see they give you the right change," she added. "Never forget that the people here are all thieves."

"Yes, Mater . . ." For a moment the boy hesitated, wondering if he dared to ask.

"If you remember everything, and bring back the right change, I might forget to tell your father about the broken pitcher and the pomegranate."

The boy smiled and, clutching the two small silver coins tightly in his fist, ran out of the house into the compound.

The guard who stood on duty at the gate removed a great wedge of wood and allowed the massive door to swing open. The boy jumped through, and grinned back at him.

"I hear you're in trouble again," the guard shouted after him.

"No, not this time," the boy replied. "I'm about to be saved."

He waved happily to the guard and started walking briskly in the direction of the village, reciting some verses from Virgil's *Aeneid*, which reminded him of home. He kept to the center of the dusty, winding path that the locals had the impudence to call a road. It seemed as if he spent half his time removing small stones from inside his sandals. If his father had been posted here for any length of time he would have made some changes; then they would have had a *real* road, straight and wide enough to allow two chariots to pass.

And Mater would have told the serving girls a thing or two. Not one of them knew how to set a table, or even to prepare food so that it was at least clean. Since they had been stationed in Judaea, he had seen his mother in a kitchen for the first time in his life. He was confident it would also be the last. Soon his father would be coming to the end of his tour of duty, and they could all return to Rome.

He had learned many things during the past year, but in particular he was now certain that when he grew up he wasn't going to be a tax collector, or work in the census office.

The village to which his mother had sent him was a few stades from the compound, and the evening sun shone down on him as he walked. It was a large, red sun, the same deep red as his father's tunic, and it was still giving out enough heat to make him sweat and long for something to drink. Perhaps there would be enough money left over to buy himself a pomegranate. He couldn't wait to take one home to show his friends how large they grew in this barbaric land. Marcus, his best friend, would probably have seen one as big, because his father had commanded a whole army in Asia Minor, but the rest of the class would be impressed.

When he reached the village, he found the narrow twisting lanes that ran between the little white houses swarming with people. They had all come from the surrounding area at his father's command to be registered for the census, so that each of them might be taxed according to their rank. His father's authority had been vested in him by the emperor himself, and once the boy had reached his sixteenth birthday, he too would serve the emperor. Marcus wanted to be a soldier and to conquer the rest of the world, but the boy was more interested in the law, and in teaching his country's customs to all the barbarians who dwelled in strange lands.

Marcus had said, "I'll conquer them, and then you can govern them."

"A sensible division between brains and brawn," he had replied. His friend didn't seem impressed, and had dunked him in the nearest bath.

The boy quickened his pace. He knew he had to be back in the compound before the sun disappeared behind the hills: His father had warned him many times that they must always be locked safely inside before sunset. He had told his son that he would be safe while it was light, as no one would dare to harm him while others could see what was going on, but that once it was dark, anything could happen. The boy was aware that his father was not a popular man with the locals, but he dismissed the plebs from his mind. (It was Marcus who had taught him to refer to all foreigners as plebs.)

When he reached the marketplace, he began to concentrate on the supplies his mother had requested. He mustn't make any mistakes this time, or he would undoubtedly end up with another leathering from his father. He ran nimbly between the stands, checking the produce carefully. Some of the local people stared at the white-skinned boy with the curly fair hair and a straight, strong nose. He displayed no imperfections or signs of disease, unlike the majority of them. Many lowered their eyes to the ground when they saw him; he had come, after all, from the land of the natural rulers. The boy did not concern himself with such thoughts. All he noticed was that their native skins were parched and lined from exposure to the sun. He knew that too much harsh light was bad for you: It made you old before your time, his tutor had warned him.

At the last stand, the boy watched an old woman haggling over an unusually plump live chicken. He marched toward her, and when she saw him she ran away in fright, leaving the fowl behind. He looked straight into the eyes of the standkeeper, refusing to bargain with such a peasant. He pointed to the chicken and handed the man one denarius. The vendor bit the silver coin, then peered at the head of Augustus Caesar, ruler of half the known world. (When his tutor had told the boy, during a history lesson, about the emperor's achievements, he remembered saying, "Magister, I hope Caesar doesn't conquer the whole world before I have a chance to join in.")

"Come on, come on. I haven't got all day," the boy said, trying to sound like his father.

The man did not reply, as he had no idea what the boy was saying. All he knew for certain was that it was never worth annoying the invaders. He held the chicken firmly by the neck and, unsheathing a knife from his belt, cut its head off in one movement. He passed the bleeding fowl over to the boy together with some local coins, which had stamped on them the image of the man the boy's father had described so often as "that useless Herod." The boy kept his hand held out, palm upward, and the man continued to place bronze talents in it until he had no more.

Once the boy had left the man talentless, he moved on to another stand, where he pointed to bags containing raisins, figs, and dates. The new standkeeper measured out a libra of each, for which he received five of the near-worthless Herod coins. The man was about to protest, but the boy stared him fixedly in the eyes, the way he had seen his father do so often. The man backed away and simply bowed his head.

Now, what else did his mother want? He racked his brains. A chicken, raisins, dates, figs, and . . . of course—two pomegranates. He walked into the next street, and searched among the stands of fresh fruit until he found the largest pomegranates on display. He selected three and immediately broke one open, dug his teeth into it, and savored the cool taste. He spat out the pips, nodded his approval to the standkeeper, and paid him with two of the three remaining bronze talents (he wanted to keep one to add to Marcus's coin collection when he returned home).

He felt his mother would be pleased that he had carried out her wishes and only spent one silver denarius. Surely even Pater would be impressed by that. He finished his pomegranate and, with his arms laden, began heading slowly out of the market and back toward the compound, trying to avoid the stray dogs that continually ran into his path, barking and sometimes snapping at his ankles. They obviously didn't realize who he was.

When the boy reached the edge of the village he noticed that the sun was already melting behind the highest hill, and, recalling his father's words about being home before dusk, he quickened his pace. As he walked up the middle of the stony path, those still on their way down toward the village stood to one side, leaving him a clear path as far as his eye could see (which wasn't all that far, because he was carrying so much in his arms).

But there was one sight he could not fail to notice. A little way ahead of him was a man with a beard—a dirty, lazy custom, his father had often told him—wearing the ragged clothing that signified that he was of the tribe of Jacob. He tugged at a reluctant donkey that was laden down with a very fat woman who was, as their custom demanded, covered from head to toe in black. The boy was about to order them out of his way when the man pulled the donkey over to the side of the road, tied it up to a post, and entered a house that, from its sign, claimed to be an inn.

In his own land such a building would never have passed the scrutiny of the local citizens' council as a place fit for paying guests, but the boy realized that for many people during this particular week, even a mat on which to lay their head would be a luxury. By the time he reached the house, the bearded man had reappeared at the door with a forlorn look on his tired face. There was obviously no room at the inn.

The boy could have told him that before he went in, and was puzzled as to what the man could possibly do next. Not that he was really all that interested: As long as they paid their taxes, both of them could sleep in the hills for all he cared. It was about all they looked fit for.

The man with the beard was telling the fat woman something, while pointing behind the inn. She nodded her agreement, and without another word he led the donkey off around the side of the building. The boy wondered what could possibly be at the back of the inn, and decided to follow them. As he turned the corner of the building, he saw the man coaxing the donkey through the open door of what looked liked a barn. The boy followed, and when he came to the open door he stopped and stared inside.

The barn was covered in filthy straw. It was full of chickens, sheep, and oxen, and smelled not unlike the sewers in the side streets back home. He held his nose, beginning to feel sick. The man was clearing away some of the dirtiest of the straw from the center of the barn, trying to make a clean patch for them to rest on—a near hopeless task. When he had done the best he could, he lifted the fat woman down from the donkey and placed her gently in the straw. Then he went over to a trough on the far side of the barn from which one of the oxen was drinking. He cupped his hands, and having filled them with water, returned to the fat woman, trying to spill as little as possible.

The boy was growing bored. He was about to leave and continue on his journey home when the woman leaned forward to drink from the man's hands. Her shawl fell from her head, and he saw her face for the first time.

He stood transfixed as he stared at her. He had never seen anyone more beautiful. Unlike the common members of her tribe, the woman's skin was almost translucent, and her eyes shone brightly. But what most struck the boy was her manner and presence. Never had he felt so in awe of anyone, even during his one visit to the Senate House to hear a declamation by Augustus Caesar.

For a moment he remained mesmerized. But then he knew what he must do. He walked through the open door toward the woman, fell on his knees before her, stretched out his hands, and presented her with the chicken. She smiled but said nothing. He offered her the two pomegranates, and she smiled again. He then dropped the rest of the food at her feet. But she remained silent.

The man with the beard was returning with some more water. When he saw the young foreigner he fell on his knees, spilling the water onto the straw, then covered his face with his hands. The boy hardly noticed but remained kneeling, staring up at the woman. Eventually he rose and walked slowly toward the barn door. When he reached it, he turned back and stared once more into that serene face. She looked into his eyes for the first time.

The young Roman hesitated for a second and then bowed his head.

It was already dusk when he ran back out onto the winding path to resume his journey home, but he was not afraid. Rather, he felt he had done something good, and that therefore no harm could possibly come to him. He looked up into the sky and saw directly above him the first star, shining so brightly in the East that he wondered why he could see no others. But his father had told him that different stars were visible in different lands, so he dismissed the mystery from his mind.

The road was now empty, and he was able to quicken his pace towards the compound. He was not far from safety when he first heard the singing and shouting. He turned quickly and looked up into the hills, to see where the danger was coming from. To begin with, he couldn't make any make sense of what he saw. Then his eyes focused on one particular field, where some shepherds were leaping up and down, singing and shouting and clapping their hands.

He had been told by Marcus that sometimes the shepherds in this country made a lot of noise at night because they believed it kept away evil spirits. How could anyone be that stupid? the boy wondered. Suddenly there was a flash of lightning across the clear black sky, and the field was ablaze with light. The shepherds fell to their knees and stared silently up into the sky, as if they were listening intently to something.

Then, just as suddenly, all was darkness again.

The boy started running toward the compound, as fast as his legs would carry him: He wanted to be inside, to hear the great gate close safely behind him, and see the guard slide the wooden wedge firmly back into place.

He would have run all the way, had his path not been blocked by the strangest sight. His father had taught him never to show any fear when faced with danger. The boy tried to breathe regularly, in case they thought he was frightened. He was frightened, but he marched proudly on, determined that he would never be forced off the road by any foreigners, however magnificently attired.

Before him stood three camels, and astride them three men, peering down at him. The first was clad in gold, and with one arm he protected something hidden beneath his cloak. By his side hung a large sword, its sheath covered in all manner of rare gems. The second man was dressed in white, and held a silver casket to his breast. The third wore red, and clung to a large wooden box.

The man in gold put up his hand and addressed the boy in a strange tongue he had never heard before, even from his tutor. Once it was clear that the boy had not understood what had been said to him, the second man tried Hebrew, and then the third yet another language.

The boy folded his arms across his chest, and stood his ground. He told them who he was and where he was going, and demanded to know where they might be bound. He hoped his piping voice did not reveal his fear. The man robed in gold replied, questioning the boy in his own tongue.

"Where is he that is born king of the Jews? For we have seen his star in the East, and are come to worship him."

"King Herod lives beyond the . . . "

"We do not speak of King Herod," said the second man, "for he is but a king of men, as we are."

"We speak," said the third, "of the King of Kings. We have come from the East to offer him gifts of gold, frankincense, and myrrh."

"I know nothing about any King of Kings," said the boy, now gaining confidence. "I recognize only Augustus Caesar, emperor of half the known world."

The man robed in gold shook his head and, pointing to the sky, inquired of the boy: "Do you observe that bright star in the East? What is the name of the village on which it shines?"

The boy looked up at the star, and indeed the village below it was now clearer to the eye than it had been in sunlight.

"That's only Bethlehem," said the boy, laughing. "You will find no King of Kings there."

"Even there we shall find him," said the second man, "for did not Herod's chief priest tell us:

> And thou Bethlehem, in the land of Judah,
> Art not least among the princes of Judah,
> For out of thee shall come a Governor
> That shall rule my people Israel."

"That's just not possible," said the boy, now almost shouting at them. "Augustus Caesar rules Israel, and half the known world."

But the three robed men did not heed his words, and left him to ride on toward Bethlehem.

Mystified, the boy set out on the last stade of his journey home. Although the sky was now pitch black, whenever he turned his eyes toward Bethlehem the village was still clearly visible in the brilliant starlight.

When he reached the great wooden gate, he banged loudly and repeatedly until the guard, his sword drawn and holding a flaming torch, came to find out who it was that dared to disturb his watch. When he saw the boy, he frowned.

"The governor is very displeased with you. He returned at sunset, and is about to send out a search party for you."

The boy darted past the guard and ran all the way to the family's quarters, where he found his father addressing a sergeant of the guard and a dozen legionnaires. His mother was standing by his side, weeping.

The governor turned when he saw his son. "Where have you been?" he said in an icily measured tone.

"To Bethlehem, sir."

"Yes, child, I am aware of that. But whatever possessed you to return so late? Have I not told you on countless occasions never to be out of the compound after dark?"

"Yes, sir."

"Then you will come to my study at once."

The boy looked helplessly toward his mother, then turned to

follow his father into the study. The guard winked at the boy as he passed by, but he realized that nothing could save him now. His father strode ahead of him, and sat down on a wooden stool behind his table. His mother followed and stood silently drying her eyes just inside the door.

"Now, tell me exactly where you have been, and why it took you so long to return. And be sure to speak only the truth."

The boy stood in front of his father and calmly told him everything that had taken place.

He told how he had gone to the village and taken great care in choosing the food for their dinner, and how in so doing he had saved half the money his mother had given him; then how on the way back he had seen a fat lady on a donkey unable to find a place at the inn. He explained why he had followed her into the barn and parted with all their food; how the shepherds had shouted and beaten their breasts until there was a great light in the sky, when they had all fallen silent on their knees; and then finally how he had come to meet the three robed men who sat astride camels and were searching for the King of Kings.

The father grew more and more angry at his son's words.

"What a story this is!" he shouted. "Do tell me more. Did you meet this King of Kings?"

"No, sir, I did not," the boy replied. His father rose and started pacing around the room.

"Perhaps there is a simpler explanation as to why your face and fingers are stained red with pomegranate juice."

"No, Pater. I did buy an extra pomegranate, but even after I had bought all the food, I still managed to save one silver denarius."

The boy handed the coin over to his mother, believing it would confirm his story. But the sight of it only made his father angrier. He stopped pacing and stared down into the eyes of his son.

"You have spent the other denarius on yourself, and now you have nothing to show for it."

"That's not true, Pater, I . . . "

"I will allow you one more chance to tell me the truth," said his father as he resumed his seat behind the table. "Fail me, boy, and I shall give you a leathering you will never forget for the rest of your life."

The boy did not hesitate. "I have already told you the truth, Pater."

"Listen to me carefully, my son. We were born Romans, born to rule the world because our laws and customs are tried and tested and have always been based on complete integrity. Romans never lie; that is our strength and the weakness of our enemies. That is why we rule while others are willing to be ruled, and as long as that is so, the Roman Empire will never fall. Do you understand what I am saying to you, boy?"

"Yes, Pater, I understand."

"Then you will also understand why it is imperative always to tell the truth, whatever the consequences."

"Yes, Pater, I do. But I have already told you the truth."

"Then there is no hope for you," said the man quietly. "You leave me no choice as to how I will have to deal with you."

The boy's mother raised her hand, wanting to come to her son's aid, but knew any protest would be useless. The governor rose from his chair, removed the leather belt from around his waist, and folded it double, with the heavy brass studs on the outside. He then ordered his son to bend down and touch his toes. The young boy obeyed without hesitation, and his father raised the belt above his head and brought it down on the child with all the strength he could muster. The boy didn't once flinch or murmur as each stroke was administered, while his mother turned away and wept.

After the father had delivered the twelfth stroke he ordered his son to go to his room. The boy left without a word and climbed the stairs to his bedroom. His mother followed. As she passed the kitchen, she stepped in and took some olive oil and ointments from a drawer.

She carried the little jars up to the boy's room, where she found him already in bed. She went over to his side, sat on the edge of the bed, and pulled the sheet back. She told him to turn onto his chest while she prepared the oils. Then she gently removed his night tunic, for fear of adding to his pain. She stared down at his naked body in disbelief.

The boy's skin was unmarked.

She ran her fingers gently over her son's unblemished body, and found it as smooth as if he had just bathed. She turned him over. There was no mark on him anywhere. Quickly she slipped his tunic back on and covered him with the sheet.

"Say nothing of this to your father," she said, "and remove the memory of it from your mind forever."

"Yes, Mater."

The mother leaned over and blew out the candle by the side of his bed, gathered up the unused oils, and tiptoed to the door. At the threshold, she turned in the dim light to look back at her son and said: "Now I know you were telling the truth, Pontius."

THE LOOPHOLE

"THAT ISN'T THE VERSION I heard," said Philip.

One of the club members seated at the bar glanced around at the sound of raised voices, but when he saw who was involved only smiled and continued his conversation.

The Haslemere Golf Club was fairly crowded that Saturday morning. And just before lunch it was often difficult to find a seat in the spacious clubhouse.

Two of the members had already ordered their second round and settled themselves in the alcove overlooking the first hole long before the room began to fill up. Philip Masters and Michael Gilmour had finished their Saturday-morning game earlier than usual and now seemed engrossed in conversation.

"And what did you hear?" asked Michael Gilmour quietly, but in a voice that carried.

"That you weren't altogether blameless in the matter."

"I most certainly was," said Michael. "What are you suggesting?"

"I'm not suggesting anything," said Philip. "But don't forget, you can't fool me. I employed you myself once, and I've known you for far too long to accept everything you say at face value."

"I wasn't trying to fool anyone," said Michael. "It's common knowledge that I lost my job. I've never suggested otherwise."

"Agreed. But what isn't common knowledge is *how* you lost your job and why you haven't been able to find a new one."

"I haven't been able to find a new one for the simple reason that jobs aren't that easy to come by at the moment. And by the way, it's not my fault you're a success story and a bloody millionaire."

"And it's not my fault that you're penniless and always out of work. The truth is that jobs are easy enough to come by for someone who can supply references from his last employer."

"Just what are you hinting at?" said Michael.

"I'm not hinting at anything."

Several members had stopped taking part in the conversation in front of them as they tried to listen to the one going on behind them.

"What I am saying," Philip continued, "is that no one will employ you for the simple reason that you can't find anyone who will supply you with a reference—and everybody knows it."

Everybody didn't know it, which explained why most people in the room were now trying to find out.

"I was let go," insisted Michael.

"In your case 'let go' was just a euphemism for 'fired.' No one pretended otherwise at the time."

"I was made redundant," repeated Michael, "for the simple reason that the company profits turned out to be a little disappointing this year."

"A little disappointing? That's rich. They were nonexistent."

"Simply because we lost one or two of our major accounts to rivals."

"Rivals who, I'm informed, were only too happy to pay for a little inside information."

By now most members of the club had cut short their own conversations as they leaned, twisted, turned, and bent in an effort to capture every word coming from the two men seated in the window alcove of the clubroom.

"The loss of those accounts was fully explained in the report to stockholders at this year's annual meeting," said Michael.

"But was it explained to those same stockholders how a former employee could afford to buy a new car only a matter of days after being fired?" pursued Philip. "A second car, I might add." Philip took a sip of his tomato juice.

"It wasn't a new car," said Michael defensively. "It was a second-hand Mini, and I bought it with part of my severance pay when I had to return the company car. And in any case, you know Carol needs her own car for the job at the bank."

"Frankly, I am amazed Carol has stuck it as long as she has after all you've put her through."

"All *I've* put her through—what are you implying?" asked Michael.

"I am not *implying* anything," Philip retorted. "But the fact is that a certain young woman, who shall remain nameless"—this piece of information seemed to disappoint most eavesdroppers—"was also let ago at about the same time, not to mention pregnant."

The bartender had not been asked for a drink for nearly seven minutes, and by now there were few members still affecting not to be listening to the altercation between the two men. Some were even staring in open disbelief.

"But I hardly knew her," protested Michael.

"As I said, that's not the version I heard. And what's more I'm told the child bears a striking resemblance—"

"That's going too far—"

"Only if you have nothing to hide," said Philip grimly.

"You know I've nothing to hide."

"Not even the blond hairs Carol found all over the back seat of the new Mini? The girl at work was a blond, wasn't she?"

"Yes, but those hairs came from a golden retriever."

"You don't have a golden retriever."

"I know, but the dog belonged to the last owner."

"That bitch didn't belong to the last owner, and I refuse to believe Carol fell for that old chestnut."

"She believed it because it was the truth."

"The truth, I fear, is something you lost contact with a long time ago. You were fired first because you couldn't keep your hands off anything in a skirt under forty, and second because you couldn't keep your fingers out of the till. I ought to know. Don't forget I had to get rid of you for the same reasons."

Michael jumped up, his cheeks almost the color of Philip's tomato juice. He raised his clenched fist and was about to take a swing at Philip when Colonel Mather, the club president, appeared at his side.

"Good morning, sir," said Philip calmly, rising for the colonel.

"Good morning, Philip," the colonel barked. "Don't you think this little misunderstanding has gone quite far enough?"

"Little misunderstanding?" protested Michael. "Didn't you hear what he's been saying about me?"

"Every word, unfortunately, like any other member present," said the colonel. Turning back to Philip, he added, "Perhaps you two should shake hands like good fellows and call it a day."

"Shake hands with that philandering, double-crossing shyster? Never," said Philip. "I tell you, Colonel, he's not fit to be a member of this club, and I can assure you that you've heard only half the story."

Before the colonel could attempt another round of diplomacy Michael sprang on Philip, and it took three men younger than the club president to pry them apart. The colonel immediately ordered both men off the premises, warning them that their conduct would be reported to the house committee at its next monthly meeting. And until that meeting had taken place, they were both suspended.

The club secretary, Jeremy Howard, escorted the two men off the premises and watched Philip get into his Rolls-Royce and drive sedately down the drive and out through the gates. He had to wait on the steps of the club for several minutes before Michael departed in his Mini. He appeared to be sitting in the front seat writing something. When he had eventually passed through the club gates, the secretary turned on his heels and made his way back to the bar. What they did to each other after they left the grounds was none of his business.

Back in the clubhouse, the secretary found that the conversation had not returned to the likely winner of the President's Putter, the seeding of the Ladies' Handicap Cup, or who might be prevailed upon to sponsor the Youth Tournament that year.

"They seemed in a jolly enough mood when I passed them on the sixteenth hole earlier this morning," the club captain informed the colonel.

The colonel admitted to being mystified. He had known both men since the day they joined the club nearly fifteen years before. They weren't bad lads, he assured the captain; in fact he rather liked them. They had played a round of golf every

Saturday morning for as long as anyone could remember, and never a cross word had been known to pass between them.

"Pity," said the colonel. "I was hoping to ask Masters to sponsor the Youth Tournament this year."

"Good idea, but I can't see you pulling that off now."

"I can't imagine what they thought they were up to."

"Can it simply be that Philip is such a success story and Michael has fallen on hard times?" suggested the captain.

"No, there's more to it than that," replied the colonel. "This morning's little episode requires a fuller explanation," he added sagely.

Everyone in the club was aware that Philip Masters had built up his own business from scratch after he had left his first job as a kitchen salesman. "Ready-Fit Kitchens" had started in a shed at the end of Philip's garden and ended up in a factory on the other side of town that employed more than three hundred people. After Ready-Fit went public, the financial press speculated that Philip's shares alone had to be worth a couple of million. When five years later the company was taken over by the John Lewis Partnership, it became public knowledge that Philip had walked away from the deal with a check for seventeen million pounds and a five-year service contract that would have pleased a pop star. Some of the windfall had been spent on a magnificent Georgian house in sixty acres of woodland just outside Haslemere: He could even see the golf course from his bedroom. Philip had been married for more than twenty years, and his wife, Sally, was chairman of the regional branch of the Save the Children Fund and a JP. Their son had just won a place at St. Anne's College, Oxford.

Michael was the boy's godfather.

Michael Gilmour could not have been a greater contrast. On leaving school, where Philip had been his closest friend, he had drifted from job to job. He started out as a trainee with Watneys, but lasted only a few months before moving on to work as a rep with a publishing company. Like Philip, he married his childhood sweetheart, Carol West, the daughter of a local doctor.

When their own daughter was born, Carol complained about the hours Michael spent away from home, so he left publishing and signed on as a distribution manager with a local soft drinks firm. He lasted for a couple of years until his deputy was promoted over him as area manager, at which decision Michael left in a huff. After his first time on unemployment, Michael joined a grain-packing company, but found he was allergic to corn and, having been supplied with a medical certificate to prove it, collected his first redundancy cheque. He then joined Philip as a Ready-Fit Kitchens rep but left without explanation within a month of the company being taken over. Another spell of unemployment followed before he took up the job of sales manager with a company that made microwave ovens. He seemed to have settled down at last until, without warning, he was let go. It was true that the company profits had been halved that year, while the company directors were sorry to see Michael go—or that was how it was expressed in their in-house magazine.

Carol was unable to hide her distress when Michael was let go for the fourth time. They could have use the extra cash now that their daughter had been offered a place at art school.

Philip was the girl's godfather.

"What are you going to do about it?" asked Carol anxiously, when Michael had told her what had taken place at the club.

"There's only one thing I can do," he replied. "After all, I have my reputation to consider. I shall sue the bastard."

"That's a terrible way to talk about your oldest friend. And anyway we can't afford to go to law," said Carol. "Philip's a millionaire and we're penniless."

"Can't be helped," said Michael. "I'll have to go through with it, even if it means selling everything."

"And even if the rest of your family has to suffer along with you?"

"None of us will suffer when he ends up paying my costs plus massive damages."

"But you could *lose*," said Carol. "Then we would end up with nothing—worse than nothing."

"That's not possible," said Michael. "He made the mistake of saying all those things in front of witnesses. There must have been over fifty members in the clubhouse this morning, including the president of the club and the editor of the local paper, and they couldn't have failed to hear every word."

Carol remained unconvinced, and she was relieved that during the next few days Michael didn't mention Philip's name once. She hoped that her husband had come to his senses and the whole affair was best forgotten.

But then the *Haslemere Chronicle* decided to print its version of the quarrel between Michael and Philip. Under the headline FIGHT BREAKS OUT AT GOLF CLUB came a carefully worded account of what had taken place on the previous Saturday. The editor of the *Haslemere Chronicle* knew only too well that the conversation itself was unprintable unless he also wanted to be sued, but he managed to include enough innuendo in the article to give a full flavor of what had happened that morning.

"That's the final straw," said Michael, when he finished reading the article for a third time. Carol realized that nothing she could say or do was going to stop her husband now.

The following Monday, Michael contacted a local solicitor, Reginald Lomax, who had been at school with them both. Armed with the article, Michael briefed Lomax on the conversation that the *Chronicle* had felt injudicious to publish in any great detail. Michael also gave Lomax his own detailed account of what had happened at the club that morning, and handed him four pages of handwritten notes to back his claims up.

Lomax studied the notes carefully.

"When did you write these?"

"In my car, immediately after we were suspended."

"That was circumspect of you," said Lomax. "Most circumspect." He stared quizzically at his client over the top of his half-moon spectacles. Michael made no comment. "Of course you must be aware that the law is an expensive pastime," Lomax continued. "Suing for slander will not come cheap, and even with evidence as strong as this"—he tapped the notes in front of him—"you could still lose. Slander depends so much on what other people remember or, more important, will admit to remembering."

"I'm well aware of that," said Michael. "But I'm determined to go through with it. There were over fifty people in the club within earshot that morning."

"So be it," said Lomax. "Then I shall require five thousand pounds in advance as a contingency fee to cover all the immediate costs and the preparations for a court case." For the first time Michael looked hesitant.

"Returnable, of course, but only if you win the case."

Michael removed his checkbook and wrote out a figure that, he reflected, would only just be covered by the remainder of his severance pay.

The writ for slander against Philip Masters was issued the next morning by Lomax, Davis & Lomax.

A week later the writ was accepted by another firm of solicitors in the same town, actually in the same building.

Back at the club, debate on the rights and wrongs of *Gilmour* v. *Masters* did not subside as the weeks passed.

Club members whispered furtively among themselves whether they might be called to give evidence at the trial. Several had already received letters from Lomax, Davis & Lomax requesting statements about what they could recall being said by the two men that morning. A good many pleaded amnesia or deafness but a few turned in graphic accounts of the quarrel. Encouraged, Michael pressed on, much to Carol's dismay.

One morning about a month later, after Carol had left for the bank, Michael Gilmour received a call from Reginald Lomax. The defendant's solicitors, he was informed, had requested a "without prejudice" consultation.

"Surely you're not surprised by that after all the evidence we've collected?" Michael replied.

"It's only a consultation," Lomax reminded him.

"Consultation or no consultation, I won't settle for less than one hundred thousand pounds."

"Well, I don't even know that they—" began Lomax.

"I do, and I also know that for the last eleven weeks I haven't been able to even get an interview for a job because of that bastard," Michael said with contempt. "Nothing less than one hundred thousand pounds, do you hear me?"

"I think you are being a trifle optimistic, in the circumstances," said Lomax. "But I'll call you and let you know the other side's response as soon as the meeting has taken place."

Michael told Carol the good news that evening, but like Reginald Lomax she was skeptical. The ringing of the phone interrupted their discussion on the subject. Michael, with Carol standing by his side, listened carefully to Lomax's report. Philip, it seemed, was willing to settle for twenty-five thousand pounds and had agreed to paying both sides' costs.

Carol nodded her grateful acceptance, but Michael only repeated that Lomax was to hold out for nothing less than one hundred thousand. "Can't you see that Philip's already worked out what it's going to cost him if this case ends up in court? And he knows only too well that I won't give in."

Carol and Lomax remained unconvinced. "It's much more touch-and-go than you realize," the solicitor told him. "A High Court jury might consider the words were only meant as banter."

"Banter? But what about the fight that followed the banter?" said Michael.

"Started by you," Lomax pointed out. "Twenty-five thousand is a good figure in the circumstances," he added.

Michael refused to budge, and ended the conversation by repeating his demand for one hundred thousand pounds.

Two weeks passed before the other side offered fifty thousand in exchange for a quick settlement. This time Lomax was not surprised when Michael rejected the offer out of hand. "Quick settlement be damned. I've told you I won't consider less than a hundred thousand." Lomax knew by now that any plea for prudence was going to fall on deaf ears.

It took three more weeks and several more phone calls between solicitors before the other side accepted that they were going to have to pay the full one hundred thousand pounds. Reginald Lomax rang Michael to inform him of the news late one evening, trying to make it sound as if he had scored a personal triumph. He assured Michael that the necessary papers could be drawn up immediately and the settlement signed in a matter of days.

"Naturally all your costs will be covered," he added.

"Naturally," said Michael.

"So all that is left for you to do now is agree on a statement."

A short statement was penned and, with the agreement of both sides, issued to the *Haslemere Chronicle*. The paper printed the contents the following Friday on its front page. "The writ for slander between Gilmour and Masters," the *Chronicle* reported, "has been withdrawn with the agreement of both sides but only after a substantial out-of-court settlement by the defendant. Philip Masters has withdrawn unreservedly what was said at the club that morning and has given an unconditional apology; he has also made a promise that he will never repeat the words used again. Mr. Masters has paid the plaintiff's costs in full."

Philip wrote to the colonel the same day, admitting perhaps he had had a little too much to drink on the morning in question. He regretted his impetuous outburst, apologized, and assured the club's president it would never happen again.

Carol was the only one who seemed to be saddened by the outcome.

"What's the matter, darling?" asked Michael. "We've won, and what's more it's solved our financial problems."

"I know," said Carol, "but is it worth losing your closest friend for one hundred thousand pounds?"

On the following Saturday morning Michael was pleased to find an envelope among his morning post with the Golf Club crest on the flap. He opened it nervously and pulled out a single sheet of paper. It read:

Dear Mr. Gilmour,

At the monthly committee meeting held last Wednesday Colonel Mather raised the matter of your behavior in the clubhouse on the morning of Saturday, April 16.

It was decided to minute the complaints of several members, but on this occasion only to issue a severe reprimand to you both. Should a similar incident occur in the future, loss of membership would be automatic.

The temporary suspension issued by Colonel Mather on April 16 is now lifted.

Yours sincerely,
Jeremy Howard (Secretary)

"I'm off to do the shopping," shouted Carol from the top of the stairs. "What are your plans for the morning?"

"I'm going to have a round of golf," said Michael, folding up the letter.

"Good idea," said Carol to herself as she wondered whom Michael would find to play against in the future.

Quite a few members noticed Michael and Philip teeing up at the first hole that Saturday morning. The club captain commented to the colonel that he was glad to observe that the quarrel had been sorted out to everyone's satisfaction.

"Not to mine," said the colonel under his breath. "You can't get drunk on tomato juice."

"I wonder what the devil they can be talking about?" the club captain said as he stared at them both through the bay windows. The colonel raised his binoculars to take a closer look at the two men.

"How could you possibly miss a four-foot putt, dummy?" asked Michael when they had reached the first green. "You must be drunk again."

"As you well know," replied Philip, "I never drink before dinner, and I therefore suggest that your allegation that I am drunk again is nothing less than slander."

"Yes, but where are your witnesses?" said Michael as they moved up on to the second tee. "I had over fifty, don't forget."

Both men laughed.

Their conversation ranged over many subjects as they played the first eight holes, never once touching on their past quarrel until they reached the ninth green, the farthest point from the clubhouse. They both checked to see there was no one within earshot. The nearest player was still putting out some two hundred yards behind them on the eighth hole. It was then that Michael removed a bulky brown envelope from his golf bag and handed it over to Philip.

"Thank you," said Philip, dropping the package into his own golf bag as he removed a putter. "As neat a little operation as I've been involved in for a long time," Philip added as he addressed the ball.

"I end up with forty thousand pounds," said Michael grinning, "while you lose nothing at all."

"Only because I pay tax at the highest rate and can therefore claim the loss as a legitimate business expense," said Philip, "and I wouldn't have been able to do that if I hadn't once employed you."

"And I, as a successful litigant, need pay no tax at all on damages received in a civil case."

"A loophole that even this chancellor hasn't caught on to," said Philip.

"Even though it went to Reggie Lomax, I was sorry about the solicitors' fees," added Michael.

"No problem, old fellow. They're also one hundred percent claimable against tax. So as you see, I didn't lose a penny and you ended up with forty thousand pounds tax free."

"And nobody the wiser," said Michael, laughing.

The colonel put his binoculars back into their case.

"Had your eye on this year's winner of the President's Putter, Colonel?" asked the club captain.

"No," the colonel replied. "The certain sponsor of this year's Youth Tournament."

THE HUNGARIAN
PROFESSOR

COINCIDENCES, WRITERS ARE TOLD (usually by the critics) must be avoided, although in truth the real world is full of incidents that in themselves are unbelievable. Everyone has had an experience that if they wrote about it would appear to others as pure fiction.

The same week that the headlines in the world newspapers read: RUSSIA INVADES AFGHANISTAN, AMERICA TO WITHDRAW FROM MOSCOW OLYMPICS, there also appeared a short obituary in *The Times* for the distinguished professor of English at the University of Budapest: "A man who was born and died in his native Budapest and whose reputation remains assured by his brilliant translation of the works of Shakespeare into his native Hungarian. Although some linguists consider his *Coriolanus* immature they universally acknowledge his *Hamlet* to be a translation of genius."

Nearly a decade after the Hungarian Revolution, I had the chance to participate in a student athletics meeting in Budapest. The competition was scheduled to last for a full week so I felt there would be an opportunity to find out a little about the country. The team flew in to Ferihegy Airport on a Sunday night and we were taken immediately to the Hotel Ifushag. (I learned later that the word meant "youth" in Hungarian). Having settled in, most of the team went to bed early since their opening-round heats were the following day.

Breakfast the next morning comprised of milk, toast, and an egg, served in three acts with long intervals between each. Those of us who were running that afternoon skipped lunch for fear that a matinee performance might cause us to miss our events completely.

Two hours before the start of the meeting, we were taken by bus to the Nép stadium and unloaded outside the dressing rooms (I always feel they should be called undressing rooms). We changed into track suits and sat around on benches anxiously waiting to be called. After what seemed to be an interminable time but was in fact only a few minutes, an official appeared and led us out on to the track. As it was the opening day of competition, the stadium was packed. When I had finished my usual warm-up of jogging, sprinting, and some light calisthenics, the loudspeaker announced the start of the 100m race in three languages. I stripped off my track suit and ran over to the start. When called, I pressed my spikes against the blocks and waited nervously for the starter's pistol. *Felkészülni, kész*—bang! Ten seconds later the race was over and the only virtue of coming last was that it left me six free days to investigate the Hungarian capital.

Walking around Budapest reminded me of my childhood days in Bristol just after the war, but with one noticeable difference. As well as the bombed-out buildings, there was row upon row of bullet holes in some of the walls. The revolution, although eight years past, was still much in evidence, perhaps because the nationals did not want anyone to forget. The people on the streets had lined faces, stripped of all emotion, and they shuffled rather than walked, leaving the impression of a nation of old men. If you inquired innocently why, they told you there was nothing to hurry for, or to be happy about, although they always seemed to be thoughtful with each other.

On the third day of the games, I returned to the Nép stadium to support a friend of mine who was competing in the semifinals of the four-hundred-meter hurdles, which was the first event that afternoon. Having a competitor's pass, I could sit virtually anywhere in the half-empty arena. I chose to watch the race from just above the final bend, giving me a good view of the home stretch. I sat down on the wooden bench without paying much attention to the people on either side of me. The race began, and as my friend hit the bend crossing the seventh hurdle with only three hurdles to cover before the finish line, I stood and cheered him heartily all the way down the home stretch. He managed to come in third, ensuring himself a place in the final the next day. I sat down again and wrote out the detailed result in my program. I was about to leave, as there were no British competitors in the hammer or the pole vault, when a voice behind me said:

"You are English?"

"Yes," I replied, turning in the direction from which the question had been put.

An elderly gentleman looked up at me. He wore a three-piece suit that must have been out of date when his father owned it, and even lacked the possible virtue that someday the style might come back into fashion. The leather patches on the elbows left me in no doubt that my questioner was a bachelor, for they could only have been sewn on by a man—either that or one had to conclude he had elbows in odd places. The length of his trousers revealed that his father had been two inches taller than he. As for the man himself, he had a few strands of white hair, a walrus mustache, and ruddy cheeks. His tired blue eyes were perpetually half closed like the shutter of a camera that has just been released. His forehead was so lined that he might have been any age between fifty and seventy. The overall impression was of a cross between a streetcar inspector and an out-of-work violinist.

I sat down for a second time.

"I hope you didn't mind my asking?" he added.

"Of course not," I said.

"It's just that I have so little opportunity to converse with an Englishman. So when I spot one I always grasp the nettle. Is that the right colloquial expression?"

"Yes," I said, trying to think how many Hungarian words I knew. "Yes," "no," "good morning," "good-bye," "I am lost," "help."

"You are in the student games?"

"Were, not are," I said. "I departed somewhat rapidly on Monday."

"Because you were not rapid enough, perhaps?"

I laughed, again admiring his command of my first language.

"Why is your English so excellent?" I inquired.

"I'm afraid it's a little neglected," the old man replied. "But they still allow me to teach the subject at the university. I must confess to you that I have absolutely no interest in sports, but these occasions always afford me the opportunity to capture someone like yourself and oil the rusty machine, even if only for a few minutes." He gave me a tired smile, but his eyes were now alight.

"What part of England do you hail from?" For the first time his pronunciation faltered, as "hail" came out as "heel."

"Somerset," I told him.

"Ah!" he said. "Perhaps the most beautiful county in England." I smiled, as most foreigners never seem to travel much beyond Stratford-upon-Avon or Oxford. "To drive across the Mendips," he continued, "through perpetually green hilly countryside and to stop at Cheddar to see Gough's caves, at Wells to be amused by the black swans ringing the bell on the cathedral wall, or at Bath to admire the lifestyle of classical Rome, and then perhaps to go over the county border and on to Devon . . . Is Devon even more beautiful than Somerset, in your opinion?"

"Never," said I.

"Perhaps you are a little prejudiced." He laughed. "Now let me see if I can recall: 'Of the western counties there are seven./But the most glorious is surely that of Devon.' Perhaps Hardy, like you, was prejudiced and could think only of his beloved Exmoor, the village of Tiverton, and Drake's Plymouth."

"Which is *your* favorite county?" I asked.

"The North Riding of Yorkshire has always been underrated, in my opinion," replied the old man. "When people talk of Yorkshire, I suspect Leeds, Sheffield, and Barnsley spring to mind. Coal mining and heavy industry. Visitors should travel and see the dales there; they will find them as different as chalk from cheese. Lincolnshire is too flat, and so much of the Midlands must now be spoiled by urban sprawl. The Birminghams of this world hold no appeal for me. But in the end I come down in favor of Worcestershire and Warwickshire, quaint old English villages nestling in the Cotswolds, and crowned by Stratford-upon-Avon. How I wish I could have been in England in 1959, while my countrymen were recovering from the scars of revolution: Olivier performing Coriolanus, another man who did not want to show his scars."

"I saw the performance," I said. "I went with a school group."

"Lucky boy. I translated the play into Hungarian at the age of nineteen. Reading over my work again last year made me aware I must repeat the exercise before I die."

"You have translated other Shakespeare plays?"

"All but three, I have been leaving *Hamlet* to last, and then I shall return to *Coriolanus* and start again. As you are a student, am I permitted to ask which university you attend?"

"Oxford."

"And your college?"

"Brasenose."

"Ah! BNC. How wonderful to be a few yards away from the Bodleian, the greatest library in the world. If I had been born in England I should have wanted to spend my days at All Souls. That is just opposite BNC, is it not?"

"That's right."

The professor stopped talking while we watched the next race, the first semifinal of the fifteen hundred meters. The winner was Anfras Patovich, a Hungarian, and the partisan crowd went wild with delight.

"That's what I call support," I said.

"Like Manchester United when they have scored the winning goal in the Cup Final. But my fellow countrymen do not cheer because the Hungarian was first," said the old man.

"No?" I said, somewhat surprised.

"Oh, no. They cheer because he beat the Russian."

"I hadn't even noticed," I said.

"There is no reason why you should, but their presence is always in the forefront of our minds, and we are rarely given the opportunity to see them beaten in public."

I tried to steer him back to a happier subject. "And before

you had been elected to All Souls, which college would you have wanted to attend?"

"As an undergraduate, you mean?"

"Yes."

"Undoubtedly Magdalen is the most beautiful college. It has the distinct advantage of being situated on the River Cherwell; and in any case I confess a weakness for perpendicular architecture and a love of Oscar Wilde." The conversation was interrupted by the sound of a pistol, and we watched the second semifinal of the fifteen meters, which was won by Orentas of the USSR. The crowd showed its disapproval more obviously this time, clapping in such a way that left hands passed right without coming into contact. I found myself joining in on the side of the Hungarians. The scene made the old man lapse into a sad silence. The last race of the day was won by Tim Johnston of England, and I stood and cheered unashamedly. The Hungarian crowd clapped politely.

I turned to say good-bye to the professor, who had not spoken for some time.

"How long are you staying in Budapest?" he asked.

"The rest of the week. I return to England on Sunday."

"Could you spare the time to join an old man for dinner one night?"

"I should be delighted."

"How considerate of you," he said, and he wrote out his full name and address in capital letters on the back of my program and returned it to me. "Why don't we say tomorrow at seven? And if you have any old newspapers or magazines, do bring them with you," he said, looking a little sheepish. "And I shall quite understand if you have to change your plans."

I spent the next morning visiting St. Matthias Church and the ancient fortress, two of the buildings that showed no evidence of the revolution. I then took a short trip down the Danube before spending the afternoon supporting the swimmers at the Olympic pool. At six I left the pool and went back to my hotel. I changed into my team blazer and gray slacks, hoping I looked smart enough for my distinguished host. I locked my door, started toward the elevator, and then remembered. I returned to my room to pick up the pile of newspapers and magazines I had collected from the rest of the team.

Finding the professor's home was not as easy as I had expected. After meandering around cobbled streets and waving the professor's address at several passers-by, I was finally directed to an old apartment house. I ran up the three flights of the wooden staircase in a few leaps and bounds, wondering how long the climb took the professor every day. I stopped at the door that displayed his number and knocked.

The old man answered immediately, as if he had been standing there, waiting by the door. I noticed that he was wearing the same suit he had had on the previous day.

"I am sorry to be late," I said.

"No matter, my own students also find me hard to find the first time," he said, grasping my hand. He paused. "Bad to use the same word twice in the same sentence. "'Locate' would have been better, wouldn't it?"

He trotted on ahead of me, not waiting for my reply, a man obviously used to living on his own. He led me down a small, dark corridor into his living room. I was shocked by its size.Three walls were covered with indifferent prints and watercolors, depicting English scenes, while the fourth was dominated by a large bookcase. I could spot Shakespeare, Dickens, Austen, Trollope, Hardy, even Waugh and Graham Greene. On the table was a faded copy of the *New Statesman*. I looked around to see if we were on our own, but there seemed to be no sign of a wife or child either in person or picture, and indeed the table was set for only two.

The old man turned and stared with childlike delight at my pile of newspapers and magazines.

"*Punch, Time,* and the *Observer*—a veritable feast," he declared, gathering them into his arms before placing them lovingly on the bed in the corner of the room.

The professor then opened a bottle of Szürkebarát and left me to look at the pictures while he prepared the meal. He slipped away into an alcove that was so small that I had not realized the room contained a kitchenette. He continued to bombard me with questions about England, many of which I was quite unable to answer.

A few minutes later he stepped back into the room, requesting me to take a seat. "Do be seated," he said. "On reflection, I do not wish you to remove the seat. I wish you to sit on it." He put a plate in front of me that had on it a leg of something that might have been a chicken, a piece of salami, and a tomato. I felt sad, not because the food was inadequate, but because he believed it to be plentiful.

After dinner, which despite my efforts to eat slowly and hold him in conversation, did not take up much time, the old man made some coffee, which tasted bitter, and then filled a pipe before we continued our discussion. We talked of Shakespeare and his views on A. L. Rowse, and then he turned to politics.

"Is it true," the professor asked, "that England will soon have a Labour government?"

"The opinion polls seem to indicate as much," I said.

"I suppose the British feel that Sir Alec Douglas-Home is not swinging enough for the sixties," said the professor, now puffing vigorously away at his pipe. He paused and looked up at me through the smoke. "I did not offer you a pipe as I assumed after your premature exit in the first round of the competition that you would not be smoking." I smiled. "But Sir Alec," he continued, "is a man with long experience in politics, and it's no bad thing for a country to be governed by an experienced gentleman."

I would have laughed out loud had the same opinion been expressed by my own tutor.

"And what of the Labour leader?" I said, forbearing to mention his name.

"Molded in the white heat of a technological revolution," he replied. "I am not so certain. I liked Gaitskell, an intelligent and shrewd man. An untimely death. Attlee, like Sir Alec, was a gentleman. But as for Mr. Wilson, I suspect that history will test his mettle—a pun which I had not intended—in that white heat and only then will we discover the truth."

I could think of no reply.

"I was considering last night after we parted," the old man

continued, "the effect that Suez must have had on a nation which only ten years before had won a world war. The Americans should have backed you. Now we read in retrospect—always the historian's privilege—that at the time Prime Minister Eden was tired and ill. The truth was he didn't get the support from his closest allies when he most needed it."

"Perhaps we should have supported you in 1956."

"No, no, it was too late then for the West to shoulder Hungary's problems. Churchill understood that in 1945. He wanted to advance beyond Berlin and to free all the nations that bordered Russia. But the West had had a bellyful of war by then and left Stalin to take advantage of that apathy. When Churchill coined the phrase 'the Iron Curtain,' he foresaw exactly what was going to happen in the East. Amazing to think that when that great man said, "If the British Empire should last a thousand years," it was in fact destined to survive for only twenty-five. How I wish he had still been around the corridors of power in 1956."

"Did the revolution greatly affect your life?"

"I do not complain. It is a privilege to be the professor of English in a great university. They do not interfere with me in my department, and Shakespeare is not yet considered subversive literature." He paused and took a luxuriant puff at his pipe. "And what will you do, young man, when you leave the university—as you have shown us that you won't be making a living as a runner."

"I want to be a writer."

"Then travel, travel, travel," he said. "You cannot hope to learn everything from books. You must see the world for yourself if you ever hope to paint a picture for others."

I looked up at the old clock on his mantelpiece only to realize how quickly the time had passed.

"I must leave you, I'm afraid; they expect us all to be back in the hotel by ten."

"Of course," he said smiling at the English public school mentality. "I will accompany you to Kossuth Square, and then you will be able to see your hotel on the hill."

As we left the apartment, I noticed that he didn't bother to lock the door. Life had left him little to lose. He led me quickly through the myriad of narrow streets that I had found so impossible to navigate earlier in the evening, chatting about this building and that, an endless fund of knowledge about his own country as well as mine. When we reached Kossuth Square he took my hand and held on to it, reluctant to let go, as lonely people often will.

"Thank you for allowing an old man to indulge himself by chattering on about his favorite subject."

"Thank you for your hospitality," I said. "And when you are next in Somerset you must come to Lympsham and meet my family."

"Lympsham? I cannot place it," he said, looking worried.

"I'm not surprised. The village has a population of only twenty-two."

"Enough for two cricket teams," remarked the professor. "A game, I confess, with which I have never come to grips."

"Don't worry," I said "Neither have half the English."

"Ah, but I should like to. What is a 'gully,' a 'no-ball,' a 'night watchman'? The terms have always intrigued me."

"Then remember to get in touch when you're next in England, and I'll take you to Lord's and see if I can teach you something."

"How kind," he said, and then he hesitated before adding: "But I don't think we shall meet again."

"Why not?" I asked.

"Well, you see, I have never been outside Hungary in my whole life. When I was young I couldn't afford to, and now I don't imagine that those in authority would allow me to see your beloved England."

He released my hand, turned, and shuffled back into the shadows of the side streets of Budapest.

I read his obituary in *The Times* once again, as well as the headlines about Afghanistan and its effect on the Moscow Olympics.

He was right. We never met again.

THE STEAL

CHRISTOPHER AND MARGARET ROBERTS always spent their summer vacation as far away from England as they could possibly afford. However, as Christopher was the classics teacher at St. Cuthbert's, a small preparatory school just north of Yeovil, and Margaret was the school matron, their experience of four of the five continents was largely confined to periodicals such as *National Geographic* and *Time*.

The Robertses' annual vacation each August was nevertheless sacrosanct, and they spent eleven months of the year saving, planning, and preparing for their one extravagant luxury. The following eleven months were then spent passing on their discoveries to the "offspring": The Robertses, without children of their own, looked on all the pupils of St. Cuthbert's as "offspring."

During the long evenings when the "offspring" were meant to be asleep in their dormitories, the Robertses would pore over maps, analyze expert opinion, and then finally come up with a shortlist to consider. In recent expeditions they had been as far afield as Norway, northern Italy, and Yugoslavia, ending up the previous year exploring Achilles' island, Skyros, off the east coast of Greece.

"It has to be Turkey this year," said Christopher after much soul-searching. A week later Margaret came to the same conclusion, and so they were able to move on to phase two. Every book on Turkey in the local library was borrowed, consulted, re-borrowed, and reconsulted. Every brochure obtainable from the Turkish Embassy or local travel agents received the same relentless scrutiny.

By the first day of the summer term, charter tickets had been paid for, a car hired, reservations made, and everything that could be insured comprehensively covered. Their plans lacked only one final detail.

"So what will be our 'steal' this year?" asked Christopher.

"A carpet," Margaret said, without hesitation. "It has to be. For over a thousand years Turkey has produced the most sought-after carpets in the world. We'd be foolish to consider anything else."

"How much shall we spend on it?"

"Five hundred pounds," said Margaret, feeling very extravagant.

Having agreed, they once again swapped memories about the "steals" they had made over the years. In Norway, it had been a whale's tooth carved in the shape of a galleon by a local artist who soon after had been taken up by Steuben. In Tuscany, it had been a ceramic bowl found in a small village where they cast and fired them to be sold in Rome at exorbitant prices: A small blemish only an expert would have noticed made it a "steal." Just outside Skopje the Robertses had visited a local glass factory and acquired a water jug moments after it had been blown in front of their eyes, and in Skyros they had picked up their greatest triumph to date, a fragment of an urn they discovered near an old excavation site. The Robertses reported their find immediately to the authorities, but the Greek officials had not considered the fragment important enough to prevent it being exported to St. Cuthbert's.

On returning to England, Christopher couldn't resist just checking with the senior classics don at his old alma mater. He confirmed the piece was probably twelfth century. This latest "steal" now stood, carefully mounted, on their living room mantelpiece.

"Yes, a carpet would be perfect," Margaret mused. "The trouble is, everyone goes to Turkey with the idea of picking up a carpet cheaply. So to find a really good one . . . "

She knelt and began to measure the small space in front of their living room fireplace.

"Seven by three should do it," she said.

Within a few days of term ending, the Robertses traveled by bus to Heathrow. The journey took a little longer than by rail but at half the cost. "Money saved is money that can be spent on the carpet," Margaret reminded her husband.

"Agreed, Matron," said Christopher, laughing.

On arrival at Heathrow they checked their baggage on to the charter flight, selected two nonsmoking seats, and, finding they had time to spare, decided to watch other planes taking off for even more exotic places.

It was Christopher who first spotted the two passengers dashing across the tarmac, obviously late.

"Look," he said, pointing at the running couple. His wife studied the overweight pair, still tan from a previous vacation, as they lumbered up the steps to their plane.

"Mr. and Mrs. Kendall-Hume," Margaret said in disbelief. After hesitating for a moment, she added, "I wouldn't want to be uncharitable about any of the offspring, but I do find young Malcolm Kendall-Hume a . . ." She paused.

"'Spoiled little brat'?" suggested her husband.

"Quite," said Margaret. "I can't begin to think what his parents must be like."

"Very successful, if the boy's stories are to be believed," said Christopher. "A string of secondhand garages from Birmingham to Bristol."

"Thank God they're not on our flight."

"Bermuda or the Bahamas would be my guess," suggested Christopher.

A voice emanating from the loudspeaker gave Margaret no chance to offer her opinion.

"Olympic Airways Flight 172 to Istanbul is now boarding at Gate Number Thirty-seven."

"That's us," said Christopher happily as they began their long march to their departure gate.

They were the first passengers to board, and once shown to their seats they settled down to study the guidebooks of Turkey and their three files of research.

"We must be sure to see Diana's Temple when we visit Ephesus," said Christopher, as the plane taxied out on to the runway.

"Not forgetting that at that time we shall be only a few kilometers away from the purported last home of the Virgin Mary," added Margaret.

"Taken with a pinch of salt by serious historians," Christopher remarked as if addressing a member of the Lower Fourth, but his wife was too engrossed in her book to notice. They both continued to study on their own before Christopher asked what his wife was reading.

"*Carpets—Fact and Fiction*, by Abdul Verizoglu, seventeenth edition," she said, confident that any errors would have been eradicated in the previous sixteen. "It's most informative. The finest examples, it seems, are from Hereke and are woven in silk and are sometimes worked on by up to twenty young women, even children, at a time."

"Why young?" pondered Christopher. "You'd have thought experience would have been essential for such a delicate task."

"Apparently not," said Margaret. "Herekes are woven by those with young eyes that can discern intricate patterns sometimes no larger than a pinpoint and with up to nine hundred knots a square inch. Such a carpet," continued Margaret, "can cost as much as fifteen, even twenty, thousand pounds."

"And at the other end of the scale? Carpets woven in old left-over wool by old leftover women?" suggested Christopher, answering his own question.

"No doubt," said Margaret. "But even for our humble purse there are some simple guidelines to follow."

Christopher leaned over so that he could be sure to take in every word above the roar of the engines.

"The muted reds and blues with a green base are considered classic and are much admired by Turkish collectors, but one should avoid the bright yellows and oranges," read his wife aloud. "And never consider a carpet that displays animals, birds, or fishes, as they are produced only to satisfy Western tastes."

"Don't they like animals?"

"I don't think that's the point," said Margaret. "The Sunni Muslims, who are the country's religious leaders, don't approve of graven images. But if we search diligently around the bazaars we should still be able to come across a bargain for a few hundred pounds."

"What a wonderful excuse to spend all day in the bazaars."

Margaret smiled before continuing. "But listen. It's most important to bargain. The opening price the dealer offers is likely to be double what he expects to get and treble what the carpet is worth." She looked up from her book. "If there's any bargaining to be done it will have to be carried out by you, my dear. They're not used to that sort of thing at Marks & Spencer."

Christopher smiled.

"And finally," continued his wife, turning a page of her book, "if the dealer offers you coffee you should accept. It means he expects the process to go on for some time because he enjoys the bargaining as much as the sale."

"If that's the case they had better have a very large pot percolating for us," said Christopher as he closed his eyes and began to contemplate the pleasures that awaited him. Margaret only closed her books on carpets when the plane touched down at Istanbul airport, and at once opened file number one, entitled "Pre-Turkey."

"A shuttle bus should be waiting for us at the north side of the terminal. It will take us on to the local flight," she assured her husband as she carefully set her watch ahead two hours.

The Robertses were soon following the stream of passengers heading in the direction of passport control. The first people they saw in front of them were the same middle-aged couple they had assumed were destined for more exotic shores.

"Wonder where they're heading," said Christopher.

"Istanbul Hilton, I expect," said Margaret as they climbed into a vehicle that had been declared obsolete by the Glasgow Corporation Bus Company some twenty years before. It spluttered out black exhaust fumes as it revved up before heading off in the direction of the local THY flight.

The Robertses soon forgot all about Mr. and Mrs. Kendall-Hume once they looked out of the little airplane windows to admire the west coast of Turkey highlighted by the setting sun.

The plane landed in the port of Izmir just as the shimmering red ball disappeared behind the highest hill. Another bus, even older than the earlier one, ensured that the Robertses reached their little guesthouse just in time for late supper.

Their room was tiny but clean, and the owner much in the same mold. He greeted them both with exaggerated gesturing and a brilliant smile that augured well for the next twenty-one days. Early the following morning, the Robertses checked over their detailed plans for day one in file number two. They were first to collect the rented Fiat that had already been paid for in England, before driving off into the hills to the ancient Byzantine fortress at Selcuk in the morning, to be followed by the Temple of Diana in the afternoon if they still had time.

After breakfast had been cleared away and they had cleaned their teeth, the Robertses left the guesthouse a few minutes before nine. Armed with their car rental form and guidebook, they headed off for Beyazik's Garage, where their promised car awaited them. They strolled down the cobbled streets past the little white houses, enjoying the sea breeze until they reached the bay. Christopher spotted the sign for Beyazik's Garage when it was still a hundred yards ahead of them.

As they passed the magnificent yachts moored alongside the harbor, they tested each other on the nationality of each flag, feeling not unlike the "offspring" completing a geography test.

"Italian, French, Liberian, Panamanian, German. There aren't many British boats," said Christopher, sounding unusually patriotic, the way he always did, Margaret reflected, the moment they were abroad.

She stared at the rows of gleaming hulls lined up like buses in Piccadilly during the rush hour; some of the boats were even bigger than buses. "I wonder what kind of people can possibly afford such luxury?" she asked, not expecting a reply.

"Mr. and Mrs. Roberts, isn't it?" shouted a voice from behind them. They both turned to see a now-familiar figure dressed in a white shirt and white shorts, wearing a hat that made him look not unlike the captain in the "Birds Eye" commercial, waving at them from the bow of one of the bigger yachts.

"Climb on board, me hearties," Mr. Kendall-Hume declared

enthusiastically, more in the manner of a command than an invitation.

Reluctantly the Robertses walked the gangplank.

"Look who's here," their host shouted down a large hole in the middle of the deck. A moment later Mrs. Kendall-Hume appeared from below, dressed in a diaphanous orange sarong and a matching bikini top. "It's Mr. and Mrs. Roberts—you remember, from Malcolm's school."

Kendall-Hume turned back to face the dismayed couple. "I don't remember your first names, but this is Melody and I'm Ray."

"Christopher and Margaret," the schoolmaster admitted as handshakes were exchanged.

"What about a drink? Gin, vodka, or . . . ?"

"Oh, no," said Margaret. "Thank you very much, we'll both have orange juice."

"Suit yourselves," said Ray Kendall-Hume. "You must stay for lunch."

"But we couldn't impose . . . "

"I insist," said Mr. Kendall-Hume. "After all, we're on vacation. By the way, we'll be going over to the other side of the bay for lunch. There's one hell of a beach there, and it will give you a chance to sunbathe and swim in peace."

"How considerate of you," said Christopher.

"And where's young Malcolm?" asked Margaret.

"He's on a scouting vacation in Scotland. Doesn't like to mess about in boats the way we do."

For the first time he could recall, Christopher felt some admiration for the boy. A moment later the engine started thunderously.

On the trip across the bay, Ray Kendall-Hume expounded his theories about "having to get away from it all. . . . Nothing like a yacht to ensure your privacy and not having to mix with the hoi polloi." He only wanted the simple things in life: the sun, the sea, and an infinite supply of good food and drink.

The Robertses could have asked for nothing less. By the end of the day they were both suffering from a mild bout of sunstroke and were also feeling a little seasick. Despite white pills, red pills, and yellow pills, liberally supplied by Melody, when they finally got back to their room that night they were unable to sleep.

Avoiding the Kendall-Humes over the next twenty days did not prove easy. Beyazik's, the garage where their little rental car awaited them each morning and to which it had to be returned each night, could only be reached via the quayside where the Kendall-Humes' motor yacht was moored like an insuperable barrier at a gymkhana. Hardly a day passed that the Robertses did not have to spend some part of their precious time bobbing up and down on Turkey's choppy coastal waters, eating oily food, and discussing how large a carpet would be needed to fill the Kendall-Humes' front room.

However, they still managed to complete a large part of their program and determinedly set aside the whole of the last day of the vacation in their quest for a carpet. As they did not need Beyazik's car to go into town, they felt confident that for that day at least they could safely avoid their tormentors.

On the final morning they rose a little later than planned and after breakfast strolled down the tiny cobbled path together, Christopher in possession of the seventeenth edition of *Carpets—Fact and Fiction*, Margaret with a tape measure and five hundred pounds in travelers' checks. Once the schoolmaster and his wife had reached the bazaar, they began to look around a myriad of little shops, wondering where they should begin their adventure. Fez-topped men tried to entice them to enter their tiny emporiums, but the Robertses spent the first hour simply taking in the atmosphere.

"I'm ready to start the search now," shouted Margaret above the babble of voices around her.

"Then we've found you just in time," said the one voice they thought they had escaped.

"We were just about to—"

"Then follow me."

The Robertses' hearts sank as they were led by Ray Kendall-Hume out of the bazaar and back toward the town.

"Take my advice, and you'll end up with one hell of a bargain," Kendall-Hume assured them both. "I've picked up some real beauties in my time from every corner of the globe at prices you wouldn't believe. I am happy to let you take full advantage of my expertise at no extra charge."

"I don't know how you could stand the noise and smell of that bazaar," said Melody, obviously glad to be back among the familiar signs of Gucci, Lacoste, and Saint Laurent.

"We rather like—"

"Rescued in the nick of time," said Ray Kendall-Hume. "And the place I'm told you have to start and finish at if you want to purchase a serious carpet is Osman's."

Margaret recalled the name from her carpet book: "Only to be visited if money is no object and you know exactly what you are looking for." The vital last morning was to be wasted, she reflected as she pushed open the large glass doors of Osman's to enter a ground-floor area the size of a tennis court. The room was covered in carpets on the floor, the walls, the windowsills, and even the tables. Anywhere a carpet could be laid out, a carpet was there to be seen. Although the Robertses realized immediately that nothing on show could possibly be in their price range, the sheer beauty of the display entranced them.

Margaret walked slowly round the room, mentally measuring the small carpets so she could anticipate the sort of thing they might look for once they had escaped.

A tall, elegant man, hands raised as if in prayer and dressed immaculately in a tailored worsted suit that could have been made in Savile Row, advanced to greet them.

"Good morning, sir," he said to Mr. Kendall-Hume, selecting the serious spender without difficulty. "Can I be of assistance?"

"You certainly can," replied Kendall-Hume. "I want to be shown your finest carpets, but I do not intend to pay your finest prices."

The dealer smiled politely and clapped his hands. Six small carpets were brought in by three assistants who rolled them out in the center of the room. Margaret fell in love with a muted green-based carpet with a pattern of tiny red squares woven around the borders. The pattern was so intricate she could not take her eyes off it. She measured the carpet out of interest: seven by three exactly.

"You have excellent taste, madam," said the dealer. Margaret, blushing slightly, quickly stood up, took a pace backward, and hid the tape measure behind her back.

"How do you feel about that lot, pet?" asked Kendall-Hume, sweeping a hand across the six carpets.

"None of them is big enough," Melody replied, giving them only a fleeting glance.

The dealer clapped his hands a second time and the exhibits were rolled up and taken away. Four larger ones soon replaced them.

"Would you care for some coffee?" the dealer asked Mr. Kendall-Hume as the new carpets lay unfurled at their feet.

"Haven't the time," said Kendall-Hume shortly. "Here to buy a carpet. If I want a coffee, I can always go to a coffee shop," he said with a chuckle. Melody smiled her complicity.

"Well, I would like some coffee," declared Margaret, determined to rebel at some point in the vacation.

"Delighted, madam," said the dealer, and one of the assistants disappeared to carry out her wishes while the Kendall-Humes studied the new carpets. The coffee arrived a few moments later. She thanked the young assistant and began to sip the thick black liquid slowly. Delicious, she thought, and smiled her acknowledgment to the dealer.

"Still not large enough," Mrs. Kendall-Hume insisted. The dealer gave a slight sigh and clapped his hands yet again. Once more the assistants began to roll up the rejected goods. He then addressed one of his staff in Turkish. The assistant looked doubtfully at his mentor, but the dealer gave a firm nod and waved him away. The assistant returned a little later with a small platoon of lesser assistants carrying two carpets, both of which when unfolded took up most of the shop floor. Margaret liked them even less than the ones she had just been shown, but as her opinion was not sought she did not offer it.

"That's more like it," said Ray Kendall-Hume. "Just about the right size for the living room, wouldn't you say, Melody?"

"Perfect," his wife replied, making no attempt to measure either of the carpets.

"I'm glad we agree," said Ray Kendall-Hume. "But which one, my pet? The faded red-and-blue, or the bright yellow-and-orange?"

"The yellow-and-orange one," said Melody without hesitation. "I like the pattern of brightly colored birds running round the outside." Christopher thought he saw the dealer wince.

"So now all we have left to do is agree on a price," said Kendall-Hume. "You'd better sit down, pet, as this may take a while."

"I hope not," said Mrs. Kendall-Hume, resolutely standing. The Robertses remained mute.

"Unfortunately, sir," began the dealer, "your wife has selected one of the finest carpets in our collection, and so I fear there can be little room for any readjustment."

"How much?" said Kendall-Hume.

"You see, sir, this carpet was woven in Demirdji, in the province of Izmir, by over a hundred seamstresses, and it took them more than a year to complete."

"Don't give me that baloney," said Kendall-Hume, winking at Christopher. "Just tell me how much I'm expected to pay."

"I feel it my duty to point out, sir, that this carpet shouldn't be here at all," said the Turk plaintively. "It was originally made for an Arab prince who failed to complete the transaction when the price of oil collapsed."

"But he must have agreed on a price at the time?"

"I cannot reveal the exact figure, sir. It embarrasses me to mention it."

"It wouldn't embarrass me," said Kendall-Hume. "Come on, what's the price?" he insisted.

"Which currency would you prefer to trade in?" the Turk asked.

"Pounds."

The dealer removed a slim calculator from his jacket pocket, tapped some numbers into it, then looked unhappily toward the Kendall-Humes.

Christopher and Margaret remained silent, like schoolchildren fearing that the headmaster might ask them a question to which they could not possibly know the answer.

"Come on, come on, how much were you hoping to sting me for?"

"I think you must prepare yourself for a shock, sir," said the dealer.

"How much?" repeated Kendall-Hume, impatiently.

"Twenty-five thousand."

"Pounds?"

"Pounds."

"You must be joking," said Kendall-Hume, walking around the carpet and ending up standing next to Margaret. "You're about to find out why I'm considered the scourge of the East Midlands car trade," he whispered to her. "I wouldn't pay more than fifteen thousand for that carpet." He turned back to face the dealer. "Even if my life depended on it."

"Then I fear your time has been wasted, sir," the Turk replied. "For this is a carpet intended only for the cognoscenti. Perhaps madam might reconsider the red-and-blue?"

"Certainly not," said Kendall-Hume. "The color's all faded. Can't you see? You obviously left it in the window too long, and the sun has got at it. No, you'll have to reconsider your price if you want the orange-and-yellow one to end up in the home of a connoisseur."

The dealer sighed as his fingers tapped the calculator again.

While the transaction continued, Melody looked on vacantly, occasionally gazing out of the window toward the bay.

"I could not drop a penny below twenty-three thousand pounds."

"I'd be willing to go as high as eighteen thousand," said Kendall-Hume, "but not a penny more."

The Robertses watched the dealer tap the numbers into the calculator.

"That would not even cover the cost of what I paid for it myself," he said sadly, staring down at the little glowing figures.

"You're pushing me, but don't push me too far. Nineteen thousand," said Mr. Kendall-Hume. "That's my final offer."

"Twenty thousand pounds is the lowest figure I could consider," replied the dealer. "A giveaway price, on my mother's grave."

Kendall-Hume took out his wallet and placed it on the table by the side of the dealer.

"Nineteen thousand pounds and you've got yourself a deal," he said.

"But how will I feed my children?" asked the dealer, his arms raised above his head.

"The same way I feed mine," said Kendall-Hume, laughing. "By making a fair profit."

The dealer paused as if reconsidering, then said, "I can't do it, sir. I'm sorry. We must show you some other carpets." The assistants came forward on cue.

"No, that's the one I want," said Mrs. Kendall-Hume. "Don't quarrel over a thousand pounds, pet."

"Take my word for it, madam," the dealer said, turning toward Mrs. Kendall-Hume. "My family would starve if we only did business with customers like your husband."

"Okay, you get the twenty thousand, but on one condition."

"Condition?"

"My receipt must show that the bill was for ten thousand pounds. Otherwise I'll only end up paying the difference in customs duty."

The dealer bowed low, as if to indicate he did not find the request an unusual one.

Mr. Kendall-Hume opened his wallet and withdrew ten thousand pounds in travelers' checks and ten thousand pounds in cash.

"As you can see," he said, grinning, "I came prepared." He removed another five thousand pounds and, waving it at the dealer, added, "and I would have been willing to pay far more."

The dealer shrugged. "You drive a hard bargain, sir. But you will not hear me complain now that the deal has been struck."

The vast carpet was folded, wrapped, and a receipt for ten thousand pounds made out while the travelers' checks and cash were handed over.

The Robertses had not uttered a word for twenty minutes. When they saw the cash change hands it crossed Margaret's mind that it was more money than the two of them earned in a year.

"Time to get back to the yacht," said Kendall-Hume. "Do join us for lunch if you choose a carpet in time."

"Thank you," said the Robertses in unison. They waited until the Kendall-Humes were out of sight, two assistants bearing the orange-and-yellow carpet in their wake, before they thanked the dealer for the coffee and in turn began to make their move towards the door.

"What sort of carpet were you looking for?" asked the dealer.

"I fear your prices are way beyond us," said Christopher politely. "But thank you."

"Well, let me at least find out. Have you or your wife seen a carpet you liked?"

"Yes," replied Margaret, "the small carpet, but . . . "

"Ah, yes," said the dealer. "I remember madam's eyes when she saw the Hereke."

He left them, to return a few moments later with the little soft-toned, green-based carpet with the tiny red squares that the Kendall-Humes had so firmly rejected. Not waiting for assistance he rolled it out himself for the Robertses to inspect more carefully.

Margaret thought it looked even more magnificent the second time, and feared that she could never hope to find its equal in the few hours left to them.

"Perfect," she admitted, quite unashamedly.

"Then we have only the price to discuss," said the dealer kindly. "How much were you wanting to spend, madam?"

"We had planned to spend three hundred pounds," said Christopher, jumping in. Margaret was unable to hide her surprise.

"But we agreed—" she began.

"Thank you, my dear, I think I should deal with this matter."

The dealer smiled and returned to the bargaining.

"I would have to charge you six hundred pounds," he said. "Anything less would be robbery."

"Four hundred pounds is my final offer," said Christopher, trying to sound in control.

"Five hundred pounds would have to be my bottom price," said the dealer.

"I'll take it!" cried Christopher.

An assistant began waving his arms and talking to the dealer noisily in his native tongue. The owner raised a hand to dismiss the young man's protests, while the Robertses looked on anxiously.

"My son," explained the dealer, "is not happy with the arrangement, but I am delighted that the little carpet will reside in the home of a couple who will so obviously appreciate its true worth."

"Thank you," said Christopher quietly.

"Will you also require a bill of a different price?"

"No, thank you," said Christopher, handing over ten fifty-pound notes and then waiting until the carpet was wrapped and he was presented with the correct receipt.

As he watched the Robertses leave his shop clinging on to their purchase, the dealer smiled to himself.

When they arrived at the quayside, the Kendall-Humes' boat was already halfway across the bay heading toward the quiet beach. The Robertses sighed their combined relief and returned to the bazaar for lunch.

It was while they were waiting for their baggage to appear on the carousel at Heathrow that Christopher felt a tap on his shoulder. He turned round to face a beaming Ray Kendall-Hume.

"I wonder if you could do me a favor, old boy?"

"I will if I can," said Christopher, who still had not fully recovered from their last encounter.

"It's simple enough," said Kendall-Hume. "The old girl and I have brought back far too many presents, and I wondered if you could take one of them through customs. Otherwise we're likely to be held up all night."

Melody, standing behind an already loaded luggage cart, smiled at the two men benignly.

"You would still have to pay any duty that was due on it," said Christopher firmly.

"I wouldn't dream of doing otherwise," said Kendall-Hume, struggling with a massive package before pushing it on the Roberts' trolley. Christopher wanted to protest as Kendall-Hume peeled off two thousand pounds and handed the money and the receipt over to the schoolteacher.

"What do we do if they claim your carpet is worth a lot more than ten thousand pounds?" asked Margaret anxiously, coming to stand by her husband's side.

"Pay the difference and I'll refund you immediately. But I assure you it's most unlikely to arise."

"I hope you're right."

"Of course I'm right," said Kendall-Hume. "Don't worry, I've done this sort of thing before. And I won't forget your help when it comes to the next school appeal," he added, leaving them with the huge parcel.

Once Christopher and Margaret had located their own bags, they collected the second cart and took their place in the red "Something to Declare" line.

"Are you in possession of any items over five hundred pounds in value?" asked the young customs official politely.

"Yes," said Christopher. "We purchased two carpets when we were on vacation in Turkey." He handed over the two bills.

The customs official studied the receipts carefully, then asked if he might be allowed to see the carpets for himself.

"Certainly," said Christopher, and began the task of undoing the larger package while Margaret worked on the smaller one.

"I shall need to have these looked at by an expert," said the official once the parcels were unwrapped. "It shouldn't take more than a few minutes." The carpets were soon taken away.

The "few minutes" turned out to be more than fifteen, and

Christopher and Margaret were soon regretting their decision to assist the Kendall-Humes, whatever the needs of the school appeal. They began to indulge in irrelevant smalltalk that wouldn't have fooled the most amateur of sleuths.

At last the customs official returned.

"I wonder if you would be kind enough to have a word with my colleague in private?" he asked.

"Is that really necessary?" asked Christopher, reddening.

"I'm afraid so, sir."

"We shouldn't have agreed to it in the first place," whispered Margaret. "We've never been in any trouble with the authorities before."

"Don't fret, dear. It will be all over in a few minutes, you'll see," said Christopher, not sure that he believed his own words. They followed the young man out through the back and into a small room.

"Good afternoon, sir," said a white-haired man with several gold stripes around the cuff of his sleeve. "I am sorry to have kept you waiting, but we have had your carpets looked at by our expert and he feels sure a mistake must have been made."

Christopher wanted to protest but he couldn't get a word out.

"A mistake?" managed Margaret.

"Yes, madam. The bills you presented don't make any sense to him."

"Don't make any sense?"

"No, madam," said the senior customs officer. "I repeat, we feel certain a mistake has been made."

"What kind of mistake?" asked Christopher, at last finding his voice.

"Well, you have come forward and declared two carpets, one at a price of ten thousand pounds and one at a price of five hundred pounds, according to these receipts."

"Yes?"

"Every year hundreds of people return to England with Turkish carpets, so we have some experience in these matters. Our adviser feels certain that the bills have been incorrectly made out."

"I don't begin to understand . . ." said Christopher.

"Well," explained the senior officer, "the large carpet, we are assured, has been spun with a crude distaff and has only two hundred *ghiordes*, or knots, per square inch. Despite its size we estimate it to be valued around five thousand pounds. The small carpet, on the other hand, we estimate to have nine hundred knots per square inch. It is a fine example of a silk hand-woven traditional Hereke and undoubtedly would have been a bargain at five hundred pounds. As both carpets come from the same shop, we assume it must be a clerical error."

The Robertses remained speechless.

"It doesn't make any difference to the duty you will have to pay, but we felt sure you would want to know, for insurance purposes."

Still the Robertses said nothing.

"As you're allowed five hundred pounds before paying any duty, the excise will still be two thousand pounds."

Christopher quickly handed over the Kendall-Humes' wad of notes. The senior officer counted them while his junior carefully rewrapped the two carpets.

"Thank you," said Christopher, as they were handed back the packages and a receipt for two thousand pounds.

The Robertses quickly bundled the large package onto its luggage cart before wheeling it through the concourse and onto the pavement outside, where the Kendall-Humes impatiently awaited them.

"You were in there a long time," said Ray Kendall-Hume. "Any problems?"

"No, they were just assessing the value of the carpets."

"Any extra charge?" Kendall-Hume asked apprehensively.

"No, your two thousand pounds covered everything," said Christopher, handing over the receipt.

"Then we got away with it, old fellow. Well done. One hell of a bargain to add to my collection." Kendall-Hume turned to bundle the large package into the trunk of his Mercedes before locking it and taking his place behind the steering wheel. "Well done," he repeated through the open window as the car drove off. "I won't forget the school appeal."

The Robertses stood and watched as the silver-gray car joined a line of traffic leaving the airport.

"Why didn't you tell Mr. Kendall-Hume the real value of his carpet?" asked Margaret once they were seated in the bus.

"I did give it some considerable thought, but I came to the conclusion that the *truth* was the last thing Kendall-Hume wanted to be told."

"But don't you feel any guilt? After all, we've stolen—"

"Not at all, my dear. We haven't stolen anything. But we did get one hell of a 'steal.'"

CHRISTINA
ROSENTHAL

THE RABBI KNEW HE couldn't hope to begin on his sermon until he'd read the letter. He had been sitting at his desk in front of a blank sheet of paper for more than an hour and still couldn't come up with a first sentence. Lately he had been unable to concentrate on a task he had carried out every Friday evening for the last thirty years. They must have realized by now that he was no longer up to it. He took the letter out of the envelope and slowly unfolded the pages. Then he pushed his half-moon glasses up the bridge of his nose and started to read.

My dear Father,

"Jew boy! Jew boy! Jew boy!" were the first words I ever heard her say as I ran past her on the first lap of the race. She was standing behind the railing at the beginning of the home stretch, hands cupped around her lips to be sure I couldn't miss the chant. She must have come from another school because I didn't recognize her, but it only took a fleeting glance to see that it was Greg Reynolds who was standing by her side.

After five years of having to tolerate his snide comments and bullying at school all I wanted to retaliate with was, "Nazi, Nazi, Nazi," but you had always taught me to rise above such provocation.

I tried to put them both out of my mind as I moved into the second lap. I had dreamed for years of winning the mile in the West Mount High School championships, and I was determined not to let them do anything to stop me.

As I came into the back stretch a second time, I took a more careful look at her. She was standing amid a cluster of friends who were wearing the scarves of Marianapolis Convent. She must have been about sixteen, and as slim as a willow. I wonder if you

225

would have chastised me had I only shouted, "No breasts, no breasts, no breasts," in the hope it might at least provoke the boy standing next to her into a fight. Then I would have been able to tell you truthfully that he had thrown the first punch, but the moment you learned that it was Greg Reynolds, you would have realized how little provocation I needed.

As I reached the back stretch I once again prepared myself for the chants. Chanting at track meetings had become fashionable in the late 1950s, when "Zat-o-pek, Zat-o-pek, Zat-o-pek" had been roared in adulation across running stadiums around the world for the great Czech champion. Not for me was there to be the shout of "Ros-en-thal, Ros-en-thal, Ros-en-thal" as I came into earshot.

"Jew boy! Jew boy! Jew boy!" she said, sounding like a a stuck record. Her friend Greg, who would nowadays be described as a preppie, began laughing. I knew he had put her up to it, and how I would like to have removed that smug grin from his face. I reached the half-mile mark in two minutes seventeen seconds, comfortably inside the pace necessary to break the school record, and I felt that was the best way to put the taunting girl and that fascist Reynolds in their place. I couldn't help thinking at the time how unfair it all was. I was a real Canadian, born and bred in this country, while she was just an immigrant. After all, you, Father, had escaped from Hamburg in 1937 and started with nothing. Her parents did not land on these shores until 1949, by which time you were a respected figure in the community.

I gritted my teeth and tried to concentrate. Zatopek had written in his autobiography that no runner can afford to lose his concentration during a race. When I reached the bend the inevitable chanting began again, but this time it only made me speed up and even more determined to break that record. Once I was back in the safety of the home straight I could hear some of my friends roaring, "Come on, Benjamin, you can do it," and the timekeeper called out, "Three twenty-three, three twenty-four, three twenty-five" as I passed the bell to begin the last lap.

I knew that the record—four thirty-two—was now well within my grasp and all those dark nights of winter training suddenly seemed worthwhile. As I reached the back stretch I took the lead, and even felt that I could face the girl again. I summoned up my strength for one last effort. A quick glance over my shoulder confirmed I was already yards in front of any of my rivals, so it was only me against the clock. Then I heard the chanting, but this time it was even louder than before, "Jew boy! Jew boy! Jew boy!" It was louder because the two of them were now working in unison, and just as I came round the bend Reynolds raised his arm in a flagrant Nazi salute.

If I had only carried on I would have reached the finishing tape and the cheers of my friends, the cup, and the record. But they had made me so angry that I could no longer control myself.

I shot off the track and ran across the grass over the long-jump pit and straight toward them. At least my crazy decision stopped their chanting, because Reynolds lowered his arm and just stood there staring pathetically at me from behind the small railing that surrounded the outer perimeter of the track. I leaped right over it and landed in front of my adversary. With all the energy I had saved for the final stretch I took an almighty swing at him. My fist landed an inch below his left eye, and he buckled and fell to the ground by her side. Quickly she knelt down and, staring up, gave me a look of such hatred that no words could have matched it. Once I was sure Greg wasn't going to get up, I walked slowly back on to the track as the last of the runners were coming round the final bend.

"Last again, Jew boy," I heard her shout as I jogged down the home straight, so far behind the others that they didn't even bother to record my time.

How often since have you quoted me those words: "Still have I borne it with a patient shrug, for sufferance is the badge of all our tribe." Of course you were right, but I was only seventeen then, and even after I had learned the truth about Christina's father I still couldn't understand how anyone who had come from a defeated Germany, a Germany condemned by the rest of the world for its treatment of the Jews, could still behave in such a manner. And in those days I really believed her family were Nazis, but I remember you patiently explaining to me that her father had been an admiral in the German navy, and had won an Iron Cross for sinking Allied ships. Do you remember me asking how you could tolerate such a man, let alone allow him to settle in our country?

You went on to assure me that Admiral von Braumer, who came from an old Roman Catholic family and probably despised the Nazis as much as we did, had acquitted himself honorably as an officer and a gentleman throughout his life as a German sailor. But I still couldn't accept your attitude, or didn't want to.

It didn't help, Father, that you always saw the other man's

point of view, and even though Mother had died prematurely because of those bastards, you could still find it in you to forgive. If you had been born a Christian, you would have been a saint.

The rabbi put the letter down and rubbed his tired eyes before he turned over another page written in that fine script he had taught his only son so many years before. Benjamin had always learned quickly, everything from the Hebrew scriptures to complicated algebraic equations. The old man had even begun to hope the boy might become a rabbi.

Do you remember my asking you that evening why people couldn't understand that the world had changed? Didn't the girl realize that she was no better than we were? I shall never forget your reply. She is, you said, far better than us, if the only way you can prove your superiority is to punch her friend in the face.

I returned to my room angered by your weakness. It was to be many years before I understood your strength.

When I wasn't pounding round that track I rarely had time for anything other than working for a scholarship to McGill, so it came as a surprise that her path crossed mine again so soon.

It must have been about a week later that I saw her at the local swimming pool. She was standing at the deep end, just under the diving board, when I came in. Her long fair hair was dancing on her shoulders, her bright eyes eagerly taking in everything going on around her. Greg was by her side. I was pleased to notice a deep purple patch remained under his left eye for all to see. I also remember chuckling to myself because she really did have the flattest chest I had ever seen on a sixteen-year-old girl, though I have to confess she had fantastic legs. Perhaps she's a freak, I thought. I turned to go into the dressing room—a split second before I hit the water. When I came up for breath there was no sign of who had pushed me in, just a group of grinning but innocent faces. I didn't need a law degree to work out who it must have been, but as you constantly reminded me, Father, without evidence there is no proof. . . . I wouldn't have minded that much about being pushed into the pool if I hadn't been wearing my best suit—in truth, my only suit with long trousers, the one I wore on days I was going to the synagogue.

I climbed out of the water but didn't waste any time looking round for him. I knew Greg would be a long way off by then. I walked home through the back streets, avoiding taking the bus in case someone saw me and told you what a state I was in. As soon as I got home I crept past your study and on upstairs to my room, changing before you had the chance to discover what had taken place.

Old Isaac Cohen gave me a disapproving look when I turned up at the synagogue an hour later wearing a blazer and jeans.

I took the suit to the cleaners the next morning. It cost me three weeks' pocket money to be sure that you were never aware of what had happened at the swimming pool that day.

The rabbi picked up the picture of his seventeen-year-old son in that synagogue suit. He well remembered Benjamin turning up at his service in a blazer and jeans and Isaac Cohen's outspoken reprimand. The rabbi was thankful that Mr. Atkins, the swimming instructor, had phoned to warn him of what had taken place that afternoon so at least he didn't add to Mr. Cohen's harsh words. He continued gazing at the photograph for a long time before he returned to the letter.

The next occasion I saw Christina—by now I had found out her name—was at the end-of-term dance held in the school gymnasium. I thought I looked pretty cool in my neatly pressed suit until I saw Greg standing by her side in a smart new dinner jacket. I remember wondering at the time if I would ever be able to afford a dinner jacket. Greg had been offered a place at McGill and was announcing the fact to everyone who cared to listen, which made me all the more determined to win a scholarship there the following year.

I stared at Christina. She was wearing a long red dress that completely covered those beautiful legs. A thin gold belt emphasized her tiny waist and the only jewelry she wore was a simple gold necklace. I knew if I waited a moment longer I wouldn't have the courage to go through with it. I clenched my fists, walked over to where they were sitting, and as you had always taught me, Father, bowed slightly before I asked, "May I have the pleasure of this dance?"

She stared into my eyes. I swear if she had told me to go out and kill a thousand men before I dared ask her again I would have done it.

She didn't even speak, but Greg leaned over her shoulder and said, "Why don't you go and find yourself a nice Jewish girl?" I thought I saw her scowl at his remark, but I only blushed like someone who's been caught with their hands in the cookie jar. I didn't dance with anyone that night. I walked straight out of the gymnasium and ran home.

I was convinced then that I hated her.

That last week of term I broke the school record for the mile. You were there to watch me but, thank heavens, she wasn't. That was the time we drove over to Ottawa to spend our summer vacation with Aunt Rebecca. I was told by a school friend that Christina had spent hers in Vancouver with a German family. At least Greg had not gone with her, the friend assured me.

You went on reminding me of the importance of a good education, but you didn't need to, because every time I saw Greg it made me more determined to win that scholarship.

I worked even harder in the summer of '65 when you explained that, for a Canadian, a place at McGill was like going to Harvard or Oxford and would clear a path for the rest of my days.

For the first time in my life running took second place.

Although I didn't see much of Christina that term, she was often in my mind. A classmate told me that she and Greg were no longer seeing each other, but could give me no reason for this sudden change of heart. At the time I had a so-called girlfriend who always sat on the other side of the synagogue—Naomi Goldblatz, you remember her—but it was she who dated me.

As my exams drew nearer, I was grateful that you always found time to go over my essays and tests after I had finished them. What you couldn't know was that I inevitably returned to my own room to do them a third time. Often I would fall asleep at my desk. When I woke I would turn over the page and read on.

Even you, Father, who have not an ounce of vanity in you, found it hard to disguise from your congregation the pride you took in my eight straight A's and the award of a top scholarship to McGill. I wondered if Christina was aware of it. She must have been. My name was painted up on the Honors Board in fresh gold leaf the following week, so someone would have told her.

It must have been three months later when I was in my first term at McGill that I saw her next. Do you remember taking me to

Saint Joan at the Centaur Theatre? There she was, seated a few rows in front of us with her parents and a sophomore called Bob Richards. The admiral and his wife looked strait-laced and very stern but not unsympathetic. In the interval I watched her laughing and joking with them: She had obviously enjoyed herself. I hardly saw Saint Joan, *and although I couldn't take my eyes off Christina she never once noticed me. I just wanted to be on the stage playing the Dauphin so she would have to look up at me.*

When the curtain came down she and Bob Richards left her parents and headed for the exit. I followed the two of them out of the foyer and into the car park, and watched them get into a Thunderbird. A Thunderbird! I remember thinking I might one day be able to afford a dinner jacket, but never a Thunderbird.

From that moment she was in my thoughts whenever I trained, wherever I worked, and even when I slept. I found out everything I could about Bob Richards and discovered that he was liked by all who knew him.

For the first time in my life I hated being a Jew.

When I next saw Christina I dreaded what might happen. It was the start of the mile against the University of Vancouver, and as a freshman I had been lucky to be selected for McGill. When I came out on to the track to warm up I saw her sitting in the third row of the stand alongside Richards. They were holding hands.

I was last off when the starter's gun fired, but as we went into the back stretch I moved up into fifth position. It was the largest crowd I had ever run in front of, and when I reached the home straight I waited for the chant "Jew boy! Jew boy! Jew boy!" but nothing happened. I wondered if she had failed to notice that I was in the race. But she had noticed because as I came round the bend I could hear her voice clearly. "Come on, Benjamin, you've got to win!" she shouted.

I wanted to look back to make sure it was Christina who had called those words; it would be another quarter of a mile before I would pass her again. By the time I did so I had moved up into third place, and I could hear her clearly: "Come on, Benjamin, you can do it!"

I immediately took the lead because all I wanted to do was get back to her. I charged on without thought of who was behind me, and by the time I passed her the third time I was several yards ahead of the field. "You're going to win!" she shouted as I ran on to reach the bell in three minutes eight seconds, eleven seconds faster than I had ever done before. I remember thinking that they ought to put something in those training manuals about love being worth two to three seconds a lap.

I watched her all the way down the back stretch, and when I came into the final bend for the last time the crowd rose to their feet. I turned to search for her. She was jumping up and down shouting, "Look out! Look out!" which I didn't understand until I was overtaken on the inside by the Vancouver number one string, who the coach had warned me was renowned for his strong finish. I staggered over the line a few yards behind him in second place but went on running until I was safely inside the dressing room. I sat alone by my locker. Four minutes seventeen, someone told me: six seconds faster than I had ever run before. It didn't help. I stood in the shower for a long time, trying to work out what could possibly have changed her attitude.

When I walked back onto the track only the ground staff were still around. I took one last look at the finish line before I strolled over to the Forsyth Library. I felt unable to face the usual team get-together, so I tried to settle down to write an essay on the property rights of married women.

The library was almost empty that Saturday evening, and I was well into my third page when I heard a voice say, "I hope I'm not interrupting you, but you didn't come to Joe's." I looked up to see Christina standing on the other side of the table. Father, I didn't know what to say. I just stared up at the beautiful creature in her fashionable blue miniskirt and tight-fitting sweater that emphasized the most perfect breasts, and said nothing.

"I was the one who shouted 'Jew boy' when you were still at high school. I've felt ashamed about it ever since. I wanted to apologize to you on the night of the prom but couldn't summon up the courage with Greg standing there." I nodded my understanding—I couldn't think of any words that seemed appropriate. "I never spoke to him again," she said. "But I don't suppose you even remember Greg."

I just smiled. "Care for coffee?" I asked, trying to sound as if I wouldn't mind if she replied, "I'm sorry, I must get back to Bob."

"I'd like that very much," she said.

I took her to the library coffee shop, which was about all I could afford at the time. She never bothered to explain what had happened to Bob Richards, and I never asked.

Christina seemed to know so much about me that I felt embar-

rassed. She asked me to forgive her for what she had shouted on the track that day two years before. She made no excuses, placed the blame on no one else, just asked to be forgiven.

Christina told me she was hoping to join me at McGill in September, to major in German. "Bit of nerve," she admitted, "since it is my native tongue."

We spent the rest of that summer in each other's company. We saw Saint Joan *again, and even lined up for a film called* Doctor No *that was all the craze at the time. We worked together, we ate together, we played together, but we slept alone.*

I said little about Christina to you at the time, but I'd bet you knew already how much I loved her; I could never hide anything from you. And after all your teaching of forgiveness and understanding you could hardly disapprove.

The rabbi paused. His heart ached because he knew so much of what was still to come, although he could not have foretold what would happen in the end. He had never thought he would live to regret his Orthodox upbringing, but when Mrs. Goldblatz first told him about Christina he had been unable to mask his disapproval. It will pass, given time, he told her. So much for wisdom.

Whenever I went to Christina's home I was always treated with courtesy, but her family were unable to hide their disapproval. They uttered words they didn't believe in an attempt to show that they were not anti-Semitic, and whenever I brought up the subject with Christina she told me I was overreacting. We both knew I wasn't. They quite simply thought I was unworthy of their daughter. They were right, but it had nothing to do with my being Jewish.

I shall never forget the first time we made love. It was the day that Christina learned she had won a place at McGill.

We had gone to my room at three o'clock to change for a game of tennis. I took her in my arms for what I thought would be a brief moment, and we didn't part until the next morning. Nothing had been planned. But how could it have been, when it was the first time for both of us?

I told her I would marry her—don't all men the first time?—only I meant it.

Then a few weeks later she missed her period. I begged her not to panic, and we both waited for another month because she was fearful of going to see any doctor in Montreal.

If I had told you everything then, Father, perhaps my life would have taken a different course. But I didn't, and have only myself to blame.

I began to plan for a marriage that neither Christina's family nor you could possibly have found acceptable, but we didn't care. Love knows no parents, and certainly no religion. When she missed her second period I agreed Christina should tell her mother. I asked her if she would like me to be with her at the time, but she simply shook her head, and explained that she felt she had to face them on her own.

"I'll wait here until you return," I promised.

She smiled. "I'll be back even before you've had the time to change your mind about marrying me."

I sat in my room at McGill all that afternoon reading and pacing—mostly pacing—but she never came back, and I didn't go in search of her until it was dark. I crept around to her home, all the while trying to convince myself there must be some simple explanation as to why she hadn't returned.

When I reached her street I could see a light on in her bedroom but nowhere else in the house, so I thought she must be alone. I marched through the gate and up to the front porch, knocked on the door, and waited.

Her father answered the door.

"What do you want?" he asked, his eyes never leaving mine for a moment.

"I love your daughter," I told him, "and I want to marry her."

"She will never marry a Jew," he said simply and closed the door. I remember that he didn't slam it; he just closed it, which made it somehow even worse.

I stood outside in the street staring up at her room for over an hour until the light went out. Then I walked home. There was a light drizzle that night, and few people were on the streets. I tried to work out what I should do next, although the situation seemed hopeless. I went to bed that night hoping for a miracle. I had forgotten that miracles are for Christians, not Jews.

By the next morning, I had worked out a plan. I phoned Christina's home at eight and nearly put the phone down when I heard the voice at the other end.

"Mrs. von Braumer," she said.

"Is Christina there?" I asked in a whisper.

"No, she's not," came back the controlled, impersonal reply.

"When are you expecting her back?" I asked.

"Not for some time," she said, and then the phone went dead.

"Not for some time" turned out to be over a year. I wrote, telephoned, asked friends from school and university, but could never find out where they had taken her.

Then one day, unannounced, she returned to Montreal accompanied by a husband and my child. I learned the bitter details from that font of all knowledge, Naomi Goldblatz, who had already seen all three of them.

I received a short note from Christina about a week later begging me not to make any attempt to contact her.

I had just begun my last year at McGill, and like some eighteenth-century gentleman I honored her wish to the letter and turned all my energies to the final exams. She still continued to preoccupy my thoughts, and I considered myself lucky at the end of the year to be offered a place at Harvard Law School.

I left Montreal for Boston on September 12, 1968.

You must have wondered why I never came home once during those three years. I knew of your disapproval. Thanks to Mrs. Goldblatz everyone was aware who the father of Christina's child was, and I felt my absence might make life a little easier for you.

The rabbi paused as he remembered Mrs. Goldblatz letting him know what she had considered was "only her duty."

"You're an interfering old busybody," he had told her. By the following Saturday she had moved to another synagogue and let everyone in the town know why.

He was more angry with himself than with Benjamin. He should have visited Harvard to let his son know that his love for him had not changed. So much for his powers of forgiveness.

He took up the letter once again.

Throughout those years at law school I had plenty of friends of both sexes, but Christina was rarely out of my mind for more than a few hours at a time. I wrote over forty letters to her while I was in Boston, but didn't mail one of them. I even phoned, but it was never her voice that answered. If it had been, I'm not even sure I would have said anything. I just wanted to hear her.

Were you ever curious about the women in my life? I had affairs with bright girls from Radcliffe who were majoring in law, history, or science, and once with a shop assistant who never read anything. Can you imagine, in the very act of making love, always thinking of another woman? I seemed to be doing my work on autopilot, and even my passion for running became reduced to an hour's jogging a day.

Long before the end of my last year, leading law firms in New York, Chicago, and Toronto were turning up to interview us. The Harvard tom-toms can be relied on to beat across the world, but even I was surprised by a visit from the senior partner of Graham, Douglas & Wilkins of Toronto. It's not a firm known for its Jewish partners, but I liked the idea of their letterhead one day reading "Graham, Douglas, Wilkins & Rosenthal." Even her father would surely have been impressed by that.

At least if I lived and worked in Toronto, I convinced myself, it would be far enough away for me to forget her, and perhaps with luck find someone else I could feel that way about.

Graham, Douglas & Wilkins found me a spacious apartment overlooking the park and started me off at a handsome salary. In return I worked all the hours God—whoever's God—made. If I thought they had pushed me at McGill or Harvard, Father, it turned out to be no more than a dry run for the real world. I didn't complain. The work was exciting, and the rewards beyond my expectation. Only now that I could afford a Thunderbird I didn't want one.

New girlfriends came and went as soon as they talked of marriage. The Jewish ones usually raised the subject within a week; the Gentiles, I found, waited a little longer. I even began living with one of them, Rebecca Wertz, but that too ended—on a Thursday.

I was driving to the office that morning—it must have been a little after eight, which was late for me—when I saw Christina on the other side of the busy highway, a barrier separating us. She was standing at a bus stop holding the hand of a little boy, who must have been about five—my son.

The heavy morning traffic allowed me a little longer to stare in disbelief. I found that I wanted to look at them both at once. She wore a long lightweight coat that showed she had not lost her figure. Her face was serene and only reminded me why she was rarely out of my thoughts. Her son—our son—was wrapped up in an oversize duffel coat and his head was covered by a baseball cap that informed me that he was a fan of the Toronto Blue Jays. Sadly, it really prevented me from seeing what he looked like. You can't be in Toronto, I remember thinking. You're meant to be in Montreal. I watched them both in my side mirror as they climbed onto a bus. That particular Thursday I must have been an appalling counselor to every client who sought my advice.

For the next week I passed by that bus stop every morning within minutes of the time I had seen them standing there, but never saw them again. I began to wonder if I had imagined the whole scene. Then I spotted Christina again when I was returning across the city, having visited a client. She was on her own, and I braked hard as I watched her entering a shop on Bloor Street. This time I double-parked the car and walked quickly across the road, feeling like a sleazy private detective who spends his life peeping through keyholes.

What I saw took me by surprise—not to find her in a beautiful dress shop, but to discover it was where she worked.

The moment I saw that she was serving a customer I hurried back to my car. Once I had reached my office I asked my secretary if she knew of a shop called "Willing's."

My secretary laughed. "You must pronounce it the German way; the W becomes a V," she explained, "thus, 'Villing's.' If you were married you would know that it's the most expensive dress shop in town," she added.

"Do you know anything else about the place?" I asked, trying to sound casual.

"Not a lot," she said. "Only that it is owned by a wealthy German lady called Mrs. Klaus Willing, whom they often write about in the women's magazines."

I didn't need to ask my secretary any more questions, and I won't trouble you, Father, with my detective work. But, armed with those snippets of information, it didn't take me long to discover where Christina lived, that her husband was an overseas director with BMW, and that they only had the one child.

The old rabbi breathed deeply as he glanced up at the clock on his desk, more out of habit than any desire to know the time. He paused for a moment before returning to the letter.

He had been so proud of his lawyer son then; why hadn't he made the first step toward a reconciliation? How he would have liked to have seen his grandson.

My ultimate decision did not require an acute legal mind, just a little common sense—although a lawyer who advises himself undoubtedly has a fool for a client. Contact, I decided, had to be direct, and a letter was the only method I felt Christina would find acceptable.

I wrote a simple message that Monday morning, then rewrote it several times before I telephoned Fleet Deliveries and asked them to hand it to her in person at the shop. When the young man left with the letter I wanted to follow him, just to be certain he had given it to the right person. I can still repeat it word for word:

Dear Christina,
 You must know I live and work in Toronto. Can we meet? I will wait for you in the lounge of the Royal York Hotel every evening between six and seven this week. If you don't come be assured I will never trouble you again.
 Benjamin

I arrived that evening nearly thirty minutes early. I remember taking a seat in a large impersonal lounge just off the main hall and ordering coffee.

"Will anyone be joining you, sir?" the waiter asked.

"I can't be sure," I told him. No one did join me, but I still hung around until seven-forty.

By Thursday the waiter had stopped asking if anyone would be joining me as I sat alone and allowed yet another cup of coffee to grow cold. Every few minutes I checked my watch. Each time a woman with blond hair entered the lounge my heart leaped but it was never the woman I hoped for.

It was just before seven on Friday that I finally saw Christina standing in the doorway. She wore a smart blue suit buttoned up almost to the neck and a white blouse that made her look as if she were on her way to a business conference. Her long fair hair was pulled back behind her ears to give an impression of severity, but however hard she tried she could not be other than beautiful. I stood and raised my arm. She walked quickly over and took the seat beside me. We didn't kiss or shake hands and for some time didn't even speak.

"Thank you for coming," I said.

"I shouldn't have, it was foolish."

Some time passed before either of us spoke again.

"Can I pour you a coffee?" I asked.

"Yes, thank you."

"Black?"

"Yes."

"You haven't changed."

How banal it all would have sounded to anyone eavesdropping.

She sipped her coffee.

I should have taken her in my arms right then, but I had no way of knowing that that was what she wanted. For several minutes we talked of inconsequential matters, always avoiding each other's eyes, until I suddenly said, "Do you realize that I still love you?"

Tears filled her eyes as she replied, "Of course I do. And I still feel the same about you now as I did the day we parted. And don't forget I have to see you every day, through Nicholas."

She leaned forward and spoke almost in a whisper. She told me about the meeting with her parents that had taken place more than five years before as if we had not been parted in between. Her father had shown no anger when he learned she was pregnant, but the family still left for Vancouver the following morning. There they had stayed with the Willings, a family also from Munich, who were old friends of the von Braumers. Their son, Klaus, had always been besotted with Christina and didn't care about her being pregnant, or even the fact she felt nothing for him. He was confident that, given time, it would all work out for the best.

It didn't, because it couldn't. Christina had always known it would never work, however hard Klaus tried. They even left Montreal in an attempt to make a go of it. Klaus bought her the shop in Toronto and every luxury that money could afford, but it made no difference. Their marriage was an obvious sham. Yet they could not bring themselves to distress their families further with a divorce, so they had led separate lives from the beginning.

As soon as Christina finished her story I touched her cheek and *she took my hand and kissed it. From that moment on we saw each other every spare moment that could be stolen, day or night. It was the happiest year of my life, and I was unable to hide from anyone how I felt.*

Our affair—for that's how the gossips were describing it— inevitably became public. However discreet we tried to be, Toronto, I quickly discovered, is a very small place, full of people who took pleasure in informing those whom we also loved that we had been seen together regularly, even leaving my home in the early hours.

Then quite suddenly we were left with no choice in the matter: Christina told me she was pregnant again. Only this time it held no fears for either of us.

Once she had told Klaus the settlement went through as quickly as the best divorce lawyer at Graham, Douglas & Wilkins could negotiate. We were married only a few days after the final papers were signed. We both regretted that Christina's parents felt unable to attend the wedding but I couldn't understand why you didn't come.

The rabbi still could not believe his own intolerance and short-sightedness. The demands on an Orthodox Jew should be waived if it meant losing one's only child. He had searched the Talmud in vain for any passage that would allow him to break his lifelong vows. In vain.

The only sad part of the divorce settlement was that Klaus was given custody of our child. He also demanded, in exchange for a quick divorce, that I not be allowed to see Nicholas before his twenty-first birthday, and that he should not be told that I was his real father. At the time it seemed a hard price to pay, even for such happiness. We both knew that we had been left with no choice but to accept his terms.

I used to wonder how each day could be so much better than the last. If I was apart from Christina for more than a few hours I always missed her. If the firm sent me out of town on business for a night I would phone her two, three, perhaps four times, and if it was for more than a night then she came with me. I remember you once describing your love for my mother and wondering at the time if I could ever hope to achieve such happiness.

We began to make plans for the birth of our child. William, if it was a boy—her choice; Deborah, if it was a girl—mine. I painted the spare room pink, assuming I had already won.

Christina had to stop me buying too many baby clothes, but I warned her that it didn't matter as we were going to have a dozen more children. Jews, I reminded her, believed in dynasties.

She attended her exercise classes regularly, dieted carefully, rested sensibly. I told her she was doing far more than was required of a mother, even the mother of my daughter. I asked if I could be present when our child was born and her gynecologist seemed reluctant at first, but then agreed. By the time the ninth month came, the hospital must have thought from the amount of fuss I was making they were preparing for the birth of a royal prince.

I drove Christina into Women's College Hospital on the way to work last Tuesday. Although I went on to the office I found it impossible to concentrate. The hospital called in the afternoon to say they thought the child would be born early that evening: Obviously Deborah did not wish to disrupt the working hours of Graham, Douglas & Wilkins. However, I still arrived at the hospital far too early. I sat on the end of Christina's bed until her contractions started coming every minute, and then to my surprise they asked me to leave. They needed to rupture her membranes, a nurse explained. I asked her to remind the midwife that I wanted to be present to witness the birth.

I went out into the corridor and began pacing up and down, the way expectant fathers do in B-movies. Christina's gynecologist arrived about half an hour later and gave me a huge smile. I noticed a cigar in his top pocket, obviously reserved for expectant fathers. "It's about to happen," was all he said.

A second doctor whom I had never seen before arrived a few minutes later and went quickly into her room. He only gave me a nod. I felt like a man in the dock waiting to hear the jury's verdict.

It must have been at least another fifteen minutes before I saw the unit being rushed down the corridor by a team of three young interns. They didn't give me so much as a glance as they disappeared into Christina's room.

I heard the screams that suddenly gave way to the plaintive cry of a newborn child. I thanked my God and hers. When the doctor came out of her room I remember noticing that the cigar had disappeared.

"It's a girl," he said quietly. I was overjoyed. "No need to repaint the bedroom immediately" flashed through my mind.

"Can I see Christina now?" I asked.

He took me by the arm and led me across the corridor and into his office.

"Would you like to sit down?" he asked. "I'm afraid I have some sad news."

"Is she all right?"

"I am sorry, so very sorry, to tell you that your wife is dead."

At first I didn't believe him, I refused to believe him. Why? Why? I wanted to scream.

"We did warn her," he added.

"Warn her? Warn her of what?"

"That her blood pressure might not stand up to it a second time."

Christina had never told me what the doctor went on to explain—that the birth of our first child had been complicated, and that the doctors had advised her against becoming pregnant again.

"Why didn't she tell me?" I demanded. Then I realized why. She had risked everything for me—foolish, selfish, thoughtless me—and I had ended up killing the one person I loved.

They allowed me to hold Deborah in my arms for just a moment before they put her into an incubator and told me it would be another twenty-four hours before she came off the danger list.

You will never know how much it meant to me, Father, that you came to the hospital so quickly. Christina's parents arrived later that evening. They were magnificent. He begged for my forgiveness—begged for my forgiveness. It could never have happened, he kept repeating, if he hadn't been so stupid and prejudiced.

His wife took my hand and asked if she might be allowed to see Deborah from time to time. Of course I agreed. They left just before midnight. I sat, walked, slept in that corridor for the next twenty-four hours until they told me that my daughter was off the danger list. She would have to remain in the hospital for a few more days, they explained, but she was now managing to suck milk from a bottle.

Christina's father kindly took over the funeral arrangements. You must have wondered why I didn't appear, and I owe you an explanation. I thought I would just drop into the hospital on my way to the funeral so that I could spend a few moments with Deborah. I had already transferred my love.

The doctor couldn't get the words out. It took a brave man to tell me that her heart had stopped beating a few minutes before my arrival. Even the senior surgeon was in tears. When I left the hospital the corridors were empty.

I want you to know, Father, that I love you with all my heart, but I have no desire to spend the rest of my life without Christina or Deborah.

I only ask to be buried beside my wife and daughter and to be remembered as their husband and father. That way unthinking people might learn from our love. And when you finish this letter, remember only that I had such total happiness when I was with her that death holds no fears for me.

Your son,
Benjamin

The old rabbi placed the letter down on the table in front of him. He had read it every day for the last ten years.

COLONEL
BULLFROG

THERE IS ONE CATHEDRAL in England that has never found it necessary to launch a national fundraising appeal.

When the colonel woke he found himself tied to a stake where the ambush had taken place. He could feel a numb sensation in his leg. The last thing he could recall was the bayonet entering his thigh. All he was aware of now were ants crawling up the leg on an endless march toward the wound.

It would have been better to have remained unconscious, he decided.

Then someone undid the knots, and he collapsed headfirst into the mud. It would be better still to be dead, he concluded. The colonel somehow got to his knees and crawled over to the stake next to him. Tied to it was a corporal who must have been dead for several hours. Ants were crawling into his mouth. The colonel tore off a strip from the man's shirt, washed it in a large puddle nearby, and cleaned the wound on his leg as best he could before binding it tightly.

That was February 17, 1943, a date that would be etched on the colonel's memory for the rest of his life.

That same morning the Japanese received orders that the newly captured Allied prisoners were to be moved at dawn. Many were to die on the march, and even more had perished before the trek began. Colonel Richard Moore was determined not to be counted among them.

Twenty-nine days later, 117 of the original 732 Allied troops reached Tonchan. Any man whose travels had previously not taken him beyond Rome could hardly have been prepared for such an experience as Tonchan. This heavily guarded prisoner-of-war camp, some three hundred miles north of Singapore and hidden in the deepest equatorial jungle, offered no possibility of freedom. Anyone who contemplated escape could not hope to survive in the jungle for more than a few days, while those who remained discovered that the odds were not a lot shorter.

When the colonel first arrived, Major Sakata, the camp commandant, informed him that he was the senior ranking officer and would therefore be held responsible for the welfare of all Allied troops.

Colonel Moore had stared down at the Japanese officer. Sakata must have been a foot shorter than himself, but after that twenty-eight-day march the British soldier couldn't have weighed much more than the diminutive major.

Moore's first act on leaving the commandant's office was to call together all the Allied officers. He discovered there was a good cross-section from Britain, Australia, New Zealand, and the United States, but few could have been described as fit. Men were dying daily from malaria, dysentery, and malnutrition. He was suddenly aware what the expression "dying like flies" meant.

The colonel learned from his staff officers that for the previous two years of the camp's existence, they had been ordered to build bamboo huts for the Japanese officers. These had had to be completed before they had been allowed to start on a hospital for their own men, and only recently huts for themselves. Many prisoners had died during those two years, not from illness but from the atrocities some Japanese perpetrated on a daily basis. Major Sakata, known because of his skinny arms as "Chopsticks," was, however, not considered to be the villain. His second-in-command, Lieutenant Takasaki ("the Undertaker"), and Sergeant Ayut ("the Pig") were of a different mold and to be avoided at all costs, his men warned him.

It took the colonel only a few days to discover why.

He decided his first task was to try to raise the battered morale of his troops. As there was no padre among those officers who had been captured, he began each day by conducting a short service of prayer. Once the service was over the men would start work on the railway that ran alongside the camp. Each arduous day consisted of laying tracks to help Japanese soldiers get to the front more quickly, so they could in turn kill and capture more Allied troops. Any prisoner suspected of undermining this work was found guilty of sabotage and put to death without trial. Lieutenant Takasaki considered taking an unscheduled five-minute break to be sabotage.

At lunch prisoners were allowed twenty minutes off to share a bowl of rice—usually with maggots—and, if they were lucky, a mug of water. Although the men returned to the camp each night exhausted, the colonel still set about setting up squads to be responsible for the cleanliness of their huts and the state of the latrines.

After only a few months, the colonel was able to arrange a football match between the British and the Americans, and following its success even set up a camp league. But he was even more delighted when the men turned up for karate lessons under Sergeant Hawke, a thick-set Australian, who had a black belt and for good measure also played the harmonica. The tiny instrument had survived the march through the jungle but everyone assumed it would be discovered before long and confiscated.

Each day Moore renewed his determination not to allow the Japanese to believe for one moment that the Allies were beaten—despite the fact that while he was at Tonchan he lost another twenty pounds in weight, and at least one man under his command every day.

To the colonel's surprise the camp commandant, despite the Japanese national belief that any soldier who allowed himself to be captured ought to be treated as a deserter, did not place too many unnecessary obstacles in his path.

"You are like the British bullfrog," Major Sakata suggested one evening as he watched the colonel carving cricket bails out of bamboo. It was one of the rare occasions when the colonel managed a smile.

His real problems continued to come from Lieutenant Takasaki and his henchmen, who considered captured Allied prisoners fit only to be considered as traitors. Takasaki was always careful how he treated the colonel personally, but felt no such reservations when dealing with the other ranks, with the result that Allied soldiers often ended up with their meager rations confiscated, a rifle butt in the stomach, or even left bound to a tree for days on end.

Whenever the colonel made an official complaint to the commandant, Major Sakata listened sympathetically and even made an effort to weed out the main offenders. Moore's happiest moment at Tonchan was to witness the Undertaker and the Pig boarding the train for the front line. No one attempted to sabotage that journey. The commandant replaced them with Sergeant Akida and Corporal Sushi, known by the prisoners almost affectionately as "Sweet and Sour Pork." However, the Japanese High Command sent a new number two to the camp, a Lieutenant Osawa, who quickly became known as "the Devil" since he perpetrated atrocities that made the Undertaker and the Pig look like church fête organizers.

As the months passed the colonel and the commandant's mutual respect grew. Sakata even confided to his English prisoner that he had requested that he be sent to the front line and join the real war. "And if," the major added, "the High Command grants my request, there will be only two NCOs I would want to accompany me."

Colonel Moore knew the major had Sweet and Sour Pork in mind, and was fearful what might become of his men if the only three Japanese he could work with were posted back to active dutiy to leave Lieutenant Osawa in command of the camp.

Colonel Moore realized that something quite extraordinary must have taken place for Major Sakata to come to his hut, because he had never done so before. The colonel put his bowl of rice back down on the table and asked the three Allied officers who were sharing breakfast with him to wait outside.

The major stood to attention and saluted.

The colonel pushed himself to his full six feet, returned the salute, and stared down into Sakata's eyes.

"The war is over," said the Japanese officer. For a brief

moment Moore feared the worst. "Japan has surrendered unconditionally. You, sir," Sakata said quietly, "are now in command of the camp."

The colonel immediately ordered all Japanese officers to be placed under arrest in the commandant's quarters. While his orders were being carried out he personally went in search of the Devil. Moore marched across the parade ground and headed toward the officers' quarters. He located the second-in-command's hut, walked up the steps, and threw open Osawa's door. The sight that met the new commandant's eyes was one he would never forget. The colonel had read of ceremonial hara-kiri without any real idea of what the final act consisted. Lieutenant Osawa must have cut himself a hundred times before he eventually died. The blood, the stench, and the sight of the mutilated body would have caused a strong-stomached Gurkha to be sick. Only the head was there to confirm that the remains had once belonged to a human being.

The colonel ordered Osawa to be buried outside the gates of the camp.

When the surrender of Japan was finally signed on board the USS *Missouri* in Tokyo Bay, all at Tonchan POW camp listened to the ceremony on the single camp radio. Colonel Moore then called a full parade on the camp square. For the first time in two and a half years he wore his dress uniform, which made him look like a Pierrot who had turned up at a formal party. He accepted the Japanese flag of surrender from Major Sakata on behalf of the Allies, then made the defeated enemy raise the American and British flags to the sound of both national anthems played in turn by Sergeant Hawke on his harmonica.

The colonel then held a short service of thanksgiving, which he conducted in the presence of all the Allied and Japanese soldiers.

Once command had changed hands Colonel Moore waited as week followed pointless week for news that he would be sent home. Many of his men had been given their orders to start the ten-thousand-mile journey back to England via Bangkok and

Calcutta, but no such orders came for the colonel and he waited in vain to be sent his repatriation papers.

Then, in January 1946, a smartly dressed young Guards officer arrived at the camp with orders to see the colonel. He was conducted to the commandant's office and saluted before shaking hands. Richard Moore stared at the young captain who, from his healthy complexion, had obviously arrived in the Far East long after the Japanese had surrendered. The captain handed over a letter to the colonel.

"Home at last," said the older man breezily, as he ripped open the envelope, only to discover that it would be years before he could hope to exchange the paddy fields of Tonchan for the green fields of Lincolnshire.

The letter requested that the colonel travel to Tokyo and represent Britain on the forthcoming war tribunal which was to be conducted in the Japanese capital. Captain Ross of the Coldstream Guards would take over his command at Tonchan.

The tribunal was to consist of twelve officers under the chairmanship of General Matthew Tomkins. Moore was to be the sole British representative and was to report directly to the General, "as soon as you find it convenient." Further details would be supplied to him on his arrival in Tokyo. The letter ended: "If for any reason you should require my help in your deliberations, do not hesitate to contact me personally." There followed the signature of Clement Attlee.

Staff officers are not in the habit of disobeying prime ministers, so the colonel resigned himself to a prolonged stay in Japan.

It took several months to set up the tribunal and during that time Colonel Moore continued supervising the return of British troops to their homeland. The paperwork was endless and some of the men under his command were so frail that he found it necessary to build them up spiritually as well as physically before he could put them on boats to their various destinations. Some died long after the declaration of surrender had been ratified.

During this period of waiting, Colonel Moore used Major

Sakata and the two NCOs in whom he had placed so much trust, Sergeant Akida and Corporal Sushi, as his liaison officers. This sudden change of command did not affect the relationship between the two senior officers, although Sakata admitted to the colonel that he wished he had been killed in the defense of his country and not left to witness its humiliations. The colonel found the Japanese remained well-disciplined while they waited to learn their fate, and most of them assumed death was the natural consequence of defeat.

The war tribunal held its first plenary session in Tokyo on April 19th, 1946. General Tomkins took over the fifth floor of the old Imperial Courthouse in the Ginza quarter of Tokyo—one of the few buildings that had survived the war intact. Tomkins, a squat, short-tempered man who was described by his own staff officer as a "pen-pusher from the Pentagon," arrived in Tokyo only a week before he began his first deliberations. The only rat-a-tat-tat this general had ever heard, the staff officer freely admitted to Colonel Moore, had come from the typewriter in his secretary's office. However, when it came to those on trial the General was in no doubt as to where the guilt lay and how the guilty should be punished.

"Hang every one of the little slit-eyed, yellow bastards," turned out to be one of Tomkins's favorite expressions.

Seated round a table in an old courtroom, the twelve-man tribunal conducted their deliberations. It was clear from the opening session that the general had no intention of considering "extenuating circumstances," "past record" or "humanitarian grounds". As the colonel listened to Tomkins's views he began to fear for the lives of any innocent member of the armed forces who was brought in front of the general.

The colonel quickly identified four Americans from the tribunal who, like himself, did not always concur with the general's sweeping judgments. Two were lawyers and the other two had been fighting soldiers recently involved in combat duty. The five men began to work together to counteract the general's most prejudiced decisions. During the following weeks they were able to persuade one or two others around the table to commute the sentences of hanging to life imprisonment for several Japanese who had been condemned for crimes they could not possibly have committed.

As each such case was debated, General Tomkins left the five men in no doubt as to his contempt for their views. "Goddam Nip sympathizers," he often suggested, and not always under his breath. As the general still held sway over the twelve-man tribunal, the colonel's successes turned out to be few in number.

When the time came to determine the fate of those who had been in command of the POW camp at Tonchan the General demanded mass hanging for every Japanese officer involved without even the pretense of a proper trial. He showed no surprise when the usual five tribunal members raised their voices in protest. Colonel Moore spoke eloquently of having been a prisoner at Tonchan and petitioned in the defense of Major Sakata, Sergeant Akida and Corporal Sushi. He attempted to explain why hanging them would in its own way be as barbaric as any atrocity carried out by the Japanese. He insisted their sentence should be commuted to life imprisonment. The general yawned throughout the colonel's remarks and, once Moore had completed his case, made no attempt to justify his position but simply called for a vote. To the general's surprise, the result was six-all; an American lawyer who previously had sided with the general raised his hand to join the colonel's five. Without hesitation the general threw his casting vote in favor of the gallows. Tomkins leered down the table at Moore and said, "Time for lunch, I think, gentlemen. I don't know about you but I'm famished. And no one can say that this time we didn't give the little yellow bastards a fair hearing."

Colonel Moore rose from his place and without offering an opinion left the room.

He ran down the steps of the courthouse and instructed his driver to take him to British HQ in the center of the city as quickly as possible. The short journey took them some time because of the melee of people that were always thronging the streets night and day. Once the colonel arrived at his office he asked his secretary to place a call through to England. While she was carrying out his order Moore went to his green cabinet and thumbed through several files until he reached the one marked "Personal." He opened it and fished out the letter. He wanted to be certain that he had remembered the sentence accurately . . .

"If for any reason you should require my help in your deliberations, do not hesitate to contact me personally."

"He's coming to the phone, sir," the secretary said nervously. The colonel walked over to the phone and waited. He found himself standing to attention when he heard the gentle, cultivated voice ask, "Is that you, colonel?" It took Richard Moore less than ten minutes to explain the problem he faced and obtain the authority he needed.

Immediately he had completed his conversation he returned to the tribunal headquarters. He marched straight back into the conference room just as General Tomkins was settling down in his chair to start the afternoon proceedings.

The colonel was the first to rise from his place when the general declared the tribunal to be in session. "I wonder if I might be allowed to open with a statement?" he requested.

"Be my guest," said Tomkins. "But make it brief. We've got a lot more of these Japs to get through yet."

Colonel Moore looked around the table at the other eleven men.

"Gentlemen," he began. "I hereby resign my position as the British representative on this commission."

General Tomkins was unable to stifle a smile.

"I do it," the colonel continued, "reluctantly, but with the backing of my Prime Minister, to whom I spoke only a few moments ago." At this piece of information Tomkins's smile was replaced by a frown. "I shall be returning to England in order to make a full report to Mr. Attlee and the British cabinet on the manner in which this tribunal is being conducted."

"Now look here, sonny," began the general. "You can't—"

"I can, sir, and I will. Unlike you, I am unwilling to have the blood of innocent soldiers on my hands for the rest of my life."

"Now look here, sonny," the general repeated. "Let's at least talk this through before you do anything you might regret."

There was no break for the rest of that day, and by late afternoon Major Sakata, Sergeant Akida and Corporal Sushi had had their sentences commuted to life imprisonment.

Within a month, General Tomkins had been recalled by the Pentagon to be replaced by a distinguished American marine who had been decorated in combat during the First World War.

In the weeks that followed the new appointment the death sentences of two hundred and twenty-nine Japanese prisoners of war were commuted.

Colonel Moore returned to Lincolnshire on November 11, 1948, having had enough of the realities of war and the hypocrisies of peace.

Just under two years later Richard Moore took holy orders and became a parish priest in the sleepy hamlet of Weddlebeach, in Suffolk. He enjoyed his calling and although he rarely mentioned his wartime experiences to his parishioners he often thought of his days in Japan.

"Blessed are the peacemakers for they shall . . ." the vicar began his sermon from the pulpit one Palm Sunday morning in the early 1960s, but he failed to complete the sentence.

His parishioners looked up anxiously only to see that a broad smile had spread across the vicar's face as he gazed down at someone seated in the third row.

The man he was staring at bowed his head in embarrassment and the vicar quickly continued with his sermon.

When the service was over Richard Moore waited by the west door to be sure his eyes had not deceived him. When they met face to face for the first time in fifteen years both men bowed and then shook hands.

The priest was delighted to learn over lunch that day back at the vicarage that Chopsticks Sakata had been released from prison after only five years, following the Allies' agreement with the newly installed Japanese government to release all prisoners who had not committed capital crimes. When the Colonel enquired after "Sweet and Sour Pork" the Major admitted that he had lost touch with Sergeant Akida (Sweet) but that Corporal Sushi (Sour) and he were working for the same electronics company. "And whenever we meet," he assured the priest, "we talk of the honourable man who saved our lives, "the British Bullfrog."

Over the years, the priest and his Japanese friend progressed in their chosen professions and regularly corresponded with each other. In 1971 Ari Sakata was put in charge of a large electronics factory in Osaka while eighteen months later Richard Moore became the Very Reverend Richard Moore, Dean of Lincoln Cathedral.

"I read in *The Times* that your cathedral is appealing for a new roof," wrote Sakata from his homeland in 1975.

"Nothing unusual about that," the Dean explained in his letter of reply. "There isn't a cathedral in England that doesn't suffer from dry rot or bomb damage. The former I fear is terminal; the latter at least has the chance of a cure."

A few weeks later the Dean received a check for ten thousand pounds from a not-unknown Japanese electronics company.

When in 1979 the Very Reverend Richard Moore was appointed to the bishopric of Taunton, the new managing director of the largest electronics company in Japan flew over to attend his enthronement.

"I see you have another roof problem," commented Ari Sakata as he gazed up at the scaffolding surrounding the pulpit. "How much will it cost this time?"

"At least twenty-five thousand pounds a year," replied the bishop without thought. "Just to make sure the roof doesn't fall in on the congregation during my sterner sermons." He sighed as he passed the evidence of reconstruction all around him. "As soon as I've settled into my new job I intend to launch a proper appeal to ensure my successor doesn't have to worry about the roof ever again."

The managing director nodded his understanding. A week later a check for twenty-five thousand pounds arrived on the churchman's desk.

The bishop tried hard to express his grateful thanks. He

knew he must never allow Chopsticks to feel that by his generosity he might have done the wrong thing as this would only insult his friend and undoubtedly end their relationship. Rewrite after rewrite was drafted to ensure that the final version of the long handwritten letter would have passed muster with the Foreign Office mandarin in charge of the Japanese desk. Finally the letter was posted.

As the years passed Richard Moore became fearful of writing to his old friend more than once a year as each letter elicited an even larger check. And, when toward the end of 1986 he did write, he made no reference to the dean and chapter's decision to designate 1988 as the cathedral's appeal year. Nor did he mention his own failing health, lest the old Japanese gentleman should feel in some way responsible, as his doctor had warned him that he could never expect to recover fully from those experiences at Tonchan.

The bishop set about forming his appeal committee in January 1987. The Prince of Wales became the patron and the lord lieutenant of the county its chairman. In his opening address to the members of the appeal committee the bishop instructed them that it was their duty to raise not less than three million pounds during 1988. Some apprehensive looks appeared on the faces around the table

On August 11, 1987, the bishop of Taunton was umpiring a village cricket match when he suddenly collapsed from a heart attack. "See that the appeal brochures are printed in time for the next meeting," were his final words to the captain of the local team.

Bishop Moore's memorial service was held in Taunton Cathedral and conducted by the archbishop of Canterbury. Not a seat could be found in the cathedral that day, and so many crowded into every pew that the west door was left open. Those who arrived late had to listen to the archbishop's address relayed over loudspeakers placed around the market square.

Casual onlookers must have been puzzled by the presence of several elderly Japanese gentlemen dotted around the congregation.

When the service came to an end the archbishop held a private meeting in the vestry of the cathedral with the chairman of the largest electronics company in the world.

"You must be Mr. Sakata," said the archbishop, warmly shaking the hand of a man who stepped forward from the small cluster of Japanese who were in attendance. "Thank you for taking the trouble to write and let me know that you would be coming. I am delighted to meet you at last. The bishop always spoke of you with great affection and as a close friend—'Chopsticks,' if I remember."

Mr. Sakata bowed low.

"And I also know that he always considered himself in your personal debt for such generosity over so many years."

"No, no, not me," replied the former major. "I, like my dear friend the late bishop, am representative of higher authority."

The archbishop looked puzzled.

"You see, sir," continued Mr. Sakata, "I am only the chairman of the company. May I have the honor of introducing my president?"

Mr. Sakata took a pace backward to allow an even smaller figure, whom the archbishop had originally assumed to be part of Mr. Sakata's entourage, to step forward.

The president bowed low and, still without speaking, passed an envelope to the archbishop.

"May I be allowed to open it?" the church leader asked, unaware of the Japanese custom of waiting until the giver has departed.

The little man bowed again.

The archbishop slit open the envelope and removed a check for three million pounds.

"The late bishop must have been a very close friend," was all he could think of saying.

"No, sir," the president replied. "I did not have that privilege."

"Then he must have done something incredible to be deserving of such a munificent gesture."

"He performed an act of honor over forty years ago and now I try inadequately to repay it."

"Then he would surely have remembered you," said the archbishop.

"Is possible he would remember me but if so only as the sour half of Sweet and Sour Pork."

There is one cathedral in England that has never found it necessary to launch a national appeal.

DO NOT
PASS GO

May 1986

Hamid Zebari smiled at the thought of his wife, Shereen, driving him to the airport. Neither of them would have believed it possible five years before, when they had first arrived in America as political refugees. But since he had begun a new life in the States, Hamid was beginning to think anything might be possible.

"When will you be coming home, Papa?" asked Nadim, who was strapped safely in the back seat next to his sister, May. She was too young to understand why Papa was going away.

"Just two weeks, I promise. No more," their father replied. "And when I get back, we'll all go on vacation."

"How long is two weeks?" his son demanded.

"Fourteen days," Hamid told him with a laugh.

"And fourteen nights," said his wife as she pulled up to the curb below the sign for Turkish Airways. She touched a button on the dashboard and the trunk opened. Hamid jumped out of the car, grabbed his luggage from the trunk, and put it on the sidewalk before climbing into the back of the car. He hugged his daughter first, and then his son. May was crying—not because he was going away, but because she always cried when the car came to a sudden halt. He allowed her to stroke his bushy mustache, which usually stopped the flow of tears.

"Fourteen days," repeated his son. Hamid hugged his wife and felt the small swelling of a third child between them.

"We'll be here waiting to pick you up," Shereen called out as her husband tipped the Skycap on the curb.

Once his six empty suitcases had been checked in, Hamid

disappeared into the terminal and made his way to the Turkish Airlines desk. Since he took the same flight twice a year, he didn't need to ask the girl at the ticket counter for directions.

After he had checked in and been presented with his boarding pass, Hamid still had an hour to wait before they would call his flight. He began the slow trek to Gate B27. It was always the same—the Turkish Airlines plane would be parked halfway back to Manhattan. As he passed the Pan Am check-in desk on B5, he observed that they would be taking off an hour earlier than him, a privilege for those who were willing to pay an extra sixty-three dollars.

When he reached the check-in area, a Turkish Airlines stewardess was slipping the sign for Flight 014, New York–London–Istanbul, onto a board. Estimated time of departure, 10:10.

The seats were beginning to fill up with the usual cosmopolitan group of passengers: Turks going home to visit their families, those Americans taking a vacation who cared about saving sixty-three dollars, and businessmen whose bottom line was closely watched by tight-fisted accountants.

Hamid strolled over to the restaurant bar and ordered coffee and two eggs sunny-side up, with a side order of hash browns. It was the little things that reminded him daily of his newfound freedom, and of just how much he owed to the United States.

"Would those passengers traveling to Istanbul with young children please board the plane now," said the stewardess over the loudspeaker.

Hamid swallowed the last mouthful of his hash browns—he hadn't yet become accustomed to the American habit of covering almost everything in ketchup—and took a final swig of the weak, tasteless coffee. He couldn't wait to be reunited with the thick Turkish coffee served in small bone china cups. But that was a tiny sacrifice when weighed against the privilege of living in a free land. He paid his bill and left a dollar on the little metal tray.

"Would those passengers seated in rows thirty-five to forty-one please board the aircraft now."

Hamid picked up his briefcase and headed for the passage-way that led to Flight 014. An official from Turkish Airlines checked his boarding pass and ushered him through.

He had been allocated an aisle seat near the back of econ-omy. Ten more trips, he told himself, and he would fly Pan Am business class. By then he would be able to afford it.

Whenever the wheels of his plane left the ground, Hamid would look out of the little window and watch his adopted country as it disappeared out of sight, the same thoughts always going through his mind.

It had been nearly five years since Saddam Hussein had dis-missed him from the Iraqi cabinet, after he had held the post of minister of agriculture for only two years. The wheat crops had been poor that autumn, and after the People's Army had taken its share, and the middlemen their cut, the Iraqi people ended up with short rations. Someone had to take the blame, and the obvious scapegoat was the minister of agriculture. Hamid's father, a carpet dealer, had always wanted him to join the family business, and had even warned him before he died not to accept agriculture—the last three holders of that office, having first been fired, later disappeared—and everyone in Iraq knew what "disappeared" meant. But Hamid did accept the job. The first year's crop had been abundant, and after all, he convinced himself, agriculture was only a stepping stone to greater things. In any case, had not Saddam described him in front of the whole Revolutionary Command Council as "my good and close friend"? At thirty-two you still believe you are immortal.

Hamid's father was proved right, and Hamid's only real friend—friends melted away like snow in the morning sun when this particular president fired you—helped him to escape.

The only precaution Hamid had taken during his days as a cabinet minister was to withdraw from his bank account each week a little more cash than he actually needed. He would then change the extra money into American dollars with a street trader, using a different dealer each time, and never exchanging enough to arouse suspicion. In Iraq everyone is a spy.

The day he was fired, he checked how much was hidden under his mattress. It amounted to $11,221.

The following Thursday, the day on which the weekend begins in Baghdad, he and his pregnant wife took the bus to Erbil. He left his Mercedes conspicuously parked in the front drive of his large home in the suburbs, and they carried no luggage with them—just two passports, the roll of dollars secreted in his wife's baggy clothing, and some Iraqi dinars to get them as far as the border.

No one would be looking for them on a bus to Erbil.

Once they arrived in Erbil, Hamid and his wife took a taxi to Sulaimania, using most of the remaining dinars to pay the driver. They spent the night in a small hotel far from the city center. Neither slept as they waited for the morning sun to come shining through the curtainless window.

The next day, another bus took them high into the hills of Kurdistan, arriving in Zakho in the early evening.

The final part of the journey was the slowest of all. They were taken up through the hills on mules, at a cost of two hundred dollars—the young Kurdish smuggler showed no interest in Iraqi dinars. He delivered the former Cabinet Minister and his wife safely over the border in the early hours of the morning, leaving them to make their way on foot to the nearest village on Turkish soil. They reached Kirmizi Renga that evening and spent another sleepless night at the local station, waiting for the first train for Istanbul.

Hamid and Shereen slept all the way through the long train journey to the Turkish capital, and woke up the following morning as refugees. The first visit Hamid made in the city was to the Iz Bank, where he deposited $10,800. The next was to the American Embassy, where he produced his diplomatic passport and requested political asylum. His father had once told him that a recently fired cabinet minister from Iraq was always a good catch for the Americans.

The embassy arranged accommodation for Hamid and his

wife in a first-class hotel, and immediately informed Washington of their little coup. They promised Hamid that they would get back to him as quickly as possible, but gave him no clue as to how long that might take. He decided to use the time to visit the carpet bazaars on the south side of the city, so often frequented by his father.

Many of the dealers remembered Hamid's father—an honest man who liked to bargain and drink gallons of coffee, and who had often talked about his son going into politics. They were pleased to make his acquaintance, especially when they learned what he planned to do once he had settled in the States.

The Zebaris were granted American visas within the week and flown to Washington at the government's expense, which included a charge for excess baggage of twenty-three Turkish carpets.

After five days of intensive questioning by the CIA, Hamid was thanked for his cooperation and the useful information he had supplied. He was then released to begin his new life in the United States. He, his pregnant wife, and the twenty-three carpets boarded a train for New York.

It took Hamid six weeks to find the right shop, on the Lower East Side of Manhattan, from which to sell his carpets. Once he had signed the five-year lease, Shereen immediately set about painting their new Americanized name above the door.

Hamid didn't sell his first carpet for nearly three months, by which time his meager savings had all but disappeared. But by the end of the first year, sixteen of the twenty-three carpets had been sold, and he realized he would soon have to travel back to Istanbul to buy more stock.

Four years had passed since then, and the Zebaris had recently moved to a larger establishment on the West Side, with a small apartment above the shop. Hamid kept telling his wife that this was only the beginning, that anything was possible in the United States. He now considered himself a fully-fledged American citizen, and not just because of the treasured blue passport that confirmed his status. He accepted that he could never return to his birthplace while Saddam remained its ruler. His home and possessions had long ago been confiscated by the Iraqi state, and the death sentence had been passed on him in his absence. He doubted if he would ever see Baghdad again.

After the stopover in London, the plane landed at Istanbul's Ataturk Airport a few minutes ahead of schedule. Hamid booked into his usual small hotel, and planned how best to allocate his time over the next two weeks. He was happy to be back among the hustle and bustle of the Turkish capital.

There were thirty-one dealers he wanted to visit, because this time he hoped to return to New York with at least sixty carpets. That would require fourteen days of drinking thick Turkish coffee, and many hours of bargaining, as a dealer's opening price would be three times as much as Hamid was willing to pay—or what the dealer really expected to receive. But there was no short cut in the bartering process, which—like his father—Hamid secretly enjoyed.

By the end of the two weeks, Hamid had purchased fifty-seven carpets, at a cost of a little over $21,000. He had been careful to select only those carpets that would be sought after by the most discerning New Yorkers, and he was confident that this latest batch would fetch almost $100,000 in the United States. It had been such a successful trip that Hamid felt he would indulge himself by taking the earlier Pan Am flight back to New York. After all, he had undoubtedly earned himself the extra $63 many times over in the course of his trip.

He was looking forward to seeing Shereen and the children even before the plane had taken off, and the American flight attendant with her pronounced New York accent and friendly smile only added to the feeling that he was already home. After lunch had been served, and having decided he didn't want to watch the in-flight movie, Hamid dozed off and dreamed about what he could achieve in the United States, given time. Perhaps his son would go into politics. Would the United States be ready for an Iraqi president by the year 2025? He smiled at the thought, and fell contentedly into a deep sleep.

"Ladies and gentlemen," a deep Southern voice boomed out over the intercom, "this is your captain. I'm sorry to interrupt the movie, or to wake those of you who've been resting, but we've developed a small problem in an engine on our starboard wing. Nothing to worry about, folks, but FAA authority rulings insist that we land at the nearest airport and have the problem dealt with before we continue with our journey. It shouldn't take us more than an hour at the most, and then we'll be on our way again. You can be sure that we'll try to make up as much of the lost time as possible, folks."

Hamid was suddenly wide awake.

"We won't be disembarking from the aircraft at any time, since this is an unscheduled stop. But you'll be able to tell the folks back home that you've visited Baghdad."

Hamid felt his whole body go limp, and then his head rocked forward. The flight attendant rushed to his side.

"Are you feeling all right, sir?" she asked.

He looked up and stared into her eyes. "I must see the captain immediately. Immediately."

The flight attendant was in no doubt of the passenger's anxiety, and quickly led him forward, up the spiral staircase into the first-class lounge, and onto the flight deck.

She tapped on the door of the cockpit, opened it and said, "Captain, one of the passengers needs to speak to you urgently."

"Show him in," said the Southern voice. The captain turned to face Hamid, who was now trembling uncontrollably. "How can I be of help, sir?" he asked.

"My name is Hamid Zebari. I am an American citizen," he began. "If you land in Baghdad, I will be arrested, tortured, and then executed." The words tumbled out. "I am a political refugee, and you must understand that the regime will not hesitate to kill me."

The captain only needed to take one look at Hamid to realize he wasn't exaggerating.

"Take over, Jim," he said to his copilot, "while I have a word with Mr. Zebari. Call me the moment we've been given clearance to land."

The captain unfastened his seatbelt and led Hamid to an empty corner of the first-class lounge.

"Take me through it slowly," he said.

During the next few minutes Hamid explained why he had had to leave Baghdad, and how he came to be living in the United States. When he had reached the end of his story the captain shook his head and smiled. "No need to panic, sir," he assured Hamid. "No one is going to have to leave the aircraft at any time, so the passengers' passports won't even be checked. Once the engine has been attended to, we'll be back up and on our way immediately. Why don't you just stay here in first class, then you'll be able to speak to me at any time, should you feel at all anxious."

How anxious can you feel? Hamid wondered, as the captain left him to have a word with the copilot. He started to tremble once more.

"It's the captain once again, folks, just bringing you up to date. We've been given clearance by Baghdad, so we've begun our descent and expect to land in about twenty minutes. We'll then be taxiing to the far end of the runway, where we'll wait for the engineers. Just as soon as they've dealt with our little problem, we'll be back up and on our way again."

A collective sigh went up, while Hamid gripped the armrest and wished he hadn't eaten any lunch. He didn't stop shaking for the next twenty minutes, and almost fainted when the wheels touched down on the land of his birth.

He stared out of the porthole as the aircraft taxied past the terminal he knew so well. He could see the armed guards stationed on the roof and at the doors leading onto the tarmac. He prayed to Allah, he prayed to Jesus, he even prayed to President Reagan.

For the next fifteen minutes the silence was broken only by the sound of a van driving across the tarmac and coming to a halt under the starboard wing of the aircraft.

Hamid watched as two engineers carrying bulky toolbags got out of the van, stepped onto a small crane, and were hoisted up until they were level with the wing. They began unscrewing the outer plates of one of the engines. Forty minutes later they screwed the plates back on and were lowered to the ground. The van then headed off toward the terminal.

Hamid felt relieved, if not exactly relaxed. He fastened his seatbelt hopefully. His heartbeat fell from 180 a minute to around 110, but he knew it wouldn't return to normal until the plane lifted off and he could be sure they wouldn't turn back. Nothing happened for the next few minutes, and Hamid became anxious again. Then the door of the cockpit opened, and he saw the captain heading toward him, a grim expression on his face.

"You'd better join us on the flight deck," the captain said in a whisper. Hamid undid his seatbelt and somehow managed to stand. He unsteadily followed the captain into the cockpit, his legs feeling like jelly. The door was closed behind them.

The captain didn't waste any words. "The engineers can't locate the problem. The chief engineer won't be free for another hour, so we've been ordered to disembark and wait in the transit area until he's completed the job."

"I'd rather die in a plane crash," Hamid blurted out.

"Don't worry, Mr. Zebari, we've thought of a way around your problem. We're going to put you in a spare uniform. That will make it possible for you to stay with us the whole time, and use the crew's facilities. No one will ask to see your passport."

"But if someone recognizes me—" began Hamid.

"Once you've got rid of that mustache, and you're wearing a flight officer's uniform, dark glasses, and a peaked hat, your own mother wouldn't know you."

With the help of scissors, followed by shaving foam, followed by a razor, Hamid removed the bushy mustache that he had been so proud of, leaving an upper lip that looked as pale as a blob of vanilla ice cream. The senior flight attendant applied some of her makeup to his skin, until the white patch blended in with the rest of his face. Hamid still wasn't convinced, but after he had changed into the copilot's spare uniform and studied himself in the toilet mirror, he had to admit that it would indeed be remarkable if anyone recognized him.

The passengers were the first to leave the plane, and were ferried by an airport bus to the main terminal. A smart transit van then came out to collect the crew, who left as a group and sheltered Hamid by making sure that he was surrounded at all times. Hamid became more and more nervous with each yard the van travelled toward the terminal.

The security guard showed no particular interest in the air crew as they entered the building, and they were left to find themselves seats on wooden benches in the white-walled hall. The only decoration was a massive portrait of Saddam Hussein in full uniform carrying a Kalashnikov rifle. Hamid couldn't bring himself to look at the picture of his "good and close friend."

Another crew was also sitting around waiting to board their aircraft, but Hamid was too frightened to start up a conversation with any of them.

"They're French," he was informed by the senior flight attendant. "I'm about to find out if my night classes were worth all the expense." She took the spare place next to the captain of the French aircraft, and tried a simple opening question.

The French captain was telling her that they were bound for Singapore via New Delhi, when Hamid saw him: Saad al-Takriti, once a member of Saddam's personal guard, marched into the hall. From the insignia on his shoulder, he now appeared to be in charge of airport security.

Hamid prayed that he wouldn't look in his direction. Al-Takriti sauntered through the room, glancing at the French and American crews, his eyes lingering on the stewardesses' black-stockinged legs.

The captain touched Hamid on the shoulder, and he nearly leaped out of his skin.

"It's okay, it's okay. I just thought you'd like to know that the chief engineer is on his way out to the aircraft, so it shouldn't be too long now."

Hamid looked beyond the Air France plane, and watched a van come to a halt under the starboard wing of the Pan Am aircraft. A man in blue overalls stepped out of the vehicle and onto the little crane.

Hamid stood up to take a closer look, and as he did so Saad al-Takriti walked back into the hall. He came to a sudden halt, and the two men stared briefly at each other, before Hamid quickly resumed his place next to the captain. Al-Takriti disappeared into a side room marked Do Not Enter.

"I think he's spotted me," said Hamid. The makeup started to run down onto his lips.

The captain leaned across to his chief flight attendant and interrupted her parley with the French captain. She listened to her boss's instructions and then tried a tougher question on the Frenchman.

Saad al-Takriti marched back out of the office and began striding toward the American captain. Hamid thought he would surely faint.

Without even glancing at Hamid, al-Takriti barked, "Captain, I require you to show me your manifest, the number of crew you are carrying, and their passports."

"My copilot has all the passports," the captain replied. "I'll see you get them."

"Thank you," said al-Takriti. "When you have collected them, you will bring them to my office so that I can check each one. Meanwhile, please ask your crew to remain here. They are not, under any circumstances, to leave the building without my permission."

The captain rose from his place, walked slowly over to the copilot, and asked for the passports. Then he issued an order which took him by surprise. The captain took the passports into the security office just as a bus drew up outside the transit area to take the French crew back to their plane.

Saad al-Takriti placed the fourteen passports in front of him on his desk. He seemed to take pleasure in checking each one of them slowly. When he had finished the task, he announced in mock surprise, "I do believe, Captain, that I counted fifteen crew wearing Pan Am uniforms."

"You must have been mistaken," said the captain. "There are only fourteen of us."

"Then I will have to make a more detailed check, won't I, captain? Please return these documents to their rightful owners. Should there happen to be anyone not in possession of a passport, they will naturally have to report to me."

"But that is against international regulations," said the captain, "as I'm sure you know. We are in transit and therefore, under UN Resolution 238, not legally in your country."

"Save your breath, captain. We have no use for UN resolutions in Iraq. And, as you correctly point out, as far as we are concerned, you are not legally even in our country."

The captain realized he was wasting his time, and could bluff no longer. He gathered up the passports as slowly as he could and allowed al-Takriti to lead him back into the hall. As they entered the room the Pan Am crew members who were scattered around the benches suddenly rose from their places and began walking around, continually changing direction, while at the same time talking at the top of their voices.

"Tell them to sit down," hissed al-Takriti, as the crew zigzagged backward and forward across the hall.

"What's that you're saying?" asked the captain, cupping his ear.

"Tell them to sit down!" shouted al-Takriti.

The captain gave a halfhearted order, and within a few moments everyone was seated. But they still continued talking at the top of their voices.

"And tell them to shut up!"

The captain moved slowly around the room, asking his crew one by one to lower their voices.

Al-Takriti's eyes raked the benches of the transit hall, as the captain glanced out onto the tarmac and watched the French aircraft taxiing toward the far runway.

Al-Takriti began counting, and was annoyed to discover that there were only fourteen Pan Am crew members in the hall. He stared angrily around the room, and quickly checked once again.

"All fourteen seem to be present," said the captain after he had finished handing back the passports to his crew.

"Where is the man who was sitting next to you?" al-Takriti demanded, jabbing a finger at the captain.

"You mean my first officer?"

"No. The one who looked like an Arab."

"There are no Arabs on my crew," the captain assured him.

Al-Takriti strode over to the senior flight attendant. "He was sitting next to you. His upper lip had makeup on it that was beginning to run."

"The captain of the French plane was sitting next to me," the senior flight attendant said. She immediately realized her mistake.

Saad al-Takriti turned and looked out of the window to see the Air France plane at the end of the runway preparing for takeoff. He jabbed a button on his hand phone as the thrust of the jet engines started up, and barked out some orders in his native tongue. The captain didn't need to speak Arabic to get the gist of what he was saying.

By now the American crew were all staring at the French aircraft, willing it to move, while al-Takriti's voice was rising with every word he uttered.

The Air France 747 eased forward and slowly began to gather momentum. Saad al-Takriti cursed loudly, then ran out of the building and jumped into a waiting jeep. He pointed toward the plane and ordered the driver to chase after it. The jeep shot off, accelerating as it wove its way in and out of the parked aircraft. By the time it reached the runway it must have been doing ninety miles an hour, and for the next hundred yards it sped along parallel to the French aircraft, with al-Takriti standing on the front seat, clinging onto the windshield, and waving his fist at the cockpit.

The French captain acknowledged him with a crisp salute, and as the 747's wheels lifted off, a loud cheer went up in the transit lounge.

The American captain smiled and turned to his chief flight attendant. "That only proves my theory that the French will go to any lengths to get an extra passenger."

Hamid Zebari landed in New Delhi six hours later and immediately phoned his wife to let her know what had happened. Early the next morning Pan Am flew him back to New York—first class. When Hamid emerged from the airport terminal, his wife jumped out of the car and threw her arms around him.

Nadim wound the window down and declared, "You were wrong, Papa. Two weeks turn out to be fifteen days." Hamid grinned at his son, but his daughter burst into tears, and not because their car had come to a sudden halt. It was just that she was horrified to see her mother hugging a strange man.

CHUNNEL
VISION

WHENEVER I'M IN NEW YORK, I always try to have dinner with an old friend of mine called Duncan McPherson. We are opposites, and so naturally we attract. In fact, Duncan and I have only one thing in common: We are both writers. But even then there's a difference, because Duncan specializes in screenplays, which he writes in the intervals between his occasional articles for *Newsweek* and *The New Yorker*, whereas I prefer novels and short stories.

One of the other differences between us is the fact that I have been married to the same woman for twenty-eight years, while Duncan seems to have a different girlfriend every time I visit New York—not bad going, considering that I average at least a couple of trips a year. The girls are always attractive, lively, and bright, and there are various levels of intensity—depending on what stage the relationship is at. In the past I've been around at the beginning (very physical) and in the middle (starting to cool off), but this trip was to be the first time I experienced an ending.

I phoned Duncan from my hotel on Fifth Avenue to let him know I was in town to promote my new novel, and he immediately asked me over for dinner the following evening. I assumed, as in the past, that it would be at his apartment. Another opposite: Unlike me, he's a quite superlative cook.

"I can't wait to see you," he said. "I've come up with an idea for a novel at last, and I want to try the plot out on you."

"Delighted," I replied. "Look forward to hearing all about it tomorrow night. And may I ask . . ." I hesitated.

"Christabel," he said.

"Christabel," I repeated, trying to recall if I had ever met her.

"But there's no need for you to remember anything about her," he added. "Because she's about to be given the heave-ho, to use one of your English expressions. I've just met a new one—Karen. She's absolutely sensational. You'll adore her."

I didn't feel this was the appropriate moment to point out to Duncan that I had adored them all. I merely asked which one was likely to be joining us for dinner.

"Depends if Christabel has finished packing," Duncan replied. "If she has, it will be Karen. We haven't slept together yet, and I'd been planning on that for tomorrow night. But since you're in town, it will have to be postponed."

I laughed. "I could wait," I assured him. "After all, I'm here for at least a week."

"No, no. In any case, I must tell you about my idea for a novel. That's far more important. So why don't you come to my place tomorrow evening. Shall we say around seven-thirty?"

Before I left the hotel, I wrapped up a copy of my latest book, and wrote "Hope you enjoy it" on the outside.

Duncan lives in one of those apartment houses on Seventy-second and Park, and though I've been there many times, it always takes me a few minutes to locate the entrance to the building. And, like Duncan's girlfriends, the doorman seems to change with every trip.

The new doorman grunted when I gave my name, and directed me to the elevator on the far side of the hall. I slid the grille doors across and pressed the button for the fourteenth floor. It was one of those top floors that could not be described as a penthouse even by the most imaginative of estate agents.

I pulled back the doors and stepped out onto the landing, rehearsing the appropriate smiles for Christabel (good-bye) and Karen (hello). As I walked toward Duncan's front door I could hear raised voices—a very British expression, born of understatement; let's be frank and admit that they were screaming at each other at the tops of their lungs. I concluded that this had to be the end of Christabel, rather than the beginning of Karen.

I was already a few minutes late, so there was no turning

back. I pressed the doorbell, and to my relief the voices immediately fell silent. Duncan opened the door, and although his cheeks were scarlet with rage, he still managed a casual grin. Which reminds me that I forgot to tell you about a few more opposites—the damn man has a mop of boyish dark curly hair, the rugged features of his Irish ancestors, and the build of a champion tennis player.

"Come on in," he said. "This is Christabel, by the way—if you hadn't already guessed."

I'm not by nature a man who likes other people's castoffs, but I'm bound to confess I would have been happy to make Christabel the exception. She had an oval face, deep blue eyes, and an angelic smile. She was also graced with that fine fair hair that only the Nordic races are born with, and the type of figure that diet advertisements make their profits out of. She wore a cashmere sweater and tapered white jeans that left little to the imagination.

Christabel shook me by the hand, and apologized for looking a little scruffy. "I've been packing all afternoon," she explained.

The proof of her labors was there for all to see—three large suitcases and two cardboard boxes full of books standing by the door. On the top of one of the boxes lay a copy of a Dorothy L. Sayers murder mystery with a torn red cover.

I was becoming acutely aware that I couldn't have chosen a worse evening for a reunion with my old friend. "I'm afraid we're going to have to eat out for a change," Duncan said. "It's been—" he paused "—a busy day. I haven't had a chance to visit the local store. Good thing, actually," he added. "It'll give me more time to take you through the plot of my novel."

"Congratulations," Christabel said.

I turned to face her.

"*Your* novel," she said. "Number one on the *New York Times* bestseller list, isn't it?"

"Yes, congratulations," said Duncan. "I haven't gotten around to reading it yet, so don't tell me anything about it. It wasn't on sale in Bosnia," he added with a laugh.

I handed him my little gift.

"Thank you," he said, and placed it on the hall table. "I'll look forward to it."

"I've read it," said Christabel.

Duncan bit his lip. "Let's go," he said, and was about to turn and say good-bye to Christabel when she asked me, "Would you mind if I joined you? I'm starving, and as Duncan said, there's absolutely nothing in the fridge."

I could see that Duncan was about to protest, but by then Christabel had passed him, and was already in the corridor and heading for the elevator.

"We can walk to the restaurant," Duncan said as we trundled down to the ground floor. "It's only Californians who need a car to take them one block."

As we strolled west on Seventy-second Street, Duncan told me that he had chosen a fancy new French restaurant to take me to.

I began to protest, not just because I've never really cared for ornate French food, but I was also aware of Duncan's unpredictable pecuniary circumstances. Sometimes he was flush with money, at other times stone broke. I just hoped that he'd had an advance on the novel.

"No, like you, I normally wouldn't bother," he said. "But it's just opened, and the *New York Times* gave it a rave review. In any case, whenever I'm in London, you always entertain me 'right royally,'" he added, in what he imagined was an English accent.

It was one of those cool evenings that make walking in New York so pleasant, and I enjoyed the stroll, as Duncan began to tell me about his recent trip to Bosnia.

"You were lucky to catch me in New York," he was saying. "I've just gotten back after being holed up in the damned place for three months."

"Yes, I know. I read your article in *Newsweek* on the plane coming over," I said, and went on to tell him how fascinated I had been by his evidence that a group of UN soldiers had set up their own underground network, and felt no scruples about operating an illegal black market in whatever country they were stationed.

"Yes, that's caused quite a stir at the UN," said Duncan. "The *New York Times* and the *Washington Post* have both followed the

JEFFREY ARCHER

story up with features on the main culprits—but without bothering to give me any credit for the original research, of course."

I turned around to see if Christabel was still with us. She seemed to be deep in thought, and was lagging a few paces behind. I smiled a smile that I hoped said "I think Duncan's a fool and you're fantastic," but I received no response.

After a few more yards I spotted a red-and-gold awning flapping in the breeze outside something called Le Manoir. My heart sank. I've always preferred simple food, and have long considered pretentious French cuisine to be one of the major cons of the eighties, and one that should have been passé, if not part of culinary history, by the nineties.

Duncan led us down a short crazy-paving path through a heavy oak door and into a brightly lit restaurant. One look around the large, overdecorated room and my worst fears were confirmed. The maître d' stepped forward and said, "Good evening, monsieur."

"Good evening," replied Duncan. "I have a table reserved in the name of McPherson."

The maître checked down a long list of reservations. "Ah, yes, a table for two." Christabel pouted, but looked no less beautiful.

"Can we make it three?" my host asked rather halfheartedly.

"Of course, sir. Allow me to show you to your table."

We were guided through a crowded room to a little alcove in the corner which had only been set for two.

One look at the tablecloth, the massive flowered plates with "Le Manoir" painted in crimson all over them, and the arrangement of lilies on the center of the table made me feel even more guilty about what I had let Duncan in for. A waiter dressed in a white open-neck shirt, black trousers, and black vest with "Le Manoir" embroidered in red on the breast pocket hurriedly supplied Christabel with a chair, while another deftly laid a place for her.

A third waiter appeared at Duncan's side and inquired if we would care for an apéritif. Christabel smiled sweetly and asked if she might have a glass of champagne. I requested some Evian water, and Duncan nodded that he would have the same.

For the next few minutes, while we waited for the menus to appear, we continued to discuss Duncan's trip to Bosnia, and the contrast between scraping one's food out of a billycan in a cold dugout accompanied by the sound of bullets, and dining off china plates in a warm restaurant, with a string quartet playing Schubert in the background.

Another waiter appeared at Duncan's side and handed us three pink menus the size of small posters. As I glanced down the list of dishes, Christabel whispered something to the waiter, who nodded and slipped quietly away.

I began to study the menu more carefully, unhappy to discover that this was one of those restaurants that allows only the host to have the bill of fare with the prices attached. I was trying to work out which would be the cheapest dishes, when another glass of champagne was placed at Christabel's side.

I decided that the clear soup was likely to be the least expensive starter, and that it would also help my feeble efforts to lose weight. The main courses had me more perplexed, and with my limited knowledge of French I finally settled on duck, as I couldn't find any sign of *"poulet."*

When the waiter returned moments later, he immediately spotted Christabel's empty glass, and asked, "Would you care for another glass of champagne, madame?"

"Yes, please," she replied sweetly, as the maître d' arrived to take our order. But first we had to suffer an ordeal that nowadays can be expected at every French restaurant in the world.

"Today our specialties are," he began, in an accent that would not have impressed central casting, "for hors d'oeuvres *gelée de saumon sauvage et caviar impérial en aigre doux,* which is wild salmon slivers and imperial caviar in a delicate jelly with sour cream and zucchini drizzled with dill vinegar. Also we have *Cuisses de grenouilles . . . la purée d'herbes . . . soupe, fricassée de chanterelles et racines de persil,* which are pan-fried frogs' legs in a parsley purée, fricassee of chanterelles and parsley roots. For the main course we have *escalope de turbot,* which is a poached fillet of turbot on a watercress purée, lemon sabayon, and a Gewürztraminer sauce. And, of course, everything that is on the menu can be recommended."

I felt full even before he had finished the descriptions.

Christabel appeared to be studying the menu with due diligence. She pointed to one of the dishes, and the maître smiled approvingly.

Duncan leaned across and asked if I had selected anything yet.

"Consommé and the duck will suit me just fine," I said without hesitation.

"Thank you, sir," said the maître. "How would you like the duck? Crispy, or perhaps a little underdone?"

"Crispy," I replied, to his evident disapproval.

"And monsieur?" he asked, turning to Duncan.

"Caesar salad and a rare steak."

The maître d' retrieved the menus and was turning to go as Duncan said, "Now, let me tell you all about my idea for a novel."

"Would you care to order some wine, sir?" asked another waiter, who was carrying a large red leather book with golden grapes embossed on its cover.

"Should I do that for you?" suggested Christabel. "Then there'll be no need to interrupt your story."

Duncan nodded his agreement, and the waiter handed the wine list over to Christabel. She opened the red leather cover with as much eagerness as if she was about to begin a bestselling novel.

"You may be surprised," Duncan was saying, "that my book is set in Britain. Let me start by explaining that the timing for its publication is absolutely vital. As you know, a British and French consortium is currently building a tunnel between Folkestone and Sangatte, which is scheduled to be opened by Queen Elizabeth on May 6, 1994. In fact, *Chunnel* will be the title of my book."

I was horrified. Another glass of champagne was placed in front of Christabel.

"The story begins in four separate locations, with four different sets of characters. Although they are all from diverse age groups, social backgrounds, and countries, they have one thing in common: they have all booked on the first passenger train to travel from London to Paris via the Channel tunnel."

I felt a sudden pang of guilt and wondered if I should say something, but at this point a waiter returned with a bottle of white wine, the label of which Christabel studied intently. She nodded, and the sommelier extracted the cork and poured a little into her empty glass. A sip brought the smile back to her lips. The waiter then filled our glasses.

Duncan continued: "There will be an American family— mother, father, two teenage children—on their first visit to En-gland; a young English couple who have just gotten married that morning and are about to begin their honeymoon; a Greek self-made millionaire and his French wife, who booked their tickets a year before, but are now considering a divorce; and three students."

Duncan paused as a Caesar salad was placed in front of him and a second waiter presented me with a bowl of consommé. I glanced at the dish Christabel had chosen. A plate of thinly cut smoked gravlax with a blob of caviar in the center. She was hap-pily squeezing half a lemon, protected by muslin, all over it.

"Now," said Duncan, "in the first chapter it's important that the reader doesn't realize that the students are connected in any way, because that later becomes central to the plot. We pick up all four groups in the second chapter as they're preparing for the journey. The reader discovers their motivations for wanting to be on the train, and I build a little on the back-ground of each of the characters involved."

"What period of time will the plot cover?" I asked anxiously, between spoonfuls of consommé.

"Probably three days," replied Duncan. "The day before the journey, the day of the journey, and the day after. But I'm still not certain—by the final draft it might all happen on the same day."

Christabel grabbed the wine bottle from the ice bucket and refilled her glass before the wine waiter had a chance to assist her.

"Around chapter three," continued Duncan, "we find the

various groups arriving at Waterloo Station to board 'le shuttle.' The Greek millionaire and his French wife will be shown to their first-class seats by a black crew member, while the others are directed to second class. Once they are all on board, some sort of ceremony to commemorate the inauguration of the tunnel will take place on the platform. Big band, fireworks, cutting of tape by royalty, etc. That should prove quite adequate to cover another chapter at least."

While I was visualizing the scene and sipping my soup—the restaurant may have been pretentious, but the food was excellent—the wine waiter filled my glass and then Duncan's. I don't normally care for white wine, but I had to admit that this one was quite exceptional.

Duncan paused to eat, and I turned my attention to Christabel, who was being served a second dollop of caviar that appeared even bigger than the first.

"Chapter five," said Duncan, "opens as the train moves out of the station. Now the real action begins. The American family are enjoying every moment. The young bride and groom make love in the rest room. The millionaire is having another row with his wife about her continual extravagance, and the three students have met up for the first time at the bar. By now you should begin to suspect that they're not ordinary students, and that they may have known each other before they got on the train." Duncan smiled and continued with his salad. I frowned.

Christabel winked at me, to show she knew exactly what was going on. I felt guilty at being made a part of her conspiracy, and wanted to tell Duncan what she was up to.

"It's certainly a strong plot," I ventured as the wine waiter filled our glasses for a third time and, having managed to empty the bottle, looked toward Madame. She nodded sweetly.

"Have you started on the research yet?" I asked.

"Yes. Research is going to be the key to this project, and I'm well into it already," said Duncan. "I wrote to Sir Alastair Morton, the Chairman of Eurotunnel, on *Newsweek* letterhead, and his office sent me back a caseload of material. I can tell you the length of the rolling stock, the number of carriages, the diameter of the wheels, why the train can go faster on the French side than the British, even why it's necessary for them to have a different-gauge track on either side of the Channel—"

The pop of a cork startled me, and the wine waiter began pouring from a second bottle. Should I tell him now?

"During chapter six the plot begins to unfold," said Duncan, warming to his theme, as one of the waiters whipped away the empty plates and another brushed a few breadcrumbs off the tablecloth into a little silver scoop. "The trick is to keep the reader interested in all four groups at the same time."

I nodded.

"Now we come to the point in the story when the reader discovers that the students are not really students, but terrorists who plan to hijack the train."

Three dishes topped by domed silver salvers were placed in front of us. On a nod from the maître d', all three domes were lifted in unison by the waiters. It would be churlish of me not to admit that the food looked quite magnificent. I turned to see what Christabel had selected: truffles with foie gras. They reminded me of a Miró painting, until she quickly smudged the canvas.

"What do you think the terrorists' motive for hijacking the train should be?" Duncan asked.

This was surely the moment to tell him—but once again I funked it. I tried to remember what point in the story we had reached. "That would depend on whether you eventually wanted them to escape," I suggested. "Which might prove quite difficult, if they're stuck in the middle of a tunnel, with a police force waiting for them at either end." The wine waiter presented Christabel with the bottle of Cheval Blanc she had chosen. After no more than a sniff of the cork she indicated that it was acceptable.

"I don't think they should be interested in financial reward," said Duncan. "They ought to be IRA, Islamic fundamentalists, Basque separatists, or whatever the latest terrorist group catching the headlines happens to be."

I sipped the wine. It was like velvet. I had only tasted such a vintage once before, in the home of a friend who possessed a cellar of old wine put down with new money. It was a taste that had remained etched in my memory.

"In chapter seven I've come up against a block," continued Duncan, intent on his theme. "One of the terrorists must somehow come into contact with the newly married couple, or at least with the bridegroom." He paused. "I should have told you earlier that in the character building at the beginning of the book, one of the students turns out to be a loner, while the other two, a man and a woman, have been living together for some time." He began digging into his steak. "It's how I bring the loner and the bridegroom together that worries me. Any ideas?"

"That shouldn't be too hard," I said, "what with restaurant cars, snack bars, carriages, a corridor, not to mention a black crew member, railway staff, and rest rooms."

"Yes, but it must appear natural," Duncan said, sounding as if he were in deep thought.

My heart sank as I noticed Christabel's empty plate being whisked away, despite the fact that Duncan and I had hardly begun our main courses.

"The chapter ends with the train suddenly coming to a halt about halfway through the tunnel," said Duncan, staring into the distance.

"But how? And why?" I asked.

"That's the whole point. It's a false alarm. Quite innocent. The youngest child of the American family—his name's Ben—pulls the communication cord while he's sitting on the lavatory. It's such a hi-tech lavatory that he mistakes it for the chain."

I was considering if this was plausible when a breast of quail on fondant potatoes with a garnish of smoked bacon was placed in front of Christabel. She wasted no time in attacking the fowl.

Duncan paused to take a sip of wine. Now, I felt, I had to let him know, but before I had a chance to say anything he was off again. "Right," he said. "Chapter eight. The train has come to a halt several miles inside the tunnel, but not quite halfway."

"Is that significant?" I asked feebly.

"Sure is," said Duncan. "The French and British have agreed the exact point inside the tunnel where French jurisdiction begins and British ends. As you'll discover, this becomes relevant later in the plot."

The waiter began moving round the table, refilling our glasses once again with claret. I placed a hand over mine—not because the wine wasn't pure nectar, but simply because I didn't wish to give Christabel the opportunity to order another bottle. She made no attempt to exercise the same restraint, but drank her wine in generous gulps, while toying with her quail. Duncan continued with his story.

"So, the holdup," said Duncan, "turns out to be nothing more than a diversion, and it's sorted out fairly quickly. Child in tears, family apologizes, explanation given by the guard over the train's intercom, which relieves any anxieties the passengers might have had. A few minutes later the train starts up again, and this time it does cross the halfway point."

Three waiters removed our empty plates. Christabel touched the side of her lips with a napkin, and gave me a huge grin.

"So then what happens?" I asked, avoiding her eye.

"When the train stopped, the terrorists were afraid that there might be a rival group on board, with the same purpose as them. But as soon as they find out what has actually happened, they take advantage of the commotion caused by young Ben to get themselves into the cabin next to the driver's."

"Would you care for anything from the dessert trolley, madame?" the maître d' asked Christabel. I looked on aghast as she was helped to what looked like a large spoonful of everything on offer.

"It's gripping, isn't it?" said Duncan, misunderstanding my expression for one of deep concern for those on the train. "But there's still more to come."

"Monsieur?"

"I'm full, thank you," I told the maître. "Perhaps a coffee later."

"No, nothing, thank you," said Duncan, trying not to lose his thread. "By the start of chapter nine the terrorists have got themselves into the driver's cabin. At gunpoint they force the *chef de train* and his co-driver to bring the engine to a halt for a second time. But what they don't realize is that they are now on French territory. The passengers are told by the loner over the train's intercom that this time it's not a false alarm, but the train has been taken over by whichever gang I settle on, and is going to be blown up in fifteen minutes. He tells them to get themselves off the train, into the tunnel, and as far away as they possibly can before the explosion. Naturally, some of the passengers begin to panic. Several of them leap out into the dimly lit tunnel. Many are looking frantically for their husbands, wives, children, whatever, while others begin running toward the British or French side, according to their nationality."

I became distracted when the maître d' began wheeling yet another trolley toward our table. He paused, bowed to Christabel, and then lit a small burner. He poured some brandy into a shallow copper-bottomed pan and set about preparing crêpes suzette.

"This is the point in the story, probably chapter ten, where the father of the American family decides to remain on the train," said Duncan, becoming more excited than ever. "He tells the rest of his tribe to jump off and get the hell out of it. The only other passengers who stay on board are the millionaire, his wife, and the young newly married man. All will have strong personal reasons for wanting to remain behind, which will have been set up earlier in the plot."

The maître d' struck a match and set light to the crêpes. A blue flame licked around the pan and shot into the air. He scooped his *pièce de résistance* onto a warm platter in one movement, and placed it in front of Christabel.

I feared we had now passed the point at which I could tell Duncan the truth.

"Right, now I have three terrorists in the cab with the chef de train. They've killed the co-driver, and there are just four passengers still left on the train, plus the black ticket collector—who may turn out to be SAS in disguise, I haven't decided yet."

"Coffee, madame?" the maître d' asked when Duncan paused for a moment.

"Irish," said Christabel.

"Regular, please," I said.

"Decaf for me," said Duncan.

"Any liqueurs or cigars?"

Only Christabel reacted.

"So, at the start of chapter eleven the terrorists open negotiations with the British police. But they say they can't deal with them because the train is no longer under their jurisdiction. This throws the terrorists completely, because none of them speaks French, and in any case their quarrel is with the British government. One of them searches the train for someone who can speak French, and comes across the Greek millionaire's wife.

"Meanwhile, the police on either side of the Channel stop all the trains going in either direction. So, our train is now stranded in the tunnel on its own—there would normally be twenty trains traveling in either direction between London and Paris at any one time." He paused to sip his coffee.

"Is that so?" I asked, knowing the answer perfectly well.

"It certainly is," Duncan said. "I've done my research thoroughly."

A glass of deep red port was being poured for Christabel. I glanced at the label: Taylor's 55. This was something I had never had the privilege of tasting. Christabel indicated that the bottle should be left on the table. The waiter nodded, and Christabel immediately poured me a glass, without asking if I wanted it. Meanwhile, the maître clipped a cigar for Duncan that he hadn't requested.

"In chapter twelve we discover the terrorists' purpose," continued Duncan. "Namely, blowing up the train as a publicity stunt, guaranteed to get their cause onto every front page in the world. But the passengers who have remained on the train, led by the American father, are planning a counteroffensive."

The maître lit a match and Duncan automatically picked up the cigar and put it in his mouth. It silenced him . . .

"The self-made millionaire might feel he's the natural leader," I suggested.

. . . but only for a moment. "He's a Greek. If I'm going to make any money out of this project, it's the American market I

285

have to aim for. And don't forget the film rights," Duncan said, jabbing the air with his cigar.

I couldn't fault his logic.

"Can I have the check?" Duncan asked as the maître d' passed by our table.

"Certainly, sir," he replied, not even breaking his stride.

"Now, my trouble is going to be the ending—" began Duncan as Christabel suddenly, if somewhat unsteadily, rose from her chair.

She turned to face me and said, "I'm afraid the time has come for me to leave. It's been a pleasure meeting you, although I have a feeling we won't be seeing each other again. I'd just like to say how much I enjoyed your latest novel. Such an original idea. It deserved to be number one."

I stood, kissed her hand, and thanked her, feeling more guilty than ever.

"Goodbye, Duncan," she said, turning to face her former lover, but he didn't even bother to look up. "Don't worry yourself," she added. "I'll be out of the apartment by the time you get back."

She proceeded to negotiate a rather wobbly route across the restaurant, eventually reaching the door that led out onto the street. The maître held it open for her and bowed low.

"I can't pretend I'm sorry to see her go," said Duncan, puffing away on his cigar. "Fantastic body, great between the sheets, but she's totally lacking in imagination."

The maître d' reappeared by Duncan's side, this time to place a small black leather folder in front of him.

"Well, the critics were certainly right about this place," I commented. Duncan nodded his agreement.

The maître bowed, but not quite as low as before.

"Now, my trouble, as I was trying to explain before Christabel decided to make her exit," continued Duncan, "is that I've done the outline, completed the research, but I still don't have an ending. Any ideas?" he asked, as a middle-aged woman rose from a nearby table and began walking determinedly toward us.

Duncan flicked open the leather cover, and stared in disbelief at the bill.

The woman came to a halt beside our table. "I just wanted to tell you how much I enjoyed your new book," she said in a loud voice.

Other diners turned around to see what was going on.

"Thank you," I said somewhat curtly, hoping to prevent her from adding to my discomfort.

Duncan's eyes were still fixed on the bill.

"And the ending," she said. "So clever! I would never have guessed how you were going to get the American family out of the tunnel alive . . . "

DOUGIE MORTIMER'S
RIGHT ARM

ROBERT HENRY KEFFORD III, known to his friends as Bob, was in bed with a girl called Helen when he first heard about Dougie Mortimer's right arm.

Bob was sorry to be leaving Cambridge. He had spent three glorious years at St. John's, and although he hadn't read as many books as he had done for his undergraduate degree at the University of Chicago, he had strived every bit as hard to come in head of the river.

It wasn't unusual for an American to win a rowing blue in the early 1970s, but to have stroked a victorious Cambridge eight for three years in a row was acknowledged as a first.

Bob's father, Robert Henry Kefford II, known to his friends as Robert, had traveled over to England to watch his son take part in all three races from Putney to Mortlake. After Bob had stroked Cambridge to victory for the third time, his father told him that he must not return to his native Illinois without having presented a memento to the University Boat Club that they would remember him by.

"And don't forget, my boy," declared Robert Henry Kefford II, "the gift must not be ostentatious. Better to show that you have made an effort to present them with an object of historic value than give them something that obviously cost a great deal of money. The British appreciate that sort of thing."

Bob spent many hours pondering his father's words, but completely failed to come up with any worthwhile ideas. After all, the Cambridge University Boat Club had more silver cups and trophies than they could possibly display.

It was on a Sunday morning that Helen first mentioned the

name of Dougie Mortimer. She and Bob were lying in each other's arms, when she started poking his biceps.

"Is this some form of ancient British foreplay that I ought to know about?" Bob asked, placing his free arm around Helen's shoulder.

"Certainly not," Helen replied. "I was simply trying to discover if your biceps are as big as Dougie Mortimer's."

Since Bob had never known a girl who talked about another man while he was in bed with her, he was unable to think of an immediate response.

"And are they?" he eventually inquired, flexing his muscles.

"Hard to tell," Helen replied. "I've never actually touched Dougie's arm, only seen it at a distance."

"And where did you come across this magnificent specimen of manhood?"

"It hangs over the bar at my dad's local, in Hull."

"Doesn't Dougie Mortimer find that a little painful?" asked Bob, laughing.

"Doubt if he cares that much," said Helen. "After all, he's been dead for over sixty years."

"And his arm still hangs above a bar?" asked Bob in disbelief. "Hasn't it begun to smell a bit by now?"

This time it was Helen's turn to laugh. "No, you Yankee fool. It's a bronze cast of his arm. In those days, if you were in the university crew for three years in a row, they made a cast of your arm to hang in the clubhouse. Not to mention a card with your picture on it in every pack of Player's cigarettes. I've never seen *your* picture in a cigarette pack, come to think of it," said Helen as she pulled the sheet over his head.

"Did he row for Oxford or Cambridge?" asked Bob.

"No idea."

"So what's the name of this pub in Hull?"

"The King William," Helen replied, as Bob took his arm from around her shoulder.

"Is this American foreplay?" she asked after a few moments.

Later that morning, after Helen had left for Newnham, Bob began searching his shelves for a book with a blue cover. He dug out his much-thumbed *History of the Boat Race* and flicked through the index, to discover that there were seven Mortimers listed. Five had rowed for Oxford, two for Cambridge. He began to pray as he checked their initials. Mortimer, A. J. (Westminster and Wadham, Oxon.), Mortimer, C. K. (Uppingham and Oriel, Oxon.), Mortimer, D. J. T. (Harrow and St. Catharine's, Cantab.), Mortimer, E. L. (Oundle and Magdalen, Oxon.). Bob turned his attention to Mortimer, D. J. T., biography page 129, and flicked the pages backward until he reached the entry he sought. "Douglas John Townsend Mortimer (St. Catharine's), Cambridge 1907, –08, –09, stroke." He then read the short summary of Mortimer's rowing career.

> Dougie Mortimer stroked the Cambridge boat to victory in 1907, a feat which he repeated in 1908. But in 1909, when the experts considered Cambridge to have one of the finest crews for years, the light blues lost to an Oxford boat that was regarded as the rank outsider. Although many explanations were suggested by the press at the time, the result of the race remains a mystery to this day. Mortimer died in 1914.

Bob closed the book and returned it to the shelf, assuming that the great oarsman must have been killed in the First World War. He perched on the end of the bed, considering the information he now possessed. If he could bring Dougie Mortimer's right arm back to Cambridge and present it to the club at the annual Blues' Dinner, it would surely be a prize that met his father's demanding criterion.

He dressed quickly and went downstairs to the pay phone in the corridor. Once directory inquiries had given him the four numbers he required, he set about trying to remove the next obstacle.

The first calls he made were to the King William—or, to be precise, the King Williams, because the directory had supplied him with the numbers of three pubs in Hull that bore that name. When he was put through to the first, he asked, "Does Dougie Mortimer's right arm hang above your counter?" He couldn't quite make out every word of the broad northern accent that replied, but he was left in no doubt that it didn't.

The second call was answered by a girl who said, "Do you mean that thing that's nailed to the wall above the bar?"

"Yes, I guess that will be it," said Bob.

"Well then, this is the pub you're looking for."

After Bob had taken down the address and checked the pub's opening hours, he made a third call. "Yes, that's possible," he was told. "You can take the 3:17 to Peterborough, where you'll have to change and catch the 4:09 for Doncaster, then change again. You'll arrive in Hull at 6:32."

"What about the last train back?" asked Bob.

"That'd be the 8:52, change at Doncaster and Peterborough. You should be back in Cambridge just after midnight."

"Thank you," said Bob. He strolled off to his college for lunch and took a place at the large center table, but proved unusually poor company for those around him.

He boarded the train to Peterborough later that afternoon, still thinking about how he could possibly relieve the pub owners of their prize possession. At Peterborough he jumped out, walked across to a waiting train on platform three, and climbed aboard, still deep in thought. When his train pulled into Hull a couple of hours later he was no nearer to solving the problem. He asked the first taxi on the rank to take him to the King William.

"Market Place, Harold's Corner, or Percy Street?" asked the cabbie.

"Percy Street, please," replied Bob.

"They don't open until seven, lad," the cabbie told him once he had dropped Bob outside the front door.

Bob checked the time. Twenty minutes to kill. He walked down a side street at the back of the pub, and stopped to watch some young lads playing football. They were using the front walls of two houses on either side of the street as goals, and showed amazing accuracy in never hitting any of the windows. Bob wondered if the game would ever catch on in America.

He became so captivated by the youngsters' skill that they stopped to ask him if he wanted to join in. He said, "No thank you," confident that if he did play with them, he would be the one person who ended up breaking a window.

He arrived back outside the King William a few minutes after seven and strolled into the empty pub, hoping no one would pay much attention to him. But at six feet four inches, and dressed in a double-breasted blue blazer, gray flannels, a blue shirt and college tie, the three people behind the bar might well have wondered if he had dropped in from another planet. He stopped himself from looking above the bar, as a young blond barmaid stepped forward and asked him what he would like.

"A half a pint of your best bitter," Bob said, trying to sound like one of his English friends when they ordered a drink from the college buttery.

The landlord eyed Bob suspiciously as he took his half-pint glass over to a small round table in the corner and sat down quietly on a stool. He was pleased when two other men entered the pub, so that the landlord's attention was distracted.

Bob took a sip of the dark liquid and nearly choked. When he had recovered, he allowed his eyes to glance above the bar. He tried to hide his excitement when he saw the bronze cast of a massive arm embedded in a large piece of varnished wood. He thought the object both dreadful and inspiring at the same time. His eyes moved down to the bold lettering printed in gold beneath it:

D. J. T. MORTIMER
1907–08–09
(ST. CATHARINE'S, STROKE)

Bob kept his eye on the landlord as the pub began to fill up, but he soon became aware that it was his wife—everyone called her Nora—who was not only in charge, but who did most of the serving.

When he had finished his drink, he made his way over to her end of the bar.

"What can I do for you, young man?" Nora asked.

"I'll have another, thank you," said Bob.

"An American," she said, as she pulled the pump and began to refill his glass. "We don't get many of you lot up 'ere, at least not since the bases closed." She placed his half pint on the counter in front of him. "So, what brings you to 'ull?"

"You do," Bob replied, ignoring his drink.

Nora looked suspiciously at the stranger, who was young enough to be her son.

Bob smiled, "Or, to be more accurate, Dougie Mortimer does."

"Now I've figured you out," said Nora. "You phoned this morning, didn't you? My Christie told me. I should 'ave guessed."

Bob nodded. "How did the arm end up in Hull?" he asked.

"Now, that's a long story," said Nora. "It was my grandfather's, wasn't it. Born in Ely 'e was, and 'e used to spend his holidays fishin' the Cam. Said it was the only catch he managed that year, which I suppose is one better than sayin' it fell off the back of a lorry. Still, when 'e died a few years back, my father wanted to throw the bloody thing out with the rest of the rubbish, but I wouldn't 'ear of it, told 'im 'e should 'ang it in the pub, didn't I? I cleaned and polished it, it came up real nice, and then I 'ung it above the bar. Still, it's a long way for you to travel just to 'ave a look at that load of old cobblers."

Bob looked up and admired the arm once again. He held his breath. "I didn't come just to look."

"Then why did you come?" she asked.

"I came to buy."

"Get a move on, Nora," said the landlord. "Can't you see there are customers waitin' to be served?"

Nora swung around and said, "Just 'old your tongue, Cyril Barnsworth. This young man's come all the way up to 'ull just to see Dougie Mortimer's arm, and what's more, 'e wants to buy it." This caused a ripple of laughter from the regulars standing nearest to the bar, but when Nora didn't join in they quickly fell silent.

"Then it's been a wasted journey, 'asn't it?" said the landlord. "Because it's not for sale."

"It's not yours to sell," said Nora, placing her hands on her hips. "Mind you, lad, 'e's right," she said, turning back to face Bob. "I wouldn't part with it for a 'undred quid," said Nora. Several others in the room were beginning to show an interest in the proceedings.

"How about two hundred," said Bob quietly. This time Nora burst out laughing, but Bob didn't even smile.

When Nora had stopped laughing, she stared directly at the strange young man. "My God, 'e means it," she said.

"I certainly do," said Bob. "I would like to see the arm returned to its rightful home in Cambridge, and I'm willing to pay two hundred pounds for the privilege."

The landlord looked across at his wife, as if he couldn't believe what he was hearing. "We could buy that little second-hand car I've had my eye on," he said.

"Not to mention a summer 'oliday and a new overcoat for next winter," Nora added, staring at Bob as if she still needed to be convinced that he wasn't from another planet. Suddenly she thrust her hand over the counter and said, "You've got yourself a deal, young man."

Bob ended up having to supply several rounds of drinks for those customers who claimed to have been close personal friends of Nora's grandfather, even if some of them looked rather obviously too young. He also had to stay overnight in a local hotel, because Nora wouldn't part with her grandfather's "heirloom," as she now kept referring to it, until her bank manager had phoned Cambridge to check that Robert Henry Kefford III was good for two hundred pounds.

Bob clung to his treasure all the way back to Cambridge that Monday morning, and then lugged the heavy object from the station to his digs in the Grange Road, where he hid it under the bed. The following day he handed it over to a local furniture restorer, who promised to return the arm to its former glory in time for the night of the Blues' Dinner.

When, three weeks later, Bob was allowed to see the results of the restorer's efforts, he immediately felt confident that he now possessed a prize not only worthy of the CUBC but that also complied with his father's wishes. He resolved not to share his secret with anyone—not even Helen—until the night of the Blues' Dinner, although he did warn the puzzled president that he was going to make a presentation, and that he required two hooks, eighteen inches apart and eight feet from the floor, to be screwed into the wall beforehand.

The University Blues' Dinner is an annual event held in the Boat House overlooking the Cam. Any former or current rowing blue is eligible to attend, and Bob was delighted to find when he arrived that night that it was a near-record turnout. He placed the carefully wrapped brown paper parcel under his chair, and put his camera on the table in front of him.

Because it was his last Blues' Dinner before returning to the United States, Bob had been seated at the top table, between the honorary secretary and the current president of doats. Tom Adams, the honorary secretary, had gained his blue some twenty years before, and was recognized as the club's walking encyclopedia, because he could name not only everyone in the room but all the great oarsmen of the past.

Tom pointed out to Bob three Olympic medalists dotted around the room. "The oldest is sitting on the left of the president," he said. "Charles Forester. He rowed at number three for the club in 1908–9, so he must be over eighty."

"Can it be possible?" said Bob, recalling Forester's youthful picture on the clubhouse wall.

"Certainly can," said the Secretary. "And what's more, young man," he added, laughing, "you'll look like that one day too."

"What about the man at the far end of the table?" asked Bob. "He looks even older."

"He is," said the Secretary. "That's Sidney Fisk. He was boatman from 1912 to 1945, with only a break for the First World War. Took over from his uncle at short notice, if I remember correctly."

"So he would have known Dougie Mortimer," said Bob wistfully.

"Now, there's a great name from the past," said Adams. "Mortimer, D. J. T., 1907–8–9, St. Catharine's, stroke. Oh, yes, Fisk would certainly have known Mortimer, that's for sure. Come to think of it, Charles Forester must have been in the same boat as Mortimer when he was stroke."

During the meal Bob continued to quiz Adams about Dougie Mortimer, but he was unable to add a great deal to the entry in Bob's *History of the boat race*, other than to confirm that Cambridge's defeat in 1909 still remained a mystery, as the light blues demonstrably had the superior crew.

When the last course had been cleared away, the president rose to welcome his guests and to make a short speech. Bob enjoyed the parts he was able to hear above the noise made by the rowdy undergraduates, and even joined in the frenzy whenever Oxford was mentioned. The president ended with the words, "There will be a special presentation to the club this year, by our colonial stroke Bob Kefford, which I'm sure we're all going to appreciate."

When Bob rose from his place the cheering became even more raucous, but he spoke so softly that the noise quickly died away. He told his fellow members how he had come to discover, and later retrieve, Dougie Mortimer's right arm, leaving out only his exact location when he first learned of its whereabouts.

With a flourish, he unwrapped the parcel that had been secreted under his chair, and revealed the newly restored bronze cast. The assembled members rose to their feet and cheered. A smile of satisfaction came over Bob's face as he looked around, only wishing his father could have been present to witness their reaction.

As his eyes swept the room, Bob couldn't help noticing that the oldest blue present, Charles Forester, had remained seated, and was not even joining in the applause. Bob's gaze then settled on Sidney Fisk, the only other person who had not risen to his feet. The old boatman's lips remained fixed in a straight line, and his hands didn't move from his knees.

Bob forgot about the two old men when the president, assisted by Tom Adams, hung the bronze arm on the wall, placing it between a blade that had been pulled by one of the Olympic crew of 1908, and a zephyr hat worn by the only blue ever to row in a Cambridge boat that had beaten Oxford four years in a row. Bob began to take photographs of the ceremony, so that he would have a record to show his father that he had carried out his wishes.

When the hanging was over, many of the members and old blues surrounded Bob to thank and congratulate him, leaving him in no doubt that all the trouble he had taken to track down the arm had been worthwhile.

Bob was among the last to leave that night, because so many members had wanted to wish him good luck for the future. He was strolling along the footpath back to his digs, humming as he went, when he suddenly remembered that he had left his camera on the table. He decided to collect it in the morning, as he was sure that the clubhouse would be locked and deserted by now, but when he turned round to check, he saw a single light coming from the ground floor.

He turned and began walking back toward the clubhouse, still humming. When he was a few paces away, he glanced through the window and saw that there were two figures standing in the committee room. He strode over to take a closer look, and was surprised to see the elderly blue, Charles Forester, and Sidney Fisk, the retired boatman, trying to shift a heavy table. He would have gone in to assist them if Fisk hadn't suddenly pointed up toward Dougie Mortimer's arm. Bob remained motionless as he watched the two old men drag the table inch by inch nearer to the wall, until it was directly below the plaque.

Fisk picked up a chair and placed it against the wall, and Forester used it as a step to climb onto the table. Forester then bent down and took the arm of the older man, to help him up.

Once they were both safely on the table, they held a short conversation before reaching up to the bronze cast, easing it off its hooks, and slowly lowering it until it rested between their feet. Forester, with the help of the chair, stepped back down onto the floor, then turned round to assist his companion again.

Bob still didn't move, as the two old men carried Dougie

Mortimer's arm across the room and out of the boathouse. Having placed it on the ground outside the door, Forester returned to switch off the lights. When he stepped back outside into the cold night air, the boatman quickly padlocked the door.

Once again the two old men held a short conversation before lifting Bob's trophy up and stumbling off with it along the towpath. They had to stop, lower the arm to the ground, rest, and start again several times. Bob followed silently in their wake, using the broad-trunked trees to conceal himself, until the elderly pair suddenly turned and made their way down the bank toward the river. They came to a halt at the water's edge, and lowered their bounty into a small rowing boat.

The old blue untied the rope, and the two men pushed the boat slowly out into the river, until the water was lapping around the knees of their evening dress trousers. Neither seemed at all concerned about the fact that they were getting soaked. Forester managed to clamber up into the little boat quite quickly, but it took Fisk several minutes to join him. Once they were both aboard, Forester took his place at the oars, while the boatman remained in the bow, clutching Dougie Mortimer's arm.

Forester began to row steadily toward the middle of the river. His progress was slow, but his easy rhythm revealed that he had rowed many times before. When the two men calculated that they had reached the center of the Cam, at its deepest point, Forester stopped rowing and joined his companion in the bow. They picked up the bronze arm and, without ceremony, cast it over the side and into the river. Bob heard the splash and saw the boat rock dangerously from side to side. Fisk then took his turn at the oars; his progress back to the riverbank was even slower than Forester's. They eventually reached land, and both men stumbled out and shoved the boat up toward its mooring, the boatman finally securing the rope to a large ring.

Soaked and exhausted, their breath rising visibly in the clear night air, the two old men stood and faced each other. They shook hands like two business tycoons who had closed an important deal, before disappearing into the night.

Tom Adams called Bob the following morning to tell him something he already knew. In fact he had lain awake all night thinking of little else.

Bob listened to Adams's account of the break-in. "What's surprising is that they only took one thing." He paused. "Your arm—or rather, Dougie's arm. It's very strange, especially since someone had left an expensive camera on the top table."

"Is there anything I can do to help?" asked Bob.

"No, I don't think so, old boy," said Adams. "The local police are making enquiries, but my bet is that whoever stole the arm will probably be halfway across the county by now."

"I think you're right," said Bob. "While you're on the line, Mr. Adams, I wonder if I could ask you a question about the history of the club."

"I'll do my best," said Adams. "But you must remember that it's only a hobby for me, old chap."

"Do you by any chance know who is the oldest living Oxford rowing blue?" There was a long silence the other end of the line. "Are you still there?" Bob asked eventually.

"Yes. I was just trying to think if old Harold Deering is still alive. I can't remember seeing his obituary in *The Times*."

"Deering?" said Bob.

"Yes. Radley and Keble, 1909–10–11. He became a bishop, if I remember correctly, but I'm damned if I can recall where."

"Thank you," said Bob. "That's most helpful."

"I could be wrong," Adams pointed out. "After all, I don't read the obituary columns every day. And I'm a bit rusty when it comes to Oxford."

Bob thanked him once again before hanging up.

After a college lunch he didn't eat, Bob returned to his digs and rang the porter's lodge at Keble. He was answered by a curmudgeonly voice.

"Do you have any record of a Harold Deering, a former member of the college?" Bob asked.

"Deering . . . Deering . . . ," said the voice. "That's a new one on me. Let me see if he's in the college handbook." Another long pause, during which Bob really did begin to think he'd been cut off, until the voice said, "Good heavens, no wonder. It was just a bit before my time. 'Deering, Harold, 1909–11, BA 1911, MA 1916 (Theology). Became Bishop of Truro.' Is that the one?"

"Yes, that's the man," said Bob. "Do you by any chance have an address for him?"

"I do," said the voice. "The Right Reverendd Harold Deering, the Stone House, Mill Road, Tewkesbury, Gloucestershire."

"Thank you," said Bob. "You've been very helpful."

Bob spent the rest of the afternoon composing a letter to the former bishop, in the hope that the old blue might agree to see him.

He was surprised to receive a call in his rooms three days later from a Mrs. Elliot, who turned out to be Mr. Deering's daughter, with whom he was now living.

"The poor old chap can't see much beyond his nose these days," she explained, "so I had to read your letter aloud to him. But he'd be delighted to meet you, and wonders if you could call on him this Sunday at 11:30, after Matins—assuming that's not inconvenient for you."

"That's fine," said Bob. "Please tell your father to expect me around 11:30."

"It has to be in the morning," Mrs. Elliot went on to explain, "because, you see, he has a tendency to fall asleep after lunch. I'm sure you understand. By the way, I'll send directions to your college."

On the Sunday morning, Bob was up long before the sun rose, and started out on his journey to Tewkesbury in a car he had rented the previous day. He would have gone by train, but British Rail didn't seem willing to rise quite early enough for him to reach his destination on time. As he journeyed across the Cotswolds, he tried to remember to keep the car on the left, and couldn't help wondering how long it would be before the British started to build some highways with more than one lane.

He drove into Tewkesbury a few minutes after eleven, and thanks to Mrs. Elliot's clear directions, quickly found the Stone House. He parked the car outside a little wicket gate.

A woman had opened the door of the house even before Bob was halfway up the scrub-covered path. "It must be Mr. Kefford," she declared. "I'm Susan Elliot." Bob smiled and shook her hand. "I should warn you," Mrs. Elliot explained as she led him toward the front door, "that you'll have to speak up. Father's become rather deaf lately, and I'm afraid his memory isn't what it used to be. He can recall everything that happened to him at your age, but not even the most simple things that I told him yesterday. I've had to remind him what time you would be coming this morning," she said as they walked through the open door. "Three times."

"I'm sorry to have put you to so much trouble, Mrs. Elliot," said Bob.

"No trouble at all," said Mrs. Elliot as she led him down the corridor. "The truth is, my father's been rather excited by the thought of an American blue from Cambridge coming to visit him after all these years. He hasn't stopped talking about it for the past two days. He's also curious about why you wanted to see him in the first place," she added conspiratorially.

She led Bob into the drawing room, where he immediately came face to face with an old man seated in a leather wing chair, wrapped in a warm plaid dressing gown, and propped up on several cushions, his legs covered by a tartan blanket. Bob found it hard to believe that this frail figure had once been an Olympic oarsman.

"Is it him?" the old man asked in a loud voice.

"Yes, Father," Mrs Elliot replied, equally loudly. "It's Mr. Kefford. He's driven over from Cambridge especially to see you."

Bob walked forward and shook the old man's bony outstretched hand.

"Good of you to come all this way, Kefford," said the former bishop, pulling his blanket up a little higher.

"I appreciate your seeing me, sir," said Bob, as Mrs. Elliot directed him to a comfortable chair opposite her father.

"Would you care for a cup of tea, Kefford?"

"No, thank you, sir," said Bob. "I really don't want anything."

"As you wish," said the old man. "Now, I must warn you, Kefford, that my concentration span isn't quite what it used to be, so you'd better tell me straight away why you've come to see me."

Bob attempted to marshal his thoughts. "I'm doing a little research on a Cambridge blue who must have rowed around the same time as you, sir."

"What's his name?" asked Deering. "I can't remember them all, you know."

Bob looked at him, fearing that this was going to turn out to be a wasted journey.

"Mortimer. Dougie Mortimer," he said.

"D. J. T. Mortimer," the old man responded without hesitation. "Now, there's someone you couldn't easily forget. One of the finest strokes Cambridge ever produced—as Oxford found out, to their cost." The old man paused. "You're not a journalist, by any chance?"

"No, sir. It's just a personal whim. I wanted to find out one or two things about him before I return to America."

"Then I will certainly try to help if I can," said the old man in a piping voice.

"Thank you," said Bob. "I'd actually like to begin at the end, if I may, by asking if you knew the circumstances of his death."

There was no response for several moments. The old cleric's eyelids closed, and Bob began to wonder if he had fallen asleep.

"Not the sort of thing chaps talked about in my day," he eventually replied. "Especially with its being against the law at the time, don't you know."

"Against the law?" said Bob, puzzled.

"Suicide. A bit silly, when you think about it," the old priest continued, "even if it is a mortal sin. Because you can't put someone in jail who's already dead, now can you? Not that it was ever confirmed, you understand."

"Do you think it might have been connected with Cambridge losing the boat race in 1909, when they were such clear favorites?"

"It's possible, I suppose," said Deering, hesitating once again. "I must admit, the thought had crossed my mind. I took part in that race, as you may know." He paused again, breathing heavily. "Cambridge were the clear favorites, and we didn't give ourselves a chance. The result was never properly explained, I must admit. There were a lot of rumors doing the rounds at the time, but no proof—no proof, you understand."

"What wasn't proved?" asked Bob. There was another long silence, during which Bob began to fear that the old man might have thought he'd gone too far.

"My turn to ask you a few questions, Kefford," he said eventually.

"Of course, sir."

"My daughter tells me that you've stroked the winning boat for Cambridge three years in a row."

"That's correct, sir."

"Congratulations, my boy. But tell me: If you had wanted to lose one of those races, could you have done so, without the rest of the crew being aware of it?"

It was Bob's turn to ponder. He realized for the first time since he had entered the room that he shouldn't assume that a frail body necessarily indicates a frail mind.

"Yes, I guess so," he eventually said. "You could always change the stroke rate without warning, or even catch a crab and fall back as you took the Surrey bend. Heaven knows, there's always enough flotsam on the river to make it appear unavoidable." Bob looked the old man straight in the eye. "But it would never have crossed my mind that anyone might do so deliberately."

"Nor mine," said the priest, "had their cox not taken holy orders."

"I'm not sure I understand, sir," said Bob.

"No reason you should, young man. I find nowadays that I think in non sequiturs. I'll try to be less obscure. The cox of the 1909 Cambridge boat was a chap called Bertie Partridge. He went on to become a parish priest in some outpost called Chersfield in Rutland. Probably the only place that would have him," he chuckled. "But when I became bishop of Truro, he wrote and invited me to address his flock. It was such an arduous journey from Cornwall to Rutland in those days that I could easily have made my excuses, but like you, I wanted the mystery of the 1909 race solved, and I thought this might be my only chance."

Bob made no attempt to interrupt, fearing he might stop the old man's flow.

"Partridge was a bachelor, and bachelors get very lonely, don't you know. If you give them half a chance, they love to gossip. I stayed overnight, which gave him every chance. He told me, over a long dinner accompanied by a bottle of nonvintage wine, that it was well known that Mortimer had run up debts all over Cambridge. Not many undergraduates don't, you might say, but in Mortimer's case they far exceeded even his potential income. I think he rather hoped that his fame and popularity would stop his creditors from pressing their claims. Not unlike Disraeli when he was prime minister," he added with another chuckle.

"But in Mortimer's case one particular shopkeeper, who had absolutely no interest in rowing, and even less in undergraduates, threatened to bankrupt him the week before the 1909 boat race. A few days after the race had been lost, Mortimer seemed, without explanation, to have cleared all his obligations, and nothing more was heard of the matter."

Once again the old man paused as if in deep thought. Bob remained silent, still not wishing to distract him.

"The only other thing I can recall is that the bookies made a killing," Deering said without warning. "I know that to my personal cost, because my tutor lost a five-pound wager, and never let me forget that I had told him we didn't have a snowball's chance in hell. Mind you, I was always able to offer that as my excuse for not getting a first." He looked up and smiled at his visitor.

Bob sat on the edge of his seat, mesmerized by the old man's recollections.

"I'm grateful for your candor, sir," he said. "And you can be assured of my discretion."

"Thank you, Kefford," said the old man, now almost whispering. "I'm only too delighted to have been able to assist you. Is there anything else I can help you with?"

"No, thank you, sir," said Bob. "I think you've covered everything I needed to know."

Bob rose from his chair, and as he turned to thank Mrs. Elliot he noticed for the first time a bronze cast of an arm hanging on the far wall. Below it was printed in gold:

H. R. R. DEERING
1909–10–11
(KEBLE, BOW)

"You must have been a fine oarsman, sir."

"No, not really," said the old blue. "But I was lucky enough to be in the winning boat three years in a row, which wouldn't please a Cambridge man like yourself."

Bob laughed. "Perhaps one last question before I leave, sir."

"Of course, Kefford."

"Did they ever make a bronze of Dougie Mortimer's arm?"

"They most certainly did," replied the priest. "But it mysteriously disappeared from your boathouse in 1912. A few weeks later the boatman was fired without explanation—caused quite a stir at the time."

"Was it known why he was fired?" asked Bob.

"Partridge claimed that when the old boatman got drunk one night, he confessed to having dumped Mortimer's arm in the middle of the Cam." The old man paused, smiled, and added, "Best place for it, wouldn't you say, Kefford?"

Bob thought about the question for some time, wondering how his father would have reacted. He then replied simply, "Yes, sir. Best place for it."

CLEAN SWEEP
IGNATIUS

FEW SHOWED MUCH INTEREST when Ignatius Agarbi was appointed Nigeria's minister of finance. After all, the cynics pointed out, he was the seventeenth person to hold the office in seventeen years.

In Ignatius's first major policy statement to Parliament he promised to end graft and corruption in public life and warned the electorate that no one holding an official position could feel safe unless he led a blameless life. He ended his maiden speech with the words, "I intend to clear out Nigeria's Augean stables."

Such was the impact of the minister's speech that it failed to get a mention in the *Lagos Daily Times*. Perhaps the editor considered that, since the paper had covered the speeches of the previous sixteen ministers *in extenso*, his readers might feel they had heard it all before.

Ignatius, however, was not disheartened by the lack of confidence shown in him, and set about his new task with vigor and determination. Within days of his appointment he had caused a minor official at the Ministry of Trade to be jailed for falsifying documents relating to the import of grain. The next to feel the bristles of Ignatius's new broom was a leading Lebanese financier, who was deported without trial for breach of the exchange control regulations. A month later came an event which even Ignatius considered a personal coup: the arrest of the inspector general of police for accepting bribes—a perk the citizens of Lagos had in the past considered went with the job. When four months later the police chief was sentenced to eighteen months in jail, the new finance minister finally made the front page of the *Lagos Daily Times*. An editorial on the center page dubbed him "Clean Sweep Ignatius," the new broom every guilty man feared. Ignatius's reputation as Mr. Clean continued to grow as arrest followed arrest, and unfounded rumors began circulating in the capital that even General Otobi, the head of state, was under investigation by his own finance minister.

Ignatius alone now checked, vetted, and authorized all foreign contracts worth over one hundred million dollars. And although every decision he made was meticulously scrutinized by his enemies, not a breath of scandal ever became associated with his name.

When Ignatius began his second year of office as minister of finance, even the cynics began to acknowledge his achievements. It was about this time that General Otobi felt confident enough to call him in for an unscheduled consultation.

The head of state welcomed the minister to Dodan Barracks and ushered him to a comfortable chair in his study overlooking the parade ground.

"Ignatius, I have just finished going over the latest budget report, and I am alarmed by your conclusion that the Exchequer is still losing millions of dollars each year in bribes paid to go-betweens by foreign companies. Have you any idea into whose pockets this money is falling? That's what I want to know."

Ignatius sat bolt upright, his eyes never leaving the head of state.

"I suspect a great percentage of the money is ending up in private Swiss bank accounts, but I am at present unable to prove it."

"Then I will give you whatever added authority you require to do so," said General Otobi. "You can use any means you consider necessary to ferret out these villains. Start by investigating every member of my cabinet, past and present. And show no fear or favor in your endeavors, no matter what their rank or connections."

"For such a task to have any chance of success I would need a special letter of authority signed by you, General."

"Then it will be on your desk by six o'clock this evening," said the head of state.

"And the rank of ambassador plenipotentiary whenever I travel abroad."

"Granted."

"Thank you," said Ignatius, rising from his chair on the assumption that the audience was over.

"You may also need this," said the General as they walked toward the door. The Head of State handed Ignatius a small automatic pistol. "Because I suspect by now that you have almost as many enemies as I."

Ignatius took the pistol from the soldier awkwardly, put it in his pocket, and mumbled his thanks.

Not another word passed between the two men. Ignatius left his leader and was driven back to his ministry.

Without the knowledge of the governor of the Central Bank of Nigeria, and unhindered by any senior civil servants, Ignatius enthusiastically set about his new task. He researched alone at night, and by day discussed his findings with no one. Three months later he was ready to pounce.

The minister selected the month of August to make an unscheduled visit abroad, as it was the time when most Nigerians went on vacation, and his absence would therefore not be worthy of comment.

He asked his permanent secretary to book him, his wife, and their two children on a flight to Orlando, and to be certain that the tickets were charged to his personal account.

On their arrival in Florida, the family checked into the local Marriott Hotel. Ignatius then informed his wife, without warning or explanation, that he would be spending a few days in New York on business before rejoining them for the rest of the vacation. The following morning he left his family to the mysteries of Disney World while he took a flight to New York. It was a short taxi ride from La Guardia to Kennedy, where, after a change of clothes and the purchase of a return tourist ticket for cash, he boarded a Swissair flight for Geneva unobserved.

Once he had arrived, Ignatius checked into an inconspicuous hotel, retired to bed, and slept soundly for eight hours. Over breakfast the following morning he studied the list of banks he had so carefully drawn up after completing his research in Nigeria: Each name was written out boldly in his own hand. Ignatius decided to start with Gerber et Cie, whose building, he observed from the hotel bedroom, took up half the Avenue de Parchine. He checked the telephone number with the concierge before placing a call. The chairman agreed to see him at twelve o'clock.

Carrying only a battered briefcase, Ignatius arrived at the bank a few minutes before the appointed hour—an unusual occurrence for a Nigerian, thought the young man dressed in a smart gray suit, white shirt, and gray silk tie who was waiting in the marble hall to greet him. He bowed to the minister, introducing himself as the chairman's personal assistant, and explained that he would accompany Ignatius to the chairman's office. The young executive led the minister to a waiting elevator, and neither man uttered another word until they had reached the eleventh floor. A gentle tap on the chairman's door elicited "*Entrez,*" which the young man obeyed.

"The Nigerian minister of finance, sir."

The chairman rose from behind his desk and stepped forward to greet his guest. Ignatius could not help noticing that he too wore a gray suit, white shirt, and gray silk tie.

"Good morning, Minister," the chairman said. "Won't you have a seat?" He ushered Ignatius toward a low glass table surrounded by comfortable chairs on the far side of the room. "I have ordered coffee for both of us, if that is acceptable."

Ignatius nodded, placed the battered briefcase on the floor by the side of his chair, and stared out of the large plate-glass window. He made some small talk about the splendid view of the magnificent fountain while a girl served all three men with coffee.

Once the young woman had left the room, Ignatius got down to business.

"My head of state has asked me to visit your bank with a rather unusual request," he began. Not a flicker of surprise appeared on the face of the chairman or his young assistant. "He has honored me with the task of discovering which Nigerian citizens hold numbered accounts with your bank."

On learning this piece of information only the chairman's lips moved. "I am not at liberty to disclose—"

"Allow me to put my case," said the Minister, raising a white palm. "First, let me assure you that I come with the absolute authority of my government." Without another word, Ignatius extracted an envelope from his inside pocket with a flourish. He handed it to the chairman, who removed the letter inside and read it slowly.

Once he had finished reading, the banker cleared his throat. "This document, I fear, sir, carries no validity in my country." He replaced it in the envelope and handed it back to Ignatius. "I am, of course," continued the chairman, "not for one moment doubting that you have the full backing of your head of state, both as a Minister and an Ambassador, but that does not change the bank's rule of confidentiality in such matters. There are no circumstances in which we would release the names of any of our account holders without their authority. I'm sorry to be of so little help, but those are, and will always remain, the bank rules." The chairman rose to his feet, as he considered the meeting was now at an end; but he had not bargained for Clean Sweep Ignatius.

"My head of state," said Ignatius, softening his tone perceptibly, "has authorized me to approach your bank to act as the intermediary for all future transactions between my country and Switzerland."

"We are flattered by your confidence in us, Minister," replied the chairman, who remained standing. "However, I feel sure that you will understand that it cannot alter our attitude to our customers' confidentiality."

Ignatius remained unperturbed.

"Then I am sorry to inform you, Mr. Gerber, that our ambassador in Geneva will be instructed to send an official communiqué to the Swiss Foreign Office about the lack of cooperation your bank has shown concerning requests for information about our nationals." He waited for his words to sink in. "You could avoid such embarrassment, of course, by simply letting me know the names of my countrymen who hold accounts with Gerber et Cie and the amounts involved. I can assure you we would not reveal the source of our information."

"You are most welcome to lodge such a communiqué, sir, and I feel sure that our Minister will explain to your ambassador in the most courteous of diplomatic language that the Foreign Ministry does not have the authority under Swiss law to demand such disclosures."

"If that is the case, I shall instruct my own Ministry of Trade to halt all future dealings in Nigeria with any Swiss nationals until these names are revealed."

"That is your privilege, Minister," replied the chairman, unmoved.

"And we may also have to reconsider every contract currently being negotiated by your countrymen in Nigeria. And in addition, I shall personally see to it that no penalty clauses are honored."

"Would you not consider such action a little precipitate?"

"Let me assure you, Mr. Gerber, that I would not lose one moment of sleep over such a decision," said Ignatius. "Even if my efforts to discover those names were to bring your country to its knees I would not be moved."

"So be it, Minister," replied the chairman. "However, it still does not alter the policy or the attitude of this bank to confidentiality."

"If that remains the case, sir, this very day I shall give instructions to our ambassador to close our embassy in Geneva, and I shall declare your ambassador in Lagos *persona non grata.*"

For the first time the chairman raised his eyebrows.

"Furthermore," continued Ignatius, "I will hold a press conference in London which will leave the world's media in no doubt of my head of state's displeasure with the conduct of this bank. After such publicity, I feel confident you will find that many of your customers would prefer to close their accounts, while others who have in the past considered you a safe haven may find it necessary to look elsewhere."

The minister waited, but still the chairman did not respond.

"Then you leave me no choice," said Ignatius, rising from his seat.

The chairman stretched out his arm, assuming that at last the minister was leaving, only to watch with horror as Ignatius placed a hand in his jacket pocket and removed a small pistol. The two Swiss bankers froze as the Nigerian minister of finance stepped forward and pressed the muzzle against the chairman's temple.

"I need those names, Mr. Gerber, and by now you must realize I will stop at nothing. If you don't supply them immediately, I'm going to blow your brains out. Do you understand?"

The chairman gave a slight nod, beads of sweat appearing on his forehead. "And he will be next," said Ignatius, gesturing toward the young assistant, who stood speechless and paralyzed a few paces away.

"Get me the names of every Nigerian who holds an account in this bank," Ignatius said quietly, looking toward the young man, "or I'll blow your chairman's brains all over his soft pile carpet. Immediately, do you hear me?" he added sharply.

The young man looked toward the chairman, who was now trembling, but who said quite clearly, "*Non, Pierre, jamais.*"

"*D'accord,*" replied the assistant in a whisper.

"You can't say I didn't give you every chance." Ignatius pulled back the hammer. The sweat was now pouring down the chairman's face, and the young man had to turn his eyes away as he waited in terror for the pistol shot.

"Excellent," said Ignatius, as he removed the gun from the chairman's head and returned to his seat. Both the bankers were still trembling and quite unable to speak.

The minister picked up the battered briefcase by the side of his chair and placed it on the glass table in front of him. He pressed back the clasps and the lid flicked up.

The two bankers stared down at the neatly packed rows of hundred-dollar bills. Every inch of the briefcase had been taken up. The chairman quickly estimated that it probably amounted to around five million dollars.

"I wonder, sir," said Ignatius, "how I go about opening an account with your bank?"

NOT FOR SALE

SALLY SUMMERS WON HER school's senior art prize at the age of fourteen. In her last four years at St. Bride's the only serious competition was for second place. When, in her final year, she was awarded the top scholarship to the Slade School of Fine Art, none of her contemporaries was at all surprised. The headmistress told the assembled parents on Speech Day that she was confident that Sally had a distinguished career ahead of her, and that her work would soon be exhibited in one of London's major galleries. Sally was flattered by all this unqualified praise, but still wasn't sure if she had any real talent.

By the end of her first year at the Slade, the staff and senior students were already becoming aware of Sally's work. Her drawing technique was regarded as quite exceptional, and her brushwork became bolder with each term. But, above all, it was the originality of her ideas that caused other students to stop and stare at her canvases.

In her final year, Sally won both the Mary Rischgitz Prize for oil painting and the Henry Tonks Prize for drawing: a rare double. They were presented to her by Sir Roger de Grey, the president of the Royal Academy, and Sally was among that tiny group who were spoken of as "having a future." But surely, she told her parents, that could be said of the top student in any year—and most of them ended up working in the creative departments of advertising agencies, or teaching art to bored schoolchildren in far-flung parts of the kingdom.

Once she had graduated, Sally had to decide whether she too would apply for a job with an advertising agency, take up a teaching appointment, or risk everything and try to put together enough original work for a London gallery to consider her for a one-woman show.

Her parents were convinced that their daughter had real talent, but what do parents know when you're their only child? thought Sally. Especially when one of them was a music teacher and the other an accountant who were the first to admit that they didn't know much about art, but they knew what they liked. Still, they seemed quite willing to support her for another year if she wanted (to use an expression of the young) to go for it.

Sally was painfully aware that, although her parents were fairly comfortably off, another year in which she produced no income could only be a burden for them. After much soul-searching she told them, "One year, and one year only. After that, if the paintings aren't good enough, or if no one shows any interest in exhibiting them, I'll be realistic and look for a proper job."

For the next six months Sally worked hours that she hadn't realized existed when she'd been a student. During that time she produced a dozen canvases. She allowed no one to see them, for fear that her parents and friends would not be frank with her. She was determined to finish her portfolio and then listen only to the toughest opinions possible, those of the professional gallery owners, and, tougher still, those of the buying public.

Sally had always been a voracious reader, and she continued to devour books and monographs on artists from Bellini to Hockney. The more she read, the more she became aware that however talented an artist might be, it was industry and dedication that ultimately marked the few who succeeded from the many who failed. This inspired her to work still harder, and she began to turn down invitations to parties, dances, even weekends with old friends, making use of every spare moment to visit art galleries or to attend lectures on the great masters.

By the eleventh month, Sally had completed twenty-seven works, but she still wasn't sure whether they displayed any real talent. Nevertheless, she felt the time had finally come to allow others to pass judgment on them.

She looked long and hard at each of the twenty-seven paintings, and the following morning she packed six of them in a large canvas folder her parents had given her the previous Christmas, and joined the early-morning commuters on their journey from Sevenoaks into London.

Sally began her quest in Cork Street, where she came across galleries exhibiting works by Bacon, Freud, Hockney, Dunston, and Chadwick. She felt overawed at the prospect of even entering their portals, let alone submitting her own humble work to the appraisal of their proprietors. She carted her canvas folder a couple of blocks north to Conduit Street, and in the windows she recognized the works of Jones, Campbell, Wczenski, Frink, and Paolozzi. She became even more discouraged and unwilling to push open any of the galleries' front doors.

Sally returned home that night exhausted, her canvas folder unopened. She understood for the first time how an author must feel after receiving a string of rejection slips. She was unable to sleep that night. But as she lay awake she came to the conclusion that she must know the truth about her work, even if it meant being humiliated.

She joined the commuters again the following morning, and this time headed for Duke Street, St. James's. She didn't bother with the galleries exhibiting old masters, Dutch still lifes, or English landscapes, and therefore walked straight past Johnny van Haeften and Rafael Valls. Halfway down the street she turned right, and finally came to a halt outside the Simon Bouchier Gallery, which was exhibiting the sculptures of the late Sydney Harpley and the paintings of Muriel Pemberton, whose obituary Sally had read in the *Independent* only a few days before.

It was the thought of death that made Sally settle on the Bouchier Gallery. Perhaps they would be looking for someone young, she tried to convince herself, someone who had a long career ahead of them.

She stepped inside the gallery and found herself in a large, empty room, surrounded by Muriel Pemberton's watercolors. "Can I help you?" asked a young woman who was sitting behind a desk near the window.

"No, thank you," Sally replied. "I was just looking."

The girl eyed Sally's canvas folder, but said nothing. Sally decided she would do one circuit of the room, and then make good her escape. She began to circle the gallery, studying the pictures carefully. They were good, very good—but Sally believed she could do just as well, given time. She would have liked to see Muriel Pemberton's work when *she* was her age.

When Sally reached the far end of the gallery, she became aware of an office in which a short, balding man, wearing an old tweed jacket and corduroy trousers, was closely examining a picture. He looked about the same age as her father. Also studying the picture was another man, who caused Sally to stop in her tracks. He must have been a little over six foot, with those dark Italian looks that people normally only come across in glossy magazines; and *he* was old enough to be her brother.

Was he Mr. Bouchier? she wondered. She hoped so, because if he owned the gallery she might be able to summon up the courage to introduce herself to him, once the little man in the scruffy jacket had left. At that moment the young man looked up and gave her a huge grin. Sally turned quickly away and began to study the pictures on the far wall.

She was wondering if it was worth hanging around any longer when the two men suddenly strolled out of the office and began walking toward the door.

She froze, pretending to concentrate on a portrait of a young girl in pastel blues and yellows, a picture that had a Matisse-like quality about it.

"What's in there?" asked a cheeky voice. Sally turned round and came face to face with the two men. The smaller one was pointing at her canvas bag.

"Just a few pictures," Sally stammered. "I'm an artist."

"Let's have a look," said the man, "and perhaps *I* can decide if you're an artist or not."

Sally hesitated.

"Come on, come on," he teased. "I haven't got all day. As you can see, I have an important client to take to lunch," he added, indicating the tall, well-dressed young man, who still hadn't spoken.

"Oh, are *you* Mr. Bouchier?" she asked, unable to hide her disappointment.

"Yes. Now, am I going to be allowed to look at your pictures or not?"

Sally quickly unzipped her canvas bag and laid out the six paintings on the floor. Both of the men bent down and studied them for some time before either offered an opinion.

"Not bad," said Bouchier eventually. "Not bad at all. Leave them with me for a few days, and then let's meet again next week." He paused. "Say Monday, 11:30. And if you have any more examples of your recent work, bring them with you." Sally was speechless. "Can't see you before Monday," he continued, "because the Royal Academy's Summer Exhibition opens tomorrow. So for the next few days I won't have a moment to spare. Now, if you'll excuse me . . . "

The younger man was still examining Sally's pictures closely. At last he looked up at her. "I'd like to buy the one of the interior with the black cat on the windowsill. How much is it?"

"Well," said Sally, "I'm not sure . . . "

"N.F.S.," said Mr. Bouchier firmly, guiding his client toward the door.

"By the way," the taller man said, turning back, "I am Antonio Flavelli. My friends call me Tony." But Mr. Bouchier was already pushing him out onto the street.

Sally returned home that afternoon with an empty canvas folder, and was prepared to admit to her parents that a London dealer had shown an interest in her work. But it was, she insisted, no more than an interest.

The following morning Sally decided to go to the opening day of the Royal Academy Summer Exhibition, which would give her the chance to find out just how good her rivals were. For over an hour she stood in the long line that stretched from the front door right across the parking lot and out onto the sidewalk. When she eventually reached the top of the wide staircase, she wished she were six feet six tall, so that she could see over the tops of the heads of the mass of people who were crowding every room. After a couple of hours strolling round the many galleries, Sally was confident that she was already good enough to enter a couple of her pictures for next year's exhibition.

She stopped to admire a Craigie Aitchison of Christ on the cross, and checked in her little blue catalog to find out the price: ten thousand pounds, more than she could hope to earn if she were to sell every one of her canvases. Suddenly her concentration was broken, as a soft Italian voice behind her said, "Hello, Sally." She swung round to find Tony Flavelli smiling down at her.

"Mr. Flavelli," she said.

"Tony, please. You like Craigie Aitchison?"

"He's superb," Sally replied. "I know his work well—I had the privilege of being taught by him when I was at the Slade."

"I can remember, not so long ago, when you could pick up an Aitchison for two, three hundred pounds at the most. Perhaps the same thing will happen to you one day. Have you seen anything else you think I ought to look at?"

Sally was flattered to have her advice sought by a serious collector, and said, "Yes, I think the sculpture *Books on a Chair* by Julie Major is very striking. She has talent, and I'm sure she has a future."

"So do you," said Tony.

"Do you think so?" asked Sally.

"It's not important what I think," said Tony. "But Simon Bouchier is convinced."

"Are you teasing me?" asked Sally.

"No, I'm not, as you'll find out for yourself when you see him next Monday. He talked of little else over lunch yesterday— 'The daring brushwork, the unusual use of color, the originality of ideas.' I thought he was never going to stop. Still, he's promised I can have *The Sleeping Cat That Never Moved* once you've both settled on a price."

Sally was speechless.

"Good luck," Tony said, turning to leave. "Not that I think you need it." He hesitated for a moment before swinging back to face her. "By the way, are you going to the Hockney exhibition?"

"I didn't even know there was one," Sally confessed.

"There's a private view this evening. Six to eight." Looking straight into her eyes he said, "Would you like to join me?"

She hesitated, but only for a moment. "That would be nice."

"Good, then why don't we meet in the Ritz Palm Court at 6:30." Before Sally could tell him that she didn't know where the Ritz was, let alone its Palm Court, the tall, elegant man had disappeared into the crowd.

Sally suddenly felt gauche and scruffy, but then, she hadn't dressed that morning with the Ritz in mind. She looked at her watch—12:45—and began to wonder if she had enough time to return home, change, and be back at the Ritz by 6:30. She decided that she didn't have much choice, as she doubted if they would let her into such a grand hotel dressed in jeans and a T-shirt of Munch's *The Scream*. She ran down the wide staircase, out onto Piccadilly, and all the way to the nearest tube station.

When she arrived back home in Sevenoaks—far earlier than her mother had expected—she rushed into the kitchen and explained that she would be going out again shortly.

"Was the Summer Exhibition any good?" her mother asked.

"Not bad," Sally replied as she ran upstairs. But once she was out of earshot she muttered under her breath, "Certainly didn't see a lot that worried me."

"Will you be in for supper?" asked her mother, sticking her head out from behind the kitchen door.

"I don't think so," shouted Sally. She disappeared into her bedroom and began flinging off her clothes before heading for the bathroom.

She crept back downstairs an hour later, having tried on and rejected several outfits. She checked her dress in the hall mirror—a little too short, perhaps, but at least it showed her legs to best advantage. She could still remember those art students who during life classes had spent more time staring at her legs than at the model they were supposed to be drawing. She only hoped Tony would be similarly captivated.

"'Bye, Mum," she shouted, and quickly closed the door behind her before her mother could see what she was wearing.

Sally took the next train back to Charing Cross. She stepped onto the platform unwilling to admit to any passerby that she had no idea where the Ritz was, so she hailed a taxi, praying she could get to the hotel for four pounds, because that was all she had on her. Her eyes remained fixed on the meter as it clicked past two pounds, and then three—far too quickly, she thought—three pounds twenty, forty, sixty, eighty . . . She was just about to ask the cabbie to stop, so she could jump out and walk the rest of the way, when he drew up to the curb.

The door was immediately opened by a statuesque man dressed in a heavy blue trench coat who raised his top hat to her. Sally handed over her four pounds to the cabbie, feeling guilty about the measly twenty pence tip. She ran up the steps, through the revolving door and into the hotel foyer. She checked her watch: 6:10. She decided she had better go back outside, walk slowly around the block, and return a little later. But just as she reached the door, an elegant man in a long black coat approached her and asked, "Can I help you, madam?"

"I'm meeting Mr. Tony Flavelli," Sally stammered, hoping he would recognize the name.

"Mr. Flavelli. Of course, madam. Allow me to show you to his table in the Palm Court."

She followed the black-coated man down the wide, deeply carpeted corridor, then up three steps to a large open area full of small circular tables, almost all of which were occupied.

Sally was directed to a table at the side, and once she was seated a waiter asked, "Can I get you something to drink, madam? A glass of champagne, perhaps?"

"Oh, no," said Sally. "A Coke will be just fine."

The waiter bowed and left her. Sally gazed nervously around the beautifully furnished room. Everyone seemed so relaxed and sophisticated. The waiter returned a few moments later and placed a fine cut-glass tumbler with Coca-Cola, ice, and lemon in front of her. She thanked him and began sipping her drink, checking her watch every few minutes. She pulled her dress down as far as it would go, wishing she had chosen some-thing longer. She was becoming anxious about what would hap-pen if Tony didn't turn up, because she didn't have any money left to pay for her drink. And then suddenly she saw him, dressed in a loose double-breasted suit and an open-neck cream shirt. He had stopped to chat with an elegant young woman on the steps. After a couple of minutes he kissed her on the cheek and made his way over to Sally.

"I am so sorry," he said. "I didn't mean to keep you waiting. I do hope I'm not late."

"No, no you're not. I arrived a few minutes early," Sally said, flustered, as he bent down and kissed her hand.

"What did you think of the Summer Exhibition?" he asked as the waiter appeared by his side.

"Your usual, sir?" he asked.

"Yes, thank you, Michael," he replied.

"I enjoyed it," said Sally. "But . . . "

"But you felt you could have done just as well yourself," he suggested.

"I didn't mean to imply that," she said, looking up to see if he was teasing. But the expression on his face remained serious. "I'm sure I will enjoy the Hockney more," she added as a glass of champagne was placed on the table.

"Then I'll have to come clean," said Tony.

Sally put down her drink and stared at him, not knowing what he meant.

"There isn't a Hockney exhibition on at the moment," he said. "Unless you want to fly to Glasgow."

Sally looked puzzled. "But you said—"

"I just wanted an excuse to see you again."

Sally felt bemused and flattered, and was uncertain how to respond.

"I'll leave the choice to you," he said. "We could have dinner together, or you could simply take the train back to Sevenoaks."

"How did you know I live in Sevenoaks?"

"It was inscribed in big bold letters on the side of your canvas folder," said Tony with a smile.

Sally laughed. "I'll settle for dinner," she said. Tony paid for the drinks, then guided Sally out of the hotel and a few yards down the road to a restaurant on the corner of Arlington Street.

This time Sally did try a glass of champagne, and allowed Tony to select for her from the menu. He could not have been more attentive, and seemed to know so much about so many things, even if she didn't manage to find out exactly what he did.

After Tony had called for the bill, he asked her if she would like to have coffee at "my place."

"I'm afraid I can't," she said, looking at her watch. "I'd miss the last train home."

"Then I'll drive you to the station. We wouldn't want you to miss the last train home, would we?" he said, scrawling his signature across the bill.

This time she knew he was teasing her, and she blushed.

When Tony dropped her off at Charing Cross he asked, "When can I see you again?"

"I have an appointment with Mr. Bouchier at 11:30—"

"Next Monday morning, if I remember correctly. So why don't we have a celebration lunch together after he's signed you up? I'll come to the gallery at about 12:30. Good-bye." He leaned over and kissed her gently on the lips.

Sitting in a cold, smelly carriage on the last train back to Sevenoaks, Sally couldn't help wondering what coffee at Tony's place might have been like.

Sally walked into the gallery a few minutes before 11:30 the following Monday to find Simon Bouchier kneeling on the carpet, head down, studying some paintings. They weren't hers, and she hoped he felt the same way about them as she did.

Simon looked up. "Good morning, Sally. Dreadful, aren't they? You have to look through an awful lot of rubbish before you come across someone who shows any real talent." He rose to his feet. "Mind you, Natasha Krasnoselyodkina does have one advantage over you."

"What's that?" asked Sally.

"She would draw the crowds for any opening."

"Why?"

"Because she claims to be a Russian countess. Hints she's a direct descendant of the last czar. Frankly, I think the Pearly Queen in the East End is about the nearest she's been to royalty, but still, she's the 'in' face at the moment—a sort of

'Minah Bird' of the nineties. What did Andy Warhol say—'In the future, everyone will be famous for fifteen minutes'? By that standard, Natasha looks good for about thirty. I see this morning's tabloids are even hinting she's the new love in Prince Andrew's life. My bet is they've never met. But if he were to turn up at the opening, we'd be jam packed, that's for sure. We wouldn't sell a picture, of course, but we'd be jam packed."

"Why wouldn't you sell anything?" asked Sally.

"Because the public is not that stupid when it comes to buying paintings. A picture is a large investment for most people, and they want to believe that they have a good eye, and that they've invested wisely. Natasha's pictures won't satisfy them on either count. With you, though, Sally, I'm beginning to feel they might be convinced on both. But first, let me see the rest of your portfolio."

Sally unzipped her bulging folder and laid out twenty-one paintings on the carpet.

Simon dropped to his knees, and didn't speak again for some time. When he eventually did offer an opinion, it was only to repeat the single word "consistent."

"But I'll need even more, and of the same quality," he said after he had risen to his feet. "Another dozen canvases at least, and by October. I want you to concentrate on interiors—you're good at interiors. And they'll have to be better than good if you expect me to invest my time, expertise, and a great deal of money in you, young lady. Do you think you can manage another dozen pictures by October, Miss Summers?"

"Yes, of course," said Sally, giving little thought to the fact that October was only five months away.

"That's good, because if you deliver, and I only say *if,* I'll risk the expense of launching you on an unsuspecting public this autumn." He walked into his office, flicked through his diary and said, "October the seventeenth, to be precise."

Sally was speechless.

"I don't suppose you could manage an affair with Prince Charles lasting, say, from the end of September to the beginning of November? That would knock the Russian countess from the Mile End Road off the front pages and guarantee us a full house on opening night."

"I'm afraid not," said Sally, "especially if you expect me to produce another dozen canvases by then."

"Pity," said Simon, "because if we can attract the punters to the opening, I'm confident they'll want to buy your work. The problem is always getting them to come for an unknown." He suddenly looked over Sally's shoulder and said, "Hello, Tony. I wasn't expecting to see you today."

"Perhaps that's because you're not seeing me," Tony replied. "I've just come to whisk Sally off to what I was rather hoping might be a celebratory lunch."

"The Summers Exhibition," Simon said, grinning at his little play on words, "will open not in June at the Royal Academy, but in October at the Bouchier Gallery. October the seventeenth is to be Sally's day of reckoning."

"Congratulations," said Tony, turning to Sally. "I'll bring all my friends."

"I'm only interested in the rich ones," said Simon, as someone else entered the Gallery.

"Natasha," said Simon, turning to face a slim, dark-haired woman. Sally's first reaction was that she should have been an artists' model, not an artist.

"Thanks for coming back so quickly, Natasha. Have a nice, you two," he added, smiling at Tony, who couldn't take his eyes off the new arrival.

Natasha didn't notice, as her only interest seemed to be in Sally's pictures. She was unable to conceal her envy as Tony and Sally walked out of the gallery.

"Wasn't she stunning?" said Sally.

"Was she?" said Tony. "I didn't notice."

"I wouldn't blame Prince Andrew if he were having an affair with her."

"Damn," said Tony placing a hand in his inside pocket. "I forgot to give Simon a check I promised him. Don't move, I'll be back in a minute."

Tony sprinted off in the direction of the gallery, and Sally waited on the corner for what seemed like an awfully long minute before he reappeared back on the street.

"Sorry. Simon was on the phone," Tony explained. He took Sally's arm and led her across the street to a small Italian restaurant, where once again he seemed to have his own table.

He ordered a bottle of champagne, "to celebrate your great triumph." As Sally raised her glass in response, she realized for the first time just how much work she would have to do before October if she was going to keep her promise to Simon.

When Tony poured her a second glass, Sally smiled. "It's been a memorable day. I ought to phone my parents and let them know, but I don't think they'd believe me."

When a third glass had been filled and Sally still hadn't finished her salad, Tony took her hand, leaned across, and kissed it. "I've never met anyone as beautiful as you," he said. "And certainly no one as talented."

Sally quickly took a gulp of the champagne, to hide her embarrassment. She still wasn't sure whether to believe him, but a glass of white wine, followed by two glasses of red, helped to convince her that she should.

After Tony had signed the bill, he asked her again if she would like to come back to his place for coffee. Sally had already decided that she wasn't going to be able to do any work that day, so she nodded her agreement. In any case, she felt she had earned an afternoon off.

In the taxi on the way to Chelsea, she rested her head on Tony's shoulder, and he began to kiss her gently.

When they arrived at his town house in Bywater Street, he helped her out of the taxi, up the steps, and through the front door. He led her along a dimly lit corridor and into the living room. She curled up in a corner of the sofa, as Tony disappeared into another room. Most of the furniture, and the pictures that covered every inch of the walls, were a blur to her. Tony returned a moment later, carrying another bottle of champagne and two glasses. Sally didn't notice that he was no longer wearing his jacket, tie, or shoes.

He poured her a drink, which she sipped as he sat down next to her on the sofa. His arm slipped around her shoulders, and he drew her close to him. When he kissed her again, she felt a little silly dangling an empty glass in midair. He took it from her and placed it on a side table, then held her in his arms, and began to kiss her more passionately. As she fell back, his hand slipped onto the inside of her thigh, and began moving slowly up her leg.

Every time Sally was about to stop him going any further, Tony seemed to know exactly what to do next. She had always felt in control in the past whenever an overenthusiastic art student had started to go a little too far in the back row of a cinema, but she had never experienced anyone as subtle as Tony. When her dress fell off her shoulders, she hadn't even noticed that he had undone the twelve little buttons down the back.

They broke apart for a second. Sally felt she ought to make a move to go, before it was too late. Tony smiled, and undid the buttons of his own shirt before taking her back in his arms. She felt the warmth of his chest, and he was so gentle that she did not complain when she realized that the clasp of her bra had come loose. She sank back, enjoying every second, knowing that until that moment she had never experienced what it was like to be properly seduced.

Tony finally lay back and said, "Yes, it has been a memorable day. But I don't think I'll phone my parents to let them know." He laughed, and Sally felt slightly ashamed. Tony was only the fourth man who had made love to her, and she had known the other three for months beforehand—in one case, years.

For the next hour they talked about many things, but all Sally really wanted to know was how Tony felt about her. He gave her no clue.

Then, once again, he took her in his arms, but this time he pulled her onto the floor and made love to her with such passion that afterward Sally wondered if she had ever made love before.

She was just in time to catch the last train home, but she couldn't help wishing she had missed it.

Over the next few months Sally devoted herself to getting her latest ideas onto canvas. When each new painting was finished, she would take it up to London for Simon to comment on. The smile on his face became broader and broader with each new picture he saw, and the word he kept repeating now was "original." Sally would tell him about her ideas for the next one, and he would bring her up to date with his plans for the opening in October.

Tony would often meet her for lunch, and afterward they would go back to his house, where they would make love until it was time for her to catch the last train home.

Sally often wished she could spend more time with Tony. But she was always conscious of the deadline set by Simon, who warned her that the printers were already proofreading the catalog, and that the invitations for the opening were waiting to be sent out. Tony seemed almost as busy as she was, and lately he hadn't always been able to fit in with her expeditions to London. Sally had taken to staying overnight and catching an early train home the following morning. Tony occasionally hinted that she might consider moving in with him. When she thought about it—and she often did—she reflected that his attic could easily be converted into a studio. But she decided that before such a move could even be contemplated, the exhibition had to be a success. Then, if the hint became an offer, she would have her answer ready.

Just two days before the exhibition was due to open, Sally completed her final canvas and handed it over to Simon. As she pulled it out of the canvas folder he threw his arms in the air, and shouted, "Hallelujah! It's your best yet. As long as we're sensible about our prices, I think that, with a touch of luck, we should sell at least half of your pictures before the exhibition closes."

"Only half?" said Sally, unable to hide her disappointment.

"That wouldn't be at all bad for your first attempt, young lady," said Simon. "I only sold one Leslie Anne Ivory at her first exhibition, and now she sells everything in the first week."

Sally still looked crestfallen, and Simon realized he had perhaps been a little tactless.

"Don't worry. Any unsold ones will be put into stock, and they'll be snapped up the moment you start getting good reviews."

Sally continued to pout.

"How do you feel about the frames and mounts?" Simon asked, trying to change the subject.

Sally studied the deep golden frames and light gray mounts. The smile returned to her face.

"They're good, aren't they?" said Simon. "They bring out the color in the canvases wonderfully."

Sally nodded her agreement, but was now beginning to worry about how much they must have cost, and whether she would ever be given a second exhibition if the first one wasn't a success.

"By the way," Simon said, "I have a friend at the P.A. called Mike Sallis who—"

"P.A.?" said Sally.

"Press Association. Mike's a photographer—always on the lookout for a good story. He says he'll come around and take a picture of you standing next to one of the pictures. Then he'll hawk the photo around Fleet Street, and we'll just have to cross our fingers and pray that Natasha has taken the day off. I don't want to get your hopes up, but someone just might bite. Our only line at present is that it's your first exhibition since leaving the Slade. Hardly a front-page splash." Simon paused, as once again Sally looked discouraged. "It's not too late for you to have a fling with Prince Charles, you know. That would solve all our problems."

Sally smiled. "I don't think Tony would like that."

Simon decided against making another tactless remark.

Sally spent that evening with Tony at his home in Chelsea. He seemed a little distracted, but she blamed herself—she was unable to hide her disappointment at Simon's estimate of how few of her pictures might be sold. After they had made love, Sally tried to raise the topic of what would happen to them once the exhibition was over, but Tony deftly changed the subject back to how much he was looking forward to the opening.

That night Sally went home on the last train from Charing Cross.

The following morning she woke up with a terrible feeling of anticlimax. Her room was bereft of canvases, and all she could do now was wait. Her mood wasn't helped by the fact that Tony had told her he would be out of London on business until the day of her opening. She lay in the bath thinking about him.

"But I'll be your first customer on the night," he had promised. "Don't forget, I still want to buy *The Sleeping Cat That Never Moved.*"

The phone was ringing, but someone answered it before Sally could get out of the bath.

"It's for you," shouted her mother from the bottom of the stairs.

Sally wrapped a towel around her and grabbed the phone, hoping it would be Tony.

"Hi, Sally, it's Simon. I've got some good news. Mike Sallis has just called from the P.A. He's coming around to the gallery at midday tomorrow. All the pictures should be framed by then, and he'll be the first person from the press to see them. They all want to be first. I'm trying to think up some wheeze to convince him that it's an exclusive. By the way, the catalogs have arrived, and they look fantastic."

Sally thanked him, and was about to call Tony to suggest that she stay overnight with him, so that they could go to the gallery together the following day, when she remembered that he was out of town. She spent the day pacing anxiously around the house, occasionally talking to her most compliant model, the sleeping cat that never moved.

The following morning Sally caught an early commuter train from Sevenoaks, so she could spend a little time checking the pictures against their catalog entries. When she walked into the gallery, her eyes lit up: Half a dozen of the paintings had already been hung, and she actually felt, for the first time, that they really weren't bad. She glanced in the direction of the office, and saw that Simon was occupied on the phone. He smiled and waved to indicate that he would be with her in a moment.

She had another look at the pictures, and then spotted a copy of the catalog lying on the table. The cover read "The Summers Exhibition," above a picture of an interior looking from her parents' living room through an open window and out onto a garden overgrown with weeds. A black cat lay asleep on the windowsill, ignoring the rain.

Sally opened the catalog and read the introduction on the first page.

> Sometimes judges feel it necessary to say: It's been hard to pick this year's winner. But from the moment one set eyes on Sally Summers's work, the task was made easy. Real talent is obvious for all to see, and Sally has achieved the rare feat of winning both the Slade's major prizes, for oils and for drawing, in the same year. I much look forward to watching her career develop over the coming years.

It was an extract from Sir Roger de Grey's speech when he had presented Sally with the Mary Rischgitz and the Henry Tonks Prizes at the Slade two years before.

Sally turned the pages, seeing her works reproduced in color for the first time. Simon's attention to detail and layout was evident on every page.

She looked back toward the office and saw that Simon was still on the phone. She decided to go downstairs and check on the rest of her pictures, now that they had all been framed. The lower gallery was a mass of color, and the newly framed paintings were so skillfully hung that even Sally saw them in a new light.

Once she had circled the room Sally suppressed a smile of satisfaction before turning to make her way back upstairs. As she passed a table in the center of the gallery, she noticed a folder with the initials N.K. printed on it. She idly lifted the cover, to discover a pile of undistinguished watercolors.

As she leafed through her rival's never-to-be-exhibited efforts, Sally had to admit that the nude self-portraits didn't do Natasha justice. She was just about to close the folder and join Simon upstairs when she came to a sudden halt.

Although it was clumsily executed, there was no doubt who the man was that the half-clad Natasha was clinging to.

Sally felt sick. She slammed the folder shut, walked quickly across the room, and back up the stairs to the ground floor. In the corner of the large gallery Simon was chatting to a man who had several cameras slung over his shoulder.

"Sally," he said, coming toward her, "this is Mike—"

But Sally ignored them both and started running toward the open door, tears flooding down her cheeks. She turned right into St. James's, determined to get as far away from the gallery as possible. But then she came to an abrupt halt. Tony and Natasha were walking toward her, arm in arm.

Sally stepped off the pavement and began to cross the road, hoping to reach the other side before they spotted her.

The screech of tires and the sudden swerve of the van came just a moment too late, and she was thrown headlong into the middle of the street.

When Sally came to, she felt awful. She blinked her eyes, and thought she could hear voices. She blinked again, but it was several moments before she was able to focus on anything.

She was lying in a bed, but it was not her own. Her right leg was covered in plaster and was raised high in the air, suspended from a pulley. Her other leg was under the sheet, and it felt all right. She wiggled the toes of her left foot: Yes, they were fine. Then she began to try to move her arms. A nurse came up to the side of the bed.

"Welcome back to the world, Sally."

"How long have I been like this?" she asked.

"A couple of days," said the nurse, checking Sally's pulse. "But you're making a remarkably quick recovery. Before you ask, it's only a broken leg, and the black eyes will have gone long before we let you out. By the way," she added, as she moved on to the next patient, "I loved that picture of you in the morning papers. And what about those flattering remarks your friend made? So what's it like to be famous?"

Sally wanted to ask what she was talking about, but the nurse was already taking the pulse of the person in the next bed.

"Come back," Sally wanted to say, but a second nurse had appeared by her bedside with a mug of orange juice, which she thrust into her hand.

"Let's get you started on this," she said. Sally obeyed, and tried to suck the liquid through a bent plastic straw.

"You've got a visitor," the nurse told her once she'd emptied the contents of the mug. "He's been waiting for some time. Do you think you're up to seeing him?"

"Sure," said Sally, not particularly wanting to face Tony, but desperate to find out what had happened.

She looked toward the swing doors at the end of the ward, but had to wait for some time before Simon came bouncing through them. He walked straight up to her bed, clutching what might just about have been described as a bunch of flowers. He gave her plaster cast a big kiss.

"I'm so sorry, Simon," Sally said, before he had even said hello. "I know just how much trouble and expense you've been to on my behalf. And now I've let you down so badly."

"You certainly have," said Simon. "It's always a letdown when you sell everything off the walls on the first night. Then you haven't got anything left for your old customers, and they start grumbling."

Sally's mouth opened wide.

"Mind you, it was a rather good photo of Natasha, even if it was an awful one of you."

"What are you talking about, Simon?"

"Mike Sallis got his exclusive, and you got your break," he said, patting her suspended leg. "When Natasha bent over your body in the street, Mike began clicking away for dear life. And I couldn't have scripted her quotes better myself: 'The most outstanding young artist of our generation. If the world were to lose such a talent . . .'"

Sally laughed at Simon's wicked imitation of Natasha's Russian accent.

"You hit most of the next morning's front pages," he continued. BRUSH WITH DEATH in the *Mail*; STILL LIFE IN ST. JAMES'S in the *Express*. And you even managed SPLAT! in the *Sun*. The punters flocked into the gallery that evening. Natasha was wearing a black see-through dress and proceeded to give the press sound bite after sound bite about your genius. Not that it made any difference. We'd already sold every canvas long before their second editions hit the street. But, more important, the serious critics in the broadsheets are already acknowledging that you might actually have some talent."

Sally smiled. "I may have failed to have an affair with Prince Charles, but at least it seems I got something right."

"Well, not exactly," said Simon.

"What do you mean?" asked Sally, suddenly anxious. "You said all the pictures have been sold."

"True, but if you'd arranged to have the accident a few days earlier, I could have jacked up the prices by at least fifty percent. Still, there's always next time."

"Did Tony buy *The Sleeping Cat That Never Moved?*" Sally asked quietly.

"No, he was late as usual, I'm afraid. It was snapped up in the first half hour, by a serious collector. Which reminds me," Simon added, as Sally's parents came through the swing doors into the ward, "I'll need another forty canvases if we're going to hold your second show in the spring. So you'd better get back to work right away."

"But look at me, you silly 'n," Sally said, laughing. "How do you expect me to—"

"Don't be so feeble," said Simon, tapping her plaster cast. "It's your leg that's out of action, not your arm."

Sally grinned and looked up to see her parents standing at the end of the bed.

"Is this Tony?" her mother asked.

"Good heavens no, Mother," laughed Sally. "This is Simon. He's far more important. Mind you," she confessed, "I made the same mistake the first time I met him."

ONE-NIGHT
STAND

THE TWO MEN HAD first met at the age of five when they were placed side by side at school, for no more compelling reason than that their names, Thompson and Townsend, came one after each other on the class register. They soon became best friends, a tie which at that age is more binding than any marriage. After passing their eleven-plus examination they proceeded to the local grammar school with no Timpsons, Tooleys, or Tomlinsons to divide them and, having completed seven years in that academic institution, reached an age when one either has to go to work or to the university. They opted for the latter on the grounds that work should be put off until the last possible moment. Happily, they both possessed enough brains and native wit to earn themselves places at Durham University to major in English.

Undergraduate life turned out to be as sociable as at primary school. They both enjoyed English, tennis, cricket, good food, and girls. Luckily, in the last of these predilections they differed only on points of detail. Michael, who was six feet two, willowy, with dark curly hair, preferred tall, bosomy blonds with blue eyes and long legs. Adrian, a stocky man of five feet-ten, with straight, sandy hair, always fell for small, slim, dark-haired, dark-eyed girls. So whenever Adrian came across a girl that Michael took an interest in or vice versa, whether she was an undergraduate or a barmaid, the one would happily exaggerate his friend's virtues. Thus they spent three idyllic years in unison at Durham, gaining considerably more than a bachelor of arts degree. As neither of them had impressed the examiners enough to waste a further two years expounding their theories for a Ph.D., they could no longer avoid the real world.

Twin Dick Whittingtons, they set off for London, where Michael joined the BBC as a trainee while Adrian was signed up by Benton & Bowles, the international advertising agency, as an accounts assistant. They acquired a small flat in the Earls Court Road which they painted orange and brown, and proceeded to live the life of two young blades, for that is undoubtedly how they saw themselves.

Both men spent a further five years in this blissful bachelor state, until they each fell for a girl who fulfilled their particular requirements. They were married within weeks of each other: Michael to a tall, blue-eyed blond whom he met while playing tennis at the Hurlingham Club; Adrian to a slim, dark-eyed, dark-haired executive in charge of the Kellogg's Corn Flakes account. Each officiated as the other's best man, and each proceeded to sire three children at yearly intervals, and in that again they differed, but as before only on points of detail, Michael having two sons and a daughter, Adrian two daughters and a son. Each became godfather to the other's first-born son.

Marriage hardly separated them in anything as they continued to follow much of their old routine, playing cricket together on weekends in the summer and football in the winter, not to mention regular luncheons during the week.

After the celebration of his tenth wedding anniversary, Michael, now a senior producer with Thames Television, admitted rather coyly to Adrian that he had had his first affair: he had been unable to resist a tall, well-built blond from the typing pool who was offering more than shorthand at seventy words a minute. Only a few weeks later, Adrian, now a senior account manager with Pearl and Dean, also went under, selecting a journalist from Fleet Street who was seeking some inside information on one of the companies he represented. She became a tax-deductible item. After that the two men quickly fell back into their old routine. Any help they could give each other was provided unstintingly, creating no conflict of interests because of their different tastes. Their married lives were not suffering—or so they convinced each other—and at thirty-five, having come through the swinging sixties unscathed, they began to make the most of the seventies.

Early in that decade, Thames Television decided to send Michael off to the United States to edit an ABC film about living in New York, for consumption by British viewers. Adrian, who had always wanted to see the eastern seaboard, did not find it hard to arrange a trip at the same time as he claimed it was necessary for him to carry out some more than usually spurious research for an Anglo-American tobacco company. The two men enjoyed a lively week together in New York, the highlight of which was a party held by ABC on the final evening to view the edited edition of Michael's film on New York, *An Englishman's View of the Big Apple.*

When Michael and Adrian arrived at the ABC studios they found the party was already well under way, and both entered the room together, looking forward to a few drinks and an early night before their journey back to England the next day.

They spotted her at exactly the same moment.

She was of medium height and build, with soft green eyes and auburn hair—a striking combination of both men's fantasies. Without another thought each knew exactly where he desired to end up that particular night, and, two minds with but a single idea, they advanced purposefully upon her.

"Hello, my name is Michael Thompson."

"Hello," she replied. "I'm Debbie Kendall."

"And I'm Adrian Townsend."

She offered her hand and both tried to grab it. When the party had come to an end, they had, between them, discovered that Debbie Kendall was an ABC floor producer on the evening news. She was divorced and had two children who lived with her in New York. But neither man was any nearer to impressing her, if only because each worked so hard to outdo the other; they both showed off abominably and even squabbled over fetching their new companion her food and drink. In the other's absence each found himself running down his closest friend in a subtle but damning way.

"Adrian's a nice chap if it weren't for his drinking," said Michael.

"Super fellow Michael, such a lovely wife, and you should see his three adorable children," added Adrian.

They both escorted Debbie home and reluctantly left her on the doorstep of her Sixty-eighth Street apartment. She kissed the two of them perfunctorily on the cheek, thanked them and said goodnight. They walked back to their hotel in silence.

When they reached their room on the nineteenth floor of the Plaza, it was Michael who spoke first.

"I'm sorry," he said. "I made a bloody fool of myself."

"I was every bit as bad," said Adrian, "we shouldn't fight over a woman. We never have in the past."

"Agreed," said Michael. "So why not an honorable compromise?"

"What do you suggest?"

"Since we both return to London tomorrow morning, let's agree whichever one of us comes back first . . . "

"Perfect," said Adrian and they shook hands to seal the bargain, as if they were both back at school playing a cricket match and had to decide on who should bat first. The deal made, they climbed into their respective beds and slept soundly.

Once back in London both men did everything in their power to find an excuse for returning to New York. Neither contacted Debbie Kendall by phone or letter, since it would have broken their gentleman's agreement, but when the weeks grew to be months, both became despondent, and it seemed that neither was going to be given the opportunity to return. Then Adrian was invited to Los Angeles to address a media conference. He remained unbearably smug about the whole trip, confident he would be able to drop into New York on the way to London. It was Michael who discovered that British Airways was offering cheap tickets for wives who accompanied their husbands on a business trip: Adrian was therefore unable to return via New York. Michael breathed a sigh of relief, which turned to triumph when he was selected to go to Washington and cover the president's State of the Union address. He suggested to the head of Outside Broadcasts that it would be wise to drop into New York on the way home and strengthen the contacts he had previously made with ABC. The head of Outside Broadcasts agreed, but told Michael he must be back the following day to cover the opening of Parliament.

Adrian phoned Michael's wife and briefed her on cheap trips to the States when accompanying your husband. "How kind of you to be so thoughtful, Adrian, but alas my school never allows time off during term, and in any case," she added, "I have a dreadful fear of flying."

Michael was very understanding about his wife's phobia and went off to book a single ticket.

Michael flew into Washington on the following Monday and called Debbie Kendall from his hotel room, wondering if she would even remember the two vainglorious Englishmen she had briefly met some months before, and if she did whether she would also recall which one he was. He dialed nervously and listened to the ringing tone. Was she in, was she even in New York? At last a click and a soft voice said hello.

"Hello, Debbie, it's Michael Thompson."

"Hello, Michael. What a nice surprise. Are you in New York?"

"No, Washington, but I'm thinking of flying up. You wouldn't be free for dinner on Thursday by any chance?"

"Let me just check my diary."

Michael held his breath as he waited. It seemed like hours.

"Yes, that seems to be fine."

"Fantastic. Shall I pick you up around eight?"

"Yes, thank you, Michael. I'll look forward to seeing you then."

Heartened by this early success, Michael immediately penned a telegram of commiseration to Adrian on his sad loss. Adrian didn't reply.

Michael took the shuttle up to New York on the Thursday afternoon as soon as he had finished editing the president's speech for the London office. After settling into another hotel room—this time insisting on a double bed just in case Debbie's children were at home—he had a long bath and a slow shave,

cutting himself twice and slapping on a little too much after-
shave. He rummaged around for his most telling tie and shirt,
and after he had finished dressing he studied himself in the
mirror, carefully combing his freshly washed hair to make the
long thin strands appear casual as well as cover the parts where
his hair was beginning to recede. After a final check, he was
able to convince himself that he looked less than his thirty-eight
years. Michael then took the elevator down to the ground floor,
and, striding out of the Plaza toward a neon-lit Fifth Avenue he
headed jauntily for Sixty-eighth Street. En route he acquired a
dozen roses from a little shop at the corner of Sixty-fifth Street
and Madison Avenue and, humming to himself, proceeded
confidently. He arrived at the front door of Debbie Kendall's
little brownstone at five past eight.

When Debbie opened the door, Michael thought she looked
even more beautiful than he had remembered. She was wearing a long blue dress, with a frilly white silk collar and cuffs,
that covered every part of her body from neck to ankles, and
yet she could not have been more desirable. She wore almost
no makeup except a touch of lipstick that Michael already had
plans to remove. Her green eyes sparkled.

"Say something," she said smiling.

"You look quite stunning, Debbie," was all he could think of
as he handed her the roses.

"How sweet of you," she replied and invited him in.

Michael followed her into the kitchen, where she hammered
the long stems and arranged the flowers in a porcelain vase.
She then led him into the living room, where she placed the
roses on an oval table beside a photograph of two small boys.

"Have we time for a drink?"

"Sure. I booked a table at Elaine's for eight-thirty."

"My favorite restaurant," she said, with a smile that revealed a
small dimple on her cheek. Without asking, Debbie poured two
whiskeys and handed one of them to Michael.

What a good memory she has, he thought, as he nervously
kept picking up and putting down his glass, like a teenager on
his first date. When Michael had eventually finished his drink,
Debbie suggested that they should leave.

"Elaine wouldn't keep a table free for one minute, even if you were Henry Kissinger."

Michael laughed and helped her on with her coat. As she unlatched the door, he realized there was no baby-sitter or sound of children. They must be staying with their father, he thought. Once on the street, he hailed a cab and directed the driver to Eighty-eighth and Second. Michael had never been to Elaine's before. The restaurant had been recommended by a friend from ABC who had assured him: "That joint will give you more than half a chance."

As they entered the crowded room and waited by the bar for the maître d', Michael could see it was the type of place that was frequented by the rich and famous and wondered if his pocket could stand the expense and, more important, whether such an outlay would turn out to be a worthwhile investment.

A waiter guided them to a small table at the back of the room, where they both had another whiskey while they studied the menu. When the waiter returned to take their order, Debbie wanted no first course, just the veal piccata, so Michael ordered the same. She refused the addition of garlic butter. Michael allowed his expectations to rise slightly.

"How's Adrian?" she asked.

"Oh, as well as can be expected," Michael replied. "He sends you his love, of course." He emphasized the word "love."

"How kind of him to remember me, and please return mine. What brings you to New York this time, Michael? Another film?"

"No. New York may well have become everybody's second city, but this time I only came to see you."

"To see me?"

"Yes, I had a tape to edit while I was in Washington, but I always knew I could be through with that by lunch today, so I hoped you would be free to spend an evening with me."

"I'm flattered."

"You shouldn't be."

She smiled. The veal arrived.

"Looks good," said Michael.

"Tastes good too," said Debbie. "When do you fly home?"

"Tomorrow morning, eleven o'clock flight, I'm afraid."

"Not left yourself time to do much in New York."

"I only came up to see you," Michael repeated. Debbie continued eating her veal. "Why would any man want to divorce you, Debbie?"

"Oh, nothing very original, I'm afraid. He fell in love with a twenty-two-year-old blond and left his thirty-two-year-old wife."

"Silly man. He should have had an affair with the twenty-two-year-old blond and remained faithful to his thirty-two-year-old wife."

"Isn't that a contradiction in terms?"

"Oh, no, I don't think so. I've never thought it unnatural to desire someone else. After all, it's a long life to go through and be expected never to want another woman."

"I'm not so sure I agree with you," said Debbie thoughtfully. "I would like to have remained faithful to one man."

Oh hell, thought Michael, not a very auspicious philosophy. "Do you miss him?" he tried again.

"Yes, sometimes. It's true what they say in the glossy magazines, it can be very lonely when you suddenly find yourself on your own."

That sounds more promising, thought Michael, and he heard himself saying: "Yes, I can understand that, but someone like you shouldn't have to stay on your own for very long."

Debbie made no reply.

Michael refilled her glass of wine nearly to the brim, hoping he could order a second bottle before she finished her veal.

"Are you trying to get me drunk, Michael?"

"If you think it will help," he replied, laughing.

Debbie didn't laugh. Michael tried again.

"Been to the theater lately?"

"Yes, I went to *Evita* last week. I loved it—" Wonder who took you, thought Michael "—but my mother fell asleep in the middle of the second act. I think I'll have to go and see it on my own a second time."

"I only wish I were staying long enough to take you."

"That would be fun," she said.

"Whereas I shall have to be satisfied with seeing the show in London."

"With your wife."

"Another bottle of wine please, waiter."

"No more for me, Michael, really."

"Well, you can help me out a little." The waiter faded away. "Do you get to England at all yourself?" asked Michael.

"No, I've only been once, when Roger, my ex, took the whole family. I loved the country. It fulfilled every one of my hopes, but I'm afraid we did what all Americans are expected to do. The Tower of London, Buckingham Palace, followed by Oxford and Stratford, before flying on to Paris."

"A sad way to see England; there's so much more I could have shown you."

"I suspect when the English come to America they don't see much outside of New York, Washington, Los Angeles, and perhaps San Francisco."

"I agree," said Michael, not wanting to disagree. The waiter cleared away their empty plates.

"Can I tempt you with a dessert, Debbie?"

"No, no, I'm trying to lose some weight." Michael slipped a hand gently around her waist. "You don't need to," he said. "You feel just perfect."

She laughed. He smiled.

"Nevertheless, I'll stick to coffee, please."

"A little brandy?"

"No, thank you, just coffee."

"Black?"

"Black."

"Coffee for two, please," Michael said to the hovering waiter.

"I wish I had taken you somewhere a little quieter and less ostentatious," he said, turning back to Debbie.

"Why?"

Michael took her hand. It felt cold. "I would like to have said things to you that shouldn't be listened to by people at the next table."

"I don't think anyone would be shocked by what they over-heard at Elaine's, Michael."

"Very well then. Do you believe in love at first sight?"

"No, but I think it's possible to be physically attracted to a person on first meeting them."

"Well, I must confess, I was to you."

Again she made no reply.

The coffee arrived, and Debbie released her hand to take a sip. Michael followed suit.

"There were one hundred and fifty women in that room the night we met, Debbie, and my eyes never left you once."

"Even during the film?"

"I'd seen the damn thing a hundred times. I feared I might never see you again."

"I'm touched."

"Why should you be? It must happen to you all the time."

"Now and then," she said. "But I haven't taken anyone too seriously since my husband left me."

"I'm sorry."

"No need. It's just not that easy to get over someone you've lived with for ten years. I doubt if many divorcées are quite that willing to jump into bed with the first man who comes along, as all the latest films suggest."

Michael took her hand again, hoping fervently he did not fall into that category.

"It's been such a lovely evening. Why don't we stroll down to the Carlyle and listen to Bobby Short?" Michael's ABC friend had recommended the move if he felt he was still in with a chance.

"Yes, I'd enjoy that," said Debbie.

Michael called for the bill—eighty-seven dollars. Had it been his wife sitting on the other side of the table, he would have checked each item carefully, but not on this occasion. He just left five twenty-dollar bills on a side plate and didn't wait for the change. As they stepped out onto Second Avenue, he took Deb-bie's hand, and they started walking downtown. On Madison Avenue they stopped in front of shopwindows and he bought her a fur coat, a Cartier watch, and a Balenciaga dress. Debbie thought it was lucky that all the stores were closed.

They arrived at the Carlyle just in time for the eleven o'clock show. A waiter, flashing a pen flashlight, guided them through the little dark room on the ground floor to a table in the corner. Michael ordered a bottle of champagne as Bobby Short struck up a chord and drawled out the words: "Georgia, Georgia, oh, my sweet . . . ." Michael, now unable to speak to Debbie above the noise of the band, satisfied himself with holding her hand, and when the entertainer sang, "This time we almost made the pieces fit, didn't we, gal?" he leaned over and kissed her on the cheek. She turned and smiled—was it faintly conspiratorial, or was it just wishful thinking?—and then she sipped her champagne. On the dot of twelve, Bobby Short shut the piano lid and said, "Goodnight, my friends, the time has come for all you good people to go to bed—and some of you naughty ones too." Michael laughed a little too loudly but was pleased that Debbie laughed as well.

They strolled down Madison Avenue to Sixty-eighth Street chatting about inconsequential affairs, while Michael's thoughts were of only one affair. When they arrived at her apartment, she took out her latchkey.

"Would you like a nightcap?" she asked without any suggestive intonation.

"No more drink, thank you, Debbie, but I would certainly appreciate a coffee."

She led him into the living room.

"The flowers have lasted well," she teased, leaving him as she went to make the coffee. Michael amused himself by flicking through an old copy of *Time*, looking at the pictures, not taking in the words. She returned after a few minutes with a coffeepot and two small cups on a lacquered tray. She poured the coffee, black again, and then sat down next to Michael on the couch, drawing one leg underneath her while turning slightly toward him. Michael downed his coffee in two gulps, scalding his mouth slightly. Then, putting down his cup, he leaned over and kissed her on the mouth. She was still clutching her coffee cup. Her eyes opened briefly as she maneuvered the cup onto a side table. After another long kiss she broke away from him.

"I ought to make an early start in the morning."

"So should I," said Michael, "but I am more worried about not seeing you again for a long time."

"What a nice thing to say," Debbie replied.

"No, I just care," he said, before kissing her again.

This time she responded; he slipped one hand onto her breast while the other one began to undo the row of little buttons down the back of her dress. She broke away again.

"Don't let's do anything we'll regret."

"I know we won't regret it," said Michael.

He then kissed her on the neck and shoulders, slipping her dress off as he moved deftly down her body to her breast, delighted to find she wasn't wearing a bra.

"Shall we go upstairs, Debbie? I'm too old to make love on the sofa."

Without speaking, she rose and led him by the hand to her bedroom, which smelled faintly and deliciously of the scent she herself was wearing.

She switched on a small bedside light and took off the rest of her clothes, letting them fall where she stood. Michael never once took his eyes off her body as he undressed clumsily on the other side of the bed. He slipped under the sheets and quickly joined her. When they had finished making love, an experience he hadn't enjoyed as much for a long time, he lay there pondering the fact that she had succumbed at all, especially on their first date.

They lay silently in each other's arms before making love for a second time, which was every bit as delightful as the first. Michael then fell into a deep sleep.

He awoke first the next morning and stared across at the beautiful woman who lay by his side. The digital clock on the bedside table showed 7:03. He touched her forehead lightly with his lips and began to stroke her hair. She awoke lazily and smiled up at him. Then they made morning love, slowly, gently, but every bit as pleasing as the night before. He didn't speak as she slipped out of bed and ran a bath for him before going to the kitchen to prepare breakfast. Michael relaxed in the hot bath, singing a Bobby Short number at the top of his voice. How he wished that Adrian could see him now. He dried himself and dressed before joining Debbie in the little kitchen, where they shared breakfast together. Eggs, bacon, toast, English marmalade, and steaming black coffee. Debbie then had a bath and dressed while Michael read the *New York Times*. When she reappeared in the living room wearing a smart coral dress, he was sorry to be leaving so soon.

"We must leave now, or you'll miss your flight."

Michael rose reluctantly, and Debbie drove him back to his hotel, where he quickly threw his clothes into a suitcase, paid the bill for his unslept-in double bed, and joined her back in the car. On the journey to the airport they chatted about the coming elections and pumpkin pie almost as if they had been married for years or were both avoiding admitting the previous night had ever happened.

Debbie dropped Michael in front of the Pan Am terminal and put the car in the parking lot before joining him at the check-in counter. They waited for his flight to be called.

"Pan American announces the departure of Flight Number 006 to London Heathrow. Will all passengers please proceed with their boarding passes to Gate Number Nine?"

When they reached the "passengers only" barrier, Michael took Debbie briefly in his arms. "Thank you for a memorable evening," he said.

"No, it is I who must thank you, Michael," she replied as she kissed him on the cheek.

"I must confess I hadn't thought it would end up quite like that," he said.

"Why not?" she asked.

"Not easy to explain," he replied, searching for words that would flatter and not embarrass. "Let's say I was surprised that—"

"You were surprised that we ended up in bed together on our first night? You shouldn't be."

"I shouldn't?"

"No, there's a simple enough explanation. My friends all told me when I got divorced to find myself a man and have a one-night stand. The idea sounded like fun, but I didn't like the thought of the men in New York thinking I was easy." She touched him gently on the side of his face. "So when I met you and Adrian, both safely living over three thousand miles away, I thought to myself, Whichever one of you comes back first . . . "

A CHAPTER OF
ACCIDENTS

WE FIRST MET PATRICK TRAVERS on our annual winter holiday to Verbier. We were waiting at the ski lift that first Saturday morning, when a man who must have been in his early forties stood aside to allow Caroline to take his place so that we could travel up together. He explained that he had already completed two runs that morning and didn't mind waiting. I thanked him and thought nothing more of it.

As soon as we reach the top my wife and I always go our separate ways, she to the A-slope to join Marcel, who only instructs advanced skiers—she has been skiing since the age of seven—I to the B-slope and any instructor who is available—I took up skiing at the age of forty-one, and frankly the B-slope is still too advanced for me though I don't dare admit as much, especially to Caroline. We always meet up again at the ski lift after completing our different runs.

That evening we bumped into Travers at the hotel bar. Since he seemed to be on his own we invited him to join us for dinner. He proved to be an amusing companion, and we passed a pleasant enough evening together. He flirted politely with my wife without ever overstepping the mark, and she appeared to be flattered by his attentions. Over the years I have become used to men being attracted to Caroline, and I never need reminding how lucky I am. During dinner we learned that Travers was a merchant banker with an office in the City and a flat in Eaton Square. He had come to Verbier every year since he had been taken on a school trip in the late fifties, he told us. He still prided himself on being the first on the ski lift every morning, almost always beating the local blades up and down.

Travers appeared to be genuinely interested in the fact that I ran a small West End art gallery; as it turned out, he was something of a collector himself, specializing in minor Impressionists. He promised he would drop by and see my next exhibition when he was back in London.

I assured him that he would be most welcome but never gave it a second thought. In fact I only saw Travers a couple of times over the rest of the vacation, once talking to the wife of a friend of mine who owned a gallery that specializes in Oriental rugs, and later I noticed him following Caroline expertly down the treacherous A-slope.

It was six weeks later, and some minutes before I could place him that night at my gallery. I had to rack that part of one's memory that recalls names, a skill politicians rely on every day.

"Good to see you, Edward," he said. "I saw the write-up you got in the *Independent* and remembered your kind invitation to the private view."

"Glad you could make it, Patrick," I replied, remembering just in time.

"I'm not a champagne man myself," he told me, "but I'll travel a long way to see a Vuillard."

"You think highly of him?"

"Oh yes. I would compare him favorably with Pissarro and Bonnard, and he still remains one of the most underrated of the Impressionists."

"I agree," I replied. "But my gallery has felt that way about Vuillard for some considerable time."

"How much is *The Lady at the Window*?" he asked.

"Eighty thousand pounds," I said quietly.

"It reminds me of a picture of his in the Metropolitan," he said, as he studied the reproduction in the catalog.

I was impressed, and told Travers that the Vuillard in New York had been painted within a month of the one he so admired.

He nodded. "And the small nude?"

"Forty-seven thousand," I told him.

"Mrs. Hensell, the wife of his dealer and Vuillard's second

mistress, if I'm not mistaken. The French are always so much more civilized about these things than we are. But my favorite painting in this exhibition," he continued, "compares surely with the finest of his work." He turned to face the large oil of a young girl playing a piano, her mother bending to turn a page of the score.

"Magnificent," he said. "Dare I ask how much?"

"Three hundred and seventy thousand pounds," I said, wondering if such a price tag put it out of Travers's bracket.

"What a super party, Edward," said a voice from behind my shoulder.

"Percy!" I cried, turning round. "I thought you said you wouldn't be able to make it."

"Yes, I did, old fellow, but I decided I couldn't sit at home alone all the time, so I've come to drown my sorrows in champagne."

"Quite right too," I said. "Sorry to hear about Diana," I added as Percy moved on. When I turned back to continue my conversation with Patrick Travers, he was nowhere to be seen. I searched around the room and spotted him standing in the far corner of the gallery chatting to my wife, a glass of champagne in his hand. She was wearing an off-the-shoulder green dress that I considered a little too modern. Travers's eyes seemed to be glued to a spot a few inches below the shoulders. I would have thought nothing of it had he spoken to anyone else that evening.

The next occasion on which I saw Travers was about a week later on returning from the bank with some petty cash. Once again he was standing in front of the Vuillard oil of mother and daughter at the piano.

"Good morning, Patrick," I said as I joined him.

"I can't seem to get that picture out of my mind," he declared, as he continued to stare at the two figures.

"Understandably."

"I don't suppose you would allow me to live with them for a week or two until I can finally make up my mind? Naturally I would be quite happy to leave a deposit."

"Of course," I said. "I would require a bank reference as well, and the deposit would be twenty-five thousand pounds."

He agreed to both requests without hesitation, so I asked him where he would like the picture delivered. He handed me a card that revealed his address in Eaton Square. The following morning his bankers confirmed that £370,000 would not be a problem for their client.

Within twenty-four hours the Vuillard had been taken to his home and hung in the dining room on the ground floor. He phoned in the afternoon to thank me, and asked if Caroline and I would care to join him for dinner; he wanted, he said, a second opinion on how the painting looked.

With £370,000 at stake I didn't feel it was an invitation I could reasonably turn down, and in any case Caroline seemed eager to accept, explaining that she was interested to see what his house was like.

We dined with Travers the following Thursday. We turned out to be the only guests, and I remember being surprised that there wasn't a Mrs. Travers or at least a resident girlfriend. He was a thoughtful host and the meal he had arranged was superb. However, I considered at the time that he seemed a little too solicitous toward Caroline, although she certainly gave the impression of enjoying his undivided attention. At one point I began to wonder if either of them would have noticed if I had disappeared into thin air.

When we left Eaton Square that night Travers told me that he had almost made up his mind about the picture, which made me feel the evening had served at least some purpose.

Six days later the painting was returned to the gallery with a note attached explaining that he no longer cared for it. Travers did not elaborate on his reasons, but simply ended by saying that he hoped to drop by some time and reconsider the other Vuillards. Disappointed, I returned his deposit, but realized that customers often do come back, sometimes months, even years later.

But Travers never did.

It was about a month later that I learned why he would never return. I was lunching at the large center table at my club, as in most all-male establishments the table reserved for members who drift in on their own. Percy Fellows was the next to enter the dining room, and he took a seat opposite me. I hadn't seen him to talk to since the private view of the Vuillard exhibition, and we hadn't really had much of a conversation then. Percy was one of the most respected antique dealers in England, and I had once even done a successful barter with him, a Charles II writing desk in exchange for a Dutch landscape by Utrillo.

I repeated how sorry I was to learn about Diana.

"It was always going to end in divorce," he explained. "She was in and out of every bedroom in London. I was beginning to look a complete cuckold, and that bloody man Travers was the last straw."

"Travers?" I said, not understanding.

"Patrick Travers, the man named in my divorce petition. Ever come across him?"

"I know the name," I said hesitantly, wanting to hear more before I admitted to our slight acquaintance.

"Funny," he said. "Could have sworn I saw him at the private view."

"But what do you mean, he was the last straw?" I asked, trying to take his mind off the opening.

"Met the bloody fellow at Ascot, didn't we? Joined us for lunch, happily drank my champagne, ate my strawberries and cream, and then before the week was out had bedded my wife. But that's not the half of it."

"The half of it?"

"The man had the nerve to come round to my shop and put down a large deposit on a Georgian table. Then he invites the two of us round to dinner to see how it looks. After he's had enough time to make love to Diana, he returns them both slightly soiled. You don't look too well, old fellow," said Percy suddenly. "Something wrong with the food? Never been the same since Harry left for the Carlton. I've written to the wine committee about it several times, but—"

"No, I'm fine," I said. "I just need a little fresh air. Please excuse me, Percy."

It was on the walk back from my club that I decided I would have to do something about Mr. Travers.

The next morning I waited for the mail to arrive and checked any envelopes addressed to Caroline. Nothing seemed untoward, but then I decided that Travers wouldn't have been foolish enough to commit anything to paper. I also began to eavesdrop on her telephone conversations, but he was not among the callers, at least not while I was at home. I even checked the mileometer on her Mini to see if she had driven any long distances, but then Eaton Square isn't all that far. It's often what you don't do that gives the game away, I decided: We didn't make love for a fortnight, and she didn't comment.

I continued to watch Caroline more carefully over the next few weeks, but it became obvious to me that Travers must have tired of her about the same time as he had returned the Vuillard. This only made me more angry.

I then formed a plan of revenge that seemed quite extraordinary to me at the time, and I assumed that in a matter of days I would get over it, even forget it. But I didn't. If anything, the idea grew into an obsession. I began to convince myself that it was my bounden duty to do away with Travers before he besmirched any more of my friends.

I have never in my life knowingly broken the law. Parking fines annoy me, dropped litter offends me, and I pay my VAT on the same day the frightful buff envelope drops through the mail slot.

Nevertheless, once I'd decided what had to be done I set about my task meticulously. At first I considered shooting Travers, until I discovered how hard it is to get a gun license, and that if I did the job properly he would end up feeling very little pain, which wasn't what I had planned for him. Then poisoning crossed my mind—but that requires a witnessed prescription, and I still wouldn't be able to watch the long slow death I desired. Then strangling, which I decided would necessitate too much courage—and in any case he was a bigger man than me so *I* might end up being the one who was strangled. Then drowning, which could take years to get the man near any water, and then I might not be able to hang around to make sure he went under for the third time. I even gave some thought to running over the damned man, but dropped that idea when I realized that opportunity would be almost nil and besides, I wouldn't be left any time to check if he was dead. I was quickly becoming aware just how hard it is to kill someone—and get away with it.

I sat awake at night reading the biographies of murderers, but since they had all been caught and found guilty, that didn't fill me with much confidence. I turned to detective novels, which always seemed to allow for a degree of coincidence, luck, and surprise that I was unwilling to risk, until I came across a rewarding line from Conan Doyle: "Any intended victim who has a regular routine immediately makes himself more vulnerable." And then I recalled one routine of which Travers was particularly proud. It required a further six-month wait on my part, but that gave me more time to perfect my plan. I used the enforced wait well because whenever Caroline was away for more than twenty-four hours, I booked a skiing lesson on the dry slope at Harrow.

I found it surprisingly easy to discover when Travers would be returning to Verbier, and I was able to organize the winter vacation so that our paths would cross for only three days, a period of time quite sufficient for me to commit my first crime.

Caroline and I arrived in Verbier on the second Friday in January. She had commented on the state of my nerves more than once over the Christmas period, and hoped the vacation would help me relax. I could hardly explain to her that it was the thought of the vacation that was making me so tense. It didn't help when she asked me on the plane to Switzerland if I thought Travers might be there this year.

On the first morning after our arrival, we took the ski lift up at about ten-thirty, and once we had reached the top, Caroline duly reported to Marcel. As she departed with him for the A-slope, I returned to the B-slope to work on my own. As always we agreed to meet back at the ski lift or, if we missed each other, at least for lunch.

During the days that followed I went over and over the plan I had perfected in my mind and practiced so diligently at Harrow until I felt sure it was foolproof. By the end of the first week I had convinced myself I was ready.

The night before Travers was due to arrive, I was the last to leave the slopes. Even Caroline commented on how much my skiing had improved, and she suggested to Marcel that I was ready for the A-slope with its sharper bends and steeper inclines.

"Next year, perhaps," I told her, trying to make light of it, and returned to the B-slope.

During the final morning I skied over the first mile of the course again and again, and became so preoccupied with my work that I quite forgot to join Caroline for lunch.

In the afternoon I checked and rechecked the placing of every red flag marking the run, and once I was convinced the last skier had left the slope for the evening I collected about thirty of the flags and replaced them at intervals I had carefully worked out. My final task was to check the prepared patch before building a large mound of snow some twenty paces above the chosen spot. Once my preparations were complete I skied slowly down the mountain in the fading light.

"Are you trying to win an Olympic gold medal or something?" Caroline asked me when I eventually got back to our room. I closed the bathroom door so she couldn't expect a reply.

Travers checked in to the hotel an hour later.

I waited until the early evening before I joined him at the bar for a drink. He seemed a little nervous when he first saw me, but I quickly put him at ease. His old self-confidence soon returned, which only made me more determined to carry out my plan. I left him at the bar a few minutes before Caroline came down for dinner so that she wouldn't see the two of us together. Innocent surprise would be necessary once the deed had been done.

"Unlike you to eat so little, especially as you missed your lunch," Caroline remarked as we left the dining room that night.

I made no comment as we passed Travers seated at the bar, his hand on the knee of another innocent middle-aged woman.

I did not sleep for one second that night, and I crept out of bed just before six the next morning, careful not to wake Caroline. Everything was laid out on the bathroom floor just as I had left it the night before. A few moments later I was dressed and ready. I walked down the back stairs of the hotel, avoiding the elevator, and crept out by the fire exit, realizing for the first time what a thief must feel like. I had a woolen cap pulled well down over my ears and a pair of snow goggles covering my eyes: Not even Caroline would have recognized me.

I arrived at the bottom of the ski lift forty minutes before it was due to open. As I stood alone behind the little shed that housed the electrical machinery to work the lift, I realized that everything now depended on Travers's sticking to his routine. I wasn't sure I could go through with it if my plan had to be moved to the following day. As I waited, I stamped my feet in the freshly fallen snow and slapped my arms around my chest to keep warm. Every few moments I kept peering round the corner of the building in the hope that I would see him striding toward me. At last a speck appeared at the bottom of the hill by the side of the road, a pair of skis resting on the man's shoulders. But what if it turned out not to be Travers?

I stepped out from behind the shed a few moments later to join the warmly wrapped man. It *was* Travers, and he could not hide his surprise at seeing me standing there. I started up a casual conversation about being unable to sleep, and how I thought I might as well put in a few runs before the rush began. Now all I needed was the ski lift to start up on time. A few minutes after seven an engineer arrived, and the vast oily mechanism cranked into action.

We were the first two to take our places on those little seats before heading up and over the deep ravine. I kept turning back to check there was still no one else in sight.

"I usually manage to complete a full run even before the second person arrives," Travers told me when the lift had reached its highest point. I looked back again to be sure we were now well out of sight of the engineer working the lift, then peered down some two hundred feet, and wondered what it would be like to land head first in the ravine. I began to feel dizzy and wished I hadn't looked down.

The ski lift jerked slowly on up the icy wire until we finally reached the landing point.

"Damn," I said, as we jumped off our little seats. "Marcel isn't here."

"Never is at this time," said Travers, making off toward the advanced slope. "Far too early for him."

"I don't suppose you would come down with me?" I said, calling after Travers.

He stopped and looked back suspiciously.

"Caroline thinks I'm ready to join you," I explained, "but I'm not so sure and would value a second opinion. I've broken my own record for the B-slope several times, but I wouldn't want to make a fool of myself in front of my wife."

"Well, I—"

"I'd ask Marcel if he were here. And in any case you're the best skier I know."

"Well, if you—" he began.

"Just this once, then you can spend the rest of your vacation on the A-slope. You could even treat the run as a warmup."

"Might make a change, I suppose," he said.

"Just this once," I repeated. "That's all I'll need. Then you'll be able to tell me if I'm good enough."

"Shall we make a race of it?" he said, taking me by surprise just as I began clamping on my skis. I couldn't complain; all the books on murder had warned me to be prepared for the unexpected. "That's one way we can find out if you're ready," he added cockily.

"If you insist. Don't forget, I'm older and less experienced than you," I reminded him. I checked my skis quickly because I knew I had to start off in front of him.

"But you know the B-course backwards," he retorted. "I've never even seen it before."

"I'll agree to a race, but only if you'll consider a wager," I replied.

For the first time I could see I had caught his interest. "How much?" he asked.

"Oh, nothing so vulgar as money," I said. "The winner gets to tell Caroline the truth."

"The truth?" he said, looking puzzled.

"Yes," I replied, and shot off down the hill before he could respond. I got a good start as I skied in and out of the red flags, but looking back over my shoulder I could see he had recovered quickly and was already chasing hard after me. I realized that it was vital for me to stay in front of him for the first third of the course, but I could already feel him cutting down my lead.

After half a mile of swerving and driving he shouted, "You'll have to go a lot faster than that if you hope to beat me." His arrogant boast only pushed me to stay ahead, but I kept the lead only because of my advantage of knowing every twist and turn during that first mile. Once I was sure that I would reach the vital newly marked route before he could I began to relax. After all, I had practiced over the next two hundred meters fifty times a day for the last ten days, but I was only too aware that this time was the only one that mattered.

I glanced over my shoulder to see he was now about thirty meters behind me. I began to slow slightly as we approached the prepared ice patch, hoping he wouldn't notice or would think I'd lost my nerve. I held back even more when I reached the top of the patch until I could almost feel the sound of his breathing. Then, quite suddenly, the moment before I would have hit the ice I plowed my skis and came to a complete halt in the mound of snow I had built the previous night. Travers sailed past me at about forty miles an hour, and seconds later flew high into the air over the ravine with a scream I will never forget. I couldn't get myself to look over the edge, as I knew he must have broken every bone in his body the moment he hit the snow a hundred feet below.

I carefully leveled the mound of snow that had saved my life and then clambered back up the mountain as fast as I could go, gathering the thirty flags that had marked out my false route. Then I skied from side to side replacing them in their correct positions on the B-slope, some hundred meters above my carefully prepared ice patch. When each one was back in place I skied on down the hill, feeling like an Olympic champion. Once I reached the base of the slope I pulled up my hood to cover my head and didn't remove my snow goggles. I unstrapped my skis and walked casually toward the hotel. I reentered the building by the rear door and was back in bed by seven-forty.

I tried to control my breathing, but it was some time before my pulse had returned to normal. Caroline awoke a few minutes later, turned over, and put her arms round me.

"Ugh," she said, "you're frozen. Have you been sleeping without the covers on?"

I laughed. "You must have pulled them off during the night."

"Go and have a hot bath."

After I had had a quick bath we made love, and I dressed a second time, double-checking that I had left no clues of my early flight before going down to breakfast.

As Caroline was pouring my second cup of coffee, I heard the ambulance siren, at first coming from the town and then later returning.

"Hope it wasn't a bad accident," my wife said as she continued to pour her coffee.

"What?" I said, a little too loudly, glancing up from the previous day's *Times*.

"The siren, silly. There must have been an accident on the mountain. Probably Travers," she said.

"Travers?" I said, even more loudly.

"Patrick Travers. I saw him at the bar last night. I didn't mention it to you because I know you don't care for him."

"But why Travers?" I asked nervously.

"Doesn't he always claim he's the first on the slope every morning? Even beats the instructors up to the top."

"Does he?" I said.

"You must remember. We were going up for the first time the day we met him, and he was already on his third run."

"Was he?"

"You are being dim this morning, Edward. Did you get out of bed the wrong side?" she asked, laughing.

I didn't reply.

"Well, I only hope it *is* Travers," Caroline added, sipping her coffee. "I never did like the man."

"Why not?" I asked, somewhat taken aback.

"He once made a pass at me," she said casually.

I stared across at her, unable to speak.

"Aren't you going to ask what happened?"

"I'm so stunned I don't know what to say," I replied.

"He was all over me at the gallery that night, and then invited me out to lunch after we had dinner with him. I told him to get lost," Caroline said. She touched me gently on the hand. "I've never mentioned it to you before because I thought it might have been the reason he returned the Vuillard, and that only made me feel guilty."

"But it's me who should feel guilty," I said, fumbling with a piece of toast.

"Oh, no, darling, you're not guilty of anything. In any case, if I ever decided to be unfaithful it wouldn't be with a lounge lizard like that. Good heavens no. Diana had already warned me what to expect from him. Not my style at all."

I sat there thinking of Travers on his way to a morgue, or even worse, still buried under the snow, knowing there was nothing I could do about it.

"You know, I think the time really has come for you to tackle the A-slope," Caroline said as we finished breakfast. "Your skiing has improved beyond words."

"Yes," I replied, more than a little preoccupied.

I hardly spoke another word as we made our way together to the foot of the mountain.

"Are you all right, darling?" Caroline asked as we traveled up side by side on the lift.

"Fine," I said, unable to look down into the ravine as we reached the highest point. Was Travers still down there, or already in the morgue?

"Stop looking like a frightened child. After all the work you've put in this week you're more than ready to join me," she said reassuringly.

I smiled weakly. When we reached the top, I jumped off the

ski lift just a moment too early, and knew as soon as I took my second step that I had sprained an ankle.

I received no sympathy from Caroline. She was convinced I was pretending in order to avoid attempting the advanced run. She swept past me and sped on down the mountain while I returned in ignominy via the lift. When I reached the bottom I glanced toward the engineer, but he didn't give me a second look. I hobbled over to the first-aid post and checked in. Caroline joined me a few minutes later.

I explained to her that the duty orderly thought it might be a fracture and had suggested I report to the hospital immediately.

Caroline frowned, removed her skis, and went off to find a taxi to take us to the hospital. It wasn't a long journey but it was one the taxi driver had evidently done many times before from the way he took the slippery bends.

"I ought to be able to dine out on this for about a year," Caroline promised me as we entered the double doors of the hospital.

"Would you be kind enough to wait outside, madam?" asked a male orderly as I was ushered into the X-ray room.

"Yes, but will I ever see my poor husband again?" she mocked as the door was closed in front of her.

I entered a room full of sophisticated machinery presided over by an expensively dressed doctor. I told him what I thought was wrong with me and he lifted the offending foot gently up on to an X-ray machine. Moments later he was studying the large negative.

"There's no fracture there," he assured me, pointing to the bone. "But if you are still in any pain it might be wise for me to bind the ankle up tightly." He pinned my X ray next to five others hanging from a rail.

"Am I the sixth person already today?" I asked, looking up at the row of X rays.

"No, no," he said, laughing. "The other five are all the same man. I think he must have tried to fly over the ravine, the fool."

"Over the ravine?"

"Yes, showing off, I suspect," he said as he began to bind my ankle. "We get one every year, but this poor fellow broke both his legs and an arm, and will have a nasty scar on his face to remind him of his stupidity. Lucky to be alive, in my opinion."

"Lucky to be alive?" I repeated weakly.

"Yes, but only because he didn't know what he was doing. My fourteen-year-old skis over that ravine and can land like a sea-gull on water. He, on the other hand," the doctor pointed to the X rays, "won't be skiing again this holiday. In fact, he won't be walking for at least six months."

"Really?" I said.

"And as for you," he added, after he finished binding me up, "just rest the ankle in ice every three hours and change the bandage once a day. You should be back on the slopes again in a couple of days, three at the most."

"We're flying back this evening," I told him as I gingerly got to my feet.

"Good timing," he said, smiling.

I hobbled happily out of the X-ray room to find Caroline head down in *Elle*.

"You look pleased with yourself," she said, looking up.

"I am. It turns out to be nothing worse than two broken legs, a broken arm, and a scar on the face."

"How stupid of me," said Caroline, "I thought it was a simple sprain."

"Not me," I told her. "Travers—the accident this morning, you remember? The ambulance. Still, they assure me he'll live," I added.

"Pity," she said, linking her arm through mine. "After all the trouble you took, I was rather hoping you'd succeed."

CHECKMATE

AS SHE ENTERED THE room every eye turned toward her.

When admiring a girl some men start with her head and work down. I start with the ankles and work up.

She wore black high-heeled velvet shoes and a tight-fitting black dress that stopped high enough above the knees to reveal the most perfectly tapering legs. As my eyes continued their upward sweep they paused to take in her narrow waist and slim athletic figure. But it was the oval face that I found captivating, slightly pouting lips and the largest blue eyes I've ever seen, crowned with a head of thick, black, short-cut hair that literally shone with luster. Her entrance was all the more breathtaking because of the surroundings she had chosen. Heads would have turned at a diplomatic reception, a society cocktail party, even a charity ball, but at a chess tournament . . .

I followed her every movement, patronizingly unable to accept that she could be a player. She walked slowly over to the club secretary's table and signed in to prove me wrong. She was handed a number to indicate her challenger for the opening match. Anyone who had not yet been allocated an opponent waited to see if she would take her place opposite their side of the board.

The player checked the number she had been given and made her way toward an elderly man who was seated in the far corner of the room, a former captain of the club now past his best.

As the club's new captain I had been responsible for instigating these round-robin matches. We meet on the last Friday of the month in a large clublike room on top of the Mason's Arms in the High Street. The landlord sees to it that thirty tables are set out for us and that food and drink are readily available.

Three or four other clubs in the district send half a dozen opponents to play a couple of blitz games, giving us a chance to face rivals we would not normally play. The rules for the matches are simple enough—one minute on the clock is the maximum allowed for each move, so a game rarely lasts for more than an hour, and if a pawn hasn't been captured in thirty moves the game is automatically declared a draw. A short break for a drink between games, paid for by the loser, ensures that everyone has the chance to challenge two opponents during the evening.

A thin man wearing half-moon spectacles and a dark blue three-piece suit made his way over toward my board. We smiled and shook hands. My guess would have been a solicitor, but I was wrong as he turned out to be an accountant working for a stationery supplier in Woking.

I found it hard to concentrate on my opponent's well-rehearsed Moscow opening as my eyes kept leaving the board and wandering over to the girl in the black dress. On the one occasion our eyes did meet she gave me an enigmatic smile, but although I tried again I was unable to elicit the same response a second time. Despite being preoccupied I still managed to defeat the accountant, who seemed unaware that there were several ways out of a seven-pawn attack.

At the half-time break three other members of the club had offered her a drink before I even reached the bar. I knew I could not hope to play my second match against the girl as I would be expected to challenge one of the visiting team captains. In fact she ended up playing the accountant.

I defeated my new opponent in a little over forty minutes and, as a solicitous host, began to take an interest in the other matches that were still being played. I set out on a circuitous route that ensured I ended up at her table. I could see that the accountant already had the better of her, and within moments of my arrival she had lost both her queen and the game.

I introduced myself and found that just shaking hands with her was a sexual experience. Weaving our way through the tables we strolled over to the bar together. Her name, she told me, was Amanda Curzon. I ordered Amanda the glass of red wine she requested and a half-pint of beer for myself. I began by commiserating with her over the defeat.

"How did you get on against him?" she asked.

"Just managed to beat him," I said. "But it was very close. How did your first game with our old captain turn out?"

"Stalemate," said Amanda. "But I think he was just being courteous."

"Last time I played him it ended up in stalemate," I told her.

She smiled. "Perhaps we ought to have a game sometime?"

"I'll look forward to that," I said, as she finished her drink.

"Well, I must be off," she announced suddenly. "Have to catch the last train to Hounslow."

"Allow me to drive you," I said gallantly. "It's the least the host captain can be expected to do."

"But surely it's miles out of your way?"

"Not at all," I lied, Hounslow being about twenty minutes beyond my flat. I gulped down the last drop of my beer and helped Amanda on with her coat. Before leaving I thanked the pub owner for the efficient organization of the evening.

We then strolled into the parking lot. I opened the passenger door of my Scirocco to allow Amanda to climb in.

"A slight improvement on London Transport," she said as I slid into my side of the car. I smiled and headed out on the road northward. That black dress that I described earlier goes even higher up the legs when a girl sits back in a Scirocco. It didn't seem to embarrass her.

"It's still very early," I ventured after a few inconsequential remarks about the club evening. "Have you time to drop in for a drink?"

"It would have to be a quick one," she replied, looking at her watch. "I've a busy day ahead of me tomorrow."

"Of course," I said, chatting on, hoping she wouldn't notice a detour that could hardly be described as on the way to Hounslow.

"Do you work in town?" I asked.

"Yes. I'm a receptionist for a firm of estate agents in Berkeley Square."

"I'm surprised you're not a model."

"I used to be," she replied without further explanation. She seemed quite oblivious to the route I was taking as she chatted on about her vacation plans for Ibiza. Once we had arrived at my place I parked the car and led Amanda through my front gate and up to the flat. In the hall I helped her off with her coat before taking her through to the front room.

"What would you like to drink?" I asked.

"I'll stick to wine, if you've a bottle already open," she replied, as she walked slowly round, taking in the unusually tidy room. My mother must have dropped by during the morning, I thought gratefully.

"It's only a bachelor pad," I said, emphasizing the word "bachelor" before going into the kitchen. To my relief I found there was an unopened bottle of wine in the larder. I joined Amanda with the bottle and two glasses a few moments later, to find her studying my chess board and fingering the delicate ivory pieces that were set out for a game I was playing by mail.

"What a beautiful set," she volunteered as I handed her a glass of wine. "Where did you find it?"

"Mexico," I told her, not explaining that I had won it in a tournament while on vacation there. "I was only sorry we didn't have the chance to have a game ourselves."

She checked her watch. "Time for a quick one," she said, taking a seat behind the little white pieces.

I quickly took my place opposite her. She smiled, picked up a white and a black bishop and hid them behind her back. Her dress became even tighter and emphasized the shape of her breasts. She then placed both clenched fists in front of me. I touched her right hand and she turned it over and opened it to reveal a white bishop.

"Is there to be a wager of any kind?" I asked lightheartedly. She checked inside her evening bag.

"I only have a few pounds on me," she said.

"I'd be willing to play for lower stakes."

"What do you have in mind?" she asked.

"What can you offer?"

"What would you like?"

"Ten pounds if you win."

"And if I lose?"

"You take something off."

I regretted the words the moment I had said them and waited for her to slap my face and leave, but she said simply, "There's not much harm in that if we only play one game."

I nodded my agreement and stared down at the board.

She wasn't a bad player—what the pros call a *patzer*—though her Roux opening was somewhat orthodox. I managed to make the game last twenty minutes while sacrificing several pieces without making it look too obvious. When I said "Checkmate," she kicked off both her shoes and laughed.

"Care for another drink?" I asked, not feeling too hopeful. "After all, it's not yet eleven."

"All right. Just a small one, and then I must be off."

I went to the kitchen, returned a moment later clutching the bottle, and refilled her glass.

"I only wanted half a glass," she said, frowning.

"I was lucky to win," I said, ignoring her remark, "after your bishop captured my knight. Extremely close-run thing."

"Perhaps," she replied.

"Care for another game?" I ventured.

She hesitated.

"Double or quits?"

"What do you mean?"

"Twenty pounds or another garment?"

"Neither of us is going to lose much tonight, are we?"

She pulled up her chair as I turned the board around and we both began to put the ivory pieces back in place.

The second game took a little longer as I made a silly mistake early on, castling on my queen's side, and it took several moves to recover. However, I still managed to finish the game off in under thirty minutes and even found time to refill Amanda's glass when she wasn't looking.

She smiled at me as she hitched her dress up high enough to allow me to see the tops of her stockings. She undid the garters and slowly peeled the stockings off before dropping them on my side of the table.

"I nearly beat you that time," she said.

"Almost," I replied. "Want another chance to get even? Let's say fifty pounds this time," I suggested, trying to make the offer sound magnanimous.

"The stakes are getting higher for both of us," she replied as she reset the board. I began to wonder what might be going through her mind. Whatever it was, she foolishly sacrificed both her rooks early on, and the game was over in a matter of minutes.

Once again she lifted her dress but this time well above her waist. My eyes were glued to her thighs as she undid the black garter belt and held it high above my head before letting it drop and join her stockings on my side of the table.

"Once I had lost the second rook," she said, "I was never in with a chance."

"I agree. It would therefore only be fair to allow you one more chance," I said, quickly resetting the board. "After all," I added, "you could win one hundred pounds this time." She smiled.

"I really ought to be going home," she said as she moved her queen's pawn two squares forward. She smiled that enigmatic smile again as I countered with my bishop's pawn.

It was the best game she had played all evening, and her use of the Warsaw gambit kept me at the board for over thirty minutes. In fact I damn nearly lost early on because I found it hard to concentrate properly on her defense strategy. A couple of times Amanda chuckled when she thought she had got the better of me, but it became obvious she had not seen Karpov play the Sicilian defense and win from a seemingly impossible position.

"Checkmate," I finally declared.

"Damn," she said, and standing up turned her back on me. "You'll have to give me a hand." Trembling, I leaned over and slowly pulled the zip down until it reached the small of her back. Once again I wanted to touch the smooth, creamy skin. She swung around to face me, shrugged gracefully, and the dress fell to the ground as if a statue were being unveiled. She leaned forward and brushed the side of my cheek with her hand, which had much the same effect as an electric shock. I emptied the last of the bottle of wine into her glass and left for the kitchen with the excuse of needing to refill my own. When I returned she hadn't moved. A gauzy black bra and pair of panties were now the only garments that I still hoped to see removed.

"I don't suppose you'd play one more game?" I asked, trying not to sound desperate.

"It's time you took me home," she said with a giggle.

I passed her another glass of wine. "Just one more," I begged. "But this time it must be for both garments."

She laughed. "Certainly not," she said. "I couldn't afford to lose."

"It would have to be the last game," I agreed. "But two hundred pounds this time and we play for both garments." I waited, hoping the size of the wager would tempt her. "The odds must surely be on your side. After all, you've nearly won three times."

She sipped her drink as if considering the proposition. "All right," she said. "One last fling."

Neither of us voiced our feeling as to what was certain to happen if she lost.

I could not stop myself trembling as I set the board up once again. I cleared my mind, hoping she hadn't noticed that I had drunk only one glass of wine all night. I was determined to finish this one off quickly.

I moved my queen's pawn one square forward. She retaliated, pushing her king's pawn up two squares. I knew exactly what my next move needed to be, and because of it the game only lasted eleven minutes.

I have never been so comprehensively beaten in my life. Amanda was in a totally different class from me. She anticipated my every move and had gambits I had never encountered or even read of before.

It was her turn to say "Checkmate," which she delivered with the same enigmatic smile as before, adding, "You did say the odds were on my side this time."

I lowered my head in disbelief. When I looked up again, she had already slipped that beautiful black dress back on and was stuffing her stockings and suspenders into her evening bag. A moment later she put on her shoes.

I took out my checkbook, filled in the name "Amanda Curzon" and added the figure "£200," the date, and my signature. While I was doing this she replaced the little ivory pieces on the exact squares on which they had been when she had first entered the room.

She bent over and kissed me gently on the cheek. "Thank you," she said as she placed the check in her handbag. "We must play again sometime." I was still staring at the reset board in disbelief when I heard the front door close behind her.

"Wait a minute," I said, rushing to the door. "How will you get home?"

I was just in time to see her running down the steps and toward the open door of a BMW. She climbed in, allowing me one more look at those long tapering legs. She smiled as the car door was closed behind her.

The accountant strolled around to the driver's side, got in, revved up the engine, and drove the champion home.

THE CENTURY

"LIFE IS A GAME," said A. T. Pierson, thus immortalizing himself without actually having to do any real work. Though E. M. Forster showed more insight when he wrote "Fate is the Umpire, and Hope is the Ball, which is why I will never score a century at Lord's."

When I was a freshman at the university, my roommate invited me to have dinner in a sporting club to which he belonged, called Vincent's. Such institutions do not differ greatly around the Western world. They are always brimful of outrageously fit, healthy young animals, whose sole purpose in life seems to be to challenge the opposition of some neighboring institution to ridiculous feats of physical strength. My host's main rivals, he told me with undergraduate fervor, came from a high-thinking, plain-living establishment that had dozed the unworldly centuries away in the flat, dull, fen country of England, cartographically described on the map as Cambridge. Now the ultimate ambition of men such as my host was simple enough: In whichever sport they aspired to beat the "Tabs" the select few were rewarded with a Blue. As there is no other way of gaining this distinction at either Oxford or Cambridge, every place in the side is contested for with considerable zeal. A man may be selected and indeed play in every other match of the season for the University, even go on to represent his country, but if he does not play in the Oxford and Cambridge match, he cannot describe himself as a Blue.

My story concerns a delightful character I met that evening when I dined as a guest at Vincent's. The undergraduate to whom I refer was in his final year. He came from that part of the world that we still dared to describe in those days (without a great deal of thought) as the colonies. He was an Indian by birth, and the son of a man whose name in England was a household word, if not a legend, for he had captained Oxford and India at cricket, which meant that outside of the British Commonwealth he was about as well known as Babe Ruth is to the English. The young man's father had added to his fame by scoring a century at Lord's when captaining the university cricket team against Cambridge. In fact, when he went on to captain India against England he used to take pride in wearing his cream sweater with the wide dark blue band around the neck and waist. The son, experts predicted, would carry on in the family tradition. He was in much the same mold as his father, tall and rangy with jet black hair, and as a cricketer, a fine right-handed batsman and a useful left-arm spin bowler. (Those of you who have never been able to comprehend the English language, let alone the game of cricket, might well be tempted to ask why not a fine right-arm batsman and a useful left-handed spin bowler. The English, however, always cover such silly questions with the words: "Tradition, dear boy, tradition.")

The young Indian undergraduate, like his father, had come up to Oxford with considerably more interest in defeating Cambridge than the examiners. As a freshman he had played against most of the English county sides, notching up a century against three of them, and on one occasion taking five wickets in an innings. A week before the big match against Cambridge, the skipper informed him that he had won his Blue and that the names of the chosen eleven would be officially announced in *The Times* the following day. The young man telegraphed his father in Calcutta with the news, and then went off for a celebratory dinner at Vincent's. He entered the club's dining room in high spirits to the traditional round of applause afforded to a new Blue, and as he was about to take a seat he observed the boat crew, all nine of them, around a circular table at the far end of the room. He walked across to the captain of boats and remarked: "I thought you chaps sat one behind each other."

Within seconds, four 180-pound men were sitting on the new

Blue while the cox poured a pitcher of cold water over his head.

"If you fail to score a century," said one oar, "we'll use hot water next time," When the four oars had returned to their table, the cricketer rose slowly, straightened his tie in mock indignation, and as he passed the crew's table, patted the five foot one inch, 102-pound cox on the head and said, "Even losing teams should have a mascot,"

This time they only laughed, but it was in the very act of patting the cox on the head that he first noticed his thumb felt a little bruised, and he commented on the fact to the wicket keeper who had joined him for dinner. A large entrecôte steak arrived, and he found as he picked up his knife that he was unable to grip the handle properly. He tried to put the inconvenience out of his mind, assuming all would be well by the following morning. But the next day he woke in considerable pain and found to his dismay that the thumb was not only black but also badly swollen. After reporting the news to his captain, he took the first available train to London for a consultation with a Harley Street specialist. As the carriage rattled through Berkshire, he read in *The Times* that he had been awarded his Blue.

The specialist studied the offending thumb for some considerable time and expressed his doubt that the young man would be able to hold a ball, let alone a bat, for at least a fortnight. The prognosis turned out to be accurate, and our hero sat disconsolate in the stand at Lord's, watching Oxford lose the match and the twelfth man gain his Blue. His father, who had flown over from Calcutta especially for the encounter, offered his condolences, pointing out that he still had two years left in which to gain the honor.

As his second Trinity term approached, even the young man forgot his disappointment and in the opening match of the season against Somerset scored a memorable century, full of cuts and drives that reminded aficionados of his father. The son had been made secretary of cricket in the closed season as it was universally acknowledged that only bad luck and the boat crew had stopped him from reaping his just reward as a freshman.

Once again, he played in every fixture before the needle match, but in the last four games against county teams he failed to score more than a dozen runs and did not take a single wicket, while his immediate rivals excelled themselves. He was going through a lean patch, and was the first to agree with his captain that with so much talent around that year he should not be risked against Cambridge. Once again he watched Oxford lose the Blues match, and his opposite number the Cambridge secretary, Robin Oakley, score a faultless century. A man well into his sixties sporting a Middlesex County Club tie came up to the young Indian during the game, patted him on the shoulder, and remarked that he would never forget the day his father had scored a hundred against Cambridge: It didn't help.

When the cricketer returned for his final year, he was surprised and delighted to be selected by his fellow teammates to be captain, an honor never previously afforded to a man who had not been awarded the coveted Blue. His peers recognized his outstanding work as secretary and knew if he could reproduce the form of his freshman year he would undoubtedly not only win a Blue but go on to represent his country.

The tradition at Oxford is that in a man's final year he does not play cricket until he has taken Schools, which leaves him enough time to play in the last three county matches before the Varsity match. But as the new captain had no interest in graduating, he bypassed tradition and played cricket from the opening day of the summer season. His touch never failed him, for he batted magnificently, and on those rare occasions when he did have an off day with the bat, he bowled superbly. During the term he led Oxford to victory over three county sides, and his team looked well set for their revenge in the Varsity match.

As the day of the match drew nearer, the cricket correspondent of *The Times* wrote that anyone who had seen him bat this season felt sure that the young Indian would follow his father into the record books by scoring a century against Cambridge: But the correspondent did add that he might be vulnerable against the early attack of Bill Potter, the Cambridge fast bowler.

Everyone wanted the Oxford captain to succeed, for he was one of those rare and gifted men whose charm creates no enemies.

When he announced his Blues team to the press, he did not send a telegram to his father for fear that the news might bring bad luck, and for good measure he did not speak to any member of the boat crew for the entire week leading up to the match. The night before the final encounter he retired to bed at seven, although he did not sleep.

On the first morning of the three-day match, the sun shone brightly in an almost cloudless sky, and by eleven o'clock a fair-sized crowd was already in their seats. The two captains in open-necked white shirts, spotless white pressed trousers, and freshly polished white boots came out to study the pitch before they tossed. Robin Oakley of Cambridge won and elected to bat.

By lunch on the first day Cambridge had scored seventy-nine for three, and in the early afternoon, when his fast bowlers were tired from their second spell and had not managed an early breakthrough, the captain put himself on. When he was straight, the ball didn't reach a full length, and when he bowled a full length, he was never straight; he quickly took himself off. His less established bowlers managed the necessary breakthrough, and Cambridge were all out an hour after tea for 208.

The Oxford openers took the crease at ten past five; fifty minutes to see through before close of play on the first day. The captain sat padded up on the pavilion balcony, waiting to be called upon only if a wicket fell. His instructions had been clear: No heroics; bat out the forty minutes so that Oxford could start afresh the next morning with all ten wickets intact. With only one over left before the close of play, the young freshman opener had his middle stump removed by Bill Potter, the Cambridge fast bowler. Oxford were eleven for one. The captain came to the crease with only four balls left to face before the clock reached six. He took his usual guard, middle and leg, and prepared himself to face the fastest man in the Cambridge side. Potter's first delivery came rocketing down and was just short of a length, moving away outside the off stump. The ball nicked the edge of the bat—or was it pad?—and carried to first slip, who dived to his right and took the catch low down. Eleven Cambridge men screamed "Howzat!" Was the captain going to be out—for a duck? Without waiting for the umpire's decision he turned and walked back to the pavilion, allowing no expression to appear on his face though he continually hit the side of his pad with his bat. As he climbed the steps he saw his father, sitting on his own in the members' enclosure. He walked on through the Long Room, to cries of "Bad luck, old fellow" from men holding slopping pints of beer, and "Better luck in the second innings" from large-bellied old Blues.

The next day Oxford kept their heads down and put together a total of 181 runs, leaving themselves only a 27-run deficit. When Cambridge batted for a second time, they pressed home their slight advantage and the captain's bowling figures ended up as eleven overs, no maidens, no wickets, 42 runs. He took his team off the field at the end of play on the second day with Cambridge standing at 167 for seven, Robin Oakley the Cambridge captain having notched up a respectable sixty-three not out, and looking well set for a century.

On the morning of the third day, the Oxford quickies removed the last three Cambridge wickets for 19 runs in forty minutes and Robin Oakley ran out of partners, and left the field with seventy-nine not out. The Oxford captain was the first to commiserate with him. "At least you notched a hundred last year," he added.

"True," replied Oakley, "so perhaps it's your turn this year. But not if I've got anything to do with it!'

The Oxford captain smiled at the thought of scoring a century when his team only needed 214 runs to win the match.

The two Oxford opening batsmen began their innings just before midday and remained together until the last over before lunch, when the freshman was once again clean bowled by Cambridge's ace fast bowler, Bill Potter. The captain sat on the balcony nervously, padded up and ready. He looked down on the bald head of his father, who was chatting to a former captain of England. Both men had scored centuries in the Varsity match. The captain pulled on his gloves and walked slowly down the pavilion steps, trying to look casual; he had never felt more nervous in his life. As he passed his father, the older man turned his sunburned face toward his only child and smiled. The crowd warmly applauded the captain all the way to the crease. He took guard, middle and leg again, and prepared to face the attack. The eager Potter who had despatched the captain so brusquely in the first innings came thundering down toward him hoping to be the cause of a pair. He delivered a magnificent first ball that swung into his legs and beat the captain all ends up, hitting him with a thud on the front pad.

"Howzat?" screamed Potter and the entire Cambridge side as they leaped in the air.

The captain looked up apprehensively at the umpire, who took his hands out of his pockets and moved a pebble from one palm to the other to remind him that another ball had been bowled. But he affected no interest in the appeal. A sigh of relief went up from the members in the pavilion. The captain managed to see through the rest of the over and returned to lunch nought not out, with his side twenty-four for one.

After lunch Potter returned to the attack. He rubbed the leather ball on his red-stained flannels and hurled himself forward, looking even fiercer than he had at the start of play. He released his missile with every ounce of venom he possessed, but in so doing he tried a little too hard, and the delivery was badly short. The captain leaned back and hooked the ball to the Tavern boundary for four, and from that moment he never looked as if anyone would pry him from the crease. He reached his fifty in seventy-one minutes, and at ten past four the Oxford team came into tea with the score at 171 for five and the skipper on 82 not out. The young man did not look at his father as he climbed the steps of the pavilion. He needed another 18 runs before he could do that, and by then his team would be safe. He ate and drank nothing at tea, and spoke to no one.

After twenty minutes a bell rang, and the eleven Cambridge men returned to the field. A minute later the captain and his partner walked back out to the crease, their open white shirts flapping in the breeze. Two hours left for the century and victory. The captain's partner only lasted another five balls, and the captain himself seemed to have lost that natural flow he had possessed before tea, struggling into the nineties with ones and twos. The light was getting bad, and it took him a full thirty minutes to reach 99, by which time he had lost another partner: 194 for seven. He remained on 99 for twelve minutes, when Robin Oakley, the Cambridge captain, took the new ball and brought his ace speed man back into the attack.

Then there occurred one of the most amazing incidents I have ever witnessed in a cricket match. Robin Oakley set an attacking field for the new ball—three slips, a gully, cover point, mid off, mid on, mid wicket, and a short square leg, a truly vicious circle. He then tossed the ball to Potter, who knew this would be his last chance to capture the Oxford captain's wicket and save the match; once he had scored the century he would surely knock off the rest of the runs in a matter of minutes. The sky was becoming bleak as a bank of dark clouds passed over the ground, but this was no time to leave the field for bad light. Potter rubbed the new ball once more on his white trousers and thundered up to hurl a delivery that the captain jabbed at and missed. One or two fielders raised their hands without appealing. Potter returned to his mark, shining the ball with even more relish and left a red bloodlike stain down the side of his thigh. The second ball, a yorker, beat the captain completely and must have missed the off stump by about an inch; there was a general sigh around the ground. The third ball hit the captain on the middle of the pad, and the eleven Cambridge men threw their arms in the air and screamed for leg before wicket, but the umpire was not moved. The captain jabbed at the fourth ball, and it carried tentatively to mid on, where Robin Oakley had placed himself a mere twenty yards in front of the bat, watching his adversary in disbelief as he set off for a run he could never hope to complete. His batting partner remained firmly in his crease, incredulous: One didn't run when the ball was hit to mid on unless it was the last delivery of the match.

The captain of Oxford, now stranded fifteen yards from safety, turned and looked at the captain of Cambridge, who held the ball in his hand. Robin Oakley was about to toss the ball to the wicket keeper, who in turn was waiting to remove the bails and send the Oxford captain back to the pavilion, run out for 99, but Oakley hesitated and for several seconds the two gladiators stared at each other, and then the Cambridge captain placed the ball in his pocket. The Oxford captain walked slowly back to his crease while the crowd remained silent in disbelief. Robin Oakley tossed the ball to Potter, who thundered down to deliver the fifth ball, which was short, and the Oxford captain effortlessly placed it through the covers for four runs. The crowd rose as one, and old friends in the pavilion thumped the father's back.

He smiled for a second time.

Potter was now advancing with his final effort and, exhausted, he delivered another short ball, which should have been dispatched to the boundary with ease, but the Oxford captain took one pace backward and hit his own stumps. He was out, hit wicket, bowled Potter for 103. The crowd rose for a second time as he walked back to the pavilion, and grown men who had been decorated in two wars had tears in their eyes. Seven minutes later everyone left the field, drenched by a thunderstorm.

The match ended in a draw.

JUST GOOD
FRIENDS

I WOKE UP BEFORE him feeling slightly horny, but I knew there was nothing I could do about it.

I blinked, and my eyes immediately accustomed themselves to the half light. I raised my head and gazed at the large expanse of motionless white flesh lying next to me. If only he took as much exercise as I did he wouldn't have that spare tire, I thought unsympathetically.

Roger stirred restlessly and even turned over to face me, but I knew he would not be fully awake until the alarm on his side of the bed started ringing. I pondered for a moment whether I could go back to sleep again or should get up and find myself some breakfast before he awoke. In the end I settled for just lying still on my side daydreaming, but making sure I didn't disturb him. When he did eventually open his eyes, I planned to pretend I was still asleep—that way he would end up getting breakfast for me. I began to go over the things that needed to be done after he had left for the office. As long as I was at home ready to greet him when he returned from work, he didn't seem to mind what I got up to during the day.

A gentle rumble emanated from his side of the bed. Roger's snoring never disturbed me. My affection for him was unbounded, and I only wished I could find the words to let him know. In truth, he was the first man I had really appreciated. As I gazed at his unshaven face I was reminded that it hadn't been his looks that had attracted me in the pub that night.

I had first come across Roger in the Cat and Whistle, a public house situated on the corner of Mafeking Road. You might say it was our local. He used to come in around eight, order a pint of mild, and take it to a small table in the corner of the room just beyond the dart board. Mostly he would sit alone, watching the darts being thrown toward double top but more often settling in one or five, if they managed to land on the board at all. He never played the game himself, and I often wondered, from my vantage point behind the bar, if he was fearful of relinquishing his favorite seat or just had no interest in the sport.

Then things suddenly changed for Roger—for the better, was no doubt how he saw it—when one evening in early spring a blond named Madeleine, wearing an imitation fur coat and drinking double martinis, perched on the stool beside him. I had never seen her in the pub before, but she was obviously known locally, and loose bar talk led me to believe it couldn't last. You see, word was around that she was looking for someone whose horizons stretched beyond the Cat and Whistle.

In fact the affair—if that's what it ever came to—lasted for only twenty days. I know because I counted every one of them. Then one night voices were raised, and heads turned as she left the small stool just as suddenly as she had come. His tired eyes watched her walk to a vacant place at the corner of the bar, but he didn't show any surprise at her departure and made no attempt to pursue her.

Her exit was my cue to enter. I almost leaped from behind the bar and, moving as quickly as dignity allowed, was seconds later sitting on the vacant stool beside him. He didn't comment and certainly made no attempt to offer me a drink, but the one glance he shot in my direction did not suggest he found me an unacceptable replacement. I looked around to see if anyone else had plans to usurp my position. The men standing round the dart board didn't seem to care. Treble seventeen, twelve, and a five kept them more than occupied. I glanced toward the bar to check if the boss had noticed my absence, but he was busy taking orders. I saw that Madeleine was already sipping a glass of champagne from the pub's only bottle, purchased by a stranger whose stylish double-breasted blazer and striped bow tie convinced me she wouldn't be bothering with Roger any longer. She looked well set for at least another twenty days.

I looked up at Roger—I had known his name for some time,

although I had never addressed him as such, and I couldn't be sure that he was aware of mine. I began to flutter my eyelashes in a rather exaggerated way. I felt a little stupid, but at least it elicited a gentle smile. He leaned over and touched my cheek, his hands surprisingly gentle. Neither of us felt the need to speak. We were both lonely, and it seemed unnecessary to explain why. We sat in silence, he occasionally sipping his beer, I from time to time rearranging my legs, while a few feet from us the darts pursued their undetermined course.

When the publican cried, "Last orders," Roger downed the remains of his beer while the dart players completed what had to be their final game.

No one commented when we left together, and I was surprised that Roger made no protest as I accompanied him back to his little semidetached. I already knew exactly where he lived because I had seen him on several occasions standing at the bus stop in Dobson Street in a silent line of reluctant morning passengers. Once I even positioned myself on a nearby wall in order to study his features more carefully. It was an anonymous, almost commonplace face, but he had the warmest eyes and the kindest smile I had observed in any man.

My only anxiety was that he didn't seem aware of my existence, just constantly preoccupied, his eyes each evening and his thoughts each morning only for Madeleine. How I envied that girl. She had everything I wanted—except a decent fur coat, the only thing my mother had left me. In truth, I have no right to be catty about Madeleine, as her past couldn't have been more murky than mine.

All that took place well over a year ago and, to prove my total devotion to Roger, I have never entered the Cat and Whistle since. He seemed to have forgotten Madeleine, because he never once spoke of her in front of me. An unusual man, he didn't question me about any of my past relationships either.

Perhaps he should have. I would have liked him to know the truth about my life before we'd met, though it all seems irrelevant now. You see, I had been the youngest in a family of four, so I always came last in line. I had never known my father, and I arrived home one night to discover that my mother had run off with another man. Tracy, one of my sisters, warned me not to expect her back. She turned out to be right, for I have never seen my mother since that day. It's awful to have to admit, if only to oneself, that one's mother is a tramp.

Now an orphan, I began to drift, often trying to stay one step ahead of the law—not so easy when you haven't always got somewhere to put your head down. I can't even recall how I ended up with Derek—if that was his real name. Derek, whose dark sensual looks would have attracted any susceptible female, told me that he had been on a merchant steamer for the past three years. When he made love to me I was ready to believe anything. I explained to him that all I wanted was a warm home, regular food, and perhaps in time a family of my own. He ensured that one of my wishes was fulfilled, because a few weeks after he left me I ended up with twins, two girls. Derek never set eyes on them: He had returned to sea even before I could tell him I was pregnant. He hadn't needed to promise me the earth; he was so good-looking he must have known I would have been his just for a night on the tiles.

I tried to bring up the girls decently, but the authorities caught up with me this time, and I lost them both. I wonder where they are now? God knows. I only hope they've ended up in a good home. At least they inherited Derek's irresistible looks, which can only help them through life. It's just one more thing Roger will never know about. His unquestioning trust only makes me feel more guilty, and now I never seem able to find a way of letting him know the truth.

After Derek had gone back to sea I was on my own for almost a year before getting part-time work at the Cat and Whistle. The publican was so mean that he wouldn't even have provided food and drink for me if I hadn't kept to my part of the bargain.

Roger used to come in about once, perhaps twice a week before he met the blond with the shabby fake fur coat. After that it was every night until she upped and left him.

I knew he was perfect for me the first time I heard him order a pint of mild. A pint of mild—I can't think of a better description of Roger. In those early days the barmaids used to flirt openly with him, but he didn't show any interest. Until Madeleine latched on to him, I wasn't even sure that it was women he preferred. Perhaps in the end it was my androgynous looks that appealed to him.

I think I must have been the only one in that pub who was looking for something more permanent.

And so Roger allowed me to spend the night with him. I remember that he slipped into the bathroom to undress while I rested on what I assumed would be my side of the bed. Since that night he has never once asked me to leave, let alone tried to kick me out. It's an easygoing relationship. I've never known him to raise his voice or scold me unfairly. Forgive the cliché, but for once I have fallen on my feet.

Brr. Brr. Brr. That damned alarm. I wished I could have buried it. The noise would go on and on until at last Roger decided to stir himself. I once tried to stretch across him and put a stop to its infernal ringing, only ending up knocking the contraption on to the floor, which annoyed him even more than the ringing. Never again, I concluded. Eventually a long arm emerged from under the blanket, and a palm dropped onto the top of the clock, and the awful din subsided. I'm a light sleeper—the slightest movement stirs me. If only he had asked me, I could have woken him far more gently each morning. After all, my methods are every bit as reliable as any man-made contraption.

Half awake, Roger gave me a brief cuddle before kneading my back, always guaranteed to elicit a smile. Then he yawned, stretched, and declared as he did every morning, "Must hurry along or I'll be late for the office." I suppose some females would have been annoyed by the predictability of our morning routine—but not this lady. It was all part of a life that made me feel secure in the belief that at last I had found something worthwhile.

Roger managed to get his feet into the wrong slippers—always a fifty-fifty chance—before lumbering toward the bathroom. He emerged fifteen minutes later, as he always did, looking only slightly better than he had when he entered. I've learned to live with what some would have called his foibles, while he has learned to accept my mania for cleanliness and a need to feel secure.

"Get up, lazybones," he remonstrated, but then only smiled when I resettled myself, refusing to leave the warm hollow that had been left by his body.

"I suppose you expect me to get your breakfast before I go to work?" he added as he made his way downstairs. I didn't bother to reply. I knew that in a few moments' time he would be opening the front door, picking up the morning newspaper, any mail, and our regular pint of milk. Reliable as ever, he would put on the kettle, then head for the pantry, fill a bowl with my favorite breakfast food, and add my portion of the milk, leaving himself just enough for two cups of coffee.

I could anticipate almost to the second when breakfast would be ready. First I would hear the kettle boil, a few moments later the milk would be poured, then finally there would be the sound of a chair being pulled up. That was the signal I needed to confirm it was time for me to join him.

I stretched my legs slowly, noticing that my nails needed some attention. I had already decided against a proper wash until after he had left for the office. I could hear the sound of the chair being scraped along the kitchen linoleum. I felt so happy that I literally jumped off the bed before making my way toward the open door. A few seconds later I was downstairs. Although he had already taken his first mouthful of corn flakes he stopped eating the moment he saw me.

"Good of you to join me," he said, a grin spreading over his face.

I padded over toward him and looked up expectantly. He bent down and pushed my bowl toward me. I began to lap up the milk happily, my tail swishing from side to side.

It's a myth that we only swish our tails when we're angry.

HENRY'S
HICCUP

WHEN THE GRAND PASHA'S first son was born in 1900 (he had sired twelve daughters by six wives) he named the boy Henry, after his favorite king of England. Henry entered this world with more money than even the most blasé tax collector could imagine, and seemed destined to live a life of idle ease.

The grand pasha, who ruled over ten thousand families, was of the opinion that in time there would be only five kings left in the world—the kings of spades, hearts, diamonds, clubs, and England. With this conviction in mind, he decided that Henry should be educated by the British. The boy was therefore despatched from his native Cairo at the age of eight to embark upon a formal education, young enough to retain only vague recollections of the noise, the heat, and the dirt of his birthplace. Henry started his new life at the Dragon School, which the grand pasha's advisers assured him was the finest preparatory school in the land. The boy left this establishment four years later, having developed a passionate love for the polo field and a thorough distaste for the classroom. He proceeded, with the minimum academic qualifications, to Eton, which the pasha's advisers assured him was the best school in Europe. He was gratified to learn the school had been founded by his favorite king. Henry spent five years at Eton, where he added squash, golf, and tennis to his loves, and applied mathematics, jazz and cross-country running to his dislikes.

On leaving school he once again failed to make more than a passing impression on the examiners. Nevertheless, he was found a place at Balliol College, Oxford, which the pasha's advisers assured him was the greatest university in the world. Three years at Balliol added two more loves to his life: horses and women, and three more ineradicable aversions: politics, philosophy, and economics.

At the end of his time *in statu pupillari*, he totally failed to impress the examiners and went down without a degree. His father, who considered young Henry's two goals against Cambridge in the Varsity polo match a wholly satisfactory result of his university career, dispatched the boy on a journey around the world to complete his education. Henry enjoyed the experience, learning more on the racecourse at Longchamp and in the back streets of Benghazi than he had ever acquired from his formal upbringing in England.

The grand pasha would have been proud of the tall, sophisticated, and handsome young man who returned to England a year later showing only the slightest trace of a foreign accent, if he hadn't died before his beloved son reached Southampton. Henry, although broken-hearted, was certainly not broke, as his father had left him some twenty million pounds in known assets, including a racing stud in Suffolk, a one-hundred-foot yacht at Nice, and a palace in Cairo. But by far the most important of his father's bequests was the finest manservant in London, one Godfrey Barker. Barker could arrange or rearrange anything, at a moment's notice.

Henry, for the lack of something better to do, settled himself into his father's old suite at the Ritz, not troubling to read the "Situations Vacant" column in *The Times*. Rather he embarked on a life of single-minded dedication to the pursuit of pleasure, the only career for which Eton, Oxford, and inherited wealth had adequately equipped him. To do Henry justice, he had, despite a more than generous helping of charm and good looks, enough common sense to choose carefully those permitted to spend the unforgiving minute with him. He selected only old friends from school and university who, although they were without exception not as well-breeched as he, weren't the sort of fellows who came begging for the loan of a fiver to cover a gambling debt.

Whenever Henry was asked what was the first love of his life, he was always hard pressed to choose between horses and women, and as he found it possible to spend the day with the one and the night with the other without causing any jealousy or recrimination, he never overtaxed himself with resolving the problem. Most of his horses were fine stallions, fast, sleek, velvet-skinned, with dark eyes and firm limbs; this would have adequately described most of his women, except that they were fillies. Henry fell in and out of love with every girl in the chorus line of the London Palladium, and when the affairs had come to an end, Barker saw to it that they always received some suitable memento to ensure that no scandal ensued. Henry also won every classic race on the English turf before he was thirty-five, and Barker always seemed to know the right year to back his master.

Henry's life quickly fell into a routine, never dull. One month was spent in Cairo going through the motions of attending to his business, three months in the south of France with the occasional excursion to Biarritz, and for the remaining eight months he resided at the Ritz. For the four months he was out of London his magnificent suite overlooking St. James's Park remained unoccupied. History does not record whether Henry left the rooms empty because he disliked the thought of unknown persons splashing in the sunken marble bath, or because he simply couldn't be bothered with the fuss of signing in and out of the hotel twice a year. The Ritz management had never commented on the matter to his father; why should they with the son? This program fully accounted for Henry's year except for the odd trip to Paris when some Home Counties girl came a little too close to the altar. Although almost every girl who met Henry wanted to marry him, a good many would have done so even if he had been penniless. However, Henry saw absolutely no reason to be faithful to one woman. "I have a hundred horses and a hundred male friends," he would explain when asked. "Why should I confine myself to one female?" There seemed no immediate answer to Henry's logic.

The story of Henry would have ended there had he continued life as destiny seemed content to allow, but even the Henrys of this world have the occasional hiccup.

As the years passed, Henry grew into the habit of never planning ahead, since experience—and his able manservant,

Barker—had always led him to believe that with vast wealth you could acquire anything you desired at the last minute, and cover any contingencies that arose later. However, even Barker couldn't formulate a contingency plan in response to Mr. Chamberlain's statement of September 3, 1939, that the British people were at war with Germany. Henry felt it inconsiderate of Chamberlain to have declared war so soon after Wimbledon and the Oaks, and even more inconsiderate of the Home Office to advise him a few months later that Barker must stop serving the grand pasha and, until further notice, serve His Majesty the King instead.

What could poor Henry do? Now in his fortieth year, he was not used to living anywhere other than the Ritz, and the Germans who had caused Wimbledon to be canceled were also occupying the George V in Paris and the Negresco in Nice. As the weeks passed and daily an invasion seemed more certain Henry came to the distasteful conclusion that he would have to return to a neutral Cairo until the British had won the war. It never crossed his mind, even for one moment, that the British might lose. After all, they had won the First World War, and therefore they must win the Second. "History repeats itself" was about the only piece of wisdom he recalled clearly from three years of tutorials at Oxford.

Henry summoned the manager of the Ritz and told him that his suite was to be left unoccupied until he returned. He paid one year in advance, which he felt was more than enough time to take care of upstarts like Herr Hitler, and set off for Cairo. The manager was heard to remark later that the grand pasha's departure for Egypt was most ironic; he was, after all, more British than the British.

Henry spent a year at his palace in Cairo and then found he could bear his fellow countrymen no longer, so he removed himself to New York just before it would have been possible for him to come face to face with Rommel. Once in New York, Henry bivouacked in the Pierre Hotel on Fifth Avenue, selected an American manservant called Eugene, and waited for Mr. Churchill to finish the war. As if to prove his continuing support for the British, on January 1 every year he forwarded a check to the Ritz to cover the cost of his rooms for the next twelve months.

Henry celebrated V-J day in Times Square with a million Americans and immediately made plans for his return to Britain. He was surprised and disappointed when the British Embassy in Washington informed him that it might be some time before he was allowed to return to the land he loved, and despite continual pressure and all the influence he could bring to bear, he was unable to board a ship for Southampton until July 1946. From the first-class deck he waved good-bye to America and Eugene, and looked forward to England and Barker.

Once he had stepped off the ship onto English soil he headed straight for the Ritz to find his rooms exactly as he had left them. As far as Henry could see, nothing had changed except that his manservant (now the servant to a general) could not be released from the armed forces for at least another six months. Henry was determined to play his part in the war effort by surviving without him for that period, and remembering Barker's words: "Everyone knows who you are. Nothing will change," he felt confident all would be well. Indeed, on the *bonheur du jour* table in his rooms at the Ritz was an invitation to dine with Lord and Lady Lympsham in their Chelsea Square home the following night. It looked as if Barker's prediction was turning out to be right: Everything would be just the same. Henry penned an affirmative reply to the invitation, happy with the thought that he was going to pick up his life in England exactly where he had left off.

The following evening Henry arrived on the Chelsea Square doorstep a few minutes after eight o'clock. The Lympshams, an elderly couple who had not qualified for the war in any way, gave every appearance of not even realizing that it had taken place, or that Henry had been absent from the London social scene. Their table, despite rationing, was as fine as Henry remembered, and, more important, one of the guests present was quite unlike anyone he could ever remember. Her name, Henry learned from his host, was Victoria Campbell, and she turned out to be the daughter of another guest, General Sir

Ralph Colquhoun. Lady Lympsham confided to Henry over the quails' eggs that the sad young thing had lost her husband when the Allies advanced on Berlin, only a few days before the Germans had surrendered. For the first time Henry felt guilty about not having played some part in the war.

All through dinner, he could not take his eyes from young Victoria, whose classical beauty was equaled only by her well-informed and lively conversation. He feared he might be staring too obviously at the slim, dark-haired girl with the high cheekbones; it was like admiring a beautiful sculpture and wanting to touch it. Her bewitching smile elicited an answering smile from all who received it. Henry did everything in his power to be the receiver and was rewarded on several occasions, aware that, for the first time in his life, he was becoming totally infatuated—and was delighted to be.

The ensuing courtship was an unusual one for Henry, in that he made no attempt to persuade Victoria to compliance. He was sympathetic and attentive, and when she had come out of mourning he approached her father and asked if he might request his daughter's hand in marriage. Henry was overjoyed when first the general agreed and later Victoria accepted. After an announcement in *The Times* they celebrated the engagement with a small dinner party at the Ritz, attended by 120 close friends who might have been forgiven for coming to the conclusion that Attlee was exaggerating about his austerity program. After the last guest had left Henry walked Victoria back to her father's home in Belgrave Mews, while discussing the wedding arrangements and his plans for the honeymoon.

"Everything must be perfect for you, my angel," he said, as once again he admired the way her long, dark hair curled at the shoulders. "We shall be married in St. Margaret's, Westminster, and after a reception at the Ritz we will be driven to Victoria Station, where you will be met by Fred, the senior porter. Fred will allow no one else to carry my bags to the last carriage of the Golden Arrow. One should always have the last carriage, my darling," explained Henry, "so that one cannot be disturbed by other travelers."

Victoria was impressed by Henry's mastery of the arrangements, especially remembering the absence of his manservant, Barker.

Henry warmed to his theme. "Once we have boarded the Golden Arrow, you will be served with China tea and some wafer-thin smoked salmon sandwiches, which we can enjoy while relaxing on our journey to Dover. When we arrive at the Channel port, we will be met by Albert, whom Fred will have alerted. Albert will remove the bags from our carriage, but not before everyone else has left the train. He will then escort us to the ship, where we will take sherry with the captain while our bags are being placed in Cabin Number Three. Like my father, I always have Cabin Number Three; it is not only the largest and most comfortable stateroom on board, but it is situated in the center of the ship, which makes it possible to enjoy a comfortable crossing even should one have the misfortune to encounter bad weather. And when we have docked in Calais you will find Pierre waiting for us. He will have organized everything for the front carriage of the Flèche d'Or."

"Such an itinerary must take a considerable amount of detailed planning," said Victoria, her hazel eyes sparkling as she listened to her future husband's description of the promised tour.

"More tradition than organization, I would say, my dear," replied Henry, smiling, as they strolled hand in hand across Hyde Park. "Although, I confess, in the past Barker has kept his eye on things should any untoward emergency arise. In any case, I have *always* had the front carriage of the Flèche d'Or, because it assures one of being off the train and away before anyone realizes that you have actually arrived in Paris. Other than Raymond, of course."

"Raymond?"

"Yes. Raymond, a servant par excellence, who adored my father. He will have organized a bottle of Veuve Clicquot '37 and a little Russian caviar for the journey. He will also have ensured that there is a couch in the railway carriage should you need to rest, my dear."

"You seem to have thought of everything, Henry darling," she said as they entered Belgrave Mews.

"I hope you will think so, Victoria; for when you arrive in Paris, which I have not had the opportunity to visit for so many years, there will be a Rolls-Royce standing by the side of the carriage, door open, and we will step out of the Flèche d'Or into the car, and Maurice will drive us to the George V, arguably the finest hotel in Europe. Louis, the manager, will be on the steps of the hotel to greet us, and he will conduct us to the bridal suite with its stunning view of the city. A maid will unpack for you while you retire to bathe and rest from the tiresome journey. When you are fully recovered we shall dine at Maxim's, where you will be guided to the corner table farthest from the orchestra by Marcel, the finest head waiter in the world. As you are seated, the musicians will strike up 'A Room with a View,' my favorite tune, and we will then be served with the most magnificent langouste you have ever tasted, of that I can assure you."

Henry and Victoria arrived at the front door of the general's small house in Belgrave Mews. He took her hand before continuing.

"After we have dined, my dear, we shall stroll into the Madeleine, where I shall buy a dozen red roses from Paulette, the most beautiful flower girl in Paris. She is almost as lovely as you." Henry sighed and concluded: "Then we shall return to the George V and spend our first night together."

Victoria's hazel eyes showed delighted anticipation. "I only wish it could be tomorrow," she said.

Henry kissed her gallantly on the cheek and said: "It will be worth waiting for, my dear, I can assure you it will be a day neither of us will ever forget."

"I'm sure of that," Victoria replied as he released her hand.

On the morning of his wedding Henry leaped out of bed and drew back the curtains with a flourish, only to be greeted by a steady drizzle.

"The rain will clear by eleven o'clock," he said out loud with immense confidence, and hummed as he shaved slowly and with care.

The weather had not improved by midmorning. On the contrary, heavy rain was falling by the time Victoria entered the church. Henry's disappointment evaporated the instant he saw his beautiful bride; all he could think of was taking her to Paris. The ceremony over, the grand pasha and his wife stood outside the church, a golden couple, smiling for the press photographers as the loyal guests scattered damp rice over them. As soon as they decently could, they set off for the reception at the Ritz. Between them they managed to chat to every guest, and they would have been away in better time had Victoria been a little quicker changing and the general's toast to the happy couple been considerably shorter. The guests crowded onto the steps of the Ritz, overflowing on to the sidewalk in Piccadilly to wave good-bye to the departing honeymooners, and were sheltered from the downpour by a capacious red awning.

The general's Rolls took the grand pasha and his wife to the station, where the chauffeur unloaded the bags. Henry instructed him to return to the Ritz, since he had everything under control. The chauffeur touched his cap and said: "I hope you and madam have a wonderful trip, sir," and left them. Henry stood on the station, looking for Fred. There was no sign of him, so he hailed a passing porter.

"Where is Fred?" inquired Henry.

"Fred who?" came the reply.

"How in heaven's name should I know?" said Henry.

"Then how in hell's name should I know?" retorted the porter.

Victoria shivered. English railway stations are not designed for the latest fashion in silk coats.

"Kindly take my bags to the end carriage of the train," said Henry.

The porter looked down at the fourteen bags. "All right," he said reluctantly.

Henry and Victoria stood patiently in the cold as the porter loaded the bags on to his trolley and trundled them off along the platform.

"Don't worry, my dear," said Henry. "A cup of Lapsang Souchong tea and some smoked salmon sandwiches and you'll feel a new girl."

"I'm just fine," said Victoria, smiling, though not quite as bewitchingly as normal, as she put her arm through her husband's. They strolled along together to the end carriage.

"Can I check your tickets, sir?" said the conductor, blocking the entrance to the last carriage.

"My what?" said Henry, his accent sounding unusually pronounced.

"Your tic-kets," said the conductor, conscious he was addressing a foreigner.

"In the past I have always made the arrangements on the train, my good man."

"Not nowadays you don't, sir. You'll have to go to the booking office and buy your tickets like everyone else, and you'd better be quick about it, because the train is due to leave in a few minutes."

Henry stared at the conductor in disbelief. "I assume my wife may rest on the train while I go and purchase the tickets," he said.

"No, I'm sorry, sir. No one is allowed to board the train unless they are in possession of a valid ticket."

"Remain here, my dear," said Henry, "and I will deal with this little problem immediately. Kindly direct me to the ticket office, porter."

"End of Platform Four, governor," said the conductor, slamming the train door, annoyed at being described as a porter.

That wasn't quite what Henry had meant by "direct me." Nevertheless, he left his bride with the fourteen bags and somewhat reluctantly headed back toward the ticket office at the end of Platform Four, where he went to the front of a long line.

"There's a queue, you know, mate," someone shouted.

Henry didn't know. "I'm in a frightful hurry," he said.

"And so am I," came the reply, "so get to the back."

Henry had been told that the British were good at standing in lines, but as he had never had to join one before that moment, he was quite unable to confirm or deny the rumor.

He reluctantly walked to the back of the line. It took some time before he reached the front.

"I would like to take the last carriage to Dover."

"You would like what?"

"The last carriage," repeated Henry a little more loudly.

"I'm sorry, sir, but every first-class seat is sold."

"I don't want a seat," said Henry. "I require the carriage."

"There are no carriages available nowadays, sir, and as I said, all the seats in first class are sold. I can still fix you up in third class."

"I don't mind what it costs," said Henry. "I must travel first class."

"I don't have a first-class seat, sir. It wouldn't matter if you could afford the whole train."

"I can," said Henry.

"I still don't have a seat left in first class," said the clerk unhelpfully.

Henry would have persisted, but several people in the line behind him were pointing out that there were only two minutes before the train was due to leave, and that they wanted to catch it even if he didn't.

"Two seats then," said Henry, unable to make himself utter the words "third class."

Two green tickets marked "Dover" were handed through the little grille. Henry took them and started to walk away.

"That will be seventeen and sixpence, please, sir."

"Oh, yes, of course," said Henry apologetically. He fumbled in his pocket and unfolded one of the three large white five-pound notes he always carried on him.

"Don't you have anything smaller?"

"No, I do not," said Henry, who found the idea of carrying money vulgar enough, without it having to be in small denominations.

The clerk handed back four pounds and a half-crown. Henry did not pick up the half-crown.

"Thank you, sir," said the startled man. It was more than his Saturday bonus.

Henry put the tickets in his pocket and quickly returned to

Victoria, who was smiling defiantly against the cold wind; it was not quite the smile that had originally captivated him. Their porter had long ago disappeared, and Henry couldn't see another in sight. The conductor took his tickets and clipped them.

"All aboard," he shouted, waved a green flag, and blew his whistle.

Henry quickly threw all fourteen bags through the open door and pushed Victoria onto the moving train before leaping on himself. Once he had caught his breath he walked down the corridor, staring into the third-class carriages. He had never seen one before. The seats were nothing more than thin worn-out cushions, and as he looked into one half-full carriage, a young couple jumped in and took the last two adjacent seats. Henry searched frantically for a free carriage, but he was unable even to find one with two seats together. Victoria took a single seat in a packed compartment without complaint, while Henry sat forlornly on one of the suitcases in the corridor.

"It will be different once we're in Dover," he said, without his usual self-confidence.

"I am sure it will be, Henry," she replied, smiling kindly at him.

The two-hour journey seemed interminable. Passengers of all shapes and sizes squeezed past Henry in the corridor, treading on his Lobb's handmade leather shoes with the words:

"Sorry, sir."

"Sorry, guv."

"Sorry, mate."

Henry put the blame firmly on the shoulders of Clement Attlee and his ridiculous campaign for social equality, and waited for the train to reach Dover Priory Station. The moment the engine pulled in, Henry leaped out of the carriage first, not last, and called for Albert at the top of his voice. Nothing happened, except that a stampede of people rushed past him on their way to the ship. Eventually Henry spotted a porter and rushed over to him, only to find he was already loading up his trolley with someone else's luggage. Henry sprinted to a second man, and then on to a third, and waved a pound note at a fourth, who came immediately and unloaded the fourteen bags.

"Where to, guv?" asked the porter amicably.

"The ship," said Henry, and returned to claim his bride. He helped Victoria down from the train, and they both ran through the rain until, breathless, they reached the gangplank of the ship.

"Tickets, sir," said a young officer in a dark blue uniform at the bottom of the gangplank.

"I always have Cabin Number Three," said Henry between breaths.

"Of course, sir," said the young man, and looked at his clipboard. Henry smiled confidently at Victoria.

"Mr. and Mrs. William West."

"I beg your pardon?" said Henry.

"You must be Mr. William West."

"I certainly am not. I am the grand pasha of Cairo."

"Well, I'm sorry, sir, Cabin Number Three is booked in the name of a Mr. William West and family."

"I have never been treated by Captain Rogers in this cavalier fashion before," said Henry, his accent now even more pronounced. "Send for him immediately."

"Captain Rogers was killed in the war, sir. Captain Jenkins is now in command of this ship, and he never leaves the bridge thirty minutes before sailing."

Henry's exasperation was turning to panic. "Do you have a free cabin?"

The young officer looked down his list. "No, sir, I'm afraid not. The last one was taken a few minutes ago."

"May I have two tickets?" asked Henry.

"Yes, sir," said the young officer. "But you'll have to buy them from the booking office on the quayside."

Henry decided that any further argument would be only time consuming, so he turned on his heel without another word, leaving his wife with the laden porter. He strode to the booking office.

"Two first-class tickets to Calais," he said firmly.

The man behind the little glass pane gave Henry a tired look. "It's all one class nowadays, sir, unless you have a cabin." He proffered two tickets. "That will be one pound exactly."

Henry handed over a pound note, took his tickets, and hurried back to the young officer.

The porter was offloading their suitcases on to the quayside.

"Can't you take them on board," cried Henry, "and put them in the hold?"

"No, sir, not now. Only the passengers are allowed on board after the ten-minute signal."

Victoria carried two of the smaller suitcases, and Henry dragged the twelve remaining ones in relays up the gangplank. He finally sat down on the deck exhausted. Every seat seemed already to be occupied. Henry couldn't make up his mind if he was cold from the rain or hot from his exertions. Victoria's smile was fixed firmly in place as she took his hand.

"Don't worry about a thing, darling," she said. "Just relax and enjoy the crossing; it will be such fun being out on deck together."

The ship moved sedately out of the calm of the harbor into the Dover Straits. Later that night Captain Jenkins told his wife that the twenty-five-mile journey had been among the most unpleasant crossings he had ever experienced. He added that he had nearly turned back when his second officer, a veteran of two wars, was violently seasick. Henry and Victoria spent most of the trip hanging over the rails getting rid of everything they had consumed at their reception. Two people had never been more happy to see land in their life than they were at the first sight of the Normandy coastline. They staggered off the ship, taking the suitcases one at a time.

"Perhaps France will be different," Henry said lamely, and after a perfunctory search for Pierre, he went straight to the booking office and obtained two third-class seats on the Flèche d'Or. They were at least able to sit next to each other this time, but in a carriage already occupied by six other passengers, as well as a dog and a hen. The six of them left Henry in no doubt that they enjoyed the modern habit of smoking in public and

the ancient custom of taking garlic in their food. He would
have been sick again at any other time, but there was nothing
left in his stomach. He considered walking up and down the
train searching for Raymond, but feared it would only result in
him losing his seat next to Victoria. He gave up trying to hold
any conversation with her above the noise of the dog, the hen,
and the Gallic babble, and satisfied himself with looking out of
the window, watching the French countryside and, for the first
time in his life, noting the name of every station through which
they passed.

Once they arrived at the Gare du Nord Henry made no
attempt to look for Maurice but simply headed straight for the
nearest taxi rank. By the time he had transferred all fourteen
suitcases he was well down the line. He and Victoria stood there
for just over an hour, moving the cases forward inch by inch
until it was their turn.

"Monsieur?"

"Do you speak English?"

"Un peu, un peu."

"Hotel George V."

"Oui, mais je ne peux pas mettre toutes les valises dans le coffre."

So Henry and Victoria sat huddled in the back of the taxi,
bruised, tired, soaked, and starving, surrounded by leather suitcases, only to be bumped up and down over the cobblestones
all the way to the George V.

The hotel doorman rushed to help them as Henry offered
the taxi driver a pound note.

"No take English money, monsieur."

Henry couldn't believe his ears. The doorman happily paid
the taxi driver in francs and quickly pocketed the pound note.
Henry was too tired even to comment. He helped Victoria up
the marble steps and went over to the reception desk.

"The grand pasha of Cairo and his wife. The bridal suite,
please."

"Oui, monsieur."

Henry smiled at Victoria.

"You 'ave your booking confirmation with you?"

"No," said Henry. "I have never needed to confirm my booking with you in the past. Before the war I—"

"I am sorry, sir, but the 'otel is fully booked at the moment. A conference."

"Even the bridal suite?" asked Victoria.

"Yes, madam. The chairman and his lady, you understand." He nearly winked.

Henry certainly did not understand. There had always been a room for him at the George V whenever he had wanted one in the past. Desperate, he unfolded the second of his five-pound notes and slipped it across the counter.

"Ah," said the reservations clerk, "I see we still have one room unoccupied, but I fear it is not very large."

Henry waved a listless hand.

The clerk banged the bell on the counter in front of him with the palm of his hand, and a porter appeared immediately and escorted them to the promised room. The clerk had been telling the truth. Henry could only have described what they found themselves standing in as a box room. The reason that the curtains were perpetually drawn was that the view, over the chimneys of Paris, was singularly unprepossessing, but that was not to be the final blow, as Henry realized, staring in disbelief at the two narrow single beds. Victoria started unpacking without a word, while Henry slumped despondently on the end of one of them. After Victoria had sat soaking in a bath that was the perfect size for a six-year-old, she lay down exhausted on the other bed. Neither spoke for nearly an hour.

"Come on, darling," said Henry finally. "Let's go and have dinner."

Victoria rose loyally but reluctantly and dressed for dinner while Henry sat in the bath, knees to nose, trying to wash himself before changing into evening dress. This time he phoned the front desk and ordered a taxi as well as reserving a table at Maxim's.

The taxi driver did accept his pound note on this occasion, but as Henry and his bride entered the great restaurant he recognized no one and no one recognized him. A waiter led them to a small table hemmed in between two other couples just below the band. As he walked into the dining room the musicians struck up "Alexander's Ragtime Band."

They ordered from the extensive menu, and the langouste turned out to be excellent, every bit as good as Henry had promised, but by then neither of them had the stomach to eat a full meal, and the greater part of both their dishes was left on the plate.

Henry found it hard to convince the new headwaiter that the lobster had been superb and that they had not purposely come to Maxim's not to eat it. Over coffee, he took Victoria's hand and tried to apologize.

"Let us end this farce," he said, "by completing my plan and going to the Madeleine and presenting you with the promised flowers. Paulette will not be in the square to greet us, but there will surely be someone who can sell us roses."

Henry called for the bill and unfolded the third five-pound note (Maxim's is always happy to accept other people's currency, and certainly didn't bother him with any change). They left, walking hand in hand toward the Madeleine. For once Henry turned out to be right, for Paulette was nowhere to be seen. An old woman with a shawl over her head and a wart on the side of her nose stood in her place on the corner of the square, surrounded by the most beautiful flowers.

Henry selected a dozen of the longest-stemmed red roses and placed them in the arms of his bride. The old woman smiled at Victoria.

Victoria returned her smile.

"Dix francs, monsieur," said the old woman to Henry.

Henry fumbled in his pocket, only to discover that he had spent all his money. He looked despairingly at the old woman, who raised her hands, smiled at him, and said:

"Don't worry, Henry, have them on me. For old time's sake."

A MATTER OF
PRINCIPLE

SIR HAMISH GRAHAM HAD many of the qualities and most of the failings that result from being born to a middle-class Scottish family. He was well educated, hardworking, and honest, while at the same time being narrow-minded, uncompromising, and proud. Never on any occasion had he allowed hard liquor to pass his lips, and he mistrusted all men who had not been born north of Hadrian's Wall, and many of those who had.

After spending his formative years at Fettes School, to which he had won a minor scholarship, and at Edinburgh University, where he obtained a second-class honors degree in engineering, he was chosen from a field of twelve to be a trainee with the international construction company TarMac (named after its founder, J. L. McAdam, who discovered that tar when mixed with stones was the best constituent for making roads). The new trainee, through diligent work and uncompromising tactics, became the firm's youngest and most disliked project manager. By the age of thirty Graham had been appointed deputy managing director of TarMac and was already beginning to realize that he could not hope to progress much farther while he was in someone else's employ. He therefore started to consider forming his own company. When, two years later, the chairman of TarMac, Sir Alfred Hickman, offered Graham the opportunity to replace the retiring managing director, he resigned immediately. After all, if Sir Alfred felt he had the ability to run TarMac, he must be competent enough to start his own company.

The next day young Hamish Graham made an appointment to see the local manager of the Bank of Scotland who was responsible for the TarMac account, and with whom he had dealt for the past ten years. Graham explained to the manager his plans for the future, submitting a full written proposal, and requesting that his overdraft facility might be extended from fifty pounds to ten thousand. Three weeks later he learned that his application had been viewed favorably. He remained in his lodgings in Edinburgh, while renting an office (or, to be more accurate, a room) in the north of the city at ten shillings a week. He purchased a typewriter, hired a secretary, and ordered some unembossed letterheaded stationery. After a further month of diligent interviewing, he employed two engineers, both graduates of Aberdeen University, and five out-of-work laborers from Glasgow.

During those first few weeks on his own Graham tendered for several small road contracts in the central lowlands of Scotland, the first seven of which he failed to secure. Preparing a tender is always tricky and often expensive, so by the end of his first six months in business Graham was beginning to wonder if his sudden departure from TarMac had not been foolhardy. For the first time in his life he experienced self-doubt, but that was soon removed by the Ayrshire County Council, which accepted his tender to construct a minor road that was to join a projected school to the main highway. The road was only five hundred yards in length, but the assignment took Graham's little team seven months to complete, and when all the bills had been paid and all expenses taken into account Graham Construction made a net loss of £143.10s.6d.

Still, in the profit column was a small reputation that had been invisibly earned, and that caused the Ayrshire Council to invite him to build the school at the end of the new road. This contract made Graham Construction a profit of £420 and added still further to his reputation. From that moment Graham Construction went from strength to strength, and as early as his third year in business, Graham was able to declare a small pretax profit, and this grew steadily over the next five years. When Graham Construction was floated on the London Stock Exchange, the demand for the shares was oversubscribed ten times and the newly quoted company was soon considered a blue-chip institution, a considerable achievement for Graham to have pulled off in his own lifetime. But then, the City likes men who grow slowly and can be relied on not to involve themselves in unnecessary risks.

In the sixties Graham Construction built highways, hospitals, factories, and even a power station, but the achievement the chairman took most pride in was Edinburgh's newly completed art gallery, which was the only contract that showed a deficit in the annual general report. The invisible earnings column, however, recorded the award of knight bachelor for the chairman.

Sir Hamish decided that the time had come for Graham Construction to expand into new fields, and looked, as generations of Scots had before him, toward the natural market of the British Empire. He built in Australia and Canada with his own finances, and in India and Africa with a subsidy from the British government. In 1963 he was named "Businessman of the Year" by *The Times* and three years later "Chairman of the Year" by *The Economist*. Sir Hamish never once altered his methods to keep pace with the changing times and, if anything, grew more stubborn in the belief that his ideas of doing business were correct whatever anyone else thought; and he had a long credit column to prove he was right.

In the early seventies, when the slump hit the construction business, Graham Construction suffered the same cut in budgets and lost contracts as its major competitors. Sir Hamish reacted in a predictable way, by tightening his belt and paring his estimates while at the same time refusing to compromise his business principles one jot. The company therefore grew leaner, and many of his more enterprising young executives left Graham Construction for firms that still believed in taking on the occasional risky contract.

Only when the slope of the profits graph started taking on the look of a downhill slalom did Sir Hamish become worried. One night, while brooding over the company's profit-and-loss account for the previous three years, and realizing that he was losing contracts even in his native Scotland, Sir Hamish reluctantly came to the conclusion that he must tender for less established work, and perhaps even consider the odd gamble.

His brightest young executive, David Heath, a stocky, middle-aged bachelor, whom he did not entirely trust—after all, the man had been educated south of the border and, worse, some extraordinary place in the United States called the Wharton Business School—wanted Sir Hamish to put a toe into Mexican waters. Mexico, as Heath was not slow to point out, had discovered vast reserves of oil off its eastern coast and had overnight become rich with American dollars. The construction business in Mexico was suddenly proving most lucrative, and contracts were coming up for tender with figures as high as thirty to forty million dollars attached to them. Heath urged Sir Hamish to go after one such contract that had recently been announced in a full-page advertisement in *The Economist*. The Mexican government was issuing tender documents for a proposed ring road around their capital, Mexico City. In an article in the business section of the *Observer*, detailed arguments were put forward as to why established British companies should try to fulfill the ring-road tender. Heath had offered shrewd advice on overseas contracts in the past that Sir Hamish had let slip through his fingers.

The next morning Sir Hamish sat at his desk listening attentively to David Heath, who felt that as Graham Construction had already built the Glasgow and Edinburgh ring roads, any application they made to the Mexican government had to be taken seriously. To Heath's surprise, Sir Hamish agreed with his project manager and allowed a team of six men to travel to Mexico to obtain the tender documents and research the project.

The research team was led by David Heath, and consisted of three other engineers, a geologist, and an accountant. When the team arrived in Mexico they obtained the tender documents from the minister of works and settled down to study them minutely. Having pinpointed the major problems, they walked around Mexico City with their ears open and their mouths shut and made a list of the problems they were clearly going to encounter: the impossibility of unloading anything at Vera Cruz and then transporting the cargo to Mexico City without half of the original consignment being stolen, the lack of communications between ministries, and worst of all the attitude of the Mexicans to work. But David Heath's most positive contribution to the list was the discovery that each minister had his own outside man, and that man had better be well disposed to Graham Construction if the firm were even to be considered for the shortlist. Heath immediately sought out the minister of works' man, one Victor Perez, and took him to an extravagant lunch at the Fonda el Refugio, where both of them nearly ended up drunk, although Heath remained sober enough to settle all the necessary terms, conditional upon Sir Hamish's approval. Having taken every possible precaution, Heath agreed on a tender figure with Perez that was to include the minister's percentage. Once he had completed the report for his chairman, he flew back to England with his team.

On the evening of David Heath's return, Sir Hamish retired to bed early to study his project manager's conclusions. He read the report through the night as others might read a spy story, and was left in no doubt that this was the opportunity he had been looking for to overcome the temporary setbacks Graham Construction was now suffering. Although Sir Hamish would be up against Costains, Sunleys, and John Brown, as well as many international companies, he still felt confident that any application he made must have a "fair chance." On arrival at his office the next morning Sir Hamish sent for David Heath, who was delighted by the chairman's initial response to his report.

Sir Hamish started speaking as soon as his burly project manager entered the room, not even inviting him to take a seat.

"You must contact our embassy in Mexico City immediately and inform them of our intentions," pronounced Sir Hamish. "I may speak to the ambassador myself," he said, intending that to be the concluding remark of the interview.

"Useless," said David Heath.

"I beg your pardon?"

"I don't wish to appear rude, sir, but it doesn't work like that anymore. Britain is no longer a great power dispensing largesse to all far-flung and grateful recipients."

"More's the pity," said Sir Hamish.

The project manager continued as though he had not heard the remark.

"The Mexicans now have vast wealth of their own, and the United States, Japan, France, and Germany keep massive embassies in Mexico City with highly professional trade delegations trying to influence every ministry."

"But surely history counts for something," said Sir Hamish. "Wouldn't they rather deal with an established British company than some upstarts from—?"

"Perhaps, sir, but in the end all that really matters is which minister is in charge of what contract and who is his outside representative."

Sir Hamish looked puzzled. "Your meaning is obscure to me, Mr. Heath."

"Allow me to explain, sir. Under the present system in Mexico, each ministry has an allocation of money to spend on projects agreed to by the government. Every secretary of state is acutely aware that his tenure of office may be very short, so he picks out a major contract for himself from the many available. It's the one way to ensure a pension for life if the government is changed overnight or the minister simply loses his job."

"Don't bandy words with me, Mr. Heath. What you are suggesting is that I should bribe a government official, I have never been involved in that sort of thing in thirty years of business."

"And I wouldn't want you to start now," replied Heath. "The Mexican is far too experienced in business etiquette for anything as clumsy as that to be suggested, but while the law requires that you appoint a Mexican agent, it must make sense to try and sign up the minister's man, who in the end is the one person who can ensure that you will be awarded the contract. The system seems to work well, and as long as a minister deals only with reputable international firms and doesn't become greedy, no one complains. Fail to observe either of those two golden rules and the whole house of cards collapses. The minister ends up in Le Cumberri for thirty years and the company concerned has all its assets expropriated and is banned from any future business dealings in Mexico."

"I really cannot become involved in such shenanigans," said Sir Hamish. "I still have my shareholders to consider."

"*You* don't have to become involved," Heath rejoined. "After we have tendered for the contract, you wait and see if the company has been shortlisted and then, if we have, you wait again to find out if the minister's man approaches us. I know the man, so if he does make contact we have a deal. After all, Graham Construction is a respectable international company."

"Precisely, and that's why it's against my principles," said Sir Hamish with hauteur.

"I do hope, Sir Hamish, it's also against your principles to allow the Germans and the Americans to steal the contract from under our noses."

Sir Hamish glared back at his project manager but remained silent.

"And I feel I must add, sir," said David Heath, moving restlessly from foot to foot, "that the pickings in Scotland haven't exactly yielded a harvest lately."

"All right, all right, go ahead," said Sir Hamish reluctantly. "Put in a tender figure for the Mexico City ring road, but be warned, if I find bribery is involved, on your head be it!" he added, banging his fist on the table.

"What tender figure have you settled on, sir?" asked the project manager. "I believe, as I stressed in my report that we should keep the amount under forty million dollars."

"Agreed," said Sir Hamish, who paused for a moment and smiled to himself before saying: "Make it $39,121,110."

"Why that particular figure, sir?"

"Sentimental reasons," said Sir Hamish, without further explanation.

David Heath left, pleased that he had persuaded his boss to go ahead, although he feared it might in the end prove harder to overcome Sir Hamish's principles than the entire Mexican government. Nevertheless he filled in the bottom line of the tender as instructed and then had the document signed by three directors, including his chairman, as required by Mexican law. He sent the tender by special messenger to the Ministry of Buildings in Paseo de la Reforma: When tendering for a contract for over thirty-nine million dollars, one does not send the document by first-class mail.

Several weeks passed before the Mexican Embassy in London contacted Sir Hamish, requesting that he travel to Mexico City for a meeting with Manuel Unichurtu, the minister concerned with the city's ring-road project. Sir Hamish remained skeptical, but David Heath was jubilant, because he had already learned through another source that Graham Construction was the only tender being seriously considered at that moment, although there were one or two outstanding items still to be agreed on. David Heath knew exactly what that meant.

A week later Sir Hamish, traveling first class, and David Heath, traveling economy, flew out of Heathrow bound for Mexico International Airport. On arrival they took an hour to clear customs and another thirty minutes to find a taxi to take them to the city, and then only after the driver had bargained with them for an outrageous fare. They covered the fifteen-mile journey from the airport to their hotel in just over an hour, and Sir Hamish was able to observe firsthand why the Mexicans were so desperate to build a ring road. Even with the windows down the ten-year-old car was like an oven that had been left on high all night, but during the journey Sir Hamish never once loosened his collar or tie. The two men checked into their rooms, phoned the minister's secretary to inform her of their arrival, and then waited.

For two days nothing happened.

David Heath assured his chairman that such a holdup was not an unusual course of events in Mexico, as the minister was undoubtedly in meetings most of the day, and after all, wasn't *mañana* the one Spanish word every foreigner understood?

On the afternoon of the third day, just as Sir Hamish was threatening to return home, David Heath received a call from the minister's man, who accepted an invitation to join them both for dinner in Sir Hamish's suite that evening.

Sir Hamish put on evening dress for the occasion, despite David Heath's counseling against the idea. He even had a bottle of *Fin La Ina* sherry sent up in case the minister's man required some refreshment. The dinner table was set, and the hosts were ready for 7:30. The minister's man did not appear at 7:30 or 7:45, or 8:00, or 8:15, or 8:30. At 8:49 there was a loud rap on the door, and Sir Hamish muttered an inaudible reproach as David Heath went to open it. He found his contact standing there.

"Good evening, Mr. Heath. I'm sorry to be late. Held up with the minister, you understand."

"Yes, of course," said David Heath. "How good of you to come, Señor Perez. May I introduce my chairman, Sir Hamish Graham?"

"How do you do, Sir Hamish? Victor Perez at your service."

Sir Hamish was dumbfounded. He simply stood and stared at the middle-aged little Mexican who had arrived for dinner dressed in a grubby white T-shirt and Western jeans. Perez looked as if he hadn't shaved for three days and reminded Sir Hamish of those bandits he had seen in B-movies when he was a schoolboy. He wore a heavy gold bracelet around his wrist that could have come from Cartier's, and a tiger's tooth on a platinum chain around his neck that looked as if it had come from Woolworth's. Perez grinned from ear to ear, pleased with the effect he was making.

"Good evening," replied Sir Hamish stiffly, taking a step backward. "Would you care for a sherry?"

"No, thank you, Sir Hamish. I've grown into the habit of liking your whiskey, on the rocks with a little soda."

"I'm sorry, I only have—"

"Don't worry, sir, I have some in my room," said David Heath, and rushed away to retrieve a bottle of Johnnie Walker he had hidden under the shirts in his top drawer. Despite this Scottish aid, the conversation before dinner among the three men was somewhat stilted, but David Heath had not come five thousand miles for an inferior hotel meal with Victor Perez, and Victor Perez in any other circumstances would not have crossed the road to meet Sir Hamish Graham, even if he'd built it. Their conversation ranged from the recent visit to Mexico of Her Majesty the Queen—as Sir Hamish referred to her—to the proposed return trip of President Portillo to Britain. Dinner might have gone more smoothly if Mr. Perez hadn't eaten most of the food with his hands and then proceeded to wipe his fingers on his jeans. The more Sir Hamish stared at him in disbelief, the more the little Mexican would grin from ear to ear. After dinner David Heath thought the time had come to steer the conversation toward the real purpose of the meeting, but not before Sir Hamish had reluctantly had to call for a bottle of brandy and a box of cigars.

"We are looking for an agent to represent the Graham Construction Company in Mexico, Mr. Perez, and you have been highly recommended," said Sir Hamish, sounding unconvinced by his own statement.

"Do call me Victor."

Sir Hamish bowed silently and shuddered. There was no way this man was going to be allowed to call him Hamish.

"I'd be pleased to represent you, Hamish," continued Perez, "provided that you find my terms acceptable."

"Perhaps you could enlighten us as to what those—hm, terms—might be," said Sir Hamish stiffly.

"Certainly," said the little Mexican cheerfully. "I require ten percent of the agreed tender figure, five percent to be paid on the day you are awarded the contract and five percent whenever you present your completion certificates. Not a penny to be paid until you have received your fee, all my payments deposited in an account at Crédit Suisse in Geneva within seven days of the National Bank of Mexico clearing your check."

David Heath drew in his breath sharply and stared down at the stone floor.

"But under those terms you would make nearly four million dollars," protested Sir Hamish, now red in the face. "That's over half our projected profit."

"That, as I believe you say in England, Hamish, is your problem. You fixed the tender price," said Perez, "not me. In any case, there's still enough in the deal for both of us to make a handsome profit, which is surely fair, as we bring half the equation to the table."

Sir Hamish was speechless as he fiddled with his bow tie. David Heath examined his fingernails attentively.

"Think the whole thing over, Hamish," said Victor Perez, sounding unperturbed, "and let me know your decision by midday tomorrow. The outcome makes little difference to me."

The Mexican rose, shook hands with Sir Hamish, and left. David Heath, sweating slightly, accompanied him down in the lift. In the foyer he clasped hands damply with the Mexican.

"Good night, Victor. I'm sure everything will be all right—by midday tomorrow."

"I hope so," replied the Mexican, "for your sake." He strolled out of the foyer whistling.

Sir Hamish, a glass of water in his hand, was still seated at the dinner table when his project manager returned.

"I do not believe it is possible that that—that that man can represent the secretary of state, represent a government minister."

"I am assured that he does," replied David Heath.

"But to part with nearly four million dollars to such an individual—"

"I agree with you, sir, but that is the way business is conducted out here."

"I can't believe it," said Sir Hamish. "I *won't* believe it. I want you to make an appointment for me to see the minister first thing tomorrow morning."

"He won't like that, sir. It might expose his position, and put him right out in the open in a way that could only embarrass him."

"I don't give a damn about embarrassing him. We are discussing a bribe, do I have to spell it out for you, Heath? A bribe of nearly four million dollars. Have you no principles, man?"

"Yes, sir, but I would still advise you against seeing the secretary of state. He won't want any of your conversation with Mr. Perez on the record."

"I have run this company my way for nearly thirty years, Mr. Heath, and I shall be the judge of what I want on the record."

"Yes, of course, sir."

"I will see the secretary of state first thing in the morning. Kindly arrange a meeting."

"If you insist, sir," said David Heath resignedly.

"I insist."

The project manager departed to his own room and a sleepless night. Early the next morning he delivered a handwritten, personal, and private letter to the minister, who sent a car around immediately for the Scottish industrialist.

Sir Hamish was driven slowly through the noisy, exuberant, bustling crowds of the city in the minister's black Ford Galaxy with flag flying. People made way for the car respectfully. The chauffeur came to a halt outside the Ministry of Buildings and Public Works in the Paseo de la Reforma and guided Sir Hamish through the long white corridors to a waiting room. A few minutes later an assistant showed Sir Hamish through to the secretary of state and took a seat by his side. The minister, a severe-looking man who appeared to be well into his seventies, was dressed in an immaculate white suit, white shirt, and blue tie. He rose, leaned over the vast expanse of green leather, and offered his hand.

"Do have a seat, Sir Hamish."

"Thank you," the chairman said, feeling more at home as he took in the minister's office; on the ceiling a large propellerlike fan revolved slowly around, making little difference to the stuffiness of the room, while hanging on the wall behind the minister was a signed picture of President José Lopez Portillo in full morning dress, and below the photo a plaque displayed a coat of arms.

"I see you were educated at Cambridge."

"That is correct, Sir Hamish, I was at Corpus Christi for three years."

"Then you know my country well, sir."

"I do have many happy memories of my stays in England, Sir Hamish; in fact, I still visit London as often as my leave allows."

"You must take a trip to Edinburgh some time."

"I have already done so, Sir Hamish. I attended the festival on two occasions and now know why your city is described as the Athens of the North."

"You are well informed, Minister."

"Thank you, Sir Hamish. Now I must ask how I can help you. Your assistant's note was rather vague."

"First let me say, Minister, that my company is honored to be considered for the city ring-road project, and I hope that our experience of thirty years in construction, twenty of them in the Third World"—he nearly said the undeveloped countries, an expression his project manager had warned him against—"is the reason you, as minister in charge, found us the natural choice for this contract."

"That, and your reputation for finishing a job on time at the stipulated price," replied the secretary of state. "Only twice in your history have you returned to the principal asking for changes in the payment schedule. Once in Uganda when you were held up by Amin's pathetic demands, and the other project, if I remember rightly, was in Bolivia, an airport, when you were unavoidably delayed for six months because of an earthquake. In both cases you completed the contract at the new price stipulated, and my advisers think you must have lost money on both occasions." The secretary of state mopped his brow with a silk handkerchief before continuing. "I would not wish you to think my government takes these decisions of selection lightly."

Sir Hamish was astounded by the secretary of state's command of his brief, the more so as no prompting notes lay on the leather-topped desk in front of him. He suddenly felt guilty at the little he knew about the secretary of state's background or history.

"Of course not, Minister. I am flattered by your personal concern, which makes me all the more determined to broach an embarrassing subject that has—"

"Before you say anything else, Sir Hamish, may I ask you some questions?"

"Of course, Minister."

"Do you still find the tender price of $39,121,110 acceptable in *all* the circumstances?"

"Yes, Minister."

"That amount still leaves you enough to do a worthwhile job while making a profit for your company?"

"Yes, Minister, but—"

"Excellent, then I think all you have to decide is whether you want to sign the contract by midday today." The minister emphasized the word "midday" as clearly as he could.

Sir Hamish, who had never understood the expression "a nod is as good as a wink," charged foolishly on.

"There is, nevertheless, one aspect of the contract I feel that I should discuss with you privately."

"Are you sure that would be wise, Sir Hamish?"

Sir Hamish hesitated, but only for a moment, before proceeding. Had David Heath heard the conversation that had taken place so far, he would have stood up, shaken hands with the secretary of state, removed the top of his fountain pen, and headed toward the contract—but not his employer.

"Yes, Minister, I feel I must," said Sir Hamish firmly.

"Will you kindly leave us, Miss Vieites?" said the secretary of state.

The assistant closed her shorthand book, rose, and left the room. Sir Hamish waited for the door to close before he began again.

"Yesterday I had a visit from a countryman of yours, a Mr. Victor Perez, who resides here in Mexico City and claims—"

"An excellent man," said the minister very quietly.

Still Sir Hamish charged on. "Yes, I daresay he is, Minister, but he asked to be allowed to represent Graham Construction as our agent, and I wondered—"

"A common practice in Mexico, no more than is required by the law," said the minister, swinging his chair round and staring out of the window.

"Yes, I appreciate that is the custom," said Sir Hamish, now talking to the minister's back, "but if I am to part with ten percent of the government's money I must be convinced that such a decision meets with your personal approval." Sir Hamish thought he had worded that rather well.

"Um," said the secretary of state, measuring his words, "Victor Perez is a good man and has always been loyal to the Mexican cause. Perhaps he leaves an unfortunate impression sometimes, not out of what you would call the 'top drawer,' Sir Hamish, but then we have no class barriers in Mexico." The minister swung back to face Sir Hamish.

The Scottish industrialist flushed. "Of course not, Minister, but that, if you will forgive me, is hardly the point. Mr. Perez is asking me to hand over nearly four million dollars, which is over half of my estimated profit on the project, without allowing for any contingencies or mishaps that might occur later."

"You chose the tender figure, Sir Hamish. I confess I was amused by the fact you added your date of birth to the thirty-nine million."

Sir Hamish's mouth opened wide.

"I would have thought," continued the minister, "given your record over the past three years and the present situation in Britain, you were not in a position to be fussy."

The minister gazed impassively at Sir Hamish's startled face. Both started to speak at the same time. Sir Hamish swallowed his words.

"Allow me to tell you a little story about Victor Perez. When the war was at its fiercest" (the old Secretary of State was referring to the Mexican Revolution in the same way that an American thinks of Vietnam or a Briton of Germany when they hear the word "war"), "Victor's father was one of the young men under my command who died on the battlefield at Celaya only a few days before victory was ours. He left a son born on the day of independence who never knew his father. I have the honor, Sir Hamish, to be godfather to that child. We christened him Victor."

"I can understand that you have a responsibility to an old comrade, but I still feel four million is—"

"Do you? Then let me continue. Just before Victor's father died, I visited him in a field hospital, and he asked only that I should take care of his wife. She died in childbirth. I therefore considered my responsibility passed on to their only child."

Sir Hamish remained silent for a moment. "I appreciate your attitude, Minister, but ten percent of one of your largest contracts?"

"One day," continued the secretary of state, as if he had not heard Sir Hamish's comment, "Victor's father was fighting in the front line at Zacatecas, and looking out across a minefield he saw a young lieutenant lying face down in the mud with his leg nearly blown off. With no thought for his own safety, he crawled through that minefield until he reached the lieutenant, and then he dragged him yard by yard back to the camp. It took him over three hours. He then carried the lieutenant to a truck and drove him to the nearest field hospital, undoubtedly saving his leg, and probably his life. So you see, the government has good cause to allow Perez's son the privilege of representing them from time to time."

"I agree with you, Minister," said Sir Hamish quietly. "Quite admirable."

The secretary of state smiled for the first time.

"But I still confess I cannot understand why you allow him such a large percentage."

The minister frowned. "I am afraid, Sir Hamish, if you cannot understand that, you can never hope to understand the principles we Mexicans live by."

The secretary of state rose from behind his desk, limped to the door and showed Sir Hamish out.

TRIAL AND
ERROR

IT'S HARD TO KNOW exactly where to begin. But first, let me explain why I'm in jail.

The trial had lasted for eighteen days, and from the moment the judge had entered the courtroom the public benches had been filled to overflowing. The jury at Leeds Crown Court had been out for almost two days, and rumor had it that they were hopelessly divided. On the barristers' bench there was talk of hung juries and retrials, as it had been more than eight hours since Mr. Justice Cartwright had told the foreman of the jury that their verdict need no longer be unanimous: A majority of ten to two would be acceptable.

Suddenly there was a buzz in the corridors, and the members of the jury filed quietly into their places. Press and public alike began to stampede back into court. All eyes were on the foreman of the jury, a fat, jolly-looking little man dressed in a double-breasted suit, striped shirt and a colorful bow tie, striving to appear solemn. He seemed the sort of fellow with whom, in normal circumstances, I would have enjoyed a pint at the local. But these were not normal circumstances.

As I climbed back up the steps into the dock, my eyes settled on a pretty blond who had been seated in the gallery every day of the trial. I wondered if she attended all the sensational murder trials, or if she was just fascinated by this one. She showed absolutely no interest in me, and like everyone else was concentrating her full attention on the foreman of the jury.

The clerk of the court, dressed in a wig and a long black gown, rose and read out from a card the words I suspect he knew by heart.

"Will the foreman of the jury please stand."

The jolly little fat man rose slowly from his place.

"Please answer my next question yes or no. Members of the jury, have you reached a verdict on which at least ten of you are agreed?"

"Yes, we have."

"Members of the jury, do you find the prisoner at the bar guilty or not guilty as charged?"

There was total silence in the courtroom.

My eyes were fixed on the foreman with the colorful bow tie. He cleared his throat and said . . .

I first met Jeremy Alexander in 1978, at a Council of British Industries training seminar in Bristol. Fifty-six British companies that were looking for ways to expand into Europe had come together for a briefing on Community law. At the time that I signed up for the seminar, Cooper's, the company of which I was chairman, ran 127 vehicles of varying weights and sizes, and was fast becoming one of the largest private road haulage companies in Britain.

My father had founded the firm in 1931, starting out with three vehicles—two of them pulled by horses—and an overdraft limit of ten pounds at his local Martins bank. By the time we became Cooper & Son in 1967, the company had seventeen vehicles with four wheels or more, and delivered goods all over the north of England. But the old man still resolutely refused to exceed his ten-pound overdraft limit.

I once expressed the view, during a downturn in the market, that we should be looking further afield in search of new business—perhaps even as far as the Continent. But my father wouldn't hear of it. "Not a risk worth taking," he declared. He distrusted anyone born south of the Humber, let alone those who lived on the other side of the Channel. "If God put a strip of water between us, he must have had good reasons for doing so," were his final words on the subject. I would have laughed, if I hadn't realized he meant it.

When he retired in 1977—reluctantly, at the age of seventy— I took over as chairman and began to set in motion some ideas I'd been working on for the past decade, though I knew my father didn't approve of them. Europe was only the beginning of my plans for the company's expansion: Within five years I wanted to go public. By then, I realized, we would require an overdraft facility of at least a million pounds, and would therefore have to move our account to a bank that recognized that the world stretched beyond the county boundaries of Yorkshire.

It was around this time that I heard about the CBI seminar at Bristol, and applied for a place.

The seminar began on Friday, with an opening address from the head of the European Directorate of the CBI. After that the delegates split into eight small working groups, each chaired by an expert on Community law. My group was headed by Jeremy Alexander. I admired him from the moment he started speaking—in fact, it wouldn't be an exaggeration to say that I was overawed. He was totally self-assured, and as I was to learn, he could effortlessly present a convincing argument on any subject, from the superiority of the Code Napoléon to the inferiority of English middle-order batting.

He lectured us for an hour on the fundamental differences in practice and procedure between the member states of the Community, then answered all our questions on commercial and company law, even finding time to explain the significance of the Uruguay Round. Like me, the other members of our group never stopped taking notes.

We broke for lunch a few minutes before one, and I managed to grab a place next to Jeremy. I was already beginning to think that he might be the ideal person to advise me on how to go about achieving my European ambitions.

Listening to him talk about his career over a meal of stargazey fish pie with red peppers, I kept thinking that, although we were about the same age, we couldn't have come from more different backgrounds. Jeremy's father, a banker by profession, had escaped from Eastern Europe only days before the outbreak of the Second World War. He had settled in England, Anglicized his name, and sent his son to Westminster. From there Jeremy had gone on to King's College, London, where he read law, graduating with first-class honors.

My own father was a self-made man from the Yorkshire Dales

who had insisted I leave school the moment I passed my O levels. "I'll teach you more about the real world in a month than you'd learn from any of those university types in a lifetime," he used to say. I accepted this philosophy without question, and left school a few weeks after my sixteenth birthday. The next morning I joined Cooper's as an apprentice, and spent my first three years at the depot under the watchful eye of Buster Jackson, the works manager, who taught me how to take the company's vehicles apart and, more important, how to put them back together again.

After graduating from the workshop, I spent two years in the invoicing department, learning how to calculate charges and collect bad debts. A few weeks after my twenty-first birthday I passed the test for my heavy goods vehicles license, and for the next three years I zig-zagged across the north of England, delivering everything from poultry to pineapples to our far-flung customers. Jeremy spent the same period reading for a master's degree in Napoleonic Law at the Sorbonne.

When Buster Jackson retired I was moved back to the depot in Leeds to take over as works manager. Jeremy was in Hamburg, writing a doctoral thesis on international trade barriers. By the time he had finally left the world of academia and taken up his first real job, as a partner with a large firm of commercial solicitors in the City, I had been earning a working wage for eight years.

Although I was impressed by Jeremy at the seminar, I sensed, behind that surface affability, a powerful combination of ambition and intellectual snobbery that my father would have mistrusted. I felt he'd only agreed to give the lecture on the off-chance that, at some time in the future, we might be responsible for spreading some butter on his bread. I now realize that, even at our first meeting, he suspected that in my case it might be honey.

It didn't help my opinion of the man that he had a couple of inches on me in height, and a couple less around the waist. Not to mention the fact that the most attractive woman on the course that weekend ended up in his bed on the Saturday night.

We met up on the Sunday morning to play squash, when he ran me ragged, without even appearing to raise a sweat. "We must get together again," he said as we walked to the showers. "If you're really thinking of expanding into Europe, you might find I'm able to help."

My father had taught me never to make the mistake of imagining that your friends and your colleagues were necessarily the same animals (he often cited the cabinet as an example). So, although I didn't like him, I made sure that when I left Bristol at the end of the conference I was in possession of Jeremy's numerous telephone and telex numbers.

I drove back to Leeds on Sunday evening, and when I reached home I ran upstairs and sat on the end of the bed regaling my sleepy wife with an account of why it had turned out to be such a worthwhile weekend.

Rosemary was my second wife. My first, Helen, had been at Leeds High School for Girls at the same time that I had attended the nearby grammar school. The two schools shared a gymnasium, and I fell in love with her at the age of thirteen, while watching her play net ball. After that I would find any excuse to hang around the gym, hoping to catch a glimpse of her blue shorts as she leaped to send the ball unerringly into the net. As the schools took part in various joint activities, I began to take an active interest in theatrical productions, even though I couldn't act. I attended joint debates and never opened my mouth. I enlisted in the combined schools orchestra and ended up playing the triangle. After I had left school and gone to work at the depot, I continued to see Helen, who was studying for her A levels. Despite my passion for her, we didn't make love until we were both eighteen, and even then I wasn't certain that we had consummated anything. Six weeks later she told me, in a flood of tears, that she was pregnant. Against the wishes of her parents, who had hoped that she would go on to university, a hasty wedding was arranged, but as I never wanted to look at another girl for the rest of my life, I was secretly delighted by the outcome of our youthful indiscretion.

Helen died on the night of September 14, 1964, giving birth

to our son, Tom, who himself only survived a week. I thought I would never get over it, and I'm not sure I ever have. After her death I didn't so much as glance at another woman for years, putting all my energy into the company.

Following the funeral of my wife and son, my father, not a soft or sentimental man—you won't find many of those in Yorkshire—revealed a gentle side to his character that I had never seen before. He would often phone me in the evening to see how I was getting on, and insisted that I regularly joined him in the directors' box at Elland Road to watch Leeds United on Saturday afternoons. I began to understand, for the first time, why my mother still adored him after more than twenty years of marriage.

I met Rosemary about four years later at a ball given to launch the Leeds Music Festival. Not a natural habitat for me, but as Cooper's had taken a full-page advertisement in the program, and Brigadier Kershaw, the high sheriff of the county and chairman of the ball committee, had invited us to join him as his guests, I had no choice but to dress up in my seldom-worn dinner jacket and accompany my parents to the ball.

I was placed at Table 17, next to a Miss Kershaw, who turned out to be the high sheriff's daughter. She was elegantly dressed in a strapless blue gown that emphasized her comely figure, and had a mop of red hair and a smile that made me feel we had been friends for years. She told me over something described on the menu as "avocado with dill" that she had just finished majoring in English at Durham University and wasn't quite sure what she was going to do with her life.

"I don't want to be a teacher," she said. "And I'm certainly not cut out to be a secretary." We chatted through the second and third courses, ignoring the people seated on either side of us. After coffee she dragged me onto the dance floor, where she continued to explain the problems of contemplating any form of work while her diary was so packed with social engagements.

I felt rather flattered that the high sheriff's daughter should show the slightest interest in me, and to be honest I didn't take it seriously when at the end of the evening, she whispered in my ear, "Let's keep in touch."

But a couple of days later she called and invited me to join her and her parents for lunch that Sunday at their house in the country. "And then perhaps we could play a little tennis afterwards. You do play tennis, I suppose?"

I drove over to Church Fenton on Sunday, and found that the Kershaws' residence was exactly what I would have expected—large and decaying, which, come to think of it, wasn't a bad description of Rosemary's father as well. But he seemed a nice enough chap. Her mother, however, wasn't quite so easy to please. She originated from somewhere in Hampshire, and was unable to mask her feeling that, although I might be good for the occasional charitable donation, I was not quite the sort of person with whom she expected to be sharing her Sunday lunch. Rosemary ignored the odd barbed comment from her, and continued to chat to me about my work.

Since it rained all afternoon we never got around to playing tennis, so Rosemary used the time to seduce me in the little pavilion behind the court. At first I was nervous about making love to the high sheriff's daughter, but I soon got used to the idea. However, as the weeks passed, I began to wonder if I was anything more to her than a "truck driver fantasy." Until, that is, she started to talk about marriage. Mrs. Kershaw was unable to hide her disgust at the very idea of someone like me becoming her son-in-law, but her opinion turned out to be irrelevant, as Rosemary remained implacable on the subject. We were married eighteen months later.

Over two hundred guests attended the rather grand county wedding in the parish church of St. Mary's. But I confess that when I turned to watch Rosemary progressing up the aisle, my only thoughts were of my first wedding ceremony.

For a couple of years Rosemary made every effort to be a good wife. She took an interest in the company, learned the names of all the employees, even became friendly with the wives of some of the senior executives. But, as I worked all the hours God sent, I fear I may not always have given her as much attention as she needed. You see, Rosemary yearned for a life that was made up of regular visits to the Grand Theatre for Opera North, followed by dinner parties with her county friends that would run into the early hours, while I preferred to work at weekends, and to be safe in bed before eleven most nights. For Rosemary I wasn't turning out to be the husband in the title of the Oscar Wilde play she had recently taken me to—and it didn't help that I had fallen asleep during the second act.

After four years without producing any offspring—not that Rosemary wasn't very energetic in bed—we began to drift our separate ways. If she started having affairs (and I certainly did, when I could find the time), she was discreet about them. And then she met Jeremy Alexander.

It must have been about six weeks after the seminar in Bristol that I had occasion to phone Jeremy and seek his advice. I wanted to close a deal with a French cheese company to transport its wares to British supermarkets. The previous year I had made a large loss on a similar enterprise with a German beer company, and I couldn't afford to make the same mistake again.

"Send me all the details," Jeremy had said. "I'll look over the paperwork on the weekend and call you on Monday morning."

He was as good as his word, and when he phoned me he mentioned that he had to be in York that Thursday to brief a client, and suggested we get together the following day to go over the contract. I agreed, and we spent most of that Friday closeted in the Cooper's boardroom checking over every dot and comma of the contract. It was a pleasure to watch such a professional at work, even if Jeremy did occasionally display an irritating habit of drumming his fingers on the table when I hadn't immediately understood what he was getting at.

Jeremy, it turned out, had already talked to the French company's in-house lawyer in Toulouse about any reservations he might have. He assured me that, although Monsieur Sisley spoke no English, he had made him fully aware of our anxieties. I remember being struck by his use of the word "our."

After we had turned the last page of the contract, I realized that everyone else in the building had left for the weekend, so I suggested to Jeremy that he might like to join Rosemary and me for dinner. He checked his watch, considered the offer for a moment, and then said, "Thank you, that's very kind of you. Could you drop me back at the Queen's Hotel so I can get changed?"

Rosemary, however, was not pleased to be told at the last minute that I had invited a complete stranger to dinner without warning her, even though I assured her that she would like him.

Jeremy rang our front doorbell a few minutes after eight. When I introduced him to Rosemary, he bowed slightly and kissed her hand. After that they didn't take their eyes off each other all evening. Only a blind man could have missed what was likely to happen next, and although I might not have been blind, I certainly turned a blind eye.

Jeremy was soon finding excuses to spend more and more time in Leeds, and I am bound to admit that his sudden enthusiasm for the north of England enabled me to advance my ambitions for Cooper's far more quickly than I had originally dreamed possible. I had felt for some time that the company needed an in-house lawyer, and within a year of our first meeting I offered Jeremy a place on the board, with the remit to prepare the company for going public.

During that period I spent a great deal of my time in Madrid, Amsterdam, and Brussels drumming up new contracts, and Rosemary certainly didn't discourage me. Meanwhile Jeremy skillfully guided the company through a thicket of legal and financial problems caused by our expansion. Thanks to his diligence and expertise, we were able to announce on February 12, 1980 that Cooper's would be applying for a listing on the Stock Exchange later that year. It was then that I made my first mistake: I invited Jeremy to become deputy chairman of the company.

Under the terms of the flotation, 51 percent of the shares would be retained by Rosemary and myself. Jeremy explained to me that for tax reasons they should be divided equally between us. My accountants agreed, and at the time I didn't give it a second thought. The remaining 4,900,000 £1 shares were quickly taken up by institutions and the general public, and within days of the company being listed on the stock exchange their value had risen to £2.80.

My father, who had died the previous year, would never have accepted that it was possible to become worth several million pounds overnight. In fact I suspect he would have disapproved of the very idea, as he went to his deathbed still believing that a ten-pound overdraft was quite adequate to conduct a well-run business.

During the 1980s the British economy showed continual growth, and by March 1984, Cooper's shares had topped the five-pound mark, following press speculation about a possible takeover. Jeremy had advised me to accept one of the bids, but I told him that I would never allow Cooper's to be let out of the family's control. After that, we had to split the shares on three separate occasions, and by 1989 the *Sunday Times* was estimating that Rosemary and I were together worth around £30,000,000.

I had never thought of myself as being wealthy—after all, as far as I was concerned the shares were simply pieces of paper held by Joe Ramsbottom, our company solicitor. I still lived in my father's house, drove a five-year-old Jaguar, and worked fourteen hours a day. I had never cared much for vacations, and wasn't by nature extravagant. Wealth seemed somehow irrelevant to me. I would have been happy to continue living much as I was, had I not arrived home unexpectedly one night.

I had caught the last plane back to Heathrow after a particularly long and arduous negotiation in Cologne, and had originally intended to stay overnight in London. But by then I'd had enough of hotels, and simply wanted to get home, despite the long drive. When I arrived back in Leeds a few minutes after one, I found Jeremy's white BMW parked in the driveway.

Had I phoned Rosemary earlier that day, I might never have ended up in jail.

I parked my car next to Jeremy's and was walking toward the front door when I noticed that there was only one light on in the house—in the front room on the first floor. It wouldn't have taken Sherlock Holmes to deduce what might be taking place in that particular room.

I came to a halt and stared up at the drawn curtains for some time. Nothing stirred, so clearly they hadn't heard the car and were unaware of my presence. I retraced my steps and drove quietly off in the direction of the city center. When I arrived at the Queen's Hotel I asked the duty manager if Mr. Jeremy Alexander had reserved a room for the night. He checked the register and confirmed that he had.

"Then I'll take his key," I told him. "Mr. Alexander has booked himself in somewhere else for the night." My father would have been proud of such thrifty use of the company's resources.

I lay on the hotel bed, quite unable to sleep, my anger rising as each hour passed. Although I no longer had a great deal of feeling for Rosemary, and even accepted that perhaps I never had, I now loathed Jeremy. But it wasn't until the next day that I discovered just how much I loathed him.

The following morning I called my secretary, and told her I would be driving to the office straight from London. She reminded me that there was a board meeting scheduled for two o'clock, which Mr. Alexander was penciled in to chair. I was glad she couldn't see the smile of satisfaction that spread across my face. A quick glance at the agenda over breakfast and it had become abundantly clear why Jeremy had wanted to chair this particular meeting. But his plans didn't matter anymore. I had already decided to let my fellow directors know exactly what he was up to, and to make sure that he was dismissed from the board as soon as was practicable.

I arrived at Cooper's just after 1.30, and parked in the space marked "Chairman." By the time the board meeting was scheduled to begin I'd had just enough time to check over my files, and became painfully aware of how many of the company's shares were now controlled by Jeremy, and what he and Rosemary must have been planning for some time.

Jeremy vacated the chairman's place without comment the moment I entered the boardroom, and showed no particular interest in the proceedings until we reached an item concerning a future share issue. It was at this point that he tried to push through a seemingly innocuous motion that could ultimately have resulted in Rosemary and myself losing overall control of the company, and therefore being unable to resist any future takeover bid. I might have fallen for it if I hadn't traveled up to Leeds the previous evening and found his car parked in my driveway, and the bedroom light on. Just when he thought he had succeeded in having the motion passed without a vote, I asked the company accountants to prepare a full report for the next board meeting before we came to any decision. Jeremy showed no sign of emotion. He simply looked down at his notes and began drumming his fingers on the boardroom table. I was determined that the report would prove to be his downfall. If only it hadn't been for my short temper, I might, given time, have worked out a more sensible way of ridding myself of him.

As no one had "any other business" to raise, I closed the meeting at 5:40, and suggested to Jeremy that he join Rosemary and me for dinner. I wanted to see them together. Jeremy didn't seem too keen, but after some bluffing from me about not fully understanding his new share proposal, and feeling that my wife ought to be brought in on it at some stage, he agreed. When I rang Rosemary to let her know that Jeremy would be coming to dinner, she seemed even less enthusiastic about the idea than he had been.

"Perhaps the two of you should go off to a restaurant together," she suggested. "Then Jeremy can bring you up to date on what's been going on while you've been away." I tried not to laugh. "We haven't got much food in at the moment," she added. I told her that it wasn't the food I was worried about.

Jeremy was uncharacteristically late, but I had his usual whiskey and soda ready the moment he walked through the door. I must say he put up a brilliant performance over dinner, though Rosemary was less convincing.

Over coffee in the sitting room, I managed to provoke the

confrontation that Jeremy had so skillfully avoided at the board meeting.

"Why are you so keen to rush through this new share allocation?" I asked once he was on his second brandy. "Surely you realize that it will take control of the company out of the hands of Rosemary and me. Can't you see that we could be taken over in no time?"

He tried a few well-rehearsed phrases. "In the best interests of the company, Richard. You must realize how quickly Cooper's is expanding. It's no longer a family firm. In the long term it has to be the most prudent course for both of you, not to mention the shareholders." I wondered which particular shareholders he had in mind.

I was a little surprised to find Rosemary not only backing him up, but showing a remarkable grasp of the finer details of the share allocation, even after Jeremy had scowled rather too obviously at her. She seemed extremely well-versed in the arguments he had been putting forward, given the fact that she had never shown any interest in the company's transactions in the past. It was when she turned to me and said, "We must consider our future, darling," that I finally lost my temper.

Yorkshiremen are well known for being blunt, and my next question lived up to our county's reputation.

"Are you two having an affair, by any chance?"

Rosemary turned scarlet. Jeremy laughed a little too loudly, and then said, "I think you've had one drink too many, Richard."

"Not a drop," I assured him. "Sober as a judge. As I was when I came home late last night and found your car parked in the driveway and the light on in the bedroom."

For the first time since I'd met him, I had completely wrong-footed Jeremy, even if it was only for a moment. He began drumming his fingers on the glass table in front of him.

"I was simply explaining to Rosemary how the new share issue would affect her," he said, hardly missing a beat. "Which is no more than is required under stock exchange regulations."

"And is there a stock exchange regulation requiring that such explanations should take place in bed?"

"Oh, don't be absurd," said Jeremy. "I spent the night at the Queen's Hotel. Call the manager," he added, picking up the telephone and offering it to me. "He'll confirm that I was booked into my usual room."

"I'm sure he will," I said. "But he'll also confirm that it was I who spent the night in your usual bed."

In the silence that followed I removed the hotel bedroom key from my jacket pocket and dangled it in front of him. Jeremy immediately jumped to his feet.

I rose from my chair, rather more slowly, and faced him, wondering what his next line could possibly be.

"It's your own fault, you bloody fool," he eventually stammered out. "You should have taken more interest in Rosemary in the first place, and not gone off gallivanting around Europe all the time. It's no wonder you're in danger of losing the company."

Funny, it wasn't the fact that Jeremy had been sleeping with my wife that caused me to snap, but that he had the arrogance to think he could take over my company as well. I didn't reply, but just took a pace forward and threw a punch at his clean-shaven jaw. I may have been a couple of inches shorter than he was, but after twenty years of hanging around with lorry drivers, I could still land a decent blow. Jeremy staggered first back-wards and then forwards, before crumpling in front of me. As he fell, he cracked his right temple on the corner of the glass table, knocking his brandy all over the floor. He lay motionless in front of me, blood dripping onto the carpet.

I must admit I felt rather pleased with myself, especially when Rosemary rushed to his side and started screaming obscenities at me.

"Save your breath for the ex–deputy chairman," I told her. "And when he comes to, tell him not to bother with the Queen's Hotel, because I'll be sleeping in his bed again tonight."

I strode out of the house and drove back into the city center, leaving my Jaguar in the hotel parking lot. When I walked into the Queen's the lobby was deserted, and I took the elevator straight up to Jeremy's room. I lay on the bed, but was far too agitated to sleep.

I was just dozing off when four policemen burst into the room and pulled me off the bed. One of them told me that I was under arrest and read me my rights. Without further explanation I was marched out of the hotel and driven to Millgarth Police Station. A few minutes after 5 A.M., I was signed in by the custody officer and my personal possessions were taken from me and dropped into a bulky brown envelope. I was told that I had the right to make one telephone call, so I rang Joe Ramsbottom, woke his wife, and asked if Joe could join me at the station as quickly as possible. Then I was locked in a small cell and left alone.

I sat on the wooden bench and tried to fathom why I had been arrested. I couldn't believe that Jeremy would have been foolish enough to charge me with assault. When Joe arrived about forty minutes later I told him exactly what had taken place earlier in the evening. He listened gravely, but didn't offer an opinion. When I had finished, he said he would try to find out what the police intended to charge me with.

After Joe left, I began to fear that Jeremy might have had a heart attack, or even that the blow to his head from the corner of the table might have killed him. My imagination ran riot as I considered all the worst possibilities, and I was becoming more and more desperate to learn what had happened when the cell door swung open and two plainclothes detectives walked in. Joe was a pace behind them.

"I'm Chief Inspector Bainbridge," said the taller of the two. "And this is my colleague, Sergeant Harris." Their eyes were tired and their suits crumpled. They looked as if they had been on duty all night, as both of them could have used a shave. I felt my chin, and realized I needed one as well.

"We'd like to ask you some questions about what took place at your home earlier this evening," said the chief inspector. I looked at Joe, who shook his head. "It would help our inquiries, Mr. Cooper, if you cooperated with us," the chief inspector continued. "Would you be prepared to give us a statement either in writing or as a tape recording?"

"I'm afraid my client has nothing to say at the moment, Chief Inspector," said Joe. "And he will have nothing to say until I have taken further instructions."

I was rather impressed. I'd never seen Joe that firm with anyone other than his children.

"We would simply like to take a statement, Mr. Ramsbottom," Chief Inspector Bainbridge said to Joe, as if I didn't exist. "We are quite happy for you to be present throughout."

"No," said Joe firmly. "You either charge my client, or you leave us—and leave us immediately."

The chief inspector hesitated for a moment, and then nodded to his colleague. They departed without another word.

"Charge me?" I said, once the cell door had been locked behind them. "What with, for God's sake?"

"Murder, I suspect," said Joe. "After what Rosemary has been telling them."

"Murder?" I said, almost unable to mouth the word. "But . . ." I listened in disbelief as Joe told me what he'd been able to discover about the details of the statement my wife had given to the police during the early hours of the morning.

"But that's not what happened," I protested. "Surely no one would believe such an outrageous story."

"They might when they learn the police have found a trail of blood leading from the sitting room to the spot where your car was parked in the drive," said Joe.

"That's not possible," I said. "When I left Jeremy, he was still lying unconscious on the floor."

"The police also found traces of blood in the trunk of your car. They seem quite confident that it will match with Jeremy's."

"Oh, my God," I said. "He's clever. He's very clever. Can't you see what they've been up to?"

"No, to be honest, I can't," Joe admitted. "This isn't exactly all in a day's work for a company solicitor like me. But I managed to catch Sir Matthew Roberts, QC, on the phone before he left home this morning. He's the most eminent criminal silk on the northeastern circuit. He's appearing in the York Crown Court today, and he's agreed to join us as soon as the court has risen. If you're innocent, Richard," Joe said, "with Sir Matthew defending you, there will be nothing to fear. Of that you can be certain."

Later that afternoon I was charged with the murder of Jeremy Anatole Alexander; the police admitted to my solicitor that they still hadn't found the body, but they were confident that they would do so within a few hours. I knew they wouldn't. Joe told me the following day that they had done more digging in my garden during the past twenty-four hours than I had attempted in the past twenty-four years.

Around seven that evening the door of my cell swung open once again and Joe walked in, accompanied by a heavily built, distinguished-looking man. Sir Matthew Roberts was about my height, but at least thirty pounds heavier. From his rubicund cheeks and warm smile he looked as if he regularly enjoyed a good bottle of wine and the company of amusing people. He had a full head of dark hair that remained modeled on the old Denis Compton Brylcreem advertisements, and he was attired in the garb of his profession, a dark three-piece suit and a silver gray tie. I liked him from the moment he introduced himself. His first words were to express the wish that we had met in more pleasant circumstances.

I spent the rest of the evening with Sir Matthew, going over my story again and again. I could tell he didn't believe a word I was saying, but he still seemed quite happy to represent me. He and Joe left a few minutes after eleven, and I settled down to spend my first night behind bars.

I was remanded in custody until the police had processed and submitted all their evidence to the Department of Public Prosecutions. The following day a magistrate committed me to trial at Leeds Crown Court, and despite an eloquent plea from Sir Matthew, I was not granted bail.

Forty minutes later I was transferred to Armley Jail.

The hours turned into days, the days into weeks, and the weeks into months. I almost tired of telling anyone who would listen that they would never find Jeremy's body, because there was no body to find.

When the case finally reached Leeds Crown Court nine months later, the crime reporters turned up in their hordes, and followed every word of the trial with relish. A multimillionaire, a possible adulterous affair, and a missing body were too much for them to resist. The tabloids excelled themselves, describing

Jeremy as the Lord Lucan of Leeds and me as an oversexed truck driver. I would have enjoyed every last syllable of it, if I hadn't been the accused.

In his opening address, Sir Matthew put up a magnificent fight on my behalf. Without a body, how could his client possibly be charged with murder? And how could I have disposed of the body, when I had spent the entire night in a bedroom at the Queen's Hotel? How I regretted not checking in the second time, but simply going straight up to Jeremy's room. It didn't help that the police had found me lying on the bed fully dressed.

I watched the faces of the jury at the end of the prosecution's opening speech. They were perplexed, and obviously in some doubt about my guilt. That doubt remained until Rosemary entered the witness box. I couldn't bear to look at her, and diverted my eyes to a striking blond who had been sitting in the front row of the public gallery on every day of the trial.

For an hour the counsel for the prosecution guided my wife gently through what had taken place that evening, up to the point when I had struck Jeremy. Until that moment, I couldn't have quarrelled with a word she had spoken.

"And then what happened, Mrs. Cooper?" prodded counsel for the Crown.

"My husband bent down and checked Mr. Alexander's pulse," Rosemary whispered. "Then he turned white, and all he said was, 'He's dead. I've killed him.'"

"And what did Mr. Cooper do next?"

"He picked up the body, threw it over his shoulder, and began walking toward the door. I shouted after him, 'What do you think you're doing, Richard?'"

"And how did he respond?"

"He told me he intended to dispose of the body while it was still dark, and that I was to make sure that there was no sign that Jeremy had visited the house. As no one else had been in the office when they left, everyone would assume that Jeremy had returned to London earlier in the evening. 'Be certain there are absolutely no traces of blood,' were the last words I remember my husband saying as he left the room carrying

Jeremy's body over his shoulder. That must have been when I fainted."

Sir Matthew glanced quizzically up at me in the dock. I shook my head vigorously. He looked grim as counsel for the prosecution resumed his seat.

"Do you wish to question this witness, Sir Matthew?" the judge asked.

Sir Matthew rose slowly to his feet. "I most certainly do, M'Lud," he replied. He drew himself up to his full height, tugged at his gown, and stared across at his adversary.

"Mrs. Cooper, would you describe yourself as a friend of Mr. Alexander?"

"Yes, but only in the sense that he was a colleague of my husband's," replied Rosemary calmly.

"So you didn't ever see each other when your husband was away from Leeds, or even out of the country, on business?"

"Only at social events, when I was accompanied by my husband, or if I dropped into the office to pick up his mail."

"Are you certain that those were the only times you saw him, Mrs. Cooper? Were there not other occasions when you spent a considerable amount of time alone with Mr. Alexander? For example, on the night of September 17, 1989, before your husband returned unexpectedly from a European trip: Did Mr. Alexander not visit you then for several hours while you were alone in the house?"

"No. He dropped by after work to leave a document for my husband, but he didn't even have time to stay for a drink."

"But your husband says—" began Sir Matthew.

"I know what my husband says," Rosemary replied, as if she had rehearsed the line a hundred times.

"I see," said Sir Matthew. "Let's get to the point, shall we, Mrs. Cooper? Were you having an affair with Jeremy Alexander at the time of his disappearance?"

"Is this relevant, Sir Matthew?" interrupted the judge.

"It most assuredly is, M'Lud. It goes to the very core of the case," replied my QC in a quiet even tone.

Everyone's gaze was now fixed on Rosemary. I willed her to tell the truth.

She didn't hesitate. "Certainly not," she replied, "although it wasn't the first time my husband had accused me unjustly."

"I see," said Sir Matthew. He paused. "Do you love your husband, Mrs. Cooper?"

"Really, Sir Matthew!" The judge was unable to disguise his irritation. "I must ask once again if this is relevant?"

Sir Matthew exploded. "Relevant? It's absolutely vital, M'Lud, and I am not being assisted by Your Lordship's thinly veiled attempts to intervene on behalf of this witness."

The judge was beginning to splutter with indignation when Rosemary said quietly, "I have always been a good and faithful wife, but I cannot under any circumstances condone murder."

The jury turned their eyes on me. Most of them looked as if they would be happy to bring back the death penalty.

"If that is the case, I am bound to ask why you waited two and a half hours to contact the police?" said Sir Matthew. "Especially if, as you claim, you believed your husband had committed murder and was about to dispose of the body."

"As I explained, I fainted soon after he left the room. I phoned the police the moment I came to."

"How convenient," said Sir Matthew. "Or perhaps the truth is that you made use of that time to set a trap for your husband, while allowing your lover to get clean away." A murmur ran through the courtroom.

"Sir Matthew," the judge said, jumping in once again. "You are going too far."

"Not so, M'Lud, with respect. In fact, not far enough." He swung back round and faced my wife again.

"I put it to you, Mrs. Cooper, that Jeremy Alexander was your lover, and still is, that you are perfectly aware he is alive and well, and that if you wished to, you could tell us exactly where he is now."

Despite the judge's spluttering and the uproar in the court, Rosemary had her reply ready.

"I only wish he were," she said, "so that he could stand in this court and confirm that I am telling the truth." Her voice was soft and gentle.

"But *you* already know the truth, Mrs. Cooper," said Sir

Matthew, his voice gradually rising. "The truth is that your husband left the house on his own. He then drove to the Queen's Hotel, where he spent the rest of the night, while you and your lover used that time to leave clues across the city of Leeds—clues, I might add, that were intended to incriminate your husband. But the one thing you couldn't leave was a body, because, as you well know, Mr. Jeremy Alexander is still alive, and the two of you have together fabricated this entire bogus story simply to further your own ends. Isn't that the truth, Mrs. Cooper?"

"No, no!" Rosemary shouted, her voice cracking before she finally burst into tears.

"Oh, come, come, Mrs. Cooper. Those are counterfeit tears, are they not?" said Sir Matthew quietly. "Now you've been found out, the jury will decide if your distress is genuine."

I glanced across at the jury. Not only had they fallen for Rosemary's performance, but they now despised me for allowing my insensitive bully of a counsel to attack such a gentle, long-suffering woman. To every one of Sir Matthew's probing questions, Rosemary proved well capable of delivering a riposte that revealed to me all the hallmarks of Jeremy Alexander's expert tuition.

When it was my turn to enter the witness box, and Sir Matthew began questioning me, I felt that my story sounded far less convincing than Rosemary's, despite its being the truth.

The closing speech for the Crown was deadly dull, but nevertheless deadly. Sir Matthew's was subtle and dramatic, but I feared less convincing.

After another night in Armley Jail I returned to the dock for the judge's summing up. It was clear that he was in no doubt as to my guilt. His selection of the evidence he chose to review was unbalanced and unfair, and when he ended by reminding the jury that his opinion of the evidence should ultimately carry no weight, he only added hypocrisy to bias.

After their first full day's deliberations, the jury had to be put up overnight in a hotel—ironically, the Queen's—and when the jolly little fat man in the bow tie was finally asked: "Members of the jury, do you find the prisoner at the bar guilty or not guilty as charged?" I wasn't surprised when he said clearly for all to hear, "Guilty, My Lord."

In fact I was amazed that the jury had failed to reach a unanimous decision. I have often wondered which two members felt convinced enough to declare my innocence. I would have liked to thank them.

The judge stared down at me. "Richard Wilfred Cooper, you have been found guilty of the murder of Jeremy Anatole Alexander . . . "

"I did not kill him, My Lord," I interrupted in a calm voice. "In fact, he is not dead. I can only hope that you will live long enough to realize the truth." Sir Matthew looked up anxiously as uproar broke out in the court.

The judge called for silence, and his voice became even more harsh as he pronounced, "You will go to prison for life. That is the sentence prescribed by law. Take him down."

Two prison officers stepped forward, gripped me firmly by the arms, and led me down the steps at the back of the dock into the cell I had occupied every morning for the eighteen days of the trial.

"Sorry, old chum," said the policeman who had been in charge of my welfare since the case had begun. "It was that bitch of a wife who tipped the scales against you." He slammed the cell door closed and turned the key in the lock before I had a chance to agree with him. A few moments later the door was unlocked again, and Sir Matthew strode in.

He stared at me for some time before uttering a word. "A terrible injustice has been done, Mr. Cooper," he eventually said, "and we shall immediately lodge an appeal against your conviction. Be assured, I will not rest until we have found Jeremy Alexander and he has been brought to justice."

For the first time I realized Sir Matthew knew that I was innocent.

I was put in a cell with a petty criminal called Fingers Jenkins. Can you believe, as we approach the twenty-first century, that anyone could still be called "Fingers"? Even so, the name had been well earned. Within moments of my entering the cell, Fingers was wearing my watch. He returned it immediately I noticed it had disappeared. "Sorry," he said. "Just put it down to 'abit."

Prison might have turned out to be far worse if it hadn't been known by my fellow inmates that I was a millionaire, and was quite happy to pay a little extra for certain privileges. Every morning the *Financial Times* was delivered to my bunk, which gave me the chance to keep up with what was happening in the City. I was nearly sick when I first read about the takeover bid for Cooper's. Sick not because of the offer of £12.50 a share, which made me even wealthier, but because it became painfully obvious what Jeremy and Rosemary had been up to. Jeremy's shares would now be worth several million pounds—money he could never have realized had I been around to prevent a takeover.

I spent hours each day lying on my bunk and scouring every word of the *Financial Times.* Whenever there was a mention of Cooper's, I went over the paragraph so often that I ended up knowing it by heart. The company was eventually taken over, but not before the share price had reached £13.43. I continued to follow its activities with great interest, and I became more and more anxious about the quality of the new management when they began to fire some of my most experienced staff, including Joe Ramsbottom. A week later I wrote and instructed my stockbrokers to sell my shares as and when the opportunity arose.

It was at the beginning of my fourth month in prison that I asked for some writing paper. I had decided the time had come to keep a record of everything that had happened to me since that night I had returned home unexpectedly. Every day the prison officer on my landing would bring me fresh sheets of blue-lined paper, and I would write out in longhand the chronicle you're now reading. An added bonus was that it helped me to plan my next move.

At my request, Fingers took a straw poll among the prisoners as to who they believed was the best detective they had ever come up against. Three days later he told me the result: Chief Superintendent Donald Hackett, known as the Don, came out top on more than half the lists. More reliable than a Gallup Poll, I told Fingers.

"What puts Hackett ahead of all the others?" I asked him.

"'e's honest, 'e's fair, you can't bribe 'im. And once the bastard knows you're a villain, 'e doesn't care 'ow long it takes to get you be'ind bars."

Hackett, I was informed, hailed from Bradford. Rumor had it among the older cons that he had turned down the job of assistant chief constable for West Yorkshire. Like a barrister who doesn't want to become a judge, he preferred to remain at the coalface.

"Arrestin' criminals is 'ow 'e gets his kicks," Fingers said, with some feeling.

"Sounds just the man I'm looking for," I said. "How old is he?"

Fingers paused to consider. "Must be past fifty by now," he replied. "After all, 'e 'ad me put in reform school for nickin' a tool set, and that was"—he paused again—"more than twenty years ago."

When Sir Matthew came to visit me the following Monday, I told him what I had in mind, and asked his opinion of the Don. I wanted a professional's view.

"He's a hell of a witness to cross-examine, that's one thing I can tell you," replied my barrister.

"Why's that?"

"He doesn't exaggerate, he won't prevaricate, and I've never known him to lie, which makes him awfully hard to trap. No, I've rarely got the better of the chief superintendent. I have to say, though, that I doubt if he'd agree to become involved with a convicted criminal, whatever you offered him."

"But I'm not . . . "

"I know, Mr. Cooper," said Sir Matthew, who still didn't seem able to call me by my first name. "But Hackett will have to be convinced of that before he even agrees to see you."

"But how can I convince him of my innocence while I'm stuck in jail?"

"I'll try to influence him on your behalf," Sir Matthew said after some thought. Then he added, "Come to think of it, he does owe me a favor."

After Sir Matthew had left that night, I requested some more lined paper and began to compose a carefully worded letter to Chief Superintendent Hackett, several versions of which ended crumpled up on the floor of my cell. My final effort read as follows:

In replying to this letter, please write on the envelope:

Number A47283 Name COOPER, R.W.

ALL INCOMING MAIL MUST
HAVE SENDERS NAME AND
ADDRESS. ANNONYMOUS
MAIL CANNOT BE ACCEPTED
NO NUMBER DELAYS MAIL.

**H.M. PRISON
ARMLEY
LEEDS LS12 2TJ**

Dear Chief Superintendent,

As you can see I am currently detained at Her Majesty's pleasure. Nevertheless, I wonder if you would be kind enough to visit me, as I have a private matter I would like to discuss with you that could affect both our futures. I can assure you that my proposal is both legal and honest, and I am confident that it will also appeal to your sense of justice. It has the approval of my barrister, Sir Matthew Roberts QC, who I understand you have come across from time to time in your professional capacity. Naturally I will be happy to reimburse any expences that this inconvenience may cause you.

I look forward to hearing from you.

Yours sincerely

I reread the letter, corrected the spelling mistake, and scrawled my signature across the bottom.

At my request, Sir Matthew delivered the letter to Hackett by hand. The first thousand-pound-a-day postman in the history of the Royal Mail, I told him.

Sir Matthew reported back the following Monday that he had

handed the letter to the chief superintendent in person. After Hackett had read it through a second time, his only comment was that he would have to speak to his superiors. He had promised he would let Sir Matthew know his decision within a week.

From the moment I had been sentenced, Sir Matthew had been preparing for my appeal, and although he had not at any time raised my hopes, he was unable to hide his delight at what he had discovered after paying a visit to the Probate Office.

It turned out that, in his will, Jeremy had left everything to Rosemary. This included over three million pounds' worth of Cooper's shares. But, Sir Matthew explained, the law did not allow her to dispose of them for seven years. "An English jury may have pronounced on your guilt," he declared, "but the hard-headed taxmen are not so easily convinced. They won't hand over Jeremy Alexander's assets until either they have seen his body, or seven years have elapsed."

"Do they think that Rosemary might have killed him for his money, and then disposed . . . "

"No, no," said Sir Matthew, almost laughing at my suggestion. "It's simply that, as they're entitled to wait for seven years, they're going to sit on his assets and not take the risk that Alexander may still be alive. In any case, if your wife *had* killed him, she wouldn't have had a ready answer to every one of my questions when she was in the witness box, of that I'm sure."

I smiled. For the first time in my life I was delighted to learn that the tax man had his nose in my affairs.

Sir Matthew promised he would report back if anything new came up. "Goodnight, Richard," he said as he left the interview room.

Another first.

It seemed that everyone else in the prison was aware that Chief Superintendent Hackett would be paying me a visit long before I was.

It was Dave Adams, an old jailbird from an adjoining cell, who explained why the inmates thought Hackett had agreed to see me. "A good copper is never 'appy about anyone doin' time for somethin' 'e didn't do. 'ackett phoned the governor last Tuesday, and 'ad a word with 'im on the Q.T., accordin' to Maurice," Dave added mysteriously.

I would have been interested to learn how the governor's trusty had managed to hear both sides of the conversation, but decided this was not the time for irrelevant questions.

"Even the 'ardest nuts in this place think you're innocent," Dave continued. "They can't wait for the day when Mr. Jeremy Alexander takes over your cell. You can be sure the long termers'll give 'im a warm welcome."

A letter from Bradford arrived the following morning. "Dear Cooper," the chief superintendent began, and went on to inform me that he intended to pay a visit to the jail at four o'clock the following Sunday. He made it clear that he would stay no longer than half an hour, and insisted on a witness being present throughout.

For the first time since I'd been locked up, I started counting the hours. Hours aren't that important when your room has been booked for a life sentence.

As I was taken from my cell that Sunday afternoon and escorted to the interview room, I received several messages from my fellow inmates to pass on to the chief superintendent.

"Give my best regards to the Don," said Fingers. "Tell 'im 'ow sorry I am not to bump into 'im this time."

"When 'e's finished with you, ask 'im if 'e'd like to drop into my cell for a cuppa and a chat about old times."

"Kick the bastard in the balls, and tell 'im I'll be 'appy to serve the extra time."

One of the prisoners even suggested a question to which I already knew the answer: "Ask 'im when 'e's going to retire, 'cause I'm not coming out till the day after."

When I stepped into the interview room and saw the chief superintendent for the first time, I thought there must have been some mistake. I had never asked Fingers what the Don looked like, and over the past few days I had built up in my mind the image of some sort of superman. But the man who stood before me was a couple of inches shorter than me, and I'm only five feet ten. He was as thin as the proverbial rake and wore pebble-lensed horn-rimmed glasses, which gave the impression that he was half blind. All he needed was a grubby raincoat and he could have been mistaken for a debt collector.

Sir Matthew stepped forward to introduce us. I shook the policeman firmly by the hand. "Thank you for coming to visit me, Chief Superintendent," I began. "Won't you have a seat?" I added, as if he had dropped into my home for a glass of sherry.

"Sir Matthew is very persuasive," said Hackett, in a deep, gruff Yorkshire accent that didn't quite seem to go with his body. "So tell me, Cooper, what do you imagine it is that I can do for you?" he asked as he took the chair opposite me. I detected an edge of cynicism in his voice.

He opened a notepad and placed it on the table as I was about to begin my story. "For my use only," he explained, "should I need to remind myself of any relevant details at some time in the future." Twenty minutes later, I had finished the abbreviated version of the life and times of Richard Cooper. I had already gone over the story on several occasions in my cell during the past week, to be certain I didn't take too long. I wanted to leave enough time for Hackett to ask any questions.

"If I believe your story," he said, "—and I only say 'if'—you still haven't explained what it is you think I can do for you."

"You're due to leave the force in five months' time," I said. "I wondered if you had any plans once you've retired."

He hesitated. I had obviously taken him by surprise.

"I've been offered a job with Group 4, as area manager for West Yorkshire."

"And how much will they be paying you?" I asked bluntly.

"It won't be full-time," he said. "Three days a week, to start with." He hesitated again. "Twenty thousand a year, guaranteed for three years."

"I'll pay you a hundred thousand a year, but I'll expect you to be on the job seven days a week. I assume you'll be needing a secretary and an assistant—that Inspector Williams who's leaving at the same time as you might well fit the bill—so I'll also supply you with enough money for backup staff, as well as the rent for an office."

A flicker of respect appeared on the chief superintendent's face for the first time. He made some more notes on his pad.

"And what would you expect of me in return for such a large sum of money?" he asked.

"That's simple. I expect you to find Jeremy Alexander."

This time he didn't hesitate. "My God," he said. "You really *are* innocent. Sir Matthew and the governor both tried to convince me you were."

"And if you find him within seven years," I added, ignoring his comment, "I'll pay a further five hundred thousand into any branch of any bank in the world that you stipulate."

"The Midland, Bradford, will suit me just fine," he replied. "It's only criminals who find it necessary to retire abroad. In any case, I have to be in Bradford every other Saturday afternoon, so I can be around to watch City lose." Hackett rose from his place and looked hard at me for some time. "One last question, Mr. Cooper. Why seven years?"

"Because after that period, my wife can sell Alexander's shares, and he'll become a multimillionaire overnight."

The chief superintendent nodded his understanding. "Thank you for asking to see me," he said. "It's been a long time since I enjoyed visiting anyone in jail, especially someone convicted of murder. I'll give your offer serious consideration, Mr. Cooper, and let you know my decision by the end of the week." He left without another word.

Hackett wrote to me three days later, accepting my offer.

I didn't have to wait five months for him to start working for me, because he handed in his resignation within a fortnight—though not before I had agreed to continue his pension contributions, and those of the two colleagues he wanted to leave the force and join him. Having now disposed of all my Cooper's shares, the interest on my deposit account was earning me over four hundred thousand a year, and as I was living rent free, Hackett's request was a minor consideration.

I would have shared with you in greater detail everything that happened to me over the following months, but during that time I was so preoccupied with briefing Hackett that I filled only three pages of my blue-lined prison paper. I should however mention that I studied several law books, to be sure that I fully understood the meaning of the legal term *autrefois acquit*.

The next important date in the diary was my appeal hearing.

Matthew—at his request I had long ago stopped calling him "Sir" Matthew—tried valiantly not to show that he was becoming more and more confident of the outcome, but I was getting to know him so well that he was no longer able to disguise his true feelings. He told me how delighted he was with the makeup of the reviewing panel. "Fair and just," he kept repeating.

Later that night he told me with great sadness that his wife, Victoria, had died of cancer a few weeks before. "A long illness and a blessed release," he called it.

I felt guilty in his presence for the first time. Over the past eighteen months, we had only ever discussed my problems.

I must have been one of the few prisoners at Armley who ever had a bespoke tailor visit him in his cell. Matthew suggested that I should be fitted with a new suit before I faced the appeal tribunal, as I had lost more than fourteen pounds since I had been in jail. When the tailor had finished measuring me and began rolling up his tape, I insisted that Fingers return his cigarette lighter, although I did allow him to keep the cigarettes.

Ten days later I was escorted from my cell at five o'clock in the morning. My fellow inmates banged their tin mugs against their locked doors, the traditional way of indicating to the prison staff that they believed the man leaving for trial was innocent. Like some great symphony, it lifted my soul.

I was driven to London in a police car accompanied by two prison officers. We didn't stop once on the entire journey, and arrived in the capital a few minutes after nine; I remember looking out of the window and watching the commuters scurrying to their offices to begin the day's work. Any one of them who'd glanced at me sitting in the back of the car in my new suit, and was unable to spot the handcuffs, might have assumed I was a chief inspector at least.

Matthew was waiting for me at the entrance of the Old Bailey, a mountain of papers tucked under each arm. "I like the suit," he said, before leading me up some stone steps to the room where my fate would be decided.

Once again I sat impassively in the dock as Sir Matthew rose from his place to address the three appeal judges. His opening statement took him nearly an hour, and by now I felt I could have delivered it quite adequately myself, though not as eloquently, and certainly nowhere near as persuasively. He made great play of how Jeremy had left all his worldly goods to Rosemary, who in turn had sold our family house in Leeds, cashed in all her Cooper's shares within months of the takeover, pushed through a quickie divorce, and then disappeared off the face of the earth with an estimated seven million pounds. I couldn't help wondering just how much of that Jeremy had already got his hands on.

Sir Matthew repeatedly reminded the panel of the police's inability to produce a body, despite the fact they now seemed to have dug up half of Leeds.

I became more hopeful with each new fact Matthew placed before the judges. But after he had finished, I still had to wait another three days to learn the outcome of their deliberations.

Appeal dismissed. Reasons reserved.

Matthew traveled up to Armley on the Friday to tell me why he thought my appeal had been turned down without explanation. He felt that the judges must have been divided, and needed more time to make it appear as if they were not.

"How much time?" I asked.

"My hunch is that they'll let you out on parole within a few months. They were obviously influenced by the police's failure to produce a body, unimpressed by the trial judge's summing up, and impressed by the strength of your case."

I thanked Matthew, who, for once, left the room with a smile on his face.

You may be wondering what Chief Superintendent Hackett—or rather ex–Chief Superintendent Hackett—had been up to while all this was going on.

He had not been idle. Inspector Williams and Constable

Kenwright had left the force on the same day as he had. Within a week they had opened up a small office above the Constitutional Club in Bradford and begun their investigations. The Don reported to me at four o'clock every Sunday afternoon.

Within a month he had compiled a thick file on the case, with detailed dossiers on Rosemary, Jeremy, the company, and me. I spent hours reading through the information he had gathered, and was even able to help by filling in a few gaps. I quickly came to appreciate why the Don was so respected by my fellow inmates. He followed up every clue and went down every side road, however much it looked like a cul-de-sac, because once in a while it turned out to be a highway.

On the first Sunday in October, after Hackett had been working for four months, he told me that he thought he might have located Rosemary. A woman of her description was living on a small estate in the South of France, called Villa Fleur.

"How did you manage to track her down?" I asked.

"Letter mailed by her mother at her local mailbox. The postman kindly allowed me to have a look at the address on the envelope before it proceeded on its way," Hackett said. "Can't tell you how many hours we had to hang around, how many letters we've had to sift through, and how many doors we've knocked on in the past four months, just to get this one lead. Mrs. Kershaw seems to be a compulsive letter writer, but this was the first time she's sent one to her daughter. By the way," he added, "your wife has reverted to her maiden name. Calls herself Ms. Kershaw now."

I nodded, not wishing to interrupt him.

"Williams flew out to Cannes on Wednesday, and he's holed up in the nearest village, posing as a tourist. He's already been able to tell us that Ms. Kershaw's house is surrounded by a ten-foot stone wall, and she has more guard dogs than trees. It seems the locals know even less about her than we do. But at least it's a start."

I felt for the first time that Jeremy Alexander might at last have met his match, but it was to be another five Sundays, and five more interim reports, before a thin smile appeared on Hackett's usually tight-lipped face.

"Ms. Kershaw has placed an advertisement in the local paper," he informed me. "It seems she's in need of a new butler. At first I thought we should question the old butler at length as soon as he'd left, but as I couldn't risk anything getting back to her, I decided Inspector Williams would have to apply for his job instead."

"But surely she'll realize within moments that he's totally unqualified to do the job."

"Not necessarily," said Hackett, his smile broadening. "You see, Williams won't be able to leave his present employment with the Countess of Rutland until he's served a full month's notice, and in the meantime we've signed him up for a special six-week course at Ivor Spencer's School for Butlers. Williams has always been a quick learner."

"But what about references?"

"By the time Rosemary Kershaw interviews him, he'll have a set of references that would impress a duchess."

"I was told you never did anything underhand."

"That is the case when I'm dealing with honest people, Mr. Cooper. Not when I'm up against a couple of crooks like this. I'm going to get those two behind bars, if it's the last thing I do."

This was not the time to let Hackett know that the final chapter of this story, as I plotted it, did not conclude with Jeremy ending up in jail.

Once Williams had been put on the shortlist for the position of Rosemary's butler, I played my own small part in securing him the job. Rereading over the terms of the proposed contract gave me the idea.

"Tell Williams to ask for fifteen thousand francs a month, and five weeks' holiday," I suggested to Hackett when he and Matthew visited me the following Sunday.

"Why?" asked the ex–chief superintendent. "She's only offering eleven thousand, and three weeks' holiday."

"She can well afford to pay the difference, and with references like these," I said, looking back down at my file, "she might become suspicious if he asked for anything less."

Matthew smiled and nodded.

Rosemary finally offered Williams the job at thirteen thousand francs a month, with four weeks' holiday a year, which, after forty-eight hours' consideration, Williams accepted. But he did not join her for another month, by which time he had learned how to iron newspapers, lay place settings with a ruler, and tell the difference between a port, sherry, and liqueur glass.

I suppose that from the moment Williams took up the job as Rosemary's butler, I expected instant results. But as Hackett pointed out to me Sunday after Sunday, this was hardly realistic.

"Williams has to take his time," explained the Don. "He needs to gain her confidence, and avoid giving her any reason for the slightest suspicion. It once took me five years to nail a drug smuggler who was only living half a mile up the road from me."

I wanted to remind him that it was me who was stuck in jail, and that five days was more like what I had in mind, but I knew how hard they were all working on my behalf, and tried not to show my impatience.

Within a month Williams had supplied us with photographs and life histories of all the staff working on the estate, along with descriptions of everyone who visited Rosemary—even the local priest, who came hoping to collect a donation for French aid workers in Somalia.

The cook: Gabrielle Pascal—no English, excellent cuisine, came from Marseilles, family checked out. The gardener: Jacques Reni—stupid and not particularly imaginative with the rose beds, local and well known. Rosemary's personal maid: Charlotte Merieux—spoke a little English, crafty, sexy, came from Paris, still checking her out. All the staff had been employed by Rosemary since her arrival in the South of France, and they appeared to have no connection with each other, or with her past life.

"Ah," said Hackett as he studied the picture of Rosemary's personal maid. I raised an eyebrow. "I was just thinking about Williams being cooped up with Charlotte Merieux day in and day out—and more important, night in and night in," he explained. "He would have made superintendent if he hadn't fooled around so much. Still, let's hope this time it turns out to our advantage."

I lay on my bunk studying the pictures of the staff for hour after hour, but they revealed nothing. I read and reread the notes on everyone who had ever visited Villa Fleur, but as the weeks went by, it looked more and more as if no one from Rosemary's past, other than her mother, knew where she was— or if they did, they were making no attempts to contact her. There was certainly no sign of Jeremy Alexander.

I was beginning to fear that she and Jeremy might have split up, until Williams reported that there was a picture of a dark, handsome man on a table by the side of Rosemary's bed. It was inscribed: "We'll always be together—J."

During the weeks following my appeal hearing I was constantly interviewed by probation officers, social workers, and even the prison psychiatrist. I struggled to maintain the warm, sincere smile that Matthew had warned me was so necessary to lubricate the wheels of the bureaucracy.

It must have been about eleven weeks after my appeal had been turned down that the cell door was thrown open, and the senior officer on my corridor announced, "The governor wants to see you, Cooper." Fingers looked suspicious. Whenever he heard those words, it inevitably meant a dose of solitary.

I could hear my heart beating as I was led down the long corridor to the governor's office. The prison officer knocked gently on the door before opening it. The governor rose from behind his desk, thrust out his hand, and said, "I'm delighted to be the first person to tell you the good news."

He ushered me into a comfortable chair on the other side of his desk, and went over the terms of my release. While he was doing this I was served coffee, as if we were old friends.

There was a knock on the door, and Matthew walked in, clutching a sheaf of papers that needed to be signed. I rose as he placed them on the desk, and without warning he turned around and gave me a bear hug. Not something I expect he did every day.

After I had signed the final document Matthew asked: "What's the first thing you'll do once they release you?"

"I'm going to buy a gun," I told him matter-of-factly.

Matthew and the governor burst out laughing.

The great gate of Armley Prison was thrown open for me three days later. I walked away from the building carrying only the small leather suitcase I had arrived with. I didn't look back. I hailed a taxi and asked the driver to take me to the station, as I had no desire to remain in Leeds a moment longer than was necessary. I bought a first-class ticket, and phoned Hackett to warn him I was on my way. During the short wait for the next train to Bradford I savored a breakfast that wasn't served on a tin plate, and read a copy of the *Financial Times* that had been handed to me by a pretty salesclerk and not a petty criminal. No one stared at me on the train—but then, why should they, when I was sitting in a first-class carriage and dressed in my new suit? I glanced at every woman who passed by, however she was dressed, but they had no way of knowing why.

When the train pulled into Bradford, the Don and his secretary, Jenny Kenwright, were waiting for me on the platform. The chief superintendent had rented me a small furnished apartment on the outskirts of the city, and after I had unpacked—not a long job—they took me out to lunch. The moment the small talk had been dispensed with and Jenny had poured me a glass of wine, the Don asked me a question I hadn't expected.

"Now that you're free, is it still your wish that we go on looking for Jeremy Alexander?"

"Yes," I replied, without a moment's hesitation. "I'm even more determined, now that I can taste the freedom he's enjoyed for the past three years. Never forget, that man stole my freedom from me, along with my wife, my company, and more than half my possessions. Oh yes, Donald. I won't rest until I come face to face with Jeremy Alexander."

"Good," said the Don. "Because Williams thinks Rosemary is beginning to trust him, and might even, given time, start confiding in him. It seems he has made himself indispensable."

I found a certain irony in the thought of Williams pocketing two pay envelopes simultaneously, and of my being responsible for one while Rosemary paid the other. I asked if there was any news of Jeremy.

"Nothing to speak of," said Donald. "She certainly never phones him from the house, and we're fairly sure he never attempts to make any direct contact with her. But Williams has told us that every Friday at midday he has to drop her off at the Majestic, the only hotel in the village. She goes inside and doesn't reappear for at least forty minutes. He daren't follow her, because she's given specific instructions that he's to stay with the car. And he can't afford to lose this job by disobeying orders."

I nodded my agreement.

"But that hasn't stopped him having the occasional drink in the hotel bar on his evening off, and he's managed to pick up a few snippets of information. He's convinced that Rosemary uses the time when she's in the hotel to make a long-distance phone call. She often drops in at the bank before going on to the Majestic, and comes out carrying a small pack of coins. The barman has told Williams that she always uses one of the two phone booths in the corridor opposite the reception desk. She never allows the call to be put through the hotel switchboard, always dials direct."

"So how do we discover who she's calling?" I asked.

"We wait for Williams to find an opportunity to use some of those skills he didn't learn at butlers' school."

"But how long might that take?"

"No way of knowing, but Williams is due for a spot of leave in a couple of weeks, so he'll be able to bring us up to date."

When Williams arrived back in Bradford at the end of the month, I began asking him questions even before he had time to put his suitcase down. He was full of interesting information about Rosemary, and even the smallest detail fascinated me.

She had put on weight. I was pleased. She seemed lonely and depressed. I was delighted. She was spending my money fast. I wasn't exactly ecstatic. But, more to the point, Williams was convinced that if Rosemary had any contact with Jeremy Alexander, it had to be when she visited the hotel every Friday and placed that direct-dial call. But he still hadn't worked out how to discover who, or where, she was phoning.

By the time Williams returned to the South of France a fortnight later I knew more about my ex-wife than I ever had when we were married.

As happens so often in the real world, the next move came when I least expected it. It must have been about 2:30 on a Monday afternoon when the phone rang.

Donald picked up the receiver and was surprised to hear Williams's voice on the other end of the line. He switched him to the speaker phone and said, "All three of us are listening, so you'd better begin by telling us why you're calling when it's not your day off."

"I've been fired," were Williams's opening words.

"Playing around with the maid, were you?" was Donald's first reaction.

"I only wish, chief, but I'm afraid it's far more stupid than that. I was driving Ms. Kershaw into town this morning when I had to stop at a red light. While I was waiting for the lights to change, a man crossed the road in front of the car. He stopped and stared at me. I recognized him immediately and prayed the lights would turn to green before he could place me. But he walked back, looked at me again, and smiled. I shook my head at him, but he came over to the driver's side, tapped on the window, and said, 'How are you, Inspector Williams?'"

"Who was it?" demanded Donald.

"Neil Case. Remember him, Chief?"

"Could I ever forget him? 'Never-on-the-Case Neil,'" said Donald. "I might have guessed."

"I didn't acknowledge him, of course, and since Ms. Kershaw said nothing, I thought I might have got away with it. But as soon as we arrived back at the house she told me to come and see her in the study, and without even asking for an explanation she dismissed me. She ordered me to be packed and off the premises within the hour, or she'd call the local police."

"Damn. Back to square one," said Donald.

"Not quite," said Williams.

"What do you mean? If you're no longer in the house, we no longer have a point of contact. Worse, we can't play the butler card again, because she's bound to be on her guard from now on."

"I know all that, Chief," said Williams, "but suspecting that I was a policeman caused her to panic, and she went straight to her bedroom and made a phone call. As I wasn't afraid of being found out any longer, I picked up the extension in the corridor and listened in. All I heard was a woman's voice give a Cambridge number, and then the phone went dead. I assumed Rosemary had been expecting someone else to pick up the phone, and hung up when she heard a strange voice."

"What was the number?" Donald asked.

"Six-four-oh-seven-something-seven."

"What do you mean, 'something-seven?' barked Donald as he scribbled the numbers down.

"I didn't have anything to write with, chief, so I had to rely on my memory." I was glad Williams couldn't see the expression on the Don's face.

"Then what happened?" he demanded.

"I found a pen in a drawer and wrote what I could remember of the number on my hand. I picked up the phone again a few moments later, and heard a different woman on the line, saying, "The director's not in at the moment, but I'm expecting him back within the hour." Then I had to hang up quickly, because I could hear someone coming along the corridor. It was Charlotte, Rosemary's maid. She wanted to know why I'd been fired. I couldn't think of a convincing reply, until she accused me of having made a pass at the mistress. I let her think that was it, and ended up getting a slapped face for my trouble." I burst out laughing, but the Don and Jenny showed no reaction. Then Williams asked, "So, what do I do now, Chief? Come back to England?"

"No," said Donald. "Stay put for the moment. Book yourself into the Majestic and watch her around the clock. Let me know if she does anything out of character. Meanwhile, we're going to Cambridge. As soon as we've booked ourselves into a hotel there, I'll call you."

"Understood, sir," said Williams, and rang off.

"When do we go?" I asked Donald once he had replaced the receiver.

"Tonight," he replied. "But not before I've made a few telephone calls."

The Don dialed ten Cambridge numbers, starting with 0223, using the digits Williams had been able to jot down, and inserting the numbers from zero to nine in the missing slot.

As it happened, 0223 640707 turned out to be a school. "Sorry, wrong number," said Donald. In short order, 717 was a chemist's shop; 727 was a garage; 737 was answered by an elderly male voice—"Sorry, wrong number," Donald repeated; 747 a newsagent; 757 a local policeman's wife (I tried not to laugh, but Donald only grunted); 767 a woman's voice—"Sorry, wrong number," yet again; 777 was St. Catharine's College; 787 a woman's voice on an answering machine; 797 a hairdresser— "Did you want a perm, or just a trim?"

Donald checked his list. "It has to be either 737, 767, or 787. The time has come for me to pull a few strings."

He dialed a local Bradford number, and was told that the new deputy chief constable of Cambridgeshire had been transferred from the West Yorkshire Constabulary the previous year.

"Leeke. Allan Leeke," said Donald, without needing to be prompted. He turned to me. "He was a sergeant when I was first promoted to inspector." He thanked his Bradford contact, then rang directory enquiries to find out the number of the Cambridge Police headquarters. He dialed another 0223 number.

"Cambridge Police. How can I help you?" asked a female voice.

"Can you put me through to the Deputy Chief Constable, please?" Donald asked.

"Who shall I say is calling?"

"Donald Hackett."

The next voice that came on the line said, "Don, this is a pleasant surprise. Or at least I hope it's a pleasant surprise, because knowing you, it won't be a social call. Are you looking for a job, by any chance? I heard you'd left the force."

"Yes, it's true. I've resigned, but I'm not looking for a job, Allan. I don't think the Cambridge Constabulary could quite match my present salary."

"So, what can I do for you, Don?"

"I need a trace on three numbers in the Cambridge area."

"Authorized?" asked the deputy chief constable.

"No, but it might well lead to an arrest on your patch," said Donald.

"That, and the fact that it's you who's asking, is good enough for me."

Donald read out the three numbers, and Leeke asked him to hang on for a moment. While we waited, Donald told me, "All they have to do is press a few buttons in the control room, and the numbers will appear on a screen in front of him. Things have changed since I first joined the force. In those days we had to let our legs do the walking."

The deputy chief constable's voice came back on the line. "Right, the first number's come up; 640737 is a Wing Commander Danvers-Smith. He's the only person registered as living in the house." He read out an address in Great Shelford, which he explained was just to the south of Cambridge. Jenny wrote the details down.

"Number 767 is a Professor and Mrs. Balcescu, also living in Great Shelford, and 787 is Dame Julia Renaud, the opera singer. She lives in Grantchester. We know her quite well. She's hardly ever at home, because of her concert commitments all over the world. Her house has been burgled three times in the last year, always when she was abroad."

"Thank you," said Donald. "You've been most helpful."

"Anything you want to tell me?" asked the deputy chief constable, sounding hopeful.

"Not at the moment," replied Donald. "But as soon as I've finished my investigation, I promise you'll be the first person to be informed."

"Fair enough," came back the reply, and the line went dead.

"Right," Donald said, turning his attention back to us. "We

leave for Cambridge in a couple of hours. That will give us enough time to pack, and for Jenny to book us into a hotel near the city center. We'll meet back here at"—he checked his watch—"six o'clock." He walked out of the room without uttering another word. I remember thinking that my father would have got along well with him.

Just over two hours later, Jenny was driving us at a steady sixty-nine miles per hour down the A1.

"Now the boring part of detective work begins," said Donald. "Intense research, followed by hours of surveillance. I think we can safely ignore Dame Julia. Jenny, you get to work on the wing commander. I want details of his career from the day he left school to the day he retired. First thing tomorrow you can begin by contacting RAF College Cranwell, and asking for details of his service record. I'll take the professor, and make a start in the university library."

"What do I do?" I asked.

"For the time being, Mr. Cooper, you keep yourself well out of sight. It's just possible that the wing commander or the professor might lead us to Alexander, so we don't need you trampling over any suspects and frightening them off."

I reluctantly agreed.

Later that night I settled into a suite at the Garden House Hotel—a more refined sort of prison—but despite feather pillows and a comfortable mattress, I was quite unable to sleep. I rose early the next morning and spent most of the day watching endless updates on Sky News, episodes of various Australian soaps, and a "Film of the Week" every two hours. But my mind was continually switching between RAF Cranwell and the university library.

When we met in Donald's room that evening, he and Jenny confirmed that their initial research suggested that both men were who they purported to be.

"I was sure one of them would turn out to be Jeremy," I said, unable to hide my disappointment.

"It would be nice if it was always that easy, Mr. Cooper," said Donald. "But it doesn't mean that one of them won't lead us to

Jeremy." He turned to Jenny. "First, let's go over what you found out about the wing commander."

"Wing Commander Danvers-Smith, DFC, graduated from Cranwell in 1938, served with Number Two Squadron at Binbrook in Lincolnshire during the Second World War, and flew several missions over Germany and occupied France. He was awarded the DFC for gallantry in 1943. He was grounded in 1958 and became an instructor at RAF Cottesmore in Gloucestershire. His final posting was as deputy commanding officer at RAF Locking in Somerset. He retired in 1977, when he and his wife moved back to Great Shelford, where he had grown up."

"Why's he living on his own now?" asked Donald.

"Wife died three years ago. He has two children, Sam and Pamela, both married, but neither living in the area. They visit him occasionally."

I wanted to ask Jenny how she had been able to find out so much information about the wing commander in such a short time, but said nothing, as I was more interested in hearing what the Don had discovered about Professor Balcescu.

Donald picked up a pile of notes that had been lying on the floor by his feet. "So, let me tell you the results of my research into a very distinguished professor," he began. "Professor Balcescu escaped from Romania in 1989, after Ceauşescu had had him placed under house arrest. He was smuggled out of the country by a group of dissident students, via Bulgaria and then on into Greece. His escape was well documented in the newspapers at the time. He applied for asylum in England, and was offered a teaching post at Gonville and Caius College, Cambridge, and three years later the chair of Eastern European Studies. He advises the government on Romanian matters, and has written a scholarly book on the subject. Last year he was awarded a CBE in the Queen's Birthday Honours."

"How could either of these men possibly know Rosemary?" I asked. "Williams must have made a mistake when he wrote down the number."

"Williams doesn't make mistakes, Mr. Cooper," said the Don. "Otherwise I wouldn't have employed him. Your wife dialed one of those numbers, and we're just going to have to find out which one. This time we'll need your assistance."

I mumbled an apology but remained unconvinced.

Hackett nodded curtly, and turned back to Jenny. "How long will it take us to get to the wing commander's home?"

"About fifteen minutes, sir. He lives in a cottage in Great Shelford, just south of Cambridge."

"Right, we'll start with him. I'll see you both in the lobby at five o'clock tomorrow morning."

I slept fitfully again that night, now convinced that we were embarked on a wild-goose chase. But at least I was going to be allowed to join them the following day, instead of being confined to my room and yet more Australian soaps.

I didn't need my 4:30 alarm call—I was already showering when the phone went. A few minutes after five, the three of us walked out of the hotel, trying not to look as if we were hoping to leave without paying our bill. It was a chilly morning, and I shivered as I climbed into the back of the car.

Jenny drove us out of the city and onto the London road. After a mile or so she turned left and took us into a charming little village with neat, well-kept houses on either side of the road. We passed a garden center on the left and drove another half mile, then Jenny suddenly swung the car round and reversed into a rest area. She switched off the engine and pointed to a small house with an RAF-blue door. "That's where he lives," she said. "Number forty-seven." Donald focused a tiny pair of binoculars on the house.

Some early-morning risers were already leaving their homes, cars heading toward the station for the first commuter train to London. The paperboy turned out to be an old lady who pushed her heavily laden bicycle slowly around the village, dropping off her deliveries. The milkman was next, clattering along in his electric van—two pints here, a pint there, the occasional half-dozen eggs or container of orange juice left on front doorsteps. Lights began to flick on all over the village. "The wing commander has had one pint of red-top milk and a copy of the *Daily Telegraph* delivered to his front door," said Donald.

People had emerged from the houses on either side of Number 47 before a light appeared in an upstairs room of the wing commander's home. Once that light had been switched on, Donald sat bolt upright, his eyes never leaving the house.

I became bored, and dozed off in the back at some point. When I woke up, I hoped we might at least be allowed a break for breakfast, but such mundane considerations didn't seem to worry the two professionals in the front. They continued to concentrate on any movement that took place around Number 47, and hardly exchanged a word.

At 10:19 a thin, elderly man, dressed in a Harris tweed jacket and gray flannels, emerged from Number 47 and marched briskly down the path. All I could see at that distance was a huge, bushy white mustache. It looked almost as if his whole body had been designed around it. Donald kept the glasses trained on him.

"Ever seen him before?" he asked, passing the binoculars back to me.

I focused the glasses on the wing commander and studied him carefully. "Never," I said as he came to a halt by the side of a battered old Austin Allegro. "How could anyone forget that mustache?"

"It certainly wasn't grown last week," said Donald, as Danvers-Smith eased his car out onto the main road.

Jenny cursed. "I thought that if he used his car, the odds would be on him heading into Cambridge." She deftly performed a three-point turn and accelerated quickly after the wing commander. Within a few minutes she was only a couple of cars behind him.

Danvers-Smith was not proving to be the sort of fellow who habitually broke the speed limit. "His days as a test pilot are obviously long behind him," Donald said, as we trailed the Allegro at a safe distance into the next village. About half a mile later he pulled into a petrol station.

"Stay with him," said Donald. Jenny followed the Allegro into the forecourt and came to a halt at the pump directly behind Danvers-Smith.

"Keep your head down, Mr. Cooper," said the Don, opening his door. "We don't want him seeing you."

"What are you going to do?" I asked, peering between the front seats.

"Risk an old con's trick," Donald replied.

He stepped out of the front seat, walked around to the back of the car, and unscrewed the gas cap just as the wing commander slipped the nozzle of a gas pump into the tank of his Allegro. Donald began slowly topping up our already full tank, then suddenly turned to face the old man.

"Wing Commander Danvers-Smith?" he asked in a plummy voice.

The wing commander looked up immediately, and a puzzled expression came over his weather-beaten face.

"Baker, sir," said Donald. "Flight Lieutenant Baker. You lectured me at RAF Locking. Vulcans, if I remember."

"Bloody good memory, Baker. Good show," said Danvers-Smith. "Delighted to see you, old chap," he said, taking the nozzle out of his car and replacing it in the pump. "What are you up to nowadays?"

Jenny stifled a laugh.

"Work for BA, sir. Grounded after I failed my eye test. Bloody desk job, I'm afraid, but it was the only offer I got."

"Bad luck, old chap," said the wing commander, as they headed off toward the pay booth, and out of earshot.

When they came back a few minutes later, they were chattering away like old chums, and the wing commander actually had his arm round Donald's shoulder.

When they reached his car they shook hands, and I heard Donald say "Good-bye, sir," before Danvers-Smith climbed into his Allegro. The old airman pulled out of the forecourt and headed back toward his home. Donald got in next to Jenny and pulled the passenger door closed.

"I'm afraid *he* won't lead us to Alexander," the Don said with a sigh. "Danvers-Smith is the genuine article—misses his wife, doesn't see his children enough, and feels a bit lonely. Even asked if I'd like to drop in for a bite of lunch."

"Why didn't you accept?" I asked.

Donald paused. "I would have, but when I mentioned that I

was from Leeds, he told me he'd only been there once in his life, to watch a test match. No, that man has never heard of Rosemary Cooper or Jeremy Alexander—I'd bet my pension on it. So, now it's the turn of the professor. Let's head back toward Cambridge, Jenny. And drive slowly. I don't want to catch up with the wing commander, or we'll all end up having to join him for lunch."

Jenny swung the car across the road and into the far lane, then headed back toward the city. After a couple of miles Donald told her to pull into the side of the road just past a sign announcing the Shelford Rugby Club.

"The professor and his wife live behind that hedge," Donald said, pointing across the road. "Settle back, Mr. Cooper. This might take some time."

At 12:30 Jenny went off to get some fish and chips from the village. I devoured them hungrily. By 3:00 I was bored stiff again, and was beginning to wonder just how long Donald would hang around before we were allowed to return to the hotel. I remembered *Happy Days* would be on at 6:30.

"We'll sit here all night, if necessary," Donald said, as if he were reading my thoughts. "Forty-nine hours is my record without sleep. What's yours, Jenny?" he asked, never taking his eyes off the house.

"Thirty-one, sir," she replied.

"Then this may be your chance to break that record," he said. A moment later, a woman in a white BMW nosed out of the driveway leading to the house and stopped at the edge of the sidewalk. She paused, looked both ways, then turned across the road and swung right, in the direction of Cambridge. As she passed us, I caught a glimpse of a blond with a pretty face.

"I've seen her before," I blurted out.

"Follow her, Jenny," Donald said sharply. "But keep your distance." He turned around to face me.

"Where have you seen her?" he asked, passing over the binoculars.

"I can't remember," I said, trying to focus on the back of a mop of fair, curly hair.

"Think, man. Think. It's our best chance yet," said Donald, trying not to sound as if he was cross-examining an old jailbird.

I knew I had come across that face somewhere, though I felt certain we had never met. I had to rack my brains, because it was at least five years since I had seen any woman I recognized, let alone one that striking. But my mind remained blank.

"Keep on thinking," said the Don, "while I try to find out something a little more simple. And Jenny—don't get too close to her. Never forget she's got a rearview mirror. Mr. Cooper may not remember her, but she may remember him."

Donald picked up the car phone and jabbed in ten numbers. "Let's pray he doesn't realize I've retired," he mumbled.

"DVLA Swansea. How can I help you?"

"Sergeant Crann, please," said Donald.

"I'll put you through."

"Dave Crann."

"Donald Hackett."

"Good afternoon, Chief Superintendent. How can I help you?"

"White BMW—K273 SCE," said Donald, staring at the car in front of him.

"Hold on please, sir, I won't be a moment."

Donald kept his eye fixed on the BMW while he waited. It was about thirty yards ahead of us, and heading toward a green light. Jenny accelerated to make sure she wouldn't get trapped if the lights changed, and as she shot through an amber light, Sergeant Crann came back on the line,

"We've identified the car, sir," he said. "Registered owner Mrs. Susan Balcescu, the Kendalls, High Street, Great Shelford, Cambridge. One endorsement for speeding in a built-up area, 1991, a thirty-pound fine. Otherwise nothing known."

"Thank you, sergeant. That's most helpful."

"My pleasure, sir."

"Why should Rosemary want to contact the Balcescus?" Donald said as he clipped the phone back into place. "And is she contacting just one of them, or both?" Neither of us attempted to answer.

"I think it's time to let her go," he said a moment later. "I need to check out several more leads before we risk coming face to face with either of them. Let's head back to the hotel and consider our next move."

"I know it's only a coincidence," I ventured, "but when I knew him, Jeremy had a white BMW."

"F173 BZK," said Jenny. "I remember it from the file."

Donald swung around. "Some people can't give up smoking, you know, others drinking. But with some, it's a particular make of car," he said. "Although a lot of people must drive white BMWs," he muttered almost to himself.

Once we were back in Donald's room, he began checking through the file he had put together on Professor Balcescu. The *Times* report of his escape from Romania, he told us, was the most detailed.

Professor Balcescu first came to prominence while still a student at the University of Bucharest, where he called for the overthrow of the elected government. The authorities seemed relieved when he was offered a place at Oxford, and must have hoped that they had seen the last of him. But he returned to Bucharest University three years later, taking up the position of tutor in politics. The following year he led a student revolt in support of Nicolae Ceauşescu, and after he became president, Balcescu was rewarded with a cabinet post, as Minister of Education. But he soon became disillusioned with the Ceauşescu regime, and within eighteen months he had resigned and returned to the university as a humble tutor. Three years later he was offered the Chair of Politics and Economics.

Professor Balcescu's growing disillusionment with the government finally turned to anger, and in 1986 he began writing a series of pamphlets denouncing Ceauşescu and his puppet regime. A few weeks after a particularly vitriolic attack on the establishment, he was dismissed from his post at the university, and later placed under house arrest. A group of Oxford historians wrote a letter of protest to

The Times but nothing more was heard of the great scholar for several years. Then, late in 1989, he was smuggled out of Romania by a group of students, finally reaching Britain via Bulgaria and Greece.

Cambridge won the battle of the universities to tempt him with a teaching job, and he became a fellow of Gonville and Caius in September 1990. In November 1991, after the retirement of Sir Halford McKay, Balcescu took over the Chair of Eastern European Studies.

Donald looked up. "There's a picture of him taken when he was in Greece, but it's too blurred to be of much use."

I studied the black-and-white photograph of a bearded middle-aged man surrounded by students. He wasn't anything like Jeremy. I frowned. "Another blind alley," I said.

"It's beginning to look like it," said Donald. "Especially after what I found out yesterday. According to his secretary, Balcescu delivers his weekly lecture every Friday morning, from ten o'clock to eleven."

"But that wouldn't stop him from taking a call from Rosemary at midday," interrupted Jenny.

"If you'll allow me to finish," said Hackett sharply. Jenny bowed her head, and he continued. "At twelve o'clock he chairs a full departmental meeting in his office, attended by all members of staff. I'm sure you'll agree, Jenny, that it would be quite difficult for him to take a personal call at that time every Friday, given the circumstances."

Donald turned to me. "I'm sorry to say we're back where we started, unless you can remember where you've seen Mrs. Balcescu."

I shook my head. "Perhaps I was mistaken," I admitted.

Donald and Jenny spent the next few hours going over the files, even checking every one of the ten phone numbers a second time.

"Do you remember Rosemary's second call, sir," said Jenny, in desperation. "'The director's not in at the moment.' Might that be the clue we're looking for?"

"Possibly," said Donald. "If we could find out who the director is, we might be a step nearer to Jeremy Alexander."

I remember Jenny's last words before I left for my room. "I wonder how many directors there are in Britain, Chief."

Over breakfast in Donald's room the following morning, he reviewed all the intelligence that had been gathered to date, but none of us felt we were any nearer to a solution.

"What about Mrs. Balcescu?" I said. "*She* may be the person taking the call every Friday at midday, because that's the one time she knows exactly where her husband is."

"I agree. But is she simply Rosemary's messenger, or is she a friend of Jeremy's?" asked Donald.

"Perhaps we'll have to tap her phone to find out," said Jenny.

Donald ignored her comment, and checked his watch. "It's time to go to Balcescu's lecture."

"Why are we bothering?" I asked. "Surely we ought to be concentrating on Mrs. Balcescu."

"You're probably right," said Donald. "But we can't afford to leave any stone unturned, and since his next lecture won't be for another week, we may as well get it over with. In any case, we'll be out by eleven, and if we find Mrs. Balcescu's phone is engaged between twelve and twelve thirty . . . "

After Donald had asked Jenny to bring the car around to the front of the hotel, I slipped back into my room to pick up something that had been hidden in the bottom of my suitcase for several weeks. A few minutes later I joined them, and Jenny drove us out of the hotel parking lot, turning right into the main road. Donald glanced at me suspiciously in the rearview mirror as I sat silently in the back. Did I look guilty? I wondered.

Jenny spotted a parking meter a couple of hundred yards away from the Department of European Studies, and pulled in. We got out of the car and followed the flow of students along the sidewalk and up the steps. No one gave us a second look. Once we had entered the building, Donald whipped off his tie and slipped it in his jacket pocket. He looked more like a Marxist revolutionary than most of the people heading toward the lecture.

The lecture hall was clearly signposted, and we entered it by a door on the ground floor, which turned out to be the only way in or out. Donald immediately walked up the raked auditorium to the back row of seats. Jenny and I followed, and Donald instructed me to sit behind a student who looked as if he spent his Saturday afternoons playing lock forward for his college rugby team.

While we waited for Balcescu to enter the room, I began to look around. The lecture hall was a large semicircle, not unlike a miniature Greek amphitheater, and I estimated that it could hold around three hundred students. By the time the clock on the front wall read 9:55 there was hardly a seat to be found. No further proof was needed of the professor's reputation.

I felt a light sweat forming on my forehead as I waited for Balcescu to make his entrance. As the clock struck ten the door of the lecture hall opened. I was so disappointed at the sight that greeted me that I groaned aloud. He couldn't have been less like Jeremy. I leaned across to Donald. "Wrong-colored hair, wrong-colored eyes, about thirty pounds too light." The Don showed no reaction.

"So the connection has to be with Mrs. Balcescu," whispered Jenny.

"Agreed," said Donald under his breath. "But we're stuck here for the next hour, because we certainly can't risk drawing attention to ourselves by walking out. We'll just have to make a dash for it as soon as the lecture is over. We'll still have time to see if she's at home to take the twelve o'clock call." He paused. "I should have checked the layout of the building earlier." Jenny reddened slightly, because she knew *I* meant *you*.

And then I suddenly remembered where I had seen Mrs. Balcescu. I was about to tell Donald, but the room fell silent as the professor began delivering his opening words.

"This is the sixth of eight lectures," he began, "on recent social and economic trends in Eastern Europe." In a thick Central European accent he launched into a discourse that sounded as if he had given it many times before. The undergraduates began scribbling away on their pads, but I became increasingly irritated by the continual drone of the professor's nasal vowels, as I was impatient to tell Hackett about Mrs. Balcescu and to get back to Great Shelford as quickly as possible. I found myself glancing up at the clock on the wall every few minutes. Not unlike my own schooldays, I thought. I touched my jacket pocket. It was still there, even though on this occasion it would serve no useful purpose.

Halfway through the lecture, the lights were dimmed so the professor could illustrate some of his points with slides. I glanced at the first few graphs as they appeared on the screen, showing different income groups across Eastern Europe related to their balance of payments and export figures, but I ended up none the wiser, and not just because I had missed the first five lectures.

The assistant in charge of the projector managed to get one of the slides upside down, showing Germany at the bottom of the export table and Romania at the top, which caused a light ripple of laughter throughout the hall. The professor scowled, and began to deliver his lecture at a faster and faster pace, which only caused the assistant more difficulty in finding the right slides to coincide with the professor's statements.

Once again I became bored, and I was relieved when, at five to eleven, Balcescu called for the final graph. The previous one was replaced by a blank screen. Everyone began looking round at the assistant, who was searching desperately for the slide. The professor became irritable as the minute hand of the clock approached eleven. Still the assistant failed to locate the missing slide. He flicked the shutter back once again, but nothing appeared on the screen, leaving the professor brightly illuminated by a beam of light. Balcescu stepped forward and began drumming his fingers impatiently on the wooden lectern. Then he turned sideways, and I caught his profile for the first time. There was a small scar above his right eye, which must have faded over the years, but in the bright light of the beam it was clear to see.

"It's him!" I whispered to Donald as the clock struck eleven. The lights came up, and the professor quickly left the lecture hall without another word.

I leaped over the back of my bench seat, and began charging down the gangway, but my progress was impeded by students who were already sauntering out into the aisle. I pushed my way past them until I had reached ground level, and bolted through the door by which the professor had left so abruptly. I spotted him at the end of the corridor. He was opening another door, and disappeared out of sight. I ran after him, dodging in and out of the chattering students.

When I reached the door that had just been closed behind him I looked up at the sign:

PROFESSOR BALCESCU
DIRECTOR OF EUROPEAN STUDIES

I threw the door open, to discover a woman sitting behind a desk checking some papers. Another door was closing behind her.

"I need to see Professor Balcescu immediately," I shouted, knowing that if I didn't get to him before Hackett caught up with me, I might lose my resolve.

The woman stopped what she was doing and looked up at me. "The director is expecting an overseas call at any moment, and cannot be disturbed," she replied. "I'm sorry, but—"

I ran straight past her, pulled open the door, and rushed into the room, where I came face to face with Jeremy Alexander for the first time since I had left him lying on the floor of my drawing room. He was talking animatedly on the phone, but he looked up and recognized me immediately. When I pulled the gun from my pocket, he dropped the receiver. As I took aim, the blood suddenly drained from his face.

"Are you there, Jeremy?" asked an agitated voice on the other end of the line. Despite the passing of time, I had no difficulty in recognizing Rosemary's strident tones.

Jeremy was shouting, "No, Richard, no! I can explain! Believe me, I can explain!" as Donald came running in. He came to an abrupt halt by the professor's desk, but showed no interest in Jeremy.

"Don't do it, Richard," he pleaded. "You'll only spend the rest of your life regretting it." I remember thinking it was the second time he had ever called me Richard.

"Wrong, for a change, Donald," I told him. "I won't regret killing Jeremy Alexander. You see, he's already been pronounced dead once. I know, because I was sentenced to life imprisonment for his murder. I'm sure you're aware of the meaning of '*autrefois acquit*,' and will therefore know that I can't be charged a second time with a crime I've already been convicted of and sentenced for. Even though this time they will have a body."

I moved the gun a few inches to the right, and aimed at Jeremy's heart. I squeezed the trigger just as Jenny came charging into the room. She dived at my legs.

Jeremy and I both hit the ground with a thud.

Well, as I pointed out to you at the beginning of this chronicle, I ought to explain why I'm in jail—or, to be more accurate, why I'm back in jail.

I *was* tried a second time; on this occasion for attempted murder—despite the fact that I had only grazed the bloody man's shoulder. I still blame Jenny for that.

Mind you, it was worth it just to hear Matthew's closing speech, because he certainly understood the meaning of *autrefois acquit*. He surpassed himself with his description of Rosemary as a calculating, evil Jezebel, and Jeremy as a man motivated by malice and greed, quite willing to cynically pose as a national hero while his victim was rotting his life away in jail, put there by a wife's perjured testimony of which he had unquestionably been the mastermind. In another four years, a furious Matthew told the jury, they would have been able to pocket several more millions between them. This time the jury looked on me with considerable sympathy.

"Thou shalt not bear false witness against any man," were Sir Matthew's closing words, his sonorous tones making him sound like an Old Testament prophet.

The tabloids always need a hero and a villain. This time they had got themselves a hero and two villains. They seemed to have forgotten everything they had printed during the previous trial about the oversexed truck driver, and it would be foolish to suggest that the page after page devoted to every sordid detail of Jeremy and Rosemary's deception didn't influence the jury.

They found me guilty, of course, but only because they weren't given any choice. In his summing up the judge almost ordered them to do so. But the foreman expressed his fellow jurors' hope that, given the circumstances, the judge might consider a lenient sentence. Mr. Justice Lampton obviously didn't read the tabloids, because he lectured me for several minutes, and then said I would be sent down for five years.

Matthew was on his feet immediately, appealing for clemency on the grounds that I had already served a long sentence. "This man looks out on the world through a window of tears," he told the judge. "I beseech Your Lordship not to put bars across that window a second time." The applause from the gallery was so thunderous that the judge had to instruct the bailiffs to clear the court before he could respond to Sir Matthew's plea.

"His Lordship obviously needs a little time to think," Matthew explained under his breath as he passed me in the dock. After much deliberation in his chambers, Mr. Justice Lampton settled on three years. Later that day I was sent to Ford Open Prison.

After considerable press comment during the next few weeks, and what Sir Matthew described to the Court of Appeal as "my client's unparalleled affliction and exemplary behavior," I ended up only having to serve nine months.

Meanwhile, Jeremy had been arrested at Addenbrookes Hospital by Allan Leeke, deputy chief constable of Cambridgeshire. After three days in a heavily guarded ward he was charged with conspiracy to pervert the course of public justice, and transferred to Armley Prison to await trial. He comes before the Leeds Crown Court next month, and you can be sure I'll be sitting in the gallery following the proceedings every day. By the way, Fingers and the boys gave him a very handsome welcome. I'm told he's lost even more weight than he did trooping backward and forward across Europe fixing up his new identity.

Rosemary has also been arrested and charged with perjury. They didn't grant her bail, and Donald informs me that French prisons, particularly the one in Marseilles, are less comfortable than Armley—one of the few disadvantages of living in the South of France. She's fighting the extradition order, of course, but I'm assured by Matthew that she has absolutely no chance of succeeding, now we've signed the Maastricht Treaty. I knew *something* good must come out of that.

As for Mrs. Balcescu—I'm sure you worked out where I'd seen her long before I did.

In the case of *Regina* v. *Alexander and Kershaw*, I'm told, she will be giving evidence on behalf of the Crown. Jeremy made such a simple mistake for a normally calculating and shrewd man. In order to protect himself from being identified, he put all his worldly goods in his wife's name. So the striking blond ended up with everything, and I have a feeling that when it comes to her cross-examination, Rosemary won't turn out to be all that helpful to Jeremy, because it slipped his mind to let her know that in between those weekly phone calls he was living with another woman.

It's been difficult to find out much more about the real Professor Balcescu, because since Ceauşescu's downfall no one is quite sure what really happened to the distinguished academic. Even the Romanians believed he had escaped to Britain and begun a new life.

The Bradford City team has been relegated, so Donald has bought a cottage in the West Country and settled down to watch Bath play rugby. Jenny has joined a private detective agency in London, but is already complaining about her salary and conditions. Williams has returned to Bradford and decided on an early retirement. It was he who pointed out the painfully obvious fact that when it's twelve o'clock in France, it's only eleven o'clock in Britain.

By the way, I've decided to go back to Leeds after all. Cooper's went into liquidation as I suspected they would, the new management team not proving all that effective when it came to riding out a recession. The official receiver was only too delighted to accept my offer of £250,000 for what remained of the company, because no one else was showing the slightest interest in it. Poor Jeremy will get almost nothing for his shares. Still, you should look up the new stock in the *F.T.* around the middle of next year, and buy yourself a few, because they'll be what my father would have called "a risk worth taking."

By the way, Matthew advises me that I've just given you what's termed "insider information," so please don't pass it on, as I have no desire to go back to jail for a third time.

THE PERFECT
GENTLEMAN

I WOULD NEVER HAVE met Edward Shrimpton if he hadn't needed a towel. He stood naked by my side staring down at a bench in front of him, muttering, "I could have sworn I left the damn thing there."

I had just come out of the sauna, swathed in towels, so I took one off my shoulder and passed it to him. He thanked me and put out his hand.

"Edward Shrimpton," he said, smiling. I took his hand and wondered what we must have looked like standing there in the gymnasium locker room of the Metropolitan Club in the early evening, two grown men shaking hands in the nude.

"I don't remember seeing you in the club before," he added.

"No, I'm an overseas member."

"Ah, from England. What brings you to New York?"

"I'm pursuing an American novelist whom my company would like to publish in England."

"And are you having any success?"

"Yes, I think I'll close the deal this week—as long as the agent stops trying to convince me that his author is a cross between Tolstoy and Dickens and should be paid accordingly."

"Neither was paid particularly well, if I remember correctly," offered Edward Shrimpton as he energetically rubbed the towel up and down his back.

"A fact I pointed out to the agent at the time, who countered by reminding me that it was my house which published Dickens originally."

"I suggest," said Edward Shrimpton, "that you remind him that the end result turned out to be successful for all concerned."

"I did, but I fear this agent is more interested in 'up front' than posterity."

"As a banker that's a sentiment of which I could hardly disapprove, as the one thing we have in common with publishers is that our clients are always trying to tell us a good tale."

"Perhaps you should sit down and write one of them for me?" I said politely.

"Heaven forbid, you must be sick of being told that there's a book in every one of us, so I hasten to assure you that there isn't one in me."

I laughed, as I found it refreshing not to be informed by a new acquaintance that his memoirs, if only he could find the time to write them, would overnight be one of the world's best sellers.

"Perhaps there's a story in you, but you're just not aware of it," I suggested.

"If that's the case, I'm afraid it's passed me by."

Mr. Shrimpton reemerged from behind the row of little tin cubicles and handed me back my towel. He was now fully dressed and stood, I would have guessed, a shade under six feet. He wore a Wall Street banker's pinstripe suit and, although he was nearly bald, he had a remarkable physique for a man who must have been well into his sixties. Only his thick white mustache gave away his true age, and would have been more in keeping with a retired English colonel than a New York banker.

"Are you going to be in New York long?" he inquired, as he took a small leather case from his inside pocket and removed a pair of half-moon glasses and placed them on the end of his nose.

"Just for the week."

"I don't suppose you're free for lunch tomorrow, by any chance?" he inquired, peering over the top of his glasses.

"Yes, I am. I certainly can't face another meal with that agent."

"Good, good, then why don't you join me and I can follow the continuing drama of capturing the elusive American author?"

"And perhaps I'll discover there is a story in you after all."

"Not a hope," he said, "you would be backing a loser if you depend on that," and once again he offered his hand. "One o'clock, members' dining room suit you?"

"One o'clock, members' dining room," I repeated.

As he left the locker room I walked over to the mirror and straightened my tie. I was dining that night with Eric McKenzie, a publishing friend, who had originally proposed me for membership of the club. To be accurate, Eric McKenzie was a friend of my father rather than myself. They had met just before the war while on vacation in Portugal and when I was elected to the club, soon after my father's retirement, Eric took it upon himself to have dinner with me whenever I was in New York. One's parents' generation never see one as anything but a child who will always be in need of constant care and attention. As he was a contemporary of my father, Eric must have been nearly seventy and, although hard of hearing and slightly bent, he was always amusing and good company, even if he did continually ask me if I was aware that his grandfather was Scottish.

As I strapped on my watch, I checked that he was due to arrive in a few minutes. I put on my jacket and strolled out into the hall to find that he was already there, waiting for me. Eric was killing time by reading the out-of-date club notices. Americans, I have observed, can always be relied upon to arrive early or late; never on time. I stood staring at the stooping man, whose hair but for a few strands had now turned silver. His three-piece suit had a button missing on the jacket, which reminded me that his wife had died last year. After another thrust-out hand and exchange of welcomes, we took the elevator to the second floor and walked to the dining room.

The members' dining room at the Metropolitan differs little from any other men's club. It has a fair sprinkling of old leather chairs, old carpets, old portraits, and old members. A waiter guided us to a corner table that overlooked Central Park. We ordered, and then settled back to discuss all the subjects I found I usually cover with an acquaintance I only have the chance to catch up with a couple of times a year—our families, children, mutual friends, work; baseball and cricket. By the time we had reached cricket we had also reached coffee, so we strolled down to the far end of the room and made ourselves comfortable in two well-worn leather chairs. When the coffee arrived I ordered two brandies and watched Eric unwrap a large Cuban cigar. Although they displayed a West Indian band on the outside, I knew they were Cuban because I had picked them up for him from a tobacconist in St. James's, Piccadilly, which specializes in changing the labels for its American customers. I have often thought that they must be the only shop in the world that changes labels with the sole purpose of making a superior product appear inferior. I am certain my wine merchant does it the other way round.

While Eric was attempting to light the cigar, my eyes wandered to a board on the wall. To be more accurate, it was a highly polished wooden plaque with oblique golden lettering painted on it, honoring those men who over the years had won the club's backgammon championship. I glanced idly down the list, not expecting to see anybody with whom I would be familiar, when I was brought up by the name of Edward Shrimpton. Once in the late thirties he had been the runner-up.

"That's interesting," I said.

"What is?" asked Eric, now wreathed in enough smoke to have puffed himself out of Grand Central Station.

"Edward Shrimpton was runner-up in the club's backgammon championship in the late thirties. I'm having lunch with him tomorrow."

"I didn't realize you knew him."

"I didn't until this afternoon," I said, and then explained how we had met.

Eric laughed and turned to stare up at the board. Then he added, rather mysteriously: "That's a night I'm never likely to forget."

"Why?" I asked.

Eric hesitated, and looked uncertain of himself before continuing: "Too much water has passed under the bridge for anyone to care now." He paused again, as a hot piece of ash fell to the floor and added to the burn marks that made their own private pattern in the carpet. "Just before the war Edward Shrimpton was among the best half dozen backgammon players in the world. In fact, it must have been around that time he won the unofficial world championship in Monte Carlo."

"And he couldn't win the club championship?"

"'Couldn't' would be the wrong word, dear boy. 'Didn't' might be more accurate." Eric lapsed into another preoccupied silence.

"Are you going to explain?" I asked, hoping he would continue, "or am I to be left like a child who wants to know who killed Cock Robin?"

"All in good time, but first allow me to get this damn cigar started."

I remained silent, and four matches later, he said, "Before I begin, take a look at the man sitting over there in the corner with the young blond."

I turned and glanced back toward the dining room area, and saw a man attacking a porterhouse steak. He looked about the same age as Eric and wore a smart new suit that was unable to disguise that he had a weight problem: only his tailor could have smiled at him with any pleasure. He was seated opposite a slight, not unattractive strawberry blond half his age who could have trodden on a beetle and failed to crush it.

"What an unlikely pair. Who are they?"

"Harry Newman and his fourth wife. They're always the same. The wives I mean—blond hair, blue eyes, ninety pounds, and dumb. I can never understand why any man gets divorced only to marry a carbon copy of the original."

"Where does Edward Shrimpton fit into the jigsaw?" I asked, trying to guide Eric back on to the subject.

"Patience, patience," said my host, as he relit his cigar for the second time. "At your age you've far more time to waste than I have."

I laughed and picked up the cognac nearest to me and swirled the brandy around in my cupped hands.

"Harry Newman," continued Eric, now almost hidden in smoke, "was the fellow who beat Edward Shrimpton in the final of the club championship that year, although in truth he was never in the same class as Edward."

"Do explain," I said, as I looked up at the board to check that it was Newman's name that preceded Edward Shrimpton's.

"Well," said Eric, "after the semifinal, which Edward had won with consummate ease, we all assumed the final would only be a formality. Harry had always been a good player, but as I had been the one to lose to him in the semifinals, I knew he couldn't hope to survive a contest with Edward Shrimpton. The club final is won by the first man to reach twenty-one points, and if I had been asked for an opinion at the time, I would have reckoned the result would end up around twenty-one to five in Edward's favor. Damn cigar," he said, and lit it for a fourth time. Once again I waited impatiently.

"The final is always held on a Saturday night, and poor Harry over there," said Eric, pointing his cigar toward the far corner of the room while depositing some more ash on the floor, "who all of us thought was doing rather well in the insurance business, had a bankruptcy notice served on him the Monday morning before the final—I might add through no fault of his own. His partner had cashed in his stock without Harry's knowledge, disappeared, and left him with all the bills to pick up. Everyone in the club was sympathetic.

"On Thursday the press got hold of the story, and for good measure they added that Harry's wife had run off with the partner. Harry didn't show his head in the club all week, and some of us wondered if he would scratch from the final and let Edward win by default as the result was such a foregone conclusion anyway. But the Games Committee received no communication from Harry to suggest the contest was off, so they proceeded as though nothing had happened. On the night of the final, I dined with Edward Shrimpton here in the club. He was in fine form. He ate very little and drank nothing but a glass of water. If you had asked me then I wouldn't have put a penny on Harry Newman even if the odds had been ten to one.

"We all dined upstairs on the third floor, as the committee had cleared this room so that they could seat sixty in a square around the board. The final was due to start at nine o'clock. By twenty to nine there wasn't a seat left in the place, and members were already standing two deep behind the square: it wasn't every day we had the chance to see a world champion in action. By five to nine, Harry still hadn't turned up and some of the members were beginning to get a little restless. As nine o'clock chimed, the referee went over to Edward and had a word with him. I saw Edward shake his head in disagreement and walk away. Just at the point when I thought the referee would have to be firm and award the match to Edward, Harry strolled in looking very dapper, adorned in a dinner jacket several sizes smaller than the suit he is wearing tonight. Edward went straight up to him, shook him warmly by the hand, and together they walked into the center of the room. Even with the throw of the first dice, there was a tension about that match. Members were waiting to see how Harry would fare in the opening game."

The intermittent cigar went out again. I leaned over and struck a match for him.

"Thank you, dear boy. Now, where was I? Oh, yes, the first game. Well, Edward only just won the first game and I wondered if he wasn't concentrating or if perhaps he had become a little too relaxed while waiting for his opponent. In the second game the dice ran well for Harry, and he won fairly easily. From that moment on it became a finely fought battle, and by the time the score had reached eleven to nine in Edward's favor the tension in the room was quite electric. By the ninth game I began watching more carefully and noticed that Edward allowed himself to be drawn into a back game, a small error in judgment that only a seasoned player would have spotted. I wondered how many more subtle errors had already passed that I hadn't observed. Harry went on to win the ninth, making the score eighteen to seven in his favor. I watched even more diligently as Edward did just enough to win the tenth game and, with a rash double, just enough to lose the eleventh, bring the score to twenty even, so that everything would depend on the final game. I swear that nobody had left the room that evening, and not one back remained against a chair; some members were even hanging on to the window ledges. The room was now full of drink and thick with cigar smoke, and yet when Harry picked up the dice cup for the last game you could hear the little squares of ivory rattle before they hit the board. The dice ran well for Harry in that final game and Edward only made one small error early on that I was able to pick up; but it was enough to give Harry game, match and championship. After the last throw of the dice everyone in that room, including Edward, gave the new champion a standing ovation."

"Had many other members worked out what had really happened that night?"

"No, I don't think so," said Eric. "And certainly Harry Newman hadn't. The talk afterwards was that Harry had never played a better game in his life, and what a worthy champion he was, all the more for the difficulties he laboured under."

"Did Edward have anything to say?"

"Toughest match he'd been in since Monte Carlo, and only hoped he would be given the chance to avenge the defeat next year."

"But he wasn't," I said, looking up again at the board. "He never won the club championship."

"That's right. After Roosevelt had insisted we help you guys out in England, the club didn't hold the competition again until 1946, and by then Edward had been to war and had lost all interest in the game."

"And Harry?"

"Oh, Harry. Harry never looked back after that; must have made a dozen deals in the club that night. Within a year he was on top again, even found himself another cute little blond."

"What does Edward say about the result now, thirty years later?"

"Do you know, that remains a mystery to this day. I have never heard him mention the game once in all that time."

Eric's cigar had come to the end of its working life and he stubbed the remains out in an ashless ashtray. It obviously acted as a signal to remind him that it was time to go home. He rose a little unsteadily, and I walked down with him to the front door.

"Good-bye, my boy," he said. "Do give Edward my best wishes when you have lunch with him tomorrow. And remember not to play him at backgammon. He'd still kill you."

The next day I arrived in the front hall a few minutes before our appointed time, not sure if Edward Shrimpton would fall into the category of early or late Americans. As the clock struck one, he walked through the door: There has to be an exception to every rule. We agreed to go straight up to lunch since he had to be back in Wall Street for a two-thirty appointment. We stepped into the packed lift, and I pressed the No. 3 button. The doors closed like a tired concertina and the slowest lift in America made its way toward the second floor.

As we entered the dining room, I was amused to see Harry Newman was already there, attacking another steak, while the little blond lady was nibbling a salad. He waved expansively at Edward Shrimpton, who returned the gesture with a friendly nod. We sat down at a table in the center of the room and studied the menu. Steak-and-kidney pie was the dish of the day, which was probably the case in half the men's clubs in the world. Edward wrote down our orders in a neat and legible hand on the little white slip provided by the waiter.

Edward asked me about the author I was chasing and made some penetrating comments about her earlier work, to which I responded as best I could while trying to think of a plot to make him discuss the prewar backgammon championship, which I considered would make a far better story than anything she had ever written. But he never talked about himself once during the meal, so I despaired. Finally, staring up at the plaque on the wall, I said clumsily:

"I see you were runner-up in the club backgammon championship just before the war. You must have been a fine player."

"No, not really," he replied. "Not many people bothered about the game in those days. There is a different attitude today with all the youngsters taking it so seriously."

"What about the champion?" I said, pushing my luck.

"Harry Newman? He was an outstanding player, and particularly good under pressure. He's the gentleman who greeted us when we came in. That's him sitting over there in the corner with his wife."

I looked obediently toward Mr. Newman's table but my host added nothing more so I gave up. We ordered coffee, and that would have been the end of Edward's story if Harry Newman and his wife had not headed straight for us after they had finished their lunch. Edward was on his feet long before I was, despite my twenty-year advantage. Harry Newman looked even bigger standing up, and his little blond wife looked more like the dessert than his spouse.

"Ed," he boomed, "how are you?"

"I'm well, thank you, Harry," Edward replied. "May I introduce my guest?"

"Nice to know you," he said. "Rusty, I've always wanted you to meet Ed Shrimpton, because I've talked to you about him so often in the past."

"Have you, Harry?" she squeaked.

"Of course. You remember, honey. Ed is up there on the backgammon honors board," he said, pointing a stubby finger toward the plaque. "With only one name in front of him, and that's mine. And Ed was the world champion at the time. Isn't that right, Ed?"

"That's right, Harry."

"So I suppose I really should have been the world champion that year, wouldn't you say?"

"I couldn't quarrel with that conclusion," replied Edward.

"On the big day, Rusty, when it really mattered, and the pressure was on, I beat him fair and square."

I stood in silent disbelief as Edward Shrimpton still volunteered no disagreement.

"We must play again for old times' sake, Ed," the fat man continued. "It would be fun to see if you could beat me now. Mind you, I'm a bit rusty nowadays, Rusty." He laughed loudly at his own joke, but his spouse's face remained blank. I wondered how long it would be before there was a fifth Mrs. Newman.

"It's been great to see you again, Ed. Take care of yourself."

"Thank you, Harry," said Edward.

We both sat down again as Newman and his wife left the dining room. Our coffee was now cold so we ordered a fresh pot. The room was almost empty and when I had poured two cups for us Edward leaned over to me conspiratorially and whispered: "Now there's a hell of a story for a publisher like you," he said. "I mean the real truth about Harry Newman."

My ears pricked up as I anticipated his version of the story of what had actually happened on the night of that pre-war backgammon championship over thirty years before.

"Really?" I said, innocently.

"Oh, yes," said Edward. "It was not as simple as you might think. Just before the war Harry was let down very badly by his business partner, who not only stole his money, but for good measure his wife as well. The very week that he was at his lowest he won the club backgammon championship, put all his troubles behind him and, against the odds, made a brilliant comeback. You know, he's worth a fortune today. Now, wouldn't you agree that that would make one hell of a story?"

À LA CARTE

ARTHUR HAPGOOD WAS DEMOBILIZED on November 3, 1946. Within a month he was back at his old workplace on the shop floor of the Triumph factory on the outskirts of Coventry.

The five years spent in the Sherwood Foresters, four of them as a quartermaster seconded to a tank regiment, only underlined Arthur's likely postwar fate, despite his having hoped to find more rewarding work once the war was over. However, on returning to England he quickly discovered that in a "land fit for heroes" jobs were not that easy to come by, and although he did not want to go back to the work he had done for five years before war had been declared, that of fitting wheels on cars, he reluctantly, after four weeks on welfare, went to see his former factory manager at Triumph.

"The job's yours if you want it, Arthur," the factory manager assured him.

"And the future?"

"The car's no longer a toy for the eccentric rich or even just a necessity for the businessman," the factory manager replied. "In fact," he continued, "management is preparing for the 'two-car family.'"

"So they'll need even more wheels to be put on cars," said Arthur forlornly.

"That's the ticket."

Arthur signed on within the hour, and it was only a matter of days before he was back into his old routine. After all, he often reminded his wife, it didn't take a degree in engineering to screw four knobs on to a wheel a hundred times a shift.

Arthur soon accepted the fact that he would have to settle

for second best. However, second best was not what he planned for his son.

Mark had celebrated his fifth birthday before his father had even set eyes on him, but from the moment Arthur returned home he lavished everything he could on the boy.

Arthur was determined that Mark was not going to end up working on the shop floor of a car factory for the rest of his life. He put in hours of overtime to earn enough money to ensure that the boy could have extra tuition in math, general science, and English. He felt well rewarded when the boy passed his eleven-plus and won a place at King Henry VIII Grammar School, and that pride did not falter when Mark went on to pass five O-levels and two years later added two A-levels.

Arthur tried not to show his disappointment when, on Mark's eighteenth birthday, the boy informed him that he did not want to go to a university.

"What kind of career *are* you hoping to take up then, lad?" Arthur enquired.

"I've filled out an application form to join you on the shop floor just as soon as I leave school."

"But why would you—"

"Why not? Most of my friends who're leaving this term have already been accepted by Triumph, and they can't wait to get started."

"You must be out of your mind."

"Come off it, Dad. The pay's good, and you've shown that there's always plenty of extra money to be picked up with over-time. And I don't mind hard work."

"Do you think I spent all those years making sure you got a first-class education just to let you end up like me, putting wheels on cars for the rest of your life?" Arthur shouted.

"That's not the whole job, and you know it, Dad."

"You go there over my dead body," said his father. "I don't care what your friends end up doing, I only care about you. You could be a solicitor, an accountant, an army officer, even a schoolmaster. Why should you want to end up at a car factory?"

"It's better paid than teaching, for a start," said Mark. "My French teacher once told me that he wasn't as well off as you."

"That's not the point, lad—"

"The point is, Dad, I can't be expected to spend the rest of my life doing a job I don't enjoy just to satisfy one of your fantasies."

"Well, I'm not going to allow you to waste the rest of your life," said Arthur, getting up from the breakfast table. "The first thing I'm going to do when I get in to work this morning is see that your application is turned down."

"That isn't fair, Dad. I have the right to—"

But his father had already left the room, and did not utter another word to the boy before leaving for the factory.

For over a week father and son didn't speak to each other. It was Mark's mother who was left to come up with the compromise. Mark could apply for any job that met with his father's approval, and as long as he completed a year at that job he could, if he still wanted to, reapply to work at the factory. His father for his part would not then put any obstacle in his son's way.

Arthur nodded. Mark also reluctantly agreed to the solution.

"But only if you complete the full year," Arthur warned solemnly.

During those last days of the summer vacation Arthur came up with several suggestions for Mark to consider, but the boy showed no enthusiasm for any of them. Mark's mother became quite anxious that her son would end up with no job at all until, while helping her slice potatoes for dinner one night, Mark confided that he thought hotel management seemed the least unattractive proposition he had considered so far.

"At least you'd have a roof over your head and be regularly fed," his mother said.

"Bet they don't cook as well as you, Mom," said Mark as he placed the sliced potatoes on the top of the Lancashire hotpot. "Still, it's only a year."

During the next month Mark attended several interviews at hotels around the country without success. It was then that his father discovered that his old company sergeant was head porter at the Savoy: Immediately Arthur started to pull a few strings.

"If the boy's any good," Arthur's old comrade-in-arms assured him over a pint, "he could end up as a head porter, even a hotel manager." Arthur seemed well satisfied, even though Mark was still assuring his friends that he would be joining them in a year to the day.

On September 1, 1959, Arthur and Mark Hapgood traveled together by bus to Coventry station. Arthur shook hands with the boy and promised him, "Your mother and I will make sure it's a special Christmas this year when they give you your first leave. And don't worry—you'll be in good hands with 'Sarge.' He'll teach you a thing or two. Just remember to keep your nose clean."

Mark said nothing and returned a thin smile as he boarded the train. "You'll never regret it . . ." were the last words Mark heard his father say as the train pulled out of the station.

Mark regretted it from the moment he set foot in the hotel.

As a junior porter he started his day at six in the morning and ended at six in the evening. He was entitled to a fifteen-minute midmorning break, a forty-five-minute lunch break, and another fifteen-minute break around midafternoon. After the first month had passed he could not recall when he had been granted all three breaks on the same day, and he quickly learned that there was no one to whom he could protest. His duties consisted of carrying guests' suitcases up to their rooms, then lugging them back down again the moment they wanted to leave. With an average of three hundred people staying in the hotel each night, the process was endless. The pay turned out to be half what his friends were getting back home, and, since he had to hand over all his tips to the head porter, however much overtime Mark put in, he never saw an extra penny. On the only occasion he dared to mention it to the head porter, he was met with the words, "Your time will come, lad."

It did not worry Mark that his uniform didn't fit or that his room was six feet by six feet and overlooked Charing Cross Station, or even that he didn't get a share of the tips; but it did worry him that there was nothing he could do to please the head porter—however clean he kept his nose.

Sergeant Crann, who considered the Savoy nothing more than an extension of his old platoon, didn't have a lot of time for young men under his command who hadn't done their national service.

"But I wasn't *eligible* to do national service," insisted Mark. "No one born after 1939 was called up."

"Don't make excuses, lad."

"It's not an excuse, Sarge. It's the truth."

"And don't call me 'Sarge.' I'm 'Sergeant Crann' to you, and don't you forget it."

"Yes, Sergeant Crann."

At the end of each day Mark would return to his little boxroom with its small bed, small chair, and tiny chest of drawers, and collapse exhausted. The only picture in the room—Hals's *The Laughing Cavalier*—was on the calendar that hung above Mark's bed. The date of September 1, 1960, was circled in red to remind him when he would be allowed to rejoin his friends at the factory back home. Each night before falling asleep he would cross out the offending day like a prisoner making scratch marks on a wall.

At Christmas, Mark returned home for a four-day break, and when his mother saw the general state of the boy she tried to talk his father into allowing Mark to give up the job early, but Arthur remained implacable.

"We made an agreement. I can't be expected to get him a job at the factory if he isn't responsible enough to keep to his part of a bargain."

During the break Mark waited for his friends outside the factory gate until their shift had ended and listened to their stories of weekends spent watching football, drinking at the pub, and dancing to the Everly Brothers. They all sympathized with his problem and looked forward to his joining them in September. "It's only a few more months," one of them reminded him cheerfully.

Far too quickly, Mark was on the journey back to London,

where he continued unwillingly to cart cases up and down the hotel corridors for month after month.

Once the English rain had subsided, the usual influx of American tourists began. Mark liked the Americans, who treated him as an equal and often tipped him a shilling when others would have given him only sixpence. But whatever the amount Mark received, Sergeant Crann would still pocket it with the inevitable, "Your time will come, lad."

One such American for whom Mark ran around diligently every day during his two-week stay ended up presenting the boy with a ten-shilling note as he left the front entrance of the hotel.

Mark said, "Thank you, sir," and turned around to see Sergeant Crann standing in his path.

"Hand it over," said Crann as soon as the American visitor was well out of earshot.

"I was going to the moment I saw you," said Mark, passing the note to his superior.

"Not thinking of pocketing what's rightfully mine, were you?"

"No, I wasn't," said Mark. "Though God knows I earned it."

"Your time will come, lad," said Sergeant Crann without much thought.

"Not while someone as mean as you is in charge," replied Mark sharply.

"What was that you said?" asked the head porter, veering around.

"You heard me the first time, Sarge."

The clip across the ear took Mark by surprise.

"You, lad, have just lost your job. Nobody, but nobody, talks to me like that." Sergeant Crann turned and set off smartly in the direction of the manager's office.

The hotel manager, Gerald Drummond, listened to the head porter's version of events before asking Mark to report to his office immediately. "You realize I have been left with no choice but to fire you," were his first words once the door was closed.

Mark looked up at the tall, elegant man in his long, black coat, white collar, and black tie. "Am I allowed to tell you what actually happened, sir?" he asked.

Mr. Drummond nodded, then listened without interruption as Mark gave his version of what had taken place that morning, and also disclosed the agreement he had entered into with his father. "Please let me complete my final ten weeks," Mark ended, "or my father will only say I haven't kept my end of our bargain."

"I haven't got another job vacant at the moment," protested the manager. "Unless you're willing to peel potatoes for ten weeks."

"Anything," said Mark.

"Then report to the kitchen at six tomorrow morning. I'll tell the third chef to expect you. Only if you think the head porter is a martinet, just wait until you meet Jacques, our *maître chef de cuisine*. He won't clip your ear, he'll cut it off."

Mark didn't care. He felt confident that for just ten weeks he could face anything, and at five-thirty the following morning he exchanged his dark blue uniform for a white top and blue and white check trousers before reporting for his new duties. To his surprise the kitchen took up almost the entire basement of the hotel, and was even more of a bustle than the lobby had been.

The third chef put him in the corner of the kitchen, next to a mountain of potatoes, a bowl of cold water, and a sharp knife. Mark peeled through breakfast, lunch, and dinner and fell asleep on his bed that night without even enough energy left to cross a day off his calendar.

For the first week he never actually saw the fabled Jacques. With seventy people working in the kitchens Mark felt confident he could pass his whole period there without anyone being aware of him.

Each morning at six he would start peeling, then hand over the potatoes to a gangling youth called Terry, who in turn would dice or cut them according to the third chef's instructions for the dish of the day. Monday sauté, Tuesday mashed, Wednesday French-fried, Thursday sliced, Friday roast, Saturday croquette . . . Mark quickly worked out a routine that kept him well ahead of Terry and therefore out of any trouble.

Having watched Terry do his job for over a week Mark felt sure he could have shown the young apprentice how to lighten his workload quite simply, but he decided to keep his mouth closed: opening it might only get him into more trouble, and he was certain the manager wouldn't give him a second chance.

Mark soon discovered that Terry always fell badly behind on Tuesday's shepherd's pie and Thursday's Lancashire hotpot. From time to time the third chef would come across to complain, and he would glance over at Mark to be sure that it wasn't him who was holding the process up. Mark made certain that he always had a spare tub of peeled potatoes by his side so that he escaped censure.

It was on the first Thursday morning in August (Lancashire hotpot) that Terry sliced off the top of his forefinger. Blood spurted all over the sliced potatoes and onto the wooden table as the lad began yelling hysterically.

"Get him out of here!" Mark heard the *maître chef de cuisine* bellow above the noise of the kitchen as he stormed toward them.

"And you," he said, pointing at Mark, "clean up mess and start slicing rest of potatoes. I 'ave eight hundred hungry customers still expecting to feed."

"Me?" said Mark in disbelief. "But—"

"Yes, you. You couldn't do worse job than idiot who calls himself trainee chef and cuts off finger." The chef marched away, leaving Mark to move reluctantly across to the table where Terry had been working. He felt disinclined to argue while the calendar was there to remind him that he was down to his last twenty-five days.

Mark set about a task he had carried out for his mother many times. The clean, neat cuts were delivered with a skill Terry would never learn to master. By the end of the day, although exhausted, Mark did not feel quite as tired as he had in the past.

At eleven that night the *maître chef de cuisine* threw off his hat and barged out of the swinging doors, a sign to everyone else they could also leave the kitchen once everything that was their responsibility had been cleared up. A few seconds later the doors swung back open and the chef burst in. He stared around the kitchen as everyone waited to see what he would do next. Having found what he was looking for, he headed straight for Mark.

"Oh, my God," thought Mark. "He's going to kill me."

"How is your name?" the chef demanded.

"Mark Hapgood, sir," he managed to splutter out.

"You waste on 'tatoes, Mark Hapgood," said the chef. "You start on vegetables in morning. Report at seven. If that *crétin* with 'alf finger ever returns, put him to peeling 'tatoes."

The chef turned on his heel even before Mark had the chance to reply. He dreaded the thought of having to spend three weeks in the middle of the kitchens, never once out of the *maître chef de cuisine*'s sight, but he accepted that there was no alternative.

The next morning Mark arrived at six for fear of being late, and spent an hour watching the fresh vegetables being unloaded from Covent Garden market. The hotel's supply manager checked every case carefully, rejecting several before he signed a receipt to show that the hotel had received over three thousand pounds' worth of vegetables. An average day, he assured Mark.

The *maître chef de cuisine* appeared a few minutes before seven-thirty, checked the menus, and told Mark to score the Brussels sprouts, trim the French beans, and remove the coarse outer leaves of the cabbages.

"But I don't know how," Mark replied honestly. He could feel the other trainees in the kitchen edging away from him.

"Then I teach you," roared the chef. "Perhaps only thing you learn is if hope to be good chef, you able to do everyone's job in kitchen, even 'tato peeler's."

"But I'm hoping to be a . . ." Mark began and then thought better of it. The chef seemed not to have heard Mark as he took his place beside the new recruit. Everyone in the kitchen stared as the chef began to show Mark the basic skills of cutting, dicing, and slicing.

"And remember other idiot's finger," the chef said on completing the lesson and passing the razor-sharp knife back to Mark. "Yours can be next."

Mark started gingerly dicing the carrots, then the Brussels

sprouts, removing the outer layer before cutting a firm cross in the base. Next he moved on to trimming and slicing the beans. Once again he found it fairly easy to keep ahead of the chef's requirements.

At the end of each day, after the head chef had left, Mark stayed on to sharpen all his knives in preparation for the following morning, and would not leave his work area until it was spotless.

On the sixth day, after a curt nod from the chef, Mark realized he must be doing something half right. By the following Saturday he felt he had mastered the simple skills of vegetable preparation and found himself becoming fascinated by what the chef himself was up to. Although Jacques rarely addressed anyone as he marched around the acre of kitchen except to grunt his approval or disapproval—the latter more commonly—Mark quickly learned to anticipate his needs. Within a short space of time he began to feel that he was part of a team—even though he was only too aware of being the novice recruit.

On the deputy chef's day off the following week Mark was allowed to arrange the cooked vegetables in their bowls, and spent some time making each dish look attractive as well as edible. The chef not only noticed but actually muttered his greatest accolade—"*Bon.*"

During his last three weeks at the Savoy, Mark did not even look at the calendar above his bed.

One Thursday morning a message came down from the undermanager that Mark was to report to his office as soon as was convenient. Mark had quite forgotten that it was August 31—his last day. He cut ten lemons into quarters, then finished preparing the forty plates of thinly sliced smoked salmon that would complete the first course for a wedding lunch. He looked with pride at his efforts before folding up his apron and leaving to collect his papers and final pay envelope.

"Where you think you're going?" asked the chef, looking up.

"I'm off," said Mark. "Back to Coventry."

"See you Monday then. You deserve day off."

"No, I'm going home for good," said Mark.

The chef stopped checking the cuts of rare beef that would make up the second course of the wedding feast.

"Going?" he repeated as if he didn't understand the word.

"Yes. I've finished my year and now I'm off home to work."

"I hope you found first-class hotel," said the chef with genuine interest.

"I'm not going to work in a hotel."

"A restaurant, perhaps?"

"No, I'm going to get a job at Triumph."

The chef looked puzzled for a moment, unsure if it was his English or whether the boy was mocking him.

"What is—Triumph?"

"A place where they manufacture cars."

"You will manufacture cars?"

"Not a whole car, but I will put the wheels on."

"You put cars on wheels?" the chef said in disbelief.

"No," laughed Mark. "Wheels on cars."

The chef still looked uncertain.

"So you will be cooking for the car workers?"

"No. As I explained, I'm going to put the wheels on the cars," said Mark slowly, enunciating each word.

"That not possible."

"Oh, yes it is," responded Mark. "And I've waited a whole year to prove it."

"If I offered you job as commis chef, you change mind?" asked the chef quietly.

"Why would you do that?"

"Because you 'ave talent in those fingers. In time I think you become chef, perhaps even good chef."

"No, thanks. I'm off to Coventry to join my mates."

The head chef shrugged. "*Tant pis*," he said, and without a second glance returned to the carcass of beef. He glanced over at the plates of smoked salmon. "A wasted talent," he added after the swing door had closed behind his potential protégé.

Mark locked his room, threw the calendar in the wastepaper basket, and returned to the hotel to hand in his kitchen clothes to the housekeeper. The final action he took was to return his room key to the undermanager.

"Your pay envelope, your cards, and your withholding tax forms. Oh, and the chef has phoned to say he would be happy to give you a reference," said the under-manager. "Can't pretend that happens every day."

"Won't need that where I'm going," said Mark. "But thanks all the same."

He started off for the station at a brisk pace, his small battered suitcase swinging by his side, only to find that each step took a little longer. When he arrived at Euston he made his way to Platform Seven and began walking up and down, occasionally staring at the great clock above the reservations hall. He watched first one train and then another pull out of the station bound for Coventry. He was aware of the station becoming dark as shadows filtered through the glass awning onto the public concourse. Suddenly he turned and walked off at an even brisker pace. If he hurried he could still be back in time to help chef prepare dinner that night.

Mark trained under Jacques le Renneu for five years. Vegetables were followed by sauces, fish by poultry, meats by pâtisserie. After eight years at the Savoy he was appointed second chef, and had learned so much from his mentor that regular patrons could no longer be sure when it was the *maître chef de cuisine*'s day off. Two years later Mark became a master chef, and when in 1971 Jacques was offered the opportunity to return to Paris and take over the kitchens of the George V—an establishment that is to Paris what the Savoy is to London—Jacques agreed, but only on condition that Mark accompanied him.

"It is wrong direction from Coventry," Jacques warned him, "and in any case they sure to offer you my job at the Savoy."

"I'd better come along, otherwise those Frogs will never get a decent meal."

"Those Frogs," said Jacques, "will always know when it's my day off."

"Yes, and book in even greater numbers," suggested Mark, laughing.

It was not to be long before Parisians were flocking to the

George V, not to rest their weary heads but to relish the cooking of the two-chef team.

When Jacques celebrated his sixty-fifth birthday, the great hotel did not have to look far to appoint his successor.

"The first Englishman ever to be *maître chef de cuisine* at the George V," said Jacques, raising a glass of champagne at his farewell banquet. "Who would believe it? Of course, you will have to change your name to Marc to hold down such a position."

"Neither will ever happen," said Mark.

"Oh, yes it will, because I 'ave recommended you."

"Then I shall turn it down."

"Going to put cars on wheels, *peut-être?*" asked Jacques mockingly.

"No, but I have found a little restaurant on the Left Bank. With my savings alone I can't quite afford the lease, but with your help . . . "

Chez Jacques opened on the rue du Plaisir on the Left Bank on May 1, 1982, and it was not long before those customers who had taken the George V for granted transferred their allegiance.

Mark's reputation spread as the two chefs pioneered "nouvelle cuisine," and soon the only way anyone could be guaranteed a table at the restaurant in under three weeks was to be a film star or a cabinet minister.

The day Michelin gave Chez Jacques its third star, Mark, with Jacques's blessing, decided to open a second restaurant. The press and customers then quarreled among themselves as to which was the finer establishment. The reservation sheets showed clearly that the public felt there was no difference.

When, in October 1986, Jacques died at the age of seventy-one, the restaurant critics wrote confidently that standards were bound to fall. A year later the same journalists had to admit that one of the five great chefs of France had come from a town in the British Midlands they could not even pronounce.

Jacques's death only made Mark yearn more for his homeland, and when he read in the *Daily Telegraph* of a new development to be built in Covent Garden, he called the site agent to ask for more details.

Mark's third restaurant was opened in the heart of London on February 11, 1987.

Over the years Mark Hapgood often traveled back to Coventry to see his parents. His father had retired long since, but Mark was still unable to persuade either parent to take the trip to Paris and sample his culinary efforts. But now that he had opened in the country's capital, he hoped to tempt them.

"We don't need to go up to London," said his mother, setting the table. "You always cook for us whenever you come home, and we read of your successes in the papers. In any case, your father isn't so good on his legs nowadays."

"What do you call this, son?" his father asked a few minutes later as noisette of lamb surrounded by baby carrots was placed in front of him.

"Nouvelle cuisine."

"And people pay good money for it?"

Mark laughed, and the following day prepared his father's favorite Lancashire hotpot.

"Now that's a real meal," said Arthur after his third helping. "And I'll tell you something for nothing, lad. You cook it almost as well as your mother."

A year later Michelin announced the restaurants throughout the world that had been awarded a coveted third star. *The Times* let its readers know on its front page that Chez Jacques was the first English restaurant ever to be so honored.

To celebrate the award, Mark's parents finally agreed to make the journey down to London, though not until Mark had sent a telegram saying he was reconsidering that job at Triumph. He sent a car to fetch his parents and had them installed in a suite at the Savoy. That evening he reserved the best table at Chez Jacques in their name.

Vegetable soup followed by steak-and-kidney pie with a plate of bread-and-butter pudding to end on were not the table d'hôte that night, but they were served for the special guests at table 17.

Under the influence of the finest wine, Arthur was soon chatting happily to anyone who would listen and couldn't resist reminding the headwaiter that it was his son who owned the restaurant.

"Don't be silly, Arthur," said his wife. "He already knows that."

"Nice couple, your parents," the headwaiter confided to his boss after he had served them their coffee and supplied Arthur with a cigar. "What did your old man do before he retired? Banker? Lawyer? Schoolmaster?"

"Oh, no, nothing like that," said Mark quietly. "He spent the whole of his working life putting wheels on cars."

"But why would he waste his time doing that?" asked the waiter incredulously.

"Because he wasn't lucky enough to have a father like mine," Mark replied.

THE CHINESE
STATUE

THE LITTLE CHINESE STATUE was the next item to come under
the auctioneer's hammer. Lot 103 caused those quiet murmur-
ings that always precede the sale of a masterpiece. The auctioneer's assistant held up the delicate piece of ivory for the packed
audience to admire while the auctioneer glanced around the
room to be sure he knew where the serious bidders were
seated. I studied my catalog and read the detailed description
of the piece, and what was known of its history.

The statue had been purchased in Ha Li Chuan in 1871 and
was referred to as what Sotheby's quaintly described as "the
property of a gentleman," usually meaning that some member
of the aristocracy did not wish to admit that he was having to
sell off one of the family heirlooms. I wondered if that was the
case on this occasion and decided to do some research to discover what had caused the little Chinese statue to find its way
into the auction rooms on that Thursday morning over one
hundred years later. "Lot Number 103," declared the auctioneer. "What am I bid for this magnificent example of . . . "

Sir Alexander Heathcote, as well as being a gentleman, was an
exact man. He was exactly six feet three and a quarter inches
tall, rose at seven o'clock every morning, joined his wife at
breakfast to eat one boiled egg cooked for precisely four minutes, two pieces of toast with one spoonful of Cooper's marmalade, and drink one cup of China tea. He would then take a
hackney carriage from his home in Cadogan Gardens at exactly
8:20 and arrive at the Foreign Office at promptly 8:59, returning home again on the stroke of six o'clock.

Sir Alexander had been exact from an early age, as became

the only son of a general. But unlike his father, he chose to serve his queen in the diplomatic service, another exacting calling. He progressed from a shared desk at the Foreign Office in Whitehall to third secretary in Calcutta, to second secretary in Vienna, to first secretary in Rome, to deputy ambassador in Washington, and finally to minister in Peking. He was delighted when Mr. Gladstone invited him to represent the government in China as he had for some considerable time taken more than an amateur interest in the art of the Ming dynasty. This crowning appointment in his distinguished career would afford him what until then he would have considered impossible, an opportunity to observe in their natural habitat some of the great statues, paintings, and drawings he had previously been able to admire only in books.

When Sir Alexander arrived in Peking, after a journey by sea and land that took his party nearly two months, he presented his seals patent to the Empress Tzu-hsi and a personal letter for her private reading from Queen Victoria. The empress, dressed from head to toe in white and gold, received her new ambassador in the throne room of the Imperial Palace. She read the letter from the British monarch while Sir Alexander remained standing at attention. Her Imperial Highness revealed nothing of its contents to the new minister, wishing him only a successful term of office in his appointment. She then moved her lips slightly up at the corners, which Sir Alexander judged correctly to mean that the audience had come to an end. As he was conducted back through the great halls of the Imperial Palace by a mandarin in the long court dress of black and gold, Sir Alexander walked as slowly as possible, taking in the magnificent collection of ivory and jade statues scattered casually around the building in much the way Cellinis and Michelangelos today lie stacked against one another in Florence.

As his ministerial appointment was for only three years, Sir Alexander took no leave, but preferred to use his time to put the embassy behind him and travel on horseback into the outlying districts to learn more about the country and its people. On these trips he was always accompanied by a mandarin from the palace staff who acted as interpreter and guide.

On one such journey, passing through the muddy streets of a small village with but a few houses, called Ha Li Chuan, a distance of some fifty miles from Peking, Sir Alexander chanced on an old craftsman's working place. Leaving his servants, the minister dismounted from his horse and entered the ramshackled wooden workshop to admire the delicate pieces of ivory and jade that crammed the shelves from floor to ceiling. Although modern, the pieces were superbly executed by an experienced craftsman, and the minister entered the little hut with the thought of acquiring a small memento of his journey. Once in the shop he could hardly move in any direction for fear of knocking something over. The building had not been designed for a six-feet-three-and-a-quarter visitor. Sir Alexander stood still and enthralled, taking in the fine-scented jasmine smell that hung in the air.

An old craftsman bustled forward in a long, blue coolie robe and flat black hat to greet him; a jet black pigtail fell down his back. He bowed very low and then looked up at the giant from England. The minister returned the bow while the mandarin explained who Sir Alexander was and his desire to be allowed to look at the work of the craftsman. The old man was nodding his agreement even before the mandarin had come to the end of his request. For over an hour the minister sighed and chuckled as he studied many of the pieces with admiration and finally returned to the old man to praise his skill. The craftsman bowed once again, and his shy smile revealed no teeth but only genuine pleasure at Sir Alexander's compliments. Pointing a finger to the back of the shop, he beckoned the two important visitors to follow him. They did so and entered a veritable Aladdin's cave, with row upon row of beautiful miniature emperors and classical figures. The minister could have settled down happily in the orgy of ivory for at least a week. Sir Alexander and the craftsman chatted away to each other through the interpreter, and the minister's love and knowledge of the Ming dynasty was soon revealed. The little craftsman's face lit up with this discovery, and he turned to the mandarin and in a hushed voice made a request. The mandarin nodded his agreement and translated.

"I have, Your Excellency, a piece of Ming myself that you might care to see. A statue that has been in my family for over seven generations."

"I should be honored," said the minister.

"It is I who would be honored, Your Excellency," said the little man, who thereupon scampered out of the back door, nearly falling over a stray dog, and on to an old peasant house a few yards behind the workshop. The minister and the mandarin remained in the back room, for Sir Alexander knew the old man would never have considered inviting an honored guest into his humble home until they had known each other for many years, and only then after he had been invited to Sir Alexander's home first. A few minutes passed before the little blue figure came trotting back, pigtail bouncing up and down on his shoulders. He was now clinging to something that from the very way he held it close to his chest, had to be a treasure. The craftsman passed the piece over for the minister to study. Sir Alexander's mouth opened wide, and he could not hide his excitement. The little statue, no more than six inches in height, was of the Emperor Kung and as fine an example of Ming as the minister had seen. Sir Alexander felt confident that the maker was the great Pen Q who had been patronized by the emperor, so that the date must have been around the turn of the fifteenth century. The statue's only blemish was that the ivory base on which such pieces usually rest was missing, and a small stick protruded from the bottom of the imperial robes; but in the eyes of Sir Alexander nothing could detract from its overall beauty. Although the craftsman's lips did not move, his eyes glowed with the pleasure his guest evinced as he studied the ivory emperor.

"You think the statue is good?" asked the craftsman through the interpreter.

"It's magnificent," the minister replied. "Quite magnificent."

"My own work is not worthy to stand by its side," added the craftsman humbly.

"No, no," said the minister, though in truth the little craftsman knew that the great man was only being kind, for Sir Alexander was holding the ivory statue in a way that already showed the same love as the old man had for the piece.

The minister smiled down at the craftsman as he handed back the Emperor Kung and then he uttered perhaps the only undiplomatic words he had ever spoken in thirty-five years of serving his queen and country.

"How I wish the piece was mine."

Sir Alexander regretted voicing his thoughts the moment he heard the mandarin translate them, because he knew only too well the old Chinese tradition that if an honored guest requests something the giver will grow in the eyes of his fellow men by parting with it.

A sad look came over the face of the little old craftsman as he handed back the figurine to the minister.

"No, no. I was only joking," said Sir Alexander, quickly trying to return the piece to its owner.

"You would dishonor my humble home if you did not take the emperor, Your Excellency," the old man said anxiously, and the mandarin gravely nodded his agreement.

The minister remained silent for some time. "I have dishonored my own home, sir," he replied, and looked toward the mandarin, who remained inscrutable.

The little craftsman bowed. "I must fix a base on the statue," he said, "or you will not be able to put the piece on view."

He went to a corner of the room and opened a wooden packing chest that must have housed a hundred bases for his own statues. Rummaging around, he picked out a base decorated with small, dark figures that the minister did not care for but that nevertheless made a perfect fit; the old man assured Sir Alexander that although he did not know the base's history, the piece bore the mark of a good craftsman.

The embarrassed minister took the gift and tried hopelessly to thank the little old man. The craftsman once again bowed low as Sir Alexander and the expressionless mandarin left the little workshop.

As the party traveled back to Peking, the mandarin observed the terrible state the minister was in, and uncharacteristically spoke first:

"Your Excellency is no doubt aware," he said, "of the old Chinese custom that when a stranger has been generous, you must return the kindness within the calendar year."

Sir Alexander smiled his thanks and thought carefully about the mandarin's words. Once back in his official residence, he went immediately to the embassy's extensive library to see if he could discover a realistic value for the little masterpiece. After much diligent research, he came across a drawing of a Ming statue that was almost an exact copy of the one now in his possession, and with the help of the mandarin he was able to assess its true worth, a figure that came to almost three years' emolument for a servant of the Crown. The minister discussed the problem with Lady Heathcote, and she left her husband in no doubt as to the course of action he must take.

The following week the minister despatched a letter by private messenger to his bankers, Coutts & Co. in the Strand, London, requesting that they send a large part of his savings to reach him in Peking as quickly as possible. When the funds arrived nine weeks later the minister again approached the mandarin, who listened to his questions and, seven days later, gave him the details he had asked for.

The mandarin had discovered that the little craftsman, Yung Lee, came from the old and trusted family of Yung Shau who had for some five hundred years been craftsmen. Sir Alexander also learned that many of Yung Lee's ancestors had examples of their work in the palaces of the Manchu princes. Yung Lee himself was growing old and wished to retire to the hills above the village where his ancestors had always died. His son was ready to take over the workshop from him and continue the family tradition. The minister thanked the mandarin for his diligence and had only one more request of him. The mandarin listened sympathetically to the ambassador from England and returned to the palace to seek advice.

A few days later the empress granted Sir Alexander's request.

Almost a year to the day the minister, accompanied by the mandarin, set out again from Peking for the village of Ha Li Chuan. When Sir Alexander arrived, he immediately dismounted from his horse and entered the workshop that he remembered so well. The old man was seated at his bench, his flat hat slightly askew, a piece of uncarved ivory held lovingly between his fingers. He looked up from his work and shuffled toward the minister, not recognizing his guest immediately until he could almost touch the foreign giant. Then he bowed low. The minister spoke through the mandarin:

"I have returned, sir, within the calendar year to repay my debt."

"There was no need, Your Excellency. My family is honored that the little statue lives in a great embassy and may one day be admired by the people of your own land."

The minister could think of no words to form an adequate reply and simply requested that the old man should accompany him on a short journey.

The craftsman agreed without question, and the three men set out on donkeys toward the north. They traveled for over two hours up a thin winding path into the hills behind the crafts-man's workshop, and when they reached the village of Ma Tien, they were met by another mandarin, who bowed low to the minister and requested Sir Alexander and the craftsman to con-tinue their journey with him on foot. They walked in silence to the far side of the village and only stopped when they had reached a hollow in the hill from which there was a magnificent view of the valley all the way down to Ha Li Chuan. In the hol-low stood a newly completed small white house of the most per-fect proportions. Two stone lion dogs, tongues hanging over their lips, guarded the front entrance. The little old craftsman who had not spoken since he had left his workshop remained mystified by the purpose of the journey until the minister turned to him and offered:

"A small, inadequate gift and my feeble attempt to repay you in kind."

The craftsman fell to his knees and begged forgiveness of the mandarin as he knew it was forbidden for an artisan to accept gifts from a foreigner. The mandarin raised the frightened blue figure from the ground, explaining to his countryman that the empress herself had sanctioned the minister's request. A smile of joy came over the face of the craftsman, and he slowly walked up to the doorway of the beautiful little house unable to resist running his hand over the carved lion dogs. The three travelers then spent over an hour admiring the little house before returning in silent mutual happiness back to the workshop in Ha Li Chuan. The two men thus parted, honor satisfied, and Sir Alexander rode to his embassy that night content that his actions had met with the approval of the mandarin as well as Lady Heathcote.

The minister completed his tour of duty in Peking, and the empress awarded him the Silver Star of China and a grateful queen added the KCVO to his already long list of decorations. After a few weeks back at the Foreign Office clearing the China desk, Sir Alexander retired to his native Yorkshire, the only English county whose inhabitants still hope to be born and die in the same place – not unlike the Chinese.

Sir Alexander spent his final years in the home of his late father with his wife and the little Ming emperor. The statue occupied the center of the mantelpiece in the living room for all to see and admire.

Being an exact man, Sir Alexander wrote a long and detailed will in which he left precise instructions for the disposal of his estate, including what was to happen to the little statue after his death. He bequeathed the Emperor Kung to his first son, requesting that he do the same, in order that the statue might always pass to the first son, or a daughter if the direct male line faltered. He also made a provision that the statue was never to be disposed of unless the family's honor was at stake. Sir Alexander Heathcote died at the stroke of midnight in his seventieth year.

His firstborn, Maj. James Heathcote, was serving his queen in the Boer War at the time he came into possession of the Ming emperor. The major was a fighting man, commissioned with the Duke of Wellington's Regiment, and although he had little interest in culture even he could see the family heirloom was no ordinary treasure, so he loaned the statue to the regimental mess at Halifax in order that the emperor could be displayed in the dining room for his brother officers to appreciate.

When James Heathcote became colonel of the Dukes, the

emperor stood proudly on the table alongside the trophies won at Waterloo and Sebastopol in the Crimea and Madrid. And there the Ming Statue remained until the colonel's retirement to his father's house in Yorkshire, when the Emperor returned once again to the living room mantelpiece. The colonel was not a man to disobey his late father, even in death, and he left clear instructions that the heirloom must always be passed on to the firstborn of the Heathcotes unless the family honor was in jeopardy. Col. James Heathcote, MC, did not die a soldier's death; he simply fell asleep one night by the fire, the *Yorkshire Post* on his lap.

The colonel's firstborn, the Reverend Alexander Heathcote, was at the time presiding over a small flock in the parish of Much Hadham in Hertfordshire. After burying his father with military honors, he placed the little Ming emperor on the mantelpiece of the vicarage. Few members of the Mothers' Union appreciated the masterpiece, but one or two old ladies were heard to remark on its delicate carving. And it was not until the reverend became the right reverend, and the little statue found its way into the bishop's palace, that the emperor attracted the admiration he deserved. Many of those who visited the palace and heard the story of how the bishop's grandfather had acquired the Ming statue were fascinated to learn of the disparity between the magnificent statue and its base. It always made a good after-dinner story.

God takes even his own ambassadors, but he did not do so before allowing Bishop Heathcote to complete a will leaving the statue to his son, with his grandfather's exact instructions carefully repeated. The bishop's son, Capt. James Heathcote, was a serving officer in his grandfather's regiment, so the Ming statue returned to the mess table in Halifax. During the emperor's absence, the regimental trophies had been augmented by those struck for Ypres, the Marne, and Verdun. The regiment was once again at war with Germany, and young Captain James Heathcote was killed on the beaches of Dunkirk and died intestate. Thereafter English law, the known wishes of his great-grandfather, and common sense prevailed, and the little emperor came into the possession of the captain's two-year-old son.

Alex Heathcote was, alas, not of the mettle of his doughty ancestors, and he grew up feeling no desire to serve anyone other than himself. When Captain James had been so tragically killed, Alexander's mother lavished everything on the boy that her meager income would allow. It didn't help, and it was not entirely young Alex's fault that he grew up to be, in the words of his grandmother, a selfish, spoiled little brat.

When Alex left school, only a short time before he would have been expelled, he found he could never hold down a job for more than a few weeks. It always seemed necessary for him to spend a little more than he, and finally his mother, could cope with. The good lady, deciding she could take no more of this life, departed it, to join all the other Heathcotes, not in Yorkshire but in heaven.

In the swinging sixties, when casinos opened in Britain, young Alex was convinced that he had found the ideal way of earning a living without actually having to do any work. He developed a system for playing roulette with which it was impossible to lose. He did lose, so he refined the system and promptly lost more; he refined the system once again, which resulted in him having to borrow to cover his losses. Why not? If the worst came to the worst, he told himself, he could always dispose of the little Ming emperor.

The worst did come to the worst, as each one of Alex's newly refined systems took him progressively into greater debt until the casinos began to press him for payment. When finally, one Monday morning, Alex received an unsolicited call from two gentlemen who seemed determined to collect some eight thousand pounds he owed their masters, and hinted at bodily harm if the matter was not dealt with within fourteen days, Alex caved in. After all, his great-great-grandfather's instructions had been exact: The Ming statue was to be sold if the family honor was ever at stake.

Alex took the little emperor off the mantelpiece in his Cadogan Gardens flat and stared down at its delicate handiwork, at least having the grace to feel a little sad at the loss of the family heirloom. He then drove to Bond Street and delivered the masterpiece to Sotheby's, giving instructions that the emperor should be put up for auction.

The head of the Oriental department, a pale, thin man, appeared at the front desk to discuss the masterpiece with Alex, looking not unlike the Ming statue he was holding so lovingly in his hands.

"It will take a few days to estimate the true value of the piece," he purred, "but I feel confident on a cursory glance that the statue is as fine an example of Pen Q as we have ever had under the hammer."

"That's no problem," replied Alex, "as long as you can let me know what it's worth within fourteen days."

"Oh, certainly," replied the expert. "I feel sure I could give you a floor price by Friday."

"Couldn't be better," said Alex.

During that week he contacted all his creditors, and without exception they were prepared to wait and learn the appraisal of the expert. Alex duly returned to Bond Street on the Friday with a large smile on his face. He knew what his great-great-grandfather had paid for the piece and felt sure that the statue must be worth more than ten thousand pounds. A sum that would not only yield him enough to cover all his debts but leave him a little over to try out his new refined, refined system on the roulette table. As he climbed the steps of Sotheby's, Alex silently thanked his great-great-grandfather. He asked the girl on reception if he could speak to the head of the Oriental department. She picked up an internal phone, and the expert appeared a few moments later at the front desk with a somber look on his face. Alex's heart sank as he listened to his words: "A nice little piece, your emperor, but unfortunately a fake, probably about 200, 250 years old, but only a copy of the original, I'm afraid. Copies were often made because . . . "

"How much is it worth?" interrupted an anxious Alex.

"Seven hundred pounds, eight hundred at the most."

Enough to buy a gun and some bullets, thought Alex sardonically as he turned and started to walk away.

"I wonder, sir . . ." continued the expert.

"Yes, yes, sell the bloody thing," said Alex, without bothering to look back.

"And what do you want me to do with the base?"

"The base?" repeated Alex, turning round to face the Orientalist.

"Yes, the base. It's quite magnificent, fifteenth century, undoubtedly a work of genius, I can't imagine how . . . "

"Lot No. 103," announced the auctioneer. "What am I bid for this magnificent example of . . . "

The expert turned out to be right in his assessment. At the auction at Sotheby's that Thursday morning, I obtained the little emperor for 720 guineas. And the base? That was acquired by an American gentleman of not unknown parentage for 22,000 guineas.

THE WINE
TASTER

THE FIRST OCCASION I MET Sefton Hamilton was in late August last year when my wife and I were dining with Henry and Suzanne Kennedy at their home in Warwick Square.

Hamilton was one of those unfortunate men who have inherited immense wealth but not a lot more. He was able quickly to convince us that he had little time to read and no time to attend the theater or opera. However, this did not prevent him from holding opinions on every subject from Shaw to Pavarotti, from Gorbachev to Picasso. He remained puzzled, for instance, as to what the unemployed had to complain about when their welfare check was just less than what he was currently paying the laborers on his estate. In any case, they only spent it on bingo and drinking, he assured us.

Drinking brings me to the other dinner guest that night— Freddie Barker, the president of the Wine Society, who sat opposite my wife and, unlike Hamilton, hardly uttered a word. Henry had assured me over the phone that Barker had not only managed to get the Society back on to a proper financial footing but was also acknowledged as a leading authority on his subject. I looked forward to picking up useful bits of inside knowledge. Whenever Barker was allowed to get a word in edgewise, he showed enough knowledge of the topic under discussion to convince me that he would be fascinating if only Hamilton would remain silent long enough for him to speak.

While our hostess produced as a starter a spinach soufflé that melted in the mouth, Henry moved round the table pouring each of us a glass of wine.

Barker sniffed his appreciatively. "Appropriate in bicentennial year that we should be drinking an Australian Chablis of

515

such fine vintage. I feel sure their whites will soon be making the French look to their laurels."

"Australian?" said Hamilton in disbelief as he put down his glass. "How could a nation of beer swiggers begin to understand the first thing about producing a half decent wine?"

"I think you'll find," began Barker, "that the Australians—"

"Bicentennial, indeed," Hamilton continued. "Let's face it, they're only celebrating two hundred years of parole." No one laughed except Hamilton. "I'd still pack the rest of our criminals off there, given half a chance."

No one doubted him.

Hamilton sipped the wine tentatively, like a man who fears he is about to be poisoned, then began to explain why, in his considered view, judges were far too lenient with petty criminals. I found myself concentrating more on the food than the incessant flow of my neighbor's views.

I always enjoy Beef Wellington, and Suzanne can produce a pastry that doesn't flake when cut and meat that's so tender that once one has finished a first helping, Oliver Twist comes to mind. It certainly helped me to endure Hamilton's pontificating. Barker managed to pass an appreciative comment to Henry on the quality of the Bordeaux between Hamilton's opinions on the chances of Paddy Ashdown reviving the Liberal Party and the role of Arthur Scargill in the trade union movement, allowing no one the chance to reply.

"I don't allow my staff to belong to any union," Hamilton declared, gulping down his drink. "I run a closed shop." He laughed once more at his own joke and held his empty glass high in the air as if it would be filled by magic. In fact it was filled by Henry with a discretion that shamed Hamilton—not that he noticed. In the brief pause that followed, my wife suggested that perhaps the trade union movement had been born out of a response to a genuine social need.

"Balderdash, madam," said Hamilton. "With great respect, the trade unions have been the single most important factor in the decline of Britain as we know it. They've no interest in anybody but themselves. You only have to look at Ron Todd and the whole Ford fiasco to understand that."

Suzanne began to clear the plates away, and I noticed she took the opportunity to nudge Henry, who quickly changed the subject.

Moments later a raspberry meringue glazed with a thick sauce appeared. It seemed a pity to cut such a creation, but Suzanne carefully divided six generous helpings like a nanny feeding her charges, while Henry uncorked a 1981 Sauternes. Barker literally licked his lips in anticipation.

"And another thing," Hamilton was saying. "The prime minister has got far too many wets in her cabinet for my liking."

"With whom would you replace them?" asked Barker innocently.

Herod would have had little trouble in convincing the list of gentlemen Hamilton proffered that the slaughter of the innocents was merely an extension of the child care program.

Once again I became more interested in Suzanne's culinary efforts, especially since she had allowed me an indulgence: Cheddar was to be served as the final course. I knew the moment I tasted it that it had been purchased from the Alvis Brothers' farm in Keynsham; we all have to be knowledgeable about something, and cheddar is my speciality.

To accompany the cheese, Henry supplied a port that was to be the highlight of the evening. "Sandeman 1970," he said in an aside to Barker as he poured the first drops into the expert's glass.

"Yes, of course," said Barker, holding it to his nose. "I would have known it anywhere. Typical Sandeman warmth but with real body. I hope you've laid some down, Henry," he added. "You'll enjoy it even more in your old age."

"Think you're a bit of an authority on wines, do you?" said Hamilton, the first question he had asked all evening.

"Not exactly," began Barker, "but I—"

"You're all a bunch of humbugs, the lot of you," interrupted Hamilton. "You sniff and you swirl, you taste and you spit, then you spout a whole lot of gobbledygook and expect us to swallow it. Body and warmth be damned. You can't take me in that easily."

"No one was trying to," said Barker with feeling.

"You've been keen to put one over on us all evening," replied Hamilton, "with your 'Yes, of course, I'd have known it any-where' routine. Come on, admit it."

"I didn't mean to suggest—" added Barker.

"I'll prove it, if you like," said Hamilton.

The five of us stared at the ungracious guest and, for the first time that evening, I wondered what could possibly be coming next.

"I have heard it said," continued Hamilton, "that Sefton Hall boasts one of the finest wine cellars in England. It was laid down by my father and his father before him, though I confess I haven't found the time to continue the tradition." Barker nodded in belief. "But my butler knows exactly what I like. I therefore invite you, sir, to join me for lunch on the Saturday after next, when I produce four wines of the finest vintage for your consideration. And I offer you a wager," he added, looking straight at Barker. "Five hundred pounds to fifty a bottle—tempting odds, I'm sure you'll agree—that you will be unable to name any one of them." He stared belligerently at the distin-guished president of the Wine Society.

"The sum is so large that I could not consider—"

"Unwilling to take up the challenge, eh, Barker? Then you are, sir, a coward as well as a humbug."

After the embarrassing pause that followed, Barker replied, "As you wish, sir. It appears I am left with no choice but to accept your challenge."

A satisfied grin appeared on the other man's face. "You must come along as a witness, Henry," he said, turning to our host. "And why don't you bring along that author johnny?" he added, pointing at me. "Then he'll really have something to write about for a change."

From Hamilton's manner it was obvious that the feelings of our wives were not to be taken into consideration. Mary gave me a wry smile.

Henry looked anxiously toward me, but I was quite content to be an observer of this unfolding drama. I nodded my assent.

"Good," said Hamilton, rising from his place, his napkin still tucked under his collar. "I look forward to seeing the three of

you at Sefton Hall on Saturday week. Shall we say twelve-thirty?"
He bowed to Suzanne.

"I won't be able to join you, I'm afraid," she said, clearing up
any lingering doubt she might have been included in the invitation. "I always have lunch with my mother on Saturdays."

Hamilton waved a hand to signify that it did not concern
him one way or the other.

After the strange guest had left we sat in silence for some
moments before Henry volunteered a statement. "I'm sorry
about all that," he began. "His mother and my aunt are old
friends, and she's asked me on several occasions to have him
over to dinner. It seems no one else will."

"Don't worry," said Barker eventually. "I'll do my best not to
let you down. And in return for such excellent hospitality perhaps both of you would be kind enough to leave Saturday
evening free? There is," he explained, "an inn near Sefton Hall
I have wanted to visit for some time: the Hamilton Arms. The
food, I'm assured, is more than adequate but the wine list
is . . ." he hesitated, "considered by experts to be exceptional."

Henry and I both checked our diaries and readily accepted
his invitation.

I thought a great deal about Sefton Hamilton during the next
ten days and awaited our lunch with a mixture of apprehension
and anticipation. On the Saturday morning Henry drove the
three of us down to Sefton Park and we arrived a little after
twelve thirty. Actually we passed through the massive wrought-
iron gates at twelve thirty precisely, but did not reach the front
door of the house until twelve thirty-seven.

The great oak door was opened before we had a chance to
knock by a tall elegant man in a tail coat, wing collar and black
tie. He informed us that he was Adams, the butler. He then
escorted us to the morning room, where we were greeted by a
large log fire. Above it hung a picture of a disapproving man
who I presumed was Sefton Hamilton's grandfather. On the
other walls were a massive tapestry of the Battle of Waterloo
and an enormous oil of the Crimean War. Antique furniture lit-
tered the room and the one sculpture on display was of a Greek

figure throwing a discus. Looking around, I reflected that only the telephone belonged to the present century.

Sefton Hamilton entered the room as a gale might hit an unhappy seaside town. Immediately he stood with his back to the fire, blocking any heat we might have been appreciating.

"Whiskey!" he bellowed as Adams appeared once again. "Barker?"

"Not for me," said Barker with a thin smile.

"Ah," said Hamilton. "Want to keep your taste buds at their most sensitive, eh?"

Barker did not reply. Before we went into lunch we learned that the estate was seven thousand acres in size and had some of the finest shooting outside of Scotland. The Hall had one hundred and twelve rooms, one or two of which Hamilton had not visited since he was a child. The roof itself, he assured us finally, was an acre and a half, a statistic that will long remain in my memory as it is the same size as my garden.

The longcase clock in the corner of the room struck one. "Time for the contest to begin," declared Hamilton, and marched out of the room like a general who assumes his troops will follow him without question. We did, all the way down thirty yards of corridor to the dining room. The four of us then took our places around a seventeenth-century oak table that could comfortably have seated twenty.

Adorning the center of the table were two Georgian decanters and two unlabelled bottles. The first bottle was filled with a clear white wine, the first decanter with a red, the second bottle with a richer white, and the second decanter with a tawny red substance. In front of the four wines were four white cards. By each lay a slim bundle of fifty-pound notes.

Hamilton took his place in the large chair at the top of the table while Barker and I sat opposite each other in the center, facing the wine, leaving Henry to occupy the final place at the far end of the table.

The butler stood one pace behind his master's chair. He nodded and four footmen appeared, bearing the first course. A fish-and-prawn terrine was placed in front of each of us. Adams received a nod from his master before he picked up the first bottle and began to fill Barker's glass. Barker waited for the butler to go around the table and fill the other three glasses before he began his ritual.

First he swirled the wine around while at the same time studying it carefully. Then he sniffed it. He hesitated and a surprised look came over his face. He took a sip.

"Um," he said eventually. "I confess, quite a challenge." He sniffed it again just to be sure. Then he looked up and gave a smile of satisfaction. Hamilton stared at him, his mouth slightly open, although he remained unusually silent.

Barker took one more sip. "Montagny Tête de Cuvée 1985," he declared with the confidence of an expert, "bottled by Louis Latour." We all looked toward Hamilton, who, in contrast, displayed an unhappy frown.

"You're right," said Hamilton. "It was bottled by Latour. But that's about as clever as telling us that Heinz bottles tomato ketchup. And, since my father died in 1984, I can assure you, sir, you are mistaken." He looked round at his butler to confirm the statement. Adams's face remained inscrutable. Barker turned over the card. It read: "Chevalier Montrachet les Demoiselles 1983." He stared at the card, obviously unable to believe his eyes.

"One down and three to go," Hamilton declared, oblivious to Barker's reaction. The footmen reappeared and took away the fish plates, to replace them a few moments later with lightly cooked grouse. While its accompaniments were being served, Barker did not speak. He just stared at the other three decanters, not even hearing his host inform Henry who his guests were to be for the first shoot of the season the following week. I remember that the names corresponded roughly with the ones Hamilton had suggested for his ideal cabinet.

Barker nibbled at the grouse as he waited for Adams to fill a glass from the first decanter. He had not finished his terrine after the opening failure, only taking the occasional sip of water.

"Since Adams and I spent a considerable part of our morning selecting the wines for this little challenge, let us hope you can do better this time," said Hamilton, unable to hide his satisfaction. Barker once again began to swirl the wine around. He seemed to take longer this time, sniffing it several times before putting his glass to his lips and finally sipping from it.

A smile of instant recognition appeared on his face and he did not hesitate. "Château la Louvière 1978."

"This time you have the correct year, sir, but you have insulted the wine."

Immediately Barker turned the card over and read it out incredulously: Château Lafite 1978. Even I knew that to be one of the finest Bordeaux one might ever hope to taste. Barker lapsed into a deep silence and continued to nibble at his food. Hamilton appeared to be enjoying the wine almost as much as the half-time score. "One hundred pounds to me, nothing to the president of the Wine Society," he reminded us. Embarrassed, Henry and I tried to keep the conversation going until the third course had been served—a lemon-and-lime soufflé that could not compare in presentation or subtlety with any of Suzanne's offerings.

"Shall we move on to my third challenge?" asked Hamilton crisply.

Once again Adams picked up a decanter and began to pour the wine. I was surprised to see that he spilled a little as he filled Barker's glass.

"Clumsy oaf," barked Hamilton.

"I do apologize, sir," said Adams. He removed the spilled drop from the wooden table with a napkin. As he did so he stared at Barker with a desperate look that I felt sure had nothing to do with the spilling of the wine. However, he remained mute as he continued to circle the table.

Once again Barker went through his ritual, the swirling, the sniffing, and finally the tasting. This time he took even longer. Hamilton became impatient and drummed the great Jacobean table with his podgy fingers.

"It's a Sauternes," began Barker.

"Any halfwit could tell you that," said Hamilton. "I want to know the year and the vintage."

His guest hesitated.

"Château Guiraud 1976," he said flatly.

"At least you are consistent," said Hamilton. "You're always wrong."

Barker flicked over the card.

"Château d'Yquem 1980," he said in disbelief. It was a vintage that I had only seen at the bottom of wine lists in expensive restaurants and had never had the privilege of tasting. It puzzled me greatly that Barker could have been wrong about the Mona Lisa of wines.

Barker quickly turned toward Hamilton to protest and must have seen Adams standing behind his master, all six feet three of the man trembling, at exactly the same time I did. I wanted Hamilton to leave the room so I could ask Adams what was making him so fearful, but the owner of Sefton Hall was now in full cry.

Meanwhile Barker gazed at the butler for a moment more and, sensing his discomfort, lowered his eyes and contributed nothing else to the conversation until the port was poured some twenty minutes later.

"Your last chance to avoid complete humiliation," said Hamilton.

A cheese board, displaying several varieties, was brought round and each guest selected his choice—I stuck to a cheddar that I could have told Hamilton had not been made in Somerset. Meanwhile the port was poured by the butler, who was now as white as a sheet. I began to wonder if he was going to faint, but somehow he managed to fill all four glasses before returning to stand a pace behind his master's chair. Hamilton noticed nothing untoward.

Barker drank the port, not bothering with any of his previous preliminaries.

"Taylor's," he began.

"Agreed," said Hamilton. "But as there are only three decent suppliers of port in the world, the year can be all that matters—as you, in your exalted position, must be well aware, Mr. Barker."

Freddie nodded his agreement. "Nineteen seventy-five," he said firmly, then quickly flicked the card over.

"Taylor's 1927," I read upside-down.

Once again Barker turned sharply toward his host, who was rocking with laughter. The butler stared back at his master's guest with haunted eyes. Barker hesitated only for a moment before removing a checkbook from his inside pocket. He filled in the name "Sefton Hamilton" and the figure of two hundred pounds. He signed it and wordlessly passed the check along the table to his host.

"That was only half the bargain," said Hamilton, enjoying every moment of his triumph.

Barker rose, paused and said, "I am a humbug."

"You are indeed, sir," said Hamilton.

After spending three of the most unpleasant hours of my life, I managed to escape with Henry and Freddie Barker a little after four o'clock. As Henry drove away from Sefton Hall neither of us uttered a word. Perhaps we both felt that Barker should be allowed the first comment.

"I fear, gentlemen," he said eventually, "I shall not be good company for the next few hours, and so I will, with your permission, take a brisk walk and join you both for dinner at the Hamilton Arms around seven-thirty. I have booked a table for eight o'clock." Without another word, Barker signaled that Henry should bring the car to a halt, and we watched as he climbed out and headed off down a country lane. Henry did not drive on until his friend was well out of sight.

My sympathies were entirely with Barker, although I remained puzzled by the whole affair. How could the president of the Wine Society make such basic mistakes? After all, I could read one page of Dickens and know it wasn't Graham Greene.

Like Dr. Watson, I felt I required a fuller explanation.

Barker found us sitting round the fire in the private bar at the Hamilton Arms a little after seven-thirty that night. Following his exercise, he appeared in far better spirits. He chatted about nothing consequential and didn't once mention what had taken place at lunchtime.

It must have been a few minutes later, when I turned to check the old clock above the door, that I saw Hamilton's butler seated at the bar in earnest conversation with the innkeeper. I would have thought nothing of it had I not noticed the same terrified look that I had witnessed earlier in the afternoon as he pointed in our direction. The innkeeper appeared equally anxious, as if he had been found guilty of serving half measures by a customs and excise officer.

He picked up some menus and walked over to our table.

"We've no need for those," said Barker. "Your reputation goes before you. We are in your hands. Whatever you suggest we will happily consume."

"Thank you, sir," he said and passed our host the wine list.

Barker studied the contents inside the leather-bound covers for some time before a large smile appeared on his face. "I think you had better select the wines as well," he said, "as I have a feeling you know the sort of thing I would expect."

"Of course, sir," said the innkeeper, as Freddie passed back the wine list, leaving me totally mystified, remembering that this was Barker's first visit to the inn.

The innkeeper left for the kitchens while we chatted away and didn't reappear for some fifteen minutes.

"Your table is ready, gentlemen," he said, and we followed him into an adjoining dining room. There were only a dozen tables, and since ours was the last to be filled there was no doubting the inn's popularity.

The innkeeper had selected a light supper of consommé, followed by thin slices of duck, almost as if he had known that we would be unable to handle another heavy meal after our lunch at the Hall.

I was also surprised to find that all the wines he had chosen were served in decanters, and I assumed that the innkeeper must therefore have selected the house wines. As each was poured and consumed, I admit that, to my untutored palate, they seemed far superior to those I had drunk at Sefton Hall earlier that day. Barker certainly seemed to linger over every mouthful and on one occasion said appreciatively, "This is the real McCoy."

At the end of the evening, when our table had been cleared,

we sat back and enjoyed a magnificent port and smoked cigars.

It was at this point that Henry mentioned Hamilton for the first time.

"Are you going to let us into the mystery of what really happened at lunch today?" he asked.

"I'm still not altogether sure myself," came back Barker's reply, "but I am certain of one thing: Mr. Hamilton's father was a man who knew his wines, while his son doesn't."

I would have pressed Barker further on the subject if the innkeeper had not arrived by his side at that moment.

"An excellent meal," Barker declared. "And as for the wine—quite exceptional."

"You are kind, sir," said the innkeeper, as he handed him the bill.

My curiosity got the better of me, I'm sorry to admit, and I glanced at the bottom of the slim strip of paper. I couldn't believe my eyes—the bill came to two hundred pounds.

To my surprise, Barker only commented, "Very reasonable, considering." He wrote out a check and passed it over to the innkeeper. "I have only tasted Château d'Yquem 1980 once before today," he added, "and Taylor's 1927 never."

The innkeeper smiled. "I hope you enjoyed them both, sir. I feel sure you wouldn't have wanted to see them wasted on a humbug."

Barker nodded his agreement.

I watched as the innkeeper left the dining room and returned to his place behind the bar.

He passed the check over to Adams the butler, who studied it for a moment, smiled, and then tore it into little pieces.

TIMEO
DANAOS . . .

ARNOLD BACON WOULD HAVE made a fortune if he hadn't taken his father's advice.

Arnold's occupation, as described in his passport, was "banker." For those of you who are pedantic about such matters, he was the branch manager of Barclays Bank in St. Albans, Hertfordshire, which in banking circles is about the equivalent of being a captain in the Royal Army Pay Corps.

His passport also stated that he was born in 1937, was five feet nine inches tall, with sandy hair and no distinguishing marks—although in fact he had several lines on his forehead, which served only to prove that he frowned a great deal.

He was a member of the local Rotary Club (hon. treasurer), the Conservative Party (branch vice-chairman), and was a past secretary of the St. Albans Festival. He had also played rugby for the Old Albanians Second Fifteen in the 1960s and cricket for St. Albans Cricket Club in the 1970s. His only exercise for the past two decades, however, had been the occasional round of golf with his opposite number from National Westminster. Arnold did not boast a handicap.

During these excursions around the golf course Arnold would often browbeat his opponent with his conviction that he should never have been a banker in the first place. After years of handing out loans to customers who wanted to start up their own businesses, he had become painfully aware that he himself was really one of nature's born entrepreneurs. If only he hadn't listened to his father's advice and followed him into the bank, heaven knows what heights he might have reached by now.

His colleague nodded wearily, then holed a seven-foot putt, ensuring that the drinks would not be on him.

"How's Deirdre?" he asked as the two men strolled toward the clubhouse.

"Wants to buy a new dinner service," said Arnold, which slightly puzzled his companion. "Not that I can see what's wrong with our old coronation set."

When they reached the bar, Arnold checked his watch before ordering half a pint of lager for himself and a gin-and-tonic for the victor, since Deirdre wouldn't be expecting him back for at least an hour. He stopped pontificating only when another member began telling them the latest rumors about the club captain's wife.

Deirdre Bacon, Arnold's long-suffering wife, had come to accept that her husband was now too set in his ways for her to hope for any improvement. Although she had her own opinions on what would have happened to Arnold if he hadn't followed his father's advice, she no longer voiced them. At the time of their engagement she had considered Arnold Bacon "quite a catch." But as the years passed, she had become more realistic about her expectations, and after two children, one of each sex, she had settled into the life of a housewife and mother—not that anything else had ever been seriously contemplated.

The children had now grown up, Justin to become a solicitor's clerk in Chelmsford, and Virginia to marry a local boy whom Arnold described as an official with British Rail. Deirdre, more accurately, told her friends at the hairdresser's that Keith was a train driver.

For the first ten years of their marriage, the Bacons had vacationed in Bournemouth, because Arnold's parents had always done so. They only graduated to the Costa del Sol after Arnold read in the *Daily Telegraph*'s "Sun Supplement" that that was where most bank managers were to be found during the month of August.

For many years Arnold had promised his wife that they would do "something special" when it came to celebrating their twenty-fifth wedding anniversary, though he had never actually committed himself to defining what "special" meant.

It was only when he read in the bank's quarterly staff magazine that Andrew Buxton, the chairman of Barclays, would be spending his summer sailing around the Greek islands on a private yacht that Arnold began writing to numerous cruise companies and travel agents, requesting copies of their brochures. After having studied hundreds of glossy pages, he settled on a seven-day cruise aboard the *Princess Corina*, starting out from Piraeus to sail around the Greek islands, ending up at Mykonos. Deirdre's only contribution to the discussion was that she would rather go back to the Costa del Sol and spend the money they saved on a new dinner service. She was delighted, however, to read in one of the brochures that the Greeks were famous for their pottery.

By the time they boarded the bus to Heathrow, Arnold's junior staff, fellow members of the Rotary Club, and even a few of his more select customers were becoming tired of being reminded of how Arnold would be spending his summer break. "I shall be sailing around the Greek islands on a liner," he would tell them. "Not unlike the bank's Chairman, Andrew Buxton, you know." If anyone asked Deirdre what she and Arnold were doing for their vacation, she said that they were going on a seven-day package tour, and that the one thing she hoped to come home with was a new dinner service.

The old coronation service that had been given to them by Deirdre's parents as a wedding gift some twenty-five years before was now sadly depleted. Several of the plates were chipped or broken, while the pattern of crowns and sceptes on the pieces that were still serviceable had almost faded away.

"I can't see what's wrong with it myself," said Arnold when his wife raised the subject once more as they waited in the departure lounge at Heathrow. Deirdre made no effort to list its defects again.

Arnold spent most of the flight to Athens complaining that the aircraft was full of Greeks. Deirdre didn't feel it was worth pointing out to him that, if one booked a flight with Olympic Airways, that was likely to be the outcome. She also knew his reply would be, "But it saved us twenty-four pounds."

Once they had landed at Hellenikon International Airport, the two vacationers climbed aboard a bus. Arnold doubted whether it would have passed its roadworthiness tests in St. Albans, but nevertheless it somehow managed to transport them into the center of Athens, where Arnold had booked them overnight into a two-star hotel (two Greek stars). Arnold quickly found the local branch of Barclays and cashed one of his traveler's checks, explaining to his wife that there was no point in changing more, since once they were on board the liner everything had already been paid for. He was sure that was how entrepreneurs conducted themselves.

The Bacons rose early the following morning, mainly because they hadn't been able to get a great deal of sleep. Their bodies had continually rolled to the center of the lumpy concave mattress, and their ears ached after a night resting on the brick-hard convex pillows. Even before the sun had risen, Arnold jumped out of bed and threw open the little window that looked out onto a backyard. He stretched his arms and declared he had never felt better. Deirdre didn't comment, since she was already busy packing their clothes.

Over breakfast—a meal consisting of a croissant, which Arnold felt was too sticky, and which in any case fell apart in his fingers; feta cheese, which he didn't care for the smell of; and an obstinately empty cup, because the management refused to serve tea—a long debate developed between them as to whether they should hire a taxi or take a bus to the liner. They both came to the conclusion that a taxi would be more sensible, Deirdre because she didn't want to be crammed into a hot bus with a lot of sweaty Athenians, and Arnold because he wanted to be seen arriving at the gangplank in a car.

Once Arnold had paid their bill—having checked the little row of figures presented to him three times before he was willing to part with another traveler's check—he hailed a taxi and instructed the driver to take them to the quayside. The longer than expected journey, in an ancient car with no air conditioning, did not put Arnold into a good humor.

When he first set eyes on the *Princess Corina,* Arnold was unable to mask his disappointment. The ship was neither as large nor as modern as it had appeared in the glossy brochure.

He had a feeling his chairman would not be experiencing the same problem.

Mr. and Mrs. Bacon ascended the gangplank and were escorted to their cabin, which to Arnold's dismay consisted of two bunks, a washbasin, a shower and a porthole, without even enough room between the bunks for both of them to be able to undress at the same time. Arnold pointed out to his wife that this particular cabin had certainly not been illustrated in the brochure, even if it had been described on the tariff by the encomium "de luxe."

The brochure must have been put together by an out-of-work estate agent, he concluded.

Arnold set out to take a turn around the deck—not a particularly lengthy excursion. On the way he bumped into a solicitor from Chester who had been innocently strolling with his wife in the opposite direction. After Arnold had established that Malcolm Jackson was a senior partner in his firm, and his wife, Joan, was a magistrate, he suggested they should join up for lunch.

Once they had selected their meal from the buffet, Arnold lost no time in telling his newfound friends that he was a born entrepreneur, explaining, for example, the immediate changes he would make to improve efficiency on the *Princess Corina* had he been the chairman of this particular shipping line. (The list, I fear, turned out to be far too long to include in a short story.)

The solicitor, who had not had to suffer any of Arnold's opinions before, seemed quite content to listen, while Deirdre chatted away to Joan about how she was hoping to find a new dinner service on one of the islands. "The Greeks are famous for their pottery, you know," she kept saying.

The conversation didn't vary a great deal when the two couples reunited over dinner that evening.

Although the Bacons were tired after their first day on board, neither of them slept for more than a few moments that night. But Arnold was unwilling to admit, as they bobbed across the Aegean in their little cabin, that given the choice he would have preferred the two-star hotel (two Greek stars), with its lumpy mattress and brick-hard pillows, to the bunks on which they were now being tossed from side to side.

After two days at sea the ship docked at Rhodes, and by then even Arnold had stopped describing it as a "liner." Most of the passengers piled off down the gangway, only too delighted to have the chance of spending a few hours on land.

Arnold and Malcolm beat a path to the nearest Barclays Bank to cash a traveler's check each, while Deirdre and Joan set off in the opposite direction in search of a dinner service. At the bank, Arnold immediately informed the manager who he was, ensuring that both he and Malcolm received a tiny improvement on the advertised rate of exchange.

Arnold smiled as they stepped out of the bank, and onto the hot, dusty, cobbled street. "I should have gone into futures trading, you know," he told Malcolm as they sauntered off down the hill. "I would have made a fortune."

Deirdre's quest for a dinner service didn't turn out to be quite so straightforward. The shops were numerous and varied in quality, and she quickly discovered that Rhodes boasted a great many potters. It was therefore necessary for her to establish which of them was the most highly regarded by the locals, and then find the shop that sold his work. This information was gained by talking to the old women dressed in black who could be found sitting silently on the street corners, about one in ten of whom, she discovered, had some broken English. While her husband was at the bank saving a few drachmas, Deirdre managed to find out all the inside information she required.

The four of them met at a small taverna in the center of the town for lunch. Over a plate of souvlakia Arnold tried to convince Deirdre that as they were visiting five islands in the course of the trip, it might perhaps be wise to wait until their final port of call, so they could purchase the dinner service at the last possible moment.

"Prices will undoubtedly fall," declared Arnold, "the closer we get to Athens." He spoke with the air of a true entrepreneur.

Although Deirdre had already seen a thirty-two-piece set she liked, at a price well within their budget, she reluctantly agreed to Arnold's suggestion. Her acquiescence was largely brought about by the fact that it was her husband who was in possession of all the traveler's checks.

By the time the ship had docked at Heraklion, on Crete, Arnold had vetted all the British nationals on board, and had permitted a major (Territorial Reserve) and his spouse to join their table for lunch—but only after discovering that the fellow held an account at Barclays. A dinner invitation followed once it had been established that the major occasionally played bridge with Arnold's area manager.

From that moment Arnold spent many happy hours at the bar explaining to the major or to Malcolm—neither of whom actually listened any longer—why he should never have taken his father's advice and followed him into the bank, since he was after all one of nature's born entrepreneurs.

By the time the ship had weighed anchor and sailed from Santorini, Deirdre knew exactly the type of dinner service she wanted, and how to establish quickly which potter she should trade with as soon as they set foot in a new port. But Arnold continued to insist that they should wait for the bigger market as they approached Athens—"More competition, forces prices down," he explained for the umpteenth time. Deirdre knew there was no point in telling him that prices seemed to be rising with each sea mile they covered on their journey back toward the Greek capital.

Paros only served as further proof of Deirdre's suspicions—if proof were still needed—as the prices there were noticeably steeper than they had been on Santorini. As the *Princess Corina* steamed on toward Mykonos, Deirdre felt that although their final port of call would probably be able to supply her with a satisfactory dinner service, it would surely no longer be at a price they could afford.

Arnold kept assuring her, with the confidence of a man who knows about such things, that all would be well. He even tapped the side of his nose with his forefinger. The major and Malcolm had reached the stage of simply nodding at him to indicate that they were still awake.

Deirdre was among the first down the gangplank when they docked at Mykonos that Friday morning. She had told her husband that she would carry out a reconnaissance of the pottery shops while he did the same with the banks. Joan and the major's wife were happy to accompany Deirdre, since by now she had become something of an expert on the subject of Greek pottery.

The three ladies began their search at the north end of the town, and Deirdre was relieved to find that there was a greater variety of shops in Mykonos than there had been on any of the other islands. She was also able to discover, with the help of several black-clad ladies, that the town boasted a potter of genuine fame, whose work could only be purchased from one shop, the House of Pétros.

Once Deirdre had located this establishment, she spent the rest of the morning inspecting all the dinner services they had to offer. After a couple of hours she came to the conclusion that the "Delphi" set, which was prominently displayed in the centre of the shop, would be a prized possession for any housewife in St. Albans. But as it was double the cost of anything she had seen on any of the other islands, she knew that Arnold would dismiss it as being out of their price range.

As the three ladies finally left the shop to join their husbands for lunch, a good-looking young man in a grubby T-shirt and torn jeans, with a couple of days' stubble on his chin, jumped out in front of them and asked, "You English?"

Deirdre stopped and stared into his deep blue eyes for a moment, but said nothing. Her companions stepped out into the cobbled road and quickened their pace, pretending it was not them to whom the stranger had spoken. Deirdre smiled at him as he stood to one side, allowing her to continue on her way. Arnold had warned her never to engage in conversation with the natives.

When they reached the restaurant at which they'd arranged to meet for lunch, the three ladies found their husbands drinking imported lager at the bar. Arnold was explaining to the major and Malcolm why he had refused to pay his subscription to the Conservative Party that year. "Not a penny will I part with," he insisted, "while they can't get their own house in order." Deirdre suspected that his unwillingness to pay had rather more to do with his recent defeat when he had run for chairman of the local branch.

Arnold passed the next hour offering his views on everything from defense cuts to New Age travelers to single-parent families, all of which he was resolutely against. When the bill for lunch was finally presented, he spent some considerable time working out what each of them had eaten, and therefore how much they should contribute toward the total.

Arnold had already resigned himself to the fact that he would have to allocate part of his afternoon to bargaining on Deirdre's behalf, now that she had finally found the dinner service she had set her heart on. Everyone else had agreed to come along and watch the born entrepreneur at work.

When Arnold entered the House of Pétros, he had to admit that Deirdre seemed to have "located the correct establishment." He kept repeating this observation, as if to prove that he had been right all along to insist that she wait until their final port of call before the big decision was taken. He seemed blissfully unaware of how the price of pottery had increased from island to island, and Deirdre made no attempt to enlighten him. She simply guided him over to the "Delphi" service displayed on a large table in the center of the room, and prayed. They all agreed it was quite magnificent, but when Arnold was told the price, he shook his head sadly. Deirdre would have protested, but she, like so many of the bank's customers over the years, had seen that look on her husband's face before. She therefore resigned herself to settling for the "Pharos" set—excellent, but unquestionably second best, and far more expensive than comparable sets had been on any of the other four islands.

The three wives began selecting the pieces they would like to buy, while their husbands gravely reminded them how much they could afford. The choices having been made, Arnold spent a considerable time haggling with the shopkeeper. He finally managed to get a 20 percent discount on the total. Once the figure had been established, Arnold was dispatched to find an English bank at which he could change the necessary traveler's checks. With passports and signed checks in hand, he left the shop to carry out his mission.

As Arnold stepped onto the sidewalk, the young man who had approached Deirdre leaped into his path and asked, "You English?"

"Naturally," replied Arnold, sidestepping him and marching on briskly in order to avoid any further conversation with such a scruffy individual. As he had told the major over lunch, "*Timeo Danaos et dona ferentis.*" It was the one snippet of Latin he could still recall from his schooldays.

When he had selected a bank, Arnold marched straight into the manager's office and changed everyone's checks at a minutely better rate than the one displayed on the board in the window. Pleased with his saving of fifty drachmas, he headed back to the House of Pétros.

He was displeased to find that the young man was still loitering on the pavement outside the shop. Arnold refused to favor the unshaven ruffian with even a glance, but he did catch the words, "You want to save money, Englishman?"

Arnold stopped in his tracks, as any born entrepreneur would, and turned to study more closely the loutish youth who had addressed him. He was about to continue on his way when the young man said, "I know where pottery is everything half price."

Arnold hesitated once again, and looked through the shop window to see his companions standing around waiting for his return; on the counter stood six large packages, already wrapped up and awaiting payment.

Arnold turned back to take a closer look at the inarticulate foreigner.

"Potter comes from village called Kalafatis," he said. "Bus journey only half hour, then everything half price."

While Arnold was digesting this piece of information, the young Greek's hand shot out hopefully. Arnold extracted a fifty-drachma note from the roll of money he had obtained at the bank, willing to speculate with the profit he had made on that particular transaction in exchange for the information he had just acquired—the act of a true entrepreneur, he thought as he marched triumphantly into the shop.

"I have made an important discovery," he announced, and beckoned them all into a corner to impart his inside information.

Deirdre did not seem at all convinced, until Arnold suggested, "Perhaps we might even be able to afford the 'Delphi' set you hankered after, my dear. In any case, why pay double, when the only sacrifice you need to make is a half-hour bus journey."

Malcolm nodded his agreement, as if listening to sage advice from senior counsel, and even the major, though grumbling a little, finally fell into line.

"Since we set sail for Athens early this evening," declared the major, "we ought to take the next bus to Kalafatis." Arnold nodded, and without another word led his little band out of the shop, not even glancing toward the packages that were left behind on the counter.

When they stepped out onto the street, Arnold was relieved to find that the young man who had given him the tipoff was no longer to be seen.

They came to a halt at the bus stop, where Arnold was a little disappointed to discover several passengers from the ship already standing in the line, but he persuaded himself that they would not be heading for the same destination. They waited in the hot sun for another forty minutes before a bus eventually pulled up. When Arnold first saw the vehicle, his heart sank. "Just think of how much money we'll be saving," he said when he noticed the looks of despair on the faces of his companions.

The journey across the island to the east coast might well have taken thirty minutes had it been in a Range Rover with no reason to slow down. But since the bus driver picked up everybody he saw along the way, without regard to official stops, they eventually arrived in Kalafatis an hour and twenty minutes later. Long before they had clambered off the ancient vehicle, Deirdre was exhausted, Joan was exasperated, and the major's wife was developing a migraine.

"Bus goes no further," said the driver as Arnold and his companions filed off. "Leave for return journey one hour. Last bus of the day."

The little band gazed up at the narrow, winding track that led to the potter's workplace.

"The journey was worth it for the view alone," gasped Arnold, as he came to a halt halfway along the path and gazed out over the Aegean. His companions didn't even bother to stop and look, let alone offer an opinion. It took them another ten minutes of determined walking before they reached their destination, and by then even Arnold had fallen silent.

As the six weary tourists finally entered the pottery, what breath they had left was taken away. They stood mesmerized by shelf after shelf of beautiful objects. Arnold felt a warm glow of triumph.

Deirdre immediately went about her business, and quickly located the "Delphi" dinner service. It looked even more magnificent than she remembered, but when she checked a little label that hung from a soup tureen's handle she was horrified to discover that the cost was only a little less than it had been at the House of Pétros.

Deirdre came to a decision. She turned to face her husband, who was toying with a pipe stand, and declared in a clarion voice that all could hear, "As everything is at half price, Arnold, presumably I can go ahead and buy the 'Delphi'?"

The other four swung around to see how the great entrepreneur would react. Arnold seemed to hesitate for a moment before he placed the pipe stand back on the shelf and said, "Of course, my dear. Isn't that why we came all this way in the first place?"

The three women immediately began selecting items from the shelves, finally gathering between them one dinner service, two tea sets, one coffee set, three vases, five ashtrays, two pitchers, and a toast rack. Arnold abandoned the pipe stand.

When the bill for Deirdre's purchases was presented to her husband, he hesitated once again, but he was painfully aware that all five of his shipmates were glaring at him. He reluctantly cashed his remaining traveler's checks, unwilling to bring himself even to glance at the disadvantageous exchange rate that was displayed in the window. Deirdre made no comment. Malcolm and the major silently signed away their own traveler's checks, with little appearance of triumph showing on either of their faces.

The goods having been paid for, the six tourists emerged from the workshop, laden down with shopping bags. As they began to retrace their steps back down the winding track, the door of the pottery was closed behind them.

"We'll have to get a move on if we're not going to miss the last bus," shouted Arnold as he stepped into the center of the path, avoiding a large cream Mercedes that was parked outside the workshop. "But what a worthwhile excursion," he added as they trundled off down the track. "You have to admit, I saved you all a fortune."

Deirdre was the last to leave the shop. She paused to rearrange her numerous bags, and was surprised to see a number of the pottery's staff forming a line at a table by the side of the shop. A handsome young man in a grubby T-shirt and torn jeans was presenting each of them in turn with a small brown envelope.

Deirdre couldn't take her eyes off the young man. Where had she seen him before? He looked up, and for a moment she stared into those deep blue eyes. And then she remembered. The young man shrugged his shoulders and smiled. Deirdre returned the smile, picked up her bags, and set off down the path after her companions.

As they clambered onto the bus, Deirdre was just in time to hear Arnold declare: "You know, Major, I should never have taken my father's advice and settled for the life of a banker. You see, I'm one of nature's born entre . . . "

Deirdre smiled again as she looked out of the window and watched the good-looking young man speed past them in his large cream Mercedes.

He smiled and waved to her as the last bus began its slow journey back to Mykonos.

NOT THE
REAL THING

GERALD HASKINS AND WALTER RAMSBOTTOM had been eating
corn flakes for over a year.

"I'll swap you my MC and DSO for your VC," said Walter, on
the way to school one morning.

"Never," said Gerald. "In any case, it takes ten boxtops to get
a VC, and you only need two for an MC or a DSO."

Gerald went on collecting boxtops until he had every medal
displayed on the back of the box.

Walter never got the VC.

Angela Bradbury thought they were both silly.

"They're only replicas," she continually reminded them, "not
the real thing. And *I* am only interested in the real thing," she
told them haughtily.

Neither Gerald nor Walter cared for Angela's opinion at the
time, both boys still being more interested in medals than the
views of the opposite sex.

Kellogg's offer of free medals ended on January 1, 1950, just
at the time when Gerald had managed to complete the set.

Walter gave up eating corn flakes.

Children of the fifties were then given the opportunity to discover the world of Meccano. Meccano demanded eating even
more corn flakes, and within a year Gerald had collected a
large enough set to build bridges, pontoons, cranes, and even
an office block.

Gerald's family nobly went on munching corn flakes, but
when he told them he wanted to build a whole town—Kellogg's
positively final offer—it took nearly all his friends in the fifth
grade at Hull Grammar School to assist him in consuming
enough breakfast cereal to complete his ambition.

Walter Ramsbottom refused to be of assistance.

Angela Bradbury's help was never sought.

All three continued on their separate ways.

Two years later, when Gerald Haskins won a place at Durham University, no one was surprised that he chose to study engineering and listed as his main hobby collecting medals.

Walter Ramsbottom joined his father in the family jewelry business and started courting Angela Bradbury.

It was during the spring break in Gerald's second year at Durham that he came across Walter and Angela again. They were sitting in the same row at a Bach cello concert in Hull Town Hall. Walter told him in the intermission that they had just become engaged but had not yet settled on a date for the wedding.

Gerald hadn't seen Angela for over a year, but this time he did listen to her opinions, because like Walter he fell in love with her.

He replaced eating corn flakes with continually inviting Angela out to dinner in an effort to win her away from his old rival.

Gerald notched up another victory when Angela returned her engagement ring to Walter a few days before Christmas.

Walter spread it around that Gerald only wanted to marry Angela because her father was chairman of the Hull City Amenities Committee and he was hoping to get a job with the council after he'd taken his degree at Durham. When the invitations for the wedding were sent out, Walter was not on the guest list.

Mr. and Mrs. Haskins traveled to Multavia for their honeymoon, partly because they couldn't afford Nice and didn't want to go to Cleethorpes. In any case, the local travel agent was making a special offer for those considering a visit to the tiny kingdom sandwiched between Austria and Czechoslovakia.

When the newly married couple arrived at their hotel in Teske, the capital, they discovered why the terms had been so reasonable.

Multavia was, in 1959, going through an identity crisis as it attempted to adjust to yet another treaty drawn up by a Dutch lawyer in Geneva, written in French, but with the Russians and Americans in mind. However, thanks to King Alfons III, its shrewd and popular monarch, the kingdom continued to enjoy uninterrupted grants from the West and non-disruptive visits from the East.

The capital of Multavia, the Haskinses were quickly to discover, had an average temperature of ninety-two degrees Fahrenheit in June, no rainfall, and the remains of a sewage system that had been indiscriminately bombed by both sides between 1939 and 1944. Angela actually found herself holding her nose as she walked through the cobbled streets. The People's Hotel claimed to have forty-five rooms, but what the brochure did not point out was that only three of them had bathrooms, and none of those had bath plugs. Then there was the food, or lack of it; for the first time in his life Gerald lost weight.

The honeymoon couple were also to discover that Multavia boasted no monuments, art galleries, theaters, or opera houses worthy of the name, and that the outlying country was flatter and less interesting than the fens of Cambridgeshire. The kingdom had no coastline and the only river, the Plotz, flowed from Germany and on into Russia, thus ensuring that none of the locals trusted it.

By the end of their honeymoon the Haskinses were only too pleased to find that Multavia did not boast a national airline. BOAC got them home safely, and that would have been the end of Gerald's experience of Multavia had it not been for those sewers—or the lack of them.

Once the Haskinses had returned to Hull, Gerald took up his appointment as an assistant in the engineering department of the city council. His first job was as a third engineer with special responsibility for the city's sewerage. Most ambitious young men would have treated such an appointment as nothing more than a step on life's ladder. Gerald however did not. He quickly made contact with all the leading sewerage companies, their advisers, and his opposite numbers throughout the county.

Two years later he was able to put in front of his father-in-law's committee a paper showing how the council could save a considerable amount of the taxpayers' money by redeveloping its sewerage system.

The committee were impressed and decided to carry out Mr. Haskins's recommendation, and at the same time appointed him second engineer.

That was the first occasion Walter Ramsbottom ran for the council; he wasn't elected.

When, three years later, the network of little tunnels and waterways had been completed, Gerald's diligence was rewarded by his appointment as deputy borough engineer. In the same year his father-in-law became mayor, and Walter Ramsbottom became a councillor.

Councils up and down the country were now acknowledging Gerald as a man whose opinion should be sought if they had any anxieties about their sewerage system. This provoked an irreverent round of jokes at every Rotary Club dinner Gerald attended, but they nevertheless still hailed him as the leading authority in his field, or drain.

When in 1966 the Borough of Halifax considered putting out to tender the building of a new sewerage system they first consulted Gerald Haskins—Yorkshire being the one place on earth where a prophet is with honor in his own country.

After spending a day in Halifax with the town council's senior engineer and realizing how much had to be spent on the new system, Gerald remarked to his wife, not for the first time, "Where there's muck there's brass." But it was Angela who was shrewd enough to work out just how much of that brass her husband could get hold of with the minimum of risk. During the next few days Gerald considered his wife's proposition, and when he returned to Halifax the following week it was not to visit the council chambers but the Midland Bank. Gerald did not select the Midland by chance; the manager of the bank was also chairman of the planning committee on the Halifax borough council.

A deal that suited both sides was struck between the two Yorkshiremen, and with the bank's blessing Gerald resigned his position as deputy borough engineer and formed a private company. When he presented his tender, in competition with several large organizations from London, no one was surprised that Haskins of Hull was selected unanimously by the planning committee to carry out the job.

Three years later Halifax had a fine new sewerage system, and the Midland Bank was delighted to be holding Haskins of Hull's company account.

Over the next fifteen years Chester, Runcorn, Huddersfield, Darlington, Macclesfield, and York were jointly and severally grateful for the services rendered to them by Gerald Haskins, of Haskins & Co PLC.

Haskins & Co. (International) PLC then began contract work in Dubai, Lagos, and Rio de Janeiro. In 1983 Gerald received the Queen's Award for Industry from a grateful government, and a year later he was made a Commander of the British Empire by a grateful monarch.

The investiture took place at Buckingham Palace in the same year that King Alfons III of Multavia died and was succeeded by his son King Alfons IV. The newly crowned king decided something finally had to be done about the drainage problems of Teske. It had been his father's dying wish that his people should not go on suffering those unseemly smells, and King Alfons IV did not intend to bequeath the problem to *his* son.

After much begging and borrowing from the West, and much visiting and talking with the East, the newly anointed monarch decided to invite tenders for a new sewerage system in the kingdom's capital.

The tender document supplying several pages of details and listing the problems facing any engineer who wished to tackle them arrived with a thud on most of the boardroom tables of the world's major engineering companies. Once the paperwork had been seriously scrutinized and the realistic opportunity for a profit considered, King Alfons IV received only a few replies. Nevertheless, the king was able to sit up all night considering the merits of the three interested companies that had been shortlisted. Kings are also human, and when Alfons discovered that Gerald had chosen Multavia for his honeymoon some twenty-five years before, it tipped the balance. By the time Alfons IV fell asleep that morning he had decided to accept Haskins & Co (International) PLC's tender.

And thus Gerald Haskins made his second visit to Multavia, this time accompanied by a site manager, three draftsmen, and eleven engineers. Gerald had a private audience with the king and assured him the job would be completed on time and for the price specified. He also told the king how much he was enjoying his second visit to his country. However, when he returned to England he assured his wife that there was still little in Multavia that could be described as entertainment before or after the hour of seven.

A few years later, and after some considerable haggling over the increase in the cost of materials, Teske ended up with one of the finest sewage systems in Central Europe. The king was delighted—although he continued to grumble about how Haskins & Co had overrun the original contract price. The words "contingency payment" had to be explained to the monarch several times, who realized that the extra £240,000 would in turn have to be explained to the East and "borrowed" from the West. After many veiled threats and "without prejudice" solicitors' letters, Haskins & Co received the final payment, but not until the King had been given a further grant from the British government, a payment which involved the Midland Bank, Sloane Street, transferring a sum of money to the Midland Bank, High Street, Hull, without Multavia ever getting its hands on it. This was after all, Gerald explained to his wife, how most overseas aid was distributed.

Thus the story of Gerald Haskins and the drainage problems of Teske might have ended, had not the British foreign secretary decided to pay a visit to the kingdom of Multavia.

The original purpose of the foreign secretary's European trip was to take in Warsaw and Prague, in order to see how glasnost and perestroika were working in those countries. But when the Foreign Office discovered how much aid had been allocated to Multavia, and after they explained to their minister its role as a buffer state, the foreign secretary decided to accept King Alfons's long-standing invitation to visit the tiny kingdom. Such excursions to smaller countries by British foreign secretaries usually take place in airport lounges, a habit the British picked up from Henry Kissinger and, later, Comrade Gorbachev; but not on this occasion. It was felt that Multavia warranted a full day.

As the hotels had improved only slightly since the time of Gerald's honeymoon, the foreign secretary was invited to lodge at the palace. He was asked by the king to undertake only two official engagements during his brief stay: the opening of the capital's new sewage system, and a formal banquet.

Once the foreign secretary had agreed to these requests the king invited Gerald and his wife to be present at the opening ceremony—at their own expense. When the day of the opening came the Foreign Secretary delivered the appropriate speech for the occasion. He first praised Gerald Haskins for a remarkable piece of work in the great tradition of British engineering, then commended Multavia for her shrewd common sense in awarding the contract to a British company in the first place. The foreign secretary omitted to mention the fact that the British government had ended up underwriting the entire project. Gerald, however, was touched by the minister's words, and said as much to the foreign secretary after the latter had pulled the lever that opened the first sluice gate.

That evening in the palace there was a banquet for over three hundred guests, including the ambassadorial corps and several leading British businessmen. There followed the usual interminable speeches about "historic links," Multavia's role in Anglo–Soviet affairs, and the "special relationship" with Britain's own royal family.

The highlight of the evening, however, came after the speeches when the king made two investitures. The first was the award of the Order of the Peacock (Second Class) to the foreign secretary. "The highest award a commoner can receive," the King explained to the assembled audience, "as the Order of the Peacock (First Class) is reserved for royalty and heads of state."

The King then announced a second investiture. The Order of the Peacock (Third Class) was to be awarded to Gerald Haskins, CBE, for his work on the drainage system of Teske. Gerald was surprised and delighted as he was conducted from his place on the top table to join the king, who leaned forward to put a large gold chain encrusted with gems of various colors and sizes over his visitor's head. Gerald took two respectful paces backward and bowed low, as the foreign secretary looked up from his seat and smiled encouragingly at him.

Gerald was the last foreign guest to leave the banquet that night. Angela, who had left on her own over two hours before, had already fallen asleep by the time he returned to their hotel room. He placed the chain on the bed, undressed, put on his pajamas, checked his wife was still asleep, and then placed the chain back over his head to rest on his shoulders.

Gerald stood and looked at himself in the bathroom mirror for several minutes. He could not wait to return home.

The moment Gerald got back to Hull he dictated a letter to the Foreign Office. He requested permission to be allowed to wear his new award on those occasions when it stipulated on the bottom right-hand corner of invitation cards that decorations and medals should be worn. The Foreign Office duly referred the matter to the palace, where the queen, a distant cousin of King Alfons IV, agreed to the request.

The next official occasion at which Gerald was given the opportunity to sport the Order of the Peacock was the mayor-making ceremony held in the chamber of Hull's City Hall, which was to be preceded by dinner at the Guildhall.

Gerald returned especially from Lagos for the occasion, and even before changing into his dinner jacket couldn't resist a glance at the Order of the Peacock (Third Class). He opened the box that held his prize possession and stared down in disbelief: the gold had become tarnished, and one of the stones looked as if it was coming loose. Mrs. Haskins stopped dressing in order to steal a glance at the order. "It's not gold," she declared with a simplicity that would have stopped the IMF in its tracks.

Gerald offered no comment and quickly fixed the loose

stone back in place with Krazy Glue but he had to admit to himself that the craftmanship didn't bear careful scrutiny. Neither of them mentioned the subject again on their journey to Hull's City Hall.

Some of the guests during the Mayor's dinner that night at the Guildhall enquired after the history of the Order of the Peacock (Third Class), and although it gave Gerald some considerable satisfaction to explain how he had come by the distinction and indeed the Queen's permission to wear it on official occasions, he felt one or two of his colleagues had been less than awed by the tarnished peacock. Gerald also considered it was somewhat unfortunate that they had ended up on the same table as Walter Ramsbottom, now the deputy mayor.

"I suppose it would be hard to put a true value on it," said Walter, staring disdainfully at the chain.

"It certainly would," said Gerald firmly.

"I didn't mean a monetary value," said the jeweler with a smirk. "That would be only too easy to ascertain. I meant a sentimental value, of course."

"Of course," said Gerald. "And are you expecting to be the mayor next year?" he asked, trying to change the subject.

"It is the tradition," said Walter, "that the deputy succeeds the mayor if he doesn't serve for a second year. And be assured, Gerald, that I shall see to it that you are placed on the top table for that occasion." Walter paused. "The mayor's chain, you know, is fourteen-carat gold."

Gerald left the banquet early that evening, determined to do something about the Order of the Peacock before it was Walter's turn to be mayor.

None of Gerald's friends would have described him as an extravagant man, and even his wife was surprised at the whim of vanity that was to follow. At nine o'clock the next morning Gerald rang his office to say he would not be in to work that day. He then traveled by train to London, to visit Bond Street in general and a famed jeweler in particular.

The door of the Bond Street shop was opened for Gerald by a sergeant from the Corps of Commissionaires. Once he had stepped inside Gerald explained his problem to the tall, thin gentleman in a black suit who had come forward to welcome him. He was then led to a circular glass counter in the middle of the shop floor.

"Our Mr. Pullinger will be with you in a moment," he was assured. Moments later Asprey's fine-gems expert arrived and happily agreed to Gerald's request to value the Order of the Peacock (Third Class). Mr Pullinger placed the chain on a black velvet cushion before closely studying the stones through a small eyeglass.

After a cursory glance he frowned with the disappointment of a man who has won third prize at a shooting range on Blackpool pier.

"So, what's it worth?" asked Gerald bluntly after several minutes had elapsed.

"Hard to put a value on something so intricately"—Pullinger hesitated—"unusual."

"The stones are glass and the gold's brass, that's what you're trying to say, isn't it, lad?"

Mr. Pullinger gave a look that indicated that he could not have put it more succinctly himself.

"You might possibly be able to get a few hundred pounds from someone who collects such objects, but . . . "

"Oh, no," said Gerald, quite offended. "I have no interest in selling it. My purpose in coming up to London was to find out if you can *copy* it."

"Copy it?" said the expert in disbelief.

"Aye," said Gerald. "First, I want every stone to be the correct gem according to its color. Second, I expect a setting that would impress a duchess. And third, I require the finest craftsman put to work on it in nothing less than eighteen-carat gold."

The expert from Asprey's, despite years of dealing with Arab clients, was unable to conceal his surprise.

"It would not be cheap," he uttered *sotto voce*. The word "cheap" was one of which Asprey's clearly disapproved.

"I never doubted that for one moment," said Gerald. "But you must understand that this is a once-in-a-lifetime honor for me. Now, when could I hope to have an estimate?"

"A month, six weeks at the most," replied the expert.

Gerald left the plush carpet of Asprey's for the sewers of Nigeria. When, a little over a month later, he flew back to London, he traveled in to the West End for his second meeting with Mr. Pullinger.

The jeweler had not forgotten Gerald Haskins and his strange request, and he quickly produced from his order book a neatly folded piece of paper. Gerald unfolded it and read the tender slowly. Requirement for customer's request: twelve diamonds, seven amethysts, three rubies, and a sapphire, all to be of the most perfect color and of the highest quality. A peacock to be sculpted in ivory and painted by a craftsman. The entire chain then to be molded in the finest eighteen-carat gold. The bottom line read: "Two hundred and eleven thousand pounds—exclusive of VAT."

Gerald, who would have thought nothing of haggling over an estimate of a few thousand pounds for roofing material or the rental of heavy equipment, or even a schedule of payments, simply asked, "When will I be able to collect it?"

"One could not be certain how long it might take to put together such a fine piece," said Mr Pullinger. "Finding stones of a perfect match and color will, I fear, take a little time." He paused. "I am also hoping that our senior craftsman will be free to work on this particular commission. He has been rather taken up lately with gifts for the queen's forthcoming visit to Saudi Arabia, so I don't think it could be ready before the end of March."

Well in time for next year's Mayor's banquet, thought Gerald. Councillor Ramsbottom would not be able to mock him this time. Fourteen-carat gold, had he said?

Lagos and Rio de Janeiro both had their sewers up and running long before Gerald was able to return to Asprey's. And he only set his eyes on the unique prize a few weeks before mayor-making day.

When Mr. Pullinger first showed his client the finished work the Yorkshireman gasped with delight. The Order was so magnificent that Gerald found it necessary to purchase a string of pearls from Asprey's to ensure a silent wife.

On his return to Hull he waited until after dinner to open the green leather box from Asprey's and surprise her with the new Order. "Fit for a monarch, lass," he assured his wife, but Angela seemed preoccupied with her pearls.

After Angela had left to wash up, her husband continued to stare for some time at the beautiful jewels so expertly crafted and superbly cut before he finally closed the box. The next morning he reluctantly took the piece around to the bank and explained that it must be kept safely locked in the vaults, as he would only be requiring to take it out once, perhaps twice, a year. He couldn't resist showing the object of his delight to the bank manager, Mr. Sedgley.

"You'll be wearing it for mayor-making day, no doubt?" Mr Sedgley enquired.

"If I'm invited," said Gerald.

"Oh, I feel sure Ramsbottom will want all his old friends to witness the ceremony. Especially you, I suspect," he added without explanation.

Gerald read the news item in the Court Circular of *The Times* to his wife over breakfast: "It has been announced from Buckingham Palace that King Alfons IV of Multavia will make a state visit to Britain between April 7th and 11th."

"I wonder if we will have an opportunity to meet the king again," said Angela.

Gerald offered no opinion.

In fact Mr. and Mrs. Gerald Haskins received two invitations connected with King Alfons's official visit, one to dine with the King at Claridge's—Multavia's London Embassy not being large enough to cater for such an occasion—and the second arriving a day later by special delivery from Buckingham Palace.

Gerald was delighted. The Peacock, it seemed, was going to get three outings in one month, as their visit to the palace was ten days before Walter Ramsbottom would be installed as mayor.

The state dinner at Claridge's was memorable, and although there were several hundred other guests, Gerald still managed to catch a moment with his host, King Alfons IV, who, he found to his pleasure, could not take his eyes off the Order of the Peacock (Third Class).

The trip to Buckingham Palace a week later was Gerald and Angela's second, following Gerald's investiture in 1984 as a Commander of the British Empire. It took Gerald almost as long to dress for the state occasion as it did his wife. He took some time fiddling with his collar to be sure that his CBE could be seen to its full advantage while the Order of the Peacock still rested squarely on his shoulders. Gerald had asked his tailor to sew little loops into his tailcoat so that the Order did not have to be continually readjusted.

When the Haskinses arrived at Buckingham Palace they followed a throng of bemedaled men and tiaraed ladies through to the state dining room, where a footman handed out seating cards to each of the guests. Gerald unfolded his to find an arrow pointing to his name. He took his wife by the arm and guided her to their places.

He noticed that Angela's head kept turning whenever she saw a tiara.

Although they were seated some distance away from Her Majesty at an offshoot of the main table, there was still a minor royal on Gerald's left and the minister of agriculture on his right. He was more than satisfied. In fact the whole evening went far too quickly, and Gerald was already beginning to feel that mayor-making day would be something of an anticlimax. Nevertheless, Gerald imagined a scene where Councillor Ramsbottom was admiring the Order of the Peacock (Third Class) while he was telling him about the dinner at the palace.

After two loyal toasts and two national anthems, the queen rose to her feet. She spoke warmly of Multavia as she addressed her three hundred guests, and affectionately of her distant cousin the king. Her Majesty added that she hoped to visit his kingdom at some time in the near future. This was greeted with considerable applause. She then concluded her speech by saying it was her intention to make two investitures.

The Queen created King Alfons IV a Knight Commander of the Royal Victorian Order (KCVO), and then Multavia's Ambassador to the Court of St. James's a commander of the same order (CVO), both being personal orders of the monarch. A box of royal blue was opened by the court chamberlain and the awards placed over the recipients' shoulders. As soon as the Queen had completed her formal duties, King Alfons rose to make his reply.

"Your Majesty," he continued after the usual formalities and thanks had been completed, "I also would like to make two awards. The first is to an Englishman who has given great service to my country through his expertise and diligence"—the king glanced in Gerald's direction. "A man," he continued, "who completed a feat of sanitary engineering that any nation on earth could be proud of and indeed, Your Majesty, it was opened by your own foreign secretary. We in the capital of Teske will remain in his debt for generations to come. We therefore bestow on Mr. Gerald Haskins, CBE, the Order of the Peacock (Second Class)."

Gerald couldn't believe his ears.

Tumultuous applause greeted a surprised Gerald as he made his way up toward their majesties. He came to a standstill behind the gilt chairs somewhere between the queen of England and the king of Multavia. The king smiled at the new recipient of the Order of the Peacock (Second Class) as the two men shook hands. But before bestowing the new honor upon him, King Alfons leaned forward and with some difficulty removed from Gerald's shoulders his Order of the Peacock (Third Class).

"You won't be needing this any longer," the king whispered in Gerald's ear.

Gerald watched in horror as his prize possession disappeared into a red leather box held open by the king's private secretary, who stood poised behind his sovereign. Gerald continued to stare at the private secretary, who was either a diplomat of the highest order or had not been privy to the king's plan, for his face showed no sign of anything untoward. Once Gerald's magnificent prize had been safely removed, the box snapped closed like a safe of which Gerald had not been told the combination.

Gerald wanted to protest, but remained speechless.

King Alfons then removed from another box the Order of the Peacock (Second Class) and placed it over Gerald's shoulders. Gerald, staring at the indifferent colored-glass stones, hesitated for a few moments before stumbling a pace back, bowing, and then returning to his place in the great dining room. He did not hear the waves of applause that accompanied him; his only thought was how he could possibly retrieve his lost chain as soon as the speeches were over. He slumped down in the chair next to his wife.

"And now," continued the king, "I wish to present a decoration that has not been bestowed on anyone since my late father's death. The Order of the Peacock (First Class), which it gives me special delight to bestow on Her Majesty Queen Elizabeth II."

The queen rose from her place as the King's private secretary once again stepped forward. In his hands was the same red leather case that had snapped shut so firmly on Gerald's unique possession. The case was reopened and the King removed the magnificent Order from the box and placed it on the shoulders of the queen. The jewels sparkled in the candlelight, and the guests gasped at the sheer magnificence of the piece.

Gerald was the only person in the room who knew its true value.

"Well, you always said it was fit for a monarch," his wife remarked as she touched her string of pearls.

"Aye," said Gerald. "But what's Ramsbottom going to say when he sees this?" he added sadly, fingering the Order of the Peacock (Second Class). "He'll know it's not the real thing."

"I don't see that it matters that much," said Angela.

"What do you mean, lass?' asked Gerald. "I'll be the laughing stock of Hull on mayor-making day."

"You should start reading the evening papers, Gerald, and stop looking in mirrors, and then you'd know Walter isn't going to be mayor this year."

"Not going to be mayor?" repeated Gerald.

"No. The present mayor has opted to do a second term, so Walter won't be mayor until next year."

"Is that right?" said Gerald with a smile.

"And if you're thinking what I think you're thinking, Gerald Haskins, this time it's going to cost you a tiara."

ONE MAN'S
MEAT . . .

COULD ANYONE BE THAT BEAUTIFUL?

I was driving round the Aldwych on my way to work when I
first saw her. She was walking up the steps of the Aldwych Theatre. If I'd stared a moment longer I would have driven into the
back of the car in front of me, but before I could confirm my
fleeting impression she had disappeared into the throng of the-
atergoers.

I spotted a parking space on my left-hand side and swung
into it at the last possible moment, without signaling, causing
the vehicle behind me to let out several appreciative blasts. I
leapt out of my car and ran back toward the theater, realizing
how unlikely it was that I'd be able to find her in such a melee,
and that even if I did, she was probably meeting a boyfriend or
husband who would turn out to be about six feet tall and
closely to resemble Harrison Ford.

Once I reached the foyer I scanned the chattering crowd. I
slowly turned 360 degrees, but could see no sign of her. Should
I try to buy a ticket? I wondered. But she could be seated anywhere—the orchestra, the dress circle, even the upper circle.
Perhaps I should walk up and down the aisles until I spotted
her. But I realized I wouldn't be allowed into any part of the
theater unless I could produce a ticket.

And then I saw her. She was standing in a line in front of the
window marked "Tonight's Performance," and was just one
away from being attended to. There were two other customers,
a young woman and a middle-aged man, waiting in line behind
her. I quickly joined the line, by which time she had reached
the front. I leaned forward and tried to overhear what she was
saying, but I could only catch the box office manager's reply:

"Not much chance with the curtain going up in a few minutes' time, madam," he was saying. "But if you leave it with me, I'll see what I can do."

She thanked him and walked off in the direction of the orchestra. My first impression was confirmed. It didn't matter if you looked from the ankles up or from the head down—she was perfection. I couldn't take my eyes off her, and I noticed that she was having exactly the same effect on several other men in the foyer. I wanted to tell them all not to bother. Didn't they realize she was with me? Or rather, that she would be by the end of the evening.

After she had disappeared from view, I craned my neck to look into the booth. Her ticket had been placed to one side. I sighed with relief as the young woman two places ahead of me presented her credit card and picked up four tickets for the dress circle.

I began to pray that the man in front of me wasn't looking for a single.

"Do you have one ticket for tonight's performance?" he asked hopefully, as the three-minute bell sounded. The man in the booth smiled.

I scowled. Should I knife him in the back, kick him in the groin, or simply scream abuse at him?

"Where would you prefer to sit, sir? The dress circle or the orchestra?"

"Don't say 'orchestra,'" I willed. "Say 'circle' . . . 'circle' . . . 'circle' . . . "

"Orchestra," he said.

"I have one on the aisle in row H," said the man in the box, checking the computer screen in front of him. I uttered a silent cheer as I realized that the theater would be trying to sell off its remaining tickets before it bothered with returns handed in by members of the public. But then, I thought, how would I get around that problem?

By the time the man in front of me had bought the ticket on the end of row H, I had my lines well rehearsed and just hoped I wouldn't need a prompt.

"Thank goodness. I thought I wasn't going to make it," I

began, trying to sound out of breath. The man in the ticket booth looked up at me, but didn't seem all that impressed by my opening line. "It was the traffic. And then I couldn't find a parking space. My girlfriend may have given up on me. Did she by any chance hand in my ticket for resale?"

He looked unconvinced. My dialogue obviously wasn't gripping him. "Can you describe her?" he asked suspiciously.

"Short-cropped dark hair, hazel eyes, wearing a red silk dress that . . . "

"Ah, yes. I remember her," he said, almost sighing. He picked up the ticket by his side and handed it to me.

"Thank you," I said, trying not to show my relief that he had come in so neatly on cue with the closing line from my first scene. As I hurried off in the direction of the orchestra, I grabbed an envelope from a pile on the ledge beside the booth.

I checked the price of the ticket: twenty pounds. I extracted two ten-pound notes from my wallet, put them in the envelope, licked the flap and stuck it down.

The girl at the entrance to the orchestra checked my ticket. "F–11. Six rows from the front, on the right-hand side."

I walked slowly down the aisle until I spotted her. She was sitting next to an empty place in the middle of the row. As I made my way over the feet of those who were already seated, she turned and smiled, obviously pleased to see that someone had purchased her spare ticket.

I returned the smile, handed over the envelope containing my twenty pounds, and sat down beside her. "The man in the box office asked me to give you this."

"Thank you." She slipped the envelope into her evening bag. I was about to try the first line of my second scene on her, when the house lights faded and the curtain rose for Act 1 of the real performance. I suddenly realized that I had no idea what play I was about to see. I glanced across at the playbill on her lap and read the words *"An Inspector Calls,* by J. B. Priestley."

I remembered that the critics had been full of praise for the production when it had originally opened at the National Theater, and had particularly singled out the performance of Kenneth Cranham. I tried to concentrate on what was taking place on stage.

The eponymous inspector was staring into a house in which an Edwardian family were preparing for a dinner to celebrate their daughter's engagement. "I was thinking of getting a new car," the father was saying to his prospective son-in-law as he puffed away on his cigar.

At the mention of the word "car," I suddenly remembered that I had abandoned mine outside the theater. Was it on a double yellow line? Or worse? To hell with it. They could have it in part-exchange for the model sitting next to me. The audience laughed, so I joined in, if only to give the impression that I was following the plot. But what about my original plans for the evening? By now everyone would be wondering why I hadn't turned up. I realized that I wouldn't be able to leave the theater during the intermission to check on my car or to make a phone call to explain my absence, as that would be my one chance of developing my own plot.

The play had the rest of the audience enthralled, but I had already begun rehearsing the lines from my own script, which would have to be performed during the intermission between Acts 1 and 2. I was painfully aware that I would be restricted to fifteen minutes, and that there would be no second night.

By the time the curtain came down at the end of the first act, I was confident of my draft text. I waited for the applause to die down before I turned toward her.

"What an original production," I began. "Quite modernistic." I vaguely remembered that one of the critics had followed that line. "I was lucky to get a seat at the last moment."

"I was just as lucky," she replied. I felt encouraged. "I mean, to find someone who was looking for a single ticket at such short notice."

I nodded. "My name's Michael Whitaker."

"Anna Townsend," she said, giving me a warm smile.

"Would you like a drink?" I asked.

"Thank you," she replied, "that would be nice." I stood up and led her through the packed huddle that was heading toward the orchestra bar, occasionally glancing back to make sure she was still following me. I was somehow expecting her no longer to be there, but each time I turned to look she greeted me with the same radiant smile.

"What would you like?" I asked, once I could make out the bar through the crowd.

"A dry martini, please."

"Stay here, and I'll be back in a moment," I promised, wondering just how many precious minutes would be wasted while I had to wait at the bar. I took out a five-pound note and held it up conspicuously, in the hope that the prospect of a large tip might influence the barman's sense of direction. He spotted the money, but I still had to wait for another four customers to be served before I managed to secure the dry martini and a Scotch on the rocks for myself. The barman didn't deserve the tip I left him, but I hadn't any more time to waste waiting for the change.

I carried the drinks back to the far corner of the foyer, where Anna stood studying her playbill. She was silhouetted against a window, and in that stylish red silk dress, the light emphasized her slim, elegant figure.

I handed her the dry martini, aware that my limited time had almost run out.

"Thank you," she said, giving me another disarming smile.

"How did you come to have a spare ticket?" I asked as she took a sip from her drink.

"My partner was held up on an emergency case at the last minute," she explained. "Just one of the problems of being a doctor."

"Pity. They missed a quite remarkable production," I prompted, hoping to tease out of her whether her partner was male or female.

"Yes," said Anna. "I tried to book seats when it was still at the National Theater, but they were sold out for any performances I was able to make, so when a friend offered me two tickets at the last minute, I jumped at them. After all, it's coming off in a few weeks." She took another sip from her martini. "What about you?" she asked as the three-minute bell sounded.

There was no such line in my script.

"Me?"

"Yes, Michael," she said, a hint of teasing in her voice. "How did you come to be looking for a spare seat at the last moment?"

"Sharon Stone was tied up for the evening, and at the last second Princess Diana told me that she would have loved to have come, but she was trying to keep a low profile." Anna laughed. "Actually, I read some of the reviews, and I dropped in on the off-chance of picking up a spare ticket."

"And you picked up a spare woman as well," said Anna, as the two-minute bell went. I wouldn't have dared to include such a bold line in her script—or was there a hint of mockery in those hazel eyes?

"I certainly did," I replied lightly. "So, are you a doctor as well?"

"As well as what?" asked Anna.

"As well as your partner," I said, not sure if she was still teasing.

"Yes. I'm a GP in Fulham. There are three of us in the practice, but I was the only one who could escape tonight. And what do you do when you're not chatting up Sharon Stone or escorting Princess Diana to the theater?"

"I'm in the restaurant business," I told her.

"That must be one of the few jobs with worse hours and tougher working conditions than mine," Anna said as the one-minute bell sounded.

I looked into those hazel eyes and wanted to say—Anna, let's forget the second act: I realize the play's superb, but all I want to do is spend the rest of the evening alone with you, not jammed into a crowded auditorium with eight hundred other people.

"Wouldn't you agree?"

I tried to recall what she had just said. "I expect we get more customer complaints than you do," was the best I could manage.

"I doubt it," Anna said, quite sharply. "If you're a woman in

561

the medical profession and you don't cure your patients within a couple of days, they immediately want to know if you're fully qualified."

I laughed, and finished my drink as a voice boomed over the P.A. system, "Would the audience please take their seats for the second act. The curtain is about to rise."

"We ought to be getting back," Anna said, placing her empty glass on the nearest window ledge.

"I suppose so," I said reluctantly, and led her in the opposite direction to the one in which I really wanted to take her.

"Thanks for the drink," she said as we returned to our seats.

"Small recompense," I replied. She glanced up at me questioningly. "For such a good ticket," I explained.

She smiled as we made our way along the row, stepping awkwardly over more toes. I was just about to risk a further remark when the house lights dimmed.

During the second act I turned to smile in Anna's direction whenever there was laughter, and was occasionally rewarded with a warm response. But my supreme moment of triumph came toward the end of the act, when the detective showed the daughter a photograph of the dead woman. She gave a piercing scream, and the stage lights were suddenly switched off.

Anna grabbed my hand, but quickly released it and apologized.

"Not at all," I whispered. "I only just stopped myself from doing the same thing." In the darkened theater, I couldn't tell how she responded.

A moment later the phone on the stage rang. Everyone in the audience knew it must be the detective on the other end of the line, even if they couldn't be sure what he was going to say. That final scene had the whole house gripped.

After the lights dimmed for the last time, the cast returned to the stage and deservedly received a long ovation, taking several curtain calls.

When the curtain was finally lowered, Anna turned to me and said, "What a remarkable production. I'm so glad I didn't miss it. And I'm even more pleased that I didn't have to see it alone."

"Me too," I told her, ignoring the fact that I'd never planned to spend the evening at the theater in the first place.

We made our way up the aisle together as the audience flowed out of the theater like a slow-moving river. I wasted those few precious moments discussing the merits of the cast, the power of the director's interpretation, the originality of the macabre set and even the Edwardian costumes, before we reached the double doors that led back out into the real world.

"Good-bye, Michael," Anna said. "Thank you for adding to my enjoyment of the evening." She shook me by the hand.

"Good-bye," I said, gazing once again into those hazel eyes.

She turned to go, and I wondered if I would ever see her again.

"Anna," I said.

She glanced back in my direction.

"If you're not doing anything in particular, would you care to join me for dinner . . . "

Author's Note

At this point in the story, the reader is offered the choice of four different endings.

You might decide to read all four of them, or simply select one and consider that your own particular ending. If you do choose to read all four, they should be taken in the order in which they have been written:

1.   RARE

2.   BURNT

3.   OVERDONE

4.   *À POINT*

RARE

"Thank you, Michael. I'd like that."

I smiled, unable to mask my delight. "Good. I know a little restaurant just down the road that I think you might enjoy."

"That sounds fun," Anna said, linking her arm in mine. I guided her through the departing throng.

As we strolled together down the Aldwych, Anna continued to chat about the play, comparing it favorably with a production she had seen at the Haymarket some years before.

When we reached the Strand I pointed to a large gray double door on the other side of the road. "That's it," I said. We took advantage of a red light to weave our way through the temporarily stationary traffic, and after we'd reached the far sidewalk I pushed one of the gray doors open to allow Anna through. It began to rain just as we stepped inside. I led her down a flight of stairs into a basement restaurant buzzing with the talk of people who had just come out of theaters, and waiters dashing, plates in both hands, from table to table.

"I'll be impressed if you can get a table here," Anna said, eyeing a group of would-be customers who were clustered round the bar, impatiently waiting for someone to leave.

I strolled across to the reservations desk. The head waiter, who until that moment had been taking a customer's order, rushed over. "Good evening, Mr. Whitaker," he said. "How many are you?"

"Just the two of us."

"Follow me, please, sir," Mario said, leading us to my usual table in the far corner of the room.

"Another dry martini?" I asked her as we sat down.

"No, thank you," she replied. "I think I'll just have a glass of wine with the meal."

I nodded my agreement, as Mario handed us our menus. Anna studied hers for a few moments before I asked if she had spotted anything she fancied.

"Yes," she said, looking straight at me. "But for now I think I'll settle for the fettucini, and a glass of red wine."

"Good idea," I said. "I'll join you. But are you sure you won't have a starter?"

"No, thank you, Michael. I've reached that age when I can no longer order everything I'm tempted by."

"Me too," I confessed. "I have to play squash three times a week to keep in shape," I told her as Mario reappeared.

"Two fettucini," I began, "and a bottle of . . . "

"Half a bottle, please," said Anna. "I'll only have one glass. I've got an early start tomorrow morning, so I shouldn't overdo things."

I nodded, and Mario scurried away.

I looked across the table and into Anna's eyes. "I've always wondered about women doctors," I said, immediately realizing that the line was a bit feeble.

"You mean, you wondered if we're normal?"

"Something like that, I suppose."

"Yes, we're normal enough, except every day we have to see a lot of men in the nude. I can assure you, Michael, most of them are overweight and fairly unattractive."

I suddenly wished I were half a stone lighter. "But are there many men who are brave enough to consider a woman doctor in the first place?"

"Quite a few," said Anna, "though most of my patients are female. But there are just about enough intelligent, sensible, uninhibited males around who can accept that a woman doctor might be just as likely to cure them as a man."

I smiled as two bowls of fettucini were placed in front of us. Mario then showed me the label on the half-bottle he had selected. I nodded my approval. He had chosen a vintage to match Anna's pedigree.

"And what about you?" asked Anna. "What does being 'in the restaurant business' actually mean?"

"I'm on the management side," I said, before sampling the wine. I nodded again, and Mario poured a glass for Anna and then topped up mine.

"Or at least, that's what I do nowadays. I started life as a waiter," I said, as Anna began to sip her wine.

"What a magnificent wine," she remarked. "It's so good I may end up having a second glass."

"I'm glad you like it," I said. "It's a Barolo."

"You were saying, Michael? You started life as a waiter . . . "

"Yes, then I moved into the kitchens for about five years, and finally ended up on the management side. How's the fettucini?"

"It's delicious. Almost melts in your mouth." She took another sip of her wine. "So, if you're not cooking, and no longer a waiter, what do you do now?"

"Well, at the moment I'm running three restaurants in the West End, which means I never stop dashing from one to the other, depending on which is facing the biggest crisis on that particular day."

"Sounds a bit like ward duty to me," said Anna. "So who turned out to have the biggest crisis today?"

"Today, thank heaven, was not typical," I told her with feeling.

"That bad?" said Anna.

"Yes, I'm afraid so. We lost a chef this morning who cut off the top of his finger, and won't be back at work for at least a fortnight. My head waiter in our second restaurant is off, claiming he has flu, and I've just had to sack the barman in the third for fiddling the books. Barmen always fiddle the books, of course, but in this case even the customers began to notice what he was up to." I paused. "But I still wouldn't want to be in any other business."

"In the circumstances, I'm amazed you were able to take the evening off."

"I shouldn't have, really, and I wouldn't have, except . . ." I trailed off as I leaned over and topped up Anna's glass.

"Except what?" she said.

"Do you want to hear the truth?" I asked as I poured the remains of the wine into my own glass.

"I'll try that for starters," she said.

I placed the empty bottle on the side of the table, and hesitated, but only for a moment. "I was driving to one of my restaurants earlier this evening, when I spotted you going into the theater. I stared at you for so long that I nearly crashed into the back of the car in front of me. Then I swerved across the road into the nearest parking space, and the car behind almost crashed into me. I leapt out, ran all the way to the theater, and searched everywhere until I saw you standing in the queue for the box office. I joined the line and watched you hand over your spare ticket. Once you were safely out of sight, I told the box office manager that you hadn't expected me to make it in time, and that you might have put my ticket up for resale. After I'd described you, which I was able to do in great detail, he handed it over without so much as a murmur."

Anna put down her glass of wine and stared across at me with a look of incredulity. "I'm glad he fell for your story," she said. "But should I?"

"Yes, you should. Because then I put two ten-pound notes into a theater envelope and took the place next to you. The rest you already know." I waited to see how she would react.

She didn't speak for some time. "I'm flattered," she eventually said, and touched my hand. "I didn't realize there were any old-fashioned romantics left in the world." She squeezed my fingers and looked me in the eyes. "Am I allowed to ask what you have planned for the rest of the evening?"

"Nothing has been planned so far," I admitted. "Which is why it's all been so refreshing."

"You make me sound like an After Eight mint," said Anna with a laugh.

"I can think of at least three replies to that," I told her as Mario reappeared, looking a little disappointed at the sight of the half-empty plates.

"Was everything all right, sir?" he asked, sounding anxious.

"Couldn't have been better," said Anna, who hadn't stopped looking at me.

"Would you like some coffee?" I asked.

"Yes," said Anna. "But perhaps we could have it somewhere a little less crowded."

I was so taken by surprise that it was several moments before I recovered. I was beginning to feel that I was no longer in control. Anna rose from her place and said, "Shall we go?" I nodded to Mario, who just smiled.

Once we were back out on the street, she linked her arm with mine as we retraced our steps along the Aldwych and past the theater.

"It's been a wonderful evening," she was saying as we reached the spot where I had left my car. "Until you arrived on the scene it had been a rather dull day, but you've changed all that."

"It hasn't actually been the best of days for me either," I admitted. "But I've rarely enjoyed an evening more. Where would you like to have coffee? Annabels? Or why don't we try the new Dorchester Club?"

"If you don't have a wife, your place. If you do . . . "

"I don't," I told her simply.

"Then that's settled," she said as I opened the door of my BMW for her. Once she was safely in I walked round to take my seat behind the wheel, and discovered that I had left my side-lights on and the keys in the ignition.

I turned the key, and the engine immediately purred into life. "This has to be my day," I said to myself.

"Sorry?" Anna said, turning in my direction.

"We were lucky to miss the rain," I replied, as a few drops landed on the windscreen. I flicked on the wipers.

On our way to Pimlico, Anna told me about her childhood in the south of France, where her father had taught English at a boys' school. Her account of being the only girl among a couple of hundred teenage French boys made me laugh again and again. I found myself becoming more and more enchanted with her company.

"Whatever made you come back to England?" I asked.

"An English mother who divorced my French father, and the chance to study medicine at St Thomas's."

"But don't you miss the south of France, especially on nights like this?" I asked as a clap of thunder crackled above us.

"Oh, I don't know," she said. I was about to respond when she added, "In any case, now the English have learnt how to cook, the place has become almost civilized." I smiled to myself, wondering if she was teasing me again.

I found out immediately. "By the way," she said, "I assume that was one of your restaurants we had dinner at."

"Yes, it was," I said sheepishly.

"That explains how you got a table so easily when it was packed out, why the waiter knew it was a Barolo you wanted without your having to ask, and how you could leave without paying the bill."

I was beginning to wonder if I would always be a yard behind her.

"Was it the missing waiter, the four-and-a-half-fingered chef, or the crooked bartender?"

"The crooked bartender," I replied, laughing. "But I sacked him this afternoon, and I'm afraid his deputy didn't look as if he was coping all that well," I explained as I turned right off Millbank, and began to search for a parking space.

"And I thought you only had eyes for me," sighed Anna, "when all the time you were looking over my shoulder and checking on what the deputy barman was up to."

"Not *all* the time," I said as I manoeuvred the car into the only space left in the mews where I lived. I got out of the car and walked round to Anna's side, opened the door and guided her to the house.

As I closed the door behind us, Anna put her arms around my neck and looked up into my eyes. I leaned down and kissed her for the first time. When she broke away, all she said was, "Don't let's bother with coffee, Michael." I slipped off my jacket, and led her upstairs and into my bedroom, praying that it hadn't been the housekeeper's day off. When I opened the door I was relieved to find that the bed had been made and the room was tidy.

"I'll just be a moment," I said, and disappeared into the bathroom. As I cleaned my teeth, I began to wonder if it was all a dream. When I returned to the bedroom, would I discover she didn't exist? I dropped the toothbrush into its mug and went back to the bedroom. Where was she? My eyes followed a trail of discarded clothes that led all the way to the bed. Her head was propped up on the pillow. Only a sheet covered her body.

I quickly took off my clothes, dropping them where they fell, and switched off the main lights, so that only the one by the bed remained aglow. I slid under the sheets to join her. I looked at her for several seconds before I took her in my arms. I slowly explored every part of her body, as she began to kiss me again. I couldn't believe that anyone could be that exciting, and at the same time so tender. When we finally made love, I knew I never wanted this woman to leave me.

She lay in my arms for some time before either of us spoke. Then I began talking about anything that came into my head. I confided my hopes, my dreams, even my worst anxieties, with a freedom I had never experienced with anyone before. I wanted to share everything with her.

And then she leaned across and began kissing me once again, first on the lips, then the neck and chest, and as she slowly continued down my body I thought I would explode. The last thing I remember was turning off the light by my bed as the clock on the hall table chimed one.

When I woke the following morning, the first rays of sunlight were already shining through the lace curtains, and the glorious memory of the night before was instantly revived. I turned lazily to take her in my arms, but she was no longer there.

"Anna?" I cried out, sitting bolt upright. There was no reply. I flicked on the light by the side of the bed, and glanced across at the bedside clock. It was 7.29. I was about to jump out of bed and go in search of her when I noticed a scribbled note wedged under a corner of the clock.

I picked it up, read it slowly, and smiled.

"So will I," I said, and lay back on the pillow, thinking about what I should do next. I decided to send her a dozen roses later that morning, eleven white and one red. Then I would have a red one delivered to her on the hour, every hour, until I saw her again.

After I had showered and dressed, I roamed aimlessly around the house. I wondered how quickly I could persuade Anna to move in, and what changes she would want to make.

Heaven knows, I thought as I walked through to the kitchen, clutching her note, the place could do with a woman's touch.

As I ate breakfast I looked up her number in the telephone directory, instead of reading the morning paper. There it was, just as she had said. Dr. Townsend, listing a surgery number in Parsons Green Lane where she could be contacted between nine and six. There was a second number, but deep black lettering requested that it should only be used in case of emergencies.

Although I considered my state of health to be an emergency, I dialled the first number, and waited impatiently. All I wanted to say was, "Good morning, darling. I got your note, and can we make last night the first of many?"

A matronly voice answered the phone. "Dr. Townsend's office."

"Dr. Townsend, please," I said.

"Which one?" she asked. "There are three Dr. Townsends in the practice—Dr. Jonathan, Dr. Anna and Dr. Elizabeth."

"Dr. Anna," I replied.

"Oh, Mrs. Townsend," she said. "I'm sorry, but she's not available at the moment. She's just taken the children off to school, and after that she has to go to the airport to pick up her husband, Dr. Jonathan, who's returning this morning from a medical conference in Minneapolis. I'm not expecting her back for at least a couple of hours. Would you like to leave a message?"

There was a long silence before the matronly voice asked, "Are you still there?" I placed the receiver back on the hook without replying, and looked sadly down at the handwritten note by the side of the phone.

Dear Michael,

> *I will remember tonight for the rest of my life.*
> *Thank you.*
> *Anna*

BURNT

"Thank you, Michael. I'd like that."

I smiled, unable to mask my delight.

"Hi, Anna. I thought I might have missed you."

I turned and stared at a tall man with a mop of fair hair, who seemed unaffected by the steady flow of people trying to pass him on either side.

Anna gave him a smile that I hadn't seen until that moment.

"Hello, darling," she said. "This is Michael Whitaker. You're lucky—he bought your ticket, and if you hadn't turned up I was just about to accept his kind invitation to dinner. Michael, this is my husband, Jonathan—the one who was held up at the hospital. As you can see, he's now escaped."

I couldn't think of a suitable reply.

Jonathan shook me warmly by the hand. "Thank you for keeping my wife company," he said. "Won't you join us for dinner?"

"That's very kind of you," I replied, "but I've just remembered that I'm meant to be somewhere else right now. I'd better run."

"That's a pity," said Anna. "I was rather looking forward to finding out all about the restaurant business. Perhaps we'll meet again sometime, whenever my husband next leaves me in the lurch. Good-bye, Michael."

"Good-bye, Anna."

I watched them climb into the back of a taxi together, and wished Jonathan would drop dead in front of me. He didn't, so I began to retrace my steps back to the spot where I had abandoned my car. "You're a lucky man, Jonathan Townsend," was the only observation I made. But no one was listening.

The next word that came to my lips was "Damn!" I repeated it several times, as there was a distressingly large space where I was certain I'd left my car.

I walked up and down the street in case I'd forgotten where I'd parked it, cursed again, then marched off in search of a phone box, unsure if my car had been stolen or towed away.

There was a pay phone just around the corner in Kingsway. I picked up the receiver and jabbed three nines into it.

"Which service do you require? Fire, Police, or Ambulance," a voice asked.

"Police," I said, and was immediately put through to another voice.

"Charing Cross Police Station. What is the nature of your inquiry?"

"I think my car has been stolen."

"Can you tell me the make, color and registration number please, sir."

"It's a red Ford Fiesta, registration H107 SHV."

There was a long pause, during which I could hear other voices talking in the background.

"No, it hasn't been stolen, sir," said the officer when he came back on the line. "The car was illegally parked on a double yellow line. It's been removed and taken to the Vauxhall Bridge Pound."

"Can I pick it up now?" I asked sulkily.

"Certainly, sir. How will you be getting there?"

"I'll take a taxi."

"Then just ask the driver for the Vauxhall Bridge Pound. Once you get there, you'll need some form of identification, and a check for one hundred and five pounds with a banker's card—that is if you don't have the full amount in cash."

"One hundred and five pounds?" I repeated in disbelief.

"That's correct, sir."

I slammed the phone down just as it started to rain. I scurried back to the corner of the Aldwych in search of a taxi, only to find that they were all being commandeered by the hordes of people still hanging around outside the theater.

I put my collar up and nipped across the road, dodging between the slow-moving traffic. Once I had reached the far side, I continued running until I found an overhanging ledge broad enough to shield me from the blustery rain.

I shivered, and sneezed several times before an empty cab eventually came to my rescue.

"Vauxhall Bridge Pound," I told the driver as I jumped in.

"Bad luck, mate," said the cabbie. "You're my second this evening."

I frowned.

As the taxi maneuvered its way slowly through the rainswept post-theater traffic and across Waterloo Bridge, the driver began chattering away. I just about managed monosyllabic replies to his opinions on the weather, John Major, the England cricket team and foreign tourists. With each new topic, his forecast became ever more gloomy.

When we reached the car pound I passed him a ten-pound note and waited in the rain for my change. Then I dashed off in the direction of a little Portakabin, where I was faced by my second line that evening. This one was considerably longer than the first, and I knew that when I eventually reached the front of it and paid for my ticket, I wouldn't be rewarded with any memorable entertainment. When my turn finally came, a burly policeman pointed to a form taped to the counter.

I followed its instructions to the letter, first producing my driver's license, then writing out a check for £105, payable to the Metropolitan Police. I handed them both over, with my check card, to the policeman, who towered over me. The man's sheer bulk was the only reason I didn't suggest that perhaps he ought to have more important things to do with his time, like catching drug dealers. Or even car thieves.

"Your vehicle is in the far corner," said the officer, pointing into the distance, over row upon row of cars.

"Of course it is," I replied. I stepped out of the Portakabin and back into the rain, dodging puddles as I ran between the lines of cars. I didn't stop until I reached the farthest corner of the pound. It still took me several more minutes to locate my red Ford Fiesta—one disadvantage, I thought, of owning the most popular car in Britain.

I unlocked the door, squelched down onto the front seat, and sneezed again. I turned the key in the ignition, but the engine barely turned over, letting out only the occasional splutter before giving up altogether. Then I remembered I hadn't switched the sidelights off when I made my unscheduled dash for the theater. I uttered a string of expletives that only partly expressed my true feelings.

I watched as another figure came running across the pound toward a Range Rover parked in the row in front of me. I quickly wound down my window, but he had driven off before I could shout the magic words "jump cables." I got out and retrieved my jumper cables from the trunk, walked to the front of the car, raised the hood, and attached the cables to the battery. I began to shiver once again as I settled down for another wait.

I couldn't get Anna out of my mind, but accepted that the only thing I'd succeeded in picking up that evening was the flu.

In the following forty rain-drenched minutes, three people passed by before a young black man asked, "So what's the trouble, man?" Once I had explained my problem he maneuvered his old van alongside my car, then raised his bonnet and attached the jump leads to his battery. When he switched on his ignition, my engine began to turn over.

"Thanks," I shouted, rather inadequately, once I'd revved the engine several times.

"My pleasure, man," he replied, and disappeared into the night.

As I drove out of the car pound I switched on my radio, to hear Big Ben striking twelve. It reminded me that I hadn't turned up for work that night. The first thing I needed to do, if I wanted to keep my job, was to come up with a good excuse. I sneezed again, and decided on the flu. Although they'd probably taken the last orders by now, Gerald wouldn't have closed the kitchens yet.

I peered through the rain, searching the sidewalks for a pay phone, and eventually spotted a row of three outside a post office. I stopped the car and jumped out, but a cursory inspection revealed that they'd all been vandalized. I climbed back into the car and continued my search. After dashing in and out of the rain several times, I finally spotted a single phone box on the corner of Warwick Way that looked as if it might just be in working order.

I dialed the restaurant, and waited a long time for someone to answer.

"Laguna 50," said an Italian-sounding young girl.

"Janice, is that you? It's Mike."

"Yes, it's me, Mike," she whispered, reverting to her Lambeth accent. "I'd better warn you that every time your name's been mentioned this evening, Gerald picks up the nearest meat ax."

"Why?" I asked. "You've still got Nick in the kitchen to see you through."

"Nick chopped the top off one of his fingers earlier this evening, and Gerald had to take him to hospital. I was left in charge. He's not best pleased."

"Oh, hell," I said. "But I've got . . . "

"The sack," said another voice, and this one wasn't whispering.

"Gerald, I can explain . . . "

"Why you didn't turn up for work this evening?"

I sneezed, then held my nose. "I've got the flu. If I'd come in tonight I would have given it to half the customers."

"Would you?" said Gerald. "Well, I suppose that might have been marginally worse than giving it to the girl who was sitting next to you in the theater."

"What do you mean?" I asked, letting go of my nose.

"Exactly what I said, Mike. You see, unfortunately for you, a couple of our regulars were two rows behind you at the Ald-wych. They enjoyed the show almost as much as you seemed to, and one of them added, for good measure, that he thought your date was 'absolutely stunning.' "

"He must have mistaken me for someone else," I said, trying not to sound desperate.

"He may have done, Mike, but I haven't. You're sacked, and don't even think about coming in to collect your pay packet, because there isn't one for a head waiter who'd rather take some bimbo to the theater than do a night's work." The line went dead.

I hung up the phone and started muttering obscenities under my breath as I walked slowly back toward my car. I was only a dozen paces away from it when a young lad jumped into the front seat, switched on the ignition, and lurched hesitatingly into the center of the road in what sounded horribly like third gear. I chased after the retreating car, but once the youth began to accelerate, I knew I had no hope of catching him.

I ran all the way back to the phone box, and dialled 999 once again.

"Fire, Police, or Ambulance?" I was asked for a second time that night.

"Police," I said, and a moment later I was put through to another voice.

"Belgravia Police Station. What is the nature of your enquiry?"

"I've just had my car stolen!" I shouted.

"Make, model and registration number please, sir."

"It's a red Ford Fiesta, registration H107 SHV."

I waited impatiently.

"It hasn't been stolen, sir. It was illegally parked on a double . . . "

"No it wasn't!" I shouted even more loudly. "I paid £105 to get the damn thing out of the Vauxhall Bridge Pound less than half an hour ago, and I've just seen it being driven off by a joyrider while I was making a phone call."

"Where are you, sir?"

"In a phone box on the corner of Vauxhall Bridge Road and Warwick Way."

"And in which direction was the car travelling when you last saw it?" asked the voice.

"North up Vauxhall Bridge Road."

"And what is your home telephone number, sir?"

"081 290 4820."

"And at work?"

"Like the car, I don't have a job any longer."

"Right, I'll get straight onto it, sir. We'll be in touch with you the moment we have any news."

I put the phone down and thought about what I should do next. I hadn't been left with a great deal of choice. I hailed a taxi and asked to be taken to Victoria, and was relieved to find that this driver showed no desire to offer any opinions on anything during the short journey to the station. When he dropped me I passed him my last note, and patiently waited while he handed over every last penny of my change. He also muttered an expletive or two. I bought a ticket for Bromley with my few remaining coins, and went in search of the platform.

"You've just about made it, mate," the ticket collector told me. "The last train's due in at any minute." But I still had to wait for another twenty minutes on the cold, empty platform before the last train eventually pulled into the station. By then I had memorized every advertisement in sight, from Guinness to Mates, while continuing to sneeze at regular intervals.

When the train came to a halt and the doors squelched open I took a seat in a carriage near the front. It was another ten minutes before the engine lurched into action, and another forty before it finally pulled into Bromley station.

I emerged into the Kent night a few minutes before one o'clock, and set off in the direction of my little terraced house.

Twenty-five minutes later, I staggered up the short path to my front door. I began to search for my keys, then remembered that I'd left them in the car ignition. I didn't have the energy even to swear, and began to grovel around in the dark for the spare front-door key that was always hidden under a particular stone. But which one? At last I found it, put it in the lock, turned it and pushed the door open. No sooner had I stepped inside than the phone on the hall table began to ring.

I grabbed the receiver.

"Mr. Whitaker?"

"Speaking."

"This is the Belgravia police. We've located your car, sir, and . . . "

"Thank God for that," I said, before the officer had a chance to finish the sentence. "Where is it?"

"At this precise moment, sir, it's on the back of a pick-up lorry somewhere in Chelsea. It seems the lad who nicked it only managed to travel a mile or so before he hit the kerb at seventy, and bounced straight into a wall. I'm sorry to have to inform you, sir, that your car's a total write-off."

"A total write-off?" I said in disbelief.

"Yes, sir. The garage who towed it away has been given your number, and they'll be in touch with you first thing in the morning."

I couldn't think of any comment worth making.

"The good news is we've caught the lad who nicked it," continued the police officer. "The bad news is that he's only fifteen, doesn't have a driver's license, and, of course, he isn't insured."

"That's not a problem," I said. "I'm fully insured myself."

"As a matter of interest, sir, did you leave your keys in the ignition?"

"Yes, I did. I was just making a quick phone call, and thought I'd only be away from the car for a couple of minutes."

"Then I think it's unlikely you'll be covered by your insurance, sir."

"Not covered by my insurance? What are you talking about?"

"It's standard policy nowadays not to pay out if you leave your keys in the ignition. You'd better check, sir," were the officer's final words before ringing off.

I put the phone down and wondered what else could possibly go wrong. I slipped off my jacket and began to climb the stairs, but came to a sudden halt when I saw my wife waiting for me on the landing.

"Maureen . . ." I began.

"You can tell me later why the car is a total write-off," she said, "but not until you've explained why you didn't turn up for work this evening, and just who this 'classy tart' is that Gerald said you were seen with at the theater."

OVERDONE

"No, I'm not doing anything in particular," said Anna.

I smiled, unable to mask my delight.

"Good. I know a little restaurant just down the road that I think you might enjoy."

"That sounds just fine," said Anna as she made her way

579

through the dense theater crowd. I quickly followed, having to hurry just to keep up with her.

"Which way?" she asked. I pointed toward the Strand. She began walking at a brisk pace, and we continued to talk about the play.

When we reached the Strand I pointed to a large gray double door on the other side of the road. "That's it," I said. I would have taken her hand as she began to cross, but she stepped off the pavement ahead of me, dodged between the stationary traffic, and waited for me on the far side.

She pushed the gray doors open, and once again I followed in her wake. We descended a flight of steps into a basement restaurant buzzing with the talk of people who had just come out of theaters, and waiters dashing, plates in both hands, from table to table.

"I don't expect you'll be able to get a table here if you haven't booked," said Anna, eyeing a group of would-be customers who were clustered round the bar, impatiently waiting for someone to leave.

"Don't worry about that," I said with bravado, and strode across to the reservations desk. I waved a hand imperiously at the headwaiter, who was taking a customer's order. I only hoped he would recognize me.

I turned round to smile at Anna, but she didn't look too impressed.

After the waiter had taken the order, he walked slowly over to me. "How may I help you, sir?" he asked.

"Can you manage a table for two, Victor?"

"Victor's off tonight, sir. Have you booked?"

"No, I haven't, but . . . "

The headwaiter checked the list of reservations and then looked at his watch. "I might be able to fit you in around 11:15—11:30 at the latest," he said, not sounding too hopeful.

"No sooner?" I pleaded. "I don't think we can wait that long." Anna nodded her agreement.

"I'm afraid not, sir," said the head waiter. "We are fully booked until then."

"As I expected," said Anna, turning to leave.

Once again I had to hurry to keep up with her. As we stepped out onto the pavement I said, "There's a little Italian restaurant I know not far from here, where I can always get a table. Shall we risk it?"

"Can't see that we've got a lot of choice," replied Anna. "Which direction this time?"

"Just up the road to the right," I said as a clap of thunder heralded an imminent downpour.

"Damn," said Anna, placing her handbag over her head for protection.

"I'm sorry," I said, looking up at the black clouds. "It's my fault. I should have . . ."

"Stop apologizing all the time, Michael. It isn't your fault if it starts to rain."

I took a deep breath and tried again. "We'd better make a dash for it," I said desperately. "I don't expect we'll be able to pick up a taxi in this weather."

This at least secured her ringing endorsement. I began running up the road, and Anna followed closely behind. The rain was getting heavier and heavier, and although we couldn't have had more than seventy yards to cover, we were both soaked by the time we reached the restaurant.

I sighed with relief when I opened the door and found the dining room was half-empty, although I suppose I should have been annoyed. I turned and smiled hopefully at Anna, but she was still frowning.

"Everything all right?" I asked.

"Fine. It's just that my father had a theory about restaurants that were half empty at this time of night."

I looked quizzically at my guest, but decided not to make any comment about her eye makeup, which was beginning to run, or her hair, which had come loose at the edges.

"I'd better carry out some repair work. I'll only be a couple of minutes," she said, heading for a door marked "Signorinas."

I waved at Mario, who was serving no one in particular. He hurried over to me.

"There was a call for you earlier, Mr. Whitaker," Mario said as he guided me across the restaurant to my usual table. "If you came in, I was to ask you to phone Gerald urgently. He sounded pretty desperate."

"I'm sure it can wait. But if he rings again, let me know immediately." At that moment Anna walked over to join us. The makeup had been restored, but the hair could have done with further attention.

I rose to greet her.

"You don't have to do that," she said, taking her seat.

"Would you like a drink?" I asked, once we were both settled.

"No, I don't think so. I have an early start tomorrow morning, so I shouldn't overdo things. I'll just have a glass of wine with my meal."

Another waiter appeared by her side. "And what would madam care for this evening?" he asked politely.

"I haven't had time to look at the menu yet," Anna replied, not even bothering to look up at him.

"I can recommend the fettucini, madam," the waiter said, pointing to a dish halfway down the list of entrées. "It's our specialty of the day."

"Then I suppose I might as well have that," said Anna, handing him the menu.

I nodded, indicating "Me too," and asked for a half-bottle of the house red. The waiter scooped up my menu and left us.

"Do you . . . ?"

"Can I . . . ?"

"You first," I said, attempting a smile.

"Do you always order half a bottle of the house wine on a first date?" she asked.

"I think you'll find it's pretty good," I said, rather plaintively.

"I was only teasing, Michael. Don't take yourself so seriously."

I took a closer look at my companion, and began to wonder if I'd made a terrible mistake. Despite her efforts in the washroom, Anna wasn't quite the same girl I'd first seen—admittedly at a distance—when I'd nearly crashed my car earlier in the evening.

Oh my God, the car. I suddenly remembered where I'd left it, and stole a glance at my watch.

"Am I boring you already, Michael?" Anna asked. "Or is this table on a time share?"

"Yes. I mean no. I'm sorry, I've just remembered something I should have checked on before we came to dinner. Sorry," I repeated.

Anna frowned, which stopped me saying sorry yet again.

"Is it too late?" she asked.

"Too late for what?"

"To do something about whatever it is you should have checked on before we came to dinner?"

I looked out of the window, and wasn't pleased to see that it had stopped raining. Now my only hope was that the late-night traffic officers might not be too vigilant.

"No, I'm sure it will be all right," I said, trying to sound relaxed.

"Well, that's a relief," said Anna, in a tone that bordered on the sarcastic.

"So. What's it like being a doctor?" I asked, trying to change the subject.

"Michael, it's my evening off. I'd rather not talk about my work, if you don't mind."

For the next few moments neither of us spoke. I tried again. "Do you have many male patients in your practice?" I asked, as the waiter reappeared with our fettucini.

"I can hardly believe I'm hearing this," Anna said, unable to disguise the weariness in her voice. "When are people like you going to accept that one or two of us are capable of a little more than spending our lives waiting hand and foot on the male sex."

The waiter poured some wine into my glass.

"Yes. Of course. Absolutely. No. I didn't mean it to sound like that . . ." I sipped the wine and nodded to the waiter, who filled Anna's glass.

"Then what did you mean it to sound like?" demanded Anna as she stuck her fork firmly into the fettucini.

"Well, isn't it unusual for a man to go to a woman doctor?" I said, realizing the moment I had uttered the words that I was only getting myself into even deeper water.

"Good heavens, no, Michael. We live in an enlightened age. I've probably seen more naked men than you have—and it's not an attractive sight, I can assure you." I laughed, in the hope that it would ease the tension. "In any case," she added, "quite a few men are confident enough to accept the existence of women doctors, you know."

"I'm sure that's true," I said. "I just thought . . . "

"You didn't think, Michael. That's the problem with so many men like you. I bet you've never even considered consulting a woman doctor."

"No, but . . . Yes, but . . . "

" 'No but, yes but'—Let's change the subject before I get really angry," Anna said, putting her fork down. "What do you do for a living, Michael? It doesn't sound as if you're in a profession where women are treated as equals."

"I'm in the restaurant business," I told her, wishing the fettucini were a little lighter.

"Ah, yes, you told me in the interval," she said. "But what does being 'in the restaurant business' actually mean?"

"I'm on the management side. Or at least, that's what I do nowadays. I started life as a waiter, then I moved into the kitchens for about five years, and finally . . . "

". . . found you weren't very good at either, so you took up managing everyone else."

"Something like that," I said, trying to make light of it. But Anna's words only reminded me that one of my other restaurants was without a chef that night, and that that was where I'd been heading before I'd allowed myself to become infatuated by her.

"I've lost you again," Anna said, beginning to sound exasperated. "You were going to tell me all about restaurant management."

"Yes, I was, wasn't I? By the way, how's your fettucini?"

"Not bad, considering."

"Considering?"

"Considering this place was your second choice."

I was silenced once again.

"It's not that bad," she said, taking another reluctant forkful.

"Perhaps you'd like something else instead? I can always . . . "

"No, thank you, Michael. After all, this was the one dish the waiter felt confident enough to recommend."

I couldn't think of a suitable response, so I remained silent.

"Come on, Michael, you still haven't explained what restaurant management actually involves," said Anna.

"Well, at the moment I'm running three restaurants in the West End, which means I never stop dashing from one to the other, depending on which is facing the biggest crisis on that particular day."

"Sounds a bit like ward duty to me," said Anna. "So who turned out to have the biggest crisis today?"

"Today, thank heaven, was not typical," I told her with feeling.

"That bad?" said Anna.

"Yes, I'm afraid so. We lost a chef this morning who cut off the top of his finger, and won't be back at work for at least a fortnight. My head waiter in our second restaurant is off, claiming he has flu, and I've just had to sack the barman in the third for fiddling the books. Barmen always fiddle the books, of course, but in this case even the customers began to notice what he was up to." I paused, wondering if I should risk another mouthful of fettucini. "But I still wouldn't want to be in any other business."

"In the circumstances, I'm frankly amazed you were able to take the evening off."

"I shouldn't have, really, and wouldn't have, except . . ." I trailed off as I leaned over and topped up Anna's wine glass.

"Except what?" she said.

"Do you want to hear the truth?" I asked as I poured the remains of the wine into my own glass.

"I'll try that for starters," she said.

I placed the empty bottle on the side of the table, and hesitated, but only for a moment. "I was driving to one of my restaurants earlier this evening, when I spotted you going into the theater. I stared at you for so long that I nearly crashed into the back of the car in front of me. Then I swerved across the road into the nearest parking space, and the car behind almost crashed into me. I leapt out, ran all the way to the theater, and searched everywhere until I saw you standing in the line for the box office. I joined the line and watched you hand over your spare ticket. Once you were safely out of sight, I told the box office manager that you hadn't expected me to make it in time, and that you might have put my ticket up for resale. Once I'd described you, which I was able to do in great detail, he handed it over without so much as a murmur."

"More fool him," said Anna, putting down her glass and staring at me as if I'd just been released from a lunatic asylum.

"Then I put two ten-pound notes into a theater envelope and took the place next to you," I continued. "The rest you already know." I waited, with some trepidation, to see how she would react.

"I suppose I ought to be flattered," Anna said after a moment's consideration. "But I don't know whether to laugh or cry. One thing's for certain; the woman I've been living with for the past ten years will think it's highly amusing, especially as you paid for her ticket."

The waiter returned to remove the half-finished plates. "Was everything all right, sir?" he asked, sounding anxious.

"Fine, just fine," I said unconvincingly. Anna grimaced, but made no comment.

"Would you care for coffee, madam?"

"No, I don't think I'll risk it," she said, looking at her watch. "In any case, I ought to be getting back. Elizabeth will be wondering where I've got to."

She stood up and walked toward the door. I followed a yard behind. She was just about to step onto the pavement when she turned to me and asked, "Don't you think you ought to settle the bill?"

"That won't be necessary."

"Why?" she asked, laughing. "Do you own the place?"

"No. But it is one of the three restaurants I manage."

Anna turned scarlet. "I'm so sorry, Michael," she said. "That was tactless of me." She paused for a moment before adding, "But I'm sure you'll agree that the food wasn't exactly memorable."

"Would you like me to drive you home?" I asked, trying not to sound too enthusiastic.

Anna looked up at the black clouds. "That would be useful," she replied, "if it's not miles out of your way. Where's your car?" she said before I had a chance to ask where she lived.

"I left it just up the road."

"Oh, yes, I remember," said Anna. "When you jumped out of it because you couldn't take your eyes off me. I'm afraid you picked the wrong girl this time."

At last we had found something on which we could agree, but I made no comment as we walked toward the spot where I had abandoned my car. Anna limited her conversation to whether it was about to rain again, and how good she had thought the wine was. I was relieved to find my Volvo parked exactly where I had left it.

I was searching for my keys when I spotted a large sticker glued to the windscreen. I looked down at the front offside wheel, and saw the yellow clamp.

"It just isn't your night, is it?" said Anna. "But don't worry about me, I'll just grab a cab."

She raised her hand and a taxi skidded to a halt. She turned back to face me. "Thanks for dinner," she managed, not altogether convincingly, and added, even less convincingly, "Perhaps we'll meet again." Before I could respond, she had slammed the taxi door closed.

As I watched her being driven away, it started to rain.

I took one more look at my immovable car, and decided I would deal with the problem in the morning.

I was about to rush for the nearest shelter when another taxi came around the corner, its yellow light indicating that it was for hire. I waved frantically and it drew up beside my clamped car.

"Bad luck, mate," said the cabbie, looking down at my front wheel. "My third tonight."

I attempted a smile.

"So, where to, guv?"

I gave him my address in Lambeth and climbed into the back.

587

As the taxi maneuvered its way slowly through the rainswept post-theater traffic and across Waterloo Bridge, the driver began chattering away. I just about managed monosyllabic replies to his opinions on the weather, John Major, the England cricket team and foreign tourists. With each new topic, his forecast became ever more gloomy.

He only stopped offering his opinions when he came to a halt outside my house in Fentiman Road. I paid him, and smiled ruefully at the thought that this would be the first time in weeks that I'd managed to get home before midnight. I walked slowly up the short path to the front door.

I turned the key in the lock and opened the door quietly, so as not to wake my wife. Once inside I went through my nightly ritual of slipping off my jacket and shoes before creeping quietly up the stairs.

Before I had reached the bedroom I began to get undressed. After years of coming in at one or two in the morning, I was able to take off all my clothes, fold and stack them, and slide under the sheets next to Judy without waking her. But just as I pulled back the cover she said drowsily, "I didn't think you'd be home so early, with all the problems you were facing tonight." I wondered if she was talking in her sleep. "How much damage did the fire do?"

"The fire?" I said, standing in the nude.

"In Davies Street. Gerald phoned a few moments after you'd left to say a fire had started in the kitchen and had spread to the restaurant. He was just checking to make certain you were on your way. He'd cancelled all the bookings for the next two weeks, but he didn't think they'd be able to open again for at least a month. I told him that as you'd left just after six you'd be with him at any minute. So, just how bad is the damage?"

I was already dressed by the time Judy was awake enough to ask why I had never turned up at the restaurant. I shot down the stairs and out onto the street in search of another cab. It had started raining again.

A taxi swung round and came to a halt in front of me.

"Where to this time, guv?"

À POINT

"Thank you, Michael. I'd like that."

I smiled, unable to mask my delight.

"Hi, Pipsqueak. I thought I might have missed you."

I turned and stared at a tall man with a mop of fair hair, who seemed unaffected by the steady flow of people trying to pass him on either side.

Anna gave him a smile that I hadn't seen until that moment.

"Hello, Jonathan," she said. "This is Michael Whitaker. You're lucky—he bought your ticket, and if you hadn't turned up I was just about to accept his kind invitation to dinner. Michael, this is my brother, Jonathan—the one who was held up at the hospital. As you can see, he's now escaped."

I couldn't think of a suitable reply.

Jonathan shook me warmly by the hand. "Thank you for keeping my sister company," he said. "Won't you join us for dinner?"

"That's kind of you," I replied, "but I've just remembered that I'm meant to be somewhere else right now. I'd better . . . "

"You're not meant to be anywhere else right now," interrupted Anna, giving me the same smile. "Don't be so feeble." She linked her arm in mine. "In any case, we'd *both* like you to join us."

"Thank you," I said.

"There's a restaurant just down the road that I've been told is rather good," said Jonathan, as the three of us began walking off in the direction of the Strand.

"Great. I'm famished," said Anna.

"So, tell me all about the play," Jonathan said as Anna linked her other arm in his.

"Every bit as good as the critics promised," said Anna.

"You were unlucky to miss it," I said.

"But I'm rather glad you did," said Anna as we reached the corner of the Strand.

"I think that's the place I'm looking for," said Jonathan, pointing to a large gray double door on the far side of the road. The three of us weaved our way through the temporarily stationary traffic.

Once we reached the other side of the road Jonathan pushed open one of the gray doors to allow us through. It started to rain just as we stepped inside. He led Anna and me down a flight of stairs into a basement restaurant buzzing with the talk of people who had just come out of theaters, and waiters dashing, plates in both hands, from table to table.

"I'll be impressed if you can get a table here," Anna said to her brother, eyeing a group of would-be customers who were clustered round the bar, impatiently waiting for someone to leave. "You should have booked," she added as he began waving at the head waiter, who was fully occupied taking a customer's order.

I remained a yard or two behind them, and as Mario came across, I put a finger to my lips and nodded to him.

"I don't suppose you have a table for three?" asked Jonathan.

"Yes, of course, sir. Please follow me," said Mario, leading us to a quiet table in the corner of the room.

"That was a bit of luck," said Jonathan.

"It certainly was," Anna agreed. Jonathan suggested that I take the far chair, so his sister could sit between us.

Once we had settled, Jonathan asked what I would like to drink.

"How about you?" I said, turning to Anna. "Another dry martini?"

Jonathan looked surprised. "You haven't had a dry martini since . . . "

Anna scowled at him and said quickly, "I'll just have a glass of wine with the meal."

Since when? I wondered, but only said, "I'll have the same."

Mario reappeared, and handed us our menus. Jonathan and Anna studied theirs in silence for some time before Jonathan asked, "Any ideas?"

"It all looks so tempting," Anna said. "But I think I'll settle for the fettucini and a glass of red wine."

"What about a starter?" asked Jonathan.

"No. I'm on first call tomorrow, if you remember—unless of

course you're volunteering to take my place."

"Not after what I've been through this evening, Pipsqueak. I'd rather go without a starter too," he said. "How about you, Michael? Don't let our domestic problems get in your way."

"Fettucini and a glass of red wine would suit me just fine."

"Three fettucini and a bottle of your best Chianti," said Jonathan when Mario returned.

Anna leaned over to me and whispered conspiratorially, "It's the only Italian wine he can pronounce correctly."

"What would have happened if we'd chosen fish?" I asked her.

"He's also heard of Frascati, but he's never quite sure what he's meant to do when someone orders duck."

"What are you two whispering about?" asked Jonathan as he handed his menu back to Mario.

"I was asking your sister about the third partner in the practice."

"Not bad, Michael," Anna said. "You should have gone into politics."

"My wife, Elizabeth, is the third partner," Jonathan said, unaware of what Anna had been getting at. "She, poor darling, is on call tonight."

"You note, two women and one man," said Anna as the wine waiter appeared by Jonathan's side.

"Yes. There used to be four of us," said Jonathan, without explanation. He studied the label on the bottle before nodding sagely.

"You're not fooling anyone, Jonathan. Michael has already worked out that you're no sommelier," said Anna, sounding as if she was trying to change the subject. The waiter extracted the cork and poured a little wine into Jonathan's glass for him to taste.

"So, what do you do, Michael?" asked Jonathan after he had given a second nod to the wine waiter. "Don't tell me you're a doctor, because I'm not looking for another man to join the practice."

"No, he's in the restaurant business," said Anna, as three bowls of fettucini were placed in front of us.

"I see. You two obviously swapped life histories during the intermission," said Jonathan. "But what does being 'in the restaurant business' actually mean?"

"I'm on the management side," I explained. "Or at least, that's what I do nowadays. I started life as a waiter, then I moved into the kitchens for about five years, and finally ended up in management."

"But what does a restaurant manager actually do?" asked Anna.

"Obviously the interval wasn't long enough for you to go into any great detail," said Jonathan as he jabbed his fork into some fettucini.

"Well, at the moment I'm running three restaurants in the West End, which means I never stop dashing from one to the other, depending on which is facing the biggest crisis on that particular day."

"Sounds a bit like ward duty to me," said Anna. "So who turned out to have the biggest crisis today?"

"Today, thank heaven, was not typical," I said with feeling.

"That bad?" said Jonathan.

"Yes, I'm afraid so. We lost a chef this morning who cut off the top of his finger, and won't be back at work for at least a fortnight. My head waiter in our second restaurant is off, claiming he has flu, and I've just had to sack the barman in the third for fiddling the books. Barmen always fiddle the books, of course, but in this case even the customers began to notice what he was up to." I paused. "But I still wouldn't want to be in any other . . ."

A shrill ring interrupted me. I couldn't tell where the sound was coming from until Jonathan removed a tiny cellular phone from his jacket pocket.

"Sorry about this," he said. "Hazard of the job." He pressed a button and put the phone to his ear. He listened for a few seconds, and a frown appeared on his face. "Yes, I suppose so. I'll be there as quickly as I can." He flicked the phone closed and put it back into his pocket.

"Sorry," he repeated. "One of my patients has chosen this particular moment to have a relapse. I'm afraid I'm going to have to leave you." He stood up and turned to his sister. "How will you get home, Pipsqueak?"

"I'm a big girl now," said Anna, "so I'll just look around for one of those black objects on four wheels with a sign on the top that reads T-A-X-I, and then I'll wave at it."

"Don't worry, Jonathan," I said. "I'll drive her home."

"That's very kind of you," said Jonathan, "because if it's still pouring by the time you leave, she may not be able to find one of those black objects to wave at."

"In any case, it's the least I can do, after I ended up getting your ticket, your dinner and your sister."

"Fair exchange," said Jonathan as Mario came rushing up.

"Is everything all right, sir?" he asked.

"No, it isn't. I'm on call, and have to go." He handed over an American Express card. "If you'd be kind enough to put this through your machine, I'll sign for it and you can fill in the amount later. And please add fifteen percent."

"Thank you, sir," said Mario, and rushed away.

"Hope to see you again," said Jonathan. I rose to shake him by the hand.

"I hope so too," I said.

Jonathan left us, headed for the bar and signed a slip of paper. Mario handed him back his American Express card.

As Anna waved to her brother, I looked toward the bar and shook my head slightly. Mario tore up the little slip of paper and dropped the pieces into a wastebasket.

"It hasn't been a wonderful day for Jonathan, either," said Anna, turning back to face me. "And what with your problems, I'm amazed you were able to take the evening off."

"I shouldn't have, really, and wouldn't have, except . . ." I trailed off as I leaned over and topped up Anna's glass.

"Except what?" she asked.

"Do you want to hear the truth?" I asked as I poured the remains of the wine into my own glass.

"I'll try that for starters," she said.

I placed the empty bottle on the side of the table, and hesitated, but only for a moment. "I was driving to one of my restaurants earlier this evening, when I spotted you going into the theater. I stared at you for so long that I nearly crashed into the back of the car in front of me. Then I swerved across the road into the nearest parking space, and the car behind almost crashed into me. I leapt out, ran all the way to the theater, and searched everywhere until I saw you standing in the line for the box office. I joined the line and watched you hand over your spare ticket. Once you were safely out of sight, I told the box office manager that you hadn't expected me to make it in time, and that you might have put my ticket up for resale. After I'd described you, which I was able to do in great detail, he handed it over without so much as a murmur."

Anna put down her glass of wine and stared across at me with a look of incredulity. "I'm glad he fell for your story," she said. "But should I?"

"Yes, you should. Because then I put two ten-pound notes into a theater envelope and took the place next to you," I continued. "The rest you already know." I waited to see how she would react. She didn't speak for some time.

"I'm flattered," she said eventually. "I didn't realize there were any old-fashioned romantics left in the world." She lowered her head slightly. "Am I allowed to ask what you have planned for the rest of the evening?"

"Nothing has been planned so far," I admitted. "Which is why it's all been so refreshing."

"You make me sound like an After Eight mint," said Anna with a laugh.

"I can think of at least three replies to that," I told her as Mario reappeared, looking a little disappointed at the sight of the half-empty plates.

"Is everything all right, sir?" he asked, sounding anxious.

"Couldn't have been better," said Anna, who hadn't stopped looking at me.

"Would you like a coffee, madam?" Mario asked her.

"No, thank you," said Anna firmly. "We have to go in search of a marooned car."

"Heaven knows if it will still be there after all this time," I said as she rose from her place.

I took Anna's hand, led her toward the entrance, back up

the stairs and out onto the street. Then I began to retrace my steps to the spot where I'd abandoned my car. As we strolled up the Aldwych and chatted away, I felt as if I was with an old friend.

"You don't have to give me a lift, Michael," Anna was saying. "It's probably miles out of your way, and in any case it's stopped raining, so I'll just hail a taxi."

"I want to give you a lift," I told her. "That way I'll have your company for a little longer." She smiled as we reached a distressingly large space where I had left the car.

"Damn," I said. I quickly checked up and down the road, and returned to find Anna laughing.

"Is this another of your schemes to have more of my company?" she teased. She opened her bag and took out a mobile phone, dialed 999, and passed it over to me.

"Which service do you require? Fire, Police, or Ambulance?" a voice asked.

"Police," I said, and was immediately put through to another voice.

"Charing Cross Police Station. What is the nature of your inquiry?"

"I think my car has been stolen."

"Can you tell me the make, color and registration number please, sir."

"It's a blue Rover 600, registration K857 SHV."

There was a long pause, during which I could hear other voices talking in the background.

"No, it hasn't been stolen, sir," said the officer who had been dealing with me when he came back on the line. "The vehicle was illegally parked on a double yellow line. It's been removed and taken to the Vauxhall Bridge Pound."

"Can I pick it up now?" I asked.

"Certainly, sir. How will you be getting there?"

"I'll take a taxi."

"Then just ask the driver for the Vauxhall Bridge Pound. Once you get there, you'll need some form of identification, and a check for £105 with a bank card—that is if you don't have the full amount in cash."

"One hundred five pounds?" I said quietly.

"That's correct, sir."

Anna frowned for the first time that evening.

"Worth every penny."

"I beg your pardon, sir?"

"Nothing, officer. Goodnight."

I handed the phone back to Anna, and said, "The next thing I'm going to do is find you a taxi."

"You certainly are not, Michael, because I'm staying with you. In any case, you promised my brother you'd take me home."

I took her hand and hailed a taxi, which swung across the road and came to a halt beside us.

"Vauxhall Bridge Pound, please."

"Bad luck, mate," said the cabbie. "You're my fourth this evening."

I gave him a broad grin.

"I expect the other three also chased you into the theater, but luckily they were behind me in the line," I said to Anna as I joined her on the back seat.

As the taxi maneuvered its way slowly through the rainswept post-theater traffic and across Waterloo Bridge, Anna said, "Don't you think I should have been given the chance to choose between the four of you? After all, one of them might have been driving a Rolls-Royce."

"Not possible."

"And why not, pray?" asked Anna.

"Because you couldn't have parked a Rolls-Royce in that space."

"But if he'd had a chauffeur, that would have solved all my problems."

"In that case, I would simply have run him over."

The taxi had travelled some distance before either of us spoke again.

"Can I ask you a personal question?" Anna eventually said.

"If it's what I think it is, I was about to ask you the same thing."

"Then you go first."

"No—I'm not married," I said. "Nearly, once, but she escaped." Anna laughed. "And you?"

"I was married," she said quietly. "He was the fourth doctor in the practice. He died three years ago. I spent nine months nursing him, but in the end I failed."

"I'm so sorry," I said, feeling a little ashamed. "That was tactless of me. I shouldn't have raised the subject."

"I raised it, Michael, not you. It's me who should apologize."

Neither of us spoke again for several minutes, until Anna said, "For the past three years, since Andrew's death, I've immersed myself in work, and I seem to spend most of my spare time boring Jonathan and Elizabeth to distraction. They couldn't have been more understanding, but they must be heartily sick of it by now. I wouldn't be surprised if Jonathan hadn't arranged an emergency for tonight, so someone else could take me to the theater for a change. It might even give me the confidence to go out again. Heaven knows," she added as we drove into the car pound, "enough people have been kind enough to ask me."

I passed the cabbie a ten-pound note and we dashed through the rain in the direction of a little Portakabin.

I walked up to the counter and read the form taped to it. I took out my wallet, extracted my driver's license, and began counting.

I only had eighty pounds in cash, and I never carry a checkbook.

Anna grinned, and took the envelope I'd presented to her earlier in the evening from her bag. She tore it open and extracted the two ten-pound notes, added a five-pound note of her own, and handed them over to me.

"Thank you," I said, once again feeling embarrassed.

"Worth every penny," she replied with a grin.

The policeman counted the notes slowly, placed them in a tin box, and gave me a receipt.

"It's right there, in the front row," he said, pointing out of the window. "And if I may say so, sir, it was perhaps unwise of you to leave your keys in the ignition. If the vehicle had been stolen, your insurance company would not have been liable to cover the claim." He passed me my keys.

"It was my fault, officer," said Anna. "I should have sent him back for them, but I didn't realize what he was up to. I'll make sure he doesn't do it again."

The officer looked up at me. I shrugged my shoulders and led Anna out of the cabin and across to my car. I opened the door to let her in, then nipped around to the driver's side as she leant over and pushed my door open. I took my place behind the wheel and turned to face her. "I'm sorry," I said. "The rain has ruined your dress." A drop of water fell off the end of her nose. "But, you know, you're just as beautiful wet or dry."

"Thank you, Michael," she smiled. "But if you don't have any objection, on balance I'd prefer to be dry."

I laughed. "So, where shall I take you?" I asked, suddenly aware that I didn't know where she lived.

"Fulham, please; forty-nine Parsons Green Lane. It's not too far."

I pushed the key into the ignition, not caring how far it was. I turned the key and took a deep breath. The engine spluttered, but refused to start. Then I realized I had left the sidelights on.

"Don't do this to me," I begged, as Anna began laughing again. I turned the key a second time, and the motor caught. I let out a sigh of relief.

"That was a close one," Anna said. "If it hadn't started, we might have ended up spending the rest of the night together. Or was that all part of your dastardly plan?"

"Nothing's gone according to plan so far," I admitted as I drove out of the pound. I paused before adding, "Still, I suppose things might have turned out differently."

"You mean if I hadn't been the sort of girl you were looking for?"

"Something like that."

"I wonder what those other three men would have thought of me," said Anna wistfully.

"Who cares? They're not going to have the chance to find out."

"You sound very sure of yourself, Mr. Whitaker."

"If you only knew," I said. "But I would like to see you again, Anna. If you're willing to risk it."

She seemed to take an eternity to reply. "Yes, I'd like that," she said eventually. "But only on condition that you pick me up at my place, so I can be certain you park your car legally, and remember to switch your lights off."

"I accept your terms," I told her. "And I won't even add any conditions of my own if we can begin the agreement tomorrow evening."

Once again Anna didn't reply immediately. "I'm not sure I know what I'm doing tomorrow evening."

"Neither do I," I said. "But I'll cancel it, whatever it is."

"Then so will I," said Anna as I drove into Parsons Green Lane, and began searching for number 49.

"It's about a hundred yards down, on the left," she said.

I drew up and parked outside her front door.

"Don't let's bother with the theater this time," said Anna. "Come at about eight, and I'll cook you some supper." She leant over and kissed me on the cheek before turning back to open the car door. I jumped out and walked quickly round to her side of the car as she stepped onto the pavement.

"So, I'll see you around eight tomorrow evening," she said.

"I'll look forward to that." I hesitated, and then took her in my arms. "Goodnight, Anna."

"Goodnight, Michael," she said as I released her. "And thank you for buying my ticket, not to mention dinner. I'm glad my other three would-be suitors only made it as far as the car pound."

I smiled as she pushed the key into the lock of her front door.

She turned back. "By the way, Michael, was that the restaurant with the missing waiter, the four-and-a-half-fingered chef, or the crooked bartender?"

"The crooked bartender," I replied with a smile.

She closed the door behind her as the clock on a nearby church struck one.